The Creektown DISCOVERIES

The Creektown Discoveries

3 HOLMES COUNTY
AMISH NOVELS

WANDA E. BRUNSTETTER

BARBOUR
PUBLISHING

Print ISBN 979-8-89151-095-1
Adobe Digital Edition (.epub) 979-8-89151-096-8

All German-Dutch words are taken from the *Revised Pennsylvania German Dictionary* found in Lancaster County, Pennsylvania.

This book is a work of fiction. Names, characters, places, and incidents are either products of the author's imagination or used fictitiously. Any similarity to actual people, organizations, and/or events is purely coincidental.

For more information about Wanda E. Brunstetter, please visit the author's website at the following internet address: www.wandabrunstetter.com

Image model photography: Richard Brunstetter III
Cover design: Buffy Cooper
Cover background photography: Doyle Yoder Photography

Published by Barbour Publishing, Inc., 1810 Barbour Drive, Uhrichsville, Ohio 44683, www.barbourbooks.com

Our mission is to inspire the world with the life-changing message of the Bible.

Member of the Evangelical Christian Publishers Association

Printed in Colombia.

CREEKTOWN DISCOVERIES

VOL ONE

The Walnut Creek WISH

Dedication

To my cousin Lois, whose joyous attitude
has always been contagious.

And to our Amish friend Orley, whose wisdom
and advice have helped so many people.

With special thanks to my granddaughter Daun, who shared
with me her personal insights regarding hotel management.

Be still, and know that I am God.
PSALM 46:10

Prologue

Walnut Creek, Ohio

"What do ya think about this old *schlidde*?" Orley Troyer held the item up for his wife's inspection. "Should we make an offer on it, Lois?"

Her brows furrowed. "It would have to be a low offer, because if you're thinking of putting the sled in our antique store for resale, I doubt you'd make much of a profit."

Orley nodded and put the item down. The old relic was not in the best shape. Not only was the paint faded, but the rope to pull the sled was missing, as well as one side of the steering controls. Lois was right—it was unlikely that anyone would want to buy the antiquated item.

"Let's see what's over there. Maybe we'll find some old dishes." Looking bright-eyed, Lois pointed to a table where none of the other people who'd come to this yard sale were looking right now.

"You go ahead," Orley responded. "I'm gonna walk around for a bit and see what else I can find."

"Okay." With her head held high and the narrow ties on her white head covering swishing from side to side, Lois headed off toward the table full of dishes and glass items.

Orley smiled. Although his sweet wife had recently turned forty-eight, in his eyes she still looked just as young and pretty as the day they'd gotten married, twenty-eight years ago. Lois was also the kindest woman he'd ever known, always thinking of others and willing to help anyone she met. He felt blessed to have married such a caring woman.

Orley glanced at some of the other tables, but almost involuntarily, his feet took him back to the sled. There was no logical reason for it, but Orley felt drawn to the item.

As he stared at the dilapidated sled, an odd feeling came over him—the one he experienced whenever he felt attracted to an item with seemingly no worth.

Orley ran his fingers over the wooden slats. *I won't be the least bit surprised if someone doesn't come into our store and buy this sled. I'm almost certain that it will have a deep meaning for that person too.*

Chapter 1

Canton, Ohio

Rhonda Davis stood in front of her bedroom window looking out at the dismal weather. Spring brought flowers but also rain. She hated wet weather and had since she was a girl, forced to walk to and from school in the rain, wind, and sometimes snow. Rhonda's father had always left for work too early to drop her off at school, and Rhonda's mother hadn't gotten her driver's license until Rhonda was in her first year of college.

"Talk about a late bloomer," she mumbled, turning away from the window. "Why'd my mom have to be afraid of everything when I was a girl?" Even now, at the age of fifty-eight, Rhonda's mother rarely did anything exciting. She preferred to stay at home and knit things that no one really wanted, rather than taking trips, getting involved in charity events, or trying a new hobby. Mom's greatest attribute was her cooking skills and the ability to play the piano.

Rhonda had always seen her mother as mousy and rather boring.

Rhonda's thirty-seven-year-old sister, Gwen, lived a boring, rather quiet life with her husband, Chad, and three children.

By the time Rhonda started high school, she had determined to make something of herself. That decision included getting a college degree and majoring in business. In her second year of college, she'd met Jeff, and two years later they were married. For the first two years, Rhonda had been satisfied with her job as assistant manager of a large hotel in Canton. But by the time she and Jeff had been married five years, Rhonda's desire to have children outweighed any accomplishments she'd made with her job. The doctor had said there was nothing physically wrong with her or Jeff that would prevent Rhonda from getting pregnant, but even after another three years, all efforts of her conceiving a child had been unsuccessful. Rhonda had finally quit hoping for a baby and thrown herself into her work at the hotel, which she now managed full time. She and Jeff had been married twelve years, and all they had to show for it was a modern townhouse, an expensive sports car, a luxury SUV, and a chasm of disinterest between them.

Rhonda figured that unless something happened to turn the tide, she and Jeff would soon be heading down the road to divorce.

"And why not?" she mumbled, picking up her hairbrush and pulling it through her shoulder-length hair. "The only thing my husband and I have in common now is that we're both married to our jobs. We can barely say a civil word to each other anymore."

She set her brush back on the dresser and laid a hand against her breastbone, releasing a heavy sigh. *If I'd known how things would turn out, I would never have married Jeff.*

Still wearing her robe, Rhonda left her room and walked to the closet in the hallway. *I wonder if that old box of junk is still in there. The one that holds some of my past. I really should dump that stuff since it doesn't serve any real purpose.*

She opened the door and looked around for a few seconds. "Yes, it's still here." Her instinct was to go through the items one more time, so she hauled the box back to the bedroom and placed it on the end of the bed. *I don't know why I've bothered to keep this stuff or go back to look at it from time to time.*

Rhonda lifted the lid and moved her hand around inside. She pulled out a silly old card from her sister that she'd made in the second grade. Rhonda couldn't help but smile. *I remember this one well. Gwen and I sure had some fun when we were kids.*

Rhonda set the card back in the box and pulled out a couple of dainty plastic red roses. *Ah, yes. . .this was on the small birthday cake Jeff got me whenwe were dating in college. Those were great days we had together back then. Of course, we were younger and had no real problems to deal with.*

Rhonda felt something soft and withdrew an embroidered handkerchief. It had been embellished with two little bells, and small bluish flowers adorned it. She held it against her chest and sighed. *This is from my wedding day, and there's the blue I needed to complete that old traditional rhyme: Something old, something new, something borrowed, something blue.*

Rhonda breathed out a puff of air. *Of course, that old saying is about bringing good luck, which I don't really believe in. A person makes their own luck, based on how hard they work to get what they want.*

She picked through a few more items and paused, holding a little book in her hand. Rhonda stared at the pocket-sized New Testament. It had been a gift from her paternal grandmother, who had since passed away. Rhonda's fingers opened it to the first page. *To my granddaughter Rhonda: May you find comfort in the words of this book. Love, Grandma Haskell.*

Rhonda's smile soon faded, because the truth was, she had no use for a Bible. Even so, she would hold on to it for sentimental reasons. Although this was her Bible, she'd never read any of it. She had, however, hoped to pass the Testament to her own daughter someday, but it looked as though all hope was lost in that department.

She placed it back in the box and felt an overwhelming urge to cry. Rhonda's frame stiffened as she got control of her emotions while carrying the box back to the closet. Then she closed the door and returned to her room.

Rhonda stepped over to her closet and picked out something presentable to wear to work. She chose a pair of gray slacks along with a colorful blouse and placed them on the bed. On her days off, Rhonda often went shopping for new clothes to add to her wardrobe, but nothing ever seemed good enough or brought any measure of satisfaction. Managing the busy hotel had become boring, and she felt like her life was going nowhere.

Downstairs in the kitchen, Rhonda found her husband sitting at the table with a cup of coffee in one hand and the newspaper spread out in front of him.

"Morning, sleepyhead. I thought maybe you were planning to spend the day in bed." He glanced up at the clock on the wall across from him, then dropped his gaze to the newspaper again.

"I don't have the luxury of sleeping all day, and you should know it. In case you forgot to look at the schedule I have posted, I need to be at work soon." Rhonda gestured to the bulletin board hanging on the wall near her desk. "And I don't usually get dressed like this to stay home for the day." Her tone was filled with sarcasm as she reached into a cabinet and withdrew a breakfast bar.

Jeff's upper lip curled slightly before he took a drink of coffee. "You and your schedules and reminder notes. Why does everything you do have to be put on paper?"

Rhonda poured herself a cup of coffee and took the seat across from him. "Without my lists, I might neglect to do something important each day." She pointed a perfectly manicured finger at him, although she wasn't sure why since his concentration seemed to be fully on whatever he was reading. "Those lists are also for your benefit, so you'll know when I'll be here and what my work schedule is. You'd do well to write some lists of your own instead of relying on your memory, which sometimes fails you."

Jeff's facial features tightened as he looked up from the newspaper and glared at her. His pale blue eyes held no sparkle, as they had when they were dating and even in the early years of their marriage. There was a time when Rhonda would have looked at her husband's face and thought he was the most handsome man on earth. But those days had faded like an old pair of jeans. These days, Rhonda barely noticed the distinguishing mark of the dimple in Jeff's chin, which she used to think was cute. Like this morning, she was more likely to observe the growth on his face, indicating that he hadn't shaved in several days.

"I don't need any stupid lists, Rhonda. I know my own daily schedule." Jeff's voice had an edge to it.

Rhonda blew on her coffee and took a sip. "Whatever you say, dear. I'm sure you never forget anything either." She unwrapped her bar and took a bite.

"I didn't say that. Just said I don't need any lists."

Rhonda continued to nibble on her meager breakfast. This was a pointless conversation and a waste of her time. She never got anywhere making suggestions to Jeff.

He finished his coffee and set the mug down with a thud. "Know what I think we should do?"

She swallowed. "About what?"

"About us and the way our life as a married couple has become."

"You mean boring and flat, devoid of the love we once felt for each other?" Rhonda couldn't keep the bitterness from her tone. She took the last bite of the bar and tossed the wrapper into the garbage.

He blinked rapidly, while the rest of his face went slack. "Surely you don't mean that."

Rhonda finished the rest of her coffee and got up from the table. "Admit it. You and I both know that there's not much left between us. You have your restaurant to run, and I have my job at the hotel. We only see each other for a short time every morning and evening, and when we're together, we hardly have a civil word to say to one another."

"It doesn't have to be that way. We could start over."

"Yeah, right." She kept her focus on the empty cup as she rinsed it out thoroughly and placed it on the top rack in the dishwasher.

"I'm serious, Rhonda, and I believe I know what we should do."

She folded her arms. "And what would that be—renew our vows so we can make more promises to love and cherish that we're not going to keep?"

He shook his head. "We oughta sell our townhouse here in Canton and move to one of the smaller, more rural communities."

Sucking air in noisily through her top teeth, she lifted her gaze to the ceiling. "You've got to be kidding. Like that would change anything."

"No, I'm not kidding." Jeff tapped the table, bringing her focus back to his unshaven face. "I've been looking at the ads for homes being sold in some of the smaller communities that are predominately made up of Amish families. You can't get any more laid back than that."

Rhonda moved back to the table and stood next to Jeff's chair. "Have you forgotten that both of our jobs are here in Canton, or do you need a reminder note for that too?"

"Very funny." He pointed to the newspaper. "Here's a nice-looking home in Walnut Creek. It has a bit of land with it, and there's going to be an open house there this Sunday. I think we should go take a look."

Rhonda carved her long fingers through the ends of her hair, holding it back away from her face and then releasing it again. "Have you not heard anything I've said? We can't move to Walnut Creek or any other rural community. Our jobs are here, and. . ."

"Yeah, but if we moved there, we could slow our pace when we're not at work. We've been arguing a lot lately, and it might be good for our marriage if we start over someplace new."

She shook her head vigorously. "I am not going to quit my job at the hotel. That would put more stress on us, because it's not likely that we could find good-paying jobs in Walnut Creek or any of the other smaller towns."

Jeff flapped his hand at her. "We can commute. Canton isn't that far from some of the smaller communities. Why don't we drive over to Walnut Creek Sunday afternoon and take the tour? There may be a few other homes for sale in the area too. Please say you'll at least think about it."

Rhonda lifted her hands so the palms pointed upward. "Okay, I'll give it some thought." She started to move away from the table but turned back to face him. "Who knows—moving might actually end up being a good thing."

Jeff offered her a half-smile. "You think so?"

"In one way at least. It would give you a reason to throw out some of that old stuff you've piled up in our garage and basement."

He shrugged. "We'll have to wait and see about that."

Chapter 2

Walnut Creek

"I can't believe I let you talk me into this," Rhonda complained as the town of Walnut Creek came into view. "It's ridiculous to think that moving here, or anywhere else for that matter, is going to improve our lives in any way."

Before Jeff could respond, Rhonda continued with her tirade. "It took us about forty minutes to get here, and there wasn't much Sunday traffic. But on weekdays the commute probably takes longer, so we'd have to get up earlier in order to be on time for work." She paused to take a breath. "So, the whole idea of moving here seems rather foolish to me."

Jeff's jaw clenched as he gripped the wheel of his SUV. "You could have said no when I suggested coming to look at the house I found in the newspaper."

"Oh sure, and listen to you gripe about it until I finally gave in and agreed to waste a perfectly good afternoon." She gave a huff. "Whenever you want something, you try to wear me down until I finally agree to it."

"Do not. You're exaggerating."

"Are you kidding me? What do you want, Jeff—some examples?"

He glanced over at Rhonda, then back at the road, waiting for his GPS to tell him when to make the next turn. "Let's change the subject, shall we?"

"Better yet, let's not say anything at all. That's safer, don't you think?" Rhonda stared out the window.

Jeff bit back a caustic retort. Hopefully, his wife's negative attitude and condemnation would improve once they toured the house. Then again, if Rhonda didn't like the place, she might be in a worse mood on the way home and would have no trouble reminding Jeff what a waste of time it had been to tour the house or make the drive to Walnut Creek.

When Jeff pulled his rig up in front of a white ranch-style house with For Sale and Open House signs, Rhonda was surprised to see how welcoming it looked. She thought the spacious front porch, low-pitched roof, and large windows made the home quite appealing. Although, since they hadn't seen the inside of the house yet, Rhonda would keep her opinion to herself. No doubt there would be things she wouldn't like about the interior, in which case she would veto the idea of making an offer on the place.

"Looks like a nice house, don't you think?" Jeff bumped Rhonda's arm, bringing her thoughts to a halt.

"Um. . .well, the exterior has a pleasing appearance."

"Right, and it has the benefit of being on one level." He scrunched up his face. "I don't know about you, but I'm kind of sick of trudging up and down all the steps in our townhouse."

Rhonda shrugged. "Stairs aren't so bad. It's a good cardio workout and helps keep us fit."

Jeff opened his door and got out of the SUV. "You coming?"

"Of course. That is why we drove all this way." Rhonda exited the vehicle and followed him up the walk leading to the house. It was an easy climb to the porch, with just two steps. A two-seated swing sat on one end of the porch with two comfy-looking throw pillows. A small bistro table with two chairs was positioned on the other end of the porch.

It was a lovely spring day, and several birds twittered from the maple tree in the front yard. Rhonda fought the temptation to take a seat on the swing and absorb the peacefulness for a while, but she reminded herself that this wasn't her home, so she had no right to take such liberties.

The front door opened, and a well-dressed, middle-aged woman greeted them with a smile. "I'm Shelly Lockhart." She handed Jeff a business card along with a flyer that listed some information about the home and property it sat upon. "Please come in and feel free to look around. I'll be in the kitchen, so if you have any questions, let me know."

"Thank you." They stepped into the foyer, and when the Realtor turned to the left, Jeff headed down the hall to the right. The first room they came to had been set up as an office, but there was a closet, so it could easily be a bedroom if whoever bought the home wanted it to be.

Of course, if we lived here, I'd keep this as my office, Rhonda thought. *It would be nice to sit in front of the window with my laptop and look out at the green grass, trees, and the field across the road, instead of staring at the row of townhouses behind ours.*

Jeff didn't say much as he perused the office space, and he didn't stay in the room long either. Rhonda figured this particular room hadn't impressed him too much.

They moved on to the next room, farther down on the left side of the hall. It was quite large, with plenty of room for the four-poster king-sized bed, two end tables, and two matching dressers. On the opposite side of the room was a small sofa and a rocking chair. A large-screen TV hung on the wall, with a gas fireplace underneath.

"Wow!" Jeff whistled. "Now this is what I call a master bedroom. I wouldn't mind coming home to this every night."

"Let's check out the master bath." Rhonda gestured to the french doors separating the bedroom from the bathroom.

Upon entering the room, she looked at each area in awe. The bathroom included a large vanity with double sinks, a deep soaking tub, a walk-in shower with two shower heads, and a smaller area for the toilet with a door for privacy.

Walking back toward the french doors, Rhonda saw another door. She opened it to reveal a spacious master closet. She couldn't think of a single negative thing about this master suite.

Jeff moved closer and gave her arm a tap. "Pretty nice, huh?"

"I'll say. I wonder what else this house has to offer."

"Well, let's go find out." Jeff stepped out of the room and led the way back down the hall. At the end, they found two more bedrooms with a nice-sized bathroom between them. While not as large as the master bath, it had a double-sink vanity, toilet, and a shower/tub combination. There was also a closet with plenty of room for linens.

One of the bedrooms had a wallpapered border, sporting colorful balloons, up where the wall met the ceiling. A crib sat against one wall, and a white dresser with some balloons painted on the drawers had been positioned on the other side of the room, which was obviously a nursery.

Rhonda swallowed against the constriction that had formed in her throat. She then looked over at Jeff and grimaced. "I wasn't expecting this."

"Neither was I." He seemed to be looking at the room with disdain. "I'm ready to move on. How about you?"

Rhonda nodded in agreement. She didn't need the reminder that they had no children. *If we did decide to buy this home, the first thing I'd do is take off the balloon border in this room and paint the walls a neutral color.*

She turned toward the door. "Let's see what other rooms are in this house."

Across from the nursery was a decent-sized laundry room with a washer and dryer, as well as a utility sink and plenty of cabinets for storage.

The final room at the end of the hall was the largest of all and had been set up with a pool table, snack bar, several comfortable-looking chairs, and another large-screen TV.

With eyes wide, Jeff lifted both hands over his head and waved them back and forth as though directing a choir. "This is it, Rhonda—my man cave!"

She rolled her eyes. "In your dreams. This place is so nice I bet we can't afford it."

He handed her the flyer the Realtor had given him. "Take a look. It's not as bad as you might think."

Rhonda studied the piece of paper. She had to admit if they sold their townhouse, buying this home might actually be doable. She turned to face Jeff. "We haven't seen the kitchen, dining room, or living room yet, so let's not get too excited about this end of the house. The rest of the home might not be to our liking at all."

"You're right, we do need to check out those rooms. I also want to see what the garage has to offer, as well as the backyard."

"Okay, then let's start with the garage since it's on this end of the house."

"Unless you'd rather check out the kitchen while I look at the garage."

Rhonda shook her head. "Since my sweet little sports car would be parked in there, along with your big vehicle, I want to see how much room we'd have."

"Okay." Jeff opened the door and went down the one step into the garage.

Rhonda followed. Because the homeowners were away during the open house, the garage was empty, but its size surprised her. A third bay meant more than enough room for two vehicles, along with plenty of shelves and cupboards for storage, as well as a large freezer, which sat near the door. Above them was a trap door, which meant there was overhead space for more storage.

"I like what I'm seeing here." Jeff's face broke into a wide grin and he rubbed his hands briskly together. "Plenty of room to display my collectibles, either here or in that TV/game room."

Rhonda bristled. "I was hoping if we moved from the townhouse that you'd get rid of all that junk."

His brows furrowed. "It's not junk. Some of my items are valuable."

"Good, then you should sell them so we'll have extra money for our savings or as a down payment for this or some other house."

Jeff pursed his lips. "I'll think about it. Right now, though, why don't we take a look at what's on the other end of this home?"

"Good idea. I'm eager to see how the kitchen is laid out." Rhonda started back down the hall and heard Jeff's footsteps behind her.

After they'd gone past the bedrooms, Rhonda looked to her right and spotted the formal living room. No TV there—that was a good thing. This cozy room was a place for visiting, with no distractions. *Of course, other than our immediate families, it's doubtful we would have many visitors, since we don't know anyone living here in Walnut Creek.*

Moving on, they came to another bathroom—this one was smaller, with just a toilet and sink. It had been cheerfully decorated with a woodsy, outdoor theme.

A few more steps down the hall, and to the left they found the formal dining room with plenty of area for the large table and china hutch that took up most of the space. It was more than adequate for serving holiday meals or giving a dinner party, should a person choose to have one.

At the end of the hall on this side of the house was the kitchen. It was another big room, with a table and chairs at one end, along with a roll-top desk and a serving cart. The stovetop, double ovens, and refrigerator were on the other end of the kitchen. In front of the sunny window was an extra-deep, two-sided sink, with plenty of counter space on both sides. Four tall chairs sat around the island in the middle of the room.

"This would be a fun kitchen to cook in," Rhonda murmured. "If I had time for that sort of thing."

"If we had this kitchen, I think we'd both make the time for cooking," Jeff responded. "Our kitchen in the townhouse pales in comparison to this one."

Rhonda couldn't argue with that. Everything about this lovely home was head and shoulders above the place they currently owned.

The Realtor joined them by the island and gestured to another room to the right of the kitchen. "Please look at the family room, and then go out the back door from there to the covered patio where you can see the one-acre yard. Feel free to wander around and explore it."

When they entered the family room, which had also been decorated with a woodsy theme, Rhonda paused to look at the gas fireplace with a wooden mantle above. *How fun it would be to decorate the area above the brick fireplace with holiday themes throughout the year. But when would I find the time for that?* she asked herself.

Jeff bumped her arm. "Let's go outside. I'm eager to see the big yard."

"It's big all right," Rhonda said after they stepped out the door. "There's a lot of lawn to be mowed." She made a sweeping gesture with her arm.

"That's what riding lawnmowers are for."

She rolled her eyes. "We don't have one of those, or any other kind of mower, since the HOAs we pay monthly cover ground maintenance for the small area of grass in our yard."

Ignoring her comment, Jeff rushed forward, leaving Rhonda on the patio. "Come on," he shouted. "You've gotta see the pond out here. It includes a waterfall, and there are some fancy-looking goldfish as well."

"Oh, boy, now he's sold." Rhonda made her way to where Jeff stood. She had to admit, the addition of the pond made this yard quite inviting. *How nice it would be to sit out here and do nothing but relax. But then when would I find the time for that? Maybe on my days off?*

While Rhonda stood by the pond, watching the fish swim around, Jeff walked the perimeter of the yard.

"There's a good-sized storage shed for tools and a lawn mower on the other side of the house," Jeff told Rhonda when he returned to her side. "The home and yard have just about everything we could want, and there's plenty of room to put in a hot tub or even a swimming pool if we wanted to."

Rhonda shook her head. "You're getting carried away, Jeff. This home and yard are too big for just the two of us."

"I want it, and if you're honest with yourself, I bet you do too. Just think how great it would be to come home from work every day to a place this peaceful."

"It is serene, but—"

"Let's put an offer on it before someone else snaps it up. A place this nice probably won't be on the market very long." Jeff put his arm around her waist. "Think about it, Rhonda—if we move here, it'll be good for our marriage." The enthusiasm in her husband's tone could not go unnoticed. Neither could the way his face seemed to light up.

"We can't make a snap decision about something so big right now. We need time to think it over—weigh the pros and cons of making such a move."

"I get that, but we don't want to lose the place either." Jeff's tone went from enthusiastic to sounding desperate. Was he really that determined to make their marriage better, or was he merely caught up in the idea of living in such a nice home in a quiet rural area?

"I cannot feel good about putting in an offer today. Can we at least sleep on it before making a decision?"

"Yeah, okay." Jeff pulled Rhonda into his arms and gave her a kiss that nearly took her breath away. It had been a long time since he'd kissed her like that, and she almost agreed to buy the house, right there on the spot. Rhonda held herself in check, though. A snap decision based on the hope that their struggling marriage would suddenly be okay was not a good idea. They both needed time to talk about this and think things through.

Chapter 3

Canton

Monday morning when the alarm buzzed by her side of the bed, it was all Rhonda could do to pull herself upright and turn it off. She'd had trouble getting to sleep last night, thinking about the home she and Jeff had looked at in Walnut Creek. So many questions and concerns had encompassed her thoughts, making it hard to come up with a decision about whether they should make an offer on the house.

Rhonda yawned as she sat remembering their drive into Walnut Creek. It was a quaint place with small businesses dotting the area, but there were many homes spaced out on large properties.

If they did get the home they'd seen, some of their extra down time would go into taking care of a yard, which they weren't used to doing. Due to her job, Rhonda's time was limited, and she'd have to adjust her new routine to include the longer commute. Even so, she couldn't help thinking about how nice the rural countryside looked and that maybe yard work could become a way to de-stress.

Rhonda couldn't get over seeing the Plain people riding in those little black buggies drawn by horses. She tapped her chin. *They sure live simply in the way they get around and even how they dress. I wonder what it would be like to get to know some of them.*

Rhonda's mind kept going over the pros and cons of moving. Their home would be great for having overnight company, and they could take guests out for the day to many places in the area. The community of

Walnut Creek was set up nicely for tourism, with its meat-and-cheese stores, Amish furniture stores, and many other Amish-owned businesses. Rhonda thought Walnut Creek would be a nice place to live, but she wasn't convinced that living there could really help her and Jeff's marriage.

She glanced over at her husband, lying on his side with his back to her. He hadn't even lifted his head from the pillow, despite the irritating buzz of the alarm clock.

Did he have a restless night too? she asked herself. *Does Jeff have as many misgivings as I do about whether to sell the townhouse and move to Walnut Creek?*

Rhonda got up and padded over to the window in her bare feet. She opened the blinds to let some sunlight in and hopefully wake her husband.

Jeff groaned and put one hand over his eyes. "Please tell me it's not morning already."

"It is, and the alarm went off. Didn't you hear it?"

"I tried not to."

She moved over to the bed and shook his leg through the covers. "Come on, we need to get ready for work or we'll be late."

He pulled the sheet over his head. "I don't care. I didn't get enough sleep last night."

"Neither did I, because my thoughts were consumed with that house we saw yesterday."

"Same here." Jeff pushed the covers aside and sat up. "I weighed the pros and cons, and I think we should get it."

Rhonda reached around and massaged the back of her neck, trying to get the kinks out. "It's not that simple, Jeff."

"It is to me. You liked the place and so did I. We need to go for it before someone else does."

"I don't see how it's possible when we haven't even put this place on the market, let alone sold it." She turned to face the window again. "In order to buy a new home, we'd have to sell the townhouse. I mean, how else would we pay for it, Jeff?"

He got out of bed and joined her at the window. "We can make a down payment with money from our savings and then take out a loan for the balance we'd owe on the house in Walnut Creek. Then as soon as this place sells, we can pay off the new place."

"That sounds simple enough, but there are two things that might get in the way of that."

He tipped his head. "Such as?"

Rhonda held up one finger. "The amount we'd get from this house might be less than what we'd need to pay off the loan."

"And the second thing?"

"There are no guarantees that our townhouse would sell right away. We might end up making payments on a loan that would take a long time to pay off and end up stuck with the townhouse and all of its expenses too."

"I doubt that would happen, but if it should, we could rent or even lease this place and use the money we'd get every month to make our payment to the bank for the loan."

Rhonda bit the inside of her cheek as she continued to rub the back of her neck. "I don't know. . .it's risky, and I'm not sure it would be smart to rent out the townhouse. I've heard horror stories about people who own rentals and how terrible the renters leave the place when it's time to move out."

Jeff took hold of Rhonda's shoulders and gave them a gentle squeeze. "Life is full of risks, but if we don't throw caution to the wind once in a while and take chances, we could miss out on something exceptional."

"Can we talk about this during breakfast? Right now, I need to take a shower and get ready for work."

"Sure, honey." Jeff smiled. "Since I don't have to be at the restaurant until almost noon, I'll fix breakfast for us this morning."

Rhonda blinked rapidly as she stared at him.

"Don't look so surprised. I do know how to cook, you know. Don't forget, that's what I used to do professionally before I bought my own restaurant."

"Of course, I know you can cook. I just can't remember the last time you offered to fix breakfast. You usually spend the time before leaving for work reading the newspaper or the antique magazine your dad subscribed to for you last Christmas."

"Well, today is different." Jeff kissed Rhonda's cheek. "I'll see you downstairs soon."

"Okay." Rhonda slipped on her robe and headed to the bathroom. *I wonder if Jeff will fix something I really like with the hope of getting me to agree to buy that house we can't really afford unless our place here sells.* She released a heavy sigh. *Decisions. . .decisions. . .decisions. . . I sure hope we make the right one.*

Jeff finished the final layer of yogurt for the parfaits he'd decided to make for breakfast, and he added a few sliced strawberries on top of each one. He sure hoped he could sway his wife into agreeing to get the house in Walnut Creek. He still couldn't get over the layout of that big home, and the large-screen television seemed to beckon him.

I'd like to come home to that place in the evenings and stretch out in my very own man cave. That room was unbelievable. I'd have a lot of fun watching all my favorite movies that Rhonda doesn't like. Jeff shook his head. *It's no fun here at the townhouse sharing the same TV—especially when we don't always want to watch the same shows.*

He set their parfaits in the refrigerator to chill and put away everything he'd used to prepare them. He then rinsed out the sponge by the sink and wiped down the messy surfaces. Except for the few dirty dishes that Jeff still needed to rinse off and wash, it looked like he hadn't done anything in the kitchen. He was pleased with the effort he had put into making breakfast so far and hoped all this would be worth it in the end.

Jeff's mind wandered as he used a sponge to scrub the small cutting board he'd used for slicing the strawberries. *I really, really hope we can get that house. I know Rhonda would like me to downsize my collection, but for now I'm gonna keep all my stuff, because I've worked hard to get them.*

Assuming Rhonda would be ready to eat soon, Jeff took out their chilled parfait glasses layered with vanilla yogurt and granola and placed them on the table—one near his spot and the other in front of Rhonda's usual place at the table. Just in time too, because a moment later, she entered the room.

He offered her his best smile. "Would you like a piece of toast or a bagel, along with your yogurt parfait?"

Eyeing the table, Rhonda gave a slow shake of her head. "You really know how to impress a woman, don't you?"

"I do my best." Jeff winked at her. "Especially for a woman as beautiful as you."

Her lips pressed together in a slight grimace as she took a seat at the table. "You wouldn't be trying to butter me up so I'll agree to buy that house, would you?"

Jeff's ears warmed. She'd found him out, and he couldn't deny it. "That did have something to do with me fixing breakfast," he admitted, "but I also wanted to do something nice for you."

She gave a quick nod. "Thank you for that."

Jeff pulled out a chair to join her at the table, but before he could sit down, his cell phone rang. He recognized the Realtor's name from yesterday in the caller ID, so he answered right away. "Hello."

"Hello, Mr. Davis. This is Shelly Lockhart. I wanted to let you know that several other people have shown an interest in the house you and your wife toured yesterday. So, if you are seriously interested in the home, I would suggest you consider putting an offer on it today."

Jeff's heartbeat raced a bit as he glanced over at Rhonda. With raised eyebrows, she leaned forward in her chair.

"Umm. . .well, I'll need to talk this over with my wife. Can I call you back in a few minutes?"

"Of course, but please don't take too long. My assistant just informed me that someone else is on the verge of making an offer on the same house."

"I'll get back to you right away."

When Jeff clicked off the phone, he sank into his chair and quickly related to Rhonda all that the Realtor had said. "So, I think we should agree to pay a bit more than the asking price, to make sure our offer is accepted."

"I'm not sure that's a good idea." Rhonda's voice sounded tense. "Maybe we should talk to your dad, or even my mom, and get their input."

Jeff lifted his gaze to the ceiling. "That's really a great idea, Rhonda. I'm sure your timid mother, who doesn't believe in taking chances, would be most helpful in giving us sound advice."

"Okay, I get what you mean, and maybe you're right. But you could talk to your dad about it. He has a level head for business."

"I've already spoken to him."

She tipped her head. "Oh? When was that?"

"Last night. You'd already gone up to bed, so I decided to give my dad a call."

"I see. What did he have to say about the situation?"

"He said the decision was ours to make, but if it were him and his business wasn't in Cleveland, he'd jump at the chance to move to Walnut Creek, where the pace is much slower."

Jeff glanced at the clock on the far wall. "We're wasting time, Rhonda. We need to give the Realtor an answer before it's too late."

She fiddled with the spoon on her placemat for several seconds. "How much more do you think we should offer?"

"How about another ten thousand dollars?"

She combed her fingers through the ends of her shiny brown hair before nodding. "Okay, let's go for it, but if our offer gets accepted, then we'd better get this place on the market right away."

At six o'clock that evening, Rhonda climbed into her car and rolled down her windows for some fresh air. It had been difficult to get through her day at work without thinking about the offer they'd made on the house of her dreams that morning after breakfast.

Although Rhonda hadn't been thrilled about taking on a mortgage payment while waiting for their townhouse to sell, the idea of living in Walnut Creek seemed like heaven right now.

Eager to get home, Rhonda started her car. She'd had a rough day at the hotel, and a few times she'd felt like quitting.

But I can't quit my job, she told herself. *We need the extra income to make ends meet, and we'll need it even more if our offer is accepted on the house.*

Rhonda would be disappointed if they lost out on the home in Walnut Creek to a higher offer. But maybe it would be for the best. At least they wouldn't be taking on a huge debt, unsure of when or if their townhouse might sell.

By the time Rhonda got home, she'd worked herself into a dither. She was glad to see Jeff's vehicle parked in the driveway and hoped that he might have started supper, because she didn't feel like cooking.

When Rhonda entered the house, Jeff greeted her with a wide grin. "The bank called me today, and we are pre-approved for the loan." He stepped forward and took hold of her hand. "And here's some even better news—Shelly Lockhart, the Realtor from Walnut Creek, called to let us know that our offer was accepted by the seller." He pulled Rhonda into his arms and gave her a strong hug. "We got the house, honey. Can you believe it? We actually got the house!"

Rhonda's thoughts became fuzzy to the point that she could hardly think or speak. "We. . .we did?"

"Yes, it's officially a done deal, and we've been approved for our loan. So now we need to get in touch with a Realtor here in Canton and get our townhouse on the market."

Perspiration broke out on Rhonda's forehead, and her stomach tightened. Although she still felt squeamish about all of this, she had to admit that she had fallen in love with that beautiful house. *And who knows,* she thought, *maybe Jeff was right when he said that moving to the rural area and owning a lovely home might be good for our marriage and improve things for us.* For the moment, at least, things looked more promising than they had in several years.

Chapter 4

"What are you doing over there on your computer? Since we both have the day off, shouldn't you be helping me pack boxes?" Jeff called across the room to Rhonda.

She looked away from her work and turned to him with a frown. "I'm responding to an important email from the hotel's corporate office, so this takes precedence over putting stuff in boxes. Besides, our townhouse hasn't sold yet, so I don't see what the rush is to get our things packed."

Jeff closed the box he'd been working on and marched across the room with both hands on his hips. "Need I remind you that by the end of this month the deal on our new home in Walnut Creek will close?"

"I realize that, but—"

"Once it closes, we will sign the final papers and get the keys. After that, we'll be free to move in."

Rhonda gave a brief nod. "Understood, but that doesn't mean we need to rush. There's some painting that will need to be done there, and I'll want to clean all the carpets." Rhonda was tempted to stop talking and get back to her unfinished email, but she decided to say something else before Jeff put in his two cents. She was too late.

"Listen, Rhonda, I don't see any reason why we can't wait till we're moved in to paint the rooms you're not happy with."

She gave a huff. "I don't want to fill rooms up with furniture and then have to move it all out to accommodate painting. It'll be much easier to paint with no furniture in the way."

"Any furniture you'll want to put in the rooms that need a fresh coat of paint can be stored in that oversized garage until the rooms are ready."

She shook her head. "That doesn't make sense, Jeff. For once, can't we do something my way instead of yours?"

His face flamed as he squinted at her. "My way, huh? As I recall, I'm the one who usually has to back down and do what you want."

"That's not true, and you know it. I agreed to buy the house in Walnut Creek even though I wasn't comfortable with the fact that our place here hasn't sold."

"True, but that's because you want the new place as much as I do."

Jeff was right. Rhonda did want that lovely home, but she wouldn't give in and admit it. Besides, her feelings about the house had nothing to do with whether they should move into the new house when the deal closed or wait until the painting could be done.

"We can talk later about what date we'll move in." Jeff got right in Rhonda's face. "But for now, what's it gonna be? Will you help me box things up in a couple of the rooms today?"

She released a heavy sigh before responding sarcastically: "Okay, okay, since you asked so nicely. Just let me finish this email and then I'll start filling a box."

He smiled. "Thank you."

She turned back to the computer. *As much as I might wish it, I seriously doubt that things will be better between me and Jeff by moving to a rural area.*

Jeff and Rhonda had been packing boxes for nearly three hours when Rhonda announced that she was hungry and stopped to fix lunch. "Would you like me to make you a sandwich?" she asked, bending down to tap Jeff's shoulder.

"Umm. . .yeah, sure. Just set it on the kitchen counter. I'll be in to get it as soon as I finish with this box."

"Okay, but what kind of sandwich do you want? There's some egg salad left from yesterday, or I can make you a ham and cheese if you prefer."

He shrugged. "I don't care. Whatever you make is fine with me."

Her brows lowered. "Really? You'll eat liverwurst if I fix it?"

Jeff wrinkled his nose. "No, not that, but I'm not worried since I haven't seen any liverwurst in our refrigerator lately."

"So, which one would you like me to make you—ham and cheese or egg salad?"

"I'll go with the ham and cheese."

"What would you like to drink?"

"A glass of water works for me."

"Okay." Rhonda exited the room, leaving Jeff to finish packing the box of old comic books he'd begun collecting since he was a teenager. There was no way he could leave those behind. Rhonda had asked him to throw them out, but he'd adamantly said no, mentioning that they were probably worth some good money.

Jeff put the last of the books into the box, sealed it with tape, and then put a label across the top. With a marking pen, he wrote the words "For Jeff's Man Cave."

Continuing to kneel in front of the box, he thought about how much bigger their new place was compared to this tiny townhouse. Regardless of what his wife thought, there would be plenty of room to display all his antiques and collectibles.

Jeff grinned and picked up a bag full of old marbles to put in the next box. He could hardly wait to visit Memory Keepers, the antique store he'd seen the day he and Rhonda had gone to their new house for the inspection. Jeff was eager to see what kind of collectibles they had that he could either buy or trade. In fact, on his first free day after he and Rhonda moved into their new place, Jeff planned to visit Memory Keepers.

Walnut Creek

"I can see why this store is called Memory Keepers," an older English woman said soon after she'd entered Lois and Orley Troyer's antique shop. "I see so many things here that remind me of my childhood and some of the things I used to see in my grandmother's house." She released a sigh. "I'll always cherish those wonderful memories."

Lois smiled from behind the front counter, where customers paid for their purchases. "Yes, many people who have visited our store have said something similar to that. I suppose all the fancy gadgets we see in our fast-paced modern world will be seen as antiques someday and people will look on them with fond memories."

The woman tipped her head to one side. "I'm surprised to hear you say that, since you Amish live a plain life, without a bunch of modern things."

"That is true," Lois said, "but I was thinking more in line with English ways rather than ours. But some Amish communities have become more progressive and have begun using cell phones, solar power, and battery-operated lights."

The woman's brows lifted. "Really? I didn't know that. But then, since I'm not from around here, I don't know much about the Amish other than what I've read or seen on TV."

"You can't believe even half of what you see or hear on TV or in the newspapers," Orley said as he strode from the back of the store up to the counter. "A lot of people have the wrong impression about us Amish. They assume without getting the facts."

The English woman's cheeks colored. "Yes, sir, I am aware of that. I only meant. . ." She stopped talking and turned toward the door. "Perhaps what I'm looking for is not here."

Certain that Orley must have hurt the woman's feelings, Lois quickly stepped out from behind the counter and apologized on her husband's behalf. "We tend to be a little touchy sometimes, whenever people criticize or misjudge our ways."

"I suppose everyone does." The woman gave a brief shrug and walked out the door.

Lois turned to face Orley. "You might want to be more careful what you say to our customers, Husband. Some folks, like that woman, won't be receptive to your blunt comments."

The wrinkles in Orley's forehead deepened. "Guess you're right. I'll work harder on my communication skills." He gave Lois's arm a gentle squeeze and shuffled off toward the back of the building again.

Lois lifted her gaze toward the ceiling. *I don't know what's gotten into that man of mine. He's usually quite friendly and all smiles with our customers, but today Orley was just the opposite. I hope he gets over whatever is bothering him before the next customer comes through our door.*

Since there were no customers at the moment, Lois went to the small room at the back of the store and grabbed her lunch. Orley had already opened his and taken a seat at the small table. He looked over at Lois with a sheepish expression. "Maybe I got a little grumpy with that English woman because I needed to eat."

She looked at him and scrunched up her nose. "Seriously?"

"Guess I need to work a little harder on my manners." He took a bite of his meat loaf sandwich and smacked his lips. "Mmm, this is good, *Fraa*. You sure make a tasty sandwich."

"*Danki.* I also brought some rich chocolate brownies with that mint frosting you like so much."

"You spoil me with your good cooking." Orley lifted the sandwich. "I'm going to enjoy this first, but I can't wait for the dessert." He tapped his insulated container. "A cup of hot *kaffi* from this thermos will go well with the brownie."

Lois couldn't help but smile, seeing the satisfied expression on her husband's face as he ate his sandwich. Sometimes, if there weren't any customers, they'd eat together in this back room. With the door to the room kept open, one of them would see if a shopper came in. They'd also be alerted by the jingle of the bell attached to the front door.

Lois reached into her lunch bag for her sandwich and took a bite. *I'm happy to say that this is good and my absolute favorite way to have leftover meat loaf.*

"If things stay slow today, would you like to head home early?" Orley asked after he'd taken another bite.

"I don't know. Why don't we wait and see how it goes?"

"That suits me just fine."

As she sat with her husband, enjoying their noon meal, Lois thought about the years they'd worked together in their antique shop. There'd been so many different items they had brought in and refurbished so that the old things could find new homes. It seemed odd to her that some people couldn't see that about their own families. Just because someone grew old didn't mean their worth was gone. Aging loved ones deserved the comfort of knowing they were loved.

Lois heard the front door open. She wiped her mouth with a napkin. "I'll take care of the customer so can you stay and finish your lunch."

"Danki." Orley grinned and reached for his bag of chips.

Lois hurried to the main floor and spotted an older man looking at a crystal vase.

"Good afternoon." Lois opened a piece of wrapped mint candy from the counter and popped it into her mouth.

"Yes, it is." He motioned to the container. "That's sure a pretty glass vase."

She nodded.

He moved ahead, looking around intently at some of the other antique merchandise.

Lois was curious, as the man seemed to be searching for something. "Are you looking for anything particular today?"

"I'm not sure. I mean, well, actually yes. I am looking for a gift for my wife." He paused for a moment. "She likes old things, so I figured I'd stop in here and see what you might have to offer."

"Does your wife collect anything in particular?" Lois questioned.

The man scratched his head. "She does have a few glass pieces around our home—like animal figurines, teacups with saucers, and plates that hang on the wall with different themes."

"We have some teacups and saucers along that wall." Lois pointed in that direction.

The man went over and picked out one of them. "Ah yes, I think my wife would like this."

Lois took the cup for him and stepped around to the back of the counter while the customer continued browsing. She thought it was nice that the gentleman was aware of what his wife liked. Apparently, he wasn't concerned about adding to one of her collections. *Some people don't appreciate their spouse's collections*, she mused. *I think we need to step back and allow our loved ones a little enjoyment in this life.*

It wasn't long before the man found two more old teacups he liked. He brought them up to the register, along with a decorative plate. "I'm going to get these for her too."

Lois rang up the amount and wrapped each of the items in heavy paper. The man got out his wallet and removed the amount of cash needed. He watched her carefully put each piece into the bag and then handed Lois the money.

Lois counted the change back to him. "I hope your wife enjoys her gifts."

He put his money away and picked up the bag. "I'm sure she will. I'm glad I came in here to have a look around. I may be back some other time. You have a nice variety of things here."

"Thank you." Lois watched the man go out the door. She then returned to the back room to finish her lunch.

Orley had eaten his food and now held open *The Budget* newspaper. "How'd it go out there?"

"Good. We sold three of those pretty teacups and saucers and a plate."

"That's nice." He rustled the paper after he'd turned the page.

Lois picked up the rest of her sandwich and started eating. Her husband was an avid reader and could pick up about anything to feed his need.

"What are you reading?"

"I'm looking at an ad for a new tractor." He winked.

"Seriously?" She popped the last bite into her mouth.

"No, but I am thinking of getting a new buggy."

"We have one already, Husband."

"*Jah*, but it's old. I have enough antiques around here." He chuckled. "I think it's time to invest in a new carriage." His gaze returned to the newspaper.

Lois shook her head and got out her brownie, placing it on a paper plate.

Orley looked up from the paper. "You'll like it, dear, I promise you."

"Are you talking about a new buggy?"

"Nope, I meant the brownie." He gave her a silly grin.

She chuckled. "You can have some of mine if you like."

"Okay, just one bite, and then I'll leave you alone." He picked up his fork, took a piece of the brownie, and popped it into his mouth. "Mmm . . . *gut* stuff."

Lois sampled hers. "You're right. It is good. I'm glad my mother gave me her recipe."

"I like her Dutch apple pie recipe too. Always good around the holidays."

She nodded. "Mom was into sweets and liked to try different desserts, so she'd get quite creative in the kitchen. Once she tried to make us a chocolate soufflé." Lois forked another bite into her mouth.

"How did it turn out?"

"It never did."

"Why?"

"Because we were too noisy, and it always fell." She laughed and finished the remainder of her brownie.

"Good one." He went back to reading again.

"Say, I was wondering if you could move that dresser for me out there in our show room."

"Which one?"

"The cherry-wood one. I'd like to add some things to it—maybe dress it up with some décor we have and see if someone takes an interest in it."

"I suppose. When do you want me to move it?"

"How about now?" Lois stood and put away her things from lunch.

Orley set aside his paper and also stood. "Sounds good."

They made their way to the dresser with Lois leading the way. It was a nice piece and in good shape for its age. Orley carefully moved it out to the place where Lois pointed. But then Lois didn't like the empty spot where it had been and wanted to move another piece of furniture to fill the space.

"Wait." Orley lifted his hand.

"What's the matter?"

"Are we going to move every piece of furniture around in this room?"

"Of course not. We're about done here. I just need you to slide that desk over a couple of feet." She pointed.

"Okay." Orley came around and pulled it into place.

"There, that's better." Lois looked at the dresser. "I'll start playing with some things to make it stand out a bit more."

"Sounds good." He turned and headed for the back room.

Lois watched him exit the main area and chuckled. *I'm sure he is going back to that paper to read it cover to cover. I'm glad we don't own a used bookstore. I'd never get any help out of him.*

Chapter 5

"There it is, hon. Aren't you excited?" Jeff pointed straight ahead as they approached their beautiful new home. "Can you believe this place is actually ours? What an awesome way to finish off the second week of May."

Rhonda couldn't mistake the excitement in her husband's voice as he drove his SUV up the driveway. She didn't want to throw cold water on their new venture, but she still had some misgivings about their hasty decision to buy this home, especially since their townhouse hadn't sold yet. Instead of voicing her thoughts, however, Rhonda smiled and said, "I wonder how long it'll be before the movers get here."

"Shouldn't be too long. I gave them good directions, and I'm sure they'll GPS it." Jeff set the brake and turned off the engine. "Let's go inside. We'll wait for them there."

"We could just wait on the front porch, since there's no furniture in the house yet." Rhonda gestured to the porch swing that the previous owners had graciously left behind for them.

Jeff shook his head. "There'll be plenty of time for sitting outside now that the warm spring weather has arrived. Right now, I'd like to go inside and walk through the whole house so we can be sure of where we want everything to go once the movers arrive."

"Good idea. I brought some signs along that I made up the other day. The numbers on them coordinate with what's written on each of the boxes we packed. I'll put the signs in the appropriate rooms so the men will know what goes where." Rhonda reached for her briefcase and stepped out of the vehicle. She'd planned to drive her car here today, but it was in the shop having some work done and wouldn't be ready until sometime next week. But that didn't matter, since she had put in for a few days' vacation in order to unpack boxes and get settled into their new home. Jeff would also be taking some time away from his restaurant, leaving it in the capable hands of his manager, Russ. Rhonda looked forward to some time away from the hotel, where she wouldn't have to deal with all the problems that went with managing the business. Times like last week, when three employees didn't show up for work without warning or explanation, left her with a pounding headache.

Rhonda hurried across the yard to catch up with Jeff. By the time she stepped onto the porch, he'd already put his newly acquired key in the lock and opened the front door. Prepared to follow him inside, Jeff caught Rhonda by surprise when he turned and swept her into his arms.

"Why—what are you doing?" she asked breathlessly.

"I'm carrying my bride across the threshold of our new forever home."

Nothing's forever, she almost said but decided not to ruin Jeff's exuberance as they entered the house.

"I can't believe it's ours." Rhonda smiled. "The empty living room seems to echo the sound made by my voice."

"For now it does, but once our furniture and the boxes start filling the empty rooms, the echoes will fade."

She couldn't wait to see this room and all the other parts of the house once they were filled with their belongings. Rhonda wondered how long it would take to unload the moving van when it arrived. The first order of business after their bedroom furniture had been put in place was to make up the bed so they could sleep in it this evening. There'd be no sleeping on a blow-up mattress, like they'd done on the night they'd moved into the townhouse at a later hour than planned.

"Now don't drop me," Rhonda murmured against Jeff's chest. "I weigh a few more pounds than I did on our wedding night."

"You're still a slender woman and just as beautiful as the day I married you."

"Thank you for saying that."

"It's the truth."

Her skin tingled beneath the warmth of his embrace. Once fully inside, and after Rhonda's feet had touched the floor, Jeff drew her into his arms and gave her such a meaningful kiss that it made Rhonda forget about the quarrel they'd had last night over another box of old things she'd asked him to get rid of. He'd ignored her, of course, and they'd ended up going to bed angry, without even saying a muffled *good night.*

Rhonda hoped there would be better days ahead, and if Jeff's heart-melting kiss was any indication of what was to come, she felt a ray of hope for them. Now if their townhouse would only sell, she could relax and enjoy the thrill of living in their beautiful new home.

Seated on the front porch with his teeth gritting so hard his jaw ached, Jeff checked the time on his cell phone. "They should've been here by now." He looked over at Rhonda, sitting beside him doing something on her iPad. "I wonder what's keeping those movers."

"If you're that worried about it, why don't you call the moving company? I'm sure they can contact the man who's driving the van," she said.

Staring out toward the road, Jeff tapped the phone against his knee. If he could will that moving van to show up right now, he sure would. "If they're not here in the next ten minutes, I will give that company a call. They need to know that the men they've hired are unreliable and more than a little tardy." He got up from the porch swing and began to pace as his agitation grew.

"For heaven's sake, Jeff, you need to calm down and try to relax."

Jeff's facial muscles tightened as he turned to face his wife. "I can't calm down. With every minute that passes without those movers showing up, I'm getting more irritated."

"That's obvious, and it's not good for your health." Rhonda pointed to the nicely greened lawn in their front yard. "Why don't you put some of your aggression to good use and jog around the house a few times?"

He frowned at the smirk on her face. "This is not funny, and I don't understand why you're so calm about the movers being late. You are the punctual one who never wants to be late for work or any appointment."

"But it's not me we're talking about—it's the movers."

"Exactly." Jeff looked at his cell phone again. "Pretty soon another hour will have passed with no moving truck in sight." He took in a few quick breaths. Normally, Jeff was the more laid back one in the family, but today was an exception. This was the kind of house he'd always wanted to own, and Jeff was eager to get their furniture and other belongings brought in so he and Rhonda could begin their new life.

He looked away from his phone and grimaced. "I don't want us to be unloading things at midnight, like we did when we moved into the townhouse. I want to have this all done today."

"We will, and you need to stop worrying. You becoming upset is not getting us anywhere."

"I can't help it. The movers should've been here by now. It's not that many miles from our townhouse in Canton to Walnut Creek, and that truck should be moving along a lot faster than one of those horse and buggies we saw on the way here."

Continuing to pace the length of the porch, Jeff paused to glance out at the road occasionally. Finally, he called the moving company, but no one answered, so he left a disgruntled message. Jeff hoped someone would return his call soon.

"Sometimes I think we oughta go back to the days when making a phone call meant you'd be likely to speak to a real person," Jeff muttered. "I'm sick and tired of always having to leave a message for someone who may or may not call back. I wish life could be less complicated, but I guess living in this century, that's not gonna happen."

Rhonda made no comment. She seemed engrossed in whatever she was doing on her iPad.

Jeff was on the verge of calling the moving company a second time when he heard the rumble of a vehicle coming down the road. A few seconds later, an oversized moving van turned up their driveway.

"Well, it's about time." Jeff turned to face Rhonda. "Would you please go inside and hit the buttons to open the garage doors? I'll direct the van to park outside, between the first and second bay. That way they can unload all the boxes into the garage."

"Sure." Rhonda left the swing and went in through the front door.

After directing the van to the spot where he wanted it parked, Jeff was tempted to storm over to the driver, who had just gotten out of the vehicle, but he held himself in check. No point in getting the man riled up when furniture and boxes needed to be unloaded in a timely and careful manner.

The middle-aged driver stepped up to Jeff, and a few seconds later, a younger man got out of the truck and joined the two. "Sorry we're late," the older one said. "We had a flat tire on the way here, and then our GPS messed us up and we took a wrong turn off the Interstate." His sweaty forehead creased, and he pulled a hanky from his back pocket to wipe off the moisture.

"It's okay. You're here now, and that's all that matters." Jeff heaved a sigh and led the way to the open garage doors. Hopefully, things would go better from this point on.

"I still think we should have painted this room before we moved all our stuff in." Rhonda felt hot tears behind her eyes as she surveyed what had once been a young child's room. *If only. . .*

Jeff slipped his arm around her waist. "Since we didn't ask the movers to put any of the boxes in this room, it shouldn't be a problem for us to get it painted soon."

"How about tomorrow? If we go after some paint in the morning, we should be able to have it done in a few hours."

"That won't fly. Tomorrow's Sunday, and you won't find much open here in Walnut Creek on what many people consider should be a day of rest." He shook his head. "I sure don't want to drive all the way to one of the bigger towns to look for paint."

"Maybe we could go to the hardware store in Millersburg tonight," Rhonda suggested. "It's not that far from here, and I'll bet it's still open."

Jeff yawned and stretched his arms over his head. "I am too tired to go anywhere, and I'm sure you must be too. We both worked hard today after the movers left, getting our bedroom furniture set up so we can sleep tonight—not to mention the things we did in the living room, dining room, and kitchen. We really got a lot done, which is why we're both beat."

Rhonda couldn't deny her fatigue. She'd forgotten how tiring moving into a new place could be. *Tiring and stressful,* she thought, looking around the nursery before turning out the light. "Guess I'll take a warm shower and get ready for bed. Maybe I'll feel more energetic in the morning."

Rhonda started down the hall toward the master bedroom. "Are you coming, Jeff?" she called over her shoulder.

"I'll be there soon. I wanna take a quick look at the news."

Rhonda halted her footsteps and turned to face him. "I assume you mean you'll be checking the news via your cell phone?"

He swiped a hand across his forehead before shaking his head. "Thought I might go out to my man cave and turn on the TV."

Her brows squished together. "Are you kidding me? When did you have time to set up your television?"

"While you were in the kitchen getting things semi-organized."

She anchored both hands firmly against her hips and frowned. "As I recall, you said you were going to see if there was room to park your vehicle in the garage. You also stated that you planned to set the grill outside on the patio so we could barbecue some steaks tomorrow afternoon."

"I did say that, and since the bay where I should be parking my vehicle is full of boxes, I parked it outside, near the third bay, which also has boxes, and came back inside." Jeff dropped his gaze to the floor. "Figured it wouldn't take long to set up the grill tomorrow afternoon, so I opted to get the TV up and running instead."

"I see." Rhonda looked upward, disparagingly shaking her head. "Don't wake me when you come to bed, because I'm sure it'll be late." She hurried into their room and closed the door before he could offer a response.

"Not that anything Jeff could say would matter anyway," Rhonda muttered as she laid a fresh towel out for the bath she'd decided to take instead of a shower. Some things would probably never change—like Jeff's addiction to his precious large-screen TV and all his nonsensical collections.

A minute later, he bounded into their bedroom with a sappy grin. "Rhonda, come see how nice the TV looks in the man cave."

"Right now?"

"Yeah, and I've got it on that home remodeling show you like so much. You know—the one with your favorite twin hosts."

"Okay, I'm coming, but I won't be watching it very long, because I want to take a bath." Rhonda followed him down the hall and into what she felt sure would be Jeff's favorite room.

Sure enough, her favorite fixer-upper program was on. It did look great on the large screen Jeff had displayed on the wall. Rhonda found herself taking a seat in one of the recliners.

"So, what do you think? Pretty cool, huh?" He grinned like a child with a new toy.

"Maybe this man cave thing isn't such a bad idea after all, as long as I—"

"I know, right?" He sat next to her for a moment, but soon his trigger finger hit the remote button, which changed what they'd watched briefly to another program.

"Hey, I thought you brought me out here to watch my remodeling program." Rhonda's brows furrowed.

"Well, I did, but there are so many other channels to watch." Jeff hit the remote button a few more times.

She stood up. "Okay, on that note, I'm going back to getting ready for my bath."

"All right, enjoy yourself. I'll be right here or, more to the point, probably in my recliner, checking out what else there is to watch."

"Have fun." Disgusted, Rhonda headed back to their room. She figured Jeff would probably end up falling asleep in that chair of his, and come morning, he wouldn't even remember the last thing he'd been watching.

Well, there was nothing she could do about it, and what she needed most right now was the opportunity to soak away the pain from working so hard all day. Hopefully, the warm water would also release some of the tension she felt in every part of her body.

Tears sprang to her eyes. *As long as Jeff puts his own needs ahead of mine, things will never get better between us. Even though we are now living in the house of my dreams, I doubt it will ever fill the void in my heart and soul.*

She moved across the bathroom as though in a daze and knelt beside the oversized tub to turn on the water. *Maybe I'm just overly tired tonight. After a good night's sleep, perhaps things will look brighter in the morning.*

Chapter 6

Canton

Sitting behind the desk in her office at the hotel, Rhonda was going over a list of things that needed to be done in several rooms on the second floor. Truth was, most of the hotel needed some upgrades, but the email Rhonda had received from the corporate office this morning informed her that only the necessary upgrades and repairs could be done at this time. So, now it was a matter of picking and choosing which rooms had priority over others.

I know the rooms with the balconies out front on the second level are normally the prime requests. And we have two larger suites with full-sized refrigerators that are popular with families. Rhonda shifted on her chair. *Too bad there isn't enough money to pay for all those rooms needing to be renovated right now.*

"I hate making decisions like these," Rhonda mumbled.

"Were you talking to yourself or me?"

Rhonda turned at the sound of the morning desk clerk's voice. She hadn't heard Lori come into her office. "I was grumbling to myself," she replied, hoping the smile she'd managed to put on her face looked sincere.

"Hotel problems, I assume?" Lori moved closer to Rhonda's desk.

"Yes, but then that's nothing new." Rhonda gave a small laugh. "It goes with the title of hotel manager, don't you know?"

The blond, curly-haired young woman gave a nod. "With me being pregnant and my crazy hormones acting up at times, I'm glad I am not in your position. My job can get pretty stressful on occasion, but I don't have nearly as many responsibilities as you're faced with each day. You must really like your job to put up with all the crazy stuff you're expected to resolve."

Rhonda shrugged. "I just do the best that I can." She watched Lori gently rubbing her stomach, wondering how it must feel to be pregnant. It was hard not to be envious of Lori's excitement over her upcoming birth. Her mild-mannered employee seemed content and cheerful as she sometimes hummed while doing the most mundane things at the hotel.

Rhonda's responsibilities here had become a part of her life. She'd enjoyed all the challenges that went with it at first. But lately, Rhonda had found herself daydreaming about how nice it would be if she could stay home all the time and enjoy the beautiful house she and Jeff had been living in for almost two weeks. With every passing day, it became more difficult to pull herself out of bed and get ready for work. What Rhonda wished she could do was putter around the yard, planting new flowers and shrubs, or recline on a lounger near the pond, absorbing the sun and listening to the gentle twitter of the birds making a home in their yard.

Pushing her wishful thoughts to the back of her mind, Rhonda turned her attention back to Lori again. "Did you come to see me for something specific, and is anyone minding the check-in desk while you're gone?"

A red hue erupted on Lori's normally pale cheeks as she shifted from one leg to the other. "I. . .uh. . .left the desk unattended, thinking I'd only be gone a few minutes and would hear the bell if anyone came to check in."

Rhonda tipped her head. "Where's Zach? He's also working today, right?"

Lori gave a quick shake of her head. "He never showed up."

"Really? Well, he didn't call in sick or let me know he wouldn't be coming in."

"I never heard anything either. Zach should have been here two hours ago, and now that leaves me at the desk by myself, with no one to fill in for me while I eat lunch or take a break."

"Well, he'd better have a mighty good excuse for his unexplained absence." Rhonda rose from her chair and gave Lori's arm a pat. "I'll help out today whenever you need to be away from the desk."

With lips parted, Lori released a noisy breath. "Thank you, Mrs. Davis. I bet you're the best manager this hotel's ever had."

"I don't know about that, but I always try to do a good job and cover all the bases."

Lori hummed a gentle melody as she went out the door and headed for the hotel lobby.

Rhonda followed. She hoped the rest of the day went quickly—she couldn't wait to go home.

Walnut Creek

Although this was not Jeff's normal day off, he'd turned the restaurant over to Russ's capable hands and taken off two hours early. There was a lot that still needed to be done in the way of unpacking boxes, but Jeff had other ideas this afternoon.

After driving a short way from his house, Jeff turned onto the street where several shops were located. He'd had his eye on one in particular and hadn't taken the time to visit there yet. With any luck, he might find something to his liking and go home with a prize to put on display somewhere in their new home.

If Rhonda knew what I was up to, she'd say a trip to the antique shop was a waste of my time and that I shouldn't spend money on something I don't need.

A short time later, Jeff pulled his rig in front of Memory Keepers Antique Store. It was an old building but appeared to be well cared for. The flower boxes outside bloomed with vibrant colors, and looking through the clear windows, he could see some of the treasures within.

Jeff's heart raced at the thought of spending the next hour or so browsing through a shop full of nostalgic things. His fascination with antiques and collectibles had begun when he was a boy, and it had never left him. In fact, the older he'd got, the more fascinated he'd become with things to collect. Some of the items he owned included vintage bottles and glass canning jars. Jeff also had a good many insulators, a few old-fashioned milk cans, and several ornate oil lamps. Then there were jars full of outdated buttons, buckles, and marbles in many sizes and colors.

Jeff got out of his SUV, and when he entered the old-style building, a slightly musty odor awakened his senses. He was greeted near the door by a middle-aged Amish man dressed in plain clothes and sporting a full beard but no mustache.

"Good afternoon. Welcome to Memory Keepers." The older man

extended his arm and gave Jeff a hearty handshake. "I'm Orley Troyer, the co-owner of this establishment. Feel free to look around and let me or my wife know if you have any questions or are looking for anything in particular."

"I will, thanks." *Between the way this man is dressed and being in here with all these antiques, I feel like I've stepped back in time.* Jeff had sometimes wondered if he would have been happier if he'd been born in a different era.

Without offering his name, Jeff turned away. He was about to wander off, when the Amish man said, "Is this your first time visiting our store? Don't think I've seen you in here before."

"My wife and I are new to the area," Jeff explained. "I'm a collector of old things and have wanted to check out your shop since we moved here almost two weeks ago."

Orley smiled as he fingered his beard. "I'm glad you stopped by. . .uh, what's your name?"

"Jeff Davis."

"Where'd ya move here from?"

"Canton. I own a restaurant there, and my wife manages a hotel in that town."

"So, you both have to commute to your jobs?"

"Yep." Jeff figured if he didn't walk away soon, the Amish guy would engage him in more unnecessary conversation. "Guess I'll take a look around now and see if anything in your store catches my eye."

"Certainly. As I said before, if you have any questions, just let me or my wife know. Lois is in the back room, but I'm sure she'll be out soon."

"Thanks." Jeff hurried off before the Amish fellow could say anything more. He wondered if all Amish men were as friendly and talkative as this one seemed to be.

Everywhere Jeff looked, he saw interesting items. A lot of old-looking trinkets hung on the high walls of the three sides of the interior. Some things had even been hung from the ceiling, like a couple of old bicycles and a few pedal cars. The owners used the shop's space effectively to house and display all its treasures.

Toward the back of the store, an old sled was propped against the wall. It was the kind Jeff and his cousin Larry used when they were boys and visited their grandparents on a snowy winter day. Being a few years older than Jeff, his brothers, Eric and Stan, hadn't shown much interest in the sled. But Jeff and his cousin used to argue over who would get the first ride down the hill behind their grandpa and grandma's house. When Grandpa died, Larry had been the recipient of the sled, as stipulated in Grandpa's will. Jeff was none too happy about it, but there wasn't much he could do. He'd had a sick feeling in the pit of his stomach the day Grandma had given the sled to Larry, while all Jeff got was a jar of old marbles to add to his collection. While he appreciated the marbles, they didn't have the same meaning for Jeff as the sled. Since Jeff's brothers didn't care about the old relic, they hadn't understood why he'd been upset when their cousin took the sled home that afternoon. While not as devastating as losing his mother to cancer the year before his grandfather's death, Jeff had mourned the loss of the old sled he'd wanted so badly.

He studied the sled here in the antique store a little closer and determined that it was very similar to the one he'd missed out on. Definitely from the same era as his grandfather's.

With a satisfied smile, Jeff picked up the sled and carried it to the front counter where the Amish man stood.

"That's an old one, and I've done a few repairs, so it's in fairly good shape," Orley commented.

"I agree. Can you hold it for me? I'd like to look around a bit more."

"Sure, no problem. I'll put it back behind the counter till you're ready to pay."

"Thanks." Jeff handed the sled to Orley and headed off to see what other goodies he could find.

Approaching a table where several items were for sale, he noticed an old yellowed plaque that quoted a Bible verse:

Be still, and know that I am God.
—Psalm 46:10

A sense of bitterness welled in Jeff's soul. He remembered the day the family's minister had read that verse before praying for Jeff's mother during the worst part of her illness.

I believed God would take away Mom's cancer, but she died anyway. A lump formed in Jeff's throat. *When the doctor told us that there was no physical reason Rhonda could not conceive, I prayed again, but no children came.* Rhonda had wanted to adopt, but Jeff said no. He had determined that if God wanted them to have children, He would have answered Jeff's prayer.

With a shake of his head, Jeff moved away from the table. *So much for praying and believing. I don't see how my dad could keep going to church and reading his Bible all these years.*

Out of the mood to look any further, Jeff made his way back to the register. "I'll pay for the sled now," he told Orley.

"Didn't see anything else that caught your fancy, huh?"

Jeff shrugged his shoulders. "I didn't look at everything, but I need to get home now anyway. Maybe I'll stop in some other time and see what else you have."

"I'll look forward to seeing you again." Orley's wide smile appeared genuine—not forced like some people's.

Jeff looked at the sled. *I can't wait to take this home and put it on display. I wonder what Rhonda will think of it. When I tell her that I've found a replacement, very much like the one my grandpa had, maybe she'll understand why I bought it.*

Jeff paid for the sled, picked it up, and said goodbye to the Amish man. There was something about the pleasant fellow that made Jeff look forward to coming back to Memory Keepers sometime soon.

After the English man left with his sled, since there was no one else in the store, Orley went to the back room to speak with Lois. She'd been in there for close to an hour, and he wondered what was taking her so long.

Upon entering the room, Orley found his wife sitting at her desk, tapping her pen, while wearing a perplexed expression.

"What have ya been up to in here? I expected you'd be out helping me soon."

"Helping do what?" She looked up at him. "Is the store full of customers right now?"

Orley shook his head. "Just one since you came back here, but he left a few minutes ago."

"Oh, then I'm sure you managed fine without me." Lois set her pen aside and scooped up whatever she'd been working on. Then she placed the notebook in a manila folder and put it in her tote bag. "Was it a new customer or someone we've met before?"

"The man's name is Jeff Davis, and it was the first time he's visited our store. Said he and his wife recently moved to Walnut Creek." Orley placed both hands on the desk. "He bought that old sled we acquired some weeks ago and said he might be back to look at other things sometime."

"That's good." Lois started for the door. "Are you coming, Husband, or do you need to stay here for a while and take a break?" She gestured to the chair she'd occupied.

"I'm fine—no need for me to sit here by myself."

"All right then. If you don't have anything else to do, would you mind helping me rearrange some of the things we put on that sale table yesterday?"

"Sure, no problem." Orley followed Lois out to the main part of the store. As they approached the table in question, he remembered how Jeff had looked at some of the items on it and scrunched up his face. Then he'd quickly made a beeline for the register to pay for the sled. *I can't be sure*, Orley thought, *but I have a feeling there's more to that fellow than just an interest in antiques. Sure hope I get the opportunity to talk to him again.*

Chapter 7

When Rhonda arrived home from work shortly before five that evening, Jeff waved at her from where he sat on the front porch swing. Since he'd said he planned to take off early in order to do some more unpacking, she figured he'd be inside doing that or at least finishing dinner preparations.

"You'll never guess what I bought today," he said when she stepped onto the porch.

"Some groceries, I hope."

Jeff shook his head. "Didn't know we needed any."

With her arms crossed, Rhonda squinted at him. "The grocery list was lying on the kitchen table. I mentioned it to you this morning."

"Sorry, I forgot." Jeff's tone of voice sounded apologetic, but his expression didn't convey any remorse.

She leaned against the porch railing, enjoying the warmth of being outside on this lovely evening in May. "If you bought something today but it wasn't groceries, where did you go shopping?"

"I made a stop at Memory Keepers Antique Store here in Walnut Creek." Jeff's eyes appeared bluer than normal as he grinned up at her. "I discovered something I've been hoping to find for a long time."

She tipped her head slightly. "What would that be?"

"A sled."

Her brows lifted. "Would you please repeat that?"

"I bought a sled." Jeff leaned forward with one hand on his knee. "It looks almost exactly like the one my grandpa used to own. In the wintertime, whenever we visited our grandparents, my cousin Larry and I would take turns sledding down the hill behind Grandpa and Grandma's house. Once in a while, my brothers would get in on the act too." Jeff paused and sat staring into the yard with a faraway look in his eyes. "Those were some good times, and I wanted a sled like that for my own."

Rhonda felt sure her husband had more to say, so she waited for him to continue.

Nearly a minute passed, and then Jeff's eyebrows pulled close and down, creating a forehead crease. "Larry got that old sled when Grandpa died, and I got a jar of marbles."

"It's nice that he left you both something. I assume his other grandchildren were recipients of some treasured item your grandfather owned too?"

Jeff gave a nod. "Eric got a pocketknife and Stan received Grandpa's harmonica."

"Did your brother know how to play it?"

"Not really, but I remember once when we were all sitting around a bonfire in my grandparents' yard, Grandpa got out the harmonica and played several songs for us." Jeff stared off into space again, and then he looked back at Rhonda. "Stan was interested in the harmonica at first, but after trying it once, he gave up and said it was too hard."

Rhonda wasn't sure what all of this had to do with the sled Jeff had just purchased, but she took a seat on the swing beside him and waited to see if he would say anything more.

"I wanted that old sled of Grandpa's really bad, and I've been on the lookout for one, but until today I've had no luck."

"You've never mentioned the sled to me before."

"I had no reason to until now." Jeff took hold of her hand. "Come inside with me and I'll show you."

Rhonda's mouth opened to ask why he'd taken it in the house, but before she could voice the question, Jeff stood and pulled her to her feet.

"It's in my man cave."

That figures. Rhonda didn't voice her thoughts. Instead, she followed Jeff into the house and down the hall. When they stepped into the room, her eyes widened. An old, worn-out-looking sled that in her opinion should have been thrown away hung in a prominent spot on the wall adjacent to where Jeff had put his large-screen TV.

"What do you think, hon? Isn't it a beauty?" The exuberance in Jeff's voice was clearly evident not to mention the satisfied-looking gleam in his eyes.

Rhonda cleared her throat before responding to Jeff's question. "There's no doubt that the sled is quite old." She pointed to the object in question. "I understand if seeing it brought back some childhood memories, but you're not a kid anymore, Jeff. Besides, since we have no children of our own, you'll have no one to pass the sled on to when you're gone."

His joyous expression faded. "I didn't need that reminder." Jeff looked up at the sled. "I can enjoy the sled while I'm here for whatever time I have left on this earth. I may even take a ride on it when the snow falls this winter."

She resisted the temptation to roll her eyes and mention that the piece of property their home sat upon had no hill for sledding. "I would prefer that you not have the old relic hanging here in the house."

"How come?"

Rhonda gestured to the sled. "Our new home is a showpiece, and there's nothing attractive about that sled."

Jeff stared at the sled for several seconds then reached up and took it off the wall. "Fine, I'll hang it in the garage on the side where I'll eventually park my rig, and you won't have to look at it."

Before Rhonda could comment, Jeff marched out of the room. She cringed when she heard the door leading to the garage open and slam shut. She'd gotten her way, but was it worth the price? Now she'd no doubt be fixing dinner by herself.

"Rhonda couldn't even say she was happy that I'd found an old sled that looks like my grandpa's or say one thing nice about it," Jeff muttered as he hung the antique on the garage wall. This wasn't the place where he wanted it to be, but Jeff got his hammer and added a nail in a decent spot so that when he pulled into the garage, the sled would be right where it could be admired. He'd brought it out here to keep the peace but saw no logical reason the sled couldn't have remained in his man cave. *I don't tell her how to decorate her home office, so I hope my wife doesn't ask me to move the TV out here too. If she does, that'll be the last straw.*

Jeff stood looking up at the sled. *Sure wish it was winter right now and I could try it out. Of course, I'd have to find the right-size hill for it without a lot of trees.* A wide smile spread across Jeff's face. *Think I'll take a drive this Sunday and check out the land that's farther out. Holmes County has lots of hills. I just need to find a suitable one that's not on someone's property. Maybe Rhonda would like to join me. It'll give us a chance to see more of the countryside. Maybe we could go right after lunch.*

A feeling of guilt crept in as Rhonda entered the kitchen to fix their evening meal. Jeff had been excited when he'd told her about the sled he'd bought, and she had thrown cold water all over his enthusiasm. Rhonda wasn't opposed to the idea of her husband having a few collectibles, but Jeff had more than he needed. The money he'd spent on them added up, and now, with a mortgage here, and a townhouse they still hadn't gotten a single offer on, she couldn't help being concerned about their finances.

An idea popped into her head, and setting the meal preparations aside, Rhonda left the kitchen. She entered the garage moments later and found Jeff on his knees in front of an open box full of collectibles. "How much do you think all the stuff you've accumulated over the years is worth?" she asked, squatting down beside him.

He jerked his head. "Umm. . .I don't know. I'd have to look up the value of each item on the internet or maybe in the antique collectors' catalog I get every month. Why do you ask?"

"Since we haven't sold the townhouse yet and there's no guarantee that an offer will come in soon, it might be a good idea if you sold some of your things, and then we could put the money into our savings account."

Jeff flinched as though he'd been injured in some way. "You're kidding, right?"

She shook her head. "We need some extra money as a buffer, Jeff."

"We're not going under financially. You have your job at the hotel, and my restaurant is doing well."

"I can't argue with that, but if the townhouse doesn't sell soon. . ."

"Let's give it another few weeks, and then I'll consider selling a few items that would bring in enough money to make it worth the sacrifice."

Rhonda looked away and gathered her thoughts. How could it be a sacrifice to part with a few old items that as far as she knew held no sentimental value? Other than the sled, of course. Jeff had made it clear that he'd bought the relic because it reminded him of the one his grandfather had owned.

Rhonda stood. "We can talk about this later. I'm hungry, so I am going back to the kitchen to get dinner finished. Are you coming, Jeff?"

"I'll be there as soon as I find a spot for the stuff in this box."

Rhonda's lips pressed together as she tromped out of the garage. *If I know my husband, he'll probably be out here for hours, and I'll end up eating my meal alone.*

Rhonda was almost to the kitchen when the doorbell rang. *Oh, great. I wonder who that could be. I hope it's not someone selling something.*

She hurried to the front door, and when she opened it, every muscle in her body tightened. "Mom! Wh–what are you doing here?" Rhonda glanced outside and saw her mother's ten-year-old gray minivan parked in the driveway. It wasn't like she needed a vehicle that big, since she lived alone and rarely had passengers.

"Is that any way to greet the woman who gave birth to you thirty-five years ago?" Rhonda's mother pushed a wayward piece of light brown hair behind her ear. "I figured it was about time I came by to see your new place." She gave Rhonda a hug. "You said you would call when you were ready for company, but I couldn't wait any longer for an invitation."

Feeling a sense of powerlessness, Rhonda forced herself to put on a happy face. "I'm glad you're here. Come in, Mom, and I'll show you around the place, but you'll have to excuse the fact that there are still some boxes sitting around we haven't unpacked yet." *Perfect timing, Mother. Now I'll feel obligated to invite you to join us for supper.* Rhonda glanced over her shoulder, hoping her husband had heard the bell. *Come out of the garage, Jeff. I could really use your support right now—especially if my mother starts asking too many questions about our reasons for choosing this home or begins nitpicking things.*

"I hope you haven't been overdoing it with all the work here that needs to be done. No doubt you and Jeff will be busy sorting through boxes for quite a while yet." Her mother paused and grabbed a hankie to wipe her nose. "Sorry about that. Spring allergies, don't you know?"

Rhonda nodded. "I hear the pollen count is higher than normal right now."

"True. It's the time of year when things are budding, but my doctor gave me something new to help with my condition."

"I hope the medicine works and you'll get some relief."

"I hope so too." Her mother glanced around. "This is quite the house. As big as it is, I'm sure it will cost a lot of money to cool in the summer and heat during the winter, not to mention your monthly payments on such a big home probably won't be cheap."

"Once we sell the townhouse, it will free us up financially."

"I'm sure it will, but until then, you two will have to pinch pennies."

"It's not that bad. I'm certain we can work through it all without a problem." No way would Rhonda admit her concerns.

Mom glanced at a nice-sized picture hanging on the wall where they stood in the hall. "Is that new?"

"Yes, Jeff got it for me."

"It looks expensive."

Rhonda reached up to rub a pulsating spot between her brows. At the moment, she wished that her mother had remained the mousy little woman who'd been afraid to take chances and didn't offer unwanted advice. But the divorce from Rhonda's dad and two years of counseling had changed all that. She still could hardly believe it, but within the last few years, Mom had gone from bashful to bold.

Chapter 8

Since it was time to eat, and Rhonda's stomach had begun to growl, she invited her mother to stay for supper with a promise of touring the house after the meal. Of course, Mom had happily agreed, saying she didn't get to see her youngest daughter often enough.

"The reason we see each other so seldom is because we both have jobs," Rhonda replied as she cut up some fresh veggies to go with the chicken and rice she'd put in the slow cooker that morning. "And when you're not working, you keep busy with Gwen and her family. If Jeff and I had children, we'd probably see you a lot more."

Mom took plates from the cupboard and set the table. "Speaking of Jeff. . .where is that good-looking son-in-law of mine? Since you asked me to set the table for three, I assume he must be joining us for supper."

"Yes, Jeff is here. He's out in the garage going through a box of antiques I am hoping he will get rid of."

"Collecting antiques can be an expensive hobby." Mom looked at Rhonda. "Now where do you keep your silverware?"

Maybe if Mom gets sidetracked, she'll drop the subject of antiques. I don't want to discuss it anymore. "They're right over there, in the drawer below the toaster." Rhonda pointed.

"Your new kitchen is the biggest I've ever been in." Mom slowly shook her head as she retrieved the utensils. "It's so full of storage. Why, I believe you have enough space for two families."

Rhonda hoped her mother wasn't dropping a hint that she'd like to move in with them. That would never work out. Besides, since Mom's house was close to Gwen's, Rhonda figured she ought to be satisfied.

"The kitchen is just right for us." Rhonda responded. "It's nice to have some elbow room."

Her mother stepped over to the table and placed the forks, knives, and spoons at each setting. "I understand. The kitchen in your townhouse was quite small."

Mom looked at the fancy clock on the far wall. "So, Jeff is out in the garage sorting his collectibles. That's got to be an expensive hobby." She returned to the cupboard for glasses. "His restaurant must be doing pretty well for him to be able to collect antiques, not to mention buying this beautiful home, which I'm sure must have been quite pricey." Her forehead creased as she turned to face Rhonda. "I hope you're not living beyond your means."

I had hoped Mom would let that subject go. I don't want to discuss this with her right now or any other time for that matter. Looking her mother straight in the eyes, Rhonda said in a low, firm voice, "Jeff and I are doing fine financially."

"Did I hear my name mentioned?" Jeff entered the room and gave Rhonda's mother a hug. "It's good to see you, June. I saw a minivan parked out front and figured it was yours. How have you been?"

She moved her head quickly up and down. "I'm doing well. How about you?"

Jeff glanced at Rhonda then back at her mother. "Can't complain. Has Rhonda shown you around the house?"

"Not yet." Rhonda spoke before her mother could respond to his question. "Dinner's ready, and I invited Mom to eat with us. I'll give her the grand tour after we finish our meal."

"Okay." Jeff moved closer to Rhonda. "Is there anything I can do to help?"

Yes, don't make my mother feel so welcome that she won't know when to go home. Rhonda shook her head. "Food's ready, so if you've washed your hands, you can go ahead and have a seat."

"I washed up in the utility room after I was done in the garage."

Rhonda wanted to ask what he'd decided to do with all the things in that box but changed her mind. It was a topic that could wait until later—when her curious mother was not around.

Jeff pulled out the chair at the head of the table and sat down. "That chicken sure smells good. I bet it will taste even better."

Rhonda forced a smile and looked at her mother. "Feel free to be seated. I just need to set the food on the table and then we'll eat."

"I can help," Mom offered.

Rhonda handed her the dish of veggies. "I'll get the rice and chicken, so you're free to sit down now."

"Okay."

Mom sat in the chair to the right of Jeff, and after Rhonda placed the rest of the food on the table, she seated herself on her husband's left.

Rhonda was about to pass the platter of chicken to Jeff when she noticed her mother's bowed head and closed eyes. *That's weird. Is she praying?* Although Rhonda and her sister had been sent to Sunday school and Bible school a few times when they'd stayed at their grandmother's house during childhood, her parents hadn't been churchgoers, and religion had never been much of a topic in their home. Rhonda and her sister hadn't even been taught to offer prayers at the table or before going to bed.

Rhonda sat quietly waiting for her mother to open her eyes and was glad that her husband did the same. Jeff did look over at Rhonda with a quizzical expression, however.

Once Rhonda's mother opened her eyes and lifted her head, Rhonda handed the chicken to Jeff. He took two pieces and set the platter next to Mom.

After each of them filled their plates, Rhonda looked at Jeff again, hoping he would get some conversation going, because she was at a loss for words. Apparently, Jeff was too. Of course, it would have been difficult to speak with his mouth full of chicken.

Mom remained quiet for a few minutes as she ate some of the rice, then she set her fork down, cleared her throat a few times, and said, "Gwen and I have been attending a Bible study at the church not far from our homes."

Rhonda nearly choked on the carrot she'd put in her mouth. She quickly washed it down with a drink of water. "Wh–when did you start going to church?"

"A few months ago. Gwen sent the kids to Sunday school at first, and then she and Scott began attending church services." Mom paused for a drink of water. "Shortly thereafter, they invited me to join them, and we've all been going ever since."

"This is the first time you've said anything about it to me. Why the big secret, Mom?" Rhonda's face heated, and her pulse began to race.

"It's no secret, really. It's just not something I wanted to discuss with you over the phone."

Rhonda shrugged. "What is there to discuss?"

"Well, I. . ."

"Let's change the subject, shall we?" Rhonda lifted the plate of veggies and held them out to her mother. "Would you like some more carrot or celery sticks?"

"No, thanks, I'm fine with what I have on my plate."

They finished their meal with minimal conversation, which was centered mostly around the pleasantly warm weather they'd been having this spring.

"From what I saw of your front yard and large front porch, it seems you'll have some nice places to relax during the summer months," Mom commented.

"Yeah, and the backyard's really great too." Jeff pushed away from the table and stood. "Rhonda, you can show your mother around the house while I put the dishes in the dishwasher. When I'm done, I'll meet you two out back by the pond."

Mom's eyes widened. "A pond? Oh, how nice that must be."

"Yep, and it's full of some colorful fish."

"I'll be eager to see it."

Rhonda left her chair and motioned for her mother to do the same. "If you'll follow me, I'll give you the grand tour."

As they went from room to room, Rhonda's mother gave several positive comments and even stated that she hoped Rhonda and Jeff would make many wonderful memories in this beautiful home.

When they entered the guest room that had been used as a nursery by the previous owners and was yet to be repainted, Mom slipped her arm around Rhonda's waist. "This would certainly make a lovely room for a baby. I wish you and Jeff would reconsider adoption."

A stab of regret shot through Rhonda like an arrow piercing its mark, but she pushed it aside. "As you already know, Jeff has never wanted to adopt, and I'd rather not talk about it." Rhonda stepped out of the room and felt relief when she saw that her mother had followed.

"Well, that concludes the tour of the house." Rhonda moved down the hall in the direction of the front door. Hopefully, her mother would take the hint and head for home without going out back to see the pond.

"I haven't seen the backyard yet. I'm sure Jeff must be waiting for us out there by now."

"Um. . .yeah, that's right." Rhonda felt more than a little rattled, especially after the mention of them adopting a baby. *Why did Mom have to bring that topic up? I wish I hadn't shown her the guest room with those balloons on the wall. For that matter, I wish Mom hadn't come here at all.*

Jeff took a seat on a wooden bench near the far end of the pond. He held a container of fish food in his hand but wouldn't feed them until Rhonda and June showed up. He thought his mother-in-law might get a kick out of watching the fish swim to the top with their mouths opened wide in eagerness to be fed. Having a pond with fish was great, but it also meant work, as the water would need to be kept clean without harsh chemicals that could harm the fish. The filter for the pump that ran the waterfall would also require regular maintenance. Even so, Jeff figured the tranquility it brought was worth all the work.

"Oh, my. . .what a lovely yard!"

Jeff turned at the sound of his mother-in-law's voice. "Come on over and see our exotic fish." He waited until June and Rhonda joined him, then he sprinkled a bit of food in the water. The fish swam over as quickly as he had expected.

June laughed. "Just look at them go after that food. They carry on like they're starving."

"Yep. It's an everyday occurrence too." Jeff handed the container to her. "Would you like to feed them?"

"Sure."

"Just be careful you don't put in too much," he warned. "Overfeeding can cause serious problems."

"Don't worry. I'll go easy."

While June fed the fish, Jeff looked over at Rhonda, who stood quietly to one side with her arms folded. Her somber expression made him wonder if something had occurred between the two women. Rhonda had mentioned several times in the past that she'd never gotten along well with her mom. Their perception of things clashed, even when Rhonda was a girl. According to Rhonda, her sister had been the favored one—at least where their mother was concerned. Rhonda had gotten along with her dad fairly well, until he'd left his wife for another woman ten years ago. Rhonda hadn't spoken to him since, and from that time on, her relationship with her mother had continued to decline. Although Jeff hadn't asked, he wondered if his wife blamed her mother for the divorce. *Could June have done something to drive her husband into the arms of another woman?*

Jeff's thoughts reverted to the present when Rhonda's mother handed him the fish food. "Thanks for letting me feed them; it was fun. I bet my granddaughters would enjoy seeing your pond and getting the chance to feed the fish."

"Sure. Anytime you're here, you're welcome to feed the fish, and so are the girls."

"If Gwen decides to bring the kids over, please tell her to call first to make sure we're at home," Rhonda stated.

"Don't worry. I'll make certain she calls you first. I probably should have done that too, instead of making an impulsive decision and showing up without an invitation."

"It's okay. We're glad we were here when you came by." Jeff looked at his wife. "Right, Rhonda?"

"Umm. . .yes, of course."

"I should be on my way home soon. No doubt my cat, Ginger, will be waiting for her evening meal." Her lips curved in a pleasant-looking smile as she looked at Jeff and then Rhonda. "I have a little housewarming gift for you, but I left it in my car. If you'd like to walk out with me, I'll give it to you."

"Okay." Rhonda's expression was one of eagerness, and Jeff figured it had more to do with the fact that June would be leaving soon than it did with whatever the gift was that she'd brought for them.

"We can walk around front rather than going through the house." Jeff led the way, and the women followed.

When they got to June's minivan, she opened the back door and withdrew a maroon-colored gift bag with white tissue paper sticking out of the opening. "I think this will go nicely in the front entrance of your home." She handed the bag to Rhonda.

"Should I open it now?"

"Yes, please do."

Rhonda reached into the sack and pulled out a beige-colored plaque with the words *God Bless Our Home* in bold, black letters.

A lock of hair fell on June's cheek as she tipped her head slightly to one side. "I hope you like it."

Jeff couldn't wait to hear his wife's response. He would let her comment before he said anything.

"It was nice of you to think of us." Rhonda had managed to put what Jeff felt sure was a fake smile on her face.

"Yes, thanks for the gift, June." Jeff hoped he sounded sincere. Seeing this wall hanging with the word *God* on it made him think about the plaque he'd seen at the antique store this afternoon. If there was one thing Jeff and Rhonda agreed upon, it was that they didn't need any part of religion in their home. While others, like Rhonda's mom and sister, might feel the need for that kind of thing, Jeff felt sure that he and Rhonda could make it through life on their own, without any help from God.

Chapter 9

"Let's go for a Sunday afternoon ride," Jeff suggested after he and Rhonda had finished eating their lunch on the back patio. "I hear tell from one of my employees that this area has a lot of nice open land. I'd like to see what some of the countryside looks like here in Holmes County."

"Seriously?" Rhonda's jaw clenched as she tapped her foot under the patio table. "What happened to our plans to open more boxes today? And don't forget that one of our guest rooms still needs to be painted."

"We unloaded several boxes this morning, and I figured we could both use a break this afternoon." Jeff finished the last of his lemonade. "Come on, honey, let's do something fun for a while. You know what they say about 'all work and no play.' "

She rolled her eyes and sighed. "Okay, but I don't want to be gone too long. There's still plenty we should get done around here, and since we both have to work tomorrow, we need to go to bed at a decent hour. No staying up till midnight, watching TV either."

Jeff bobbed his head. "No problem. We won't be gone more than a few hours."

"Promise?"

"Of course. When you're ready to come back home, just say the word."

"It's nice to sit out here on the front porch and relax, jah?" Orley smiled at Lois.

She nodded. "I can't think of anyone I'd rather spend my Sunday afternoon with."

He reached across the short span between them and took hold of her hand. "My feelings exactly. I knew the day we got married that I was one lucky fellow."

Heat rushed to Lois's cheeks, and she fanned her face with her free hand. Orley's compliments always made her blush—especially when he looked at her with such a tender expression, the way he was now.

"Our church service was good today, wasn't it?" she asked.

"Jah," Orley agreed. "The minister's sermon on loving our neighbors was a good reminder of how we should treat others."

Lois gave a decisive nod. "I appreciated his use of 1 John 4:12: 'If we love one another, God dwelleth in us, and his love is perfected in us.' "

"That's a good one, all right. But then there are many other fine verses that speak of love for others."

Lois glanced out toward the road in front of their property. "Did you notice how that vehicle slowed down in front of our place? I thought for a minute that it was going to stop or drive on in here, but then it finally moved on."

"I did make a mental note of it," Orley said. "Figured it was probably someone out taking a leisurely Sunday drive or heading somewhere they weren't familiar with. That can happen when people from out of the area don't know the back roads."

"True." Lois let go of Orley's hand and stood.

"Where ya goin'?"

"In the house to get some refreshments." Lois moved her brows up and down. "When we first got home from church, I saw you eyeballing those brownies I made yesterday."

He snickered and gave his belly a thump. "I wouldn't say no if you brought some of those tasty morsels out for us to enjoy."

"No problem, Husband. I'll pour us some iced tea as well." Lois stepped into the house and closed the screen door behind her. What a nice day this was turning out to be.

"It's sure pretty out here in the country," Jeff commented as he turned onto County Road 172. He glanced over at Rhonda, and she gave a noncommittal shrug.

"There are a lot of Amish farms out this way, and the ones I'm seeing so far are very well kept."

"I've noticed too and am amazed at the large gardens alongside or out in front of all the white homes we've driven by already," Rhonda said. "There were also no electrical wires running to their homes, and I've seen several houses with black carriages parked outside."

"Did you see those horses and buggies pulling out of that driveway a ways back?"

"How could I have missed them? They were all driving so slow." Rhonda spoke in a tone of agitation.

Jeff grimaced. His wife was obviously not having the good time he'd hoped she would on their little jaunt. "Those Amish must have been heading home from church."

"I didn't see any church buildings."

"They take turns holding Sunday services in each member's home, barn, or other large building on their property," Jeff explained.

"Who told you that?"

"No one. I read about it on the internet when I was looking up information on the Amish way of life."

"Why would you want to know about that?" she questioned.

"Just curious is all. Since we live in the heart of Amish country, I thought it would be a good idea to learn something about the culture of the Plain people who reside here."

"I see."

They rode in silence for a while, until Jeff noticed a house on the right side of the road with a nice-sized hill that looked perfect for sledding. He slowed the SUV for a better look and was tempted to stop. On second thought, he decided to keep going.

Jeff glanced over at Rhonda. Her eyes were closed, with her head leaning against the headrest of her seat. He wondered if she was bored or trying to take a nap.

After traveling a bit farther, he turned the vehicle around and headed in the direction from which they'd come. When his rig approached the place where he'd seen the nice hill, Jeff noticed a man and a woman dressed in plain clothes sitting on the front porch.

On an impulse, Jeff pulled his SUV into the yard. At the same time, Rhonda opened her eyes and leaned forward. "Wh–where are we, and why are you stopping here?"

"See that hill over there?" Jeff pointed.

"Yes. What about it?"

"I'm pretty sure it's part of the property that belongs to the people who live here." Jeff's anticipation mounted. "I'm gonna stop and talk to them about it."

Rhonda blinked rapidly as her dark brows squished together. "Why would you want to talk to complete strangers about a hill on their property?"

"Because it would be the perfect place to try out my old sled, and I'll need to get their permission to use it."

"Have you lost your mind, Jeff? Winter is six months away, and there won't be snow on the ground until then, if we get any at all this year."

He frowned at her. "Don't ya think I know that? I just want to pave the way so that when the time comes, I'll have a place to go sledding."

She wrinkled her nose. "Okay, Jeff, whatever you say."

Ignoring his wife's sarcasm, Jeff drove his rig up the driveway. As he drew closer to the house, Jeff was surprised to discover that the Amish man on the porch was Orley Troyer, the owner of the antique store he had visited. He chuckled. "What are the odds?"

Rhonda looked at Jeff with a curious expression. "What are you talking about?"

"That's the man who sold me the sled, and I bet the woman sitting beside Orley is his wife. What a coincidence. I can't wait to talk to them." Jeff opened the door and got out. "You coming, Rhonda?"

She shook her head. "I'll wait here, but please don't take too long. We need to get home soon so we can—"

Without waiting for his wife to finish her sentence, Jeff sprinted for the house. He was almost there when Orley stepped off the porch and greeted him. "Well, hello there, Jeff." With a wide smile, Orley extended his hand.

Jeff shook it eagerly. "You remember me?"

"Of course. I remember most of my customers—especially the ones who buy old sleds." Orley's smile remained fixed as he gave a quick wink. "Come on up to the porch. I want you to meet my wife."

Jeff glanced back at his vehicle, where Rhonda waited, wondering if he should include her too. After a few second's deliberation, he gave a wave and then motioned for her to join them on the porch. Based on the sour-grapes expression on Rhonda's face when she got out of his rig, Jeff figured if he didn't find a way to redeem himself, he might be sleeping in a recliner in his man cave tonight. In all honesty, though, sleeping out there wouldn't be the worst thing, because he liked his little getaway room. But Jeff thought better of the idea and decided to do something nice for Rhonda to keep the peace.

When Rhonda joined him on the porch, Orley and Jeff introduced their wives.

"Please take a seat and join us for some iced tea and brownies." Lois offered them a pleasant smile as she motioned to the two empty chairs next to the ones she and Orley now occupied.

"I'll get your beverages." Lois rose from her seat.

"Oh, don't bother on our account. We can't stay long anyhow. Right, Jeff?" Rhonda's question was spoken in a near whisper.

Before Jeff could respond, Lois went inside, and Orley spoke up. "Surely you can stay long enough for a glass of cold tea and some of these." He lifted the plate of brownies that had been sitting on the small table between his and Lois's chairs.

"Sounds good to me." Jeff plucked a chocolate goody off the plate and took a bite. "Yum. . .this is sure tasty. You should try one, Rhonda."

"No, thanks. I'm not hungry right now. I'm also trying to avoid eating too many sweets." She sat with her arms crossed and a stoic expression.

Jeff brushed some brownie crumbs off the front of his shirt. *Yep. I'm probably gonna be sleepin' in the man cave tonight. I wish my uptight wife could just relax and enjoy herself with these nice folks.*

Lois returned a few minutes later and handed Rhonda and Jeff each a glass of iced tea. Jeff took a drink and smacked his lips. "Thanks. This sure hits the spot."

Rhonda drank her tea too, and Jeff felt relieved when she looked at Lois and said, "Thank you."

"You're probably wondering why we dropped by, since I had no idea you lived here." Jeff directed his statement to Orley.

The older man smiled as he gave a nod. "I'll admit, I was surprised to see you."

With no hesitation, Jeff made known his desire to go sledding on their hill when winter brought snow. He ended by asking if they would mind.

"I'm guessing you're eager to try out that old sled?" The twinkle in Orley's eyes said he already knew the answer.

Jeff nodded enthusiastically.

"I have no problem with it, and I might be tempted to try a little sledding myself." Orley looked over at Lois. "What do you say, Fraa?

Would you have any objections to me and Jeff going sledding on our hill?"

"Of course not," she quickly answered.

"Maybe you womenfolk would like to join us."

Lois gave her husband what Jeff felt sure was a playful pinch. "No, thanks. I'll just watch from the sidelines and warm your insides with some hot chocolate when you're done having fun."

Jeff wasn't about to ask Rhonda if she'd like to go sledding—not with the way her posture had slumped.

In need of a change of subject, Jeff observed, "This is a nice place you have here."

"Thanks. Lois and I have lived in this home since we got married."

"Do you have a big family to help take care of your home and yard?" The question came from Rhonda and seemed to be directed to Lois.

The middle-aged woman shook her head. "It's just Orley and me. We've never been blessed with children."

"Neither have we." Rhonda placed one hand against her chest and released an audible sigh. "But I keep busy managing a hotel in Canton, and Jeff has his own restaurant to occupy his time. We also recently purchased a new home in the area and still have a lot of unpacking to do, so our lives are plenty busy." Rhonda nudged Jeff's arm. "We should go and let these two enjoy the rest of their Sunday in peace and quiet."

Jeff knew he'd better do as she'd suggested or he could end up sleeping outside on a chaise lounge tonight instead of in the comfort of his favorite recliner. It was nice to visit with the Amish couple. They seemed like good folks. But Rhonda had a point—Orley and Lois could probably use some time alone.

He stood and thanked Orley and his wife for taking time out to visit with them and also for the refreshments Lois had provided.

"You're welcome," the Troyers said in unison.

"Come by here or stop in at the store anytime you like," Orley added.

Jeff gave a nod. "Thanks, I will."

Once their goodbyes had been said, Rhonda and Jeff got into his all-wheel-drive vehicle. As they headed in the direction of home, Rhonda decided it would be best if she remained quiet. She was irritated that they'd wasted so much time at the Amish couple's home when they should have been unpacking more boxes. Rhonda also thought it was ridiculous that

Jeff had thought he needed to find a hill so he could go sledding. He wasn't a little kid anymore, and he ought to grow up and face his responsibilities as a man. Rhonda hoped that by the time winter arrived, her impetuous husband would forget about the silly notion of going sledding with the Amish man.

She rubbed her throbbing temples. Between her mother dropping by unannounced a few days ago and Jeff's unexpected stop at the Amish couple's home, Rhonda felt more stressed than ever.

Jeff bumped Rhonda's arm. "Aren't the Troyers a nice couple?"

She shrugged. "They seem to be, but then first impressions are not always accurate. The Troyers may not be as nice as you think."

"Don't be so judgmental, Rhonda. I believe they are genuine people. Remember, I spoke to Orley at his antique store, and he acted the same way toward me then as he did today."

She pursed her lips. "Oh yes, I'm sure. He wanted your business, after all."

"No, I'm certain it was more than that. Orley seemed genuinely—"

"I hope you don't keep making trips to that store—unless it's to sell off some of your antiques or collectibles that have some monetary value." She tapped Jeff's arm. "I assume they buy items at their store as well as sell."

"Probably, but I haven't decided if or when I'd be willing to part with any of my collections." Jeff kept his focus straight ahead.

Rhonda's fingers clenched her purse straps. *We'll see about that.*

Chapter 10

Canton

Monday morning Jeff arrived at his restaurant an hour before opening in order to put a few of his collectibles on display. He couldn't help being a little excited about doing this and hoped for some possible feedback from his employees and the patrons who would see his antiques. And by bringing the items to his business, Jeff would still be able to enjoy them.

Rhonda might not be too thrilled when she finds out I haven't sold any of my collectibles, he thought. *I don't intend to at this point either.*

Last night, Jeff had told Rhonda that he would be clearing out some of his memorabilia this morning, and she seemed relieved. Jeff had not specified, however, that he'd be taking them to his restaurant to put on display. He assumed his wife thought he planned to sell the items. His announcement, plus a little bit of time spent unpacking some more boxes after they'd gotten home from the Troyers had apparently been enough to keep him from having to sleep in the man cave. Of course, sleeping there would have meant more time to watch TV.

"Mornin', Boss," his manager said. "Do you have any more boxes to bring in?"

"Nope, this is all for now, Russ. I brought some of my antiques to put out on display." Jeff opened the lid and showed his faithful employee the contents. "Some will go on this shelf, and I'll place the milk bottles on the tables as a decoration."

Russ leaned in closer. "Those look like nice pieces."

"Thanks. It's taken me awhile to collect all these bottles." Jeff set the big box down and carefully took out one item at a time, arranging several of them on the shelf. When finished, he stood back and eyed his work. *I like how this looks. It wasn't such a bad idea after all.*

"Hey Boss, can you come over and take a look at the new menus we had printed?"

Jeff turned at the sound of Russ's voice. "Oh, yeah, I've been so busy I kinda forgot about those." He joined the middle-aged man he'd hired three years ago and looked at the counter where one of the menus had been set out.

"They look pretty good." Jeff smiled. "Hopefully, the new breakfast items we've added will be a favorite with our morning customers."

"Don't see why they wouldn't be. All the items we've currently offered have sold well." Russ bobbed his balding head. "The locals and many from outside the area come here to enjoy the downhome cooking we serve."

"I'd like to think so. That is what my restaurant is noted for—nothing fancy, just simple but tasty, nourishing meals like down-to-earth folks would get at home."

"Only better. Right, Boss?"

Before Jeff could respond to his manager's question, he heard the rumble of a truck out back. "I bet that's the delivery we've been waiting for. Would you mind opening the back doors for them to bring in the boxes?"

"Sure, I'll take care of it right now." Russ hurried toward the back of the restaurant.

Jeff picked up an old milk bottle from the box and placed it in the center of one of the tables. With the proper amount of water and some fresh-cut flowers placed inside, the glass bottle would make a nice centerpiece. Since Jeff had brought several other bottles like this one from home, he could put them on most of the tables. Those that didn't get a milk bottle would get something else—either a different kind of old bottle or a small glass canning jar.

Or, he thought, *I might drop by the Troyers' antique store on the way home this afternoon and see if they have some other kinds of milk bottles.*

Jeff cringed when his mind shifted gears, taking him back to a day when he was a boy, and he'd searched for and found an old soda-pop bottle in one of his grandpa's sheds, set way back on his grandparents' property. Jeff hadn't realized it until later, but the overgrown path he'd followed to the shed had left him with a nasty case of poison ivy. Due to the severe itching he'd dealt with for several days, Jeff had almost given up on the idea of collecting old bottles. But his fascination with antiques and collectibles had won out, and he'd kept pursuing his hobby, sometimes taking risks to dig up or scrounge around in search of old things.

The business phone rang, putting Jeff's thoughts on hold. He hurried over and answered, "Jeff's Red Barn Restaurant."

"Hey, Son, how's it going?"

Jeff reached up and rubbed the bridge of his nose. "Everything's fine, Dad. How come you're calling me on the business line instead of my cell phone?"

"I tried that number and all I got was your voice mail, so I figured I might catch you at the restaurant."

"And so you did. Anything new with you?" Jeff wasn't about to admit to his father that he'd left his cell phone at home that morning. *He might think I'm irresponsible.*

"Actually, there is something new in my life, but I'd like to wait and tell you in person. Is it okay if I drive down this weekend? I'd like to see your new place and spend a little time visiting with you and your lovely wife."

Jeff shifted the receiver to his other ear. "I'll be busy most of Saturday, painting one of our guest rooms, but Sunday is free. At least I hope it is, unless Rhonda comes up with some other project for me."

"The drive from Cleveland will take me about an hour and a half, and I wouldn't be able to come until church is over, which wouldn't give us as much time to talk as I'd like. How about if I come Saturday morning? I'll help you do the painting."

Jeff tapped his fingers on the countertop as he thought about the promise he'd made to his wife last night, agreeing to paint the guest room this coming weekend. "Yeah, Dad, Saturday would be fine, and I appreciate your offer to help paint. Between the two of us, we can get the job done twice as fast as I would painting the room by myself."

"Great. I'll see you around 9:00 a.m. on Saturday. Or is that too early?"

"Nine's fine. Talk to you soon, Dad."

After Jeff said goodbye, he bonked his head. *Sure hope I did the right thing. Since Dad and I don't see eye-to-eye on his Christian viewpoints, I'll have to be careful what I say if that topic comes up. I don't want to end the day feeling stressed out, the way Rhonda did after her mother dropped by our house unannounced.*

Jeff picked up another antique milk bottle to set on the next table.

At least my wife and I are like-minded when it comes to our lack of religious beliefs. If I could just make her understand how important old relics like this are to me. Sure wish she shared my interest in antiques.

A knock sounded on Rhonda's office door, and she looked up from her paperwork. "Come in."

A few seconds later, Lori stepped into the room, wearing a deep frown. "I. . .I have some bad news." With fluttery hand movements, she spoke in an emotion-choked voice.

"What is it? You're obviously upset."

"Thirty mattresses and box springs were just delivered, and they're sitting in the middle of the hotel lobby."

"Did you tell the people who delivered the mattresses what rooms they should be put in?"

"I. . .I couldn't; they unloaded them quickly and then took off." Lori's hands dropped limply to her sides. "I didn't even know the mattresses were being delivered today. Did you?"

"No, I did not. All the corporate office told me was that the company they had ordered them from would let me know when they had a firm delivery date." Rhonda gathered her wits about her and stood. "Please get ahold of the maintenance man and all the housekeepers. You can watch the desk while the rest of us haul the mattresses and box springs to their appropriate rooms."

"Okay." Lori placed both hands on her belly as she hurried from the office.

Rhonda leaned against her desk and brought a shaky hand to her forehead. Last night she'd been upset with Jeff when he'd quit helping her unpack boxes and gone in to watch TV, and now this? *How much more stress can I handle?* At the moment, she wished she could walk away from this job, go home, and sit by the pond for the rest of the day with a cold drink in her hands.

But I can't quit, Rhonda told herself. *We'd never be able to make the mortgage payment every month if I weren't working. If we'd just get an offer on the townhouse, it would help.*

With a determination she didn't feel, Rhonda forced herself to leave the room and head for the lobby to face the items waiting for her and the rest of the employees.

Walnut Creek

Orley had been talking with an Amish man named Jake Miller from their church district, when he caught sight of Lois wearing her dark outer bonnet and carrying one of her larger purses as she headed for the front door.

He excused himself from Jake and hurried over to Lois. "Are you going somewhere?"

She gave a brief nod. "I. . .I have an errand to run."

"How long will you be gone?"

"It shouldn't take long." Lois offered Orley a close-lipped smile and rushed out the door.

His brows furrowed. *I wonder why my fraa always has so many errands to run. She's seemed a bit preoccupied here of late too. I hope Lois isn't keeping anything from me.* He watched out the window as she walked briskly down the sidewalk. *Maybe she hasn't been feeling well and has gone off to see the doctor without telling me. Think I'm gonna come right out and ask her about it when she gets back to the store.*

Orley returned to his customer, who now had an antique clock in his possession. "Would you take fifty dollars less for this than what you have on the sticker?" Jake asked.

Orley reached up and gave his earlobe a tug. "I could knock twenty-five off for you. Would that be agreeable?"

The man tilted his head from side to side a few seconds then grinned and said, "It's a deal."

Orley got out a cardboard box and some packing material and met Jake up front at the register. He wrapped the clock securely and placed it carefully inside the box.

Jake pulled out his wallet and paid Orley in cash. "My fraa's *gebottsdaag* is next week, and this will be a nice gift for her."

Orley smiled. "I hope Edna likes it, and please tell her happy birthday from me and Lois."

"I will." Jake picked up the box, and with a little whistle, he strode out the front door.

Since there were no other customers in the store, Orley decided this would be a good time to go into the back room and get himself a snack. He'd only made it halfway there when the bell above the door jangled. He turned and saw Jeff Davis step in.

"Well, this is a pleasant surprise," Orley said. "I was hoping I would get to see you again. Just didn't expect it would be this soon."

Jeff smiled. "I'm on a mission."

Orley tipped his head. "And what would that be?"

"I'm giving my restaurant a facelift and need some old milk bottles for the rest of my tables that currently have no centerpiece."

"I believe I can help with that." Orley pointed to a shelf on the left side of the room. "There are plenty of milk bottles in different sizes and shapes to pick from."

"Sounds good. I'll take a look." Jeff moved to the other side of the room, and Orley followed.

"Lois and I enjoyed our brief visit with you and your wife yesterday."

"I appreciated it too."

"And your wife? Did Rhonda like visiting with us?" It was probably a bold question, but the words slipped off Orley's tongue before he thought it through.

Jeff's cheeks reddened. "I believe she did, but she was a little put out with me for staying at your place too long and then not getting enough unpacking done at home."

"Sunday is supposed to be a day of rest," Orley stated. "Maybe some time away from unloading boxes was good for both of you."

"Yeah, that's how I felt, but Rhonda tends to be a workaholic. And I had promised her that we'd get a lot of unpacking done over the weekend, which didn't happen, even though I did get a few boxes unloaded." Jeff sighed as he rubbed the back of his neck. "Things have been strained between me and my wife for some time, and I had hoped by moving to a more relaxed atmosphere and settling into a new home that things would get better. I sure wish there was something I could do to make things better between us and cause Rhonda to smile whenever she looks at me."

Orley leaned in closer. "Would you like my advice?"

"Uh. . .sure."

"Maybe you should give your wife a nice gift or a pretty bouquet. Lois has always responded favorably whenever I've given her special gifts or flowers."

Jeff slowly nodded. "That's not bad advice. Thanks for the suggestion."

Orley grinned. "You're most welcome. You'll have to drop by again and let me know if your wife responded well to your gesture."

"I'll do that, and before going home, I think I will go to the local flower shop and get a nice bouquet for Rhonda."

Orley gave Jeff's shoulder a few taps. "Next time you come by the store, you should bring your wife with you. I'm sure Lois would enjoy getting better acquainted with Rhonda."

"Okay, I'll give her that invitation." Jeff pointed to the shelf overhead. "Now about those bottles. . ."

Soon after Jeff left the store, Lois returned.

"Are you feeling okay?" Orley asked, stepping up to her.

Tipping her head to one side, Lois pursed her lips. "I'm fine. Why do you ask?"

"Oh, no particular reason. You just haven't seemed like yourself here of late. If there was something wrong, you'd tell me, wouldn't you?"

Lois gave Orley's arm a gentle squeeze. "There's nothing wrong, Husband. If I didn't feel well, I would speak up."

Although Orley felt relieved, he still wondered why Lois always had so many errands to run and why she never explained where she planned on going. It seemed like a mystery to him—one he had no answers for.

Before Orley got the chance to ask Lois anything more, an English man and a woman came into the store. They didn't appear to be together, so Orley asked the man if he needed assistance while Lois spoke with the woman.

Once Orley directed the man to the section where old tools were displayed, he stood off to one side with his arms folded. *If I don't get busy with something this evening and end up forgetting about it, I plan to ask Lois a few more questions. I don't want to be suspicious, but I do have a feeling she's hiding something from me.*

Chapter 11

When Jeff pulled his rig in front of the garage, he was disappointed to see that Rhonda's car wasn't there. Since he'd taken the time to stop at the antique store and then the flower shop, he figured his wife would be home from work by now.

Maybe something came up at the hotel and she had to work later than usual, he reasoned. *Or she might have made a stop on the way home to pick up some groceries or a take-out meal for our supper.*

Jeff got out of his vehicle and reached into the backseat to get the dozen red roses he'd purchased for Rhonda. The florist had placed the flowers inside cone-shaped plastic wrap, and Jeff wanted to put them in a vase with some water as soon as possible.

He hurried up the walk and stepped onto the porch then put his key in the door and turned the knob. Upon entering, Jeff headed straight for the kitchen to look for a vase. After searching through all the cupboards, Jeff came to the conclusion that there were no vases in the kitchen. Most likely they were still in a box in the garage.

"We've gotta get the rest of those boxes opened and things put away," he muttered. "They're taking up the space where we should be parking our vehicles."

Jeff snapped his fingers when an idea popped into his head. *An old canning jar would make the perfect vase for the flowers.* He left the roses on the table and hurried out to the garage.

When Rhonda drove into the yard, she saw Jeff's SUV parked outside the garage. "Good, he's home. I hope he got supper started."

Every muscle in Rhonda's body ached. She couldn't wait to spend some time in the soaking tub. Hauling mattresses and box springs into guest rooms was not on her list of managerial duties. When Rhonda had been hired for the job, she'd been told that she would be responsible for recruiting, training, and supervising the staff. She would also be expected to manage budgets, maintain financial records, plan maintenance work, set up hotel events, and book rooms. In addition to all that, Rhonda would need to handle customer complaints, promote and market the business, and make sure the hotel complied with health and safety regulations and licensing laws. There was no question about it—Rhonda had a lot on her plate. But the job provided a decent salary, and keeping busy helped take her mind off troubles at home or conflicts with her mother and sometimes her sister.

Rhonda reached for the carnations, protected by plastic wrap, and got out of the car. The flowers at the check-in counter had been replaced today. Since they still had some life left in them, Rhonda had brought them home to enjoy and add a little brightness to the rest of her day rather than throw the flowers out.

When Rhonda entered the kitchen, she was surprised to see red roses on the kitchen table.

Now how did those get there? Could Jeff have bought them? She poked her tongue against the inside of her cheek. *Today's not my birthday, our anniversary, or any other special occasion, so what would have prompted him to buy flowers?*

Opening the door under the kitchen sink, she took out two cut-glass vases. After filling them with water, she put the carnations in one vase and the roses in the other. Then, placing them both on the table, she headed down the hall in search of Jeff.

Rhonda was halfway between the kitchen and living room when she saw Jeff coming toward her with an old canning jar in his hand.

"Oh, good, you're home; I have something for you." Jeff gave Rhonda a kiss on the cheek.

"You mean the roses?"

"Yeah. I picked them up at the flower shop in town. Do you like them?"

"They're beautiful, and as you know, my favorite flower." She tipped her head back to give him better eye contact. "Was there any particular reason you bought me flowers?"

"Just wanted to do something special for you."

"Thank you."

He smiled and held up the jar. "I couldn't find any vases, so I went out to the garage and found this in one of the boxes."

"No need for that now. I had put a couple of vases under the kitchen sink."

"I never thought to look there." Jeff thumped the side of his head. "Dummy me."

Rhonda shook her head. "You're not dumb. Guess I should have mentioned that I had put them there, but since you rarely buy me flowers. . ." Her voice trailed off. "Sorry, I just meant that. . ."

"It's okay. I'll work a little harder at being more attentive." He caressed her cheek with his thumb. "You look tired. Did you have a rough day at the hotel?"

She touched both temples while closing her eyes. "You have no idea."

"What happened?"

Rhonda opened her eyes and clasped his hand. "Let's go to the kitchen. I'll tell you about it while I fix supper."

"I have a better idea." Jeff gave Rhonda what appeared to be a heartfelt smile. "You can sit at the table, and I'll fix us something to eat."

Rhonda pressed a palm against her chest. "Thank you, Jeff. I would appreciate that very much."

When they entered the kitchen, Jeff's gaze went to the table where she'd set the two vases filled with flowers. "You bought yourself some flowers too?" His brows lifted high on his forehead.

"No, they came from the hotel lobby and were replaced by a new bouquet," she explained. "Since the carnations had a few days' life left in them, I didn't want to throw the pretty flowers out. Besides, I'd hoped their lovely aroma and soft, muted pink color might help me relax."

Jeff set the glass jar on the counter, pulled Rhonda into his arms, and gently patted her back. "I'm sorry you had a rough day. I wish we both had jobs that could be done from home so we'd have more time to be here at our beautiful place."

Rhonda took a seat at the table. "This house and property are like a sanctuary for me. At the end of a workday, I find myself more eager than ever to come home." She released a lingering sigh. "Although working from home is a pleasant thought, it's not likely to happen since both of our jobs require us to be in Canton."

"True." Jeff opened the refrigerator and took out two bison-burger patties from the bottom freezer. "I'll thaw these in the microwave and then cook 'em on the outdoor grill. How's that sound?"

"Delicious." Rhonda's stomach growled, reminding her that she'd missed lunch today due to all the craziness with the mattresses and a few other disturbances.

"You went in a little earlier than usual this morning. How did your day go at the restaurant?" she asked, keeping her focus on Jeff.

"Not too bad. And I'll get to the reason why I went to work earlier, but first I'll mention something else. We got our new menus, and the fresh items we offered seemed to be well liked by the customers who ordered them."

"That's good. A little change is always nice. It gives people a reason to keep coming back."

"Yeah." Jeff placed the meat patties on a plate. "And now the reason as to why I went to work earlier. I wanted to spend some time changing things up a bit, to give the restaurant a more country feel. I decided that the decor should go along with what folks might expect when they come into a restaurant that resembles an old barn."

"What did you do to accomplish that?"

"I set some of my old bottles and jars on the tables as centerpieces. I also put some on a few shelves up on the walls." He glanced over at her and grinned. "Now you won't have to worry about lookin' at those old relics sitting around here."

While Rhonda would have preferred that her husband had sold some of his bottles and jars, at least he had taken them out of the garage and most likely emptied another box in the process. Determined not to say anything negative that could spoil this pleasant time of being together, Rhonda kept her thoughts to herself.

He cleared his throat. "Did you hear what I said, Rhonda?"

"Umm. . .you mean about the old relics?"

"No, actually I had moved on to another topic."

"What about?"

"I was telling you that if I hadn't left my cell phone at home this morning, I could have gotten some pictures of the tables and you could have seen how nice they look now."

"You'll be there tomorrow, so you can take some pictures then."

"Good point." Jeff put the plate in the microwave and set the timer to defrost the patties. "I got a phone call from my dad today."

"That's nice."

"Being caught off guard, I asked him why he was calling me on the business line instead of my cell phone."

"Did you explain that you'd left it at home?"

"No. I felt embarrassed and dumb at the same time when Dad said all he'd gotten was my voice mail, which was why he called the restaurant's number."

"Don't let it bother you. We all forget things at times." Rhonda shifted in her seat. "How's everything going with him?"

"Okay, I guess. He asked if he could come here on Saturday, and when I mentioned that I'd be painting the guest room, he volunteered to help." Jeff moistened his lips with the tip of his tongue. "Are you okay with that?"

"Certainly. Especially since it means that spare room will get done, and we can finally use it for overnight guests." She sucked in her lower lip. "Although, I can't imagine who would ever spend the night. With my mom and sister living in New Philly, it's not likely that they'd ever need to stay all night with us."

"What about your nieces?" Jeff asked. "It might be fun to have Megan and Kimberly sleep over some weekends."

"I'll give that idea some thought." Rhonda leaned close to the vase filled with roses and inhaled deeply of their fragrant aroma. *Having Gwen's girls stay here for even one night would only remind me that Jeff and I have no children of our own.* She clenched her fingers while holding them in her lap. *Do I really need that reminder?*

Redirecting her thoughts, Rhonda focused on the beautiful bouquet from Jeff. It had been a long time since he'd given her flowers, and she appreciated the sweet gesture.

I need to make an effort to do more thoughtful things for him too. She tapped her fingers. *Let's see now. . .should I make a list. . .*

"This is a mighty good chicken-and-rice casserole you fixed for our *nachtesse* this evening." Orley looked across the table at Lois and smiled.

"Danki. I made our supper dish this morning before we left for the store, so when we got home, all I had to do was warm it in the oven."

He wiped his mouth on a napkin and leaned a bit closer to her. "There's something I've wanted to ask you."

She quirked an eyebrow. "What's that?"

"Do you still enjoy working at the store, like you did when we first opened the business? Or have you become bored with it?"

"Of course, I'm not bored. What made you ask such a question?"

"For the past month or so, you've been gone from the store more than usual, running errands and who knows what else? When we first opened Memory Keepers, you seemed to like it, but here lately you appear to be preoccupied with other things."

Lois waved his question aside. "Everything is fine. I've just had more errands to run lately."

Orley decided to be more direct with his next question. "What kind of errands have you had to run that've taken you away from the store several times a week for the past few months?"

Small circles of red erupted on Lois's cheeks. "Why would you care about that? Are you worried that I may have been buying things I don't need?"

He shook his head vigorously. "Of course not. I'm just curious since you are gone a lot."

"Oh, I go here and there. It seems like there's always so many things to be done."

"Well, um. . ."

Their conversation was interrupted when a knock sounded on the front door. Orley rose from his seat. "I'll go see who that is." He hurried from the room.

Lois got up and cleared the table. During the couple trips made back and forth from the dining room, she glanced at her mending basket. *My, my, that basket of mine has a pile of work needing to be done. With so many other things I'm expected to do, I don't know when I'll get around to doing any mending.*

After placing all the dishes and silverware on the counter, she ran warm water and liquid detergent into the kitchen sink. She'd only gotten the dishes put into the water when Orley returned to the kitchen and announced that their closest neighbor's cows had gotten out, and some of them were roaming around in their yard.

"So, I'm going out to help Abe round up the cows and get them herded back over to his pasture."

"I hope it goes well, and please be careful."

"I will. Don't worry. See you soon." Orley quickly exited the room.

As Lois washed the dishes, she thought about the brief conversation she and Orley had at the table. It appeared that her husband didn't trust her and felt the need to ask those questions. She wished there were something she could do to put his mind at ease.

As Lois sloshed the sponge across one of the plates and scrubbed it thoroughly, she looked out the window at Orley and their neighbor herding the cows out of their yard. *No matter how busy I am with other things, I'll make a concentrated effort to spend more time with him, either here at home or at the shop. Hopefully, that will put my husband's concerns to rest.*

Chapter 12

At nine o'clock sharp, Jeff glanced out the kitchen window and saw his dad's convertible pull into the yard. The sporty-looking vehicle he drove was an eye catcher for a man in his midfifties.

What's up with my dad? I don't get it. When he and Mom were together, he drove an older sedan, and he seemed okay with it. Why the sudden change? Jeff shook his head and tried to compose himself.

"My dad's here," he called to Rhonda.

She stepped into the kitchen from the dining room, where she'd been unloading a box of her good dishes into the hutch. "Should I let him in, or did you want to greet your dad at the door?"

"Guess we could do it together." Jeff moved closer to Rhonda and put his arm around her waist. They walked down the hall, and he opened the front door.

Jeff watched as his father got out of the car and came up the walkway carrying a canvas satchel. Dad's trim but muscular body and full head of dark hair made him look much younger than his fifty-seven years. Jeff hoped he would look that good when he reached his father's age.

"It's good to see you, Son," Dad said when he'd stepped onto the porch. "And you as well, Rhonda." He greeted Jeff with a hearty handshake and a hug and then hugged Rhonda.

"Hi, Dad. Nice to see you too." Jeff invited his father inside.

"Welcome to our home, Don." Rhonda motioned to the three boxes stacked in the entryway. "As you can see, we haven't fully unpacked yet. It's my goal today to open these and find a suitable place for everything inside."

Jeff's father gave an ample, white-toothed smile. "As big as this place looks from the outside, I'm guessing there'll be more than enough room for all of your things." He set his satchel on the floor. "How about giving me a tour of the house before we begin painting?"

Just look at his teeth. I've never seen them look so white. Jeff tried not to stare and gave a hearty nod. "Of course. That's what I'd planned to do." He couldn't help wondering if his wife had also noticed his dad's bright smile.

"I have some laundry to do, so I'd better get that out of the way before I start unloading more boxes." Rhonda smiled at Jeff and his dad. "By the time you two finish painting the guest room, it'll probably be time for lunch, so I'll have something ready for you to eat around one."

"Sounds good to me," Jeff's dad said. "No doubt we'll be hungry by then."

While Rhonda headed off to the utility room, Jeff's first stop was to show his dad the dining room and kitchen.

"Pretty nice. Looks like this place has a lot to offer," Dad commented after seeing both rooms.

"Yeah, but wait till you see the rest of the house." Jeff couldn't help feeling a bit proud. To his way of thinking, having a home this nice was proof of his success as a businessman. And to be honest, he wanted to impress his father. Although Jeff's younger brothers, Eric and Stan, were both married with three children apiece, neither of them lived in above-average houses. Eric was a journeyman electrician, but he didn't own the business. Stan taught choir and band at a high school in Cleveland. There was nothing extraordinary about his home either.

Jeff continued with the tour of his house. The whole time, Dad commented on how big the place was and mentioned all the work it would take to keep it up, not to mention the expenses involved.

"I hope you and Rhonda didn't bite off more than you can chew by buying this place," he said, looking at Jeff with a serious expression.

"I'm not concerned about the extra work. In fact, it's relaxing to putter around in the yard." Jeff reached around to rub the back of his hot neck. *Can't my dad just be happy for me without having to make unnecessary comments?*

"Too bad your job isn't closer to home," Dad said. "I imagine the commute will get old after a while."

Jeff's features tightened as he shook his head firmly. "I don't mind the drive. Gives me time to think about things while I'm heading to and from work." *If my dad were the Christian he always says he is, then he shouldn't be so critical. I wonder if Dad throws cold water on anything Eric or Stan chooses to do. Guess it's a good thing I don't live close to him anymore, or we might butt heads the way we often did in the past.*

"Let's take a look at the garage now," Jeff said, moving their conversation in another direction. "There's something I'd like to show you."

When they entered the garage, Jeff pointed out the old sled hanging on the farthest wall.

"Say, that looks like your grandpa's old sled." Dad moved closer and seemed to be scrutinizing the item. "But that makes no sense. When my dad died, his will stated that he wanted your cousin Larry to have it." He put his hand on Jeff's shoulder. "I remember how disappointed you were when Larry walked off with the sled and you got a jar of old marbles."

Jeff lowered his head and shuffled his feet against the concrete floor. "It may seem silly to you, but I've always searched for a sled like the one Grandpa used to have and hoped I'd find one."

"It's not silly, Son. You enjoyed using the old relic when you were a kid, and I'm glad you found one so similar."

Jeff looked up. "Really, Dad?"

"Of course. I'm also happy that you and Rhonda have this nice home." Dad looked directly at Jeff. "Sorry if I came off earlier as though I didn't support your decision to move here. I'm just concerned that you may have taken on too much—especially since you now have a mortgage plus a townhouse that hasn't sold yet."

"It's okay. Our old place will sell soon." Jeff placed one hand against his belly. "I feel it in my gut."

"That's good, but a little prayer wouldn't hurt either."

Here we go. Am I now going to get the religious talk? Jeff felt a tingling in his chest. If there was one thing he didn't need, it was to hear anything about God. The man upstairs had taken Jeff's mother, and Jeff didn't think he could ever forgive God for that. Truth was, he wasn't even sure there was a God.

If God's real, then He could have healed her from the ravages of cancer, Jeff thought. *If God is love, then why would He take a mother away from her young boys when they needed her so much? Dad needed her too.*

Jeff had never understood why, after his mother's death, his father had continued going to church, praying, and reading his Bible. Wasn't he angry about losing his wife?

Eric and Stan, though not as open about their faith, had kept going to church after Mom died. But not Jeff. The moment they'd lowered his mother's casket into the ground, he'd vowed never to pray again, pick up a Bible, or step one foot in church. He wanted nothing to do with God. Dad had tried to get Jeff to attend church many times over the years. But even as a boy, Jeff had refused, shouting that he'd run away from home if his father forced him to attend church or pray out loud at the table. His father must have known Jeff meant it, for he'd never forced him to do either of those things. Dad did, however, continue to pray at the table and talk about God. After Jeff married Rhonda and moved to Canton, his father had sent them religious birthday and Christmas cards. Jeff wondered if Dad thought he could wear him down and Jeff would eventually forgive God and start going to church like he had before Mom's death.

Jeff's fingers clenched into the palms of his hands, causing his nails to bite into his skin. *Well, if that's what he thinks, then he doesn't know me very well.*

"Do you still have the old marbles from your grandpa?" Dad asked, halting Jeff's contemplations.

"Yeah, sure. I keep them in a jar over there on my workbench." Jeff pointed in that direction. "Feel free to take a closer look if you want to."

His dad wandered over to the worktable, and Jeff followed. "I've learned a lot about marbles since I inherited these."

"Oh yeah? Like what?"

"Well, to begin with, no one really knows when the first marble was made or used in a game." Jeff reached into the jar and plucked out one of the older marbles from the nineteenth century. "This one is known as a 'Lutz.' See how the transparent glass has stripes of fillings around the center core that make it sparkle?"

Dad nodded.

"It was named after a New England glassmaker, but many believe it was made in Germany."

"That's interesting."

"There are other types of marbles with different kinds of swirls." Jeff pointed to another marble. "This is called a clambroth. It has striped swirls on a creamy background and was mostly produced in the United States at the turn of the century."

"You seem to know a lot about marbles."

"Yeah, I've studied up on them, and there's a lot more I could tell you, but we need to get busy painting that spare room, so why don't we head there now?"

"I'm willing, but I would like to see your backyard."

"How about we save that tour until after lunch? In fact, when the time comes, maybe we could eat lunch out on the patio."

Dad bobbed his head. "Sounds great to me. Fresh air and sunshine go well with food."

While Dad got his satchel and went to the guest bathroom to change into the work clothes he'd brought along, Jeff went to the master bath and put on a grubby pair of jeans and a light blue, stained T-shirt. He walked past the mirror in his room and stopped to take a second glance at his reflection. While what he wore wasn't the best, he thought his form looked pretty good. Then he opened his mouth wide. *Hmm. . .my teeth aren't as nice looking as my dad's though.* Jeff frowned. *Maybe I should do something to brighten my own smile.*

He closed his mouth with a snap of his teeth. *I wonder what is going on with my dad. Is there some reason he's driving a fancy car and has whitened his teeth?*

Jeff moved away from the mirror. *Guess I'd better make sure I have everything we'll need for painting laid out in the guest room.*

A short time later, Jeff and his father got to work.

"By the looks of those balloons painted on the wall, I'd have to say that this must have been a young child's bedroom for the previous owners," Dad commented as he stirred the beige-colored paint in the large bucket setting close to him.

Jeff offered a brief nod.

"If you would reconsider adopting a baby or even a toddler, the room could still be put to good use."

Jeff's face heated. "We've been through this before, Dad, and you know my reasons for not adopting."

"Yes, I remember. At first you said that you couldn't afford to adopt, but later, after you were making a decent living, you stated that you wanted a child who would be biologically connected to you and Rhonda."

Jeff merely shrugged in response. He really didn't want to talk about this. If Dad kept pressing, Jeff might end up blurting out the real reason he didn't want children, and then he'd be in for a big lecture. No, it was best that he kept his thoughts to himself—especially since he hadn't admitted the truth to Rhonda for fear of her reaction.

Jeff grabbed two paintbrushes and handed one to his father. "Let's change the subject, shall we?"

"Sure, no problem." Dad cleared his throat a couple of times, the way a person might do if they were about to make an announcement. "Remember when we spoke on the phone the other day, and I said there was something I wanted to tell you?" Dad dipped his brush into the paint can and began to paint his side of the room.

Jeff's brows furrowed as he turned to look more fully at his father. "You look so serious. Is something wrong?"

Dad shook his head. "Not wrong, but it's kind of a sensitive subject."

"Sensitive for who—you or me?"

"Maybe for both of us. Me in the telling and you in the hearing."

Jeff tipped his head. "What do you mean?"

"A few weeks ago, I logged onto the internet and joined a Christian dating site for people fifty-five and older."

Jeff nearly dropped his paintbrush. "Are you kidding?" *Now that explains the white teeth and fancy car. He's trying to make an impression on the opposite sex. I sure never expected my father would be interested in anyone but Mom. I'm not sure if I'm ready to see him with another woman—or even hear about his pursuit in finding someone compatible to date.*

"No, Son, I'm not kidding. There aren't any single women my age at the church I attend, so I decided—"

"Why, after all these years, would you want to get married again?"

"I didn't say anything about getting married. All I'm looking for is companionship right now. If something were to develop later, then—"

"Why don't you get a dog? They make good companions, you know."

"That would not be the same as a person-to-person friendship." Dad moved closer to Jeff and gave his arm a poke.

Jeff lifted his gaze to the ceiling to keep from rolling his eyes. "A dog won't make caustic remarks or give you the silent treatment if you say or do the wrong things."

Dad's forehead wrinkled. "Are you and Rhonda having marriage problems?"

Jeff was quick to shake his head. He had never let on to his dad or anyone but Russ that things weren't perfect in his marriage, and he wasn't about to admit it now. Besides, things had been going a little better between him and Rhonda since they'd moved to Walnut Creek—especially after Jeff gave her that bouquet of roses.

"Please take the worried look off your face," Jeff said as he resumed painting. "Everything's fine between me and my wife."

Chapter 13

After Rhonda put all the food on the picnic table, she took a seat beside Jeff, which put her across from his father.

"Would you two mind if I offered a blessing, or would you prefer to pray silently like some folks do?" Don asked.

Why does Jeff's dad think every time he has a meal it needs to be prayed over before we can eat? Rhonda held her tongue and looked at Jeff, hoping he would respond, because she wasn't about to tell his dad that he couldn't offer a prayer at their table.

"Umm. . .yeah, sure, Dad. Go ahead and pray if you want to." Jeff's tone sounded flat, but at least he hadn't said no, which would have been rude.

Although Rhonda didn't believe in prayer herself, she had no objections to others praying. To her way of thinking, offering prayers to God was a waste of time and about as useless as wishing on a star or hunting for a four-leaf clover. She'd tried praying when things first went sour for her parents. But no matter how hard Rhonda pleaded with God, her prayers had gone unanswered when Dad left Mom for another woman.

Pushing the painful memory aside, Rhonda lowered her head as Don began to pray.

"Heavenly Father, thank You for the meal set before us and for the hands that prepared it. Please bless this food to the needs of our bodies. Amen."

Rhonda was glad her father-in-law had kept his prayer short and did not mention her or Jeff. There had been times in the past when he'd said a lengthy prayer, asking God to bless and protect each of his family members.

If we're blessed, it's not God's doing, Rhonda thought as she passed the bowl of macaroni salad to Don. *The blessings we've received came about from hard work and the determination to succeed.*

"Here, Dad, have some cold fried chicken." Jeff passed the platter to his father. "I brought it home from the restaurant last night. There's also baked beans with bacon in that bowl with the foil. It's one of the customers' favorite sides at the restaurant. You should give it a try."

Rhonda took the foil off the beans and spooned some onto her plate.

Don nodded and forked a piece of chicken then handed the platter back to Jeff. "I'll try those baked beans and see how good they are too." He paused. "I guess having food to bring home is one of the fringe benefits of owning your own place to eat."

"Yep, but I don't bring food home for us every night. Rhonda and I both like to cook, so we prepare most of our meals here in our new kitchen."

Rhonda watched his father taste the beans. His eyebrows shot up as he smiled and commented on how tasty they were. She was pleased that their meal was good and hoped the conversation would be as well.

As Jeff's dad worked on his drumstick, he looked out into their yard. "This is some place you have here. With all this green grass, plus a beautiful pond, you'll probably be content to stay right here and never take a vacation."

Rhonda spoke up before Jeff could say anything. "It's a nice oasis, but I would still enjoy leaving the state of Ohio and going to the Bahamas or maybe one of the Hawaiian Islands sometime."

"Me too," Jeff agreed. "But running my business keeps me pretty tied down, so we're not likely to take any long vacations."

Her husband's comment didn't set well with Rhonda, but with Jeff's dad sitting there, she chose not to say anything. *Surely Jeff could take time away from his restaurant long enough to take me on a real vacation, which we haven't had in a long while.*

"You know, I bet Eric and Stan's kids would get a kick out of feeding the fish in your pond." Don looked over at Jeff. "During the time we spent painting the guest room this morning, didn't you mention that there were goldfish in the pond?"

"Yep." Jeff spooned some garlic dip onto his plate and added several potato chips.

"And with a nice big yard like this, the children would enjoy having so much space to run and play," Don added after he'd taken a drink of lemonade.

"Maybe later this summer, when we're more settled, we could have the whole family here for a get-together," Jeff responded.

"That's a great idea, Son. Everyone could bring something for a potluck picnic. You've certainly got the perfect place for that." He looked over at Jeff and smiled. "Let me know when you're ready to do it, and I'll spread the word."

The tightness in Rhonda's jaw and facial muscles caused her discomfort. *Why would Jeff have said that without talking to me first? A decision to have his family or mine over to our place is something we should discuss before extending an invitation.*

She took a deep breath to give herself a few seconds to think of what she wanted to say. "If we are able to make it happen, we can send out invitations," Rhonda spoke up. "I'll include a list of what each family should bring."

"Sounds like a plan." Don grinned at Rhonda. "My son's lucky to have married you. You're an organizer, just like my sweet Sharon was." His facial muscles slacked. "Even though it's been a good many years since she passed, I still miss her."

Rhonda glanced at Jeff to see if he would say something, but he kept quiet, and his focus remained on his unfinished plate of food.

"I've never lost a spouse, so I can't say that I understand how you feel, but I'm sure that losing your wife had to be difficult."

"You're right. And although the pain has lessened with time, it's never gone completely away." Don placed one hand over his heart. "The love I felt for Sharon will always stay with me."

Jeff's cheeks reddened, as though he'd been exposed to the sun too long. "Maybe now that you're putting both feet in the dating world again, you'll forget about Mom."

Don shook his head. "No, I won't, Jeff. But life goes on, so don't you think it's about time I started living again?"

Jeff lifted his shoulders in a brief shrug. "You're a grown man. You can do whatever you want."

Although Rhonda hadn't been aware that her father-in-law had started dating, she realized that he must have said something to Jeff about it before they'd come outside to eat lunch. It was obvious Jeff was unhappy about his dad's decision to start dating again.

Jeff's dad has been acting different than he normally does, Rhonda thought. *Like driving a sporty car here today and caring far more about his appearance than I remember him doing. And he's been whitening his teeth.*

Knowing they needed to get the conversation back onto smoother ground, Rhonda smiled at Don and said, "Thank you for helping Jeff paint the guest room—I've wanted it done since we first bought the place."

"You're welcome. Glad I could help, and I enjoyed the opportunity to visit with Jeff." Don offered Jeff what Rhonda thought looked like a hopeful expression. The poor man was obviously looking for some confirmation of his son's love and appreciation. If only Jeff would give an affirmative nod or say something positive. But Jeff just sat with a placid expression while he finished the food on his plate.

Rhonda had toyed with giving his leg a swift kick from under the table, but instead, she kept her composure and fiddled with the napkin in her lap. She'd thought things had been going fairly well between Jeff and his dad, but then the topic of his mother had been brought up. Jeff's obvious frustration had increased when he'd mentioned that his dad had begun dating.

Maybe he should have kept that news to himself or at least waited until his dad headed home to tell me. Rhonda pursed her lips. *How are we going to host a Davis family get-together if Jeff can't even be civil to his dad?*

"Ha! Ha! Ha! This is hilarious!"

Lois walked over to Orley, who sat behind the counter Monday morning, reading the paper. She gave his arm a poke. "What's so funny?"

"This. It's just plain laughable." He pointed to the "Dear Caroline" column.

She leaned a bit closer. "What does it say that you find so amusing?"

"Just listen to this: 'Dear Caroline: I have a pet pig that I let in the house. My mother is afraid of it. Should I put the pig outside when my mother comes to visit, or should I tell Mother she will either have to get over her fear of little piggy or stop coming to my house? Sincerely, In a Pig Dilemma.'"

Tears rolled down Orley's cheeks as he held his sides and rocked back and forth. "Can you imagine having a pet pig and letting it be in the house?"

Lois gave a shake of her head. "Well, I certainly couldn't, but—"

"And wait till ya hear what Dear Caroline said in response." He grabbed a tissue from the box on the counter and dried his face.

"What did she say?"

"'Dear In a Pig Dilemma, You may need to ask yourself this question: Who is more important to you—your mother or the pig?'" Orley reached under his reading glasses and wiped the moisture from beneath his eyes. "Why would anyone write to a complete stranger and ask such a ridiculous question? And why would Dear Caroline even bother to answer?"

"Well, maybe—"

"And who is this 'Dear Caroline' person that she thinks she has all the answers to people's problems?"

"Perhaps she—"

Orley closed the paper and slapped his hand on the countertop. "I can't believe the woman—if it is actually a woman who writes this column—gets paid to give advice to people who send her letters in care of the newspaper." He puffed out his chest a bit. "I sometimes give advice to people who come into our place of business and don't charge a penny."

Lois gave him another poke, this one on the middle of his back. "Go on with you now. The folks you give advice to haven't asked for it, and some may not appreciate your comments either."

"Jeff Davis, that young fellow who bought the old sled, seemed to appreciate it when he came by the store earlier this week. He mentioned that things have been strained in his marriage."

"What kind of advice did you give him?"

"I suggested that he buy his wife a nice gift or get her a pretty bouquet." Orley winked at Lois. "That's worked well whenever you've been put out with me."

"That's because you've always included an apology with it."

"Maybe Jeff did too." Orley leaned both elbows on the countertop. "Sure wish I could have been at their house when he gave his wife the flowers. I would've liked to have seen her reaction."

Lois clicked her tongue against the roof of her mouth. "That's because you're such a romantic at heart."

He slipped his arm around her waist. "That's absolutely true. I wish all married couples could be as happy together as we are."

She leaned her head against his shoulder. "We're very fortunate, jah?"

"Most definitely. But one of the reasons we're happily married is because we talk things through and don't keep secrets from each other."

Lois pointed to the antique clock on the wall across the room. "Would you look at the time? It's past one o'clock, and we haven't had lunch. Should I go get our sandwiches and bring them up here so we can eat, or would you rather we took turns eating in the back room? Since it's been busy today, we probably shouldn't leave the main part of the shop unattended. One or both of us need to be here in case a customer comes in."

"You're right, so why don't you bring our lunches up here? Then we can read some more of the Dear Caroline column while we eat." He snickered.

Lois gave her husband a third poke before grabbing the newspaper and folding it up. "Enough about Dear Caroline. I'm sure there are plenty of other things we can find to talk about."

"All right, Fraa. While you go after our lunches, I'll sit here and think about what our next topic of conversation should be."

"You're so predictable."

"That's right, but you should keep a close eye on me, 'cause one of these days I might say or do something totally unpredictable." Orley gave Lois another wink.

She chuckled, gave him a hasty peck on the cheek, and headed for the back room. *How fortunate I was when he came into my life. I wouldn't trade my special man for anything in the world.*

Orley and Lois had no more than finished their lunch when she announced that she had an errand to run.

He frowned. "What, again? Who's gonna help me run this store if you're off doing who-knows-what kind of errand?"

"I'll only be making one stop, and I shouldn't be gone more than thirty minutes or so." She made a sweeping gesture with her arm. "Since the store is devoid of customers at the moment, you should be fine by yourself for a short while."

He folded his arms and gave an exaggerated huff. "Okay, but if we get flooded with customers while you're gone, I'll be a nervous wreck. We are going into the peak of tourist season, you know."

Lois gave his shoulder a tender pat. "I doubt many people will come in, but if it should happen, then you'll have to stick to business and forget about sticking your *naas* into other people's business while trying to solve their personal problems."

Orley grunted and touched the end of his nose. "Very funny. For your information, I do not stick my nose into anyone's business unless they open up and share their problems with me."

Lois gave him another pat. "I know, dear husband. I know, and I respect you for that." She picked up her purse and outer bonnet and hurried out the door.

Orley smiled, pulling his fingers through the ends of his long, full beard. *The best day of my life was when I met my sweet Lois. I wouldn't trade that dear woman for anything.*

Chapter 14

"Before you leave for work, there's something I'd like to talk to you about," Rhonda said as she and Jeff finished eating breakfast Monday morning.

He glanced up from the newspaper he'd been reading. "Sure, what's up?"

"I've been thinking about the way things went between you and your dad on Saturday."

Jeff gave no response. His concentration seemed to be on the paper again. Either that or he'd chosen to ignore her statement.

Rhonda tried again. "The way you talked to your father while we were eating lunch out back sounded disrespectful."

"You don't understand, do you?" The skin around Jeff's eyes tightened as he squinted.

"He accepted my mother's death as God's will, and even though Dad says he still loves Mom, he's looking—on the internet, no less—for another woman."

"I don't think it's wrong for him to seek love again, Jeff. After all—"

"Well, if he's gonna do it, then why mess around with an online matchmaking site? Probably more than half of the people who have signed up there are scammers."

"But if it's a Christian site—"

Jeff lifted his gaze toward the ceiling while shaking his head. "Like that really matters. Some people call themselves Christians to give the impression that they're good people."

She looked at her well-groomed husband's clean-shaven face. "You're right. I can't argue with that. Even so, your dad is a grown man, capable of making his own decisions." Rhonda placed her hand on his arm. "Why don't you give him a call and apologize in case you hurt his feelings?"

"I'm not gonna apologize for saying something I believe is the truth. Besides, my dad isn't the type to carry grudges. He probably hasn't given much thought to the things I said."

"Maybe not, but in case he was upset, maybe you should call just to clear the air."

Jeff shoved the newspaper aside, drank the rest of his coffee, and stood. "I'm done with this conversation, and I need to get on the road. I'll see you this evening, Rhonda. I hope you enjoy your day off." He hurried from the room without giving her a kiss goodbye.

Rhonda remained at the table until she heard Jeff's vehicle leave the yard. Although she needed to unpack a few more boxes, she really needed to calm down and get her mind off Jeff and his stubborn attitude.

I think after I put the dishes in the dishwasher, I'm going to grab the newspaper and go out back to relax on one of the patio chairs for a while. Most of the time, my life is about work either here or at the hotel, so I deserve to take a break and enjoy the sunshine and fresh air.

Rhonda reclined on the chaise longue, listening to the sweet melody of the birds chirping as they flitted back and forth among the trees in their yard. The aroma of roses mingling with the light scent of clipped grass from the mowing Jeff had done yesterday was an added bonus. The only thing that disturbed the tranquility of it all was when a plane flew overhead.

She looked up and shielded her eyes from the glare of the sun. *I wonder where that plane is off to—maybe some of the passengers are on their way to a tropical place for a vacation.* Rhonda lowered her arm and heaved a sigh. *I wish Jeff and I could be taking a trip this summer or fall. Oh, well, at least we have this beautiful yard to enjoy.*

She'd almost forgotten the newspaper lying in her lap until a light breeze rustled the pages. Rhonda picked up the paper and scanned a few pages, and then her gaze fell on the Dear Caroline column. "Hmm... It might be interesting to read some of the letters and see what kind of a response Caroline offered."

After reading a few of the problems and complaints people had written about, Rhonda realized that she wasn't the only person facing situations they didn't know how to deal with. One letter spoke of a problem with a nosey neighbor who kept peeking over the fence and making snarky comments. Caroline's suggestion to the person who'd written was to either ask the neighbor nicely to refrain from spying on her or build a higher fence.

"Good answer," Rhonda murmured. "This Caroline, or whoever she is, must have a lot of wisdom to be giving such good advice."

She folded her hands beneath her chin and contemplated. *Think I might write a letter to Caroline and see what she has to say about Jeff's and my situation. In fact, I'm going to do it right now while I'm thinking about it.*

Rhonda got off the chaise longue and hurried inside to her desk. *"Dear Caroline,"* she wrote on a piece of lavender stationery. *"My husband and I are having marital problems."* She paused and lifted her pen, unsure of what to write next. It wasn't enough to say they were having problems with their marriage. Rhonda needed to be more specific.

She tapped her pen against the desktop. *Let's see now. . .what specific question should I ask Caroline? Okay, maybe I'll add this to my opening line: "I won't say it's all my husband's fault, although I think it mostly is. You see, he thinks he can say whatever he wants and is sometimes rude—like he was to his father the other day."*

Rhonda drew a line through her last sentence. *If I wrote that and Jeff would read the "Dear Caroline" column, he might realize it was me who sent the letter.*

Rhonda started again on another sheet of paper. *"Dear Caroline: My husband and I are having some marital problems and can't seem to agree on anything. When he doesn't want to talk about something, he retreats to another room and shuts me out. What can I do to get him to listen to me and be willing to talk through our problems? Unhappy Wife."*

Satisfied with her question, Rhonda folded the paper and slipped it inside an envelope. After writing the address of the newspaper on the front of the envelope and making it "in care of Dear Caroline," she sealed and stamped it but didn't include her return address. If the person who wrote the column did respond to Rhonda's question, it would be published sometime within the next few weeks.

And so I shall wait and try to be patient, Rhonda told herself. *I just hope Dear Caroline answers.*

Canton

When Jeff arrived at his restaurant, he found Russ washing the front windows.

"Where's Wally?" Jeff asked. "He's the one I hired to keep the restaurant clean, and that includes windows."

Russ glanced over his shoulder. "He called in sick, so I'll fill in for him today."

"Seriously? You're supposed to manage things here, not do the job of a janitor."

"I don't mind, Boss, really."

"Okay. Guess I'll be doing double duty too."

"We all appreciate it when you chip in. You're a great guy, Jeff."

"Thanks. Too bad my wife doesn't think so."

"What do you mean?"

Jeff took a seat and signaled for Russ to do the same. He spent the next fifteen minutes grumbling about his father's visit.

"I still can't believe, after all these years since my mom died, that my dad wants to start dating. The fact that he bought a convertible and has even whitened his teeth makes me wonder if Dad's lost it."

Russ chuckled. "Maybe he's in some sort of midlife crisis."

"Yeah, could be—only he's a little past midlife."

"Well, not to worry. Your dad will either give up on his quest or find the perfect woman."

Jeff frowned. What his manager had just said didn't set well with him. *I wish now I'd never said anything.*

He rose from his chair. "Well, it's time to get to work. The morning crowd will soon be pouring into the restaurant. I'll be in my office for the next hour or so. Give a holler if you need me."

Russ gave a nod and left his seat too. "Will do."

When Jeff entered his office, tucked away near the back of the restaurant, a thought entered his head. *Think I'll stop by Memory Keepers Antique Store on the way home this evening.* He picked up the remote to his television and clicked it on while taking a seat in the overstuffed office chair. "Ah, that feels better." Jeff relaxed into its soft cushioning and put his feet up on the desk. He surfed through the channels and then turned it off. "I don't have time for this. I need to look at my work list." He grabbed the paper, but before he started to read it, the Amish-owned antique shop reentered his thoughts. *Just being among all those old things might make me feel better, and it'll be nice to talk to Orley Troyer again.*

Walnut Creek

Orley watched from across the room as Lois talked with an elderly Amish woman from another church district. The way those two had their heads together made it appear as if they knew each other well and were good friends.

That's my sweet Lois, Orley mused. *She's friendly and outgoing and gets along with most people.* He gave his beard a little tug. *Of course, she says that about me too.*

Orley was about to rearrange some things he'd put on display earlier, when he spotted Jeff Davis entering the store.

"It's good to see you again." Orley approached the young man and shook his hand. "Where's your wife? I thought you were going to bring her along the next time you came in."

"I'd hoped to do that, but I got off work a short time ago and on a whim decided to stop here. Besides, Rhonda's not into antiques the way I am."

"Oh, I see." Orley gave his beard another tug. *Jeff seems kind of down in the dumps today. I wonder if everything's okay.*

"Speaking of Rhonda. . ." Jeff leaned against one of the tables where several old books had been displayed. "I gave her some flowers like you had suggested."

"Did she like them?"

"Yeah. I got her red roses, and she said she liked them, but now she's barely talking to me."

Orley tipped his head. "Oh? Why's that?"

"Well, it's like this. . ."

Orley listened as Jeff complained that his wife expected too much from him and often gave lengthy lectures whenever he did or said something she thought was wrong. "I oughta have the right to feel the way I do about certain things and say whatever I want in regard to those things without her getting on my case."

Orley said a quick silent prayer asking God to give him the right words to say. "You know, Jeff, there are times when we need to listen when our wives chastise us."

Jeff blinked. "You—you think so?"

Orley gave a decisive nod then glanced at Lois, where she still stood talking with Mary Schrock. "I'll admit I haven't always listened to my wife, but I've learned to give whatever she says my consideration, because she is often right."

Jeff reached around and rubbed both sides of his neck. "That might be true with Rhonda, as well, but not when it concerns my dad."

"Are you having some issues with your father?" Orley questioned.

"Yeah, but I won't bore you with my problems."

"I don't mind listening if you want to talk about it."

Jeff shook his head. "Not today." He glanced toward the front of the store, where two more people had come in. "You have other customers to look after, so I'll let you take care of business." Jeff turned in the opposite direction and wandered off to another area in the store.

Orley went to see if he could help the man and woman who'd come in, but they didn't stay long, saying they'd only come to look around.

When the couple left a short time later, Orley noticed Jeff looking at the plaque with the Bible verse on it from Psalm 46:10. Believing Jeff might be interested in purchasing the item, Orley stepped up to him and said: "If you're interested in buying that plaque you're looking at, I can offer you a good deal on it. How about half price?"

"Thanks anyway, but my wife and I are not into that kind of a decoration." Jeff was quick to set the plaque back on the table.

"The religious kind, you mean?"

"Yeah. We're not the churchgoing type of people."

Orley's brows drew together as he made strong eye contact with Jeff. "Do you believe in God?"

Jeff's gaze darted in another direction, as though he was unable to look Orley in the eye. Then, just as quick, a sheen of sweat broke out on his forehead. "Can we talk about something else? Religion, like politics, is not the best topic."

Orley would have liked Jeff to have answered his question about whether he believed in God, but he didn't want to push it, so he asked a different question. "Is there anything specific I can help you with today?"

"Not really." Jeff gestured to an area where several old household items had been displayed. "This may seem weird, but there's something about being around so many things from the past that makes me feel kind of settled inside."

"It doesn't seem strange to me," Orley said. "I always feel a sense of nostalgia when I am around old things here in Memory Keepers or at home, where we have some old items that were passed on to us from deceased relatives."

"I bet you don't have a bunch of antiques piled up in boxes inside a rented storage shed, the way I did before we moved to our new place that has a big garage."

Orley chuckled. "No, but I do have some boxes like that in my barn."

Jeff's facial muscles seemed to relax as he broke into a wide smile. "You know what, Mr. Troyer?"

Orley shook his head.

"After coming into this store and talking to you, I feel better than I have all day."

Orley placed his hand on Jeff's shoulder and gave it a squeeze. "I'm glad. Feel free to stop by anytime, and if you're out for a drive near our home on a Sunday afternoon, don't hesitate to stop and say hello."

"Thanks, I'll keep that in mind."

As Orley moved away from Jeff and up front toward the counter, where another customer now stood, he said a second prayer on Jeff's behalf. *Heavenly Father, Please give me more opportunities to speak with Jeff. And if You do, then I'll be asking for the right words to say to him, because I'm certain that he's facing some difficulties and needs a personal relationship with You.*

Chapter 15

It had been two weeks since Rhonda sent Dear Caroline a letter, and upon opening the newspaper during breakfast, she was pleased to discover that Caroline had responded.

"*Dear Unhappy Wife,*" she silently read, "*It's a given that all married couples have disagreements. Some might argue about money, family problems, the best way to raise their children, or any number of things. No two people will see eye-to-eye all the time. But if disagreements happen often, it could threaten the strength of your marriage. If you and your husband are having serious marital problems and are unable to communicate and talk things through, then perhaps you should consider discussing your situation with a marriage counselor. It would be best if you could see the counselor together, but if your husband won't go, then you might benefit from going there alone.*"

Rhonda put the paper down and massaged her throbbing temples. She had suggested counseling to Jeff when they first started having problems, but he'd given her a definite no, saying he would not discuss their problems with a stranger. Fortunately, neither of their families knew about the conflict in her and Jeff's marriage. Somehow, they'd managed to keep it a secret, and Rhonda hoped to keep it that way, because if either Jeff's father or her mother found out, they'd no doubt offer their unwanted advice on the subject.

Rhonda glanced across the kitchen table, where Jeff sat reading an antique collector's magazine. *Why would it be any different now if I suggested counseling? Besides, it's not up to me to solve the problems between Jeff and his dad. Between the craziness of my job at the hotel and dealing with other issues between me and Jeff, I have enough things to worry about, and I won't be going to see a counselor by myself.*

Rhonda folded the newspaper and laid it aside. *So much for asking Dear Caroline's advice. I might have been better off talking to some stranger on the street—anyone who would listen to what I had to say. Maybe they would have given me better advice.*

"Is everything all right?" Jeff looked across the table at Rhonda. "You haven't said more than a few words to me this morning."

"It's nothing. I just have a lot on my mind." She picked up her glass of tomato juice and took a drink.

Jeff didn't bother to ask what was on his wife's mind. If she'd been thinking about him and the situation with his dad, he didn't want to open the topic and rehash it again.

He took a sip of his steaming coffee and then bit into his toast spread heavily with peanut butter. *Maybe Rhonda isn't happy with me because I haven't gotten all the boxes unpacked in the garage. Those flowers I got her seemed to help, but if I gave her another bouquet this soon, she'd probably think something was up.*

Jeff continued to eat his breakfast while picturing how awesome the man cave would look with the antiques he still had in the garage, but the thoughts fleeted with Rhonda's brisk sigh.

"I dread going to work this morning." She set her juice glass down and placed both elbows on the table.

"How come?"

"Part of the hotel is still under renovation, and because of it, many areas are in disarray." Rhonda's nose wrinkled as she frowned. "I'll be glad when it's all completed and things get back to semi-normal."

"You sound a little overwhelmed."

"I am. Sometimes I wish I had a twin, because lately, some of my employees have been absent from work, which means there's more for me to do."

"I'm sure that adds stress to your day, and I'm sorry you have to deal with it." Jeff tilted his head. "Would you like me to bring something home from the restaurant this evening, so you don't have to cook supper?"

Her eyes brightened some. "I'd appreciate that. Thank you."

"No problem." *Good. At least she's speaking to me now.* He smiled at her. "Is there anything specific you'd like me to bring?"

Rhonda shook her head. "Whatever you choose is fine with me, especially if it's chicken."

He let out a chuckle and nodded. "Okay, great. I'll see what my head cook has planned for the special of the day, and if there's plenty of it left by the time I head for home, I'll bring some of that."

Jeff got up from the table, put his dishes in the sink, and leaned down to give Rhonda a kiss on the cheek. "I'm heading out now. I hope you have a good day."

"You too."

Jeff hesitated a moment, wondering if he should say anything more, but Rhonda had picked up the newspaper again, so he said goodbye and went out the door.

While Lois worked on her grocery list, Orley sat across the table from her reading the Dear Caroline column in the newspaper again.

"So many people with so many problems." He frowned. "I wonder how many readers of the Dear Caroline column actually take her advice."

Lois shrugged. "I suppose it all depends on whether they believe the things she says will help them or not."

"I suppose." Orley pointed to the newspaper. "One person Caroline responded to is having marital problems, and Caroline suggested professional counseling. It's a shame how many couples seem to be struggling in their marriage these days."

Lois glanced at Orley but said nothing.

His brow furrowed. "From the few things Jeff Davis has told me, I believe that he and his wife are struggling in their marriage."

"That's a shame." Lois added a bit of cream to her coffee and gave it a few stirs.

"I think the biggest reason is that Jeff and Rhonda do not have a personal relationship with God."

Lois tipped her head. "How do you know that?"

"When Jeff was in the store the other day, he pretty much came right out and said so."

"How did you respond?"

"Well, noticing his curiosity in that old decorative item with the verse of scripture on it, I said, 'If you're interested in buying that plaque you're looking at, I can offer you a good deal on it. How about half price?'"

"How did Jeff respond to that?"

"He said, 'Thanks anyway, but my wife and I are not into that kind of a decoration.' Jeff was quick to set the plaque back on the table too." Orley gave his beard a tug. "He also said that he and Rhonda are not churchgoing people."

Lois pursed her lips. "That's a shame."

"Jah, and I then asked if he believed in God."

"What did he say?"

"He avoided my question and asked if we could talk about something else. So rather than push for an answer, I went in a different direction and asked if there was anything I could help him with."

"It's too bad he didn't want to discuss anything about God with you." Lois picked up her cup of coffee to take a drink, but then she set it back down. "But I suppose it was best not to push."

"I wish we could've talked about what might be troubling him. But it must be in the Lord's time, and apparently Jeff wasn't ready yet." Orley rapped on the tabletop with his knuckles. "The next thing Jeff said to me was that being in our store, around so many things from the past, made him feel kind of settled inside. I have to wonder if being in our store made him think of someone or something from his past, so seeing all the antiques brought him some measure of comfort."

"Do you think something from Jeff's past put a deep hurt in his heart?"

He shrugged. "Could be."

Lois clasped both hands under her chin. "Perhaps that young man is under conviction and therefore is trying to deny that God exists. Jeff needs to know that the only way he can find true happiness is to have a personal relationship with the Lord."

"Absolutely." Orley drank the last of his coffee. "I want to make it easy for Jeff to talk with me about God whenever he feels the need, but I won't force the issue. I feel that it's vital to reach out to Jeff, as well as others we meet, and share the love of God with them."

"You're right," Lois agreed. "As Christians, it's our duty to show them the way to salvation and a life of faith."

"As you stated, I shouldn't push," Orley said. "But I will continue to minister to Jeff as I see the need." He pushed his chair away from the table. "And now, my dear fraa. . ." He paused and glanced at the kitchen clock. "I believe it's time that we get our bicycles out and head over to the shop."

"All right. I'll be ready as soon as I rinse out our cups and put them in the sink." She smiled at Orley. "You never know who God might send our way on this bright, sunny day."

Canton

"I'm not feeling too well," Lori said when Rhonda joined her behind the hotel's reception desk. "Would you be able to fill in for me if I went to the break room and rested awhile?"

Rhonda leaned closer to Lori. "You're not having contractions, I hope."

"No, just some nausea and heartburn."

"Your shift will be over in two more hours anyway, so why don't you go home, where you can rest more comfortably?"

"But my replacement won't be here until close to the end of my shift, which would leave you here to manage things behind the desk on your own."

Rhonda patted Lori's shoulder. "There are only a few people with reservations for this afternoon, so I'll be fine."

Lori's lips parted, and she released a puff of air. "Thank you, Mrs. Davis. You're the best."

Rhonda smiled as Lori gathered her things and headed out the door. She envied the young woman's pregnancy, even though it meant sometimes not feeling well.

Rhonda's shoulders slumped as she stood behind the counter waiting for the next guests to check in. *If Jeff and I could have had a child, our lives would be complete, and we'd have peace in our home instead of quarreling so much of the time.*

Rhonda swallowed against the lump in her throat. She wasn't sure if Jeff truly wanted children. He had said that he did early on in their marriage, but as more time passed, and Rhonda didn't get pregnant, Jeff said he'd accepted the fact and figured maybe he and Rhonda weren't meant to have kids. He'd repeated that when she'd brought up the topic of adoption and added that he wouldn't feel comfortable raising a child who wasn't biologically theirs. This made no sense to Rhonda, for she could have easily loved and nurtured an adopted child. *If only Jeff could.*

Rhonda's self-pity increased when a young couple with a baby came through the front door and walked into the lobby. Their smiling faces and the sight of the fair-haired infant caused Rhonda to choke up. She moistened her lips and drew a couple of quick breaths, hoping she wouldn't give in to the tears pushing the back of her eyes. It certainly wouldn't appear professional if she allowed herself to cry.

"Hello. My name is Lewis McDowell, and we have a reservation," the young blond-haired man said when he stepped up to the counter.

The auburn-haired women beside him nodded. "I hope you have a crib available for our little girl. We forgot to bring her folding playpen when we left home this morning."

"It won't be a problem," Rhonda said. "We have a few cribs in our storage room, so I'll have one brought up to your room."

She processed the man's credit card and handed him two keycards. "Your room is on the third floor, and the elevator is down that hall a short way." Rhonda pointed in that direction. "Oh, and if you need a cart for your luggage, they're near the front door. Unfortunately, there is no one available to take your baggage up to your room."

"It's not a problem. I can manage," Mr. McDowell said before walking away.

Everyone from housekeeping had gone home, so Rhonda paged the maintenance man, but he didn't answer her call. She tried several more times and finally gave up. *Guess I'd better go get the crib myself.*

Rhonda hurried to the storage room, put the key card in, and stepped inside. When the door shut behind her, she grasped the handle, but the door did not open. It was then that she realized the strike plate and panic bar that could complete the electronic connection to the lock on the inside of the door were missing. Since the door worked electronically, turning the handle wouldn't do anything to help her get out of the cramped room.

Her heart began to pound as she drew a sharp intake of breath. *Oh no! I'm trapped in here! Now what am I going to do?*

Rhonda took a few more deep breaths and tried to think. *All I need to do is call someone to come and rescue me.*

Rhonda reached for her cell phone, which she normally kept in the pocket of whatever outfit she wore to work, but it wasn't there. That's when she remembered that she'd left it on the shelf under the welcome desk when she'd decided to come in here to get the crib herself.

Rhonda had always prided herself on having the key skills for hotel management, which included reliability, having stamina, and making good decisions. But since first coming to work here, she had never been locked in a room barely larger than a closet. At the moment, the prospect of being trapped in this stuffy small space for what could be a lengthy amount of time left Rhonda with nothing to do but pound on the door and scream.

Chapter 16

Rhonda continued to pummel the door and call for help. She'd been stuck in the storage room for over an hour, getting more frustrated and claustrophobic with each passing moment. The key card she'd used to get into the storage room was useless on the inside, so she'd put it in her skirt pocket. Her hope of getting out of the storage closet wasn't looking too good, but surely someone would hear her calls for help.

Rhonda wiped at the sweat on her forehead. *If anyone rescues me at this point, I'll give them a hug. I'm getting desperate, waiting to get out of this room, and oh, how I wish someone would hear my cries for help.*

Rhonda placed both arms behind her back, gripping one wrist with the other hand as she began to pace. *If I only had my cell phone with me and could call someone for help, I wouldn't be in this pickle. How could I have been so careless?*

The musty odor in the room had given her a headache, and the small size caused Rhonda to feel as if the walls were closing in on her. If she didn't get out soon, she feared she might faint or at the very least have a major panic attack.

Although Rhonda wasn't normally prone to anxiety attacks, she'd had a bad one when she'd been trapped in an elevator that had stalled a few years ago. At least there had been a call button inside the confined space, and thankfully she'd reached someone for help right away. But it had taken awhile for the repairman to arrive and get the elevator working again. By the time the door finally opened, Rhonda was drenched in sweat, and her heart felt like it might explode. She had wanted to run someplace and hide, but there'd been nowhere to go. When the elevator walls had seemed to close in on her, Rhonda had become hysterical.

I can't let that happen again, she told herself. *I must keep control of my emotions and try to keep a clear head.*

Rhonda pounded on the door again for what seemed to be the hundredth time and jumped back when the door abruptly opened. She was so thrilled that she threw both arms around Bill, the desk clerk who had obviously come on duty and stood holding the door open. "Thank you! Thank you! I'm so glad I am freed."

Heat flushed Rhonda's face as she quickly released him and stepped back. Normally, she wouldn't have hugged a staff member, but in this case, who could blame her?

Bill cleared his throat and brushed at his shirt. "I—I wasn't expecting anyone to be in here—at least not till I heard pounding on the door. You surprised me in more ways than one. Are you all right, Mrs. Davis?"

"Yes. But the fact that this room access has issues doesn't set well with me." Rhonda drew in a deep breath and released it slowly. "I used a key card to get into the storage room, but after the door closed, I saw that the plate and panic bar were missing on the inside, so turning the handle did nothing, which meant there was no way to open the door." She stepped out into the hall to breathe in some fresh air. "That's when I realized I was trapped. And since I had foolishly left my cell phone behind the check-in counter, I couldn't call anyone for help."

"Good thing I showed up when I did then, huh?"

"Yes, most definitely. I was stuck in that room over an hour, and no amount of pounding or hollering for help rousted anyone until you came along. You're the hero of the hour, that's for sure." Rhonda felt so grateful that he'd opened the door, she could've given him another hug but thought it best not to do so. "I'm not sure how much longer I could've handled being locked inside there, so thank you, thank you for rescuing me."

His cheeks reddened. "No thanks needed, Mrs. Davis. I'm just glad you're okay."

"Me too. How'd you know to look for me in there?"

"A man who said he'd checked in earlier came down to the front desk, asking about a crib. He said you had told him and his wife that you were going to get one and have it brought up to their room. But they'd been waiting a long time, and you never showed up, so he came to me to ask for assistance."

Rhonda drew her fingers through the ends of her hair, tucking it behind her ears. "I'm glad you mentioned the crib just now. I felt so relieved to be out of the room that I forgot about that young couple's request."

"If you'll stand here and hold the door, I'll get the crib and take it up to them," Bill offered.

"Thank you. That would be much appreciated. I'll have to get someone here soon to fix the lock on this door so it doesn't happen to anyone else." Rhonda held the door open and watched as her employee picked up the crib and hauled it out of the room.

"I agree with you, Mrs. Davis. Being locked in this small area isn't a good thing, and it could have happened to any of us."

Rhonda let the door close behind her and walked with Bill to the elevator. "I will stay at the front desk while you're gone, and when you get back, I'll go up to that couple's room and extend my apologies. Oh, and one more thing," she was quick to add. "Until we can get the problem resolved, we'll need to make all the other hotel employees aware of the situation with this storage room so that none of them goes in without propping it open."

When Rhonda knocked on the couple's door a short time later, she heard the baby crying. Soon the door opened, and she was greeted by the child's father.

"I came to apologize for the delay in getting a crib up to your room." She gave a nervous laugh. "I am embarrassed to admit it, but I got locked in the storage room, and it was over an hour before one of the hotel desk clerks came and rescued me."

"Oh, that's terrible," the woman said, joining her husband near the open door. She held the baby in her arms, patting the crying infant's back. "I'm sure that must have been frustrating."

"It was." Rhonda glanced at the crib that had been set in place near the king-sized bed and then she looked at the fussy baby. "I don't mean to be forward, but would it be all right if I held your baby?"

"Of course. Maybe you'll have better luck getting her to calm down than her father or I have had." The woman handed Rhonda the baby and asked if she would like to come inside.

Feeling a bit like an intruder yet eager to hold the young child, Rhonda entered the room and took a seat in the comfortable chair near the window. As she held the infant, she felt the little one's tears against her cheek. The aroma of baby lotion caused Rhonda's muscles to relax, and her nerves were soothed in the process. *After what I've just been through, this is like a tonic. I think mothers are truly blessed by their little ones.*

She patted the baby's back, like the child's mother had done, all the while gently rocking back and forth. Within minutes, the crying stopped and the baby's eyelids closed. Rhonda held the little one a while longer, until she felt certain the child had fallen asleep. Then she stood up slowly and placed the precious bundle into the crib.

"Thank you," the baby's mother whispered. "You must have children of your own, for you certainly have a mother's touch."

Rhonda slowly shook her head. "My husband and I have not been blessed with children." Before the man or woman could comment, she hurried over to the door. "I need to get back downstairs now, but don't hesitate to call the front desk if you need anything."

"Thanks, we will." The man opened the door for Rhonda, and she stepped out. When the door shut behind her, she walked slowly down the hall toward the elevator. Holding the couple's baby had brought back memories of how she had felt when her sister's girls were babies and she'd held them in her arms. Although it had been a painful reminder that she and Jeff had no children of their own, Rhonda had cuddled Gwen's babies as often as she could.

I can't think about that right now, she chided herself. *I need to return to my office and get some paperwork done before it's time to go home.*

The thought of returning to her and Jeff's sanctuary gave Rhonda some measure of comfort. *We may not have any children, but the house Jeff and I live in is a lot nicer than Gwen and Scott's place.*

Rhonda stepped into the elevator and pushed the button for the first floor. *Who am I kidding? I'd sooner live in a humble dwelling with one child than be childless and live in a palace.*

Walnut Creek

When Jeff entered the house that evening, he found Rhonda stretched out and asleep on the living-room couch. It wasn't like his wife to take a nap this late in the day. He figured she must have had a rough day at the hotel and had come home feeling exhausted, which was a common occurrence for Rhonda. It seemed like things were always hectic at the hotel. He often wondered how she functioned so well as the manager, dealing with so many stressful situations and events.

Of course, my job can be demanding and hectic, Jeff reasoned. *In addition to supervising my employees, I assist in the planning and managing of menus, oversee inventory, take care of finances, promote the restaurant, and develop business strategies.* He thumped the top of his head. *Sometimes it feels like I'm going in a hundred directions and my noggin is about to explode.*

Careful not to wake Rhonda, Jeff quietly made his way to the kitchen with the meat loaf and mashed potatoes he'd brought home from the restaurant. He then turned the oven on low and put the food in to stay warm while he made a leafy tossed salad to go with the main dish.

I sure wish I had time to grow a big garden. If I could be around here more, I'd be able to get a lot of things done. Jeff took out a cucumber, tomato, and some red cabbage to add to the salad. *Maybe I should give Russ more authority at the restaurant so I can be at home more hours.* He took out a sharp knife to cut up the veggies. *Of course, that would mean I'd have to hire someone else to take over some of Russ's responsibilities. Yeah, I'll definitely give it some thought.*

Jeff washed and sliced the veggies to begin the process of making the salad. *Maybe I can talk Rhonda into working fewer hours at the hotel too. I bet things would go better between us if we spent more time together, like we did when we were newlyweds. Boy, I sure miss those carefree days.*

He glanced out the kitchen window and smiled when two finches landed on the feeder he'd put up over the weekend. *I would like it if Rhonda and I had fewer hours at work and more time to spend at home doing things together.*

Jeff's musings were set aside when Rhonda entered the kitchen and joined him at the window. "What are you looking at?" She yawned and rubbed her eyes.

"Just watching the birds and wishing we could both spend more time at home."

"That's a nice thought, Jeff, but clearly not possible since we are up to our ears in debt with this house. And I'm beginning to think our townhouse is never going to sell."

"It will sell, Rhonda. The right buyer just hasn't come along."

"I wish I had your optimism." When she looked at Jeff, he saw in her eyes the depth of her fatigue.

"Rough day at work?" he asked. "Is that why you were sleeping on the couch when I got home?"

"Yes. I'll tell you about it while we're eating supper." She glanced at the stove. "Speaking of which...what's that delicious aroma coming from the oven?"

"Meat loaf and mashed potatoes—my chef's special today." He gestured to the wooden bowl on the counter. "I'm making a nice tossed salad to go with it."

Rhonda smiled, although it didn't quite reach her eyes. "That was thoughtful of you."

Jeff slipped his arm around her waist. "I hate it when we argue, and I've been thinking about what you said to me this morning concerning my dad."

"Oh?"

"I'm gonna give him a call after supper and apologize for anything I may have said that might have hurt his feelings while he was here."

"I'm glad."

"I'm still not okay with the idea of him looking for a woman to date—especially via the internet."

"You never know, Jeff. It could work out."

He shrugged and returned to his salad-making duties. "We'll see."

"Do you think we should make plans to have your dad and the rest of your family over for a picnic soon?"

"I suppose. I'll bring it up to Dad while we're on the phone."

"When would you want to do it?"

"How about the Fourth of July? That'll give us a few weeks to make our plans for the event."

"Okay." Rhonda opened the cupboard door and took out two plates and two tall glasses. After setting them on the table, she got their silverware. "Would you be okay if I invited my family too? If we don't include them, my sister will probably end up dropping by here unannounced sometime soon, the way Mom did." Rhonda pressed her lips together in a grimace. "I'd rather host one big family get-together than have people showing up here at inopportune times."

"Agreed." Jeff grabbed a couple of pot holders and removed the meat loaf and potatoes from the oven. "Since that's settled, we can eat, and you can share with me about your day. Once we're done with our meal, we can both call our parents and extend the invitation."

After Jeff sat down, and Rhonda had taken a seat, he leaned slightly forward and massaged his forehead. *Sure hope we're not making a mistake having both of our families here on the same day.*

Chapter 17

"Are you ready to go yard-saling with me?" Orley asked Lois the morning of the last Saturday in June.

She looked up from the letter she'd been writing and frowned. "I don't understand why you'd want to close Memory Keepers on a day when we're usually quite busy to go traipsing all over town from one yard sale to another."

"Well, for one thing, my youngest sister, Martha, is having a yard sale today, and I told her we would probably stop by. Also, whenever we've gone yard-saling, we have always come back with something we can fix up or sell as is in our antique store. And if we go early, we're more likely to get the best deals." Orley's words were rushed as he grabbed his straw hat off the wall peg in the kitchen.

"Not only that, but stopping at yard sales gives us a chance to visit with people we might never have met. And you never know whose lives we might touch." He picked up the newspaper and held it out to her. "There are a lot of good ones listed today, so what do you say? Should we go by horse and buggy, hire a driver, or ride our bikes?"

Lois saw the determined look on her husband's face and figured he was not going to give up the idea of checking out some yard sales today. Since she had no desire to be at the antique store by herself, she decided she might as well go with Orley on his treasure hunt.

"I'll go with you, Husband, but let's take our bikes. It'll be good exercise, and we won't have to pay a driver or take the time to hitch our *gaul* to the carriage."

"Good thinking." Orley bobbed his head. "And if we find anything too big to put in our bike baskets or the cart I'll hook up to the back of my bicycle, we can call a driver to pick up any larger items."

"All right," Lois agreed. "I'll get my purse and outer bonnet, and we can be on our way."

"I don't know why I agreed to do this today," Rhonda complained as she and Jeff left one yard sale and headed for another. "With all the things that need to be done at our place, we shouldn't be out looking at other people's junk."

"Well, you know what they say. One man's junk is another man's treasure."

"Right." She folded both arms across her chest and stared straight ahead. *I am already dreading this silly outing. Knowing my husband, if he sees an antique or some collectible, he'll want to buy it.* Rhonda's back stiffened. *I'll have to watch Jeff like a kid and try to talk him out of buying whatever old thing he finds. As it is, my husband still hasn't sold any of his own antiques to help with our finances like I've asked him to do. And here we go again possibly adding more junk to an existing problem.*

"Look at it this way," Jeff continued, "if we were at home this morning, you'd probably be inside the house doing laundry or cleaning, and I'd either be in the garage or outside mowing the lawn and pulling weeds." Jeff reached across the front seat in his SUV and gave Rhonda's arm a gentle squeeze. "This way we're getting some together time, which I like."

Rhonda enjoyed being with Jeff too—when they weren't quarreling. "Okay, but let's not stay out too long or go to many more sales. When we get home, I'll help you with the yard work, which means we'll be together while getting something done."

"Just a few more places, and then I'll take you out to lunch. After that, we'll go home and spend a good part of the afternoon working in our beautiful yard."

So far Jeff hadn't found anything he seemed interested in. Rhonda was thankful, and she hoped the place they went next wouldn't have anything eye-catching either. She had to admit that the kinds of things people sold at yard sales were interesting. Some of the items still had original price tags on them, indicating they'd never been used.

Why would a person buy furniture, clothing, or appliances and not use them? she wondered. It seemed like a waste of money. Rhonda thought about her mother and how she had always been frugal, seldom wasting money on unnecessary things. Of course, Rhonda's father had been the opposite—spending money whenever he had a whim.

"We don't need to go out for lunch, Jeff." She uncrossed her arms. "Let's save the money, and I can fix us a salad or sandwich when we get home."

"No way! We rarely go out to eat anymore. Besides, there's that Amish-style restaurant not far from our home that we still haven't tried. I hear they serve pretty good food." He looked over at Rhonda and winked. "It's always good to keep a check on the competition."

She poked his arm. "Yeah, right, Jeff. Your restaurant's in Canton, and it doesn't serve Amish food."

"No, but we do offer home-style cooking, and I might get a few ideas for some things we could add to the menu at the Red Barn Café."

"Okay, fine," Rhonda conceded. "We can go out to lunch when we're done yard-saling."

"Wow, look at all the great stuff they have for sale here." Jeff made a sweeping gesture with his arm. "I bet there are some antiques and collectibles too."

Rhonda moaned and shook her head. "You bought some old marbles at the last yard sale we stopped at, so please don't get carried away here."

"Who said anything about getting carried away?" Jeff's eyes appeared wide and rounded as he licked his lips in anticipation.

Rhonda held her ground. "I mean it, Jeff. We're on a tight budget, and we can't afford to spend money on unnecessary things."

He put his hand on the small of her back and gave it a few taps. "Don't worry. I'm just gonna take a look and see what's available."

Yeah, right. Rhonda figured she'd better stick close to her husband or he would end up buying some antique or collectible that he most certainly didn't need. "Let's start over on the right side of the yard." She clasped his hand.

He hesitated but finally went along. As they approached one of the tables, Jeff halted. "Look over there." He pointed across the yard. "That's Orley and Lois Troyer."

"So it is." Although Rhonda had only met them the one time when she and Jeff stopped at the Troyers' home, she recognized the Amish couple.

"They're probably on the lookout for things they can buy at a reasonable price and resell in their antique store."

"Let's go over there and say hello." Jeff let go of Rhonda's hand and turned in that direction.

"Wait. Maybe we shouldn't bother them right now. They seem to be talking to another Amish couple."

"We can just meander over that way, and I'll wait to speak to them until they end their conversation with the other couple." Jeff took hold of Rhonda's hand again and started moving in the Troyers' direction. Rhonda had no choice but to go with him.

As they approached the Troyers, the other Amish couple moved off in another direction. Orley looked over at Jeff and Rhonda and smiled. "Well, hello there, you two. Looks like Lois and I aren't the only ones out yard-saling today." He stepped forward and shook Jeff's hand.

Jeff grinned back at him. "Yep, but this will be the last one we stop at, because when we leave here, I'm taking my wife out to lunch."

"How good it is to see you both." Lois greeted Rhonda with a hug, which took her by surprise. She wasn't used to hugging people she barely knew.

"Umm. . .yes, it's nice to see you too." Rhonda stepped back, surprised by the warmth and comfort she'd felt from Lois's greeting. She still couldn't get over how plain Lois and Orley dressed. It was funny how simple the Amish seemed, having no electricity in their homes or a car to drive. Rhonda had heard from Jeff that they didn't have televisions either. She glanced at her husband. *The way he watches TV in his man cave all the time, I think I could welcome not having that electronic inconvenience.*

"Say, Jeff, there are some nice-looking collectibles on that table over there." Orley gave his beard a quick tug. "Why don't the two of us check it out and let our wives visit for a while?"

Jeff hurried off with Orley.

Rhonda pinched the skin between her thumb and forefinger, unsure of what to say. It wasn't like she and this Amish woman had anything in common, so there wasn't much to talk about. And now that Jeff had run off with Orley, there was no telling what he might buy. As an antique dealer, Mr. Troyer might be a bad influence on her husband.

"How have you been?" Lois asked. "Are you and Jeff getting settled into your new home?"

"For the most part, but there are still some boxes in the garage we haven't gone through." Rhonda glanced across the way to see where Jeff and Orley had gone and cringed inwardly when she saw her husband pick up what looked like some sort of vintage tool. She wanted so badly to go over and check on things but didn't want to be rude to Lois.

"Jeff mentioned that you work at a hotel in Canton. I imagine that keeps you pretty busy."

Rhonda turned to face Lois again. "Yes, it does." She was on the verge of mentioning how stressful her job could be, when two young children—a girl and a boy—ran past, each with a toy in their hands. Their laughter rang out, and Rhonda felt compelled to watch them. On the other hand, it was one more reminder that she and Jeff would never have any kids of their own. She looked at Lois and then Orley. *They have no children either. I suppose in that way, she and I do have something in common. But would Lois mind if I brought up that sensitive topic?*

"Those children seem to be having a good time," Lois said. "I've always enjoyed watching my nieces and nephews when they run and play. In fact, Orley and I saw some of them earlier today when we stopped by to check out my sister's yard sale."

"Do you miss not having children of your own?" Rhonda questioned.

Lois grew quiet for a minute, as she pressed her lips together and looked down. Then, just as quick, she looked up at Rhonda and smiled. "My husband and I have learned to take pleasure in spending time with other people's children. We also enjoy the quality time we have together as husband and wife."

"I see." Rhonda thought about her own nieces and nephews and wondered how things would go on the Fourth of July during their combined family get-together. Lois's statement made Rhonda wonder if she could find joy in spending time with her sister's daughters, as well as her brother and sister-in-law's children. She also questioned why spending time with Jeff had never been enough for her. It wasn't that she didn't love him. She just felt incomplete without a family to care for and dote over, the way Gwen did with her two children.

All I can do is try to enjoy my nieces and nephews, Rhonda told herself. *It would be better than spending the Fourth feeling sorry for myself.*

"Wow, would you look at that?" Orley pointed to a vintage oil lamp made of thick glass with a cranberry red hue. "I've done my research on oil lamps, and I'm 100 percent sure that this one was made in the mid-1800s."

Jeff studied the lamp for several seconds. "It's beautiful, but how do you know it's not a newer lamp made to look old?"

"For one thing, it doesn't have a base that is glued to the font, which is another piece of glass. They were fused together while the glass was still hot." Orley fingered the base of the lamp. "A newer one would most likely be glued together."

"That's interesting. As you can probably tell, I don't know much about antique lamps other than that I assume they burned kerosene."

"That's true, but at one time they used animal oils. Then in the 1800s, kerosene replaced the oils from animals." Orley held the lamp up toward the sunlight, looking it over thoroughly. "The price isn't bad, and if I buy it, I'm sure I could turn a profit."

"I'll bet you could too." Jeff's gaze went to several pieces of vintage jewelry. One in particular caught his eye. It was an enamel daisy pin priced at ten dollars, although he was sure it was worth more than that. "I think Rhonda might like that," he said, pointing to the piece of jewelry.

"Then why don't you get it for her?"

Jeff drew in his lower lip as he weighed the issue. "I'd like to, but she might say no if I show it to her."

"Maybe you should buy the pin and surprise her with it." Orley grinned. "Most women like surprises—at least the good kind."

"You know, now that I think about it, our wedding anniversary is coming up in September, and the pin might make a nice gift for Rhonda." Jeff gave a decisive nod. "While she's over there talking with Lois, I'm going to go pay for the item."

"I'll go with you," Orley said. "And I'm definitely getting this old lamp."

Jeff picked up the daisy pin and looked around. This yard sale was a good-sized one compared to the others they'd been to today. People were looking over the goods, and some carried different items with them to purchase. Thankfully, no one was up at the cashier at the moment, so he and Orley could be waited on quickly. *I would sure like to keep this pretty pin a surprise for Rhonda.* Jeff glanced Rhonda's way to be sure she wasn't watching, and once he was certain that Lois had his wife's full attention, he headed over to the table near the garage door to pay for the item. *When we get home, I'll need to find a good place to hide the pin until our anniversary.* He scratched his chin. *It just needs to be someplace where I don't forget it.*

Chapter 18

"I hope we didn't make a mistake by inviting both your family and mine to celebrate the Fourth of July with us today," Jeff said as he and Rhonda set up folding tables in their backyard.

Rhonda had been having some reservations about the day's event too. She wanted to have everything perfect, but so far, her planning had been pretty much guesswork. "Should we have the tables lined up in one row so we're all sitting together, or should they be nearby each other but separate?" She stood with one hand on her hip.

Jeff slowed his work. "You seem to be overthinking this."

"I want everything to go as smoothly as possible, and I'm hoping we will all have a pleasant day." Rhonda reached back to make sure her ponytail was secure. "I hope we have enough folding chairs. I'm only seeing fourteen out here."

"The others are still in the garage, and there are four more leaning up against the wall by the door going into the house."

Rhonda looked at her soiled hands. "All the chairs still need to be wiped down; they're quite dusty."

"Don't worry, honey. I'll stop what I'm doing here and go grab the remaining chairs and a rag for cleaning them."

"Thank you." Rhonda watched as Jeff headed inside. *I wish we hadn't had to dip into our spare money to buy these three tables for this Fourth of July gathering. It will set us back even further than we need to be with the big debt we're living with right now. It probably would have been cheaper in the long run if we'd just rented some tables.* She slid a few of the folding chairs near one of the new tables and stood back to get a good look.

A short time later, Jeff came out with the last of the chairs and a rag dangling from his back pocket. "That's all of them, so we can start wiping off each chair now."

Rhonda pointed at what she'd just set up. "Do you think these chairs will look okay with the new tables?"

Jeff shrugged his shoulders. "I don't see why not."

"They don't seem to go together that well."

"I believe you're overthinking it again. No one is going to care about whether the chairs perfectly match the tables. Let's just get this all set up and be done with it."

If everyone they'd invited came today, there would be a total of eighteen people. That could create a lot of mayhem, especially with eight children running around. Rhonda could see one of the children falling into the pond and getting wet. Or a couple of kids might get carried away and overfeed the fish, leaving waterlogged food floating all over the surface of the water.

I shouldn't think about things like that happening on such a nice day. I'm sure the children's parents will keep a close eye on their kids. She set up the next folding chair and tried to shake off any bad vibes.

Rhonda looked over at Jeff. "The only time our families have ever been together was the day of our wedding, and that was briefly, so they are basically strangers to one another." She rubbed the small of her back, where a kink was trying to form. "I wonder if our two families will even have anything to say to each other. It would be awkward if nobody did much talking."

"Let's not borrow trouble, Rhonda. It will work out fine." Jeff paused from what he was doing to wipe the sweat from his forehead. "Sure is a hot one today. Makes me wish we had a swimming pool instead of a pond full of fancy-looking fish."

Using the handkerchief he'd pulled from his short's pocket, he gave his forehead another swipe. "Maybe when the townhouse finally sells, we can have a pool put in. Think how nice that would be during the hot summer months."

"With our jobs, we're gone most of the time, so it wouldn't be worth it to have a pool we wouldn't use regularly." Rhonda grimaced as the muscle in her back tightened a bit more. Since they'd been shorthanded at the hotel again yesterday, she had ended up having to help haul some boxes of bedding into some of the rooms that had recently been renovated. Rhonda figured the unwanted sensations in her back had something to do with yesterday. She hoped it wouldn't go out on her today, of all times.

"You okay? You look like you might be in pain." Jeff stood from his squatting position and came over to stand beside Rhonda.

"My back's acting up a bit, and I hope it's nothing to worry about. Once we get the rest of these tables set up, I can sit down and rest awhile."

"Go ahead and take a break now. There's just one table left, and I can finish it." Jeff pointed to a chaise longue. "I'll get an ice pack from the freezer, and you can stretch out for a bit. Our company won't be here for two more hours, so you have enough time to rest your back."

"Okay, but if I fall asleep, please wake me in plenty of time before they get here."

"Sure thing, honey." Jeff kissed her cheek. "After I get your ice pack, I'll set out the paper plates and plastic utensils we'll use for our afternoon meal and make sure the frozen ground beef patties have thawed sufficiently."

Although their guests had volunteered to bring something to contribute to their meal, Jeff had insisted that he and Rhonda would supply all the food. Fortunately, the only cooking involved barbecuing the burgers and hot dogs. Jeff had brought potato and macaroni salads home from the restaurant last night, and Rhonda had picked up several bags of chips at the grocery store. For dessert, they would serve ice cream and cookies, so there really wasn't a lot of work involved.

Rhonda smiled. "Thank you, Jeff, for being so helpful."

"No problem," he said before going into the house.

Rhonda was pleased that things had been going better between them lately. It seemed like Jeff had been trying harder to please her. *Perhaps there's some hope for our marriage after all*, she thought as she reclined on the chaise longue. *Maybe Jeff has figured out that he needs to be more attentive to my needs.*

After Jeff got out the paper plates and plastic utensils, he opened the back door to see how Rhonda was doing. He'd given her an ice pack fifteen minutes ago and hoped it was helping.

Seeing her eyes were closed and that she wore a peaceful expression, Jeff decided not to disturb her. After her day at the hotel yesterday, his wife deserved a little downtime. He hoped Rhonda's back would feel better by the time everyone arrived.

Jeff closed the door quietly and went back to the kitchen. When he looked at the clock and saw they had ninety minutes to go until their guests arrived, he decided to head down the hall to his man cave and see what was on TV.

Although Jeff wouldn't have admitted it to Rhonda, he too had a few misgivings about having his family here to visit and hoped everything would go well. His and Rhonda's old place hadn't been set up well for entertaining, and get-togethers were always at Dad's or one of his brothers' homes, so this would be a new experience for them.

Jeff pulled his fingers through the back of his thick hair and puffed out his chest. *I bet my brothers will be envious when I show them my private oasis. If Eric and Stan lived closer, they'd probably be over here all the time.* He frowned. *I doubt Rhonda would approve of that. And truthfully, I probably wouldn't appreciate it either, because my brothers and I would most likely be arguing over what program we wanted to watch on my large-screen TV.*

After Jeff entered his man cave and took a seat in his recliner, he waited a bit to turn on the TV, reflecting instead on the relationship he had with his brothers. Eric, being two years older than Jeff, had always tried to be the leader, telling his younger brothers what to do. Jeff had tried to stand his ground, but Stan, who was two years younger than Jeff, was more compliant and went along with whatever Eric said. Consequently, some of the things Jeff and his brothers did as boys had gotten all three of them in trouble with their parents.

Jeff leaned his head back and closed his eyes. He dozed off for a while, and when he came fully awake, an image of his mother came to mind. She'd been a kind, soft-spoken woman and hadn't deserved to die when her boys weren't even fully raised. Eric had been fourteen; Jeff, twelve; and Stan, ten. Although Jeff's dad had done his best to see to Jeff and his brothers' needs, it hadn't filled the empty spot in their home left by his mother's death. Even now, twenty-three years later, Jeff missed his mother's gentle spirit. He'd never heard her say an unkind word about anyone.

The day of Mom's funeral, Jeff had heard several people say that Sharon Davis had always set a Christian example for her family as well as everyone else who knew her. The minister had stated during the eulogy that Jeff's mother loved the Lord and had served Him well.

Jeff's jaw clenched. *Then why didn't God make her well so she could continue to serve Him?*

The doorbell rang, and Jeff nearly catapulted out of his chair. Glancing at his watch, he grimaced. *Oh, no—they're here! How could I have lost track of the time?*

Jeff rushed out of the room and down the hall. He had to rouse Rhonda before he opened the door to their company. *Oh, boy—I bet she's gonna be mad.*

"Honey, wake up. Some of our guests are at the front door."

Rhonda's eyes flew open, and she jerked her head. "They came early?"

"No, they showed up on time. Sorry, Rhonda, but I messed up and didn't keep an eye on my watch."

Rhonda got off the lounger, being mindful of her back. At the moment, it felt better than when she'd lain down, and she wanted to keep it that way. "I need to go check my appearance. Would you please answer the door?"

"Okay, sure. . .no problem." Jeff took the ice pack from her, which was now quite warm. "I'll drop this off in the kitchen and then go see which of our family members is waiting on the front porch."

"Please hurry, Jeff. If you leave them standing there too long, they might think we're not home."

"I'm sure no one will believe that since we specifically invited them here today."

Rhonda went inside and made her way down the hall to their room. Her clothes were wrinkled, and she felt a wet spot on the back of her shorts where the ice inside the cold pack had melted.

Her back felt a bit better, and she hurriedly undressed and put on a clean, rose-colored tank top with a pair of beige capris. Then she touched up her makeup and redid her ponytail. It was time to greet her guests.

A few minutes later, she saw Jeff in the entryway talking with his father and two brothers. Beside them stood Eric's wife, Monica, and their children, Susan, Billy, and Steve. Stan's wife, Connie, along with their kids, Tim, Debbie, and Nina, were also there.

Looking at the size of this group, crowded in the hall and all talking at once, Rhonda was glad none of her family had arrived yet. It was bound to become even more hectic when they got here.

Once everyone had been sufficiently greeted, Jeff's dad offered to take the kids out back, while Jeff gave his brothers and their wives a tour of the house. Rhonda appreciated Don's suggestion but cautioned him to keep an eye on the children because of the pond.

"No worries," he was quick to say. "I'll make sure none of my grandkids fall in."

Soon after Jeff headed down the hall to give his brothers and sisters-in-law the house tour, Don and the kids went out the back door. Rhonda was tempted to go with them, but someone needed to stay close to the front door to let her family in when they arrived.

Her back had begun to knot up again, so she took a seat on the bench in the entryway. A short time later, Rhonda heard a vehicle pull in. Opening the door, she saw Gwen and her husband, Scott, exit the front seat of their van. Then the back doors opened, and Rhonda's mother, along with Gwen and Scott's daughters, Kimberly and Megan, ages nine and eleven, got out.

Rhonda waited until they stepped onto the front porch to greet them. "Welcome. It's nice to see all of you." She looked down at the girls. "You two have sure grown since the last time I saw you."

They both giggled and nodded.

Gwen gave Rhonda a hug, then she turned to their mother and said, "You were right, Mom, this place is a palace."

"I'd hardly call it that, but our new home is pretty good-sized." Rhonda hugged her mother then shook Scott's hand. "Come on in everyone, and I'll show you around."

After they'd entered the house, Rhonda told the girls that Jeff's nieces and nephews were out back with his father. "Maybe you'd like to go out there while I show your parents the rest of the house."

"I wanna see it too." Megan's lower lip protruded.

"You girls can see it later," their father said. "Right now, I think you should go outside and say hello to the other kids."

"Okay, Daddy," the girls said in unison.

"I'll take them out back," Rhonda's mother spoke up. "Since I've been there before, I know the way."

"Thanks, Mom." Gwen gave a wide smile.

After Mom ushered the girls out the back door, Rhonda led the way down the hall. When they entered Jeff's man cave, where he and his brothers and sisters-in-law had gone, Scott gave a whistle. "Wow, the lucky dog. I'm so jealous."

Rhonda was about to comment, when Gwen leaned closer to her and whispered, "Did Mom tell you what she's been up to lately?"

Rhonda shook her head.

"You're not going to believe this, but she's recently decided to. . ."

Gwen's sentence was cut short when Megan came running into the room. "Mommy! Daddy! Come quick! Kimberly fell in the pond, and I think she's drowning!"

Gwen and Scott raced out of the room, and with her heart pounding, Rhonda followed. She couldn't even comprehend how her sister and brother-in-law would feel if their little girl drowned.

Chapter 19

Rhonda's back tightened even more, and her heart continued to pound as she dashed out the back door behind her sister and brother-in-law. To her surprise, there were two people in the pond—Megan and Jeff's father. Holding the waterlogged girl around her waist, Don moved toward the edge of the pond. Meanwhile, Rhonda's mother stood by with her hands cupped around her mouth, shouting directions at him. By the time everyone reached the pond, Megan and Don were out of the water.

Gwen rushed forward and hugged her wet child. "Are you all right, my darling girl?"

"I'm fine, Mommy. Just really wet is all."

"What were you doing in the pond? Weren't you warned to stay away from there?" Scott bent down so he was eye level with his daughter.

"I leaned forward to look at the fish, and then the next thing I knew, I was in the water with 'em." Her teeth chattered as she briskly rubbed her arms.

"Let's get you inside and out of those wet clothes." Rhonda took hold of the young girl's hand.

"I didn't bring either of the girls a change of clothes today," Gwen was quick to say. "But now I wish I had."

"It's okay," Rhonda responded. "I'm sure I can find something she can wear while her clothes are being washed and dried."

"My clothes aren't dirty; they're just wet." Megan lifted her chin and looked up at Rhonda with a determined expression.

"The pond water is dirty, so your clothes aren't clean now." Rhonda turned her attention to Jeff's dad. "I'm sure Jeff has something you can wear while your clothes are being washed and dried."

Don looked at Jeff and jiggled his brows. "I don't know. . . I've been working out at the gym lately and getting in shape, so your clothes might be too big for me."

Jeff's cheeks reddened. "Very funny, Dad."

Rhonda held her breath and waited for her father-in-law's response. She felt sure Don was only kidding and hoped no tension would develop between Jeff and his dad.

Don poked Jeff's arm and said, "Just kidding, Son. I do think, however, that I can probably fit into a pair of your shorts."

"Okay then, follow me." Jeff headed back to the house, and his father followed. Rhonda and Gwen, with Megan in tow, went in behind them.

When Rhonda stepped inside, she paused at the door and hollered back to those still outside, "Relax and enjoy yourselves. We'll be back soon, and then Jeff will get the grill heated so we can cook the meat and eat."

After putting the clothes in the washer, Rhonda provided Megan with a T-shirt and her terry cloth robe. They were too big for the young girl, but at least her body was covered. Jeff loaned his dad a button-down shirt and a pair of his shorts, so at least no one would have to sit through their meal wearing wet clothes.

Jeff noticed that his wife seemed agitated as she flitted around, asking several times if Megan was okay. He hoped the incident wouldn't get her down since she wanted this whole family gathering to go well. He also was concerned that the tension might make his wife's back worse.

When they returned to the patio, everyone found a seat to visit while Jeff got the grill going. Jeff's brother, Stan, offered to help, but Jeff said he could manage and told Stan to relax and enjoy himself.

Jeff looked around his barbecue grill for the tool to clean off the grilling surface.

Rhonda came over to him and tilted her head. "What are you looking for?"

"I found it." He held up the nasty-looking scraper.

She grimaced. "Is that all you have to clean the grill with?"

"Yeah, and there's nothing wrong with it." Jeff smiled and in a low voice he asked, "How are you doing?"

"Okay. At least my back seems to be holding out."

He winked and began scraping at the grill. "I'm glad."

"I'll go inside and grab the rolls." She turned and headed into the house.

Jeff paused his cleaning and closed the lid on the grill. The temperature gauge climbed higher, as he set his tool down and went inside to get the meats. When Jeff returned, he was pleased to see that their guests looked content as they chatted with each other.

While the hot dogs and ground beef patties cooked, Jeff looked out at the beautiful yard. The grass had been freshly cut, and there wasn't a weed in sight. He felt kind of puffed up being able to show his family his and Rhonda's new home. Jeff hoped it was an indication to them—especially Stan—that as a business owner, he'd become successful. It probably shouldn't matter what anyone thought, but Jeff needed the reassurance that he had made something of himself.

Shaking his thoughts aside, Jeff concentrated on cooking the beef patties and hot dogs, while Rhonda took care of setting out the chips, condiments, and eating utensils. The salads and other cold items wouldn't be taken from the refrigerator until the meat had finished cooking.

Half an hour later, everyone took their seats at the tables. Although Jeff wasn't thrilled about it, he wasn't surprised when his dad asked if he could offer a prayer before they began eating.

"Sure, Dad." Jeff nodded. What else could he say? His father was a churchgoer, and so were Stan and Eric, not to mention that Rhonda's mother had told her previously that she'd begun attending church with Gwen and her family. There was no question about it: Jeff and Rhonda were outnumbered when it came to their nonreligious beliefs.

When everyone bowed their heads, Jeff did the same. Instead of praying, he allowed his mind to wander. *Sure am glad Megan didn't drown. No doubt Rhonda and I would have gotten the blame for not having a fence around the pond, and of course, we'd have felt guilty about it. And who knows—Rhonda's sister and her husband might have filed a lawsuit against us.*

He shifted uneasily on his folding chair. *I'm surprised no one from either of our families made any comments about the lack of a fence.*

Since the front of their property had an iron gate that usually remained closed when they were home, Jeff hadn't seen the need to put a fence around the pond. Apparently, neither had the previous owners.

Things are different now, Jeff told himself. *If we continue to have family with young children over or in the event that some neighbor kids should wander onto our property, we need to be proactive in protecting anyone from the potential of drowning in our pond.*

Jeff made a mental note to see about the cost of getting a fence put up. He grimaced. *Rhonda and I are away from home a good deal of the time because of our jobs. If we aren't here and the gate is closed, no deliveries would ever get made. Maybe it's a good thing we don't have any kids of our own,* he reasoned. *Then we'd really have to be worried about the pond.*

When an elbow connected to his ribs, Jeff's eyes snapped open. He looked at Rhonda, sitting beside him, and saw that her eyes were open too, as were the others who sat at the tables.

"Did you have a lot to tell God about, Uncle Jeff?" The question came from Eric's youngest son, Billy, who was six.

Jeff's face warmed. "Uh, yeah. . .I guess." He got up, grabbed the pan of hot dogs and burgers, and took them over to the serving table, where all the other food had been placed. Pointing to the table, Jeff hollered, "Come on, everyone, it's time to fill your plates!"

When the people sitting at the first table got up, Jeff saw his dad look over at Rhonda's mother and heard him say, "If you'd like to sit tight, I'd be happy to get your food, June."

She shook her head, barely making eye contact with him. "Thanks anyway, but I'm kind of a fussy eater, so I'd better do my own choosing."

Fussy eater? This was the first time Jeff had heard his mother-in-law say anything like that. *Maybe June's too independent to let anyone wait on her—especially someone she barely knows. Or maybe she doesn't care for my dad. From the way she hollered at him when Megan was in the pond, I'd have to say that's probably the case.*

After both of their families had filled their plates, Jeff and Rhonda went over to the serving table. "I wonder if everyone will go home after they eat," he whispered to her. "Or should we invite them to stay longer and set out some outdoor games to play?"

"You know, we still have dessert to serve our guests."

"Oh, yeah, I almost forgot about that."

"Instead of playing outdoor games, maybe we should invite everyone into your man cave to watch a family-oriented DVD on your large-screen TV," she suggested. "It might be less stressful than worrying about one of the other kids getting too close to the pond."

Jeff bobbed his head. "Good point. I'll extend the invitation after everyone is done eating. And in addition to serving ice cream and cookies, I'll offer to pop a big batch of buttery popcorn."

"Whew! I don't know about you, but I'm exhausted." Jeff flopped onto the living-room couch beside Rhonda. "Our company stayed longer than I expected."

She nodded and rubbed her stomach. "I definitely ate way more than I should have today. The food was so good. Everyone seemed to enjoy themselves, and I can't believe we all sat through two movies. There was only a little ice cream left over, but those cookies we served were devoured. And who knows how much popcorn and soda pop you served?"

Jeff chuckled and gave his middle a pat. "I agree, the meal was tasty, and I got carried away and ate more than I should have." He reached for her hand. "I'm glad my man cave is big enough to accommodate them all, but we couldn't have done it without bringing in several folding chairs. Makes me wonder if we ought to buy a few more recliners or even a sectional."

"That's not necessary," Rhonda said, following a yawn. "We probably won't have that many people here all at one time very often."

"True. Except for Megan falling in the pond, I believe things went pretty well today."

"I suppose, but that accident really scared me." Rhonda's voice lowered to a near whisper. "I shudder to think of what could have happened if your dad had not jumped in and rescued her."

"If we have another family get-together here this summer, it should probably be with just one of our families at a time. Things were pretty hectic today, and it was hard to visit one-on-one with anybody."

"I agree, but I'm not sure I'll be up to another get-together this summer—with your family or mine." Rhonda reached around and massaged her lower back. "It was a bit too much for me."

"I'm sorry. How's your back holding up?" Jeff asked. "Did the stress of today make it worse?"

"A couple of times, like during the pond incident, it started to spasm, but it seemed to work itself out." She winced. "At least until now."

"Would you like me to massage it for you? Or how about taking a warm bath with Epsom salts? I'd be happy to fill the tub for you."

"A relaxing bath does sound nice. Thanks for offering."

He pulled her close and rubbed the small of her back for a few seconds. "I'll get the water running right now."

When Jeff left the room, Rhonda followed him down the hall. She heard the water running in the tub and took a seat on the edge of their bed to wait until Jeff told her it was ready.

Maybe I should write a letter to the Dear Caroline column again and let her know that she was wrong. My husband and I don't need counseling, because things are getting better between us now that he's being more attentive.

Once Jeff had the tub filled, Rhonda went into the bathroom to prepare for her bath. After stepping into the tub of warm water, she felt herself begin to relax.

I wonder what Gwen was going to tell me about Mom before Kimberly rushed in to tell us Megan had fallen into the pond. In all the excitement, I forgot to bring the topic up before everyone went home. The next time Gwen and I talk, I'll ask her about it.

Chapter 20

Rhonda stood on the porch, holding the remote that opened and closed their front gate, while watching her husband pull his SUV out of the yard. She wished her day off could be easy, with nothing to do but relax in the chaise longue out back. The outside temperature was pleasantly warm, without a cloud in the sky.

What a bummer to waste such a beautiful day stuck indoors working, but I have an agenda to follow. Rhonda leaned against the doorjamb and looked down at her feet. *My toenails could sure use some fresh polish, but those dumb boxes in the garage won't take care of themselves.*

Rhonda looked up and watched her husband give a wave as he pulled his rig onto the street. When he was out of sight, she clicked the button that closed the gate. It had been three weeks since their family get-together, and the decision Rhonda and Jeff had made two weeks ago was to put a large waterproof tote box outside of their front gate for any packages that might be delivered. Thankfully, their mailbox was the locking kind, and it also sat outside the front gate.

After much discussion, Rhonda and Jeff had agreed that they couldn't afford to put up a fence around the pond at this time. Besides, Rhonda didn't like the idea of having one there. It would take away from the pleasant look of the pond and waterfalls. This meant if they did have company with small children, they would need to watch carefully, making sure none of them got close to the pond unless an adult was nearby.

We probably shouldn't have bought this house, Rhonda thought as she opened the front door and went inside. *It's really too big for just the two of us, and since our townhouse still hasn't sold, I'm more concerned about our finances than ever.*

She placed the gate remote on the table in the entryway. *The sensible thing would be to move back into the townhouse and put this place on the market. Though that would be difficult to do, because Jeff and I like it here so much. No, there's got to be some other way.*

Last night, Rhonda had pleaded with Jeff to sell some of his antiques that were valuable and put the money in their savings. He'd refused and suggested instead that they should lower the price of the townhouse. Rhonda's response was that they had already lowered it once, and if they continued to lower the price, they wouldn't break even, let alone make a profit. The subject came up again at breakfast this morning, and Jeff had left for work with nothing resolved. She wondered if they would ever truly get their marriage back on track. Jeff had been more attentive lately, which helped, but this topic seemed to make him more stubborn than a mule.

I need answers, and I'm running out of ideas. My husband doesn't seem worried about our financial situation.

Rhonda made her way to the kitchen to fix a cup of tea. "One step forward and two back. Maybe there's no hope for us at all."

She took a seat at the kitchen table with her cup of tea while she went through yesterday's mail and read the newspaper. "Nothing but bills and a few junk catalogs," she muttered. "Sure don't need those."

Rhonda had vowed not to buy anything they didn't need until their townhouse sold and they could pay off the mortgage on their new place, which would leave them free of any major debt. But with their anniversary coming up, she would make an exception and get her husband a gift.

She heaved a sigh. *If I had known that we'd be in this position right now, I never would have agreed to buy this place. We both thought this endeavor might help our marriage, but we sure called it wrong. When the topic of money comes up, we end up in an argument every time.*

How often had she been over this? She'd said it to herself so many times, not to mention all the discussions that had occurred between her and Jeff. The way his face would tighten whenever she brought up the subject of money let Rhonda know it was not something her husband wanted to discuss.

She doodled on the envelope flap from a utility bill, making a frowny face. *My husband's pride has always gotten in the way of his making good decisions, and I'm just as guilty for going along with it.*

Rhonda tapped her pen and drew another upside-down smile. *I need to think of some ways to make extra money so we can pay off some credit card bills and add some to our savings account. If Jeff would be willing to sell some of his collectibles and other things he doesn't need, we could have a yard sale.*

Rhonda's lips pressed together as she gave a shake of her head. *Hosting a yard sale entails a lot of work, and neither of us has the time for that. Besides, it's doubtful that I could talk Jeff into parting with much of anything.*

Rhonda rested both arms on the table and blew out a puff of air. *If I'd seen that side of him when we were dating in college, I would have run the other way.*

She gave a soft shake of her head. *Who am I kidding? I was drawn to Jeff's outgoing personality and all the compliments and gifts he showered me with. Even if I had known about his compulsion to collect old things, I probably would have looked the other way.*

Rhonda closed her eyes and reflected on the fun times she and Jeff had shared during their two years of dating before he'd asked her to marry him. Even though he'd said she could take time to think it over, Rhonda had given him her answer right away. She'd fallen deeply in love with Jeff and couldn't wait to be his wife. Now, nearly thirteen years later, Rhonda was filled with doubts. Perhaps if she'd waited and dated more men, she would have found someone to whom she was better suited.

Desperately needing to clear her mind of these thoughts, Rhonda opened the newspaper to the Dear Caroline column. Maybe reading about some other people's problems would make her situation seem minor.

"Dear Caroline," the first one read. "My sister hasn't spoken to me for the last five years. We had an argument after our father died about who would get his guitar and harmonica. It was clearly stated in his will that he wanted my son, who plays in a band, to have both of his musical instruments. My sister didn't think it was fair for Dad to choose my son over hers—never mind that her son isn't interested in music at all. The discussion led to us parting ways. When I tried calling her a few months later, she hung up on me, but not before she said a few choice words and made it clear that she wanted nothing more to do with me. I've tried calling her a couple of other times, but she refuses to talk to me. Is there anything I can do to restore the relationship with my sister? Frustrated and Deeply Hurt."

Eager to know what Caroline's response was, Rhonda read on.

"Dear Frustrated and Deeply Hurt: Since your sister won't take any of your calls, you might consider writing her a letter or asking another family member to talk to your sister on your behalf. Perhaps an impartial person might be able to help the two of you work things out. If, however, your sister is still unwilling, you may have to respect her wishes and move on with your life without a resolution."

"Guess I'm not the only one with unresolved problems." Rhonda set the paper aside and stood. It was time to quit stalling and get something practical done.

Shortly after noon, Rhonda wandered out to the garage to empty a few more boxes. These had been in the storage unit they'd rented while living in the townhouse, and she had no idea what was in any of them.

"Probably more of Jeff's collectibles he didn't want me to know about." Her knuckles whitened when she tore open the lid and saw two glass oil lamps. "Why does my husband have to be so eccentric when it comes to his hobby? With all the stuff he's collected, he could start his own antique store."

Rhonda's forehead wrinkled as she studied the intricate lamps. She could only imagine how much money they must have cost. Was it any wonder they had so little left in their savings account?

"This has gone on long enough," Rhonda grumbled. "If Jeff won't sell some of his things, then maybe I will. There are so many items in these boxes, I doubt he would miss one or two."

Rhonda stood in front of Memory Keepers, wondering if she should go in. She'd come here with the idea of asking if they would buy the ornate oil lamp she'd placed in the trunk of her car, but now Rhonda had second thoughts. If she left the lamp here to be sold on consignment or even sold it outright to the Troyers, what would happen if Jeff came in and saw it sitting there?

A warm breeze came up, blowing several strands of Rhonda's hair to one side, and she pushed them back in place with her hand.

Suddenly, a thought came to mind, and she smiled. *I won't take the lamp inside or see if they will buy it. Instead, I'll ask them not to sell Jeff anything else if he comes into their store.*

Lois got out a dust rag to clean an empty shelf that Orley would be putting some newly acquired items on soon. Their busy morning had stretched into the noon hour, with more customers coming in than normal. Although they'd made several sales, Lois hoped things would slow down a bit for the rest of the afternoon so she could get some paperwork done.

She glanced toward the front of the store, where Orley stood behind the register, waiting on a customer. He seemed in his element here, always smiling and chatting with the people who visited their store. Her husband was definitely an extrovert, whereas Lois kept to herself a bit more. Of course, at times she was quite talkative, especially when she suspected someone was hurting emotionally and needed to talk.

The bell above the door jangled, and Lois glanced in that direction. She was surprised to see Rhonda Davis enter the store. Lois looked past the young woman to see if Jeff was with her but saw no sign of him.

Since Orley was still busy with his customer, Lois set the dust rag aside and went over to greet Rhonda. "Good afternoon." She smiled and gave the young woman a hug. "What brings you into our store today? Did you come to buy something for your husband?"

Rhonda's hand movements appeared flighty as she fiddled with the straps on her purse. "No, I. . .uh. . .came to ask you a favor."

"Of course. What is it you would like me to do?"

Rhonda shifted her purse to the other arm and lowered her voice. "If my husband comes in here again and wants to buy something, would you and your husband kindly refuse to sell it to him?"

Lois's eyes widened. She'd never had a request such as this and wasn't sure how best to respond.

"I know it might seem like a strange thing to ask, but there's a reason for it."

Lois leaned closer and listened as Rhonda explained that the home they'd left in Canton several months ago had not sold yet, and money was tight.

"And so," Rhonda continued, "we can't afford for him to be coming in here buying antiques he does not need."

"Orley and I cannot force any customer who comes into our store to leave without buying anything, but we can certainly try to dissuade him."

Rhonda pressed a palm to her chest. "Thank you. I appreciate your help with this."

Before Lois could offer a response, the young woman said, "I'd better head out now. I need to go home and get supper started before Jeff gets home from work." She turned and was out the door before Lois could form the word *goodbye*.

Lois's mind raced as she struggled with doubt. *I certainly hope I said the right thing to Rhonda. I also hope that Orley and I can talk Jeff out of buying anything if he does show up here again.*

Chapter 21

"Our driver's here. Are you about ready to head out?" Orley asked Lois from the front door.

She nodded. "I'll get my outer bonnet and be right there."

"Sounds good. I'm going out to the barn to make sure I closed the horse's stall door, then I'll join you in Rick's van."

"Okay. I'll be in the backseat waiting for you."

Orley left the house, and Lois went to get her bonnet. After putting it on over her white head covering, she stepped into the living room to get her purse. She had previously placed it on the small table next to her rocking chair, but to her surprise, it was not there now.

She looked around the room and rubbed her forehead. *I can't go without my purse. It has the money in it that we'll need for our shopping trip to Millersburg. I'll look in a few other rooms for it, but first I'd better run outside and let Orley and our driver know that I am going to be a few more minutes.*

Lois opened the front door and stepped onto the porch. *Now that's strange. There's no van in sight. I wonder if Rick drove around back, thinking I'd be coming out that door.*

Lois hurried through the kitchen and spotted her handbag sitting on the table. *At least I found my purse; now I just need to find out where those men are.* She grabbed the purse on her way to the back door and stepped out. "This doesn't make sense. There's no van here either. Did they leave without me?" She grimaced. "For goodness' sake, why would they do that? Orley knows there were some things I needed to shop for." Lois patted her purse. "I have the money right here."

Feeling a bit put out, she took off her black bonnet and placed it on the kitchen table. It was strange to be forgotten when she and Orley had talked during breakfast about going to Millersburg.

Lois stood there, looking out the window in hopes that the van would roll back into the yard to pick her up. But the longer she waited for the vehicle to return, the more the anticipation of that happening faded. *I really wanted to go with him and have some fun shopping today, but since it looks like I'll be stuck here all morning, I may as well get something done.*

Lois went to her sewing room and opened the middle drawer of her desk. *Think I'll catch up on my letter writing, and then maybe I'll bake some bacon-cheese muffins.*

After Lois finished writing the first letter to her once-widowed father, who had remarried twenty years ago and lived in Pennsylvania, her thoughts went to the visit she'd had from Rhonda yesterday. After the young woman left the antique store, Lois had waited to tell Orley about Rhonda's request until he'd finished with his customer. He had been as surprised as she was about the situation but agreed that if Jeff came in looking to buy something, he would try to talk him out of it. Of course, Lois knew, from being married to a determined man, that if Jeff really wanted to buy one of the antiques in their shop, there would be nothing she or Orley could say or do to dissuade him.

Shaking her concerns aside, Lois returned to her letter writing.

A short time later, after she'd finished the last one and was about to head for the kitchen to fix a cup of tea, Lois heard a horn honk in the front yard. She hurried to look out the living-room window and was surprised to see her husband get out of Rick's van and approach the house.

Lois opened the door and greeted him on the porch, but before she could say anything, Orley spoke first. "I'm sorry we left you behind. You'd said you'd be right out, and when I came out of the barn, I assumed you'd gotten into the back of the van." He paused and swiped at the trickle of sweat running down his forehead. "When I took my seat in the front of the van, I never thought to look in the back. Then Rick started talkin' to me and away we went. We were halfway to Millersburg when I turned in my seat to ask you a question. Imagine my surprise when I realized you weren't there." A crimson flush swept across his cheeks. "I feel like a *dummkopp*. Will you forgive me, Lois?"

She stepped forward and gave him a hug, unmindful of whether Rick might be watching them from the van. "You are not a dunce, and of course

I forgive you, dear husband. Next time, however, please make sure that I'm with you before you let our driver take off."

Orley thumped his forehead. "I guarantee it will not happen again."

Canton

Rhonda sat at her desk, going over the checklist of things that had been done in the hotel's renovation so far. Only half of the rooms were finished, but the lobby had been completely refurbished, which made it more appealing when guests checked in. Some of the older rooms were decent enough and could still be rented, but most were in the process of being repainted or having tile replaced in the bathrooms, so they were not available to guests right now. That meant less money coming in; but once the renovations were completed, the entire hotel would be more appealing, and they would hopefully make up the difference in income with more reservations from people booking rooms.

Rhonda reached around to rub a spot on her back where a muscle wanted to spasm. *I wish there was something I could do about Jeff's and my personal finances. It would help if I could talk him into selling some of his antiques.*

Rhonda reflected on how she had stopped by the Troyers' antique store yesterday. She hoped Lois had remembered to tell her husband about the request to discourage Jeff from buying any antiques. Hopefully, the Amish couple would honor that appeal.

She doodled on the edge of her paperwork. *I'm glad I made it home before Jeff did and was able to put the fancy kerosene lamp back in the box where I found it. I hate to think of what he would have said if he'd discovered the lamp was missing and questioned me about it. Of course, he would have been more upset if I'd actually sold the antique without his knowledge or permission.*

Rhonda often felt as if she were walking on eggshells around her husband when she tried to discuss their finances. Since she and Jeff had been getting along better for a while, she didn't want to do anything that might make things worse. But keeping quiet on the topic of money only meant prolonging their problem, and it almost drove her crazy. *What can I do? I wish I had some answers.*

Her desk phone rang, ending Rhonda's contemplations. When she picked up the receiver and heard Susan's voice from the corporate office, she cringed. Whenever there was something unpleasant to relate, it was usually Susan who called. She was good at what she did, and perhaps that was why she'd been hired for the job, but Susan could also come off as demanding and rude.

"Good morning, Susan. How are you?" Rhonda tried to keep her tone pleasant and upbeat.

"I'd be doing a lot better if the most recent reviews written about our hotel were not so negative."

Rhonda could almost visualize Susan's wrinkled forehead and squinted eyes. "Which reviews are you referring to?"

"The ones that were posted yesterday."

"I wasn't here then. It was my day off."

"You could have checked them from home. You do have a computer there, right?"

"Well, yes, but—"

"For heaven's sake, haven't you looked at them today?"

"No, actually, I've been working on—"

"Need I remind you that part of your job is reading the reviews and responding to them promptly?"

"I am aware of that, but as you know, I have many other responsibilities here."

"Regardless, you are supposed to check for reviews first thing every morning and respond to them in a timely manner." There was a pause, then Susan spoke again. "If you'll get on your computer right now and go to the page that lists reviews of our hotel, you will see a very negative complaint about the hot tub not working. I want you to see that it gets fixed right away. Is that understood?"

Rhonda's body heat rose as she went online and to the page Susan had directed her to. "Yes, I see that review, but it makes no sense because we don't have a hot tub at this hotel." *You should know that, Susan.* "Maybe the person who posted the review stayed at some other hotel and got it mixed up with ours."

"I don't care if they did mix it up. The review is under our hotel listing, and it needs to be dealt with right away."

"Okay, Susan, I'll take care of it."

"And remember that you need to respond positively to any and all reviews—even those that are negative."

Rhonda's pulse quickened as her muscles quivered. She felt like a child being told what to do. *Doesn't Susan believe I'm a responsible person who can think for herself? Maybe I should remind her that I do have a bachelor's degree in hotel management and one in marketing.*

"I've always responded correctly whenever we've gotten positive or negative reviews, Susan, and I will continue to do so," Rhonda said.

"Good. And don't forget to check for reviews regularly."

"I will. Is there anything else you wish to speak with me about?"

"That's all for now. You'll be hearing from me if there are any other problems, though. Goodbye, Rhonda."

When Rhonda hung up the phone, she stared at the computer screen with her teeth and fingers clenched. She wished those who worked at the corporate office—especially Susan—would be a little kinder and more understanding.

Rhonda had worked for another hotel before taking this job, and no one from the head office had ever spoken to her so harshly or condescendingly. She wished she could either quit her job here and find something closer to home or, better yet, stop working all together and make her career as a homemaker.

Rhonda bit down on her bottom lip so hard that she tasted blood. *If Jeff and I had even one child and we weren't in debt up to our necks, I could stay home and be a full-time mother.*

Tears pricked the back of her eyes. *But with Jeff refusing to adopt and our finances being so tight, there is no way I can stop working right now.*

Walnut Creek

Jeff entered the house and placed his car keys on the narrow table in the entryway. He'd had a busy day at the restaurant and was glad to be home where he could unwind.

Rhonda had called earlier to tell him that she would be working a few hours later than usual today. Some new tables and chairs had been delivered to the hotel for the breakfast room, and she needed to make sure they were set up correctly.

"I believe my wife's job is more stressful than mine," Jeff said to his reflection in the mirror above the entry table. "Too bad neither of us is old enough to retire. It would be nice to stay home all the time and enjoy our place here."

He stroked the stubble on his chin, realizing for the first time all day that he'd forgotten to shave this morning. "Guess I'd better take care of that before Rhonda gets home. She wouldn't appreciate a kiss from a prickly pear."

Jeff headed down the hall to their bedroom. When he stepped into the master bath and picked up his shaver, a thought popped into his head. *Since Rhonda's not here, I should get out that daisy pin I bought for her at that yard sale awhile back. I'll put it in a nice box and wrap it in some of that fancy paper Rhonda keeps in one of the guest room closets, along with some craft items she rarely finds time to use.*

After Jeff finished shaving, he went to his closet to change into a pair of shorts and a T-shirt. It felt good to lounge around in comfortable clothes when he was at home.

"Okay now, where did I put that daisy pin? Did I hide it in one of my dresser drawers?"

He opened each one and rummaged through the clothes, but there was no sign of the pin. He scrunched up his face then relaxed it, trying to remain calm. *It hasn't been that long since I brought the piece of jewelry home. I ought to remember where I put it.*

Jeff walked to the front door. *I'll try retracing my steps from that day. I just need to recall where I'd feel the surest of a place that Rhonda wouldn't find the pin.*

He went back to the walk-in closet and looked through some shoe boxes on the top shelf of his side. Nothing there but shoes, and some boxes were empty. Jeff didn't know why he'd saved the ones with nothing in them, but he didn't want to take the time to discard those boxes now.

Hmm. . .I'm still not remembering where I hid her gift. His shoulders slumped as he stared at his top shelf in the closet. *This isn't good at all. How can I be so absentminded or careless? Rhonda could arrive home any minute, and I wouldn't feel good about spoiling her surprise. Since our anniversary is a week away, if I can't find that pin, I'll need to buy Rhonda something else,* Jeff told himself.

Jeff remembered seeing several pieces of vintage jewelry for sale at Memory Keepers, so if he couldn't locate the daisy pin, he would stop by the Troyers' store within the next few days. Hopefully, he'd be able to find something there that Rhonda might like. Otherwise, he'd have to come up with a gift for her that didn't include vintage jewelry.

Chapter 22

It was down to the wire. Jeff and Rhonda's thirteenth anniversary had arrived, and he still hadn't found the vintage daisy pin he'd planned to give her. He had called Russ this morning to let him know that he wouldn't be at the restaurant when it first opened and might not arrive until closer to noon. He'd wished his wife a happy anniversary and reminded her that they had dinner reservations at the Chalet in the Valley restaurant for seven o'clock that evening. Jeff had also given Rhonda a kiss before she headed out the door for work half an hour ago. Since that time, he'd searched for the pin again but had finally given up and was now heading down the road toward the Troyers' Memory Keepers.

Jeff looked forward to this evening and the meal he and Rhonda would share. Although the restaurant's address was in Millersburg, the building was actually closer to the quaint village of Charm and overlooked the Doughty Valley. Jeff hoped things would go well tonight and that he and Rhonda would have a memorable evening.

A short time later, Jeff pulled up in front of Memory Keepers. When he entered the building and saw Orley sitting on a stool behind the front counter, he gave a wave and went directly to the spot where he'd last seen the vintage jewelry. But the items he'd hoped for were not there. Thinking they might have been moved, Jeff looked at the nearby tables but saw nothing there either. After a few minutes of moving things around and checking more places, he stepped up to Orley and asked if they still had some vintage jewelry in the store.

The pleasant Amish man shook his head. "Sorry, but we sold the last few pieces yesterday."

Jeff felt sweat leaching out of him from the frustration he felt and sagged against his side of the counter. "That's a disappointment. I had hoped to buy my wife a special piece of jewelry from what I'd seen in here before. Our anniversary is today, and I want to give her a nice gift when we go out to dinner this evening."

Orley's eyebrows rose slightly as he leaned both elbows on the counter. "I thought you were going to give Rhonda that antique daisy pin you found at the yard sale the four of us attended."

"I had planned to, but now I can't remember where I put it." Jeff drew in a quick breath. "Guess now I'll have to give Rhonda something else."

"Does it have to be vintage?" Orley questioned.

Jeff shrugged. "I suppose not, but since she likes daisies, I thought..."

"You might find something nice in one of the gift shops here in Walnut Creek or the village of Berlin." Orley drummed his fingertips on the countertop. "With all those stores catering to the tourists, you're bound to find something to choose from."

"Yeah, I guess." Jeff glanced around, allowing his gaze to roam over the various tables, shelves, and cabinets filled with numerous antiquated items. "Have you gotten anything new in the store lately?"

Orley rubbed the bridge of his nose before nodding. "Just some bigger pieces of antique furniture. Nothing you'd be interested in, I'm sure."

"You're right. We've already got enough furniture in our house." Jeff pulled his fingers through the back of his hair. "Since our new place is bigger than our old one, we had to buy a few extra chairs for the living room after we moved in. We also purchased a pull-out sofa for the second guest room to accommodate extra overnight guests, should we have any. Our townhouse in Canton had a spare bedroom, so fortunately we already had furniture to put in the other guest room at our new place."

"I assume your townhouse still hasn't sold?"

"No, and I'm beginning to wonder if it ever will."

Orley stepped around from the register and placed his hand on Jeff's shoulder. "I can understand your feelings of discouragement, but you can't give in to despair or let negative thoughts overtake you."

That's easy for you to say. You're not the one in my predicament. Jeff didn't voice his thoughts. Instead, he forced a smile and said, "I'd better get going and see if I can find something for Rhonda at one of the shops in Berlin before I head to my restaurant in Canton."

He was almost to the front door when Orley called out to him. "Wait a minute, Jeff. There's something I'd like to give you and Rhonda for your anniversary."

Jeff turned around to face the bearded man. "I appreciate the thought, but there's no need for that."

"Please don't say no. I'd really like to give you something, and I'm sure if my wife wasn't in the back room doing some paperwork, she'd agree with me." Orley walked over to one of the tables in the center of the room, picked up something Jeff couldn't distinguish, and placed it in a small box he'd taken from under the table. Then Orley came back to where Jeff stood and handed it to him. "Happy anniversary. Perhaps you and your wife can open this tonight, either before or after you go out for supper."

A warm flush crept across Jeff's cheeks. "Thank you." Gripping the box in his hands, he hurried out the door. *That surely was unexpected.*

Canton

"I'm surprised you're still here," Lori said when Rhonda met her in the hotel's downstairs hallway at four o'clock that afternoon.

"Why wouldn't I be?" Rhonda asked.

"With today being your wedding anniversary and figuring you and your husband would have made plans for this evening, I assumed you'd be getting off work early this evening." Lori brushed a loose curl aside and smiled.

Rhonda shook her head. "I got here a little later than normal this morning so I could pick up something I had ordered for Jeff at the jewelry store. Now I have to make up the time I lost." She glanced at her watch. "I'll be leaving by five, which should give me plenty of time to get home, change into something nicer, and still make our seven o'clock dinner reservations."

"Where are you going to eat? I assume it's not Jeff's restaurant?"

Rhonda shook her head. "I don't know where it is, but Jeff said it's someplace close to home and has a very nice atmosphere."

Lori smiled. "I'll be eager to hear about your evening, and I hope you and Jeff have a wonderful anniversary."

"Thank you, Lori. I hope so too."

Rhonda watched her ever-pleasant employee amble toward the front desk as a couple came in through the front entrance with their suitcases in tow. Rhonda listened to Lori greet them with a cheerful tone. Even though at times the young woman complained of some discomfort from her pregnancy, she nearly always seemed to be in good spirits. Lori had said once that despite the distresses that went with being pregnant, it was worth it and that she couldn't wait to be a mother to her precious baby.

Rhonda bit the inside of her lip. *If only I could be in her shoes.*

Walnut Creek

"You look beautiful in that color," Jeff said when Rhonda stepped out of their master bathroom wearing a pale yellow dress with white trim around the collar.

"Thanks."

Jeff liked to see his wife dressed up, but even more than that, he loved to spend quality time with her. He watched her go to the closet and pick out two pairs of shoes—a white pair of heels and black flats.

"Which shoes should I wear?" Rhonda turned toward him.

He shrugged. "Either one looks fine to me."

Rhonda slid on the heels and stood in front of the full-length mirror. "I should probably go with these. What do you think?"

"They look nice, but wouldn't the others be more comfortable?"

"Yes, that's true." She removed them and slipped on her leather flats, gazing back at the mirror. "These are dressy enough, and they are more comfortable on my feet."

Rhonda put the white ones away in their closet. Then she stood in front of the mirror fussing with her hair a bit before walking over to Jeff. "I'm ready to go."

"Okay, but before we leave, I'd like to give you something." *Sure wish I could have found that dainty daisy pin. It would have looked great on Rhonda's yellow dress.* Jeff handed her a peach-colored gift bag. "This isn't what I'd originally planned to give you, but I hope you'll like it just the same. Happy anniversary, honey."

Rhonda opened the bag, and when she reached inside, a smile spread across her lovely face. "A picture-framed alarm clock. What a clever idea. And you even thought to put one of our wedding pictures in it. Thank you, Jeff."

"I'm glad you like it." He felt a head-to-toe release of all tension.

She placed his gift on her nightstand and stepped over to her side of the dresser. "Now it's your turn." Rhonda opened her top dresser drawer and took out a gift box with a green bow stuck to the top. "I ordered this for you from the jewelry store in Canton. I hope you like it."

Jeff lifted the lid off the box and grinned when he withdrew a wristwatch. "Wow, honey, this is great. I especially like that it has the logo for my favorite football team in the center of the watch. This will be fun to wear on game days."

Her gaze remained fixed on him as he set the time and put the watch on his left arm. "It cost a little more than some of the other watches I looked it, but I've been saving up to get it, so I hope you like it."

"I love it, and I love you even more." Jeff bent his head and gave her a lingering kiss. When they broke away from each other, he looked at the watch again. "We'd better go or we're gonna miss our reservations."

"Okay. I just want to check my makeup and get my purse, and then I'll meet you in the car."

"Sounds good, and if you have no objections, we'll take your sporty car tonight. It's classier looking and a lot more fun to drive than my SUV."

Rhonda offered him another pleasant smile and nodded before going over to her makeup table.

Jeff whistled as he headed out the door with a spring in his step. He hoped the rest of their evening would go as well as the beginning had.

Millersburg

"This restaurant is so quaint and lovely." Rhonda smiled at Jeff from across the table. "It's like a hidden gem here in the heart of Amish country."

He nodded. "You're right. I chose this place because it offers Swiss, Austrian, and American cooking, which gives us a varied menu to choose from. The atmosphere is also nice."

"I agree." Rhonda studied the rich wooden decor throughout the dining room. It had a warm, cozy feeling and made her feel as if she were in another country. "Those spunky goats we saw in the fenced-in area outside the restaurant when we arrived were pretty cute too."

"Yeah." Jeff chuckled. "I really got a kick out of the biggest one and the way he sat up there on the hill, like he was a king overlooking his domain."

She laughed. "That was pretty funny."

"Do you know what you're going to order?" Jeff pointed to Rhonda's menu.

She pressed her lips together and studied the entrées. "Nearly everything listed here appeals, but I think I'll go with the chicken schnitzel. It comes with either asparagus or broccoli and one side."

"Which of the sides sounds good to you?"

"Think I'll try the hot German potato salad. I've never had it served that way before. What are you going to order, Jeff?"

"I'm goin' with the Reuben schnitzel, topped with sauerkraut and Guggisberg Swiss cheese. It's also served with broccoli or asparagus, covered with hollandaise sauce. For my side, I'll get either the mashed potatoes and gravy or some applesauce."

"There are a lot of carbs in mashed potatoes, and the gravy would also be fattening."

Watching Jeff's face tighten as he rubbed the back of his neck caused Rhonda to wish she hadn't said anything negative about the potatoes and gravy. "I—I didn't mean to imply that you need to watch your weight, I just thought. . ." *I suppose I shouldn't have thrown cold water on his choice for this evening's meal. It's not like he normally eats like that. Tonight's a special occasion for us.*

Their waitress, wearing a Bavarian-style dress, arrived at their table and asked if they had any questions about the menu.

"No questions on my part," Jeff was quick to say. "I think we're both ready to order." He looked at Rhonda. "Why don't you go first?"

Rhonda told the young woman what she wanted, and then Jeff placed his order. After the waitress left, they sat quietly, drinking their water. When Rhonda couldn't stand the silence any longer, she said, "Are you upset with me, Jeff, for reminding you about the carbs in the potatoes?"

"No. You were right. I don't need the extra carbs, and I'm sure I'll enjoy the applesauce."

"Okay. I just don't want to spoil your evening."

"Don't worry—you haven't. And unless the food is either cold or not cooked to our liking, the meal won't be spoiled either."

"That sure was a good dinner. I enjoyed every bite of food on my plate." Rhonda reached across the leather seat of the sports car and placed her hand on Jeff's arm.

"Mine was good too," he agreed as he shifted it into fifth gear, being careful to keep his eyes on the road. Now that the sun had set and they were driving on a curvy road, Jeff needed to give driving his full attention.

Jeff felt like he owned the road, shifting with pleasure and having all the vehicle's power at his fingertips. His SUV had an automatic transmission, which he didn't mind, but Rhonda's sporty-looking vehicle was more fun to drive.

Rhonda turned on the radio, and the pleasant music was no distraction at all. In fact, Jeff felt quite content and relaxed. In addition to the tasty meal they'd eaten, the conversation at the table between him and Rhonda had been pleasant and upbeat. Neither of them had mentioned their jobs or said anything negative to the other. Jeff was convinced that their marriage had gotten back on track and without much effort from either of them.

We have hit a few bumps in the road of our marriage, Jeff admitted to himself, *but I'm glad Rhonda and I didn't seek counseling like some other couples we know. The next time I see Orley, I'll let him know that things are going better between me and Rhonda.*

Thinking about Orley caused Jeff to remember the anniversary gift the Amish man had given him this morning. When he'd arrived home from work this afternoon, Jeff had set the box on the kitchen table after going through the mail. He still couldn't figure out why Orley would give them anything for their anniversary, since the Amish couple didn't know Jeff and Rhonda that well. Even so, the gift was a nice gesture, and Jeff was eager to find out what was inside that small box. He'd forgotten about it until now and hadn't mentioned it to Rhonda yet.

Guess I'll wait till we get home, and then I'll show her the gift and we can open it together.

"Jeff, look out!"

His wife's shout along with the two eyes shining in the road made him jump. Jeff gripped the steering wheel and hit the brakes, but it was too late. The sickening thump when Rhonda's sporty car hit the deer was deafening to Jeff's ears.

Chapter 23

"I don't know why you're so upset with me. It's not my fault a deer ran in front of our car." Jeff's shoulders slumped. "I feel terrible about hitting the poor thing. I've never run into an animal before, and I hope I never have to live through something like that again."

"It was *my* car, Jeff, and it's probably totaled." Tears sprang to Rhonda's eyes and ran down her hot cheeks as they stood on the shoulder of the road waiting for help to arrive.

"It will be okay. We have insurance, and I'll get them called right away." Jeff reached for her hand. "It could have been worse. At least neither of us is hurt like that poor animal." He pointed to the small doe lying dead by the side of the road. "I'm sorry our lovely evening had to end with me hitting the deer."

"I read in a magazine someone left at the hotel a few weeks ago that over one million deer are killed each year from getting hit by a car." Rhonda shivered even though the evening air was quite warm. "I shudder to think of how many people have been killed when their vehicle has hit a deer."

"Any loss of human life is a tragedy." Jeff let go of Rhonda's hand and slipped his arm around her. "You're trembling. Are you cold?"

"No, just shook up over what happened to the deer and my car."

"I get it. My legs are kinda shaky too."

Rhonda looked at him and grimaced. "How am I going to get to work in the morning?"

"I'll drive you there and pick you up when you're ready to leave for the day. We may have to rely on my rig alone until we can get a new one.

It is doubtful that yours can be fixed."

Rhonda brought a shaky hand to her forehead. "This is one more thing that we didn't need to happen."

"I agree, but since you have full coverage on your car, we'll either be reimbursed for the repairs or given the money to buy a new vehicle."

Rhonda moved closer to her car, noticing some fur left by the animal where the dents showed. She looked down, saw that her shoe rested in the blood spot from the doe, and groaned. "I wish this part of our evening had never happened. I feel so bad for that poor animal." Rhonda tried to stave off more tears as she continued to stare at her damaged vehicle. "I really liked my car, and I hope it can be repaired, but if it's not fixable, and we have to wait to buy a new one, you'll be stuck taking me to and from the hotel five days a week."

"I don't mind driving you, but it might be best if we see about renting a car. Since you have good coverage, I think our insurance company will pay for that too."

"No, they won't. With our finances being tight, I called a few weeks ago and lowered our premium by cutting back on a few things we had on our policy, including reimbursement for renting a car in the case mine was ever out of commission."

Jeff folded his arms and groaned. "You should have consulted me before you did that, Rhonda. Doesn't my input count for anything?"

"Of course, it does, but. . ."

Rhonda's words trailed off when two vehicles pulled up almost simultaneously. One was a sheriff's car and the other a tow truck. For now, their discussion was over, but no doubt it would be dealt with again when they got home.

Walnut Creek

Lois looked away from the to-do list she'd been working on and glanced at the grandfather clock across the room. It was getting close to ten o'clock—definitely time for bed.

She nibbled on one of the homemade snickerdoodles she'd made after work. It went well with the warm cup of chamomile tea she had brewed for herself. A little snack before bed wouldn't hurt anything, and it sure was tasty.

Lois's day had been busy. She'd had time to do a few chores before she and Orley went to work at the antique shop this morning. Soon after they'd opened their business, a few elderly English people, possibly tourists, had come in. Lois had introduced herself, saying that if they needed anything to let her know. She figured the ladies must be from out of town because she'd never seen them around before.

Even now, Lois had to chuckle when she thought about how those three ladies browsed as they chatted about the different things the antique shop offered. The tallest woman had pointed to an old train set and commented that it looked like the one her dad used to have.

Not wanting to wake Orley while he rested, Lois suppressed a snicker. *When a certain piece stirs up memories for a person, I guess they can't help but want to talk about it.*

Her gaze went to her husband, slouched in his favorite chair. His eyes were closed, and soft snores vibrated from his nose.

Lois couldn't figure out how Orley could doze for a few hours in his chair and go right to sleep when they went to bed. She would have to be sick or overly tired to sleep in her chair.

She finished the last cookie and drank the remainder of her tea. Then she rose from her chair and went to the kitchen to rinse the dishes and pull down the window shades. *I should put the cookie tin away first and then do up these dishes.* Lois ran the water and added some detergent in the sink while pondering a few things: *I wonder how Jeff and Rhonda are doing? I hope they are able to work things out.* While the warm water ran, she began washing the few dishes. *That young couple needs prayer, and I'll be sure to do that before I go to sleep tonight.*

Lois finished her task and went back to where Orley slept. She looked out the front-room window and saw the lights of a buggy going by. Soon it slowed to make the turn into the neighbor's driveway. *I thought so. It's the Millers. They must have been out visiting this evening. They're good people, such a nice young family, and their three little ones are so sweet.*

A lump formed in her throat. *If Orley and I could have had children, I would have tried to be the very best mother. I'm sure Orley would have been a good father too.*

Shaking her thoughts aside, Lois waited until the clock chimed ten times. When her husband didn't budge, she left her chair, walked over to him, and gave his arm a nudge. "Wake up, sleepyhead. It's time for bed."

Orley's nose twitched slightly, but his eyes remained closed.

"Ich geh noch em bett." She shook his arm with a little firmness this time.

His eyelids opened just a crack, but he made no effort to move. "Okay, you go ahead to bed. I'll be there soon."

She shook her head. "If I leave you here in this chair and go to bed by myself, you'll wake up in the morning in the same place you are right now."

Orley yawned and sat up a little straighter. "You're right as always, my dear fraa."

She snickered. "Jah, sure. I'm only right when I'm agreeing with you on something."

"That's not true. You're right at least fifty percent of the time."

She gave his arm a poke. "Come now, silly *mann*. We can talk about this pointless subject another time when you're not half asleep."

He got up from his chair and turned to face her. "I'll have you know that I'm wide awake."

"I'll bet you won't be once your *kopp* hits the pillow on our comfortable bed."

Orley bent his head and kissed her cheek. "Right again, Fraa."

She rolled her eyes then began to move away from his chair, but he caught hold of her hand.

"Wait a minute, Lois. There's something I've been meaning to tell you."

"Oh? What's that?"

"This morning, while you were busy doing paperwork in the back room, Jeff Davis came into our store, wanting to buy a piece of vintage jewelry for his wife because it was their anniversary."

She clutched the sides of her apron. "Oh dear. What did you tell him?"

"I said all the antique jewelry had sold, which was the truth."

"Was he satisfied with your answer?"

Orley shrugged. "I think so, but I could tell from the way his shoulders sagged that he wasn't happy about it."

"As I recall, you mentioned the day we met the Davises at one of the yard sales we'd stopped at that Jeff had bought an old but pretty pin to give his wife."

"True, but he couldn't remember where he put it, so he was looking to find something to replace the daisy pin."

"Did he look at anything else in the store or mention wanting to buy something?"

Orley shook his head. "Nope. When I suggested that he might be able to find something suitable for Rhonda in one of the gift shops here in town or perhaps Berlin, Jeff was ready to head out the door." Orley gave his beard a quick tug. "Before he left, I gave him an anniversary gift from us."

She tilted her head to one side. "Oh, what did you give him?"

"Remember that old plaque with Psalm 46:10 written on it: 'Be still, and know that I am God'? You know, the one that had been lying on one of the center display tables."

"Jah. We've had it in the store for a long time. I kept thinking someone would buy it, but the plaque's pretty much been ignored." Lois tapped her chin with her index finger. "Maybe we should put it in a more prominent place so it's more visible."

"There's no need for that now, because I put the plaque in a box and handed it to Jeff before he went out the door."

Lois's lips parted slightly before they formed a full-fledged smile. "That was a good gift to give the young couple whose marriage seems to be struggling. If they'd come to know God personally, He would be there to help them deal with any problems that might come their way."

Orley nodded. "My thoughts exactly, and for that, I'll continue to pray."

Jeff entered the house behind Rhonda and paused in the hallway. "Does it seem warmer than normal in here, or am I just overheated from dealing with the ordeal of hitting that deer?"

Rhonda stood beside him a moment and nodded. "It is quite warm. It hasn't been this uncomfortable in the house before, and it seems a little odd to me. What did you set the thermostat on before we left to go out to dinner?"

"Like usual, seventy-two."

"And did you make sure that it was set for the air-conditioning to run and not the furnace for heat?"

She must think I'm an idiot or something. Jeff's body temperature came up a notch as his jaw tightened. "It's only the first week of September, and we haven't had any cold weather yet, so why would you think I'd be stupid enough to turn on the heat?"

"I didn't say you were stupid."

"Sounded like it to me. I feel like you are treating me like a child."

"Don't be so defensive, Jeff. I was only asking if—oh, never mind. I'll go look at the thermostat myself."

"If you don't believe me, go ahead and look all you want." Jeff put both hands on his hips.

"I didn't say that."

"Don't bother checking. I'll take a look at it myself." He moved past her and hurried down the hall, although the sound of her footsteps told him she was close behind.

When Jeff viewed the thermostat, his eyes widened. "What in the world?"

"What's wrong?" Jeff felt his wife's warm breath as she peered over his shoulder.

"It's set to seventy-two, like I said, and it's in AC mode. Even so, the temperature here in the house is up to eighty. It's no wonder we feel hot."

Rhonda sagged against the wall. "This is not good, Jeff. Now we're going to have to call someone to check it out, and we'll probably end up with an expensive repair bill—or worse yet, discover that we need a whole new air-conditioning unit." She sighed. "I dread trying to sleep in this overly warm house tonight. We're going to be miserable."

"Maybe it won't be so bad. For starters, we should open some windows, which oughta help, since the outside air felt cooler than it does in here. And there's a box fan in the garage I can bring in."

"All right, but before we get started with that, I really need something cold to drink."

"Same here. Let's go to the kitchen and open those windows first, and then we can take the pitcher of lemonade out of the refrigerator."

"Okay." Rhonda turned and trudged down the hall as if in slow motion.

Jeff felt bummed about the way this evening had turned out. He'd wanted their anniversary celebration to go well. It had been so pleasant during their meal at the restaurant, but hitting the deer had put a damper on things. To make matters worse, Jeff felt sure Rhonda blamed him for the accident. Despite the lateness of the evening, Jeff had already notified their insurance company about the accident and was told that someone would be by the house tomorrow around noon to pick up Rhonda's vehicle.

The ride home with the tow truck driver as they'd brought her pathetic-looking car back to their yard hadn't helped either. While the driver talked nonstop to Jeff the whole way, Rhonda sat silent, staring straight ahead with her arms crossed.

When they entered the kitchen, Jeff opened both kitchen windows, while Rhonda got out two glasses and filled them with ice cubes. The air coming through the open windows was a little cooler than the stuffy kitchen, but there wasn't much of a breeze. No doubt, it would be a miserable night trying to sleep, even if they opened every window in the house.

Once Rhonda poured lemonade into their glasses, they both took a seat.

"What's this?" she asked, gesturing to the cardboard box on the table.

"Oh, yeah; I almost forgot about that. Orley gave it to me when I stopped at Memory Keepers this morning."

Rhonda's forehead wrinkled. "You bought something from the antique store?"

"No. He put some item in a box before I left and said it was an anniversary gift for us from him and Lois."

She took a drink from her glass and placed it back on the table. "That's odd. Orley doesn't know you or me very well. Why would he give us anything?"

Jeff shrugged. "I don't know, but even though his wife wasn't in the room at the time, he said he was sure she would also want us to have the gift."

"Have you opened it to see what's inside?"

Jeff shook his head. "I was waiting so we could open the gift together."

Rhonda glanced at the clock on the far wall. "We may as well do it now, because in another twenty minutes, it'll be past midnight and it will no longer be our anniversary."

"Yeah, right." He pushed the box in her direction. "Why don't you do the honors?"

Rhonda pulled the flaps open and reached into the box. When she withdrew the gift, she wasn't smiling. "Why would Orley give us this?" She turned the antiquated plaque to face Jeff.

His pulse quickened and his chest tightened. "Be still, and know that I am God." He leaned back in his chair and groaned. "I thought I'd made it clear to that determined Amish man that you and I are not religious."

"Apparently, you didn't make it clear enough." She placed the unwanted gift on the table. "So now what are we supposed to do with this?"

"Beats me." Jeff turned his hands palms up. "Guess we could pitch it in the garbage."

Her mouth twisted as though she'd eaten something distasteful. "We probably shouldn't do that, in case Orley asks you about it, but I'm certainly not going to hang it on any wall in our house."

"Agreed. I'm going out to the garage and get that box-fan to use in our bedroom tonight." Jeff picked up his glass and drank the sweet liquid in just a few gulps. He had half a notion to return the old plaque but didn't want to hurt Orley's feelings. *Guess for now at least, I'll stick it out in the garage someplace where I won't have to see it.*

Chapter 24

A loud thump followed by a yelp caused Lois to sit straight up in bed. A quick glance at her husband's side of the bed told her exactly what had happened. Orley had a habit of sleeping close to the edge of the bed and had fallen out on more than one occasion. This morning was a repeat performance.

She sprang out of bed and went around to where he lay on the floor. "Are you all right?"

"I'm fine." He turned over, got up slowly, and took a seat on the bed.

"You always say you're fine even when you're not." Lois followed the comment with a click of her tongue.

"Well, it's true. All I feel is a little *glumpe* on my kopp." Orley touched his forehead.

Lois placed her fingers on the spot he had touched. "Feels more like a goose egg has formed than just a little lump."

"No matter. It's nothing for you to worry about. Now that we're awake, we'd better get dressed, do our chores, and eat breakfast so I can get out our bikes. Since we're having another sale, we don't want to be late opening the store today."

Lois glanced at the clock on Orley's bedside table to check the time. "You're right. The alarm will be going off soon anyway." She placed her hand on his arm. "I think we should call one of our drivers to take us to the store today, though."

He tipped his head back and looked up at her. "How come?"

"You always peddle fast and furious when we're biking, and with that lump you earned when you hit the floor, you might feel light-headed, or you could even faint. Then you'd be making a trip to see the doctor."

Orley stood up, planting his feet in a wide stance. "I am fine, I tell you. We do not need a driver or a doctor. When the weather turns cold and we want to stay warm, then I'll call on someone to take us to the store in their motorized vehicle."

Lois lifted her shoulders in a halfhearted shrug. "Okay, Husband, whatever you say."

Canton

When Jeff pulled into the hotel parking lot, Rhonda told him goodbye and got out of his vehicle. It seemed so odd not to be driving her own car today, and she couldn't help but feel sorry for herself.

"I hope your day goes well," Jeff called through the open window on the passenger's side.

With a backward wave, Rhonda nodded and hurried inside.

A few seconds after entering the hotel, she was approached by Gayle, the night desk clerk. "Lori's husband called awhile ago. She went to the hospital with heavy contractions during the night, and her baby girl was born early this morning."

Rhonda's eyes widened. "Is everything all right? Lori's due date wasn't supposed to be for another two weeks."

"Both mother and daughter are doing fine," Gayle responded. "But she obviously will not be working today, so someone will need to take the next shift."

"That someone will have to be me." Rhonda took in a few deep breaths. She was exhausted, having gotten to bed so late last night, and wished now that she had hired someone to take Lori's place earlier, since she wouldn't be coming back to work at the hotel anytime soon if at all.

"Can you stay a little longer while I go to my office and make some phone calls?"

Gayle bit down on her bottom lip. "I could stay another hour, but then I'll need to go because I have a dental appointment."

"Okay, that's fine." Rhonda hurried to her office and took a seat at the desk, where she pulled out a list of people who had recently applied for a job at the hotel. She was about to call one of them to set up an interview, when her cell phone rang. Seeing who the caller was, she felt compelled to answer. "Sorry, Gwen, but I'm at the hotel, and I really don't have time to talk."

"This will only take a few minutes," her sister said. "It's about our mother."

Rhonda sat up straight. "Is something wrong with Mom? Is she sick or has she been in an accident?"

"No, she's fine physically." There was a pause. "Remember on the Fourth of July when I was about to tell you something concerning our mother?"

"Oh, yeah. . .you never finished your sentence because Megan fell into the pond."

"Right. And I've been meaning to call you ever since but haven't gotten around to it until now."

"I meant to call you as well." Rhonda was on the verge of telling her sister about Jeff hitting a deer and how their AC had gone out, but Gwen spoke first.

"Mom has been doing something out of character for her lately."

"In what way?"

"She's entered the dating game."

Rhonda's mouth nearly fell open. "Say what?"

"Yeah, she's gone out with two different men so far."

"You're kidding, right?"

"No, I'm telling the truth."

Rhonda set the phone on her desk and placed both hands against her ever-warming cheeks. *Where did Mom meet these guys? This is so unlike her to be dating. It's hard to picture this happening.*

After a long pause, her sister spoke again. "Are you still there, Rhonda?"

She picked up the phone and held it close to her ear. "Yes, I'm here. Just in shock is all."

"It was a surprise for me too, but I've come to accept the idea because Mom deserves to be happy."

Rhonda figured with Mom going all religious these days that she must have lost her good sense. The acceptance she heard from Gwen about their mother's actions only deepened the betrayal she felt, which lit her fuse.

"Our mother deserved to be happy with Dad too, but he made sure her life and ours were miserable." Rhonda felt a tightness around her eyes, and it was all she could do to keep her voice down. "Did you forget the vow our badly shaken mother made after he walked out on her for another woman?"

"No, I haven't forgotten. Mom said she would never get involved with another man because after Dad had cheated on her not once but three times that we know of, she lost faith in men."

"And with good reason." Rhonda's head began to pound. "What brought on this sudden need for a man in her life? Mom lives close to you and gets to see her granddaughters nearly every day, so she shouldn't be lonely."

"Spending time with a man who has similar interests and is kind enough to take her on dates isn't the same as being with the girls."

"But which man? We all had to deal with the mistakes our mother made in choosing our father," Rhonda was quick to say. "And has she really learned her lesson? What if the next guy she chooses isn't any better than Dad?"

"Remember, she's just getting started in this dating phase."

"Yes, but if either of the two men she's seen are merely pretending with her, and Mom doesn't see through their lies, then things may move faster than you think."

"I don't believe she's considering marriage. Not at this time, at least. I mean, I haven't picked up on anything. She's only gone out with the one man twice and the other fellow just once."

Many questions rolled around in Rhonda's head. "Who are these men? I hope she's not involved in internet dating, like Jeff's father has recently started doing."

"No, not at this point anyhow. The two men both go to our church, and they seem very nice. I must add there seems to be a good-sized group of single, middle-aged men who belong to our congregation."

Oh great. This just gets better. My sister should be keeping a close eye on our mother. "Anyone can attend church or proclaim to be a Christian, but that doesn't mean they are. Take our father, for example. He went to church at Christmas and Easter and came to our Bible school programs. And what did that prove?" Rhonda's voice had risen a little higher, and if she didn't get off the phone with her sister soon, she might end up yelling.

"Listen, Gwen, I really do need to go. Things are hectic for me right now."

"Oh, I'm sorry. Is there anything I can do?"

"Not unless you have a magic wand to wave and make everything better in my life."

"What's wrong?"

"It's nothing you can help with, and I have to hang up now so I can take care of hotel business."

"Okay, but I want you to know that I'll be praying for you."

"Don't bother. God's never answered any of my prayers. But if you want to ask God for something, pray that Mom gets out of the dating game and concentrates on something that won't leave her with low esteem and a broken heart." Rhonda didn't give her sister a chance to respond. "Bye, Gwen," she said and clicked off the phone.

Rhonda sat several minutes, trying to digest the conversation she'd just had with Gwen. It couldn't have happened at a worse time than now, with everything else falling from the sky. *How can my sister be so casual about this?* She brought a shaky hand up to her throbbing brows and began to massage them. The pain in Rhonda's head had increased, but she forced herself to pick up the phone and call the first name on her list of employee prospects.

Jeff hoped things would go well for himself and Rhonda today. Since he was the one who'd wrecked Rhonda's car, he wanted to figure out a way to make things better.

He parked his SUV in the parking lot and headed for his restaurant. Shortly after Jeff entered the building and had talked to Russ, he went to his office to check for any messages he may have gotten on his cell phone that morning. He saw there was a missed call from his dad, but he hadn't left a message. He decided to return the call before things got busy. Hopefully, since Dad ran his own computer repair business and might not be open yet, he would have a few minutes to talk.

Jeff punched in his dad's number and wasn't surprised when he answered right away. "Hey, Dad. I saw that you called me last night, but there was no message."

"Another call came in I needed to answer, so I didn't bother to leave a message. Figured I'd call again this morning, but you beat me to it."

"So, what's up?"

"Nothing much. We haven't talked since the Fourth of July, so I wanted to see how things are going with you and Rhonda and wish you a happy anniversary."

"I should've called you too, but things got busy here at the restaurant, and now everything's kind of crazy for me and Rhonda. Our anniversary was pretty much ruined."

"What happened?"

Jeff explained about hitting the deer and mentioned that the air conditioner at their house had quit working. "Someone is coming out to look at it later today."

"I'm sorry to hear about your problems. Is there anything I can do to help? I'd be happy to pay for the AC repairs or—"

"No thanks, Dad. I can manage this on my own."

"Are you sure?"

"Yeah."

"Well, let me know if you change your mind. In the meantime, I'll be praying that things work out and you don't end up having to get a new air-conditioning unit. Those can be pretty expensive, you know."

Jeff grimaced. "I'm well aware."

"If you'd like to borrow my truck until you get a new car, let me know. I will see if one of your brothers would be free to follow me down to your place in their vehicle sometime this weekend."

Jeff lifted his gaze to the ceiling. *Rhonda would never drive that old truck.* "Umm. . .I appreciate the offer, but if we can't get another car right away, we'll probably rent one for Rhonda."

"Why throw your money away on a rental?" Dad questioned.

"I don't want to put you out. I'm sure I'll come up with something."

"It's no big deal, and it's a parent's right to help out their children."

Jeff's tone softened. "Okay, thanks for the offer. I'll let you know if I change my mind. Talk to you later, Dad."

When Jeff ended the call, he put both hands behind his head and leaned back in his chair with a groan. It was nice of his father to offer money or the loan of his truck, but Jeff wished Dad hadn't mentioned the word *prayer*.

Walnut Creek

Feeling winded and hot, Lois had a hard time keeping up with her husband as they rode their bikes along the shoulder of the road. Apparently, the bump on his head hadn't affected his ability to ride a bike at rapid speed.

And she wasn't that surprised about it either. But in this extreme heat, she wished he would slow down. They'd been going so quickly, she couldn't enjoy the passing scenery, as she normally would. The only good thing about traveling this fast was that they'd probably get to the store with time to spare before they needed to put the Open sign in the front window. That would give Lois a little time to sit at her desk in the back room and write a few letters. She didn't like getting behind on things, but it seemed to be happening more often than not these days.

I need to figure out some way to get more organized and schedule the things I need to accomplish in a better way, she told herself. *There are just not enough hours in a day to get everything done.*

By the time they'd reached the store and had their bicycles brought into one of the back rooms where they kept them during business hours, Lois felt quite winded and more than ready to sit and rest awhile. Orley too appeared to be out of breath, so they took seats in their little office area. Lois found both of them a cold bottle of water, which had been in the small cooler in Orley's bicycle basket.

"How are you feeling?" She wiped some perspiration from above her brows and looked over at her husband.

"Hot and tired, but otherwise I'm fine and dandy." He touched his forehead. "The lump from this morning's mishap has gone down some, and it doesn't hurt at all."

"I'm glad to hear it." She leaned closer to him. "I've said this before and I'll say it once again—you really shouldn't sleep so close to the edge of the bed."

"I can't help it. I don't start out that way, but sometime during the night, my body shifts to the right. I guess I like to travel, especially in my sleep." Orley chuckled.

"Maybe we should get a bigger bed. You know—a king size."

"I'll give it some thought." He chugged on his water and wiped the sweat from his forehead with a tissue he'd pulled from the little box on Lois's desk. "So, I've been thinking. . ."

"About what?"

"Jeff Davis. I'm worried that I did the wrong thing by giving him that religious plaque."

"Is it ever wrong to share the good news with others? And by the way, those doubts after doing something good aren't from Him." She pointed upward.

Orley tapped a finger against the bridge of his nose. "I suppose not, but that young man is struggling, and I don't want to do anything that might push him further from finding a personal relationship with God."

"I can relate with what you've said, and I'm trying to remember to pray regularly for Jeff and Rhonda. I understand certain things, especially when I. . ." Lois stopped talking and drank some more water. It was not the right time for this discussion. She had a letter to finish writing, and Orley should be in the front part of their store, ready to greet customers when it was time to open. They could continue their discussion about the correct way to tell others about Jesus some other time.

Chapter 25

Canton

"How'd your day go?" Jeff asked when Rhonda got into his SUV at six o'clock that evening.

"Not well."

"How come? I hope you didn't get locked in the storeroom again."

After fastening her seatbelt, Rhonda shook her head. "That door's been fixed."

"What kind of problems did you encounter?"

"To begin with, Lori's baby came early, so she couldn't work today, which meant I had to fill in for her at the desk."

"It's great that she had her baby, but I'm sorry you had a rough day." Jeff turned down the music playing on the radio. "Couldn't you have called one of your other employees to take Lori's place?"

"I tried, but everyone had either made other plans for the day or didn't answer their phone."

Jeff pulled out of the parking lot. "Guess you'll need to hire someone to replace Lori now, huh?"

The traffic was busy at that time of the evening, and instead of responding to her husband's comment, Rhonda cried out, "Jeff, watch out for that van!"

"I see him." Jeff braked and tooted his horn. "What an impatient driver. He shouldn't be allowed to drive. I wonder how he got his license."

"You need to be more careful. Remember the deer? We don't need to wreck another vehicle."

Why did she have to bring that up? "I don't need the reminder, and please stop critiquing my driving. I'm doing fine. It was the other guy who messed up. We'll be home soon and out of this dumb traffic, so try to relax."

Rhonda didn't respond.

Jeff repeated his question about hiring a new employee.

"Yes, I will need to find a replacement for Lori. I made several calls from my list of recent applicants, so tomorrow I'll be conducting a few interviews." Rhonda sighed. "Hopefully, I will find someone suitable soon, because there are many things I need to do that won't get done if I'm at the reception desk too many hours."

"I hate to tell you this, but I have some news that won't make your day any brighter."

"Is it about my car or the air-conditioning?"

"Both. I went home around noon and met with the cooling-and-heating technician."

"What did he say?"

"The compressor went out, and since it's an older one, they can't get new parts to repair it. So, our only alternative is to get a new air-conditioning unit, which of course will be expensive."

"And impossible at this time."

"Are you willing to sleep in a sweatbox like we did last night with only a few open windows and a box fan that didn't cool our bedroom enough?"

"The Amish do it, and they survive."

"We're not Amish, Rhonda, and we aren't used to sleeping in an overly hot room."

"We'll have to get used to it because we have no extra money to put out for a new AC."

Jeff couldn't miss the determination in his wife's voice. *Should I say something about my dad's offer to help?* Although he didn't want to accept money from his father, for the sake of keeping the house cool until winter set in, he might do it. Since the furnace hadn't been affected, only the air-conditioning unit, they should be fine for heat all winter.

"We could put a new AC unit on one of our credit cards," Jeff suggested.

"No way!"

His wife's shrill tone caused Jeff to have second thoughts about telling her the second piece of news he had to report. But she needed to know what they were faced with, so Jeff plunged ahead.

"We can discuss the AC situation later, but on another note, while I was at the house, our insurance company sent someone out to pick up your car, and they hauled it away to wherever they do their estimates. They'd called first and said when they'd be coming, which was good since our gate is kept closed when we aren't there." Jeff grimaced. "Now it's the waiting game until we find out if the car's totaled or by some chance can be fixed."

"I doubt it can be repaired, Jeff. You know how terrible it looked. Either way, this is really putting a hardship on us." Rhonda's voice broke, and Jeff figured she was close to tears.

He glanced her way. Sure enough, tears rolled down her flushed cheeks.

"Ah, honey, don't cry." Jeff let go of the steering wheel with one hand and reached over to touch her arm. "We'll figure something out, but let's wait till we get home to talk more about it. Okay?"

She swiped her hand across her face and gave a brief nod.

With a determined set of his jaw, Jeff focused on the road ahead.

Walnut Creek

As Rhonda and Jeff sat out back on their patio, eating sandwiches and chips for supper, neither of them said much at first. They'd agreed earlier that they didn't feel like cooking anything and did not want to heat up the kitchen any more than it already was from the house being closed all day. Jeff had offered to put some meat on the grill, but Rhonda said she'd rather eat something cold, so she'd made ham and cheese sandwiches.

Rhonda was nearly finished with her sandwich, when she pushed her plate aside and told Jeff about the phone call she'd had from Gwen. "I can't even express how surprised I was to learn that my mother has begun dating. If she's not careful, she could end up going from the frying pan into the fire with one of those men, who I doubt she knows very much about." Rhonda paused to put a few chips on her paper plate. "Just because they go to her church doesn't mean they can be trusted."

"My dad goes to church, and he's trustworthy," Jeff said.

Rhonda pointed a finger at him. "We're not talking about your dad. We're talking about two strangers we've never met."

"Okay, but there's nothing you can do about it. Your mother's a grown woman and can make her own decisions."

She glared at him but chose to say nothing. *I wouldn't expect you to understand.*

Jeff ate quietly for a while, and Rhonda picked at her food.

"My dad called me today, and after I told him about hitting a deer and our AC going out, he offered us some money and also the loan of his truck."

With determination, Rhonda shook her head. "I am not interested in driving your father's truck, but if you don't mind using it, then I'm willing to drive your SUV."

Jeff tugged on his lower lip. "Why don't you talk to your mom and see if she would loan you her car? Since she lives close to your sister, she probably has transportation available to her whenever she needs to go someplace. You should at least call and tell her what's happened."

"I don't see the point. She'd probably do like your dad did and offer to loan us some money. Besides, Mom needs her car to go to and from the dentist's office where she works as a receptionist."

"I'm not sure Dad's offer was a loan," Jeff said, giving no response to Rhonda's last comment.

"We're not charity cases, Jeff, and as responsible adults, we need to figure something out on our own."

"That's what I thought at first too, but now that I've had more time to think about it, maybe we shouldn't let our pride get in the way. I think we oughta go ahead and at least accept his offer to loan us the truck. Like you said, I can drive it and let you have my rig."

Rhonda mulled over what Jeff had suggested. Her facial muscles relaxed a bit as she finished her iced tea and set the glass down. "That will help, and with access to two vehicles again, we will be freed up to go about our normal routines." She looked toward their house and frowned. "But it doesn't take care of the situation with our air conditioner. I dread going back into the house, where it's so uncomfortably warm."

"You said it yourself—we can't afford to buy a new one, and I'm sure you don't want to max out our credit cards."

"No, I don't, but you could part with some of your antiques."

Jeff looked at her with raised brows. "You've gotta be kidding, Rhonda. Even if I could find a buyer for any of my old things, a new central air unit, plus installation, would cost anywhere from five to ten thousand dollars. I don't have any antiques valued at that amount."

"Then we'll just have to get by without AC until sometime next year and hope that our townhouse has sold by then."

Jeff thumped the tabletop with his knuckles. "It should've sold by now. I think we should get a new Realtor."

"How's that going to help? If homes like ours aren't selling, another Realtor wouldn't have any better luck than the one we have now." She pursed her lips. "We made a mistake buying this place—let's face it."

He shook his head vigorously. "No, we didn't, Rhonda. We're just dealing with a rough spot right now, and we need to work our way through it."

Her eyes narrowed as she swatted at the air. "I'm working. . .you're working. . .but nothing's working out for us. One problem crops up, and another one's right on its heels."

Jeff heaved a heavy sigh and got up from his chair. This discussion was getting them nowhere, and he needed to be by himself for a while. His first thought was to go watch TV in the man cave, but it was too hot in there to enjoy watching anything. So, Jeff headed for the pond and took a seat on one of the benches to watch the fish swim around. He needed to feed them but didn't feel like going to the shed to get the food right now. It would have to be done before he went back to the house, however. Although having a pond with fish was nice, it also meant more work.

Maybe after I've sat here awhile, I'll feel better. Jeff leaned forward with his elbows on his knees and closed his eyes. *How can I make things better? Is there anything I can do to solve our financial problems? Maybe Rhonda's right—we probably should have been satisfied to stay at our townhouse in Canton. The question is, where do we go from here?*

New Philadelphia, Ohio

June had taken a seat at her kitchen table to eat the shrimp salad she'd made for her supper, when someone rapped on the back door. A few seconds later, Gwen stepped into the room.

"How many times have I told you to keep your doors locked, Mom?" She stood in front of June with both hands on her hips. "Some stranger could walk right in, uninvited."

"You just did." June cracked a smile.

Gwen scrunched up her face. "I am not a stranger, Mom. And I only turned the doorknob to see if it was locked. Of course, when I found out it wasn't, I came in." She pulled out a chair at the table and took a seat. "You really should be more careful."

Ignoring her daughter's pointed expression, June said, "I'm surprised to see you here at this time of the day. Shouldn't you be fixing supper for your family?"

"We've already eaten. My considerate hubby brought pizza on his way home from work." Gwen gestured to June's salad. "Looks like you're eating light tonight."

"Yes. I didn't feel like cooking."

"Sorry, Mom. I should have invited you to join us for pizza."

"That's okay. This nice cold salad is fine for me." June drank some water. "So, what's the reason for your visit? I'm sure it has to be more than checking to see if my door was locked."

Gwen nodded. "I wanted to talk to you about Rhonda."

"What about your sister?"

"I spoke to her today, and she sounded pretty stressed."

"Did she explain why?"

"No, but she mentioned that things were hectic at the hotel."

June poked a shrimp with her fork. "That's nothing new. Ever since your sister began working there, things have been crazy."

"True, and she's probably used to all the challenges of being a hotel manager by now, but I think something else may be stressing her."

"Such as?"

Gwen shrugged. "I don't know, but maybe if you give her a call, she'll tell you what's bothering her."

June placed her fork on the plate without eating the shrimp. "It has been awhile since I talked to Rhonda. I'll give her a call as soon as I finish my salad." She looked at Gwen. "Would you like to be here when I call, so you can hear what she says? I can put it on Speaker mode, and then you could ask her a few questions too."

"No, I'd better not stay for that. Rhonda might not appreciate me asking questions or putting in my two cents."

"Okay. I'll make the call after you're gone, or if you'd like to stay, I just won't put it on Speaker."

"I really should go." Gwen pushed back her chair and stood. "I promised the girls that we could roast marshmallows this evening, and they're probably waiting for me in front of the firepit, along with their dad."

June got up and gave her daughter a hug. "Thanks for dropping by. If what Rhonda has to say is anything important, I'll let you know."

"Okay, Mom. I'll talk to you again soon."

After Gwen went out the back door, June finished her salad and put the dishes in the sink. Then she picked up her cell phone and punched in Rhonda's number.

Walnut Creek

Rhonda was about to enter the master bedroom when her cell phone rang. She didn't feel like answering, but if it was hotel business, she probably should.

She looked at the caller ID, and seeing that it was her mother, she answered. "Hi, Mom. How are you?"

"I'm fine. In fact, I'm more than fine."

Rhonda couldn't miss the bubbly tone of her mother's voice. "That's good. Sure wish I could say the same."

"What's wrong?"

"Pretty much everything right now."

"I'm sorry to hear that. Do you want to explain?"

Rhonda began by telling her mother about the need to find a new front-desk clerk at the hotel, then she brought up the subject of their air-conditioning going out. "And if that's not bad enough, Jeff hit a deer last night when we were leaving a restaurant near Charm, where we'd gone to celebrate our anniversary."

"Oh my, I forgot it was your anniversary. I hope neither of you were hurt."

"We're both fine, but my car is probably totaled. The front end doesn't look good at all."

"I'm sorry to hear it. Is there anything I can do?"

"Not unless you have a lot of money lying around."

"I could help a little, but I don't have enough to buy you a new car or. . ."

"I am not expecting your help, Mom. Our insurance will pay to either fix the car or replace it, and we're not going to worry about the AC until next year when the hot weather hits."

"But it's warm right now. And from what I saw on the weather channel the other day, it sounds like the heat wave might continue for a few weeks. I may have a fan or two around here I could lend you. Do you have any fans you can use there now?"

Rhonda entered her bedroom and took a seat on the edge of the bed. "Yes. We have a box fan in our room, and I'll tell Jeff about your offer of the extra fans. We plan to open all the windows once the sun goes down each evening. So, we'll pretend we're Amish for the rest of September." She gave a forced laugh. "Can you picture that—me dressed in plain Amish clothes, sitting in a rocking chair and reading a book by a gas lantern?"

"No, I certainly cannot. You're used to having a cell phone, computer, and many other modern things."

"Yeah, and up until now—air-conditioning."

"Are you sure I can't help by chipping in on that?"

"Yes, Mom, I'm sure, but thank you for offering." *If Jeff wouldn't accept money from his dad, I certainly can't take my mother up on her offer. We'll just have to deal with this on our own.*

"Gwen mentioned that she'd talked to you earlier today."

Her mother's comment pushed Rhonda's thoughts aside. "Uh, yeah, that's right. She called while I was at the hotel, so we didn't talk long."

"Did she tell you that I've gone out a couple of times with two men who go to our church?"

"Yes, she mentioned it."

"She thinks it's good that I'm dating again. What are your thoughts, Rhonda?"

"If that's what you have chosen to do, then my opinion really doesn't matter."

"Yes, it does. I'm open to your input, just as I was to Gwen's."

"Okay, then, here goes. . . After what my father pulled on you, I think it's a mistake to get involved with another man." There, it was out, and Rhonda felt better for having said it.

"These men aren't like your dad. They are kind, Christian men."

"People who call themselves Christians are not perfect, Mom."

"I didn't mean to imply that they were. It's just that—"

"Look, I don't want to throw cold water on your excitement over dating, but you need to be careful. Either one of the men you've been seeing might appear to be nice, but they could be wolves in sheep's clothing."

There was a long pause before Rhonda's mother spoke again. Rhonda figured she was either mulling over her statement and giving it some consideration or had become irritated because Rhonda hadn't shared in her excitement over entering the dating game again.

"I appreciate your concern, dear, but I am being cautious. Now, I have to go, but I'll talk to you again soon."

I can't be excited for her, Rhonda told herself after she'd said good-bye and clicked off the phone. *And I won't put my stamp of approval on Mom dating anyone—Christian or not.*

Chapter 26

Jeff stretched out on his patio lounge chair, placing both hands behind his head. "I'm glad our weather's finally cooled down. Looks like fall is here to stay."

Rhonda took a deep breath and released it slowly. "At least it solves one of our problems. We just need to pinch our pennies and try to save up for a new AC before the hot weather takes over next year."

Jeff's cell phone rang from where he'd laid it on the table beside his chair. He picked it up and looked at the caller ID. "It's our Realtor. Maybe she has some good news."

Rhonda sat quietly as he conversed with the woman they'd hired to sell their townhouse. They needed an offer, and soon. She folded her arms. *I hope our townhouse sells for the price we're asking. It's hard not to be impatient over this since we've been waiting for several months without even a nibble.*

When Jeff got off the phone a few minutes later, he looked over at Rhonda and smiled. "We have an offer."

She sat up straight. "Really? Is it a good one?"

"Well, yes and no. The couple interested in purchasing the townhouse wants to be in there within thirty days, which is a good thing. The downside is that they want us to lower the price by ten thousand dollars."

"You're kidding."

"I wish I were, but that's the buyer's offer."

Rhonda's stomach clenched as her eyes widened. "That's a lot less money than our asking price, Jeff. What are those people thinking?"

"They probably can't pay the full price and are hoping we'll come down so they can buy the place."

How disappointing. I wish they would've accepted our offer. Instead, all this will do for us is add more frustration and stress as we decide what to do. Rhonda shook her head. "We can't lower the price that much. We need to make enough money so we can pay off the loan on this place."

"If we accept their offer, it'll give us enough to knock the balance down here, which would mean we could pay off the rest of this mortgage sooner."

Rubbing her arms briskly, she leaned forward. "I think we should make a counteroffer and agree to sell the townhouse for five thousand dollars less."

Jeff thumbed his ear. "I don't know, Rhonda. They could decline our offer and walk away. As you keep reminding me, we need to get our old place sold."

"Of course we do, but we can't give it away. Don't forget, in addition to wanting to pay off this house, we'll need money for a new air-conditioning unit next year."

"I'm well aware, but we'll have even less money if we don't sell the townhouse." Jeff looked directly at her. "And don't forget, we've been saving quite a bit of money because I'm borrowing my dad's truck, and we didn't have to rent a car for you to drive while we're waiting for insurance money to come through."

"Yes, I know." Using her fingertips, Rhonda closed her eyes and made little circles all over her tight forehead. She remembered how two days after their accident, Don and Eric had driven down to deliver Don's truck. She'd been grateful and had fixed them a nice meal before they headed home in Eric's vehicle.

Jeff nudged her arm. "You okay? You're not dealing with another headache, I hope."

"Not yet, but it may be forthcoming."

"Want me to massage the back of your neck?"

"No, that's okay. I'll feel better once we resolve this problem." She tilted her head from side to side, weighing their choices. "What if we give a counteroffer of eight thousand dollars less than our asking price? Does that sound reasonable to you?"

Jeff bobbed his head. "The couple who want our townhouse may not think so though." He picked up his cell phone. "Should I call our Realtor back and let her know of our decision?"

"Yes, please do."

While Jeff made the call, Rhonda leaned her head against the back of the chaise longue and closed her eyes. If she believed in the power of prayer, Rhonda would say one right now, asking that the prospective buyers would accept their counteroffer.

Canton

The following morning, Rhonda sat in her office at the hotel, looking at a list of supplies the head of housekeeping had turned in. The number of items looked larger than the previous month and had thrown her off guard.

I'm sure that's because of the renovation work and that for a while we were shy ten to fifteen rooms to put up our guests for the night.

Rhonda had always worked hard, and she carried the weight of her job. The stress of it meant a headache most of the time, however.

I'm so tired of dealing with all this. I'd much rather be at home making out my grocery list right now. Rhonda pursed her lips. *There are too many responsibilities here, and I'm tired of it.*

One of those responsibilities was hiring new employees when needed. After going through ten potential desk clerks, Rhonda had finally hired one last week. It was a relief not to have the extra responsibility of working behind the front desk.

A knock sounded on the office door, and Rhonda called, "Come in." She was surprised when Lori entered the room with a baby in her arms.

"I came by to show you my little sweet pea." Lori smiled as she moved closer to Rhonda's desk. "I hope you're not too busy to take a peek at her."

"No, of course not." Rhonda's throat swelled as she gazed at the wee infant in the young mother's arms. "She's beautiful, Lori. Congratulations."

"Thank you. Derek and I are so happy we've become parents."

"What did you name her?"

"Natalie—after my great-aunt. She's the sweetest lady."

When the baby stirred and emitted a sweet cooing sound, Rhonda's throat tightened to the point she could barely swallow. Although she was happy for Lori, she couldn't help feeling envious. After all these years of being unable to have children, she did not understand why it still hurt so much when she saw other people's babies.

"Would you like to hold her?" Lori asked.

"Umm. . .I feel like a cold might be coming on, and I don't want to expose your little girl, so I'd better not."

"Oh, okay. Maybe some other time."

Rhonda nodded. Then, realizing she hadn't thought to buy the baby a gift, she retrieved her checkbook and wrote a check for fifty dollars. "Please use this to buy the baby something." She handed the check to Lori.

Lori's soft brown eyes filled with an inner glow. "Thank you so much. That's very kind of you."

"You're welcome." Rhonda glanced at the paperwork on her desk. She needed to get busy working but didn't want to be rude. Besides, the longer Lori stood here, the more Rhonda's heart filled with regrets.

"I'm not sure when or if I'll be returning to work for you." Lori looked at her and then at the baby. "As busy as this place is, you'll no doubt need to hire another person, and I certainly understand."

"Yes, and someone has been hired to take your place. However, if at a later date you choose to come back to work here, there will hopefully be a spot for you. Or at the very least, I'll be happy to give a good reference if you should ever decide to apply for another job."

"Thank you, Rhonda," Lori responded. "I'd better go and let you get back to work."

Rhonda smiled, despite the tears she struggled to hold back. "Feel free to come by some other time."

"I will, but next time I'll call before I drop by." Lori said goodbye and turned toward the door.

She is so blessed with her sweet newborn. If only I could be a mother. It was difficult for Rhonda to shake away the desire of having her own child. She could hardly hold back the idea as it resonated within her.

After Lori left, Rhonda booted up her computer. Although she still had paperwork to do, not to mention answering review comments, she went to the internet and typed in "What are the reasons a couple can't get pregnant?"

Several sites came up, and she clicked on the first one that caught her interest, listing several reasons for an inability to conceive. "Number one," she said quietly. "A woman's cycle and ovulation might be irregular. Number two: the younger a woman is, the easier it is for her to get pregnant."

Rhonda continued to read more reasons. Being either overweight or underweight. The man might be sterile. Endometriosis could contribute to fertility problems. A woman's Fallopian tubes could be blocked due to scar tissue or adhesions. An endocrine disorder or some underlying medical condition. Uterine fibroids. Too much stress.

Rhonda paused to drink some of her lukewarm coffee and groaned. She and Jeff had been tested, and the doctor hadn't found anything physically wrong with either of them. He had mentioned stress, though, and said that they should both eat a balanced diet, exercise regularly, and look for ways to lower their stress.

"Yeah, right." She tapped her left foot and frowned. *How's a person supposed to ease their stress when it keeps on coming? Even waiting to hear something back from our Realtor is causing me stress. If the people who are interested in our townhouse don't accept our counteroffer, I don't know what we're going to do.*

Rhonda clicked out of the page she'd been looking at and found another one that pertained to eating a healthy diet. The doctor who'd written the article recommended eating plenty of vegetables, fruits, whole grains, lean protein, and healthy fats. He also stated that there were several specific nutrients a woman should focus on to support her fertility. The main ones he'd listed were folate, CoQ10, iron, vitamin D, zinc, and omega-3 fatty acids.

Maybe I should make an effort to eat healthier and take the supplements listed here, Rhonda told herself. *Although I don't know why. After thirteen years of not conceiving, I doubt that eating healthier and taking certain supplements would make any difference.* She shifted on her chair. *If I do decide to make some changes regarding my health, I won't say anything to Jeff. He'd probably say what I read was a bunch of hooey and give me a lecture on learning to be content without children.*

Walnut Creek

When Rhonda arrived home that evening, she found Jeff in the kitchen, talking on his cell phone. She put her things away and took a seat at the table to wait until he was done. *I'm guessing it isn't his father. It sounds more like he's speaking to our Realtor about the townhouse.*

Rhonda looked down at her nails and picked at a hangnail. *If only we could be free from our old place and focus all our attentions on this new home.*

She let her mind go blank while her husband continued to talk.

"That was our Realtor," Jeff said when he'd clicked off his phone. "The people who want our townhouse have agreed to our terms."

Rhonda heaved an audible sigh. "What a relief. That's one less thing we'll have to worry about now. Did she say anything else?"

"Just that the deal should close within the next thirty days, and once it does, we'll have our share of the money."

Her face scrunched a bit. "If we could have sold it ourselves, we wouldn't have been obliged to pay a commission."

"True, but we're both too busy to be bothered with trying to sell a home on our own. We did the right thing by hiring her."

"I suppose." Rhonda heaved another sigh. "Whew! I'm exhausted."

"Rough day at the hotel?"

"Just the usual, but the biggest stress of my day was when Lori came by to show me her baby."

He raised his brows. "Why would that be stressful?"

"You know how much I want children. Seeing Lori's beautiful little girl was just another reminder that we will never become parents or have the privilege of raising a child."

Jeff looked at her pointedly. "It's wrong for you to be jealous of everyone who has a child. You should find something to get your mind off it and quit harping on the topic so you can focus on other things."

Hurt by his comment, Rhonda stood up and moved over to the refrigerator to take out something for supper. *How can Jeff be so unfeeling? Is he really content not to have children?* She took out a bag of premade salad ingredients. *I wonder if Jeff would change his mind if I ever did get pregnant.*

Rhonda woke up the next morning with a pounding headache. She'd been dreaming when the alarm went off, nearly jolting her out of bed. In the dream, Rhonda and Jeff were parents. She held a fair-skinned, curly-headed girl on her lap, while watching Jeff play on the floor with their dark-haired son. Even now, fully awake, Rhonda remembered the joy she'd felt when the little girl had called her "Ma-ma." *If only it were true and not a dream.*

She figured that the events of yesterday had made an impact on her. Rhonda had tried not to be jealous or harbor any regrets about her life without a child, but it seemed impossible to shake those feelings. She rubbed her forehead and sat up in bed, but when the room began to spin, she laid back down. *What's going on? Why do I feel like this? Did the cold I felt coming on yesterday become a reality? Could my sinuses and ears be so plugged that it's affected my equilibrium?*

Rhonda turned her head slowly to the left and realized that her husband was not on his side of the bed. She lay there a few moments, wondering if he might be in the kitchen fixing breakfast. Her stomach roiled at the thought of food. Although she'd been hungry enough last night when they ate supper, Rhonda had no appetite for food right now. Between the nausea and headache, she felt certain that she'd never be able to get dressed and go to work this morning. In fact, Rhonda didn't think she could even get out of bed. *Could this be a migraine, or have I come down with the flu?*

She called out to Jeff several times, but he didn't answer. *Maybe when I don't show up in the kitchen, he'll come back to our room to check on me.* Rhonda closed her eyes, which did nothing for the headache, but at least it helped the dizziness subside.

I need to call my assistant manager and let her know that I won't be coming in to work today. She rolled onto her side and reached for her cell phone, but before she could punch in the number, Jeff entered the room.

"How come you're still in bed? I figured you'd be up and dressed by now."

Rhonda moaned, and through half-closed eyelids, she looked at him standing by her side of the bed. "I'm sick, Jeff. There's no way I'll be going to work today." She held the phone out to him. "Would you call my assistant manager and let her know that I won't be in today?"

"Sure, honey." He placed his hand on her forehead. "Your head feels hot. You must have a fever."

"I wouldn't be surprised. My head is also pounding, and I'm real woozy and nauseous."

"I'll make the call and then fix you a cup of ginger tea. That should help your stomach settle." He took a seat on the edge of the bed and clasped her hand. "It sounds like you must have the flu. Would you like me to take the day off and stay home with you? I don't feel right about leaving you here alone when you're not feeling well."

"No, don't do that; I'll be okay. Just bring me the tea and a few bottles of water. I'll spend the day in bed, and hopefully by the time you get home this evening, I'll feel better."

"Are you sure you don't want me to stay?"

"Yes, and there's no need for you to worry."

"Okay, but if you take a turn for the worse, please give me a call and I'll come right home."

"I will." Rhonda closed her eyes again. Her head hurt less when she didn't have to see any light in the room. *At least I know Jeff cares about me. Guess that's something to be grateful for. I just wish. . .* Her thoughts gave way to slumber.

Chapter 27

Berlin, Ohio

On the way home from work that afternoon, Jeff decided to stop at the pharmacy to pick up a few things he hoped would make Rhonda feel better. He had called her several times during the day and always felt bad if he awakened her. The last time Jeff called to let her know he would be leaving the restaurant soon, she had mentioned having a sore throat. He'd mentally added throat spray and lozenges to the list of things to buy.

Pulling into the pharmacy parking lot, Jeff noticed several horses and buggies at the hitching rail. It was nice that the shopping complex, which the pharmacy was a part of, had provided a place for the Plain people to park while they shopped.

Jeff parked his dad's truck and got out of the vehicle. He would be glad when he got the SUV back. Their insurance company had pronounced Rhonda's car totaled, but it could be a few more weeks before they received a settlement check. They would wait till then to begin looking at new cars, and Jeff hoped his wife would find one to her liking. She'd enjoyed her sporty vehicle, so it might be a difficult decision to choose another car unless it was comparable to her previous one.

Jeff pushed those thoughts out of his mind and entered the building. He'd gone down the first aisle when someone tapped his shoulder. Jeff turned and was surprised to see Orley behind him.

"It's good to see you." The Amish man smiled. "Lois and I were talking about you and your wife the other day and wondered if you had a nice anniversary."

"It wasn't the best." Jeff dropped his gaze to the floor.

"Mind if I ask why it wasn't the best?"

"On the way home from dinner at the Chalet in the Valley restaurant, I hit a deer." Jeff raised his head and looked at Orley, hoping his negative outlook wasn't too obvious.

"Sorry to hear that. Were either of you hurt?"

"No, but the front end of Rhonda's car sure was, and the impact killed the young doe."

Orley gave a slow shake of his head. "That's a shame, but praise God neither of you was hurt."

Ignoring Orley's comment, Jeff said, "To top it off, when we finally got home that night, it didn't take us long to realize that our air-conditioning unit had a problem. The house was so hot, we weren't sure we could sleep inside."

"We did have some warmer than normal evenings a few weeks ago."

"How do you and your wife cope with hot weather?"

"We open several windows for a cross-breeze and set a battery-operated fan near our bed."

"We used an electric box fan, but it didn't do much good. We're used to sleeping with a cooler temperature, so we were both pretty miserable." Jeff reached around to rub the back of his neck.

"Our weather has cooled considerably now," Orley stated. "I'm sure you must be more comfortable."

"Weather-wise, yes, but this morning Rhonda woke up sick. I think it's some type of flu." Jeff gestured to a bottle of aspirin and other medicines. "That's why I'm here. I came for something to take away Rhonda's headache and to help her throat."

"You might also consider stopping by the health food store in town. There's a homeopathic remedy specifically used to help alleviate symptoms of the flu."

Jeff's interest was piqued. "What's the name of it?"

Orley scratched behind his left ear. "Sorry, but I can't remember what it's called. I'm sure someone who works at the health food store could help you with that though."

"Okay, I'll stop by there after I leave here." Jeff was about ready to say goodbye and move on down the aisle, when Orley spoke again.

"Did you and your wife like the anniversary gift I gave you from me and Lois?"

Jeff shuffled his feet nervously. He felt trapped and uncertain about how best to answer. He didn't want to admit that they were none too thrilled with the religious plaque, but at the same time, it would be a lie to say that they liked it. Some quick thinking kicked in and Jeff replied, "It was kind of you to think of us."

Orley produced a wide smile in response. "Just remember, Jeff, that a personal relationship with God is the only way to find peace and true happiness."

Jeff held his arms tightly at his sides, feeling as though he'd been backed into a corner. *Why does this Amish man have to be so persistent? Doesn't he realize I have no need of his religious beliefs? Why can't he leave well enough alone?*

"I'd better get the things I came in for now and head for home. Rhonda's probably wondering what's taking me so long." Jeff took a few steps away from Orley.

"Please tell your wife that Lois and I will be praying for her to get better soon. Oh, and don't forget about stopping by the health food store."

"Yeah, thanks. See you around, Orley." Jeff grabbed a bottle of aspirin and hurried to the next aisle, where remedies for coughs and sore throats were sold. The last thing he'd needed today was a push from Orley Troyer in the direction of God.

Walnut Creek

After Jeff entered the house that evening, he put some of the things away that he'd purchased in Berlin, picked up the rest of the items he thought might help Rhonda feel better, and went to check on her. He found his pale wife propped up in bed, drinking from a bottle of water.

"How are you feeling?" Jeff took a seat on the edge of the bed, holding the bag of remedies.

She held up her hand. "Better not get too close to me. I'm pretty sure what I have is the flu, and it's no doubt contagious. We don't need you getting sick too and missing work."

"I'm not worried about it, and even if I do get sick, Russ will cover for me at the restaurant until I'm better."

Rhonda peered at the bag Jeff held. "What did you bring me?"

"I got some cold-and-flu remedies that I hope will help you feel better."

Setting the bag aside, he placed his hand on her forehead. "I think you have a fever. Have you taken your temperature today?"

She shook her head.

"I'll get the thermometer." Jeff went to the bathroom and took the digital thermometer from the medicine cabinet. When he returned, he handed it to her. "Please put this under your tongue."

"I know what to do with it." Rhonda quirked a smile and did as he'd asked. When it beeped, she removed the item and handed it to Jeff.

"Not too bad. Just a little over one hundred."

"I think it was higher than that earlier today because I did a lot of sweating, and then I got the chills." She moaned. "I hate being sick and missing time off work."

"As frustrated as you've become with work, I wouldn't think you'd miss it."

"I can't argue the point that my job is usually frustrating." She squinted at him. "If we were on a relaxing vacation, it would be one thing, but taking sick days off is no fun."

He smoothed back Rhonda's damp hair from her face. "Most of the items I picked up after work are from the pharmacy in Berlin, and at Orley's suggestion, I dropped by the health food store and bought a homeopathic remedy that is supposed to help curtail flu symptoms."

"Where did you see Orley?"

"At the pharmacy. It was there that he told me about the all-natural remedy." Jeff grimaced. "He also asked if we liked the anniversary gift they'd given us."

Rhonda covered her cough with the palm of her hand. "What'd you tell him?"

"I didn't provide a direct answer. Just skirted around it by saying we appreciated their gesture." He glanced at the thermometer still in his hand then back at Rhonda. "Can you imagine what he would have thought if I'd told him that I put the old plaque inside a cupboard in our garage?"

"He'd probably be offended."

"I'm sure. Now enough about the gift. I'm going to the kitchen to open a can of chicken noodle soup. I got you some saltines to nibble on too. It's the one food that seems to be more tolerated when a person feels nauseated. Oh, and I bought a box of real fruit ice pops and organic chocolate-covered ice-cream bars from the health food store. Those should help your sore throat feel better." Jeff stood. "I'm going back to the kitchen now and heat the soup."

"I'm not hungry, Jeff, but thanks for offering."

"You need the nourishment, Rhonda. Now please rest, and I'll be back soon to check on you."

"I saw Jeff Davis at the pharmacy today," Orley said when Lois took a seat next to him at the dining-room table, where they'd chosen to have their dessert after supper.

"How are he and Rhonda doing?" Lois cut into her piece of apple pie and took a bite.

"They're going through a rough time right now."

"In what way?"

"First of all, he mentioned their anniversary."

Lois drank her tea. "Did they like the plaque you gave them?"

"I'm not sure. When I asked him that question, Jeff just said he appreciated our thoughtfulness. He also mentioned that he'd hit a deer on the way home from their anniversary dinner."

"Oh, no! Were either of them hurt?"

Orley shook his head. "Only the deer and Rhonda's car. Actually, the doe died." He paused to eat a bite of his pie then continued. "To make matters worse, when they returned home that evening, they discovered that their air-conditioning had quit working. So, of course, they spent a miserable night trying to sleep in an overly warm house."

Lois wiped her mouth with a napkin before speaking again. "We are not used to having air-conditioning, so we've come up with ways to deal with the heat, but most English people—especially those who rely on air-conditioning—have a hard time staying cool when the weather is hot and muggy."

"Jah, that's right." Orley used his napkin to wipe up a bit of coffee that had spilled on the table. "It's good that the weather has cooled now, though, because Jeff mentioned that Rhonda has the flu. She'd no doubt be even more miserable in a hot, stuffy house."

Leaning both wrists against the table, Lois sat with her hands lightly folded. "We need to continue praying for that couple. They seem to be having more than their share of trials."

"I agree. We do need to keep praying for them." Orley's lips pressed together. "Wish I'd thought to ask for Jeff's phone number so I could call and check up on them."

"That would be a good idea. Maybe Jeff will drop by Memory Keepers again, and you can ask for it then."

"I hope so. I don't know all the reasons, but I'm sure the Lord directed that young man to our store for a purpose beyond looking at antiques."

"I believe you're right, Husband." Lois pushed her chair back and stood. "I'm going to do up these dishes and join you in the living room, where we can relax for a while before it's time for bed."

"Sounds good to me. Think I'll take a look at the newspaper while you're doing that." Orley rose too.

"All right, I'll be in there soon."

When Lois entered the living room a short time later, she found Orley in his favorite chair, wearing his reading glasses, and holding the newspaper near his face.

"Let me get a light going in here so you're not straining to see." Lois grabbed a lighter and lit the kerosene lamp. "How's that?"

"Much better. Danki."

Lois took a seat in the chair beside him, where she often sat when she wanted to chat. But she wasn't sure how much talking they would get done this evening since her husband seemed engrossed in whatever he was reading.

She reached into the wicker basket on the other side of her chair and withdrew her knitting needles and a ball of yarn. Maybe when Orley finished reading the paper, they could talk. If not, then Lois would be content to begin a new knitting project, as she'd wanted to make a winter stocking cap for her husband.

Lois had barely begun to knit when Orley gave a deep chuckle. "You've gotta be kidding."

She turned her head in his direction. "What was that?"

He rapped the paper with his knuckles and rolled his eyes. "I've been reading that Dear Caroline column, and I can't believe some of the dumb things people can come up with to write her about."

She leaned closer to him. "Such as?"

"Well, here's one that I'm sure you'll get a kick out of. Listen to what it says: 'Dear Caroline: My husband leaves his clothes lying around on the floor and never puts them in the hamper, like I've asked him to do many times. On a few occasions, I have tripped over them. What should I do about this? Fed Up.'" He looked over at Lois and lifted a single eyebrow while closing his opposite eye. "How *lecherich*! Can you believe anyone would waste the time to write a letter to someone they didn't even know about something so trivial?"

Lois poked her tongue against the inside of her cheek and inhaled a long breath. "I don't think it's ridiculous at all. The woman who wrote that letter is obviously upset about her husband's carelessness and most likely hoped that Caroline could offer some suggestions."

"Well, listen to what the columnist said in response. 'Dear Fed Up, Nagging probably won't help, so my suggestion is don't continue to pick up your husband's clothes. Don't launder them even if they are dirty. Eventually, he will run out of clean clothes to wear, so he will have no choice but to pick them up himself.'"

Orley grunted. "That's just common sense. Doesn't take a genius or someone like Caroline, who thinks she is a counselor, to come up with something so sensible. I've spoken to people with bigger problems than that and—"

"You are not the only person who can give out advice, you know." Lois followed her statement with a noisy huff. "I am sure that Caroline is trying to do her best and give sensible answers to those who have asked her advice."

Orley's chin jutted out. "Why are you defending that woman? It's not like you know her personally."

Lois took a deep breath and blurted, "Actually, I am well acquainted with Caroline."

"Oh?" He tipped his head, looking at her with a curious expression.

Lois pointed to herself. "Caroline is me."

Orley snickered. "Jah, right. Are you pullin' my leg?"

She gave a slow shake of her head. "I've been writing that column for nearly a year."

His eyes widened, making them appear bulged. "B–but how can that be? Until now, you've never said a word about this to me."

Lois slid her finger around the rim of her teacup as she searched for the right response to her husband's question. "I didn't want you to know that the paper had hired me to write the column."

"So, they know who the author is, but no one else—not even me?" Orley's gaze flicked upward, and then he looked at Lois with a glassy stare. "I feel betrayed."

Her chin quivered as she reached over and touched his arm. "I'm sorry, Orley, but I wasn't sure you would approve. I wanted to do something meaningful that could hopefully help people who are hurting and need guidance."

"Oh, and you can't accomplish that in our store like I do when I recognize that someone needs a bit of mentoring?"

Lois sucked in her cheeks as she pulled her hand back. "I have done that many times, but my newspaper column reaches a lot more people than the few that come into our store and open up about their problems."

Orley sat quietly, staring into his coffee cup. Then he looked back at Lois and frowned. "It hurts that you made an agreement with our local newspaper to pose as Caroline and chose not to tell me."

"I was going to tell you but wanted to give it a try first and see how things worked out." She swallowed hard. "After the first issue came out and you made some joke about the column, I couldn't muster up the courage to tell you. You've done that several times since, so I felt certain that you would ask me to quit writing as Caroline."

"You're right, I probably would have discouraged you, but if that's what you really want to do, then you have my blessing."

"Really?"

"Jah."

"Danki." She smiled and clasped Orley's hand. "Again, I am sorry for not telling you, and I hope you'll forgive me."

Orley gave her fingers a gentle squeeze. "I do, and I'm glad we've had this discussion. Keeping things from one another is not healthy for a marriage." He paused a moment and then spoke to her in a calm, gentle tone. "All those times when you had errands to do, and I didn't know where you were headed off to, it was because of Dear Caroline, right?"

"Jah."

Orley gave a brief nod and went back to reading the paper.

Lois sighed with relief. Although there were a few things from her past that she hadn't told him about, since the day she and Orley had gotten married, this was the first time she'd deliberately deceived him. How thankful she was that he'd forgiven her and given his blessing to continue writing as Dear Caroline.

Chapter 28

Cleveland

Rhonda kept her eyes on the road as she followed Jeff in his dad's truck. Driving her new silver compact car with its soft leather interior was nice, and she'd been getting more familiar with its options. While she missed her old vehicle, this one would be a good replacement. They'd bought her new car yesterday, and Jeff said he felt it was best not to keep his dad's truck any longer. Rhonda appreciated Don loaning them the rig, and she was aware that Jeff was eager to get his SUV back from her. She was equally eager to drive something more to her liking. The car she'd chosen wasn't as sporty as her previous one, but it was cute and got good gas mileage. That was a plus since she commuted to and from the hotel five days a week.

Rhonda was glad that she felt like her old self again. The flu bug she'd contracted had lasted for over a week. Fortunately, Jeff had not gotten sick. Either his immune system had been stronger than hers, or it was because, at her request, he'd slept in the room set up for their overnight guests. Things were pretty much back to normal now and would be even better once the deal closed on their townhouse. It was set to happen in two weeks. What a relief it would be to hand over the keys for their old place to the new owners. Even better would be receiving the check.

Jeff changed lanes, and Rhonda followed, easing in behind the truck. Traffic wasn't too bad for a Saturday, which was nice. Hopefully, not many cars would be on the road when they returned home later today. Maybe they could stop for a bite to eat at one of their favorite restaurants.

Rhonda had already decided that she would let Jeff drive back to Walnut Creek. It would give him a chance to get a feel for her new car, and she could relax in the passenger's seat. Since they'd be leaving Don's place before it got dark, they'd be able to see anything that might be on the road, including deer.

Rhonda thought about the information she'd read online about the importance of looking for ways to de-stress. Suggestions included doing deep breathing exercises, drinking calming herbal teas, and soaking in a bathtub filled with warm water. Another idea was to take a cold shower to relieve anxiety. Rhonda hoped she'd be able to implement a few things that might help her relax.

She gripped the steering wheel a little tighter and frowned. *With a job like mine, I'll probably never be free of stress. And dealing with traffic when I have to commute to work all the time sure doesn't help.*

Jeff's blinker came on again, only this time he took an exit. Rhonda followed him off the ramp and through some streets leading to his dad's place. Although the trip to Cleveland didn't take long, she was ready to get out of the car and stretch her legs.

For some reason, her mother came to mind. *I wonder how things are going with her these days?* It had been several weeks since she'd found out from Gwen about her mom dating. *I don't like the idea of Mom going out with strange men, and I can't believe she's entered the dating scene and is willing to try again.* She gripped the steering wheel tighter. *Knowing Mom, she'll probably end up liking the wrong guy and have her heart broken.*

Rhonda dreaded the time when she'd have to talk to Mom about her dating again. It seemed Jeff's relationship issues with his father paled in comparison to her problem with Mom. Rhonda hoped things would go well during their brief visit with Don. It always upset her whenever Jeff became defensive around his dad.

Of course, Rhonda reminded herself, *more often than not, I'm the same way with my mother.* Her jaw clenched. *I would never put up with a cheating man the way Mom did when she kept giving my dad second chances and more.*

At times Rhonda's mother got on her nerves—especially if she tried to cram religion down Rhonda's throat. *She ought to know that I'm not about to start going to church or attend some Bible study. I mean, why should I? That God she talks about has done nothing for me.*

Jeff looked in his rearview mirror and was glad to see that Rhonda's new car was behind him. He'd been keeping an eye on her vehicle ever since they'd merged onto the main highway. Although the silver-tone car she had chosen to buy wasn't her first choice, it was the best they could do with the amount of money they'd received from their insurance company.

At least it's nice looking and seems to handle well on the road. Hopefully, Rhonda has enjoyed driving it today.

Jeff turned left at the next intersection, drove a few more blocks, and pulled the truck into his father's driveway. He made sure to park close to the garage, leaving enough room for Rhonda's car to pull in behind him.

Jeff and Rhonda had no sooner gotten out of their vehicles than Jeff's dad came out of the house. He came right over and gave Rhonda a hug then stepped up to Jeff and did the same.

"How was your trip?" Dad questioned. "Were you slowed by traffic?"

Jeff shook his head. "There were fewer vehicles on the road than I thought there'd be." He gestured to Rhonda's car. "What do you think of my wife's new set of wheels?"

"Looks good." Dad went over and gave the car a quick once-over. "Does it drive well?" he asked, directing his question to Rhonda.

"Yes, it handles quite nicely." She smiled. "It's not as sporty as my other car, but I think it's going to work out okay for me."

"That's good." Dad looked back at Jeff. "How'd my truck work out for you? Did you have any problems with it?"

"Nope, none at all. It got me to and from my restaurant with no problems as well as to all the other places I needed to go."

"Glad to hear it." Dad clasped Jeff's shoulder. "Come inside and I'll fix you both something cold to drink. It'll be nice to sit and visit awhile."

Jeff looked at Rhonda, and when she gave him an approving nod, he said, "Sure, Dad. But we can't stay too long."

"Do you have someplace else you need to go?"

Jeff couldn't miss his dad's look of disappointment. "No, just home, but we'd like to get back before dark," he replied.

"That's several hours from now." Dad motioned them to follow him onto the front porch. When he opened the door, a yappy little terrier darted out and pawed at Jeff's leg.

He bent down and gave the hyper animal a few pats. "When did you get a dog, Dad?"

"He showed up at my place a few weeks ago with no collar or identification tags. I ran an ad and asked around, trying to find his rightful owner, but had no luck." Dad looked down at the dog and shook his head. "The little fellow worked his way right into my heart."

"What'd you name him?" Jeff asked.

"Dancer." Dad grinned. "He's a smart little guy and dances on his back feet whenever he wants a doggie treat."

Jeff resisted the urge to roll his eyes. He figured Rhonda was probably amused by the statement too.

They entered the house, and Dad invited them to take a seat in the living room, saying they should make themselves comfortable while he went to the kitchen to get some cold apple cider. "Unless you'd rather have it warm?" he added.

Jeff looked at Rhonda, and when she shook her head, he replied for both of them. "Cold is fine, Dad."

"Okay, I'll be right back."

After his father left the room, Jeff seated himself on the couch. Rhonda had no more than taken a seat beside him when Dancer leaped into her lap and began licking her hand. She wasted no time in picking up the dog and setting him on the floor. A few seconds later, Dancer jumped up again. This time the mutt put his paws on her chest and slurped her chin.

"Eww. . ." Rhonda's nose wrinkled as she looked over at Jeff. "If this keeps up, we'll be leaving a lot sooner than your father expects."

"Sorry, hon." Jeff took the dog from her and placed him back on the floor. "Go lay down, Dancer." He pointed to the doggie bed that had been positioned near his dad's recliner.

The stubborn animal made no effort to move. He sat looking up at Jeff with his head cocked to one side. *"Yip! Yip! Yip!"*

Jeff looked at Rhonda to see her reaction, but she sat silently with her arms crossed. He figured she might be trying to protect herself in case the dog tried to jump up on her again.

"What do you think of my pooch?" Dad asked when he entered the living room with a jug of apple cider and three paper cups.

Jeff glanced at the dog. "Well, um. . ."

"Would you like to see him dance?"

"Sure."

Dad set the cider and cups on the small table near the couch, reached into his shirt pocket, and pulled out a small doggie biscuit. As soon as

Don held the biscuit, Dancer scurried over, stood up on his hind legs, and danced around. The crazy animal yipped and yapped until Dad let the treat fall. With one quick snap, Dad's furry companion snatched the biscuit then dashed out of the room.

"Where's he going?" Jeff asked.

"He'll either eat the treat or hide it someplace to consume later." Dad chuckled as he poured them each a glass of cider. "I've found biscuits in some mighty strange places."

"It seems as though you've taken an eccentric dog under your wing," Rhonda spoke up. "Where do you put Dancer when you're at your business or out making calls?"

"I put plenty of old newspapers on the floor and barricade him on the utility porch, with enough food and water so he can get by till I get home. I'm not about to let him have free rein of the house while I'm gone." Dad took a seat in his recliner. "Eventually, I'll build Dancer a dog run outside, but with the weather turning colder, I wouldn't feel right about leaving him outside for too long. A bigger dog could take it but not a little terrier like mine." He took a drink of cider and smacked his lips. "Boy, this sure is good."

Jeff's brows drew together. He didn't know what to think. He'd never seen his dad this hyper before. Was it acquiring a new dog or something else? He was about to ask when Dad posed a question.

"How are things going with the sale of the townhouse? It's been a few weeks since you called and said you had a buyer."

"We do, and we're supposed to close in two weeks," Rhonda said before Jeff could respond.

"That's great!" Dad's smile stretched wide. "It just goes to show what the power of prayer can do."

Yeah, right. What good did prayers do on Mom's behalf to keep her from dying? Jeff wanted to say the words out loud, but what good would that do? His dad would probably say something lame like, "It must have been your mother's time to die." Jeff had heard that line before, and it only made him angrier. He wasn't sure he could forgive God for taking a sweet woman like his mother away from her family.

In order to temper the fury boiling inside him, Jeff lifted his glass of cider and took a drink. The tangy, cold liquid helped cool Jeff's parched throat. Too bad it couldn't do the same for the hot anger churning in his soul. Whenever Jeff was at the restaurant, overseeing things and visiting with customers, his anger at God would dissipate, or at least he didn't think about it so much. The same held true when he was at home with Rhonda, enjoying their private retreat. But a few minutes spent in his father's presence or even talking with him on the phone often opened Jeff's old wounds. If only he could find some way to let them go permanently.

"So, you have a new car now, and you'll soon receive the money from the sale of your old place, but what about your air-conditioning? Have you been able to get that replaced?" Dad directed his question to Jeff.

"No, and we're not going to do anything about it until spring, when we have a better feel for our finances," Jeff replied.

Dad bobbed his head like a woodpecker attacking the bark on a tree. "That's smart thinking." He looked at Rhonda and grinned. "Aren't you glad I raised my boy to think things through?"

"Well, actually—"

"So, Dad, other than acquiring a dog, what else is new with you these days?" Jeff set his paper cup down and leaned slightly forward. It was definitely time for a topic change.

Dad moved to the edge of his recliner, with his shoulders straight and pulled back. "Well, Son, I'm glad you asked. As I've mentioned to you previously, I'm back in the dating scene."

Jeff slowly nodded his head.

"After going on a few dates and looking at many women's profiles on the dating site I've been using, I have finally found one that I feel could be my soulmate. Of course, I haven't met her on a date yet."

This sounds utterly ridiculous! I don't know how my dad could get a good feeling about a person without even meeting her. "Better not get your hopes up, Dad," Jeff was quick to say. "If none of the other women worked out for you, this one you're so excited about might not be the one for you either."

"Don't be so negative, Son. I've been praying about this, and if it's the Lord's will for me to find another helpmate, He will lead me to the right one, and I'll have an assurance about it."

Jeff's gaze flicked upward. *Right, Dad. Of course, you will.*

New Philadelphia

June picked up her purse and was almost to the door, when it swung open and Gwen stepped in.

Gwen shook her finger like June was a child. "For goodness' sakes, Mom, when are you going to remember to lock your doors?"

"And when are you going to remember to knock?"

Ignoring June's question, Gwen said, "The girls and I are heading out to do some shopping, and I was wondering if you'd like to join us."

June shook her head. "I can't today because I'm going to get my hair done. After that, I have a manicure appointment."

"Let me guess—you have another date tonight with Walt. Or is it Robert this time?"

June's face heated up. "Neither. This man's name is Andy. I met him on a Christian dating site a few weeks ago, but tonight will be the first time we've met in person."

Gwen frowned. "Do you think that's a good idea?"

"I don't see why not."

"I don't trust those dating sites, Mom. This fellow could be some kook, pretending to be something he's not."

"That's why I'm meeting the man tonight, so I can get to know him better and find out more about his relationship with the Lord. And if it doesn't work out, I'll try someone else whose profile is a closer match to what I'm looking for."

"And what would that be?"

"He has to have the same standards and similar interests as me."

Gwen pulled in her bottom lip then released it. "Does Rhonda know you've visited a dating site?"

"No, but then I haven't talked to her in a few weeks."

"What do you think she'd have to say about it?"

June shrugged.

"She wouldn't approve, Mom, and you know it."

"You're right, but not because I'm connecting with a man on a Christian dating site. Your sister doesn't want me to date anyone, and it has nothing to do with whether he's religious or not. She's worried that if I got married again, my husband might cheat on me the way your father did."

"She may be wrong about that, but I think you ought to be cautious and not—"

June opened her purse and withdrew her car keys. "I don't have time to debate this with you, Gwen. If I don't leave now, I'll be late getting to the styling salon."

"Okay, I'll let you go. We can talk about this some other time."

June smiled and gave her daughter a hug. "Try not to worry about me. I'm a grown woman, and whether you and your sister realize it or not, I am perfectly capable of taking care of myself. I'm also relying on God to help me make good decisions."

Chapter 29

Walnut Creek

Rhonda glanced over at Jeff and noticed how tightly he gripped the steering wheel. She reached over and placed her hand gently on his arm. "Are you stressed from all the traffic we encountered after leaving your dad's place or is it something else?"

"The traffic didn't bother me so much. It's Dad's foolish behavior."

"Him having a dog or the idea that he's seeking women to date?"

"Both. Dad hasn't been the same since he bought that flashy-looking convertible." Jeff groaned. "I'm convinced that he's dealing with some sort of midlife crisis."

"My mother must be going through one too because she's definitely not thinking straight these days."

"At least she hasn't bought a convertible or taken in some hyper mutt." Jeff let go of the steering wheel with his right hand and reached up to rub the back of his neck—one more hint that he felt stressed out.

"Please use both hands on the wheel. You don't have good control with just one hand."

His brows furrowed. "I do too. A lot of people drive with one hand on the wheel."

"But they're not driving my car."

"Should I pull over so you can drive?"

Rhonda couldn't miss her husband's sarcastic tone. "Don't be silly; we're almost home."

Jeff put his hand back on the steering wheel. "There, are you happy now?"

She combed her fingers through her hair and flipped it back behind her ears. "Are you angry about what I said, Jeff, or just taking your frustrations over your dad's actions out on me?"

"Guess it's mostly my feelings about Dad. Sorry for snapping at you, honey. I think we'll both feel better once we're in our own home where we can fully relax."

"You're right," Rhonda agreed. "I'll fix us a snack, and then maybe we can watch a movie together in your man cave."

He glanced her way and grinned before looking back at the road. "That sounds great. Since we stopped for an early dinner on the way home, I'm not all that hungry, but in an hour or so, a snack might be nice. I'll make some popcorn to go with whatever you fix."

"That would be nice."

As they approached their home, he reached for the remote to open the gate. "And the best part is that the two of us will be spending some quality time together."

"It was nice we had a chance to spend some time fellowshipping with your brother, Samuel, and his wife, Esther, after the rest of the people went home today," Lois commented as she and Orley headed for home in their buggy. "I still have some of my snack mix left over. It's setting behind my seat in the red container."

"There were plenty of snacks to nibble on earlier today, but I can always make room for a little more." He chuckled.

"It was good to visit with some familiar faces while we ate and even afterward during the cleanup time in the kitchen."

He bobbed his head. "Jah, since today is our off-Sunday, I'm glad we could attend church services with my brother's church district this morning. It was also nice that it was held at Samuel and Esther's home."

"Speaking of homes. . .that one there is certainly beautiful." Lois pointed up ahead.

Orley squinted. "And you know what? I believe that is Jeff and Rhonda Davis in the car going into that yard through the open gate."

"How do you know it's them?"

"The woman in the passenger's side turned her head to the right, and I recognized her face."

As Orley's horse, Biscuit, approached the gate, he pulled back on the reins to make the gelding stop. "Jah, it's them all right. Jeff parked the car by that big garage, and now he's getting out. If I had a horn, I would give it a few toots."

"Since you don't, we should keep going."

"Nope." Orley handed the reins to Lois and climbed down from the buggy.

"What are you doing?" she called to him.

Ignoring his wife's question, he stood outside the closed gate, cupped his hands around his mouth, and hollered, "Hello, Jeff Davis!"

A few seconds passed before Jeff looked his way and waved.

"He sees us." Orley glanced over his shoulder at Lois before turning to look back at Jeff, who was now headed his way.

When the young man stepped up to the gate, Orley smiled and reached his hand over the top of the barrier. Jeff followed suit and gave Orley's hand a firm shake.

"It's nice to see you again," Orley said. "I have driven by here many times but didn't realize this was your place." He gestured to the house. "It certainly looks grand from the outside."

"Yeah, the inside's pretty awesome too. If you have the time, you're welcome to come in for a tour."

"We have plenty of time. Lois and I are on our way home from my brother's place, where church was held this morning, but we're in no hurry to get home."

"Okay then. I'll open the gate and let you in." Jeff pulled a remote from his shirt pocket, and when his thumb came down on it, both sides of the gate swung open. "You can pull your rig in and secure the horse to a section of our fence."

"Sounds good." Orley climbed back in the buggy and turned to face Lois with a grin. "We're goin' in."

She tipped her head. "Into the Davises' yard?"

"Jah, and then into their house. Jeff is gonna give us a tour."

"But they just got home from somewhere," she responded. "They might not appreciate us barging in."

"Jeff extended the invitation, so I'm sure it's okay." He took the reins from Lois and guided his horse into the yard. When Jeff pointed to the place along the fence where he wanted him to go, Orley directed Biscuit to that spot, gave Lois the reins again, and got out. After the horse was secured, he waited for Lois to climb down from the carriage. Then they both walked with Jeff up to the house, where Rhonda stood on the front porch.

"Hello." She offered them a smile, but it appeared as though it may have been forced. Or perhaps the pretty young woman was just tired. "Jeff said you would like to see our house."

"That would be lovely," Lois was quick to say, "but if this isn't a good time, we can come by some other day."

"No, it's okay." Jeff unlocked and opened the front door. "We just got back from Cleveland, where we went to return my dad's truck that he loaned us after I hit the deer I told Orley about."

"I was sorry to hear the sad story," Lois said as she and Orley stepped into the spacious entryway behind Rhonda and Jeff.

"Is the vehicle you were driving to replace the car you wrecked when you hit the deer?" Orley questioned.

"Yes, it is," Rhonda spoke up. "But I don't like it as much as the one I used to have."

Orley could not miss the disappointment in her tone, and he didn't understand why she would be dissatisfied with such a nice car. Then again, many things confused him about the way some English people thought, not to mention all the modern, fancy gadgets they owned.

"Okay now, if you're ready for the tour, we'll start on the left side of the house." Jeff's comment pushed Orley's thoughts aside.

"Yes, we are ready to see what your home looks like." Orley glanced at Lois and was pleased when she gave a nod.

As the Davises showed them through each room in their beautiful home, Lois was astounded. She'd never been in a house so fancy before and wondered why this young couple had bought such a large place for just the two of them.

Each to his or her own, she thought. *Unless Orley and I had a big family, I sure wouldn't want a house that large.*

When Jeff showed them a room at the end of the long hall he'd said was his "man cave," Lois held both hands against her cheeks. "I've never seen such a large television screen." She pointed to the place where it hung on the wall.

"I didn't realize you Amish had TVs in your homes," Jeff commented.

"We don't," Orley spoke up. "But we've seen the television sets in some of our English neighbors' homes. But none were as large as yours."

Jeff shrugged his shoulders. "What can I say—I like to see what I'm seein' in a big way."

"He's not kidding about that," Rhonda interjected. "If there was a bed in here, I think my husband might sleep in this room."

Jeff nudged his wife's arm. "Very funny, Rhonda."

His eyes narrowed into tiny slits, and Lois couldn't mistake the look of irritation on the young man's face.

"Now that you've had the full tour of the inside of our home, let's go out back and I'll show you around the yard." Jeff looked at his wife. "Would you mind fixing us that little snack you had talked about before we pulled into our yard awhile ago? We can eat it on the back patio."

"That's okay. Don't go to any trouble on our account." With a shake of her head, Lois held up her hand.

"It's fine," Rhonda said. "There's a container of creamy cucumber dip that I made yesterday in the refrigerator. We can have it with some cut-up veggies and crackers if that sounds good to everyone."

"It's fine with me." Orley was the first to respond and then looked at Lois. "We have your snack mix out in the buggy that we could contribute. Let me go grab it." He turned and went out the front door.

While he was gone, Lois looked around some more. She noticed that while they'd toured the home, there were only a few antiques on display. Most of their furnishings were modern pieces that fit nicely with the house's upscale designs. Lois asked Jeff when the house was built.

"When our Realtor showed us the place, she said it was five years old," Jeff responded.

Soon Orley came back inside with the container and handed it to Lois. "Here you go."

Lois thanked him and turned to look at Rhonda. "It's filled with a few different types of crackers with nuts mixed in."

"That sounds good." Rhonda smiled.

"Is there anything I can help you with in the kitchen?" Lois asked.

Rhonda shook her head. "I can manage. Why don't you go out with the men and look at our yard? There's a table on the patio you can set your snack mix on so you can be hands-free while you take a look around."

Lois hesitated a few seconds but finally nodded. As she stepped out the back door behind the men, her breath caught in her throat. "This yard is beautiful. The grass is so green, the flowers are lovely, and there's even a pond with waterfalls." She placed her container on the patio table and pointed in that direction.

"Let's take a walk out there so you can see our fancy fish." Jeff led the way.

Lois stood between Orley and Jeff, barely able to take it all in. The fish swam near the edge of the pond as though begging to be fed, and the cascading waterfalls, which Jeff had turned on, made Lois feel as if she were near a mountain stream.

"If I had a place like this, I'd never need to go anywhere for a vacation," Orley commented. "Think I could set up a hammock and lie out here all day, listening to the gurgling water as it cascades into the pond."

Lois had to agree. This yard was so relaxing. *If Orley and I had a yard like this, during warmer weather, I'd sit outside and answer the letters that are forwarded to me from the newspaper for my Dear Caroline column. I bet I could think more clearly and give better answers if I had a place this serene to do my writing. Of course*, she reminded herself, *I'd probably never get any work done in the house or at our store. So, I will not allow myself to long for something that really isn't necessary.*

"Shall we go back up to the patio now and wait for Rhonda to bring the snacks out?" Jeff's question broke into Lois's thoughts.

"You two go ahead and relax," she said. "I'd like to help Rhonda bring the refreshments out." She hurried up to the house.

When she entered the kitchen, Lois said to Rhonda, "Your yard is beautiful and such a relaxing place to spend time outdoors."

Rhonda set a tray of veggies on the table and turned to face Lois. "Yes, the yard and pond were one of the reasons we bought this home, but there's a lot of upkeep that goes with taking care of it. Since both Jeff and I work five days a week, it's hard for us to do all the things that need to be done in the yard or here in the house."

"Have you considered hiring someone to help with the chores?"

"Oh, we've considered it all right, but it would be one more expense we don't need at this time."

"I understand." Lois gestured to the paper plates and napkins on the counter. "Should I take those out to the patio?"

"Yes, please. You can set them on the table."

"What else can I bring out?"

"Plastic cups are in that cupboard." Rhonda pointed. "And there's a jug of apple cider in the refrigerator. I'll get a tray and bring out the crackers, dip, and cut-up vegetables."

"Okay." Lois gathered the items and took them outside to the picnic table, where the men sat talking. They glanced her way, smiled, and continued their conversation on the topic of antique clocks. Rather than interrupt them, she went back inside.

"Our husbands are talking about vintage clocks," she told Rhonda.

The young woman lifted her gaze to the ceiling. "That figures. I've never been able to understand Jeff's fascination with old things."

"You don't care for antiques?"

Rhonda shrugged her slender shoulders. "They're okay, but a lot of them—at least the ones Jeff's interested in—are quite expensive." She moved closer to Lois. "Jeff hasn't been back in your store looking to buy anything else, I hope."

"Just that time when Orley mentioned that Jeff had come in, looking for an old piece of jewelry to give you for your anniversary, but Orley informed him that all the vintage jewelry had sold."

Rhonda pressed her lips together a few seconds before speaking. "I believe my husband is addicted to old things, and it hasn't done anything to help our marriage. Quite the opposite. His obsession has made things between us more stressful because he refuses to part with any of his collectibles."

Lois was on the verge of saying something, when Jeff stepped into the kitchen, looking directly at Rhonda. "Are you about ready with the snacks?"

"They're right there on the table. I was just getting ready to bring them out."

"Great!" He grabbed the tray filled with crackers, dip, and veggies. "I'll take them out for you."

"Thanks." Rhonda grabbed a few bananas and apples from the fruit bowl. "I'm trying to eat a healthier diet, which includes plenty of fruits and vegetables," she told Lois as they followed Jeff out the back door.

Lois smiled. "Orley and I enjoy healthy snacks too."

As they ate and drank their refreshments, Jeff noticed that Rhonda directed most of her conversation to Lois and barely looked at him, even when he asked her a question. *Is she upset with me because I invited the Troyers in for a tour of our home? Or maybe she's put out with me for suggesting that she fix us some snacks.* Jeff chomped on an apple. *But that makes no sense, since we'd already agreed that we would enjoy having snacks while we watched TV. Of course, it was supposed to be just the two of us. Maybe Rhonda resents the intrusion of two people neither of us knows very well.*

"Say Jeff, I was wondering about that plaque I gave you for your anniversary. I didn't see it hanging on the wall in any of the rooms we walked through on the tour of your house. Did you not like the gift?"

Orley's question jolted Jeff out of his contemplations. "Um. . .no, it was a nice gift. I just haven't had the time to hang it yet."

"I can understand why," Lois interjected. "Between working full time at your restaurant and taking care of this big home and yard, I doubt you have much free time at all."

"You're right about that," Jeff agreed. "Sometimes I wish I could sell my business and find a job closer to home." He glanced at Rhonda, who sat with her arms folded. "You wish that too, right?"

She gave a noncommittal shrug and reached for her glass of cider.

"We should probably get going and let these two have what's left of the day to themselves." Lois gave her husband's arm a nudge.

"Yeah, sure." Orley pushed his chair back and stood. "Before we go though, I was wondering if I could get your phone number, Jeff. That way we can keep in touch."

"Sure thing." Jeff reached into his pocket and pulled out a pen and small tablet. After he'd written his cell number down, he tore off the paper and handed it to Orley.

"Thanks. If I don't call before, I'll definitely let you know when winter sets in and there's enough snow on our hill for sledding." Orley grinned. "It'll be fun to watch you try out that old sled you bought the first day you visited our store."

Jeff smiled. "That'd be great. I'll look forward to that call."

Chapter 30

Autumn's chilly fingers had blown away the colorful leaves on the trees in Jeff and Rhonda's yard. Now the smell of an early winter drifted on the brisk breeze that had whooshed in last night and covered their yard with a blanket of fluffy white snow.

"Oh, boy." Jeff rubbed his hands together in the anticipation of finally getting to try out his old sled on the Troyers' hill. Of course, he wouldn't go there without checking with Orley first.

This would be a good day for sledding, Jeff thought, looking up at the heavy snow coming down. *Since I'm not working today, maybe I could drop by their house and see if Orley might be home.*

"How come you've been standing in front of the kitchen window so long?" Rhonda asked, stepping up to him.

"Just watching the snow come down and wishing I could try out my sled." He turned his head in her direction. "Since neither of us has to work today, why don't we bundle up in warm clothes and take a ride over to the Troyers' place?"

Her thick lashes fluttered like a bird in flight. "You're kidding, right?"

Jeff gave a quick shake of his head. "Orley said when it snowed, I could try out my sled on that hill at the back of his property." He rubbed his hands together again. "I'm just itching to give my old sled a try."

"This is only the third week of November, Jeff. It won't officially be winter until December twenty-first."

"It looks and feels like winter, and by next month there might not be any snow, so I'd like to take advantage of it now." He clasped her arm. "Come on, Rhonda, please say you'll take a ride with me to the Troyers' place."

"I don't feel right just going over there unannounced. Shouldn't you try and call Orley first? What if they're not home?"

"It will be okay, and come to think of it, that day he asked me for my number, I should have gotten his as well. Don't know why I didn't."

Rhonda muttered something under her breath.

"What was that?"

"Oh nothing."

"I'm gonna get my sled and go over there. Please come along and keep me company. Besides, the scenery will be pretty as we take a drive out to their place." Jeff gave a quick pout and followed it with a grin. "Then we'll come back here, turn on the gas fireplace, and veg out the rest of the day."

"If Orley and Lois are at home, what am I supposed to do while you're sledding? We have so few days when we're both not working, and I'd hoped we could do something fun today."

"And so we shall. We can take turns sledding down the Troyers' hill." Jeff's excitement mounted as he continued to gaze out the window at the freshly fallen snow.

"I'm not interested in sledding, Jeff." Rhonda bumped his arm with her elbow. "The last time I got on a sled, I lost control and ended up in a snowbank with icy-cold snow up my nose."

"If you don't want to sled, you can stand on the sidelines and cheer me on." Jeff slipped his arm around Rhonda's waist and pulled her close.

"The last thing I want to do is stand around in the snow and shiver while I watch you act like a big kid on that antiquated sled of yours. Which, by the way, might not even be safe."

"It's not in that bad a shape. I mean, I've dusted the sled off and looked it over. I'd like to do some minimal work on it so that it doesn't take away from its original look, but it's all cosmetic, and I'm sure I can still make it work." Jeff turned to face Rhonda and gave her a kiss. "There's no need to worry. I'll be fine, honey. You'll see."

"It sure is nice having a day at home together," Orley said when he entered the small room he and Lois used as their home office.

She looked up from where she sat at the desk and nodded. "I always appreciate the days off we take from the store. It gives me a chance to catch up with things around here." Lois gestured to the stack of letters lying before her. "Not to mention being able to get some of these letters answered that were sent to my newspaper column. There doesn't seem to be enough hours in a day for me."

Orley frowned. "I'd kinda hoped we could go play in the *schnee* together."

She swatted the air. "Go on with you now. I have work to do here, and we're too old to be playing in the snow."

Orley shook his head vigorously. "One is never too old to play in the snow, and if you're too busy answering letters, then allow me to help, and you can get it done quicker."

Her brows lifted. "Let me get this straight. You want to help me come up with answers to the people who have written to Caroline?"

"Jah, that's right."

"Okay then, how would you respond to this one?" Lois picked up the letter on top and read it to him. " 'Dear Caroline: I have a finicky cat that won't eat unless I'm holding her in my lap. It's probably my fault because I began feeding her like this when she was a kitten. I've tried everything to get her to eat from her dish while it's on the floor. Is there anything I can do to break my cat's habit? Powerless Pet Owner.' "

Orley's eyes widened. "Is that the kind of letter you normally get?"

"Sometimes. Of course, there are other letters involving more serious issues like this one: 'Dear Caroline: My father left my mother for another woman when I was a teenager. Now she's in her fifties and has begun dating. I'm afraid she'll make a mistake and end up getting involved with the wrong man. How can I make her listen to reason? Desperate Daughter.' "

She looked at him with squinted eyes. "Any ideas how I should respond to either of those letters?"

Orley gave his beard a couple of pulls. "Well, for the first one, I'd tell that person to put food in the *katz*'s dish, set it on the floor, and walk out of the room. I bet in no time the furry critter would be gobbling up that food."

Lois pursed her lips and gave her chin a few taps. "Hmm. . .I will definitely consider that. Now what about the second letter?"

Orley gave his beard a couple more tugs. "That one's a little more difficult since it involves a daughter and her mother. I might need to think about that awhile. I'll ponder it while I step outside and check the weather."

"Okay, but I may have come up with a reply to the letter by the time you return." Lois gave him a sly little grin.

"I wouldn't be one bit surprised." He winked and left the room to get his jacket and stocking cap.

When Orley went out the door and stepped onto the porch, he breathed in the chilly air as a few birds chattered at a nearby feeder. It was always nice to enjoy the serenity of a quiet day.

Orley soon saw a familiar vehicle drive into the yard. After it stopped near the house, he went out to greet Jeff and his wife, who had both gotten out of the SUV.

"Hello." He extended his hand to Rhonda and then to Jeff. "This is a nice surprise."

Grinning widely, Jeff shook Orley's hand. "I couldn't remember what days the antique store was closed, so I wasn't sure if you'd be home."

"Yep, today is one of our day's off," Orley responded. "I assume both of you must not be working today either."

"That's right, and since we have all this unexpected beautiful snow, I was hoping I might be able to try out my sled on your hill." Jeff pointed in that direction.

"Sounds like a good idea, and I'd like to join you." Orley gestured to the house. "Let's go inside, and I'll let Lois know you're here. Maybe the four of us can take turns sledding."

Rhonda shook her head. "I only came along to watch."

"Okay, well maybe you'll change your mind once you see how much fun Jeff and I have." Orley opened the door and invited them in. "I'll get Lois and see if she'd like to do any sledding or would rather stand on the sidelines and watch."

When Orley entered the room where he'd left his wife a short time ago, he found her still hard at work on her letters. "The Davises are here," he said. "Jeff and I are going to do a little sledding, but Rhonda said she'll watch. How about you, Lois? Would you like to join us men on the hill or wait down below with Rhonda?"

Lois splayed her hands out wide and flexed her fingers. "I'm not finished here yet, but I probably do need a break." She rose from her chair. "I'll bundle up and come outside to watch and visit with Rhonda while you and Jeff play in the snow."

He wrinkled his nose at her. "We won't be playing, Fraa. We'll be sledding."

She snickered. "Same difference."

"Those two sure seem to be having fun, don't they?" Lois commented as she and Rhonda stood off to one side at the bottom of the hill, watching Orley and Jeff carrying on like a couple of kids.

"I'll say." Rhonda slipped her gloved hands inside her jacket pocket. "It would be a lot more fun if Jeff and I had a child and I was witnessing him or her sliding down that hill."

"So, you're unable to have children?"

"Apparently, although we've never been given a logical reason, not even after all the tests we'd had run."

"And you're sad about that?"

Rhonda nodded. "Don't you feel the same because you and Orley have no children?"

Lois moved closer to her. "I learned some time ago that I could have a happy life even if I couldn't have children. I had to be willing to accept life with its conditions and on its terms not my own. And I decided that my life was a gift from God, and my happiness was not dependent upon children, a husband, or any of the other things I had once thought were the source of happiness. It's about being able to accept the bitter and sweet parts of life."

Rhonda bit her lower lip. "I've had plenty of bitter."

"Do you associate not having children with feelings of failure?" Lois asked.

Rhonda nodded.

Lois gently patted her arm. "I understand, and it's normal to feel that way, but it's not true. The first step is to find other things that bring you happiness without having children."

"I've tried, but nothing, not even my busy managerial position at the hotel, makes me feel fulfilled."

"Perhaps you might consider taking up a hobby you enjoy or doing some charitable work."

"Maybe, if I had the time. My job is quite demanding."

"I understand. Mine can be as well."

Rhonda couldn't imagine that owning an antique store could be demanding, but she chose not to voice her thoughts.

"Another thing you can do," Lois continued, "is to talk about your feelings of pain and loss. Have you done that, Rhonda?"

"I have, but only to Jeff." Rhonda looked down as her eyes filled with tears. "He gets upset when I bring up the topic, so I try not to mention it to him anymore."

"Perhaps it's a touchy subject because he too is hurting."

"I thought he was at first, but now I'm not so sure. Jeff seems to find his fulfillment in other things—like collecting antiques that we can't afford and watching favorite programs on his large-screen TV."

Lois's forehead wrinkled. "Oh, I see." She leaned closer to Rhonda. "May I ask you another question?"

"Sure."

"Do you have a personal relationship with God?"

Rhonda bristled. *Now why is she asking me that? And what business is it of hers anyway?* "Jeff and I aren't the religious types," she mumbled. "We don't go to church either."

"I'm sorry to hear that. A permanent feeling of peace and acceptance is what we all need, and it can only come from a relationship with God. The Bible tells us that. . ."

Rhonda was glad when Orley yelled down to Lois, asking her to fix them something warm to drink. It had felt good to discuss the way she felt about not having children until Lois brought up the topic of God.

Rhonda shivered, pulling the scarf around her neck a little closer. *If I'm going to discuss anything of a serious nature again, I'll write another letter to the Dear Caroline column. At least she doesn't try to cram religion down my throat.*

"One last trip down the hill, and we'll be ready for hot chocolate," Orley hollered.

"Let's watch his final run with the sled, and then we'll go inside," Lois said. "By the time the men come in, I'll have something hot ready for us all to drink."

"Okay." Rhonda was sure Jeff would want a hot beverage, so she really couldn't say no to Lois's invitation. She stood silently watching as both Jeff and Orley pushed off on their sleds and sailed down the hill. Jeff's sled did fine, but Orley's must have gotten hung up on a clump of snow or something else. In a split second, he was off the sled and lying face-down, unmoving in a pile of snow.

"Oh dear! I believe he might be hurt." Lois tromped through the snow and dropped to her knees next to her husband.

With her heart pounding, Rhonda followed. By the time she reached them, Orley had rolled over and was laughing so hard, tears rolled down his rosy cheeks. "What a ride that was! Reminds me of when I was a boy and lost control of the sled one time. I ended up hitting a tree and breakin' my naas."

Frowning, Lois shook her finger at him. "That's not funny, Orley. When you were lying there, unmoving, I thought you had been seriously hurt."

He shook his head. "Nope. Just couldn't catch my breath for a few seconds. And with the snow being so cold and seeping into my boots and up my sleeves, I didn't think I could move."

"I'm glad you're okay." Rhonda looked over at Jeff. "The way you two were carrying on, either one of you could have been hurt."

Jeff shrugged his shoulders. "We were just having fun. Right, Orley?"

The men said they'd be in after a few more runs down the hill, so the ladies went into the house. Jeff couldn't believe how much fun it was to be out playing like a kid again on his old sled, and he had a nice friend to keep him company. He was glad he'd discovered the relic in Orley's shop. And what were the odds of finding one just like his grandfather's?

"If we continue to have snowy days all winter, I'd like to come back and do this again sometime," Jeff said as he and Orley pulled their sleds back up the hill.

Orley grinned. "Same here. Maybe next time we can talk our wives into joining us."

Jeff shook his head. "I doubt Rhonda would be willing."

"Speaking of your wife, did you ever find that daisy pin you'd wanted to give her?"

"No, but hopefully one of these days it'll turn up."

Orley nodded and brushed some snow off his leg. "When we go inside and have the chance, I'd like to show you some of the treasures I've found."

"That'd be great." Jeff positioned his sled, sat down on it, but didn't push off.

"I found a few of the better ones at an auction. The one my wife likes, we got a few years ago at an auction in Florida. Have you been to any of the auctions locally?"

"No. I'm sure that would be interesting though."

Orley took a seat on his sled and looked over at Jeff. "It is a good way to find some nice pieces. And there's usually food to eat, so you can recharge your energy."

"Sounds like fun."

"It is. Lois and I like to go from time to time. We often see familiar faces and enjoy visiting with new people too. My wife and I like being together, and when we go to auctions, we sometimes make a whole day out of it."

"Think I'd like that too." Jeff looked off toward the horizon. *I wish my wife were as interested in antiques and collectibles as I am. Also wish I knew what we need in our lives to have a better marriage. I can't help wondering how Orley and Lois seem so content with each other.*

Orley cleared his throat. "Are you ready to go?"

"Yes, let's do it." Jeff pushed off the hill.

His companion did the same, and they slid quickly downward. At the bottom, they came to a stop, both wearing smiles. Orley looked toward the neighbors' place and waved. An Amish man with a couple of little boys waved back, and the neighbor called out some words in Pennsylvania Dutch. Orley answered him back. Jeff was curious about what was being said, but he felt no need to inquire on the topic.

They headed back up the hill again and came down at the same time. Jeff was happy with his sled. It rode well, and he decided it was worth every penny he'd spent. He glanced over at Orley, with his pink cheeks and big smile. It was obvious that this man liked to have fun. He also conveyed a sense of peace that came from within.

Jeff heard his wife call his name. "We're ready for you guys to come in now."

He cupped his hands around his mouth and hollered in response, "Be right there!"

"And now," Orley said, "let's put our sleds away and head to the house for hot chocolate. I bet my wife has some of her tasty banana bread set out for us too."

As Jeff pulled his sled toward the house, he listened as Orley whistled a pleasant tune. *Sure wish I knew where that man's joyful attitude and peaceful expression comes from. I'd like a taste of it myself.*

Chapter 31

"Here's the newspaper." Jeff handed it to Rhonda. "It's a very nice Thanksgiving edition, and after a quick glance through it, I saw ads from plenty of stores that will be having big sales tomorrow morning."

"I won't be one of those frenzied shoppers." Rhonda shook her head. "Dealing with all the crowds is too stressful, and I've been looking for ways to lower my stress levels."

"Is that why your yoga mat is on the floor in the spare guest room?"

She nodded. "I decided to put that room to good use as a place where I can unwind."

"Good idea. And speaking of unwinding. . .since we don't have to be at your mom's place for dinner till two o'clock, I'm going out front to build a snowman." He rested his hand on the kitchen table. "It'll be fun. You wanna join me?"

"No thanks. I had enough exposure to the snow the day I stood beside Lois, watching you and Orley sledding down that snowy hill behind their house."

Jeff chuckled. "That was a fun day. Made me feel like a kid again, when my cousins and I used to slide down the hill at my grandpa's place."

With a small laugh, she rolled her eyes. "I never would have guessed."

He bent his head and kissed her. "If you change your mind, I'll be outside creating Mr. Snowman."

When Jeff left the room, Rhonda fixed herself a cup of peppermint tea and took a seat at the table to read the paper. She heard the front door open and close, and a short time later, she saw Jeff through the window, beginning his task of rolling a small snowball across the yard.

She watched him for a couple more minutes. *I'm satisfied staying inside and keeping cozy warm. Knowing Jeff, he'll want some hot cocoa when he's finished playing out there.*

Looking back at the newspaper, Rhonda scanned through the ads and went straight to the Dear Caroline column, hoping a reply to her recent letter might be there. Sure enough, there it was.

"Dear Caroline," she silently read. *"My father left my mother for another woman when I was a teenager. Now she's in her fifties and has begun dating. I'm afraid she'll make a mistake and end up getting involved with the wrong man. How can I make her listen to reason? Desperate Daughter."*

Rhonda's gaze went to Caroline's response. *"Dear Desperate Daughter, Although it's often difficult for a grown child to see their single parent begin dating, it's important to remember that your mother is an adult. She needs to feel that she has your support and is given the opportunity to make her own decisions. Your mother may be lonely or feel the need for male companionship. In all fairness, you need to give her the freedom to make her own decisions. It's also important that you be there to support her if those decisions don't turn out well."*

Rhonda sat quietly, sipping her tea and pondering Caroline's response. She reflected on how it would be if she were in her mother's place and had a grown daughter who opposed her desire to start dating.

If Jeff ever left me for another woman, she thought, *I don't think I could ever trust another man. Of course, Mom and I are different, and what feels wrong to me obviously doesn't to her. Guess I need to stop worrying about it and just be there for Mom if and when she needs me.*

New Philadelphia

"What would you like me to do next, Mom?" Gwen asked after she'd finished cutting dill pickle slices.

June gestured to the stack of her good plates on the kitchen table. "Why don't you take those to the dining room and ask your girls to set the table in there? They'll need to include silverware, napkins, and glasses."

"No problem. I'll oversee them to be sure the chore is done correctly." Gwen picked up the plates and left the room.

June opened the oven door to check on the turkey. When she pulled back the foil covering the big bird, a tantalizing aroma drifted up to her nose. Soon, the whole kitchen smelled delicious. The thermometer she'd placed in the turkey's breast showed that the meat was done, so she turned down the heat and covered it again, before closing the oven door. She would leave the bird there until everyone she'd invited arrived.

June rubbed a sweaty palm against the fabric of her apron. *Perhaps I should have told Gwen and Rhonda about the other guest I invited today rather than keeping it a surprise.*

Although it was unlike June to be so impulsive, she'd invited a man she had met on the internet dating site to join them for dinner today and couldn't help feeling a bit apprehensive. Would both of her daughters approve of him? Would they mind that she'd included him in their Thanksgiving plans? *Maybe I have made a mistake.* June closed her eyes and sent up a little prayer.

Hearing the sound of a vehicle pull into the yard, June opened her eyes and looked out the kitchen window. *Guess I'll know soon enough, because he's here, so there's no turning back now.* She removed her apron and headed for the front door. *Now if Rhonda and Jeff would just get here, we can eat our Thanksgiving meal.*

When Jeff pulled into Junc's yard, his eyebrows squished together as he peered out the front window of his SUV.

"What's wrong?" Rhonda questioned.

"That looks like my dad's truck parked over there. In fact, I know it is because I recognize the license plate." He pointed. "What would he be doing here? Last I heard, he'd made plans to be at Eric's place today."

"Did he know we were invited to my mom's for Thanksgiving?"

Jeff shrugged. "I'm not sure. I may have mentioned it when we talked on the phone the other day, but he never said anything about coming down."

"Maybe he wanted to surprise you."

"Oh, I'm surprised all right. And I hope he got your mom's permission and didn't just barge in unannounced." Jeff tapped his knuckles on the steering wheel. "My father's been quite impulsive lately and acting kind of weird ever since he bought that convertible."

Rhonda nodded. "He and my mom would make a good pair. They've both been acting out of character for the last several months."

Jeff rolled his eyes. "Yeah, right. Now wouldn't that be something to talk about—your mother and my father. They barely know each other, and as far as I can tell, they have nothing in common."

Rhonda laughed. "Well, we can't sit here any longer, talking about such a ridiculous scenario. We need to get the food I brought and go inside."

"You're right." Jeff opened his door and Rhonda did the same. When they got out, he reached into the back and took out the box of food Rhonda had prepared.

Walking up to the house, she looked over at him and smiled. "Try to relax, Jeff. If your dad is here, I'm sure he has a good explanation."

They stepped onto the porch, but before either of them could lift a hand to knock, the door swung open. Rhonda's mother greeted them with a pleasant smile. "Happy Thanksgiving!"

"Same to you, Mom," Rhonda said.

"How were the roads between Walnut Creek and here?"

"Not too bad," Jeff responded. "Since we haven't had any heavy snowfall for a couple of days, the roads were mostly clear."

"That's good to hear." Mom glanced at the box Jeff held. "If that's the food you brought, I can take it to the kitchen." She held out her hands.

"No, that's all right," Jeff said. "I'll do the honors."

"Okay."

Jeff started for the kitchen but stopped and turned to face Rhonda's mother again. "Is that my dad's truck parked in your yard?"

Circles of pink erupted on her cheeks. "Umm. . .yes, as a matter of fact it is. Don's in the kitchen, carving the turkey for me."

Rhonda expected Jeff to ask why his dad was here, but instead he headed down the hall, straight for the kitchen. Rhonda's mother followed, and Rhonda was right behind her. She wasn't about to miss out on Jeff greeting his dad.

Jeff entered the kitchen, set the box on the table, and stepped up to the counter, where his father stood carving the turkey. "What are you doing, Dad?"

"I'm carving a turkey, Son." Grinning, he bumped Jeff's arm with his elbow. "And it's a tender one too. See how it falls right off the bone?"

Reaching up to rub the back of his hot neck, Jeff said, "I can see that. What I'd like to know is, what are you doing here?"

"Rhonda's mother invited me." Dad turned and motioned for her to join him at the counter.

Smiling, June did as he'd asked. "Today is our first official date."

"What?" Jeff and Rhonda said simultaneously. He looked at his wife and noticed that her eyes had widened and her mouth hung slightly open. No doubt, she was as shocked as he was.

"We met on that Christian dating site I told you about," Dad explained.

June bobbed her head. "It was a surprise to both of us when our profile pictures came up and we realized that we already knew each other."

"Yeah, and we were equally surprised to discover that we have several things in common. So, rather than meet somewhere for our first date, June invited me to join her family for Thanksgiving dinner today." Dad turned back to his job of cutting the turkey.

Meanwhile, Rhonda pulled out a chair at the table and sat down. She either didn't have anything to say or had decided it was best not to voice her thoughts. Jeff felt certain, though, that his wife could not be happy about this unexpected development. Rhonda had stated many times that she didn't think her mother ought to be dating. He was sure she hadn't changed her mind about that, even if it was his dad her mother had suddenly taken an interest in. This whole thing of their parents entering the dating world again had become more surprising.

Although there was plenty he wanted to say, Jeff decided to keep quiet—at least until he had a chance to speak to his dad alone. *There's no point in me getting upset and ruining everyone's holiday*, Jeff told himself. *But at some point, I will express my feelings to Dad. Even though I've known June since Rhonda and I got married, and she's a nice enough person, no woman can ever replace my mom.*

A short time later, everyone gathered in the dining room, and Don led the family in prayer. Rhonda chanced a peek at Jeff, who sat beside her, looking down but with his eyes open. She couldn't miss the way a vein on the side of his neck protruded. *He's unhappy about my mother and his father dating. Although it does seem a bit odd, at least Mom didn't invite some stranger to join us today. Guess that's something to be grateful for.* Rhonda reached over and clasped Jeff's hand, and he gave her fingers a little squeeze. *I wonder if his thoughts are the same as mine.*

When Don's prayer ended, the platters and bowls of food were quickly passed around, and everyone began eating. Rhonda was careful about what she ate, choosing only healthy items, like the fruit salad, cut-up veggies, and cucumber dip she'd made to bring along. She also chose a piece of turkey, but no gravy or stuffing, and just a dab of potatoes.

"For goodness' sakes, Rhonda, you're certainly not eating much," Mom commented. "Are you on a diet to lose weight, because if that's the case, you're already thin enough."

Rhonda grimaced. "No, Mom, I am not on a diet. I'm just trying to eat healthier these days."

"I heard from Mom that your townhouse has sold," Gwen interjected. She glanced at Jeff and then settled her gaze on Rhonda. "I bet you're relieved."

Rhonda nodded. "We had to lower the price some, but we were glad when the deal finally closed and we received our check. Now we'll be able to buy a new air conditioner in the spring and hopefully pay off the mortgage on our new place in Walnut Creek."

"I still don't understand why you need a house and yard that big. It would make more sense if you had children, but for just the two of you, it seems like a waste of space to me."

Gwen's comment hurt, and Rhonda struggled not to make a caustic response. *It's none of my sister's business how big our place is. She's probably jealous because her home isn't as spacious.* Rhonda's fingers curled into the palms of her hands as she held them firmly in her lap. *And did Gwen have to remind me that we have no children? Doesn't she care how much it hurts me to be unable to have babies?*

As though sensing her irritation, Rhonda's mother reached over and gave her arm a gentle pat. Then she looked across the table at Gwen and stated firmly, "That comment was unnecessary. Jeff and Rhonda have both worked hard ever since they got married, and they deserve to have a large home if that's what they want. They also didn't need the reminder that they are unable to have children."

"Sorry." Gwen dropped her gaze. "I didn't mean to put a damper on the otherwise nice day. Will you forgive me?"

Rhonda nodded. What else could she do with everyone staring at her?

On the way home that evening, Rhonda brought up the subject of Jeff's dad and her mother dating. "It was a surprise to find out that our parents met on a dating site and that today was their first date."

Jeff kept his gaze straight ahead and said nothing.

"I don't particularly like the idea, but at least they're dating someone we both know, so we don't have to worry what kind of person they are seeing socially."

Still no response from Jeff.

Sensing his reservations, Rhonda decided not to push. She thought about the letter she'd sent to Caroline and reflected on the columnist's reply. *Perhaps I do need to follow Caroline's advice and accept my mother's decision to try dating again. If it doesn't work out, Mom will learn from her mistakes. She doesn't need me telling her what to do.*

Walnut Creek

"That was some tasty meal we had at my *bruder*'s house today." Orley yawned and patted his belly. "But now I'm ready to settle into my favorite chair and take a *leie*."

"Nap, nothing." Lois tapped his shoulder. "If you're that tired, you should go to bed."

"Jah, maybe I will." He gave another noisy yawn. "You coming too?"

"I'll be there in a little while. I need to put my pie pans away, and I may do a little reading before I turn in."

"Okay." Orley pulled Lois into his arms and gave her a warm hug. "I love you."

"I love you more." She poked his stomach teasingly. "That's why I made your favorite chocolate cream pie to take to our family gathering today."

"I appreciated your kind gesture." He tweaked Lois's nose and followed it with a kiss on her lips. "If I'm asleep when you come to our room, would ya turn out the lamp on my side of the bed?"

"Of course," she replied, "but there's no need for you to leave it on. If I use my flashlight, I'll be able to see just fine coming into the room without you having to burn more batteries on the lamp."

"All right." Orley kissed her again and ambled out of the room.

Lois went to the kitchen, and after putting the pie pans away, she got out her Bible and took it over to the table. Their house was silent, with her husband already in bed.

She read a few passages from the book of Psalms and bowed her head for prayer. *"Heavenly Father,"* Lois silently prayed. *"Thank You for the many blessings You have given to me and Orley, which include our extended family. It was a joy to spend time with the adults who attended the function, but talking to our nieces and nephews was also most pleasant."*

Lois paused from her prayer and opened her eyes. *I wonder what it would be like if Orley and I had children of our own.*

With her elbows on the table, she placed both hands against her cheeks and reminded herself of the things she'd told Rhonda that snowy day when Orley and Jeff went sledding on their hill. Lois had to admit that she'd always wanted to raise a child or maybe several, but she had never let on to Orley. She didn't want to hurt his feelings or cause him to think that she blamed him because they couldn't have children.

Maybe it's best that we have no children, she thought. *While I don't think we would have been too strict, Orley and I might have been too permissive and ended up spoiling our kinner.* A few tears seeped from her eyes and rolled onto the table. *But oh, what a joy it would have been to be able to hold a boppli—a baby we could call our own.*

Chapter 32

The resonance of a rooster crowing pulled Jeff out of a fitful sleep. But that made no sense; they didn't have any chickens, and neither did any of their closest neighbors. Could one have somehow wandered into their yard?

Then, as Jeff came more fully awake, he remembered fooling with his ringtone last night and setting it to the sound of a rooster crowing to see if he would like it. Well, he didn't. It was annoying!

Groggily, Jeff reached over to his nightstand, and when he picked up the phone, he saw the time and recognized Russ's number. *What's he doing calling me in the middle of the night?*

Jeff pulled himself up and padded into the bathroom to take the call. "What's up, Russ? Have you no idea what time it is?"

"Yeah, Boss. It's two o'clock in the morning, and I'm calling with bad news."

"What's wrong? Are you sick? Have you been hurt?" Jeff's mind raced with all sorts of negative possibilities.

"I'm fine, but your restaurant caught fire. It burned fast, and there isn't much left."

"What?" Jeff blinked rapidly as he tried to process what he'd heard. "How'd you find out, and why wasn't I notified by the authorities?"

"It happened a short time ago. The sirens woke me up. Since my apartment is near the restaurant and the sirens sounded close, I got dressed and headed over there." Russ's voice cracked with the emotion he obviously felt. "There are emergency vehicles up and down the block, and they're sure it was arson because three other businesses in the area also burned down."

Jeff's heart pounded, and his legs felt like sticks of rubber. He had to lean against the counter for support and couldn't help seeing his shocked expression in the mirror. *Who would do such a thing, and why'd they target my business?* Jeff frowned. *And why would God allow this to happen?*

"Are you still there, Boss?"

"Yeah, just trying to come to grips with what you've told me and wondering why this happened."

"Who can say? There are a lot of crazy people in our world who don't care about others and just want to wreak havoc."

Jeff leaned forward and massaged his forehead. He sure never expected anything like this to occur. Just when things seemed to be going better in his life, and now he had this to deal with!

"I'll get dressed and head your way. I need to see for myself how bad it is, and I'm sure the authorities will want to ask me some questions."

"Okay. I'll be here waiting for you. I'll also let the fireman in charge and the police know that you've been told and will be on your way."

"Thank you. I'll see you as soon as I can get there." Jeff clicked off his phone and went to the walk-in closet to get dressed. He'd picked out a pair of jeans to put on when Rhonda came in.

"What's going on?" Her sleepy eyes squinted against the well-lit bathroom light. "Who was on the phone, and why are you getting dressed at this time of the morning?"

Speaking rapidly, Jeff told her what Russ had said.

Rhonda's eyes widened, and she covered her mouth with the palm of her hand. "That's terrible, Jeff. What are you going to do?"

"Russ's waiting for me, and I'm going to Canton to see for myself how bad it is. Then my next step will be to contact my insurance company and file a claim for the loss of my restaurant."

Tears rolled down Rhonda's cheeks as she moved closer and gave him a hug. "I'll get dressed and go with you."

Jeff inhaled through his nose and exhaled through his mouth. "There's nothing you can do there, and there's no point in both of us losing sleep." He gave her arm a pat. "Please go back to bed. I'll wake you when I get home."

Rhonda shook her head. "I'm fully awake now, and after hearing this devastating news, there's no way I can go back to bed and sleep."

"Well, whatever you do, try not to worry. I'll call you when I get there." Jeff finished getting dressed, gave Rhonda a kiss, and hurried out of the room.

After Jeff left, Rhonda sat on the edge of their bed, filled with disbelief. How could something like this have happened? Without the income from Jeff's restaurant, how were they going to make it financially? In addition to her concern over losing the restaurant, Rhonda felt hurt that Jeff didn't want her to go with him. Did he not need her support? Or had her distraught husband been in such a hurry to get to Canton that he didn't want to wait for Rhonda to get dressed?

There was no way Rhonda could go back to bed now, so she slipped her robe on and plodded out to the kitchen to brew a cup of calming herbal tea. Fortunately, she didn't have to go to work until Monday, as she'd taken Thanksgiving, plus three more days off to get a few things done and rest when needed.

As she sat at the kitchen table, staring into her cup of tea, tears sprang to her eyes. She'd thought that, with determination, she and Jeff could get through anything in their own strength, but now she realized they couldn't. Certain things, like Jeff's restaurant burning down, were out of their control. The insurance policy Jeff had taken out on his business would no doubt pay enough so he could build a new restaurant, but that would take time. And since they'd have to pay their deductible first, what money they did receive might not be enough to build a new restaurant.

Rhonda sipped her tea. *I never imagined this kind of trouble would happen to Jeff and me.* She wished she could talk to someone about this right now, but she didn't want to wake her mother or sister during the middle of the night. She couldn't call Lois, either, because the good-natured Amish woman would surely be in bed. In addition to that, the Troyers didn't have a phone in their house. Even if she called and left a message on the answering machine in their phone shed, they probably wouldn't listen to it until later today.

At this moment, Rhonda desperately needed to talk to someone, so she did the only thing she could think of—she prayed. It was the first prayer Rhonda had uttered since she'd begged God to keep her dad from leaving home. That prayer had gone unanswered, because Dad had walked away from Mom and his daughters without looking back. Although he had paid child support, he'd rarely come around. He cared more about his new wife and the stepdaughter he'd inherited than he did his own girls.

As more tears fell, Rhonda prayed out loud, "Lord, if You're listening, and if You care about me, would You please provide answers and let Jeff and me know what direction to take now? We can't make it on my income alone, and it could be several months before Jeff is able to rebuild and get his restaurant open for business again."

Rhonda paused and pulled a tissue from the pocket of her robe to dry her eyes and blow her nose. Although she still felt concern, a small sense of peace pervaded her soul.

I wonder where that Bible is that I received for perfect attendance when I went to Bible school as a girl. Maybe I should look for it and do some reading while I'm waiting for Jeff to return.

An hour later, Rhonda sat on the living-room sofa with a Bible in her lap. After searching through several boxes in her closet, she had located the book.

Unsure of where to begin reading, Rhonda opened the New International Version of the Bible to a section where a purple ribbon had been placed by one of the Bible school teachers. It was the book of Romans, chapter 10. As an adult, she had never read from the Bible, but she remembered reading it and even memorizing some verses when she was a girl.

Maybe it's time for me to read it now, she told herself.

Rhonda began reading out loud with the first verse. When she came to verse 9, her throat clogged, and she had to swallow several times before going on. "If you declare with your mouth, 'Jesus is Lord,' and believe in your heart that God raised him from the dead, you will be saved."

Rhonda thought about the question Lois had asked her when they'd stood out in the snow, watching Orley and Jeff on their sleds. *"Do you have a personal relationship with God?"*

Rhonda had admitted that she and Jeff weren't the religious type and didn't go to church. She could still picture the look of concern on the Amish woman's face as she'd expressed her sorrow over hearing Rhonda's admission. She had tried to block out Lois's next statement about everyone needing a permanent feeling of peace and acceptance, which could only come from a relationship with God. But now, after reading the verse found in Romans, she realized that to have a relationship with God, one must first accept His Son as their Lord and Savior.

Rhonda bowed her head and closed her eyes as she prayed a heartfelt prayer: "Jesus, I believe that You are Lord, and I believe in my heart that God raised You from the dead. Please fill my life with Your peace and strengthen my faith no matter what trials I might face." Rhonda ended her prayer by asking God to keep Jeff safe and to provide for their needs.

As she sat holding the Bible in her lap, Rhonda felt such a sense of peace that she wanted to share it with someone right now. She wished it could be Jeff, but knowing how adamant he was about having nothing to do with religion, she had second thoughts. In fact, the more Rhonda thought about it, the more she realized the best thing she could do was say nothing—at least for now. It would not be good to get him any more riled up than he was already, and she didn't want anything to come between them. Perhaps if Jeff saw a change in her, she would feel free to share her conversion with him.

Canton

Jeff had given Rhonda a call once he'd arrived, and now he stood in his restaurant's parking lot next to Russ, staring at the remains of his restaurant while slowly shaking his head. "I can't believe this happened not only to me but to three other businesses as well."

"I know. It makes my blood boil to think that anyone could do such a horrible thing."

"There's absolutely nothing salvageable. That fire had to be really hot to do this kind of damage." Jeff continued to eye the smoking rubble while slowly shaking his head. "It feels like my whole world's crashed in on me."

"I can say this with certainty—I believe we are put through trials for a reason." Russ spoke with a softened tone.

Jeff's brows furrowed, but he didn't verbalize his thoughts. *Trials? But I'm a good person. Why does God allow bad things to happen to people like me?*

Russ placed his hand on Jeff's shoulder. "What are you gonna do, Boss? Do you plan to rebuild?"

Jeff's shoulders slumped, and he leaned slightly forward as he massaged his pulsating forehead. "I honestly don't know. There's so much to think about, and I'm feeling pretty overwhelmed right now."

"Of course, you are. Anyone would be if they'd just lost their business."

Jeff sucked in a deep breath and let it out slowly. "There are so many things to consider—how much my insurance will pay—how long it will take until the claim is settled—how much money it would take to rebuild—and what to do about my employees who are now out of a job."

Russ gave a nod. "You do have a lot to think about."

"What about you?" Jeff asked. "Will you take unemployment and hold out, hoping you'll get your job as manager back? Or would you rather move on and find something else?"

"Well, I. . .uh. . ." Russ put his hands in his jacket pockets as he rocked back and forth. "Guess I could get by on unemployment if I knew for sure you were going to reopen within a reasonable timeframe. Otherwise. . ."

"I wish I could offer you, as well as my other employees, a guarantee that you'd be returning to work soon, but I can't." Jeff's voice wavered. "Right now, all I can think about is the need to contact my insurance company with the bad news that my restaurant is gone, and I'll proceed from there." He looked once again at the pile of rubble before him and swallowed against the lump that had formed in his throat. When he'd arrived on the scene nearly two hours ago, he'd talked to the police and firemen and answered all their questions, but now it was time to go home. Jeff had hoped that after he'd left, Rhonda could go back to bed and fall asleep. But when he'd called earlier to let her know he'd arrived, she had answered right away. During their brief chat, she'd told him that she was too upset to go back to bed. Jeff asked her to try and get some sleep and told her not to worry. If he found her asleep when he arrived home, he'd go to bed too rather than try to think things through with a foggy brain.

Walnut Creek

When Jeff arrived home, he found Rhonda asleep on the couch in the living room. She looked so peaceful, he didn't want to wake her. He made his way quietly down the hall but didn't stop at the master bedroom. He was no longer tired, so instead of going to bed, Jeff headed for the garage to take care of some business.

Skirting around Rhonda's car, Jeff made his way over to the spot where his SUV should have been parked, had it not been for all the boxes of antiques and collectibles yet to be unpacked. He'd planned to put up more shelves in order to display his old bottles and jars but hadn't gotten around to it yet. Now, it no longer seemed important. Instead of sleeping, Jeff would go through each box and pick out the items he thought would bring in the most money.

Rhonda woke up and glanced at the antique clock on the mantel above the fireplace. It was 6:00 a.m., which meant she'd been sleeping at least three hours.

She pulled herself off the couch and went to the front window, relieved to see that Jeff's rig was parked outside. *I bet he went to bed after he got home from Canton, but I wonder why he didn't wake me.*

Rhonda looked in their room, but there was no sign of her husband. *He must be in his man cave.* She hurried down the hall and opened the door, but Jeff wasn't there either. *Could he be in the garage?*

When Rhonda entered the garage a few minutes later, she was surprised to see Jeff squatted next to several opened cardboard boxes. "What on earth are you doing?" she questioned.

He looked up at her and grimaced. "I'm doing what I should have done a long time ago. I'm going to sell most of my antiques if I can find the right buyers."

Rhonda blinked rapidly as she stared at him. "How come?"

"I won't be getting a settlement from the insurance company for at least thirty days, and we need money more than I need a bunch of old things sitting around collecting dust. So, my plan is to take most of these old things over to the Troyers' antique store and see if they will buy them. I may also run an ad in the paper."

Rhonda stood with her mouth slightly open.

"With Christmas just a month away, some people might be interested in buying some of my collectibles to give as gifts or even to keep for themselves." Jeff stood up and walked over to where she stood. "So, I'm gonna head over to Memory Keepers after breakfast. They should be open by then. Would you like to go with me?"

She shook her head. "But I would like you to tell me how bad the fire was and what happened while you were in Canton earlier this morning."

"I'll go over all that with you while we're eating breakfast."

"Okay." Rhonda gave Jeff a hug. "We've been through rough times before, and we'll get through this too. We just need to. . ." She stopped talking and gave his shoulder a pat. "I'll go get breakfast started while you finish what you're doing."

"Okay. Let me know when you're ready to eat."

She gave a brief nod. *Oh, how I wish I could share Jesus with Jeff right now. But I'm sure he would not be receptive.*

Jeff scratched the back of his head. He couldn't put his finger on it, but there was something different about Rhonda today. Despite the uncertainty of their future, there was a sense of calmness about her. In fact, her expression, which often revealed stress, was one of peace.

How odd, Jeff thought as he knelt again and pulled another box over to him. *It's not like my wife to appear so calm when we're in the middle of a crisis. Maybe it's all that relaxing herbal tea she's been drinking lately. Yep, that must be it.*

Chapter 33

"You look different this morning," Jeff said when he took a seat at the breakfast table. "Are you wearing different makeup?"

She shook her head. "I'm not wearing any makeup."

"Maybe it's the way you're wearing your hair."

"It's a ponytail, Jeff. There's nothing special about my hair." She took a bite of her scrambled eggs. *My husband appears to be avoiding the topic of what happened to his business. I'm sure he's holding in his thoughts and feelings.* "Are you going to talk about the fire now?"

"Yeah, sure." Jeff drank some of his coffee then set the mug down. "There's not much left of my restaurant. Nothing salvageable at least. It's hard to come to grips with what's happened to my livelihood, not to mention my employees, who will now be out of work." His eyes misted. "I had the awful job of calling the cooks and waitresses to let them know they'll need to go on unemployment or begin looking for new work elsewhere. Russ and I even drove around and looked at the other buildings that had burned, and they were all destroyed too." He pounded his fist on the table, causing some of his coffee to spill over. "It's not fair! I'm out of business and my employees have no jobs."

"But you'll rebuild and start over, right?"

"I—I don't know." Jeff's forehead wrinkled as he pushed his hair off his forehead. He needed a haircut, but that was not a priority—at least not today. The first order of business was to see Orley Troyer.

"Have you called your dad and told him what happened?"

"Not yet. How about your mom? Does she know?"

"No, but I plan to call her sometime today."

"I may have to ask Dad for a loan."

"Are you sure? In the past you haven't wanted to ask him for money."

"True, but I've never needed it this bad before." Jeff ate the last of his toast and pushed back his chair. "I'm gonna load all the boxes I've filled and head over to Memory Keepers now. Hopefully, I'll be able to sell some of the things today, and I won't have to ask my dad for as much money to borrow." He gave Rhonda a kiss before hurrying out of the room.

After Jeff's SUV pulled out of the yard, Rhonda put their breakfast dishes in the dishwasher and went to her home office to boot up the computer. Using her browser, she searched for a women's Bible study in her area. She found one listed and bookmarked it. As nice as it would be to fellowship with other Christian women, it would mean being gone from home, which would also mean she'd have to come up with an explanation to Jeff if he asked where she was going. *I'd like to tell him everything, but he'd be shocked at my change of heart—especially since we've agreed for a long time that neither of us wanted anything to do with religion.*

Rhonda was pleased when she discovered an online Bible study she could take, which might work better since it wouldn't compete with her work schedule or take her away from home. The topic Rhonda was most interested in was prayer, and they certainly needed a lot of that right now.

Rhonda turned away from the computer, picked up the phone, and called her mother. "Hi, Mom, there's something I need to tell you."

"What is it, Rhonda? You sound excited about something."

"I'm a Christian now, Mom. In the early hours this morning, I prayed and accepted the Lord as my Savior."

"Oh, Rhonda, that's wonderful. It's such an answer to prayer."

"Please don't say anything about it to Jeff, because he'd be upset if he knew."

"I won't mention it to him, but I don't think you should keep such an important occurrence from your husband."

"I'll tell him when I feel the time is right." Rhonda paused and drank some of her sparkling mineral water. "There's something else I need to tell you."

"What is it, Rhonda? Is it more good news?"

"No, just the opposite. In the wee hours of this morning, Jeff's restaurant was destroyed by fire."

Rhonda heard the intake of her mother's breath. "Oh no! How did it happen?"

Rhonda told her what little she knew and ended by saying that three other businesses had also been burned. "The officials told Jeff that they're sure it was arson, so of course there will be an investigation."

"I hope they find out who did it. A crime like that should not go unpunished."

"If there were no witnesses, we might never know who was responsible."

"I would assume that Jeff has good insurance on the building."

"Yes, but it could be a month or even longer before the claim is settled."

"Will you be able to manage financially until then?" Mom asked.

"I—I think so. Jeff's going to sell some of his antiques, and he may talk to his dad about borrowing some money."

"I'm sure Don would loan it to him too." Mom spoke in an uplifted tone. "He's such a nice man. I still can't get over the way we found each other on that Christian dating site."

"Any plans to see him again?" Rhonda questioned.

"Yes. Before Jeff's dad left after our Thanksgiving gathering, he asked if he could take me out to dinner at a restaurant here in New Philly next Friday evening. I guess he doesn't mind the commute."

Hearing the excitement in her mother's voice, Rhonda smiled. "I'm sure you'll have a pleasant evening, Mom."

"Yes, I'm certain of it."

"Will you be seeing Don exclusively now or continue to see other men as well?"

"Our relationship is too new for me to speak for him, but as far as I'm concerned, I have no desire to date anyone else right now. Even during our family gathering on the Fourth of July, I enjoyed visiting with Jeff's father. It may be too soon to say this, but I have a good feeling about the possibility of a permanent relationship with Don."

Rhonda drank some more water and tried to picture Jeff's father and her mother as a married couple. *I wonder if it will ever come to that.*

"I hate to end this conversation, Mom, but I need to get some laundry done, so I'd better hang up."

"Okay. Thanks for calling, and remember, I'll be praying for both you and Jeff. I don't have a lot of money saved up, but if there's anything I can do to help, please let me know."

"Thanks, Mom. Have a good day."

When Rhonda hung up, she rose from her desk and walked over to the window to look out. The clouds had parted, and the sun shone brightly, making the snow that was left in their yard look like tiny diamonds that had been scattered about. Although their future was uncertain, she felt an inner peace that hadn't been there until she'd found a personal relationship with the Lord. Now if only Jeff would do the same.

Carrying one cardboard box in his hands, Jeff entered Memory Keepers and placed it on the front counter, which Orley stood behind.

"What have ya got in there?" the Amish man asked.

"Old milk bottles I'd like to sell. I have more in my vehicle, along with some canning jars, a few gas lamps, and some insulators."

Orley tipped his head and looked at Jeff through squinted eyes. "You want to put all those items on consignment here?"

Jeff opened the flap on the box so that the items inside could be seen. "I need some money right now and was hoping you might be able to buy some or all of them outright."

Orley slipped both thumbs under his suspenders and gave them a light snap. "With it being this close to Christmas, some of these items could sell right away, but I'm not in a position to buy everything from you today."

"Oh, I see." Jeff dropped his gaze.

"Whatever I'm not able to pay you for can be left here on consignment, though. Could be those might sell between now and the holiday as well."

"Okay. I'll go get the other boxes, and after you've looked through them, you can let me know which items you're able to buy from me today." Jeff started to move away from the counter but stopped when Orley posed another question.

"Mind if I ask why you're in need of money? Are you looking to buy something special for your wife's Christmas present?"

Jeff shook his head. "Somebody set fire to my restaurant last night, so I'm out of business, which means, except for what Rhonda makes, there's no other income for us right now."

Orley's eyes widened. "I am sorry to hear this. Do you know what started the fire?"

"Three other businesses in the area were also burned down, so it was obviously arson."

"That's a shame. It's hard to understand why a person would do something so hateful."

"Tell me about it." Jeff's fingernails bit into his palms as he curled his fingers into them.

"I'll tell you what. . . I'll pay you a fair price for the items in this box, and when you bring the rest in, I will write them up to be sold on consignment." Orley leaned closer to Jeff. "My wife and I will be praying for you and Rhonda during this difficult time."

Prayers, prayers, prayers. Jeff gritted his teeth. *Why do Christians believe that prayer is the answer for everything?*

After Jeff left the Troyers' antique store with a few hundred dollars, he decided it was time to give his dad a call. Still sitting in the parking lot, he picked up his cell phone and clicked Dad's number.

"Hey, Son, I was about to call your number, but you beat me to it." A short pause ensued. "I heard what happened to your restaurant, and I wanted you to know how sorry I am."

"Who told? Did my wife call and let you know?"

"No, I heard it from Rhonda's mother. She called me awhile ago."

"I see. Guess Rhonda must have called her after I left the house."

"You're not at home?"

"No, I just left the antique store here in Walnut Creek."

"You went out shopping for antiques?"

Jeff's facial muscles tightened. "No, Dad, I was not shopping. I need money right now, so I went there to sell off some of my collectibles."

"You don't need to do that, Son. I'm more than happy to provide whatever money you'll need to get by on until your insurance pays and you're able to rebuild the restaurant."

"I appreciate the offer, Dad, and I'll pay you back just as soon as I can. The only thing is, I may not build a new restaurant."

"How come?"

"For one thing, I'm getting tired of the commute. I'd like to find some other kind of work closer to home."

"What type of job?"

"I don't know. There are quite a few restaurants in our area. Maybe one of them is hiring."

"Doing what, Jeff?"

"Beats me. I'll wait tables or cook if I have to. I started out that way, remember?"

"Of course I do, but I can't imagine you going from owning your own business to working for someone else in any position."

"One does what one has to when the going gets rough." Jeff gripped his cell phone a little tighter.

"Don't let bitterness take control and keep you from making wise decisions."

"I don't need any lectures, Dad. The only help I need right now is. . ."

"Just give me a number, and I'll put a check in the mail for you. Or would you rather that I come down there and give it to you in person?"

"No, that's okay. You can mail the check." Jeff stated the amount he needed and was about to say goodbye when his dad spoke again.

"Ever since June called and told me what happened, I've been praying for you—that God will provide for your needs and bring you back to Him."

Great! More prayer and more preaching. What's my dad trying to do—make me feel guilty for turning my back on God?

Jeff gritted his teeth. "Okay, Dad, thanks in advance for your willingness to help out. I need to go now, but I'll let you know when the check arrives."

"All right then. I'll talk to you again soon. Oh, and please tell Rhonda I said hello and that my prayers are with her too."

"I'll give her the message. Bye, Dad."

Jeff clicked off his phone and put his key in the ignition. It was time to go home and give Rhonda the news that, thanks to his father, they'd be okay financially until the insurance check came in.

As Jeff drove out of the parking lot, his stomach knotted. *First Orley and now my dad trying to cram their religious views down my throat. I don't know why they won't let up, but I wish they'd keep their opinions to themselves. Makes me want to avoid them both, but it wouldn't be right to ignore my own father.* He rapped his knuckles on the steering wheel. *And in spite of Orley's religious inclinations, he's a nice guy and we have our enjoyment of antiques in common.* Jeff hated to admit it, but the truth was he liked hanging around the Amish man.

A few miles down the road, Jeff spotted a sign nailed to a fence post bordering someone's land. As he drew closer, the words came fully into his view: YOU MATTER TO GOD.

He groaned. "Sure don't remember seeing that sign before."

A little farther on, he saw another sign. This one read: ARE YOU

Having Problems? Give Them to God.

Disgusted, Jeff looked away and kept his focus on the road. *What kind of a religious fanatic would tack signs like that along this country road?*

He could hardly believe it, but one more sign came into view: Trust in God at All Times.

"This is getting ridiculous! Is someone trying to tell me something?" Jeff shook his head. Maybe he was seeing things because of fatigue. After all, he'd only had a few hours of sleep last night before that crazy rooster crow tone woke him. *I need to go home and take a nap*, Jeff told himself. *I'm bound to feel better after a few hours of sleep.*

Rhonda's stomach growled. *Could it be lunchtime already?* She glanced at the clock near the bottom of her computer screen and was surprised to see that it was half past noon. She'd been so engrossed in the Bible study for new Christians that she'd found online, time had gotten away from her. She'd learned a lot so far—from the scriptures listed as well as the study leader's comments. One of those statements was that when a person receives Jesus, they become a child of God.

I don't have to dwell on the failures of my earthly father anymore, Rhonda thought. *From now on, my focus should be on my heavenly Father, who loved me so much that He sent His Son to earth to die for me.* A lump formed in her throat. *I only wish Jeff would accept God's gift of salvation too. I need to keep praying for him until he does.*

Hearing their front gate open, Rhonda looked out the window and saw Jeff's SUV pull into the yard. *Oh, good, he's home. I hope everything went okay.*

She left her office and headed down the hall. A short time later, Jeff entered the house and took off his boots, leaving them in the hall near the coat tree. "How'd it go at the antique store?" Rhonda asked. "Did Orley buy any of the items you'd brought?"

"Just one box. The rest he took on consignment." He released a heavy sigh. "I called my dad, and he's agreed to loan us some money. Said he'd put a check in the mail."

"That was good of him, but we could have driven up to his place to get it."

"I thought of that, and he even mentioned coming here with the money, but I asked him to mail it instead."

"How come?"

Jeff scrunched up his face. "Because I didn't want to hear more of his religious babble. I've had enough religion crammed down my throat for one day."

Rhonda cringed inwardly. Now was definitely not the time to tell her husband about the prayer she'd uttered early this morning. If Jeff knew she'd given her heart to Jesus, he'd pull away from her emotionally and maybe even physically.

"Are you hungry?" she asked. "Shortly before you arrived, I was thinking about fixing some lunch."

Jeff shook his head. "I don't want anything to eat, but I am exhausted, and I need to take a nap."

"Of course you do. It's been too many hours since you've slept." Rhonda put her arms around Jeff and rubbed the small of his back. "Sleep well, and if you're hungry when you wake up, I'll fix you something to eat."

"Thanks." He kissed her forehead then pulled away and shuffled down the hall.

Rhonda remained in the entrance. Taking a seat on the bench near the door, she bowed her head. *Heavenly Father, Please soften my husband's heart and open his eyes to the truth. Show Jeff how much You love him, and please bring him to a saving knowledge of Christ. In Jesus' name, Amen.*

Chapter 34

"What's all this?" Lois asked when she came out of the back room and found Orley kneeling beside several cardboard boxes in the middle of their store.

He looked up at her with eyebrows drawn together. "Jeff Davis came by awhile ago and asked if I could buy all this from him." Orley pointed to each of the boxes.

Lois tapped a finger against her lips. "That seems odd. As much as he likes antiques, I'm surprised he'd be willing to part with any of his collectibles."

"Under normal circumstances, I don't think he would, but his restaurant in Canton burned down, and he's in need of money right now."

"I'm so sorry to hear that." Lois knelt on the floor beside her husband. "Were you able to buy everything from him?"

He shook his head. "We don't have that much cash on hand, and I would never have done that anyway without consulting you. So, I bought one box, but the rest of the items he left on consignment, and I'm hoping for his sake they will all sell."

Lois put both hands against her cheeks. "I feel bad for Jeff and Rhonda. They've been through a lot the past few months, and I'm sure it's been hard on their marriage as well as their finances."

Orley nodded and rose to his feet. Then he reached out his hand and helped Lois up. "When Jeff was here, he seemed so despondent, wearing an almost hopeless expression. I told him we'd be praying for them, but I don't believe my words meant that much to Jeff."

"I think he's trying to bear the burden of all this on his own shoulders." Lois pinched the skin just above the neckline of her dress. "What that young couple needs the most is a personal relationship with the Lord. If only one of them could make a commitment to the Lord, maybe the other one would in time."

"I agree, but it's not something we can force them to do. They must both come to a place where they realize their need for Jesus."

"Very true. So, we'll keep praying for them like we have been—that something will happen to open their eyes—and in the meantime, we'll ask God to show us if there's anything more we can do to help out."

He bent his head and rubbed noses with her. "Sure am glad the Good Lord brought such a *schmaert* woman into my life."

She smiled and gave his belly a little poke. "I had to be smart to choose a wonderful Christian man like you."

Jeff stood in front of the bathroom mirror, a pained expression staring back at him. The skin around his eyes bunched, and he felt a deep ache at the back of his throat, making it difficult to swallow. *I'm glad Dad was willing to loan us some money, but if I don't rebuild the restaurant, I'll need to find a job so we have two incomes to make it through. My wife doesn't need the extra stress of thinking she'll have to work longer hours to compensate for my lack of income either.*

Jeff massaged his temples while he lingered in front of the mirror. He figured he and Rhonda could get caught up with their debts, but now losing the restaurant had set them back. He'd worked hard to make his restaurant a success, and for what—to see it lying in a heap of rubble and ashes?

Maybe this is God's way of punishing me for turning my back on Him and denying that He even exists. Jeff clenched his jaw until it throbbed. *I have every right to be angry at God. He took my mother when I needed her the most.*

How many times had he told himself this? One hundred—maybe more? Sometimes the anger Jeff tried so hard to hold in caused him to explode over little things, which of course had not been good for his and Rhonda's marriage.

There had been times when his wife had compared the situation with her dad walking out on her family to him losing his mother to cancer. As far as Jeff was concerned, there was no comparison. Although Rhonda's father had abandoned his family, he was still alive. Jeff's mother's body had died, and maybe her spirit had too. He wasn't sure that the people who'd professed Christianity while they were alive went to heaven when they died. Jeff didn't know if there really was a heaven. Some people believed that when a person passed away, their consciousness died along with their body, and they just evaporated into nothingness like vapor.

To stifle his disconcerting thoughts and give himself a boost, Jeff grabbed a washcloth and wet it with cool water then rubbed it all over his face. Normally, this would have revived him but not today—he was too exhausted.

I need to sleep and quit thinking about things, Jeff told himself. *All the speculation in the world won't change the fact that my mother is gone and so is my restaurant. I can rebuild my place of business, but I'll never see Mom again.*

Jeff's shoulders curled forward as he shuffled wearily out of the bathroom. He grabbed the folded blanket at the foot of the bed, flopped down, and covered himself with it. It wasn't long before Jeff drifted off to sleep.

"Jeff. . . Jeff. . . Jeff. . . Come to me, Son. Follow the light."

Jeff recognized his mother's voice, but he couldn't see her face. It was as though he had fallen into a black hole or had gotten trapped in some dark cave.

He turned his head to the right and then the left, searching for some sign of light, but there was none. Jeff groped around with both hands, hoping to find something familiar he could grasp, but it was useless. No matter how hard Jeff tried, he couldn't get his bearings and saw no sign of light.

"Let go of your fear and take a step forward."

Jeff did as the voice asked.

"That's right. Now take another step and then two more. Soon you will see the light."

Once more, Jeff did as he was told. To his relief, he saw a tiny ray of light in the distance. In desperation, he kept moving forward. "Mom, is that you?"

"Yes, Son, keep moving toward the light."

Jeff continued, until he was bathed in a glorious radiance like he had never seen before. He blinked against the brightness and stood in awe at the sight before him. There stood his mother, dressed in white and holding a gold-plated sign etched with elegant lettering in one hand. It read: Be Still, and Know That I Am God.

But Mom's not God. Why is she holding that sign? It resembled the one

Orley had given him, only this was more elaborate and beautiful.

Jeff's mother turned to her left, making a sweeping gesture with her other hand.

He inhaled a deep breath as his gaze became fixed on a magnificent city—every building and all the streets were made of gold. Could this be heaven? Jeff gulped in another breath. Am I dead?

He shook his head. No, I can't be. I don't remember dying. But if I am dead, then I don't deserve to be in heaven because I turned my back on God and rejected His Son.

"Please, Jeff, don't be mad at God for taking me away. I'm in a much better place." His mom spoke in a pleading tone.

Hot tears rolled down Jeff's cheeks and spilled onto his shirt as his mother's image began to fade. "Don't go, Mom," he shouted. "Please don't leave me like you did before."

"If you accept Christ as your Savior, I promise, we will see each other again. Goodbye, Son. I love you very much." As quickly as she'd appeared, Jeff's mother vanished.

"I love you too." Jeff dropped to his knees and sobbed. Is it true, Mom? If I accept Christ, will we be reunited when I die?

Jeff's eyes snapped open, and he blinked multiple times. He sat up straight, his body drenched in sweat. *Was it a dream? A figment of my imagination? Or did I actually speak to my mom?* It had seemed so real. Whatever it was, Jeff felt certain that God's hand had been in it. For the first time since his mother died, Jeff knew without reservation that God was real, and when his mom's soul left her body, she had gone to heaven.

"I want to go there someday too." With assurance, he spoke out loud.

Jeff got up and knelt on the floor along his side of the bed. As he prayed and gave his heart to the Lord, tears flowed down his face. "Forgive me, Father," he murmured. "I know that Your Son died on the cross for my sins, and I'm sorry that I have been breaking Your commandments while living in this world." Jeff paused a few seconds and swallowed hard. "Please fill my life with Your love and peace."

Jeff remained on the floor in prayer for several more minutes before standing up. He remembered how he'd been so desperate at the Troyers' shop and hoped Orley could come through for him. Calling on his dad to rescue him from his financial situation had also shown how worried

Jeff was. Yet all the while, God had waited for Jeff to call upon Him and pray for his needs. *I'm glad my heavenly Father is so patient and forgiving.*

He combed a hand through his tousled hair. As much as Jeff wanted to share the wonderful experience he'd just had with Rhonda, he couldn't do it today. If he told her that he had given his heart to the Lord, she would be upset and think Jeff was trying to pull her into Christianity. So for now, at least, he would keep his conversion a secret.

This experience felt right, and he remembered how, back in his youth, he'd enjoyed going to Sunday school and learning about Jesus. Jeff remembered praying before going to sleep and at the beginning of their meals with his family. It was good reuniting himself with that, and this time he would make sure not to turn his back on Jesus ever again. It would be hard not to share his return to Jesus with Rhonda, but for now he'd try. Someday, however, when he felt the time was right, Jeff would witness to his wife. He hoped when that time came, she would be open to the idea of accepting Christ as her Savior too.

Rhonda had opened the door a crack and peeked into their bedroom a short time ago. The room was quiet except for the familiar soft rhythm of breathing that was soothing to her ears. She'd found Jeff sprawled out on the bed sound asleep. He had changed into some sweatpants and looked content while he slept there. It was good that he'd gone in to take a nap. Between lack of sleep and dealing with the stress of losing his restaurant, she felt sure he'd been on the verge of collapse. If only he could experience the sense of peace in his heart that she'd felt since accepting Christ as her Savior. Rhonda struggled with the desire to tell him about it, but if he reacted negatively, their marriage could suffer even more than it had in the past. She couldn't chance it right now.

Rhonda closed the door to insure that her husband continued to receive the rest that he needed. She turned to leave, and out of the blue, the words of the plaque the Troyers had given them popped into her mind. *I'd almost forgotten about that. It should still be out in the garage where Jeff put it. I hope one day we can agree to hang our anniversary gift from Orley and Lois in a special place here in our home.*

Rhonda tiptoed down the hall and went into her office. Since Jeff was asleep, this was a good time to read more scripture. As she entered the room, her nose wrinkled. "My office seems a little stuffy. I need to let in some fresh air." She stepped over to open the window and paused to watch some birds feeding at a nearby feeder. *They sure are fun to observe.*

Rhonda took in enough air to fill her lungs and then released it slowly. *I do feel at peace. . .thank You, Lord.*

She moved from the window, took a seat at the desk, and opened her Bible to a list of topics at the back. Perhaps there would be some verses that would help her know exactly how to pray for their situation right now. Before she got started, the strong need for a snack led her to reach into her desk drawer for the protein bar she'd put there the other day. After removing the wrapper, she indulged herself with its sweet chocolate covering and the rich peanut butter center. *I'm glad there was only one of these in my drawer*, she mused, *or I'd be tempted to eat more.*

As Rhonda enjoyed her treat, she thought about the positives in her life. *I'm married to a hard-working man; I am healthy; I have a job that pays well; and the best thing of all is I have the Lord in my life.* She reached for a tissue and wiped off her hands before grabbing the Bible again.

As Rhonda turned several pages and looked at the different topics, her gaze came to rest on the word *Forgiveness*. Underneath it was written: "Un-forgiveness is like a cancer—if you do not take care of it, the disease will eat away at your soul."

Rhonda wrote down some of the passages about forgiving that were listed, and then she turned in her Bible to Matthew 6:14–15 (NIV). A feeling of guilt crept into her soul as she read the words silently: *"For if you forgive other people when they sin against you, your heavenly Father will also forgive you. But if you do not forgive others their sins, your Father will not forgive your sins."*

Rhonda's thoughts went to her father, and she realized that she had never forgiven him for what he'd done to her mother, which in turn had affected her and Gwen's lives as well.

"So, if I don't forgive my dad, my Father in heaven will not forgive me," Rhonda whispered, nearly choking on the words.

Tears pooled in her eyes and dripped onto her hot cheeks. *I can't call myself a Christian if I'm unable to forgive.*

Rhonda closed her eyes and bowed her head. *Dear Lord: Forgive me for harboring ill feelings toward my dad all these years. Although what he did was wrong, I have been guilty of not being willing to forgive him.* She paused to swipe at her tears. *Forgive me, Jesus, for every bad thought I've had about my dad. Please give me the courage and the right words to write Dad a letter, letting him know that I have forgiven him.*

Rhonda had finished her prayer and was about to look at some other Bible passages, when she heard footsteps coming down the hall. Quickly wiping her eyes, she put the Bible in her desk drawer and left her office. As Jeff approached Rhonda in the hall, she was surprised to see his unfocused gaze. His face and neck were flushed with color. Perhaps he was still groggy from having just gotten up.

"You didn't sleep very long," she said. "Did you get enough rest?"

"I slept as long as I needed to." Jeff kept walking. "I need my cell phone. Think I left it in the kitchen."

"Are you sure? I don't recall seeing it there when I heated some soup for my lunch."

"It's okay. I'll find it." Jeff stopped walking and looked at Rhonda.

She tipped her head. *Is that a look of peace I see on my husband's face? Could a short nap have been all that he needed to calm down?*

Jeff slipped his arm around Rhonda's waist. "There's no need to worry about anything, honey. I'm confident that it's all going to work out."

Rhonda stood speechless. Could this be the same man who'd trudged down the hall nearly two hours ago with a look of defeat? She had no idea what had happened between then and now to lift Jeff's spirits, but it didn't really matter. She was pleased to see the improvement.

Chapter 35

Monday morning when Jeff went to the mailbox, there was an envelope from his father. Much to his relief, the check had made it. Jeff waited until he was back in the house to open it. Dad's check should get them by for at least a month. He had also included a note saying that if Jeff needed more to let him know.

Should I tell Dad about the dream I had a few days ago? Jeff felt the need to tell someone, and he was sure his father would be happy to hear that he'd given his heart to the Lord. He'd just have to make it clear that he didn't want Rhonda to know.

Since she had gone to work at the hotel, Jeff had the house to himself. That gave him the chance to make the call to his dad and not have to worry about her hearing what he said.

Jeff took off his jacket, hung it on the clothes tree, and headed to the kitchen to get coffee. It felt strange being home on a workday, knowing he no longer had a restaurant to run. He'd have to adjust to not seeing his employees and visiting with the customers who came in.

Jeff grabbed a mug from the cupboard and filled it with the steaming brew. Once that was done, he got his cell phone and took a seat at the table. Jeff punched in his dad's number and was disappointed when a voice message came on, saying Dad was unavailable now and to please leave a message.

"Hey, Dad. It's Jeff. I got the check today and wanted to say thanks. I'll pay you back as soon as I can." Jeff paused, trying to decide whether to say anything about his dream but decided to wait until he could speak directly to his dad. "Please give me a call when you have the time. There's something else I want to tell you."

Jeff hung up, grabbed his coffee, and headed down the hall to his man cave. This time, though, instead of watching TV, he planned to spend some time praying about the future. After that, he would make a trip to the Christian bookstore in town to buy a study Bible. Afterward, he might drop by the Troyers' house to talk with Orley. He certainly needed to tell someone about his good news. Since Memory Keepers was usually closed on Mondays, he hoped he would find the kindly Amish man at home.

Orley had just finished chopping and stacking firewood when a vehicle pulled into the yard. He smiled after the driver got out and began walking toward the house.

Orley extended his hand. "It's good to see you, Jeff."

The young man nodded. "I'm glad to see you too. I have some good news I want to share." Jeff grinned widely. "Actually, there are two pieces of good news."

"I'm always eager to hear positive news." Orley gestured to the house. "Let's go inside where it's warmer, and you can tell me about it."

"Sounds good."

Orley led the way, and when they entered the house, Lois greeted them at the entryway. She shook Jeff's hand. "It's nice to see you. Is your wife along?"

"No, Rhonda's working at the hotel today."

"Orley told me what happened to your restaurant. I was sorry to hear about it." Lois spoke in a soothing tone of voice. There was no mistaking the sympathy she felt.

"Yeah, it was a real shock," Jeff said. "But in the long run, it could turn out to be a blessing."

"Let's take a seat and you can tell me about it." Orley gestured to the living room.

"Would you two like some coffee or hot chocolate?" Lois asked.

"Hot chocolate sounds good," Jeff replied.

"I'd like some too." Orley smiled and gave his wife's arm a pat. "Danki."

"You are most welcome."

When Lois headed to the kitchen, Orley and Jeff seated themselves in two adjacent chairs with a small table between them.

"I'm eager to hear your good news," Orley said.

"For one thing, my dad loaned me enough money to get by until my insurance pays the claim I put in for the loss of my restaurant."

"Good to hear. Your father sounds like a nice man."

"He is. Unfortunately, I haven't always appreciated him the way that I should."

"Sometimes we tend to take people—especially family members included—for granted. It's important for us to focus on their good qualities instead of looking for things we don't like about them."

"True, and I've been guilty of doing that in the past—especially where my dad is concerned." Jeff shook his head. "But not anymore. From now on, I'm going to focus on his positive traits and try to show my appreciation."

"Good thinking. If I had a son or daughter, I'd hope they would feel that way too."

Jeff sat quietly for a few minutes before he spoke again. "I've been thinking about my restaurant and whether or not I should rebuild it."

"Is there a reason why you wouldn't want to?"

"For one thing, I'm getting tired of the commute." Jeff crossed his feet at the ankles. "It's also a big responsibility to provide jobs for my employees and oversee everything that needs to be done."

"What would you do if you didn't rebuild?" Orley questioned.

Jeff shrugged. "I'm not sure. Maybe see if I can find a job closer to home or even something I can do while working from our house."

"I see."

Lois came into the room, carrying a tray with cookies and two mugs of hot chocolate. She set the tray on the table between them and started to leave the room.

"Aren't you going to join us?" Orley asked.

"I have some things I need to do at my desk, but you two go ahead and enjoy the snacks while you visit." She looked over at Jeff. "Please tell your wife I said hello, and I'll look forward to seeing her sometime soon."

Jeff smiled and reached for a cookie. "Thanks, I'll give her your message."

After Lois left the room, Orley picked up his mug and took a drink. "Ah…there's nothing quite like hot chocolate to warm a body on a chilly day such as this."

"I agree. Now would you like to hear my other good news?"

"Of course."

Jeff leaned closer to Orley's chair and whispered, "Can you keep what I'm about to say a secret—at least from my wife?"

Taken by surprise, all Orley could do was give a brief nod. He did not like keeping secrets but didn't want to hurt Jeff's feelings. And if Orley said no, most likely Jeff would not open up and say whatever was on his mind.

"When I came back from Canton after looking at what little remained of my restaurant, I felt exhausted and went to the bedroom to take a nap."

Orley listened as Jeff went on to say that he'd had a dream—one that felt as though it was actually happening.

"I saw my mother," Jeff said. "She talked to me, and I responded. It seemed like we were standing on the outskirts of heaven." He paused and took a drink from his mug. "She held a sign with the same verse of scripture on it as the one you gave Rhonda and me for our anniversary."

" 'Be still, and know that I am God?' "

"Yeah."

Orley couldn't help wondering where this was leading, but he remained quiet and listened as Jeff went on to tell him all the things that his mother had said.

"I believe God gave me that dream or whatever it was for a reason. He wanted me to understand, without a doubt, that He is God and there is a heaven where believers go after they die." Jeff's voice cracked, and tears welled in his eyes. "When I woke up, I got on my knees and prayed. I asked God to forgive my sins and told Him that I believe His Son, Jesus, died for me." Jeff reached into his pocket, pulled out a handkerchief, and blew his nose. "I'm a believer now, Orley, and for the first time since my mother died, I feel a sense of peace."

Overcome with emotion, Orley had a hard time holding back his own tears. How thankful he was that God had answered his prayers for Jeff. It gave him the reassurance that whenever there was a need, a Christian should never quit praying. "Pray without ceasing," the Bible said.

"Thank you for sharing this wonderful news with me," Orley stated with conviction. "I'm just a bit confused as to why you don't want your wife to know about your conversion."

"Rhonda is against all things that involve religion. Well, let me back up a bit. We both used to be against religion for our own reasons. Rhonda and I felt justified in feeling that way because we felt that God had let us down in the past." He wiped away an escaped tear. "If you don't mind,

I'll share my wife's story with you. It won't take long."

When Orley nodded, Jeff continued speaking. "She used to go to Bible school when she was a girl, but when her dad divorced her mother and married another woman, Rhonda became bitter and angry with God for not answering her prayers."

"I see."

"If Rhonda knew that I, who used to feel the same way she does, now have a personal relationship with Jesus, she would be very upset." Jeff took another drink and set his mug down. "We've had our share of marital problems, and I'm sure many of them were my fault." He reached up and rubbed the back of his neck. "I feel certain that if she knew I was a Christian, it would put an even bigger strain on our relationship. She might walk away from the marriage. So, I do not see any option but to keep it a secret. Don't you agree?"

Orley felt as though he was on the hot seat right now. He remembered the things their bishop had said to him and Lois before pronouncing them man and wife. The minister had stated that they needed to practice good communication in their marriage and divorce was not an option. It didn't make sense to Orley that anyone would leave their spouse because they said they'd become a Christian. Their belief in Christ had always been an important part of his and Lois's marriage. In fact, Orley looked forward to the time of devotions they had together after supper each evening. No way would their religious views put a wedge between him and his wife. *But unlike me, Jeff is English and in a different situation with his wife. It's clear that he's trusting my character enough to share what's on his heart. For that I feel honored.*

Speaking kindly but with every assurance that what he was saying was true, Orley said, "I will not repeat anything you have said to me today to your wife, but personally, I think you are wrong to not tell her."

Jeff stiffened. "You don't understand. Rhonda is as adamant about having nothing to do with God as I was before I had that dream. Which, by the way," he added. "I'm sure was ordained by God."

Orley reached over and placed one hand on Jeff's knee. "As I stated previously, I won't mention any of what you have said to Rhonda, but I will be praying that God gives you the courage to tell her when you feel the time is right."

Jeff slowly nodded. "I hope I'll eventually be able to do that, because it's not easy holding in something that was life changing for me. In the meantime, though, I want to be a good husband and try to make up for all the times I said hurtful things to Rhonda."

"That should add strength to your marriage, and perhaps after she sees the change in you, she'll be more open to hearing about your new relationship with the Lord."

"That's what I'm hoping." Jeff took another cookie and dunked it in what was left of his hot chocolate.

Orley pulled his fingers through his beard as he tried to reason things out. *Although Jeff said he didn't want me to tell Rhonda, he said nothing about Lois. I'd like her to be praying for Jeff and Rhonda too, so after he leaves, I'm going to tell her what he said.*

Jeff had just pulled into his own yard when his cell phone rang. Seeing that it was his dad, he shut off his SUV and took the call. "Hey, Dad, did you get my message?"

"Yes, I sure did. Glad to know the check got there okay."

"I'll pay you back as soon as I get my insurance check."

"No problem. I'm not worried about it." There was a slight pause on Dad's end. "You mentioned in your message that there was something else you wanted to talk to me about."

"Yep, there is." Taking a deep breath, Jeff launched into the story about his dream and what had followed when he'd awakened.

He heard his dad's quick intake of breath. "Wow, Jeff, that's amazing! I'm so happy for you. This is certainly an answer to prayer."

"I wish you could have seen her, Dad. Mom was absolutely beautiful. Her face appeared to be glowing."

"You are blessed to have had a dream like that."

"I know, and since I have plenty of time to myself these days, I'm going to check around and see if there are any men's Bible study classes near me that I could attend."

"Sounds like a good plan. Spending time in the Word will help to strengthen your faith."

"I made a trip to our local Christian bookstore earlier today and bought a study Bible."

"That's great. So, what did Rhonda say when you told her about turning your life over to Christ?"

"I–I haven't said anything to her about the dream or my prayer afterward. She has no idea I accepted the Lord as my Savior."

"Shouldn't you tell her something as important as that? Wouldn't it be great if your testimony led her to Christ?"

"Yes, it would, but to be honest, before my conversion, Rhonda and I both felt that God had let us down in big ways. We agreed it was best to stay away from anything of a religious nature. But now that's behind me, and I'm ready to pursue a new life with Jesus. My biggest concern, though, is that my wife needs the Lord too. Rhonda's always been adamant about her feelings toward God. When she was a girl, she used to pray that her father and mother would stay together, but her prayers were not answered in the way she wanted. Since that time, she's held a lot of bitterness in her heart toward God as well as her father."

"Wasn't that the way you felt before your conversion?"

"Yeah, I was angry at God for taking Mom. But now I feel different. I have a new understanding of things."

"I'm sure you do, which is why you might be the one who can reach your wife."

"But she might get angry and accuse me of trying to cram religion down her throat. That's how I used to feel when people stated that they were praying for me or said preachy things that did nothing but irritate me."

"I understand your apprehension where Rhonda is concerned, but I wish you would give it more thought."

"I will, Dad. I really do want to share Jesus with her, but now is not the right time."

"Any time's the right time to share God's love and the redemption He offers because of His Son. Pray for the right words to say, and speak them from the heart with love."

Jeff looked in his rearview mirror and saw Rhonda's car pulling in. "I'd better go, Dad. My wife just got home."

"Okay, I'll talk to you again soon. And if we don't see each other before, I'm hoping we can enjoy each other's company on Christmas Day."

"Umm. . .Rhonda and I haven't made any plans yet for Christmas."

"I figured you hadn't, so I was thinking it might be nice if you came here to my place for Christmas this year. I'm planning to invite June as well."

"I'll talk to Rhonda about it and get back to you, okay?"

"Sure, Son. Oh, and Jeff. . ."

"Yeah, Dad?"

"I love you."

"Love you too."

When Jeff hung up, he got out of his rig, waved at Rhonda before she pulled her car into the garage, and went inside to wait for her. Jeff didn't know whether he had the courage to speak to Rhonda about God today, but he looked forward to spending time with her.

Chapter 36

Jeff left the Christian bookstore whistling and with a spring in his step. Inside the bag he carried was a daily devotional, which he would keep hidden in a safe place in his man cave since Rhonda rarely came in there anymore.

Jeff still hadn't figured out what was going on with his wife. When she wasn't cooking or doing some chore around the house, she often retreated to her office. Jeff figured she was either doing hotel work from home or playing some computer game. Her favorite was a word game that claimed to help strengthen a person's brain. So, whenever Rhonda was holed up in her office, Jeff took advantage of the time to read the Bible, which helped to bolster his faith.

It had been two weeks since Jeff's restaurant burned down, and with each passing day, he became more convinced that he did not want to rebuild. It had been a difficult decision, but yesterday Jeff had called each of his employees and given them the news. Most said they understood and had already begun looking for new jobs, but Russ had been a little put out with Jeff's decision. Jeff apologized, and after explaining his reason in detail, Russ finally said he understood and wished his boss well in whatever he decided to do for employment.

Jeff unlocked his SUV and put his purchase on the passenger seat. *Even though I'm going through rough times right now, the Lord is giving me hope.* He glanced again at the bag. *I can't wait to start using my new devotional this evening.*

Since the Christian bookstore wasn't far from the antique store, Jeff decided to make that his next stop. He hadn't talked with Orley since he'd dropped by his house to share the news that he'd become a Christian, so it would be nice to connect with the kindly Amish man again and let him know what he'd decided. Hopefully, his new friend wouldn't be too busy with customers and would have some time to talk.

When Jeff entered Memory Keepers a short time later, he saw Orley talking with an elderly Amish man at the counter, while Lois visited with an Amish woman, who Jeff figured might be the older man's wife.

Since they were both busy at the moment, Jeff wandered around the store, looking at the few milk bottles on display. He didn't see any of the ones he'd brought in and left on consignment, so he hoped that meant they had sold. Although the money he'd put in the bank from his dad's check would keep them afloat as far as paying bills and buying gas for their vehicles as well as grocery items, it would be nice to have some cash to buy Christmas presents. The holiday was getting closer, and after discussing it with Rhonda, they had decided to accept the invitation they'd received to spend Christmas Day at his dad's place in Cleveland. Jeff looked forward to it, but he wasn't sure about Rhonda. She'd been acting out of character ever since his restaurant burned. Although she was much nicer to him than she had been previously, Jeff had a feeling his wife was keeping something from him. He wanted to ask but didn't want to start a discussion that could end up in an argument.

When Orley and Lois's customers left the shop, Jeff smiled and walked over to Orley. "Do you have a few minutes to talk?" he asked.

"Sure do." Orley grinned in his usual friendly manner. "Why don't we go in the back room where it's private?"

"Are you sure? What if more customers come in?"

"It won't be a problem. I'll ask Lois to let me know."

Before Orley had a chance to speak to his wife, she spoke up. "I heard what you said, and don't worry, I'll let you know if things get busier than I can handle." She glanced around and smiled at Jeff. "Looks like you came here alone again today."

"Yeah, Rhonda's at work."

"How's she doing?"

"From what I can tell, Rhonda's okay. She's been working longer hours than normal so she can take a few extra days off the week of Christmas.

The extra money is nice, but we don't get to spend as much time together as I would like."

Lois gave a sympathetic smile along with an understanding nod. Then she motioned to the door of the back room. "You two go on now and enjoy your chat. There are bottles of water in the cold bag I brought from home this morning, as well as some mighty good apples to snack on."

"Thanks," Jeff said. "I might take you up on that offer."

When they entered the small room, Orley invited Jeff to take one of the chairs, and then he placed the cooler bag on the desk and seated himself in the other chair. "I have some good news for you."

"Good news is always welcome," Jeff said.

"Nearly everything you brought in on consignment has sold. So, you have money coming."

"That's great. It'll give me some cash to buy a few Christmas presents." Jeff took the bottle of water Orley held out to him.

"Would you like an apple?" Orley asked.

"Are you going to have one?"

"You bet."

"Guess I will then too."

Orley reached into the cooler and withdrew two perfectly shaped red apples. "These are not only sweet, they're nice and crispy."

Jeff took a bite and drank some water. "I've made a decision, Orley."

"About what?"

"The business I lost. I've decided not to rebuild the restaurant."

"Mind if I ask why?"

"I'd like to find a job closer to home. Eventually, I hope Rhonda will be able to do the same." Jeff stopped talking long enough for another bite of apple and more water, and then he spoke again. "When we're gone so much from home, it's hard to keep up with everything that needs to be done in and outside the house. There's also the problem of Rhonda and me having less time to spend together."

Orley gulped down most of the water in his bottle and set it on the table. "I know a lot of people in the area. Would you like me to put my feelers out and see what jobs are available right now?"

"Sure, that'd be great." Jeff twisted the gold wedding band around his finger. "I still haven't told Rhonda about the dream I had or that I committed my life to Christ. There doesn't seem to be a right time to tell her."

"The longer you wait, the harder it will be."

"I know, but I'm afraid of her reaction."

"I assume you've prayed about it?"

"Yes, but I haven't gotten a clear answer yet."

"You will. The Lord always answers in His time." Orley pointed upward. "I remind myself daily that He knows what's best for me."

"I know that I need to trust Him."

"Right." Orley glanced at the newspaper lying on the desk. Lois had been looking at it earlier to see if her most recent column had been included. Out of curiosity, he turned to the page that gave listings for homes and places of business for sale. One jumped out at him. "Now here's something that might interest you, Jeff." He pointed to the page.

Jeff left his seat and came over to stand beside Orley's chair. "What is it?"

"Seems there is an inn for sale right here in Walnut Creek. If becoming an innkeeper is something you think you might enjoy, here's the name of the Realtor to contact." Orley pointed to the woman's name and the telephone number to call.

Jeff rolled his neck from side to side, rubbing it as he did so. "Hmm...that does sound like an interesting prospect. I could cook meals or at least breakfast for the guests, and Rhonda could handle the business end of things. Managing the hotel in Canton has given her plenty of experience."

Orley wrote the name of the Realtor and her phone number on a piece of paper and handed it to Jeff. "If you decide to talk to this woman, please let me know how it turns out. In the meantime, I'll be praying about the situation."

Jeff gave Orley a wide smile. "Don't know what I'd do without a friend like you. You're so positive about things, and it's been a real encouragement to me."

Orley smiled and gave Jeff a pat on the back. "I think of you as a friend too. Now, my friend, let's go up front to the cash register, and I'll pay you the money you have coming."

Canton

As Rhonda entered her office at the hotel and took a seat at the desk, her thoughts went to Jeff. Ever since his restaurant burned down, Rhonda had been concerned about him. He was gone more than usual, and when she would ask where he'd been, he usually gave little explanation. Whenever they talked, Jeff acted upbeat, but she suspected that he was trying to hide his real feelings about what had happened to his business. If that was the case, Rhonda wouldn't push, but she hoped Jeff would eventually open up to her about it. She knew from experience that it wasn't good to hold things in.

Last night, Jeff had told Rhonda that he had decided not to rebuild his restaurant. The announcement had come as a shock, and when she'd asked why, his response was even more surprising. Jeff had stated that he was tired of the commute to Canton and wanted to find a job closer to home. This seemed strange to Rhonda, because when Jeff had tried to convince her to sell their townhouse and move to Walnut Creek, he'd said he didn't mind commuting to the restaurant.

Why the sudden change? she asked herself. Rhonda had to admit that she would also prefer to work somewhere closer to home. She had even looked into the possibility. Unfortunately, none of the local hotels was in need of a manager at this time, and all the other positions had been taken.

Rhonda's biggest concern was their finances. If Jeff didn't rebuild his restaurant and wasn't able to find a decent paying job near home, they'd never be able to live off her income alone.

Refocusing, Rhonda turned on her computer. While waiting for it to boot up, she closed her eyes for a silent prayer. *Dear Lord, Please help me not to worry about the future and to trust You to provide for all of our needs. Give me the wisdom to know when I should tell Jeff that I'm a Christian, and help him to be receptive to the idea.*

Rhonda's prayer was interrupted when Marian, the new desk clerk she'd hired after Lori left, came into the room.

"Good morning, Mrs. Davis. I thought you might like a cup of coffee." Marian placed the steaming cup of strong-smelling brew on Rhonda's desk. The pungent odor wafted up to Rhonda's nose and caused her stomach to churn. *What's going on? The smell of coffee has never done this to me before. Maybe it's a new brand, or I may have lost my desire for coffee since I've been drinking more herbal tea lately.*

"Thank you, Marian." Rhonda forced a smile as another wave of nausea swept through her. She placed both hands against her stomach, hoping to halt the unpleasant feeling.

"You don't look well, Mrs. Davis." Marian put her hand on Rhonda's shoulder. "Are you sick?"

"I don't think so. For some reason, the strong coffee odor made me feel queasy. I'm sure it'll pass, but would you please take the cup back with you? I haven't had coffee in a while, and I don't think I can drink any right now."

"Oh, I'm sorry." The young employee picked up the mug and started for the door.

"I appreciate the gesture," Rhonda called out to her. "And please let me know if you need anything or any problem arises at the front desk. I'll be in here working on a spreadsheet for a few hours, but feel free to let me know if anything comes up that you can't handle."

Marian turned to Rhonda and smiled. "Thanks, I will."

After the young woman left, Rhonda opened the spreadsheet she'd been working on the day before. The document was related to budget cuts, and it was Rhonda's job to decide what the hotel did or didn't need.

She made a few notations in column B when another wave of nausea hit. With this one, Rhonda knew that if she didn't get to the bathroom quickly, she'd have to use the garbage can to empty her stomach.

Hurrying out of the room and rushing down the hall, Rhonda made it to the women's restroom just in time. Once she'd finished vomiting, she went to the sink to wash her face and rinse out her mouth. Now that she thought about it, Rhonda remembered dealing with a queasy feeling yesterday morning and the day before too. She'd also missed her period but figured it was from stress. Was it possible. . .

No, it can't be, she told herself. *After all these years of hoping for a baby, there's no way I could be pregnant.*

Although the odds were slim, she had been trying to eat healthier in addition to taking several nutritional supplements she'd found at the health food store in Berlin.

Rhonda blotted her face on a paper towel. *If I'm pregnant, it would be no less than a miracle.*

It was probably a waste of time and money, but Rhonda decided she would go to the pharmacy near the hotel during her lunch hour and pick up a pregnancy kit. By this time tomorrow morning, she would hopefully know the truth. *No doubt pregnancy will be ruled out, and I'll have to accept the fact that I have a touch of the flu.*

The following morning, Rhonda woke up early and slipped quietly out of bed, being careful not to wake Jeff. After putting on her robe and slippers, she left their room and went down the hall to the guest bathroom to take the pregnancy test. Not wanting Jeff to see the kit, when Rhonda got home from work yesterday, she'd put her pharmacy purchase in the guest vanity. She wasn't trying to be sneaky, but she didn't want him to know about her suspicions until the test either confirmed or denied them. There was no point in getting Jeff's hopes up only to disappoint him if the test turned out to be negative.

Five minutes later, Rhonda stepped out of the bathroom with a smile on her face. The test had shown a positive result. After all these years, she was going to become a mother. Rhonda couldn't wait for her husband to get out of bed so she could share this super good news with him.

She hurried to the kitchen to start breakfast. Jeff liked bacon and eggs, but the thought of smelling greasy bacon cooking or looking at runny egg whites made Rhonda's stomach lurch. So instead, she would opt for fruit and yogurt parfaits.

As Rhonda reached for the parfait glasses, she heard a crazy rooster crow and realized that Jeff had left his cell phone on the counter. Thinking it might be something important, she picked up the phone to answer, but it went to voice mail. Rhonda typed in Jeff's password to listen to the message.

"Hello, Jeff. This is Reba Sterling, returning your call. I'm available to see you today, so please call me at this number. I look forward to talking to you again."

Rhonda's gaze flitted around the room. *Who is this woman, and why is she calling my husband? I've never heard Jeff mention her name.*

Rhonda saved the message and would tell Jeff about it when he woke up. Surely, he would tell her who Reba Sterling was.

Jeff came into the kitchen a few minutes later, wearing a pair of black slacks and a pale blue dress shirt. "I hope you didn't fix a big breakfast, because I don't have time to eat much this morning. In fact, don't bother to fix anything at all. I'll just grab a cup of coffee for the road."

"Oh? Is there somewhere you need to go?"

His chin dipped slightly, and he looked away. "Yeah, I have an appointment and a few errands to run."

"What appointment is that?"

"It's nothing you need to worry about." Jeff kissed the back of Rhonda's neck. "Is there any coffee made?"

Nearly gagging at the prospect of smelling the strong brew, Rhonda shook her head.

"That's okay. I'll stop somewhere for coffee on the way." He grabbed his cell phone and started for the door. "See you later. I hope you have a good day." Jeff was gone before Rhonda could think of what to say. She'd wanted to ask who the woman was who'd left the message for him. Even more so, Rhonda wanted to tell Jeff about the pregnancy test she'd taken.

Maybe it's best if I don't tell him about the results of the test right now, she thought. *I think it would be better for me to make an appointment with my doctor in Canton and get a blood test. Then I'll know for sure whether I'm really pregnant. In the meantime, I'll keep all this to myself.*

Chapter 37

Canton

Rhonda had reached the supply room at the hotel and was about to open the door when her cell phone rang. Recognizing her doctor's number, she quickly answered. She'd gotten in to see Dr. Gates three days ago and had been anxiously waiting to hear the results of her blood test. Rhonda's heart pounded as she listened to the woman on the other end, and she had to lean against the wall for support when she was given the news that the blood test was positive. Rhonda was indeed pregnant. If everything went according to schedule, the baby would be born during the first week of August.

"Thank you for calling," Rhonda said, barely able to speak around the constriction in her throat. *I can't believe it! This is such a wonderful confirmation, and now I know why I've been feeling so odd lately.* She felt relieved, happy, excited all at once. *Boy, Jeff is going to be surprised when I tell him. Or will he be overwhelmed with losing his business recently and our having a lack of funds on hand?*

"I'll schedule an ultrasound appointment soon, as well as any other appointments I'll need during my pregnancy," she said, refocusing.

After Rhonda ended her call, she entered the supply room and took a seat on the wooden stool near the door. She was thrilled about the child growing in her womb but couldn't help feeling some concern. In addition to the fact that she was approaching her mid-thirties and hoping she wouldn't have any complications, she was worried about telling Jeff. He'd been acting so strange lately—like he was keeping something important from her. A week ago, when she'd finally been able to ask him about the woman who'd left a message on his cell phone, he'd been evasive, saying he couldn't tell her right now.

Can't tell me? Rhonda's skin prickled. *If Jeff is involved with another woman and wants to end our marriage, why doesn't he come right out and tell me the truth?*

Either way, Rhonda needed to know, and she planned to question him about it after she got home. In addition, she would need to pray about these matters beforehand. Only then would she feel ready to give Jeff the news that she was pregnant. An overwhelming need to pray swept over her.

She bowed her head. *"Dear Lord, I'm really stressed out right now. Things were going along fairly well until Jeff lost his restaurant, but he hasn't been himself since then. I'm afraid he doesn't love me anymore and may have found someone else."* Rhonda paused a few seconds to wipe away the tears rolling down her cheeks. *"Please give me the courage to talk to Jeff about this, as well as my pregnancy. And I pray that he will be receptive when I tell him that I'm a Christian now."*

Walnut Creek

Lois had been baking Christmas cookies all morning and would need to start lunch soon. Their sixteen-year-old neighbor, Gary, and his twin sister, Gayle, had invited Orley to ice skate with them on their parents' pond. Lois had tried to talk him out of it, saying at the age of fifty-five, he wasn't as young as he used to be and could fall and get hurt, but he'd insisted that he would be fine.

"That husband of mine always says he's fine," she murmured. "He could end up with two broken legs, and he'd still proclaim that he was just fine."

The wind-up timer went off, and Lois hurried to open the oven door. The cutout cookies were lightly brown, which meant they were done. She removed the tray and set it on a cooling rack. Once the cookies were cool enough, Lois would frost them with white icing. In addition to the cookies, she'd made some fudge and divinity. They were Orley's favorite candies, so Lois would have to hide them away until Christmas Day, when they would go to Orley's brother Ezra's house for dinner.

Lois had always loved Christmas. In addition to the delicious meal that was served and all the goodies available for snacking and dessert, she liked reading the Bible and focusing on Christ's birth. Although she didn't know for sure the exact date Jesus was born, it was nice to set aside December 25 to celebrate and reflect upon the most wonderful gift God had given when He'd sent His Son to earth.

Lois had often wondered how Jesus' mother, Mary, must have felt when she first held her precious baby. Although Lois had never had an opportunity to hold a child of her own, she'd held many other people's babies, and it was always a joy.

As Lois placed the next batch of cutouts onto the cookie sheet in readiness to be baked, her thoughts went to Rhonda and the conversation they'd had the day Orley and Jeff had enjoyed sledding on their hill. Rhonda's deep yearning for a baby had been obvious, from her pained expression and also the things she'd said. *I hope some of the things I said to her that day helped. I felt bad seeing her so troubled.*

The heavy stomping of boots on the back porch interrupted Lois's thoughts. A few minutes later, Orley stepped into the kitchen, red-cheeked, bright-eyed, and apparently with no injuries.

"How did it go?" she asked.

"It was great. The three of us had a *gut* time, and I never fell once."

"I'm glad to hear that."

He rubbed his hands together briskly and reached for one of the cookies that were done.

Lois shook her finger at him. "Only one, please. The rest I am saving for Christmas."

His bottom lip protruded like a pouty little boy. "But that's almost a week away. How do you expect me to stay away from all these goodies that long?"

She lifted her gaze to the ceiling. "You are incorrigible."

Orley's forehead wrinkled. "What's with the big word? Do I need to get the dictionary to figure out what you mean?"

Lois chuckled. "*Incorrigible* means 'hopeless,' and I read the word you think is big in the newspaper."

"You mean the paper that publishes your Dear Caroline column?"

She nodded.

"How's that going, anyway? You haven't said much about it lately."

Lois paused to put the next tray of cookies into the oven. "It's going okay. I just wish I knew what the people do when they read the answers

I give to their questions."

"Hopefully, they listen to your good advice and do what you've suggested."

"I hope so too." Lois grabbed one of the finished cookies and gave another one to Orley. "Let's eat these first, and then I'll fix us some lunch."

He kissed her cheek. "You're a good fraa. I'm sure glad I was smart enough to marry you."

Lois's face warmed at his compliment. "I'm glad I married you too."

Jeff whistled as he set the dining-room table. An organically grown chicken baked in the oven, along with two medium-sized russet potatoes. He'd also bought some fresh broccoli to steam, which he would start cooking as soon as Rhonda got home.

Jeff placed the water glasses on the table as well as napkins and silverware. *I can only imagine what Rhonda's expression will be when I tell her my news. I hope she isn't too upset with me for not telling her before what I've been up to these past few weeks. But it's time, and she deserves to know the truth about everything.*

When Rhonda pulled her car into the yard, she was relieved to see Jeff's SUV parked in the driveway. He'd been gone so much lately, she hadn't expected him to be home. Rhonda was exhausted from working all day and didn't relish the idea of having to cook anything. *Maybe I'll make us some toasted cheese sandwiches and heat a can of tomato soup to go with it.* While it might not be the healthiest meal, it would be quick and easy, and that's all Rhonda had the strength for this evening.

She drove her vehicle into the garage, picked up her purse and briefcase, and made her way into the house. As Rhonda approached the guest room that had once been a nursery, she gave a slow, disbelieving shake of her head. *It doesn't seem possible that by August of next year, this will be a baby's room once again. Her hands tingled as she placed them against her stomach. Oh, thank You, Lord. A thousand times, thank You for the wonderful miracle within me. I only hope that when I tell my husband, he will be as excited as I am.*

Rhonda made her way down the hallway and stopped at her office to put her briefcase and purse in the chair by her desk. When she stepped back into the hall, she couldn't miss the smell of food cooking. Approaching the dining room, Rhonda was surprised to see that the table had been set with their best dishes. Two lit candles had been placed on either side of a vase filled with white roses.

"What's going on?" Rhonda asked when she entered the kitchen where Jeff stood at the stove. "Why is the dining-room table set with our best dishes?"

"Because we have things to talk about, and I wanted to do it in a relaxed atmosphere with good food."

She sniffed the air. "So, you've cooked our meal?"

"Yep. Roasted chicken, baked potatoes, and broccoli."

Her stomach growled at the thought of eating the home-cooked meal, and that was a lot better than the nausea she'd felt earlier today. She moistened her lips with the tip of her tongue. "Thank you for cooking tonight. I'm exhausted and wouldn't have had the energy to fix anything nearly as good as what you've made." She took a few steps closer to him. "I. . .uh. . .have a few things I want to talk to you about too."

"That's good. I'm eager to hear what you have to say." Jeff gestured toward the dining room. "Why don't you take a seat? The broccoli should be done, so I'll bring in the food shortly."

"Okay."

Why is Jeff being so nice to me? Rhonda asked herself as she entered the dining room and took a seat at the table. *Is this his way of preparing me for bad news?* Rhonda glanced around the spacious room. *If Jeff leaves me, I'll have to raise the baby by myself, and I'll never be able to keep this big house.*

She gulped in some air, trying to calm her nerves. There'd been a time when Rhonda thought ending their marriage might be the best thing for both of them, but now, with a baby coming, she couldn't imagine raising their child without his or her father. Besides, she still loved Jeff with all her heart and had hoped by her actions she could win him to the Lord.

"Here we go." Jeff set a plate of succulent-looking chicken on the table. "Be right back."

He returned a few minutes later with two baked potatoes and a bowl of steaming broccoli. "Hang tight. I just have to get the sour cream, butter, and chives."

Rhonda waited for his return. The longer they put off talking, the more apprehensive she became. She wanted desperately to get this conversation over with so she would know where she stood with Jeff.

Jeff returned with the potato toppings and took a seat across from her.

Great. Now I'll have to look right at him while we're talking. Rhonda clasped her hands together in her lap, wanting so badly to pray out loud.

"I hope you don't mind, but I'd like to offer a prayer before we begin eating," Jeff said.

Her heart skipped a beat. "Did I hear that right? You want to pray before our meal?"

"Yeah. Is that okay with you?"

All Rhonda could manage was a quick nod. In the thirteen years of their marriage, she'd never heard her husband offer a prayer for anything.

Jeff bowed his head, and Rhonda did the same. "Heavenly Father, Rhonda and I have some serious things to talk about this evening and some decisions will need to be made. Please bless this time of us being together and help us to make wise decisions. Amen."

Rhonda lifted her head and looked at Jeff. Were those tears she saw in his eyes? Or perhaps the glow from the candlelight had caused his eyes to appear watery.

Jeff cleared his throat. "Would you like to go first, or shall I?"

"I guess I can. Unless you'd rather wait to discuss things until after we've eaten."

"No, we can eat and talk." Jeff forked a piece of chicken onto his plate and pushed the platter closer to her. "Sorry, I should have let you serve yourself first."

Rhonda helped herself to a piece and then moved the platter back to him. After they both had their plates full of food, she drank some water and spoke. "I have two very important things to tell you."

"Okay."

"First of all, you probably won't like this, but a few weeks ago, I accepted Christ as my personal Savior."

His brows shot up. "Seriously?"

"Yes."

"Why didn't you say something sooner?"

"Knowing how you felt about religious things, I was afraid of your reaction."

"I understand."

Rhonda wished she could read Jeff's uncertain expression, as he rubbed the back of his neck.

"I will comment on this," he said, "after you've told me the other thing you wanted to say."

Rhonda's muscles quivered as she drew in several quick breaths and released them slowly. "I'm pregnant."

"What?" His quick exhale through his nose came out sounding like a snort. "After all these years—that's impossible."

"Nothing is impossible with God."

"Are. . .are you sure about this?"

She nodded. "I took a home pregnancy test, and it was positive. Just to be certain that it was accurate, I followed up by getting a blood test at my doctor's office. I got a call while I was at the hotel today, and the doctor said it was positive." Rhonda touched her stomach and gave it a few pats. "The baby will be born in early August."

A wide grin spread across Jeff's face. "Wow, Rhonda, how exciting! It's a miracle."

"I agree."

"So now are you ready for my news?"

"Yes, please." Rhonda steeled herself for what he might say. She hoped the continued smile on his face meant it wasn't bad news.

"First off—I too am a Christian."

"You are?"

"Yeah. Let me tell you how it happened."

Rhonda ate some of her potato and listened with interest as Jeff told her about the dream he'd had of seeing his mother and how he'd prayed and accepted the Lord afterward.

"Why didn't you tell me about this right away?" she asked.

"For the same reason you didn't say anything to me about becoming a Christian. I was afraid telling you would affect our marriage in a negative way."

Rhonda's thoughts scrambled as she tried to digest all that Jeff had said. It hardly seemed possible that they'd both given their hearts to the Lord and neither of them had caught on.

"Now there's something else I want to say, and I hope you'll be in agreement with what I want to do, because if you are, we'll have to move fast, before it's too late." Jeff looked at Rhonda with a most serious expression.

"What is it?" Her mind raced, searching for answers. "What are you talking about, Jeff?"

"There's an inn for sale here in Walnut Creek, and I've had several meetings with the Realtor, Reba Sterling, in regard to it."

"Did you say Reba Sterling?"

"Yeah, that's right."

Rhonda pushed tightly against the back of her chair and released a sigh of relief. "I listened to a message that a woman named Reba had left on your cell phone one morning while you were still in bed. I didn't know who she was, but I thought. . ." Her voice trailed off.

"What did you think, honey?"

"Oh, nothing. It's not important now." She placed both elbows on the table and leaned closer to Jeff. "So, tell me about this inn and why you met with the Realtor about it."

"We could sell this place and move there. We'd have our own living quarters, and there are several spacious guest rooms. You could take care of the business end of things, and I'd cook the guests a nice breakfast every morning. Since I won't be rebuilding my restaurant, this would be the perfect setup for us."

Jeff had spoken so fast, Rhonda could hardly keep up with him. "Whoa! Wait a minute, please. What about my position at the hotel?"

"How much do you really like that job, Rhonda—not to mention the commute I've heard you complain about?"

"True, but I really like this house, and I thought you did too."

"I do, but I think you might like the living quarters at the inn just as well. And you should see the beautiful grounds that come with the place. It's like one giant park. Will you at least agree to go look at it with me and talk with Reba about the possibilities? I spoke with her again this afternoon, and she said she'd be available to show it to us tomorrow morning."

"I don't have to be at work until noon, so I suppose we could look at the inn around nine, if that's doable." Rhonda couldn't believe she was agreeing to look at the place. The whole idea was a bit overwhelming.

"Great! I'll call Reba and set it up as soon as we finish eating our supper." Jeff reached out a hand, like he was going to take a piece of chicken. Instead, he pushed his chair back and came around to her side of the table. Then, pulling Rhonda gently to her feet, he wrapped his arms around her in a warm embrace. "Even if we don't buy the inn, I want you to know that I love you very much, and I am super excited about becoming a dad. So now, the most important thing we can do is pray and ask God to reveal His will to us so that we'll know with a certainty whether we should make an offer on the inn."

"I agree. Now that we're both believers, we should seek God's will together in all things."

Jeff nodded and placed his hand against Rhonda's belly. "Have you thought of a name for our baby yet?"

She rolled her eyes. "Of course not, silly. We don't even know if it's a boy or a girl."

Rhonda definitely saw moisture in her husband's eyes, just as she felt tears in her own eyes. "Our parents are going to be thrilled when we tell them that we're expecting a baby."

"You're right. Should we wait till Christmas to make the announcement?"

Rhonda nodded. "I think it would be a great Christmas present. I'd also like to stop by the Troyers' and tell them the exciting news."

Jeff nodded. "Let's plan to do that on Christmas Eve. The last time I talked with Orley, he mentioned that he and Lois would be at his brother's house Christmas Day, so I'm sure they'll be home the night before Christmas. I'll give him a call and see if they'll be home Christmas Eve."

"That sounds like a plan." Rhonda gestured to the food on the table. "I'm sure everything is cold by now. Should we heat things up in the microwave?"

He grinned and gave her a kiss. "Yeah, I suppose we should."

As they picked up their plates and headed to the kitchen, Rhonda sent up a silent prayer. *Thank You, Lord, for answered prayer and making my wish for a baby come true.*

Chapter 38

"This is so relaxing." Rhonda breathed in and out as she leaned her head against the back of the sofa and closed her eyes. "Between the warmth of the cozy fire in our gas fireplace and the lull of Christmas music from the CD player, I could almost fall asleep."

She felt the warm touch of her husband's hand. "Better sit up then because I have a gift for you to open."

Rhonda's eyes snapped open, and she giggled. "I thought we'd decided not to open any Christmas gifts until tomorrow morning." She sat forward, looking at his gift and wondering what was inside.

"This one's an exception, because I'd like you to wear it tonight when we go over to the Troyers' for supper." Jeff handed Rhonda a small white box with a red bow stuck on the lid.

"Thank you." She gave the gift a little shake.

"This is the gift I'd planned to give you for our thirteenth anniversary. But I couldn't remember where I'd put it until yesterday, when I was in the garage going through some things to get rid of. I felt really foolish when I found the gift in my toolbox." Jeff chuckled. "I remember thinking it was a safe place to hide it since you probably wouldn't look there, but then I didn't look there either until yesterday."

Rhonda opened the lid and smiled as she removed the pretty daisy pin. "It's lovely, Jeff. Is it a vintage piece of jewelry?"

He nodded. "I bought it at the yard sale we went to this past summer, and don't worry, it wasn't expensive."

"Thank you again. It's beautiful." Rhonda reached over and gave his hand a gentle squeeze.

"Would you like to wear it tonight? Since Orley was with me when I bought the pin and knew that I had lost it, he'll be pleased to see that I finally found it."

"Of course, I want to wear it." She handed the piece of jewelry to Jeff. "Would you pin it on for me?"

"Sure thing." Jeff took hold of the antique pin and secured it close to the neckline on Rhonda's blue solid-colored blouse. "It looks great, honey. I'm glad you like it."

"Definitely." She held her hand against the piece of jewelry and fingered each petal on the daisy. "Would you like to open your gift now?"

"Sure thing. You know me—I'm like a kid at Christmas—always eager to open presents."

Rhonda got up and went over to the tree to retrieve his package from underneath, where their gifts for family members had also been placed. Smiling, she handed him the box. "I hope you like it."

Jeff tore off the paper and then opened the cardboard flaps. His eyes widened when he withdrew the old milk bottle inside. "Wow, thanks! This looks like one that I had put on display at the restaurant before the fire. Did you get it at Memory Keepers?"

She shook her head. "I checked there, but Orley said he didn't have any antique milk bottles at this time. Guess he sold the last of them a week ago. So, I searched the internet and bought the bottle from an antique dealer." Rhonda sat next to Jeff, and he leaned over and gave her a kiss.

"I really appreciate it, but I hope you didn't have to break the bank to get the bottle."

"No, the seller gave me a pretty good deal."

"I'm glad. We need to keep unnecessary spending to a minimum now that we are going to become parents."

Joyful tears sprang to her eyes. "I still can hardly believe the miracle God gave us. It will be exciting to share the news with your dad and my mom tomorrow. I also plan to call my sister, but not until after Mom's been told."

"Same here with my brothers, since they'll be at their in-laws Christmas Day. It'll be a different kind of holiday having it at Dad's and with just us and our parents."

"It'll be quieter than if our nieces and nephews were there, but I'm kind of looking forward to just the four of us enjoying Christmas Day together."

"Same here. Guess it'll be sort of a double date."

"Next year will be different, though. We'll have a son or daughter, so things might be more hectic but oh so fun." Rhonda rubbed both hands against her stomach. "I can hardly wait, and I'm going to do the best I can to be a good mother." She smiled at Jeff. "I'm sure you'll be a good father too."

Jeff slid a little closer to Rhonda. "I have something to confess. Something I should have told you a long time ago."

Fear gripped Rhonda's heart like a vise. She wasn't sure if she wanted to hear his confession.

"Before I say this, I want you to know that I don't feel this way any longer."

"What way? During the worst of our marital problems, did you feel that you no longer loved me?"

He shook his head vigorously. "No, it was never that. I've always loved you, Rhonda, even when I didn't like you too well."

She grimaced. "Thanks for that candid remark."

"You know what I mean, honey. I'm sure there were times when I was being a pain in the neck that you didn't care much for me either."

Rhonda slowly nodded. "Guilty as charged."

Jeff sat quietly for a few seconds before speaking again. "This is what I've never told you before. Early on in our marriage, when you wanted to adopt and I refused, it wasn't for any of the reasons I told you."

"Oh?" She tipped her head. "Why then, Jeff?"

"It was a selfish reason. I wanted you all to myself. I was afraid if we had a baby that you would be consumed with the child and wouldn't have time for me anymore. Quality time is my love language," he added. "And I've always wanted to spend that time with you." Jeff remained silent after admitting how he'd felt and stared at their Christmas tree with its pretty packages underneath.

Meanwhile, the only noise in the room was the soft Christmas music playing in the background.

Rhonda sat, too stunned to say anything. With the way her husband had immersed himself in TV and his hobby of collecting antiques, she never would have guessed that he desired to have more quality time with her. When she could find her voice, she looked at him and said, "Do you still feel that way, Jeff? Do you wish we weren't having this baby?"

"Of course not. I'm excited about becoming a dad. Since becoming a Christian, I've asked God to help me be a loving husband and to not put my selfish needs ahead of yours." Jeff's eyes appeared to be watery as he put his hands against her belly and gave it a few pats. "Please believe me, Rhonda, I want this baby very much."

"I'm so glad you do. I am sure we will make some mistakes while raising our child, just as our parents did, but with God's help, we'll do our best to raise him or her in a Christian home."

"I agree wholeheartedly." Jeff glanced at his watch. "I told Orley that we'd be there by six, so we'd better leave now or we're going to be late."

"You're right. I'll go to the kitchen and get the cucumber dip and veggies from the refrigerator. When the Troyers were here, Lois commented on how much she enjoyed the dip, so I made a big batch this morning. Some I will take to your dad's tomorrow, and the rest I'm taking tonight to enjoy with whatever Lois is planning for supper."

"I'm sure it'll be appreciated."

When Rhonda stood, Jeff did too. Then he pulled her close and gave her a kiss—this one even more meaningful than the last. "I love you, Mrs. Davis."

"I love you too."

"I heard a vehicle pull into our yard. Could you please go see if it's Rhonda and Jeff?" Lois asked as she opened the refrigerator door to take out some lunchmeat and cheese for open-faced sandwiches.

"Jah, I'm sure it must be them," Orley responded. "Jeff said they'd be here around this time. I hope you have some cookies or candy to share with them."

"I have both, but not until we've all eaten our sandwiches."

"Of course, I knew that." He gave her a smirk and quickly left the room.

Lois giggled as she shook her head. "That husband of mine is such a kidder, not to mention a tease."

She opened the packages from the refrigerator. The selections of meats and cheeses looked mouthwatering to put on the slices of bread. Once Lois had tossed the discarded packaging away, she began slicing the olives on the cutting board. She heard the front door open and the sounds of her husband and their guests exchanging greetings. She felt joy in her heart knowing that the Lord had moved in their new friends' marriage. *I'm thankful that God hears our prayers. And I'm glad He can use those who want to serve Him.*

Lois got out a loaf of french bread, as well as the condiments to put on the sandwiches. It wasn't long before Orley returned to the kitchen along with Rhonda and Jeff. She stopped working at the counter and wiped the juice from the olives onto her apron. It was good to see them and spend time together on this joyous holiday.

Rhonda had a rosy glow about her, and Lois wondered if it was the chilly evening air or something else. Perhaps the young woman felt the joy that went with it being Christmas Eve.

"Merry Christmas. We're so glad you could join us for supper this evening." Lois gave both Rhonda and Jeff a hug. Normally, she and Orley didn't befriend customers who came into the store unless they already knew them personally, but this couple was different. They'd formed an attachment to them, especially since Jeff had informed Orley the other day that both he and Rhonda had become Christians.

"Thank you for inviting us." Rhonda handed Lois two plastic containers. "I brought some cucumber dip along with cut-up veggies."

"How thoughtful." Lois smiled. "It'll go well with our open-faced sandwiches."

"Are those the kind of sandwiches that have no lids?" Jeff asked.

Orley thumped Jeff's back. "Yes, and Lois makes 'em look and taste so good."

"I'll be eager to try some," Jeff said.

"What can I do to help?" Rhonda asked.

"You can spread mayonnaise on each piece of bread, and then I'll put the slices of lunchmeat and cheese on." Lois gestured to Orley. "The table's all set in the dining room, so why don't you and Jeff relax in the living room until the sandwiches are ready?"

"All right, if you're sure you don't need me for anything."

Lois waved him away. "Rhonda and I can handle things just fine. I'll call you when we're ready to eat."

"Alrighty then." Orley clapped Jeff on the back. "We've had our orders, so to the living room we shall go."

A short time later, they were all seated at the table. Following their silent prayer, Lois passed the tray of sandwiches around as well as the cut-up vegetables, chips, and dip.

"These sandwiches sure look enticing," Jeff commented. "Makes it hard to know which one to pick."

"Don't choose one, take several." Orley reached for a sandwich with ham and cheese. Sliced olives decorated the top, along with a sliver of tomato. On top of that, squiggles of mayonnaise and mustard gave the sandwiches a final, festive touch.

"Lois showed me how to make the fancy sandwiches," Rhonda said. "So, Jeff, anytime you want me to make some, just say the word."

He grinned over at her. "Good to know."

They visited about several topics as they ate their meal, and when they were finished, Jeff looked over at Rhonda and said, "Should we tell them now?"

She nodded. "You can do the honors."

Orley leaned forward with an eager expression. "I'm all ears. What is it you want us to know?"

"We'd like to share two things with you and Lois." Jeff paused and drank some water. "The first and most important announcement we have to make is that Rhonda is expecting a baby. He or she will be born the first part of August."

Lois's fingers touched her parted lips, and Orley's brows shot up. "That's wonderful news," they said simultaneously.

"Yes, we consider it a miracle from God." Jeff looked at Rhonda with an endearing expression. "We are both so happy and can't wait to become parents."

"And well you should be," Orley said. "We are equally happy for you. Right, Lois?"

She smiled while nodding her head. "The good Lord has looked upon you with favor."

Rhonda felt certain that Lois was sincere in her statement, but she couldn't help wondering if the sweet Amish woman might be a bit envious. A couple as kind and loving as Orley and Lois would have certainly made wonderful parents. Rhonda wished the Troyers would have been able to have at least one child.

"Now what's your other piece of news?" Orley questioned. "I'm sure it can't compare to your first announcement."

"On a personal level, it doesn't," Rhonda spoke up, "but it does have to do with the future for us and our baby."

"Rhonda and I made an offer on that inn you told me about, Orley." Jeff's face broke into a wide smile. "Our offer was accepted, and the same day, I got word from my insurance company that they would be processing the claim I made when my restaurant burned down. So, we'll be using that money to purchase the inn."

Lois clapped her hands, and Orley followed suit. "That is truly wonderful news."

"Will you be selling the home you're living in now?" Lois asked.

"Yes, and we'll miss the place, but our living quarters at the inn, although a bit smaller, are equally nice," Rhonda replied.

"I'm going to do all the cooking for the guests who stay at our inn," Jeff said. "And Rhonda will take care of the business end of things." He reached for her hand and gave her fingers a tender squeeze. "We're excited to not only be a married couple but business partners too."

Orley began to ply Jeff with more questions, and Rhonda and Lois got up to clear the table. When they entered the kitchen and had placed the dishes in the sink, Lois gave Rhonda a hug. "I truly am happy for both of you, and I hope we can continue to keep in touch."

"Of course, we will. Jeff and I want our child to get to know you as we have. Also, we want you to know how much we appreciate all the advice you've given us. I believe your prayers and the things you've shared with us are a big part of the reason we both realized how much we needed the Lord in our lives. So, thank you for that."

"No thanks are needed," Lois said. "Orley and I take no credit for anything. We are just God's instruments and want to share His love and goodness with others."

Holding one hand against her heart, Rhonda said, "I no longer have to wish for things, because now when I have a problem too difficult for me, I'll remember that God is just a simple prayer away."

Epilogue

Eight Months Later

"Oh, Jeff, isn't our sweet Emily the most beautiful baby you've ever seen?"

"Absolutely!" He took a seat on the couch next to Rhonda and leaned over to kiss the top of their daughter's downy head. "She is adorable, and she has her mother's dark hair."

"I enjoy watching her." Rhonda fussed with Emily's soft blanket covered in printed pastel butterflies.

Jeff smiled. "She's melting my heart."

Rhonda had given birth to their precious little girl four days ago with no complications, and they'd come home from the hospital the following day. They had finished setting up the nursery in time for their little one's homecoming. Jeff and his dad had done the majority of the work, painting and setting up the furniture, while her mom helped hang the curtains and took care of anything else that was needed.

Things were falling into place for them better than Rhonda could have ever imagined. They'd sold their house a week after it went on the market and had been living in their private accommodations at the inn ever since. Their new business was doing well, with plenty of satisfied clientele. Rhonda's responsibilities weren't nearly as great as they had been at the hotel, and Jeff seemed to enjoy cooking breakfast for their guests. He also liked visiting with many of the people and talking about some of the antiques he had on display. Running the inn was a big change for them but in a positive way. It brought a lot less stress than their previous jobs had entailed.

"I still can't believe the news my dad and your mom gave us when they stopped by last evening to see the baby."

Jeff's comment pulled Rhonda out of her musings. "I know. Since they've been dating close to a year now, we should have expected that they would end up getting engaged, but their announcement still took me by surprise."

"You're okay with it though, right?"

She bobbed her head. "It strikes me kind of funny, however, to know that my father-in-law will soon become my stepfather."

Jeff laughed. "Yeah, and my mother-in-law will be my stepmom. It's sort of weird but good. I'm happy they found each other." He got up from the couch, left the room for a few minutes, and returned with two plaques in his hands. "I found these when I was going through more boxes we haven't opened yet and figured we should find a place to hang them, either here in our home or in the entryway where our guests come into the inn."

Rhonda smiled as she read the first plaque: God Bless Our Home. It had been a housewarming gift from her mother after they'd moved into their previous home. "I think we should hang that one here, where we live," she responded.

Jeff gave a nod. Then he held up the other one that read: Be Still, and Know That I Am God. "What about this?"

"Let's hang that plaque so that everyone who enters our inn can see it. As Christians, we should let others know what we believe."

"I agree." Jeff smiled. "And if they ask any questions about the scripture, it'll open the door so we can tell them what that verse truly means to us."

"For sure." Rhonda put the baby over her shoulder and gently patted the infant's back. "I'm glad the Troyers were able to drop by here earlier today to visit with us and greet our daughter. I will think of those two every time I see the Bible verse on that plaque."

"Same here."

Rhonda closed her eyes, listening to her daughter's slow, even breathing. *This sweet child is a wonderful blessing from God, and so are Lois and Orley. I wonder who, in need of mentoring, will walk through the doors of Memory Keepers next.* Rhonda smiled. *Whoever they are, I'm sure that dear Amish couple will be as much of a blessing to them as they have been to us.*

RHONDA'S CREAMY CUCUMBER DIP

1 (8-ounce) package cream cheese, softened

1 cup sour cream

2 tablespoons Miracle Whip salad dressing

½ teaspoon Worcestershire sauce

1 medium cucumber, chopped

¼ cup chopped green pepper

1 rounded tablespoon chopped onion

In mixing bowl, stir together cream cheese, sour cream, Miracle Whip, and Worcestershire sauce. Add cucumber, green pepper, and onion. Refrigerate two hours before serving with your favorite crackers or veggies.

LOIS'S BACON CHEESE MUFFINS

2 cups flour

1 cup shredded Cheddar cheese

8 bacon strips, fried and crumbled

2 tablespoons sugar

½ teaspoon garlic powder

3 teaspoons baking powder

¼ teaspoon salt

1 egg

1 cup milk

¼ cup vegetable oil

Preheat oven to 400 degrees. In large bowl, combine flour, cheese, bacon, sugar, garlic powder, baking powder, and salt. In another bowl, beat egg, milk, and oil. Stir liquid mixture into dry ingredients just until moistened. Fill greased muffin pans two-thirds full. Bake for 15 to 20 minutes or until toothpick inserted in center comes out clean. Cool for 5 minutes before removing from pan. Yield: 1 dozen

Discussion Questions

1. When Rhonda and Jeff first got married, they got along well; but as the years went on, conflict erupted, causing marriage problems. What do you think is the biggest reason some married couples don't get along? Is there anything a husband and wife can do to prevent marital problems?

2. When Rhonda and Jeff's marriage problems first began, she'd wanted him to go with her to see a counselor, but he'd refused. Is it possible for a couple having marriage problems to get help without professional counseling? What other things might they try to get their marriage back on track?

3. Jeff was a collector of antiques, which was a cause of dissension between him and Rhonda because his hobby was expensive. Have you ever known someone who collected high-priced things even when they couldn't afford them? Is there a way this problem can be dealt with?

4. Rhonda desperately wanted a baby, and when it appeared that she and Jeff would not become parents, she threw herself into her work to the point that she was gone more than she was at home. How did this play into the problems she and her husband experienced?

5. In the early part of their marriage, Jeff didn't care about having children because he wanted Rhonda all to himself. He'd never admitted this to her, though, making excuses about why he did not want to adopt. Should he have admitted the real reason, or was he right not to tell his wife the truth until years later?

6. Although Orley and Lois enjoyed selling vintage items and even kept some for themselves, their main focus was on mentoring people who came into the store and seemed to be burdened with a problem. What are some ways we can help others who are troubled and need a touch from God?

7. Lois had been writing a column for the local newspaper for a while before she admitted it to her husband. Why do you think she didn't want him to know? Is there ever a time when a husband or wife should keep a secret from his or her spouse?

8. The relationship Jeff had with his father had been strained since the death of Jeff's mother. Things got worse when Jeff's dad began dating. Even though Jeff was a grown man, he couldn't deal with the possibility of his father getting married again. Have you ever been in a similar situation—either as the adult child of a widowed parent who wanted to begin dating again or as the widowed parent with an adult child who was opposed to the idea? Were you able to work things out so that everyone involved was comfortable with the idea?

9. When Rhonda's mother, June, became a Christian, Rhonda felt uncomfortable around her because she wanted nothing to do with God. It didn't help that June, eager to have her daughter accept Christ, brought up the topic of religion whenever she talked to Rhonda. How can a Christian witness to a family member who is not a believer without making them feel pressured or uncomfortable about the topic?

10. Rhonda didn't approve of her mother using a dating site to choose a man she might be willing to see socially. She also didn't like the idea of her dating men she'd met at church. Why do you think Rhonda felt this way? Should she have been more understanding of her mother's desire to go out with a Christian man?

11. Jeff felt a bit puffed up when he and Rhonda bought a new house. He wanted to show his brothers that he'd made something of himself. What usually happens when a person takes on more than they can handle financially in order to impress others?

12. In this story, Rhonda experienced what she believed to be a miracle. Has God ever performed a miracle in your life, or have you witnessed a miracle in someone else's life? How did seeing a miracle strengthen your faith?

13. What was Jeff's reason for keeping his conversion to Christianity a secret from Rhonda? Is there a reason or a time when we should not share our Christian beliefs with others? Why?

14. Rhonda was also afraid to tell Jeff that she'd become a Christian. Were her reasons legitimate? Should she have told him right away and given him the chance to accept or reject what she had done?

15. Were there any scriptures in this story that you particularly liked? If so, how do they apply to your own situation?

CREEKTOWN DISCOVERIES

VOL TWO

The Sugarcreek SURPRISE

Dedication

To my Amish friend LeAnne, a dedicated schoolteacher.

For God hath not given us the spirit of fear;
but of power, and of love, and of a sound mind.
2 Timothy 1:7

Prologue

Walnut Creek, Ohio

Lois Troyer took a seat at the kitchen table to read the letters she had received this morning from her newspaper column, Dear Caroline. The antique store she and her husband, Orley, owned was closed for the day, and Orley had gone fishing with his friend Lester. The house was quiet, and this was the perfect time for her to get some of the letters answered and sent back to the newspaper for publication.

Lois took a sip of peppermint tea, then slit open the envelope on top of the pile. "Dear Caroline," she read out loud. "My granddaughter is twenty-five years old and has never had a serious boyfriend. Whenever a young man takes an interest in her, she pulls away. I am concerned about her, because she works all the time and has a limited social life. I have tried to coax her into doing more social things, but to no avail. Is there anything I can do to help her? —Worried Grandma."

Lois pursed her lips. "Now, how should I respond to this letter?"

Chapter 1

Sugarcreek, Ohio

Lisa Miller rubbed her chilly arms against September's nippy breeze as she stood on the front porch of the Amish schoolhouse, ready to greet her young students, ages six to ten. The view from where she stood looked beautiful this time of the year, encompassing the resting farmlands surrounding the one-room schoolhouse. In the distance, trees had started turning gold, and the intense morning light made them appear to have a gilded glow. While Lisa breathed in the crisp air, she glanced at the neatened lawn in the schoolyard that was still being mowed weekly. It wouldn't be too many more weeks before winter would be upon them, and then the task of mowing would be finished for the year.

When Yvonne Yoder, the teacher who taught the higher grades, rang the bell, all the children from grades one to eight filed into the building.

Lisa smiled as each one came past. "Good morning," she said cheerfully.

"*Guder mariye*, Teacher." Six-year-old Nancy Burkholder looked up at Lisa and grinned.

"*Mir hen unser middaagesse mitgnumme*," said her twin brother, Nathan, as he held up his lunch pail.

Lisa nodded and spoke to the siblings in English, because it was important for all Amish children to learn a second language in their early years of school. "Yes, I see that you carried your dinner, Nathan. Now both of you should put your lunch pails away, take off your wraps, and be seated at your desk."

The twins nodded and went obediently inside.

Keeping her smile in place, Lisa greeted the rest of the students, then stepped inside behind the last one and shut the door. What a privilege it was to be teaching at this school. Each of the pupils she taught filled her life with such joy. She couldn't imagine doing anything else. Since Lisa had no plans of getting married, she hoped she'd be able to teach right here at this school for a good many years. Although she'd had no formal training, Lisa, like all young Amish women chosen to teach at a one-room Amish schoolhouse, had been an excellent scholar back when she'd attended this school. How fortunate she felt to have been chosen by the school board to teach here seven years ago. The time had gone quickly, and she'd enjoyed every year.

After Lisa stepped into the main part of the schoolhouse, she was pleased to see that each of the children now sat at their desk with hands folded. Yvonne took her place at the front of the room and read a portion of scripture from the Bible. Following that, everyone stood to recite the Lord's Prayer. Afterward, Lisa led the students in singing a few songs. She enjoyed this part of the day so much—not just in the pleasure of singing herself but in listening to the children's blended voices as they sang with enthusiasm. Although school had only been in session a little over a month so far, the entire classroom seemed quite cooperative.

When the singing ended, Lisa worked with the fifteen younger ones on their reading, using the Dick and Jane series that was popular in the middle years of the 1900s. Lisa's scholars opened their reading material to the page where they'd left off from yesterday's lesson.

Meanwhile, Yvonne taught the twenty older children, ranging in ages from eleven to fifteen. Considering the size of the class, the children were well behaved and attentive. Not like last year when Lisa had dealt with two unruly eight-year-olds who talked out of turn and interrupted with questions that had nothing to do with the lesson. Those actions had been quite unnerving at times.

Things went well with the reading lesson until Lisa saw something furry out of the corner of her eye. Apparently the children must have seen it too, for several giggles, whispers, and snickers ensued.

The fluffy orange cat let out a loud meow. Then it darted close to where eight-year-old Gina Schlabach sat. The blond-haired girl bent down to pet the cat and squealed when it jumped up and onto her lap. But the skittish animal didn't stay there long and was soon on the floor again.

Lisa groaned. *A little unexpected excitement is not what we need this morning. Well, at least it's not a mouse. That would have really caused a stir—especially for me, since I have no love whatsoever for rodents.* Lisa had always been glad that her grandparents had several outdoor cats to keep the mice down.

She reached for the cat, but before her hands could touch the animal's furry coat, it zipped between her legs and made a dash toward the front entrance. The kids were all shouting, "Get it! Get it!" while Yvonne hurried to open the door. Instead of going out, as Lisa had hoped, the determined cat whipped around and raced to the front of the room.

David Stutzman, who'd recently turned fourteen, got up from his seat and took off after the cat. "I'll get him!" the boy hollered. The chase began, and soon two more of the older boys joined in.

There was no way Lisa or Yvonne could resume their lessons right now, so they stood on either side of the room and waited. A short time later, Johnathan Graber, the oldest boy in the class, got ahold of the cat, and everyone cheered. Lisa felt relief when the furry animal had been taken outside and everyone was back in their seats. *So much for a quiet start to the day.*

Things went smoothly the rest of the morning, and at eleven thirty, it was time for lunch. The students washed their hands before getting out their lunch pails. Then everyone took a seat at their desk. Following a silent prayer, the children and teachers began to eat.

From her teacher's desk, Lisa listened to the children visit with one another as they ate the food their mothers had packed for them. Most included sandwiches, but some children had a thermos filled with warm soup, as well as crackers and sometimes cheese. Most often an apple, orange, or cupcake was included for dessert.

Lisa's lunch today consisted of a swiss cheese and turkey sandwich, which her grandmother had insisted on making for her. The kindly woman had also included a thermos full of Lisa's favorite cinnamon herbal tea, as well as a lemon-flavored fry pie for dessert. Lisa appreciated her grandmother's thoughtfulness in choosing some of her favorite things. Grandma and Grandpa Schrock had been good to Lisa ever since she first came to live with them when she was seven years old, after her parents and paternal grandparents had been killed in a tragic accident.

Lisa couldn't remember much about the part of her childhood that had taken place before the accident eighteen years ago. She did remember the horrible sense of loss she'd felt, waking up in the hospital with Grandpa and Grandma Schrock at her side and being told that she was the only one who'd survived when the van she'd been riding in with her parents and other grandparents had been hit by another vehicle. Even their English driver had died in the crash. Lisa's maternal grandparents had told her often that it was a miracle she hadn't been killed, and they'd said they felt blessed being able to raise Lisa.

A lump formed in Lisa's throat, and she tried to push it down with a drink of water. Even all these years later, it still hurt to think about her loss. She had no siblings, and when her parents died, she'd become an orphan. How grateful Lisa was that Grandma and Grandpa Schrock had gone to Indiana and brought her to their home in Ohio. She'd been shy around them at first and tried hard not to become attached, for fear of losing them too. But it had been impossible to live in the same house and not form an attachment with such a sweet, caring couple. Even so, Grandma and Grandpa had been the only people Lisa had allowed herself to get close to. Even Lisa's friendship with Yvonne was superficial, although the other schoolteacher had often said she considered Lisa to be her good friend.

Sometimes Lisa found herself envying others who were involved in their friendships, as they spent time together doing fun things and talking about their plans and dreams for the future. The emptiness inside could be disheartening at moments, but Lisa would always manage to push those feelings of envy aside, trying to refocus on anything else to take her mind off the sadness she felt.

I should be thankful for what the Lord has provided for me. And why am I so unsure about my future? Why can't I be like other people my age? Lisa took a few sips of her soothing, warm cinnamon tea. *What will I do someday when my grandparents are gone and I'm all alone? Will I be able to manage on my own without them?*

Lisa's attention refocused when Yvonne announced that it was time for the scholars to clear off their desks and go outside for the remainder of their lunch break.

Lisa looked at her half-eaten sandwich. Where had the time gone? *Guess that's what I get for doing too much thinking when I should have been eating,* she told herself.

"I see you're not finished with your lunch yet," Yvonne said when she approached Lisa's desk. "Why don't you go ahead and finish eating while I take the children outside?"

Lisa nodded. "Yes, thank you so much. As soon as I finish I'll be outside to join you."

"Take your time." Yvonne gave Lisa's shoulder a pat and followed the students out the front door.

Lisa felt guilty seeing her co-teacher go out alone with the children, so she hurried to finish her lunch and then slipped into her sweater and rushed out the front door.

Several of the older children had started a game of baseball, while some of the younger ones used the playground equipment. Lisa stood nearby, watching and remembering her days of playing in this same schoolyard. She'd been a shy child back then and was still shy when around adults—especially those she didn't know very well.

Soon recess was over, and it was story time, which Lisa had enjoyed as a young girl and still did as the teacher. She was reading the second book of a five-book series about a set of boy-and-girl twins who lived in Ohio. The children enjoyed the stories about the high-spirited twins, who seemed to find some sort of adventure at every corner.

Lisa wished she had a sibling—someone with whom she could share her innermost feelings and deepest desires. But then, if she had a brother or sister, they too may have died as a result of the accident that had taken four people from Lisa's family. One thing Lisa had never understood was why her life had been spared and not the others who'd been riding in the van that fateful day. It didn't make sense that she was alive but her parents and grandparents weren't. Grandma Schrock had told Lisa on more than one occasion that God must have a special purpose for Lisa's life. What it was, she couldn't imagine, but like her grandpa had said not long ago during their family devotions, no one should question why God allows what He does. Lisa hadn't fully accepted that idea though. Over the years, she'd questioned on more than one occasion the reason why God would allow certain things to happen.

"Teacher, when are ya gonna start readin' to us?"

Caught off guard by Nathan Burkholder's question, Lisa realized that although she held the children's book in her hands, she still had not opened it or begun to read.

She quickly opened the book to the page she'd marked with a ribbon the last time she'd read to the students and cleared her throat. The children seemed spellbound as she read to them about another adventure the fictional twins experienced. Truthfully, Lisa found herself enjoying the story right along with her young pupils.

After story time ended, Lisa taught an English lesson to her students and helped them work on their spelling.

The school day ended at three thirty, and Lisa and Yvonne said goodbye to their students.

"Feel free to go home whenever you're ready," Lisa told Yvonne. "I will do a few things to prepare for tomorrow's lessons, and then I'll close and lock the schoolhouse before going home."

Yvonne looked a bit hesitant at first but finally nodded. "*Danki.* I'll see you tomorrow morning, Lisa."

Half an hour later, as Lisa was about to pick up her things and leave the schoolhouse, a knock sounded on the front door.

I wonder who that can be. I bet one of the scholars forgot to take their lunch box or something else home with them.

Lisa went to the door. When she opened it, she was surprised to see a young, beardless Amish man with a crop of thick brown hair on the porch. She didn't recognize him and wondered if he was new to the area or visiting someone here in Sugarcreek.

"Hello." He offered her a friendly smile and reached out his hand. "My name's Paul, and I'm here to see about the work that needs to be done on the schoolhouse."

Lisa's brows furrowed. She had no idea what this man was talking about. "I—I am not aware of any work that needs to be done here at this time. Some repairs were done at the schoolhouse this summer, while school was not in session, so—"

"Oh, no," he interrupted. "This has to do with the window that got broken during a baseball game last week."

Lisa's forehead wrinkled. She felt more confused than ever. "We have no broken windows here. I'm one of the teachers, and if a baseball had hit one of our windows I would most certainly have known about it."

He reached under his straw hat and scratched the side of his head. "To ease my curiosity and to make sure there's absolutely no broken window at this schoolhouse, would ya mind if I walk around the outside of the building and take a look? Maybe the window got broke when you weren't here."

She was on the verge of arguing further with him, but his determined expression made Lisa believe that the best approach was to let him look. But she needed to see for herself as well. "I'll go with you."

"Sure, no problem." He stepped off the porch, and Lisa followed. They walked around the entire building, and sure enough, just as Lisa had said, none of the windows were broken.

Paul rubbed his chin. "Hmm. . .that's sure strange. I wonder why my uncle would ask me to come here if there were no broken windows." His cheeks colored as he eyed Lisa with a look of confusion. "Sorry to have bothered you, Teacher. . . . Uh, what is your name?"

"I'm Lisa. I teach the younger grades here."

"Nice to meet you. I'm new to the area, so maybe I misunderstood what my uncle said and came to the wrong schoolhouse."

She gave a slow nod. "*Jah,* that must be what happened all right." Lisa's skin prickled as Paul tipped his head and stared at her in a peculiar sort of way. She wished he would leave the schoolyard so she could get her bike and be on her way home.

"Well," he said after a few more seconds passed, "guess I'd better head back to my uncle Abe's shop and find out where I went wrong." Paul moved toward his horse and buggy, secured at the hitching rail. "It was nice meeting you," he said once more, only this time he called it out over his shoulder.

She gave a quick nod. "I hope you find the schoolhouse you're looking for."

"Danki."

Lisa watched as he climbed into his buggy and guided his horse out of the schoolyard. It was nerve racking enough that she'd been forced to talk to a complete stranger, but the fact that he was such a nice-looking man made her feel even more rattled.

Chapter 2

When Lisa rode her bicycle into her grandparents' yard that afternoon, she spotted Grandma pulling weeds in the garden. A good-sized pile of debris sat off to one side near the patch of flowers planted in a nice, tidy row. Lisa pedaled a little farther toward her grandparents' large white home with a wraparound porch. *It looks like Grandma's already gotten a good amount of the task completed. I shouldn't be surprised. I hope she still needs my help after I took so long to get home.*

Lisa's grandmother was a hard worker and liked to spend time in her garden. Sometimes it seemed Grandma could be a little obsessed with it. Like last year when she'd talked about getting a certain type of strawberry plant. A week later, she'd hired a driver and hunted at some different places around town until finally finding the ones she wanted.

Lisa parked the bike by the barn and hurried over to the garden. "Sorry I'm late, Grandma. I'd hoped to be here earlier, but I got waylaid at the schoolhouse."

Grandma's blue eyes appeared as sincere as ever when she looked up at Lisa and slowly shook her head. "Not a problem. I'm almost finished here, so why don't you go inside and rest a bit? I'm sure you're tired from teaching all day, not to mention the ride home on your bike."

Before Lisa could form a response, her grandmother quickly added, "When we start supper you can tell me all about your day."

Lisa hesitated but finally nodded. "I'll go get changed and meet you in the kitchen."

"Take your time. I still have one more row to weed, and then I'll be in."

"Are you sure I can't help? I can hurry and get changed and be right back." Lisa paused to wipe her damp forehead.

Grandma shook her head a second time. "There's no need for that. You look hot and tired. I think a cold drink and a little time to rest would be good for you right now."

Lisa couldn't deny it. She'd pedaled hard coming home and had worked up a sweat.

"Danki," she said. "You always seem to know what I need—often before I realize it myself."

Grandma's brows furrowed as she cast a knowing look in Lisa's direction. "Now if I could just convince you to socialize more with young people your age. . ."

Here we go again. Grandma's always nudging me to get out there and spend more time with my peers. Lisa lowered her head and kicked at a small stone with the toe of her shoe. She knew exactly what her grandmother was leading up to. "I keep busy enough with my teaching job, and I don't need a boyfriend." *I honestly don't want to discuss this subject.*

She stepped onto the porch and hurried into the house before her well-meaning grandmother could say anything more. They'd had this conversation too many times, and Lisa didn't want to discuss it again. Although she felt sure that Grandma meant well, Lisa did not like to be pushed in a direction she didn't want to go—especially if it involved falling in love and getting married. Although a few young men, like Aaron Wengerd, had been interested in her, Lisa never allowed herself to get close to any of them. At her grandmother's insistence, she had attended a few young people's singings and other events but had always declined when any young man asked if he could take her home in his carriage. Since Lisa had no plans of getting married, it wouldn't make sense to lead on any would-be suitor.

She went to the kitchen and grabbed a bottle of water from the refrigerator. After touching her face with the cold bottle, Lisa twisted off the cap and took a long drink. *That sure hits the spot. Grandma was right when she said a cold drink is what I needed.* She closed the refrigerator door and headed out of the room to the hallway with the unfinished water in her hand.

Feeling more tired than she had realized, Lisa slowly climbed the stairs to her room. After shutting the door, she set her book bag on the floor by the desk.

Lisa liked the bedroom she had fixed up with a beach theme. It faced the sunny west side of the house and felt warm and comfy in the afternoon. But some days her room became too warm, like today. So she opened the window to allow air to flow in. It felt nice to soak up the quiet of her personal space as she stood looking out at the view of the countryside beyond her grandparents' property.

Lisa took another refreshing drink of water before moving away from the window and setting the bottle on her nightstand. *I can take my time since Grandma said she'd be awhile yet.*

She slipped off her shoes and padded across the room to the closet to find one of her work frocks. Lisa picked one out, laid it on the bed, and plopped down beside it. She thought back to Grandma's comment before coming inside from the garden. *Grandma likes to encourage me to go and do things with people my age. I wish she'd realize that I'm not interested in doing that. Surely by now she must know that I'm not outgoing.*

Lisa stared at the tote she'd brought in with her. In addition to a few books, it held papers she needed to grade this evening. *My students are my focus. That's the way things have been for the last seven years. Even though my life isn't complicated and full of social obligations, that's fine with me. But I have to admit that sometimes it can be a little boring to spend so much time by myself.*

Every now and then, Yvonne would talk to Lisa about her plans and she'd try to include Lisa in them. But Lisa would always have some excuse as to why she couldn't join her fellow teacher. For now at least, all she needed to think about was resting a few minutes, getting changed, and going down to the kitchen to begin supper preparations.

"So now tell me about your day," Grandma said as she cut up some beets she'd brought in from the garden earlier and precooked.

Lisa turned from her place at the stove, where she'd been tending a skillet of fried chicken. "Things went along well until a *wusslich katz* got into the schoolhouse and created quite a stir when it didn't want to be caught."

Grandma chuckled. "A frisky cat would be enough to cause some excitement, all right." She took out a kettle and put the beets inside, then added some water and placed the pot on the back burner of the propane stove. "Were you able to get it out of the building without too much trouble?"

"Jah. One of the boys finally caught the critter."

Grandma got a faraway look in her eyes before going to the refrigerator to take out some carrots and celery. "Even though I'm sure I've told you this story in the past, I can't help retelling it. One day back when I taught school, my *hund*, Nipper, followed me to the schoolhouse and slipped in through the open door before I could stop her. The *kinner* thought it was great to have a dog attend school, and they made it clear they didn't want me to take her out." Grandma washed the veggies and began cutting them up. "Of course, if I'd let Nipper stay, she would have been a distraction, so I took her outside and told her to go home."

"Did she?" Lisa asked.

"No. That determined animal curled up on the front porch and waited for me till school was out for the day. I even caught some of the students giving her pieces of their sandwiches during lunch."

I remember this story. Lisa snickered. She liked how animated Grandma's voice had become and could almost picture the look of surprise Grandma must have had on her face. No doubt she felt a bit irritated, but most likely Grandma had thought it was kind of funny. That was how it usually went around here whenever one of their farm animals did something humorous or out of character.

"Did anything else unusual happen today?" Grandma asked.

Lisa poked a fork into the chicken to check for tenderness before responding. "The only other thing that caught me off guard was when a young Amish man came to the schoolhouse as I was getting ready to leave. I didn't recognize him and assumed he must be new to the area."

"Did he give his name or say why he was there?"

"He said he was Paul but didn't state his last name. He also informed me that he'd come to the schoolhouse to see about fixing a broken window."

Grandma's brows lifted. "What happened? Did someone throw a ball through one of the building's windows?"

Lisa shook her head. "There are no broken windows, and I told him so. But then he insisted on walking around the schoolhouse to check, just in case." She frowned. "So I went with him."

"How did that go?"

"Just like I expected. There were no broken windows."

"What happened after that?"

"He looked kind of embarrassed and said he must be at the wrong schoolhouse."

"I assume he left then?"

"Jah, but before he got into his buggy, he gave me a really strange look." Lisa scrunched up her nose. "It made me feel *naerfich.*" She didn't mention that Paul had asked her name.

Grandma paused from her job. "Did he say anything specific that made you nervous, or was it just his *ausdruck*?"

"It was only his expression." Lisa lifted her shoulders in a brief shrug. "But maybe I was being too sensitive. Sometimes when people look at me a certain way, I imagine that they are thinking something about me, which may not be true."

Grandma pursed her lips. "Granddaughter, you worry too much about what others think."

Lisa gave no reply as she turned back to face the stove. She was fully aware of what her grandmother thought, so there was no point in talking about it.

Walnut Creek

"Are those some of the old milk bottles you got at the flea market the other day?" Lois peered over her husband's shoulder as he placed two of the more unusual ones on a shelf that had been built on one side of their antique store. She stepped back and grabbed out a tissue from her apron band to catch a sneeze.

"Bless you, *fraa*. Are you coming down with a *kalt*?"

"Danki for the blessing, and no, it's not a cold. My allergies act up sometimes when I've been dusting."

"That makes sense." Orley turned his head in her direction and pointed at the milk bottles. "Do you like them?"

She bobbed her head and stuffed her hankie back under the apron band. "From what I can tell, they look very nice."

"I think so too."

The bell on the front door jingled, interrupting their conversation. Lois turned to see who had come into the store and smiled as their friend Jeff Davis walked in. "Hello, Jeff."

"Hey, it's good to see you." Orley had a big grin on his face too as he stepped away from the milk bottle display and went to greet Jeff. "How have you, Rhonda, and that sweet baby girl of yours been?" He extended his hand.

"We're all doing well, and our precious Emily keeps us smiling every day. I have to admit, she has Rhonda and me in the palm of her little hand." Jeff gave Orley a hearty handshake then came over and encompassed Lois in a friendly hug. "How are you folks getting along these days?"

Orley bobbed his head. "Fine and dandy. We're still keeping busy buying and selling antiques."

Lois couldn't miss the twinkle in her husband's eyes. He loved the kind of work they were in and probably wouldn't know what to do if they ever had to give up their store. Lois enjoyed it too, but not nearly as much as Orley did. He often commented that just the smell of old things here in the shop gave him a sense of satisfaction. "Makes me feel in touch with the past," he'd said on more than one occasion.

"How are things going at the inn, Jeff?" Lois asked. "Is your new business doing well?"

He nodded. "It certainly is. We have reservations booked clear through the end of this year and into the next as well."

"That's good to hear." Orley gave Jeff's back a few pats. "We're glad things are working out well for you and Rhonda." He looked at Lois. "Isn't that right, fraa?"

"Absolutely."

"So now, what brings you into our store this afternoon?" Orley asked Jeff.

"I was in town picking up a few things for Rhonda and thought I'd drop by to see how you folks are doing."

"We're gettin' along well and keeping plenty busy." Orley gestured to the milk bottles he'd placed on the shelf. "I got those in recently, in case you're interested."

"I'm always interested in looking," Jeff said, "but I'd better not buy anything right now."

"No problem," Orley responded. "Feel free to come by anytime just to look around."

"Maybe one of these days you two can come over to our place again for another visit."

"That would be nice."

Lois stepped closer to her husband. "And perhaps you, your wife, and that little one of yours could come by one evening soon for supper. We would love to have you over, Jeff."

"I'll talk to Rhonda about doing that." He offered Lois a wide grin.

Orley ran a thumb and finger along his left suspender. "It would be real nice to take the time and do some catching up."

"I agree." Jeff paused and looked toward the door. "I'd like to look around to see what you've added here, but I'd better save it for another time. I have more errands to run right now."

"I'll give you a call to let you know what evening might work best for us and see what your schedule looks like."

"Thanks. I'd better get going." Jeff gave Lois another hug and shook Orley's hand again.

"Tell your wife we said hello, and give that precious baby girl a kiss from us," Lois said.

"I'll be sure and do that, and feel free to drop by the inn anytime to say hello when you're not working here and are in our area. I'm sure Rhonda would like to see you."

"We will." Lois watched as Jeff headed out the door; then she turned to face Orley. "What a nice surprise to see Jeff today. It's always good when someone we know and have mentored comes in to say hello."

Orley nodded.

"I'm glad we were given the opportunity to befriend them and see how the Lord worked things out for their marriage. We as humans can only do so much, but Jesus can work out any problem no matter how big it is."

"Jah." Orley pressed a palm against his chest. "I'm kind of disappointed, though, that no one since Jeff and Rhonda has come into the shop with a problem we can try to help them with."

"Husband, that's one of your special qualities that I've admired for a good many years. You have a wonderful gift for helping those in need, and it's made me grow in my walk with the Lord too." Lois touched his arm and gave it a few pats. "If it's meant to be, someone who is dealing with a problem and needs a touch from God will come into Memory Keepers." She pointed upward. "We just need to pray and be ready to share the good news."

"Agreed."

"And while we are waiting for that person, or maybe more than one person, I will continue to try to help people who write letters to the Dear Caroline column. I so enjoy writing answers for their problems."

Orley leaned close to Lois and brushed a kiss across her cheek—something he would never do if a customer had been in the store. "I appreciate the fact that on occasion you have read me some of those letters and allowed me to offer a few suggestions."

"That's right," Lois said. "Together we make a good team, always trying to stay true to what the Lord has taught us in His Word."

"And relying on Him to help us respond out of love and kindness to those people who are hurting because of life's problems," Orley added. "So we'll wait patiently and be ready for the day when God sends someone into the store who may need our help."

Chapter 3

Sugarcreek

"We'd better hurry, or we're going to be late for church," Grandma announced as she and Lisa entered the kitchen Sunday morning. "I can't believe all three of us overslept. Guess that's what we get for staying up late last night to finish that thousand-piece puzzle."

"I think we were all determined to see the puzzle finished." Lisa reached for the multivitamin container and removed the lid. "It was a nice evening though." She took out a chewable tablet and replaced the lid. "I especially enjoyed snacking on popcorn and some of those yummy, lemon-filled *kichlin* you made yesterday morning."

"Those cookies did turn out well." Grandma laughed. "If I hadn't moved the plate away from your *grossdaadi*, I believe he would have eaten every last one." She opened the refrigerator and took out a bottle of milk. "I think since we're running late that we should all have a bowl of cold cereal this morning. We can eat as soon as your grandpa comes in from getting the horse and buggy ready to go."

"I'll get out the cereal and set the table," Lisa offered.

"I'm going to use up the blueberries that are left in the refrigerator. Those should go well with our food this morning." Grandma smiled. "While you're doing that, I'll also make some *kaffi*. We'll need some good, strong brew to help us stay awake this morning. Sure wouldn't want to fall asleep in the middle of one of our ministers' sermons. Not only would we miss a good message, but it would be most embarrassing if anyone saw us dozing off."

Lisa nodded, but her thoughts turned to other things. Grandma had gotten out the berries, rinsed them, and then placed them into a bowl. As Lisa went about getting the dishes and cereal on the table, she reflected on how things had gone during the three-hour church service she and her grandparents had attended two weeks ago. It had been held in their neighbor's barn, which was nice because they could walk over and didn't have to travel by horse and buggy. This morning, however, the service would be at the home of Yvonne's parents, two miles away.

Lisa had never voiced her thoughts, but attending church was one of the few Amish gatherings in her community that she didn't dread attending. The men and women sat on opposite sides of the building and ate at separate tables during the noon meal when the service concluded. She didn't have to worry about someone like Aaron Wengerd striking up a conversation with her or, worse yet, asking if he could take her out someplace, like he'd done at the last young people's singing. Lisa hadn't wanted to attend the event, but after Grandma kept insisting that she go, Lisa had finally given in. Unfortunately, other than singing, she hadn't enjoyed much else—especially the socializing that had occurred before and then after everyone was done singing. Since Lisa had come to the event with Yvonne, she'd had to wait until her co-teacher had finished mingling before she could go home. She'd promised herself that evening that she would not attend any more young people's social gatherings, even if Grandma pestered her about going.

Today, during church at least, as long as Lisa didn't make the mistake of looking directly at anyone on the men's side of the room, she would not have to worry about any of the young men making eye contact with her. And of course Lisa would do her best to keep her eyes on the songbook while they were singing and on the ministers when they spoke.

The aroma of fresh-brewed coffee caused Lisa's contemplations to dissolve like a puff of smoke. A few seconds later, Grandpa entered the kitchen via the back door. "The horse and buggy are all set to go, so as soon as we've eaten we can leave for church." He looked at Grandma. "Is breakfast about ready?"

She pointed to the table. "It's all set out, and we kept things simple so we could eat quickly. I rinsed off the last of the blueberries so we can have them with our cereal."

"Good to hear." Grandpa went over to the sink and washed his hands.

After he'd dried them on a kitchen towel, they all took their seats at the table and bowed their heads.

Dear Lord, Lisa prayed silently, *thank You for our food and for my grandparents. Without them, I'd be all alone in the world.* She swallowed against the constriction that had formed in her throat. *Please keep Grandma and Grandpa healthy and safe from all harm.*

Paul sat on one end of a backless wooden bench next to his seventeen-year-old cousin, Kevin, making an effort to keep his focus on the sermon being preached. Although the topic on the importance of humility was a good one, he found it difficult not to keep glancing at the women's side of the room, where a pretty blond schoolteacher sat. Although Paul knew nothing about the young woman other than that she taught at the schoolhouse where he'd mistakenly shown up, for some strange reason he felt drawn to her. He glanced toward the preacher then back at Lisa again. *Since she's not sitting by anyone her age, I wonder if she's kind of shy. I hope I'll be given a chance to talk to Lisa again. I'd like to find out more about her.*

He picked up his comb that had slipped from his black trouser pocket and put it away. At the same time, a baby across the room began to cry, and the mother tried to console it, but she soon got up to go take care of the little one.

Paul's attention was pulled back to the sermon when the minister, whose name he did not know, practically shouted, "There is no place for haughtiness in a Christian's life. The Bible tells us in Philippians 2:3–4, 'Let nothing be done through strife or vainglory; but in lowliness of mind let each esteem other better than themselves. Look not every man on his own things, but every man also on the things of others.'"

Paul understood the importance of thinking more about others than oneself. He'd always tried to do that, even as a child when it came to sharing his toys. Unfortunately, some people, like his so-called used-to-be friend Ervin Yoder, didn't care whose feelings he trampled on. If Ervin had cared about the friendship they'd had since childhood, he wouldn't have stolen Paul's girlfriend. Paul had gone steady with Susan Lambright nearly two years, and he'd hoped to marry her. Then the night before he had planned to propose, he'd caught Susan in the arms of Ervin. Paul would never forget the feeling of betrayal that had smacked him in the gut like an angry wave when Ervin announced that he and Susan had been secretly seeing each other for the past three months. Paul had learned right then that things didn't always go the way a person had planned. He'd learn to be wary and keep up his guard.

Paul's lips pressed tightly together as he envisioned Susan holding Ervin's hand when she'd told Paul that although she had agreed to let him court her, she'd never really thought of him as anything more than a good friend.

Good friend? Are you kidding me? Good friends don't hold hands, kiss each other, and talk about their future together. Paul pulled his fingers into the palms of his hands. *I need to accept the bitter with the sweet and move on, no matter what disappointments life throws at me. That is the main reason I left Indiana and came here to Ohio. I just need to trust God and follow His direction. I'm sure He has a plan for my life that doesn't include getting married.*

During the noon meal that followed the church service, Paul's cousin Kevin introduced him to all the young men in attendance. Most of them, except for one fellow by the name of Aaron Wengerd, had welcomed him warmly. But when Aaron simply mumbled, "Hello," before leaving, Paul figured there must be something about him that Aaron didn't like, or maybe the fellow was on the shy side.

Once they'd set up tables inside the building for the noon meal, the women brought out the different choices of bread, cheese, peanut butter, pickles, and beverages. Paul couldn't wait to grab a cup of coffee to recharge his battery. The men and children began to take their seats at the tables, and it wasn't long before the ladies did the same. Soon one of the ministers said it was time to pray, and the room quieted for silent prayer.

Afterward, the people rose, and lines began to form at the different tables; some were getting their drinks first, while others went for the food that had been set out.

Paul felt somewhat awkward, not knowing anyone besides his uncle, aunt, and two cousins at this nice-sized gathering. The church district Paul had been part of back in Indiana wasn't as large as this one. Paul would have to get used to its size since he'd chosen to live here. But he hoped after being here today he'd get to meet a good share of people. Paul had picked out his food and found a place to sit with the men. He saw the pretty young schoolteacher again, sitting beside an older woman with mostly gray hair. Paul's attentions were quickly diverted, however, when a young man sitting across from him said, "Hi, my name's Steven." He gestured to the teenage boy who sat next to him. "And this is my brother, Samuel."

Paul shook both of their hands. "It's nice to meet you. My name's Paul Herschberger, and I moved to Ohio to work as a carpenter for my uncle Abe."

Steven nodded. "We heard Abe's nephew was coming here. When Abe told our *daed*, he seemed excited about it."

Paul smiled. It felt good to know his dad's brother wanted him to be here. "So what do you fellows do for a living?" he questioned.

Steven opened his mouth, but Samuel spoke first. "Our parents live near your uncle's place, and the two of us work with our daed as horse trainers."

"Sounds like an interesting occupation."

"That's for sure," Steven put in. "There's never a dull moment when you're workin' with horses."

The conversation went well as they covered several topics. Paul felt as if he was getting to know them a little and felt pleased when Steven invited him to come by and visit sometime.

The awkwardness Paul had felt earlier began to subside. He finished what was on his plate before excusing himself to get a refill of coffee. A while after he returned to his place with Steven and Samuel, Paul's uncle came and got him, saying he wanted to introduce Paul to some of the older men. When they approached a short, stocky man with mostly gray hair, Uncle Abe made the introductions. "This is my nephew Paul Herschberger. He recently moved here from Indiana."

The older man grinned as he gave Paul a hearty handshake. "I'm Jerold Schrock, but most everyone calls me Jerry."

"It's good to meet you, Jerry."

"Likewise."

"My nephew's a carpenter, and he'll be working for me, unless he finds something else he'd rather be doing." Uncle Abe put his hand on Paul's shoulder.

"I doubt that I'd want to work for anyone else or do anything other than carpentry work," Paul said with a shake of his head.

"Your uncle does good work, and he treats his customers well," Jerry interjected.

Paul nodded. "I feel fortunate that in addition to providing me with a job, my aunt and uncle have invited me to stay with them and their family."

Uncle Abe leaned closer to Paul and spoke quietly. "Just a reminder, nephew, that since this is Sunday, our day of rest, we shouldn't be talking about work."

Paul struggled with the urge to remind his uncle that he'd brought up the subject, but he held his tongue and gave an agreeable nod instead.

Jerry looked over at Paul. "What made you decide to leave Indiana and move to Ohio?"

Paul shifted his stance as he cleared his throat. "Well, I—uh—needed a change of pace. Thought it'd be nice to make a new start." He paused and looked over at his uncle. "So when Uncle Abe suggested that I move here, I jumped at the chance."

"Sometimes it's good to start over in a new place," Jerry said. "I did that after I met my fraa at a mutual friend's wedding." He glanced over at a group of older women sitting together across the yard. Paul assumed one of them must be Jerry's wife, but since the older man didn't point her out, Paul thought it would be impolite to ask.

"Where'd you live before moving to Sugarcreek?" Paul asked instead.

"I grew up in a town on the western side of Pennsylvania, not far from Pittsburgh." Jerry looked over at the older women again. "My wife, Marlene, lived in Sugarcreek, and I decided it would be a nice place to live too. So I found a job and moved here even before I asked her to marry me."

Uncle Abe chuckled. "You'd have been in for a big surprise if she'd said no."

Jerry gave a vigorous shake of his head. "I knew Marlene was the woman for me, so I wouldn't have taken no for an answer."

Paul couldn't help noticing the older man's determined expression. It made him wonder if he should have tried harder to woo Susan back instead of giving up and taking off for what he hoped would be greener pastures. Well, he was here now, and one way or another, Paul planned to make a new life for himself. Of course, he would probably remain a bachelor, because if there was one thing Paul knew, he could not allow himself to fall in love with any woman and set himself up for the possibility of getting hurt again.

While Lisa walked leisurely behind her grandparents as the three of them headed for their buggy, she heard Grandma ask Grandpa a question that made her ears perk up: "Who was that young man you were talking to after the meal?"

"His name is Paul, and he's new to the area. Fact is, the young man's Abe Herschberger's nephew."

"I see," Grandma responded as they picked up their pace a bit.

"Paul's a carpenter, and he'll be working for Abe."

"He's the same man I told you about that stopped at the schoolhouse a few days ago when I was getting ready to leave," Lisa spoke up. "I—I was surprised to see him in church."

Grandma stopped walking and turned to face Lisa. "Did you have a chance to talk to him today?"

"No, but he looked my way several times, and it made me feel naerfich."

"He probably recognized you from when he stopped by the schoolhouse." Grandpa, who'd also turned to face Lisa, gave her a quick wink. "Paul seems like a nice man, so there was nothin' for you to feel nervous about."

Lisa offered no response. There was no point in trying to explain how she felt. Grandma always pressured her to be more social, and Grandpa sometimes made comments about her shyness, often saying that Lisa needed to quit acting like a turtle and come out of her shell. His words stung like the prick from a rosebush. So whenever possible, Lisa tried to avoid the topic of her not wanting to socialize. No one, not even her grandparents, understood how Lisa felt deep inside, and since she didn't want to talk about her inner feelings, Lisa would make sure it stayed that way.

Chapter 4

Lisa stood in front of the classroom, looking at the bulletin board her co-teacher had planned for some of the older students to decorate. Yvonne had developed a nagging toothache yesterday and had no choice but to go to the dentist this morning, leaving Lisa to teach all eight grades on her own. Lisa figured Yvonne would be back sometime this afternoon, and it would be good to save the harder subjects until then and do something creative during the morning session. So while the upper classes did their reading assignment, Lisa had her younger students color some leaves that the older students had drawn previously. Once the coloring was done, the third- and fourth-grade children cut the leaves out. When those had been finished, the fifth-grade girls put the leaves on the bulletin board while Lisa read her lower-grade students a story about a boy who liked to rake the leaves in his backyard and then jump into the pile. She'd taken the book about the twins home with her over the weekend and had forgotten to bring it back this morning, so she hoped the children would enjoy this book instead.

"Of course," Lisa said as she neared the end of the story, "when the boy jumped, the leaves scattered, so he had to rake them all up again."

A few hands went up, and Lisa allowed the pupils to ask questions.

"What would you like to know, Johnny?" Lisa pointed to the dark-haired boy from the second grade.

"Have you ever jumped in a pile of leaves?"

Lisa smiled. "Yes, when I was a girl I did that many times."

"Do you still jump in the leaves?" the same boy questioned.

She shook her head. "But I do enjoy walking through leaves that have fallen from the trees this time of the year. I like to hear the crunch, crunch, crunch beneath my feet."

Another hand shot up. Lisa gestured to the first-grade girl. "What is your question, Linda?"

"Can we walk through the crunchy leaves after lunch during our outside recess time?"

"Yes, you certainly can, and I'd be happy to walk along with you."

"Can we rake the leaves and jump in the big pile?" This question came from eight-year-old Abner.

"If there's a rake in the toolshed out back, you can take turns raking the leaves," Lisa replied. "But you'll have to rake them in a pile again after you've taken turns jumping in."

All heads in the lower grades bobbed eagerly as the children looked at their teacher with happy smiles.

Just thinking about walking through the fallen leaves and watching the children rake and jump into the pile made Lisa feel like a kid again. She looked forward to the noon recess and walking briskly through the leaves with some of her scholars. The cool, refreshing autumn air would be an added bonus.

At lunchtime, since Yvonne had not shown up yet, Lisa told the children, according to their ages, to go wash up and get their lunches then bring them back to their desks.

While they ate, Lisa sat at her own desk, eating the first half of the ham and cheese sandwich her grandmother had prepared for her this morning.

Grandma's so good to me, she thought, savoring each bite. *Ever since I came to live with her and Grandpa, she's always been attentive to my needs. Grandpa's thoughtful too. I bet they treated my mother well when she lived with them. Maybe they're raising me the same way they did her.*

A lump formed in Lisa's throat, and when she took another bite of her sandwich, she could barely get it down. Although she remembered very little about the accident that had taken her parents' and paternal grandparents' lives, the pain of what had happened often crept to the surface of her thoughts. Lisa wouldn't know what to do if her mother's parents were taken from her too. She loved them both so dearly and knew without a doubt that they missed their only daughter. Despite the horrible pain they must have felt, Grandma and Grandpa Schrock had remained strong for Lisa and always tried to be cheerful and encouraging. She didn't understand where their strength came from.

Lisa reached for her bottle of water and was about to take a drink when little Anna Troyer, who sat in the front row, shrieked so loud Lisa nearly jumped out of her chair.

"What's wrong, Anna?" Lisa asked, approaching the child's desk.

"Look, Teacher—*iemense*!" Anna's chin quivered as she pointed at several ants crawling around on the surface of her desk.

"I'll take a look and see what I can do." Leaning over Anna's desk, Lisa peered into the child's lunch box and discovered that there were also ants in there. She tried not to let on, but the sight of them made her skin crawl.

Anna continued to howl, and Lisa quickly picked up the lunch box and took it outside after instructing one of the older boys to take care of the ants on Anna's desk and any that might have made their way to the floor.

After removing the sandwich, cookies, and apple from Anna's lunch box, Lisa placed them on the wide porch railing. At least it appeared that all of Anna's lunch, held in plastic bags, had been protected from the ants.

Being careful not to touch any, Lisa dumped the little insects out of the lunch box and onto the ground. Anna came outside with tears on her face and stood beside her. She pointed and watched the little black insects on the ground crawling away. "Look at them, Teacher. Did any get inside the wrappers and eat my food?"

Lisa gave Anna what she hoped was a soothing smile. "Nope, your lunch items seem sealed and you should be able to eat your food."

Lisa saw that a few of the more determined bugs remained and appeared to be stuck to the sides of the lunch box. Upon closer inspection, she saw that the pesky insects were trapped in a drizzle of amber-colored honey.

"Did your mama make you a peanut butter and honey sandwich this morning?" Lisa asked Anna, who remained close to her.

Sniffling, the little girl nodded.

When Lisa sat on the porch step and looked up from her angle at the wrapping of the peanut butter and honey sandwich again, she noticed a small hole in the bag housing the bread. Apparently the honey had leaked out through the hole, and the ants saw it as an invitation to take up residence in the lunch box and enjoy a free meal.

"I don't want my sandwich now," Anna said with a whimper. "It might be full of iemense." She wrinkled her freckled nose. "Sure wouldn't wanna eat some icky bugs."

"I don't think any of the ants got into the bag, but if you don't want to eat your bread, I'd be happy to give you half of my ham and cheese sandwich. Does that sound good to you?"

"Jah." Anna took a seat on the porch step beside Lisa and leaned her head against Lisa's shoulder. "I like you, Teacher. You're real nice."

"Thank you." Lisa smiled. "I like you too."

At a tender moment like this, Lisa felt a strong desire to become a mother. But it would mean getting married, and that was something she would never do, no matter how much she loved being with children. So Lisa's only recourse was to keep teaching school for as long as possible and enjoy spending time with other people's children.

A few moments later, the same older boy Lisa had asked for help inside the classroom came out to let her know that the ants had been taken care of.

"Thank you for helping out."

"No problem. Besides, I've gotten rid of many spiders at home for my *mamm*. I catch 'em and then put the creepy crawlers outside for her."

"I'm sure she appreciates you doing that." Lisa reached up and put the rest of Anna's food in her lunch box.

He nodded then turned and headed back inside of the schoolhouse.

Lisa took Anna by the hand. "Let's go back to our desks now and finish eating."

As soon as everyone had cleared away their lunch boxes and cleaned off their desks, they all went outside to play. The older boys, and a few of the girls, showed no interest in frolicking in the leaves, so they got a game of baseball going. While they hooted, hollered, and cheered each other on, Lisa watched the younger ones have fun playing in the piles of leaves two of the third-grade boys had raked up. Although Lisa was tempted to jump in too, she held herself in check and stuck to walking back and forth in the crackling leaves. Several of the young girls trotted along with her, laughing and singing a silly song one of the children had made up as they walked along.

When recess was about to conclude, Yvonne showed up. "Looks like everyone's having a good time," she said.

"For sure." Lisa noticed a bit of swelling in her friend's jaw. "How'd it go at the dentist's? Did he figure out what was wrong with your tooth?"

Yvonne grimaced. "It's infected and I was given antibiotics."

"Oh, sorry to hear."

"The worst part is that I'll need to have a root canal done next Wednesday. So do you think you'll be able to handle all of the classes, or should I see about getting you a helper?"

"I managed fine this morning, so I'm sure it won't be a problem for me to teach all eight grades that day."

"Thank you." Yvonne released a deep sigh. "As much as I dislike the idea of going back to see the dentist, I'll sure be glad when the appointment is over with and my throbbing gum feels better."

Lisa nodded. Although she'd never had an abscessed tooth or a root canal, she'd heard from others that it wasn't the most pleasant thing.

Lisa continued to watch the children play with the leaves. One of the boys picked up an armful and tossed them into the air. The brilliant colors floated back down. Some landed on a boy's head, and the rest fell to the ground. He laughed and tossed some more. His act encouraged one of the other children to do the same thing. Lisa enjoyed hearing them laughing at one another, each wearing a few leaves on some area of their clothing. But soon the merriment ended as they'd brushed themselves off and walked together, visiting before going in for more lessons.

Lisa glanced at her co-teacher, who was also watching the children. *I'll be praying that things will continue to get better for Yvonne. We all can use prayer in our lives, and it's good to pray for those in need.*

She gave Yvonne's arm a few pats. "Recess is about over now. I guess we'd better let the children know it's time to go inside."

Since Paul's uncle was out of town and had given him the day off, Paul had decided to take advantage of this beautiful fall day and check out a few yard sales in the area. Because he was new to Sugarcreek, Paul would keep local for now, giving him a chance to get used to his surroundings.

So far he'd been adjusting well to living at his uncle and aunt's house. They had made the transition from his parents' home to their place pretty easy. Paul had told them right away that he would help out with the animals and anything else he could do to repay their generosity. He also let it be known that he was thankful for the job Uncle Abe had offered him. The pay wasn't bad either. In fact, Paul would be earning more than what he'd previously made working for his dad.

As Paul guided his aunt's horse and buggy down the road, he looked at the different houses, farms, and lay of the land along the way. Soon he saw a wooden sign that read Horse Training. *That must be where those two brothers live who I met after church last Sunday. One of these days I'll have to pop in to visit them and get a close look at how they train horses for pulling buggies, pony carts, and wagons.* Paul looked over in that direction again and saw someone working with a horse. Then he looked back at the road as a couple of cars were coming, reminding him that he needed to stay focused.

Paul saw a Yard Sale sign at the end of the next driveway, so he guided Aunt Emma's horse and buggy onto the property. It was probably wishful thinking, but Paul thought it would be great if he could find a specific old milk bottle that he'd been searching for. Although the chances were slim, it was worth looking.

Paul secured his aunt's horse to a fence post and entered. It didn't take long before he spotted an Amish man, who looked to be in his late fifties, walking up and down between the row of tables. He'd never seen this man before and figured he must not be from his uncle's church district because he hadn't seen him at church last Sunday. When the bearded man glanced his way, Paul gave a nod and moved in the direction of the first table. There were some fancy glasses and cups but nothing vintage, so Paul moved on to the next table.

"Looking for anything specific?" the Amish man questioned as he approached Paul.

"Yeah, but I probably won't find it here." He brushed a hand across his damp forehead. "Uh. . .is this your place? Are you the one hosting this yard sale?"

"Nope, I'm just here looking." He moved closer to Paul. "Mind if I ask what it is that you are seeking?"

"An old milk bottle like my grandmother used to have. It was an unusual one and she really liked it, but thanks to my clumsiness, the bottle got broken. I'd like to replace it for her, but it's doubtful that I'll ever find another one like it."

The man pulled a business card from his pocket and handed it to Paul. "My wife and I own an antique store, Memory Keepers, in Walnut Creek. Why don't you drop by sometime when you're in the area? We often have quite a few old milk bottles for sale, and some are available right now."

Paul's interest was piqued. "I just might do that." Even though anything he might buy in an antique store would no doubt be higher priced than a yard sale item, Paul didn't mind. He'd be willing to pay more if he could surprise his grandmother with a milk bottle identical to—or even almost like—the one he'd broken.

Marlene Schrock pulled out a chair and took a seat at the kitchen table. The house seemed quiet, since she'd finished using the washer for the day and the clothes were outside drying on the line. Lisa was teaching at the school, and Marlene's husband, Jerry, was away today, seeing a friend who'd had foot surgery, and no doubt he'd be awhile visiting the man.

Marlene glanced at the three loaves of fresh bread sitting on the counter. Between doing laundry and baking bread, she had spent a good portion of the morning working. Now it was time to take a much-needed break with a cup of coffee and the chance to read this morning's newspaper.

I wouldn't mind a softer chair to sit on, though. She rose and pushed in the wooden seat. *I think I'll move out to the living room and relax in the recliner.* Marlene grabbed her things and got comfortable in the cozy living-room chair.

She did a quick read-through of some news articles and scanned a few ads, then turned to the page that featured the Dear Caroline column. Marlene was pleased to see her letter had been printed and Caroline had responded. After a few sips of coffee, she set the mug on the end table and eagerly read the message from Caroline out loud.

"Dear Worried Grandma: If your granddaughter isn't responding to any of the men who have shown an interest in her, she may not have met the right one. If you know a man you believe could be right for her, you might consider trying to get them together. Sometimes all it takes is a little nudge from a well-meaning matchmaker."

Marlene smiled and picked up her coffee mug for another drink. *Playing matchmaker is a good idea. Don't know why I didn't think of it myself. Now all I need to do is find the right man for Lisa.*

Chapter 5

"I'm going into town to run a few errands this morning. Would you like to go with me?" Lisa's grandfather asked her after they'd finished eating breakfast the first Saturday of October.

She looked across the table at her grandmother, but before Lisa could voice the question that had come to mind, Grandma smiled and said: "Now don't you worry about the *gschaar*. I am perfectly capable of washing and drying the dishes myself. You and your grossdaadi don't get much one-on-one time, and I think you should go along with him." She bobbed her head a couple of times for emphasis. "It'll be a nice outing for both of you." Grandma stood and picked up the juice container to put away in the refrigerator.

Lisa's mind raced as she thought of a few more excuses, but knowing her grandmother, nothing would be convincing enough. Even when debating about something with Grandpa, Grandma could be very persuasive and quite often won out. While Lisa had no desire to go to town today, where she would likely have to make conversation if she and Grandpa ran into someone they knew, Lisa figured she might as well give in.

Her grandmother moved to the sink and began to rinse out the bowl used to prepare their scrambled eggs.

With a slow nod, Lisa looked over at Grandpa and gave a forced smile. "I'll be ready to go with you as soon as I help Grandma clear the breakfast dishes. It's the least I can do to help out so she doesn't have to do everything herself."

"No problem," he said. "I'll get the horse and buggy ready and be waiting for you outside."

When Lisa entered the barn a short time later, the odor of sweet-smelling hay assaulted her senses. She paused by the door, listening to the crackle of dry straw being spread in a stall. Apparently Grandpa wasn't ready to go yet.

Lisa headed in the direction of the sound and found him raking fresh straw across the floor in her horse's stall. The gentle mare she had named Pet stood in the corner of the cubicle, munching on what was left of the oats Lisa had fed her earlier this morning.

Grandpa looked away from his chore and smiled at Lisa. "I'll get my horse out as soon as I'm done here. You can wait for me in the buggy if you want to."

She shook her head. "I'd rather do something more meaningful than stand around wasting time. How about if I take Benny out of his stall and get him hitched to the buggy?"

He grinned at her. "Danki, Lisa. I appreciate your willingness to help."

"I'm happy to do it." Lisa lingered as he resumed his work. *Maybe we could do something fun together while we're out today.* "Grandpa, while we are in town maybe we could look for another puzzle to work on."

He chuckled. "Sure, we can check out a couple of places I know of that usually have a variety of them." He stepped out of the stall to bring in more bedding.

"I've got a little spending money on me. I was also thinking maybe we could stop and get some ice cream."

"I might be up for a treat while we're out shopping. You know me. . . . I never turn down a dish of ice cream," he teased.

"Okay, I better get busy hooking Benny to the buggy." Lisa hurried to the next stall, where Grandpa's horse waited. Given all that her grandparents had done for her, offering to help whenever needed was the least she could do.

Walnut Creek

Paul secured his uncle's horse, Cinnamon, at the hitching post outside the antique store and stepped down from the open buggy he'd also borrowed from his uncle. When Paul left Indiana, his own horse and buggy had remained behind under the care of his folks. Paul's intent was to have them brought out here once he felt certain that he liked living in Ohio and wanted to stay. Paul hadn't even been here a month yet, so he couldn't be sure; but he liked the lay of the land, and working for his uncle had been going well. Unless something came up to change his mind, he would most likely be staying. Before winter set in, he hoped to have his own horse and buggy with him. When Paul felt ready, he would either buy or rent a place of his own. He wouldn't feel right about staying with his aunt and uncle indefinitely—especially since they still had two children living at home.

Paul let his thoughts drift away and focused on the antique store he was about to enter. He'd been eager to come here ever since he'd met the Amish man who owned the business. The building sat in a good location, and the fact that it was on a main street made it quite visible. Paul couldn't help but notice the vintage-looking WELCOME sign on the front door. When he opened the door, a bell near the top jangled.

Paul's senses awakened as he entered the building and breathed in the distinct odors of leather, wood, and something else, mixed with a musty aroma. His eyes scanned many kinds of old items. *I'm guessing this shop is pretty good sized. There must be plenty of interesting things in this store.*

Paul glanced around at the narrow aisle for walking between the table displays on both sides. A glimmer of sunlight shining through one of the windows made the silver and crystal vases look more appealing. Antique wooden cabinets had been filled with collectible plates, china cups, and thimbles in various sizes and colors. Rusty and paint-distressed signs advertising various businesses hung on one wall. Old clocks and musical instruments decorated another wall, and another area of the shop was full of old farm tools. Rustic-looking furniture had been scattered about the room, along with cedar chests, trunks, vintage kitchen items, and stacks of old books. There were so many things Paul hardly knew where to look first. But one thing was certain: he wouldn't leave here before seeing what their old milk bottles looked like. Paul hoped that among the bottles they had in the store there'd be the one he'd been searching for.

"Well, hello there." Orley Troyer stepped out from behind the front counter and shook Paul's hand. "You're the young man I met at a yard sale a few weeks ago, aren't you?"

Paul nodded. "I was the person looking for a particular old milk bottle, and you invited me to stop by your shop and see what kinds of bottles you have for sale."

"Yes indeed. The old milk bottles I have are right over there." Orley pointed to a shelf on one wall. "There are some nice ones too, so maybe one of 'em will catch your eye."

"Thanks. I'll go take a look." Paul headed in that direction. When he reached the shelf, he looked each of the bottles over carefully. He had to admit there were some nice ones for sale but nothing quite like the one his grandma used to own.

He turned to face Orley. "Sorry, but I don't see the one I've been looking for here. Are these the only milk bottles you have?"

The older man nodded. "I'm always on the lookout for more, however. So if you'd like to provide me with a phone number where you can be reached, I'd be happy to give you a call if I get more in."

"Thanks, I'd appreciate that." Paul reached into his jacket pocket for the notebook and pen he usually carried but found nothing except a hankie. "Would you have something I can write my phone number on?"

"Of course. There's a stack of writing pads on the counter up front."

Paul followed Orley, and when they reached the checkout counter, an Amish woman joined them.

"I'd like you to meet my wife, Lois." Orley gestured to the auburn-haired lady.

Paul shook the smiling woman's hand. "It's nice to meet you. I'm Paul Herschberger."

"This young man and I met at a yard sale a few weeks ago," Orley explained. "He came in to check out the antique milk bottles here in our store, but none of the ones we have resemble the bottle he's been looking for."

"That's too bad. We can let you know if we get any more in," she said in a kindly tone.

"I told him the same thing." Orley handed Paul one of the tablets and a pen.

After he wrote down his uncle's phone number, he handed the tablet back.

Orley tore off the piece of paper with the phone number and gave the remainder of the notebook to Paul. "You're welcome to keep this. Oh, here's a pen too. We recently had them made with our business name—Memory Keepers—to give out to our customers."

With a "thank you," Paul accepted the tablet, noting that in addition to the name of the store, it included a phone number and address. "I'd best get going. I have a few other stops I need to make today. Again, it was nice to meet you, Lois, and good to see you again, Orley."

Lois nodded, and Orley grinned. "It was nice seeing you as well," they said almost at the same time.

Although a bit disappointed about not finding the right milk bottle, Paul was glad he'd stopped by Memory Keepers. The Troyers were a friendly couple, and he'd enjoyed seeing their store. Something about being among so many vintage items gave Paul a sense of peace and satisfaction.

Sugarcreek

"Fall is sure a pleasant time of the year," Lisa's grandfather commented as they drew closer to town.

"Jah, I enjoy seeing all the pretty-colored leaves." As they approached an Amish farm, Lisa looked to her left, noticing that the grain silo had recently been filled. A herd of cows grazed inside a fenced pasture, and several chickens ran about in the yard. She fought the urge to wave at the homemade scarecrow wearing a black hat, standing tall in the field of corn that had already been harvested. No doubt that scraggly scarecrow would be torn down before the harsh winds of winter blew in.

In some ways Lisa dreaded the cold winter months. But there were good things to look forward to, such as sledding when the ground was covered with snow, ice-skating on frozen ponds, and caroling a few days before Christmas. Lisa also looked forward to the annual Christmas program put on by the schoolchildren for their families.

"You've grown awfully quiet all of a sudden." Grandpa nudged Lisa's arm.

"Just thinking is all," she responded.

"About anything in particular?"

"It was nothing important. I was having a few thoughts about the upcoming winter months. It'll be here before we know it."

"That's for sure. When I was a boy, time seemed to drag on, but the older I've gotten, the quicker the days seem to go flying by."

Lisa didn't think time moved much differently than when she was young, but then she hadn't thought that much about it either. Her schedule could be busy while teaching the children, but usually weekends were pretty laid back and she had time to do the things she wanted, like help out her grandparents, read one of her newest novels, or enjoy a stroll down the road, appreciating the sounds and views of nature.

As the horse clippity-clopped into town at a pretty good pace, Grandpa pulled back on the reins to slow the gelding.

When the hardware store came into view, Grandpa guided his horse to the closest hitching rail. Lisa climbed down and secured the animal. After Grandpa joined her, they went inside the store. "As soon as I find the paint, I'll see what they've got for puzzles here." He smiled.

"Okay, I think I'll take a look around and see what else they have in the store. There could be something new since the last time I was here." Lisa headed in the opposite direction.

While Grandpa looked for paint and a new puzzle plus a few other supplies, Lisa wandered up and down the aisles, although not searching for anything in particular. She wished the Christian bookstore in town were closer. If it were, she'd go there to browse around while Grandpa did his shopping here.

I should have asked him to drop me off there before coming here, Lisa thought. *Oh well, I'm in this store now, so I may as well make the best of it. Maybe Grandpa would like my opinion on the paint he's getting for the kitchen.*

Lisa pivoted to head back to the paint section, but she came face-to-face with Aaron Wengerd.

"Hello, Lisa. How are you doin' today?" He offered her a wide smile.

Her cheeks heated as she dropped her gaze to the floor. "I–I'm fine." Remembering her manners, she quickly added, "How are you?"

"Doin' okay." Aaron cleared his throat loudly. "Say, I have a question to ask."

Lisa forced herself to look at him. "What?"

"There's a young people's singing planned for tomorrow evening. I was wondering if you're planning to go."

Lisa shook her head. "Probably not."

"How come?"

She merely shrugged in response.

"I'd be happy to come by your grandparents' place and get you."

She glanced around, hoping her grandpa would show up and come to her rescue. "I. . .uh. . .well, if I do go to the singing, I'll probably walk, since the people hosting the event don't live far from Grandma and Grandpa's house. But danki for asking."

"It's not safe for you to be walking alone, especially after the singing when it's dark."

"I'll be fine. I've walked by myself many times."

"But I don't think—"

"There you are, Lisa," Grandpa said, carrying the bucket of paint in one hand as he started down the aisle toward her. In his other hand he toted a basket with a puzzle he'd found along with a few other items. "I've got what I need, and I'm ready to go." He gave Aaron a nod. "Sorry to interrupt your conversation with my granddaughter, but we have some other stops and need to get going."

Aaron opened his mouth as if he might say something, but in a hurry to get away from him, Lisa mumbled a quick goodbye. Then she took hold of her grandfather's arm and hurried away.

"I see you found a puzzle for us to start on." Lisa stayed in step with him.

"Jah, this one is a fall scene, and it caught my eye right away." He raised the basket toward her.

"That's a nice one. I'm sure it will be fun to put together."

Grandpa nodded and began speaking in Pennsylvania Dutch. "What'd Aaron want?" Grandpa asked as they approached the checkout counter, where someone else was being waited on with a shopping basket.

"He asked if he could pick me up for the singing tomorrow evening."

"What'd you tell him?"

"I said I probably wouldn't go, but if I did, I'd walk."

"Did he press the issue?"

"No, but only because you came along at just the right time."

Grandpa made a little grunting sound. "That fellow is persistent. I would be surprised if he doesn't show up at our house tomorrow evening and try to persuade you to go with him to the singing."

Lisa's jaw clenched. "He'd better not," she whispered. "Because if he does, I'll refuse to go."

Grandpa chuckled. "If anyone's going to take you, it'll be me. Aaron's right about one thing—you shouldn't be out walking alone."

Chapter 6

"Are you going to the young people's singing tonight?" Yvonne whispered to Lisa after they'd taken their seats on the women's side of the room before church started Sunday morning.

Lisa shrugged. "How about you?"

"Jah. I missed the last one, so I thought it'd be nice to attend this singing." Yvonne gave Lisa's shoulder a little bump. "I hope you can make it."

"Maybe so." Lisa glanced at the men's side of the room and noticed Aaron staring at her. She quickly dropped her gaze. *If it weren't for Aaron, it would be easier for me to attend that singing tonight. I really wish he'd stop pursuing me. Surely by now he must realize that I'm not interested in a relationship with him.*

Lisa had been around Aaron throughout most of their school years, and she'd never been a fan of his pushy demeanor. At least that's how she perceived him to be. Yvonne, on the other hand, had mentioned him in passing a while ago, saying she thought he was easy to get along with and quite good looking. Lisa wished Aaron would set his sights on her friend and forget about pursuing her, but she figured it wasn't her place to suggest it.

If by some chance Lisa were to ever fall in love, it would have to be with a very special person. She frowned. *I can't believe that by now Aaron hasn't figured out that I do not want to date him.* She twisted her fingers around the ties on her head covering. *Or anyone else for that matter.*

The room fell silent when the church district's three ministers entered the building and headed to the front of the congregation, where they took their seats. Lisa felt relief when the service started and she could focus on the first songs from their church hymnal, the Ausbund. She loved to sing, and she always felt encouraged by the words.

About halfway through the sermon, Lisa made the mistake of glancing across the room again. Her face heated when she saw that carpenter fellow, Paul, looking at her with a curious expression. At least she thought it was her he'd been focused on. Maybe it was just her imagination. But there was something about the fellow that sparked a little curiosity. She felt certain that he was nothing at all like Aaron. Although Lisa didn't know him that well, Paul seemed quieter and more polite than Aaron. But she figured it didn't really matter what Paul was like, since he was a stranger to their community and might not even be staying.

Pulling her attention back to the preacher's message, Lisa reflected on Proverbs 22:6, the scripture verse the minister had quoted: "Train up a child in the way he should go: and when he is old, he will not depart from it."

Although Preacher Sam spoke primarily to the parents, Lisa felt that the message was appropriate for her and Yvonne since they were teachers. Every child in their classroom needed guidance, not only to gain a sound education but also to shape their behavior. It was a privilege for Lisa to take part in training the young children who were in her care during school hours. It was a privilege to see her students gain knowledge and acquire good study habits. A solid education and good work ethic would be necessary when the children grew up, learned a trade, and got a job. Lisa thought about how most Amish young people, including herself, contributed to their family's income. This showed their sense of responsibility for those they lived with and cared for.

Being careful to keep her eyes on the minister who was still speaking, and not on any of the young men across the room, Lisa's focus returned to the elderly man's sermon.

When church ended and everyone filed out of the buggy maker's shop, Lisa heard her name being called. She glanced to her right and saw one of her students, Nancy Burkholder, heading her way.

"Teacher, guess what I got for my *gebottsdaag* yesterday?" the child asked with all the enthusiasm of a seven-year-old.

Lisa leaned down so that she was eye level with the young girl. "What did you get for your birthday?"

"I got a pony." Nancy glanced at her twin brother, Nathan, who stood near their ten-year-old brother, Simon. She looked at Lisa again and blinked a couple of times. "Uh. . .guess the little horse isn't really mine. It belongs to me and my *bruder*, since *Mamm* and Daed gave it to the both of us."

Her twin brother approached. "Our pony is real friendly, and she likes to be petted."

Lisa smiled. "A pony is a nice gift. I hope you and your sister will take good care of it."

Nathan grinned from ear to ear.

Nancy bobbed her head. "We're gonna brush and feed her whenever our daed says. And someday when we get older, Daed's gonna teach us how to train her to pull a cart with us in it."

"I can't wait to help train our pony." Her brother's voice grew louder.

"Me too." Nancy stepped closer to Lisa.

"Sounds like something for you to look forward to." Lisa gave the little girl's shoulder a gentle squeeze. "Did she have a name when you got her, or did you and Nathan get to choose a name?"

"Daed said we could choose." Nancy wrinkled her nose. "Nathan wanted to call her Slowpoke, on account of she don't move too fast. But I said we should name her Brownie, 'cause she's the color of chocolate."

Nathan looked at his sister. "I liked the name Slowpoke. You wanted to name our pony after food, and that's kinda *dumm*."

"That's okay. Other animals are named after food—like Abe Herschberger's horse named Cinnamon." Nancy pointed toward the fenced-in field where all the buggies and horses were held. "I thought Brownie was a cute name."

"Which name did you end up with for the pony?"

"Neither. When we couldn't decide, Mamm stepped in and said the pony should be called Daisy, which was the name of the pony she had when she was a *maedel*."

"Did your daed suggest a name for the pony?" Lisa questioned.

Nathan shook his head with a defeated expression. "Nope. Daed said the name Mamm wanted would stand."

Nancy's lower lip protruded. "So now we're stuck callin' the pony somethin' neither of us like. Mamm said if Nathan and I had agreed on a name, she wouldn't have stepped in."

"That was a good lesson to learn, jah?"

Nancy nodded. "I hope when I'm a *mudder* someday, I don't have *zwilling* babies." She wrinkled her nose for the second time.

"How come?" Lisa questioned.

"Cause if I had twins, then they'd hafta share their birthdays like me and Nathan do every year."

Nancy's twin didn't comment about the possibility of her having twins someday. He just shrugged his shoulders and headed back over to where his father sat, visiting with some of the other men.

Since I'm never getting married and having children, giving birth to twins is something I'll never have to worry about, Lisa told herself. She figured raising twin babies would be more difficult than having a single baby. And she could definitely see where twins having to share a birthday, and even their gift, would be hard.

Nancy bumped Lisa's hand and tipped her head to one side. "Think I hear my mamm callin' me, so I'd better go. See you at school tomorrow, Teacher."

Lisa gently squeezed the young girl's hand. "You can count on it."

Nancy grinned before turning away and skipping off to see what her mother wanted.

A moment later, Yvonne stepped up to Lisa and said, "Have you made up your mind yet about going to the singing tonight?"

Lisa drew in a breath of air and released it slowly. "Unless I change my mind between now and then, guess I will go, but only because I enjoy singing."

"I like it too," her friend said, "but I wouldn't mind if some nice-looking young man asked if he could take me home when the singing is over."

"Are you thinking of anyone in particular?"

Yvonne gave a slow shake of her head. "No, not really."

"Are you sure about that?"

A flush of pink swept across Yvonne's cheeks as she tucked her arms in close to her sides. "I'd rather not say."

"Okay." Lisa gestured to the barn, where the men had been busy turning the wooden benches they'd sat upon during church into tables. "Guess we'd better go inside and help the other women get the light meal set out on the tables."

"What time should I pick you up?" Grandpa asked when he dropped Lisa off that evening at the home where the singing was taking place.

"It should be over by nine," she replied.

"All right I'll come back to get you then. Unless," he added with a wink, "some handsome young fellow should ask if he can bring you home. If that happens, just call and leave me a message. I'll go out to the phone shack at a quarter to nine to see if you have called."

Lisa shook her head vigorously. "That won't happen, Grandpa, because I have no intention of riding home with anyone but you."

"All right then, have a good time." He reached across the buggy seat and gave her arm a tender squeeze.

Lisa stepped down from the buggy and hurried toward the oversized buggy shed where she saw Yvonne and some other young people heading. She had almost caught up to Yvonne when Aaron came alongside her.

"Hey, Lisa." He grinned at her, and in a most pleasant voice, he said, "I'm glad you could make it tonight."

She gave a brief nod and hurried on. By the time Lisa joined Yvonne, she had already gone into the building and was talking to David and Katie Hostetler, who had hosted the event.

Lisa held back, not wanting to interrupt. Feeling timid and out of her comfort zone, she stood off to one side near the beverage table. Hopefully Yvonne would see her once she had finished talking to the Hostetlers.

Fidgeting with the ties on her head covering, Lisa glanced around the spacious room where several tables and benches had been set out to accommodate those who had come for the pre-singing meal.

I hope no one says anything to me about why I haven't been to the last couple of singings, Lisa thought. *In fact, I'd be happy if nobody but Yvonne said anything to me this evening. I just want to eat, sing, and go back to the comfort and safety of my grandparents' home.*

"I'm glad you could make it," Yvonne said when she joined Lisa a few minutes later.

"Well, I do enjoy singing." Lisa spoke quietly.

"Jah, me too." Yvonne gestured to a group of young people across the room. "Looks like we have a good turnout tonight for our young people's gathering."

Before Lisa could comment, their hostess announced that it was time to eat. She then explained which side of the room the young men would sit on, which, of course, was across from where the women would sit to eat and also sing.

Once everyone had a paper plate and had made their way through the line, Lisa took a seat at the end of one table, next to Yvonne. After the young people were seated, all heads bowed for silent prayer, and then everyone began to eat. In addition to plenty of pizza, several fresh vegetables had been cut up to enjoy along with three flavored dips—ranch, onion, and garlic. The beverages consisted of individual bottles of water, several jugs of homemade root beer, and tall pitchers of lemonade.

Lisa had chosen two slices of Hawaiian pizza, which included ham and pineapple in addition to onions and cheddar cheese. This was one of Lisa's favorite kinds of pizza, and as she savored each bite, she came to the conclusion that coming here had been worth it, if only for the food.

Paul hadn't been to a singing in some time—ever since Susan broke up with him—and was enjoying this introduction to singings in Sugarcreek. He'd visited with a few of the young men before and during supper. Everyone seemed friendly and welcoming, for which he was glad. It helped to make the transition of moving from Indiana to Ohio a bit easier. He really wanted to fit in but knew it would take time before he established any close relationships in this Amish community.

Paul opened the songbook he'd been given and turned to the page that the song leader announced. The words to the song "Just a Little Talk with Jesus" blurred on the page as his thoughts led him in another direction. *I bet once the singing is over, a good many of the fellows here tonight will be offering to give certain young women a ride home in their buggy.* He shifted on his chair. *Well, I won't be one of them. Besides the fact that I'm new here and don't know any of the girls well enough to invite them to take a ride in my buggy, I would not want to lead any woman to believe that I might be interested in courting her. No, that would not be fair.*

After the singing ended and Lisa, with a strained voice from singing so many songs, had said goodbye to Yvonne, she went outside to wait for her grandfather. She hoped he would get here soon, because the wind had picked up and the chill in the air caused her to shiver.

"What are ya doin' out here in the cold?"

Lisa turned at the sound of Aaron's voice. "I'm waiting for my grossdaadi," she said. "He will be picking me up soon."

"There's no need for that. I'd be happy to give you a ride." He leaned closer to her ear—so close she could feel his warm breath.

Lisa shook her head determinedly. "I told you—Grandpa's coming for me."

"What time did he say he'd be here?"

"Nine o'clock."

"Well, it's only eight thirty, so there's no sense in your standin' out here for half an hour. If we go now, I can have you home before your grandpa even leaves his house."

"No thanks."

"Oh, come on, Lisa. Stop playing so hard to get. Most young women your age are married by now, and you're not even going steady with anyone."

Lisa's facial muscles tightened as she pressed her lips together in a grimace. "Please, Aaron, stop bothering me."

"Aw, don't be like that." He got right in her face. "You know you want to."

"Are you deaf? Didn't you hear what she said? Please stop badgering Lisa."

Aaron tuned to face Paul, the newcomer, who had stepped between them. "You're new here, aren't you?"

"Jah," Paul replied. "I came in September."

"So what gives you the right to stick your *naas* in where it's not wanted? Whatever I say to Lisa is none of your business."

Lisa held up a trembling hand and shook her head. "There's no need to argue about this." She turned to face Paul. "As I've already told Aaron, my grossdaadi is picking me up, and he should be here soon." She moved quickly away from the men and rushed out to one of the hitching posts to wait there. As much as Lisa had enjoyed the meal and time of singing after they'd eaten, she wished she hadn't let her grandparents or Yvonne talk her into coming here tonight. Unless something happened to change her mind, this would be the last singing she would ever attend.

Chapter 7

"How did the singing go last night?" Marlene asked, sitting next to Lisa during breakfast the following morning. "Since you went straight to bed when you got home, I didn't have the chance to ask." She couldn't help being curious about the event. Marlene hoped that Lisa had enjoyed her time there and that maybe one of the young men may have taken an interest in her.

Lisa's neck bent slightly forward, and her voice cracked when she spoke. "The food and singing were okay, but afterward. . ."

"What happened, Lisa? Did something occur that upset you?"

"Jah." Lisa took a sip of apple juice and set the glass down. "Aaron wanted to give me a ride home, and after I told him that Grandpa would be coming to get me, he kept insisting." She paused to take another drink. "Then that new fellow, Paul, came along and put Aaron in his place."

"Oh dear, that must have been quite embarrassing for you." Marlene spoke in a soothing tone as she gave her granddaughter's arm a gentle pat.

"Jah, it was. I appreciated the newcomer's concern for me, but it really was not his place to say anything to Aaron." Lisa straightened her shoulders. "I was doing fine by myself."

Hmm. . .it's interesting that the new fellow would do something like that—pretty bold, in fact. It may not be appreciated, but I'm just going to come right out and say what I'm thinking to Lisa. "I wonder if Paul might be interested in you."

Lisa gave a quick shake of her head, and her expression collapsed as if it were a pricked balloon. "Of course not, Grandma. We barely even know each other. I'm surprised you would even think such a thing."

Marlene glanced over at Jerry as he chewed on a piece of his buttered toast. She wasn't through with this topic and hoped he would say something to help.

Her husband winked at her and took a sip of coffee. "Paul seems like a nice person," he said from his place at the head of the table. "His uncle speaks highly of him."

Marlene couldn't help feeling pleased with her husband's effort at continuing this topic. She hoped they could bring about a spark in their granddaughter's way of thinking about Paul. If there was a possibility that he might be interested, maybe Lisa would give him a chance in the future.

"When did you last talk to Abe?" Marlene questioned.

He picked up the salt shaker and sprinkled some salt on his poached eggs. "When he came into my harness shop last Friday."

"Oh? What did he have to say?" Marlene's interest was piqued.

"He mentioned that Paul has a good work ethic, not to mention some mighty fine woodworking skills."

"Is Paul planning to remain in Sugarcreek permanently, or is he only here temporarily?"

"I'm not sure, but from the sound of things, I believe that Abe thinks his nephew plans to stay. But you can never tell with a young, single man. Paul might have an *aldi* back home, or he may find a girlfriend while he's living here."

"What do you mean by that?"

He tugged on his beard. "If whatever he's looking for here in Ohio happens, then I'm sure he'll want to stay. But if things don't go right, and Paul isn't as happy as he'd hoped to be, then he'll probably return to Indiana at some point."

"I suppose that makes sense." Marlene looked over at Lisa to see her reaction, but to her disappointment, her granddaughter said nothing, apparently absorbed in finishing her meal. As her granddaughter continued to eat and then poured herself more apple juice, Marlene wondered what exactly Lisa had on her mind.

Marlene rose from her chair. "I'd like another cup of coffee. Husband, would you like another one too?"

"Sure, that sounds good, since I'm not quite finished with my eggs."

She refilled their cups and brought them back, taking her seat again. A little more small talk transpired between her and Jerry, while their granddaughter continued to eat in silence.

Finally, when her scrambled eggs and toast had been eaten, Lisa bowed her head for a final silent prayer then cleared her dishes and put them in the sink. "It's later than I thought, and I need to get to the schoolhouse, Grandma. Would you mind doing the dishes without my help this morning?"

"Not at all," Marlene responded. "You go on ahead, and I hope you have a good day."

"Danki. I hope Grandpa's and your day goes well too."

As soon as Lisa went out the door, Marlene looked over at her husband and said, "What would you think about hiring Abe's nephew to build and install some new kitchen cabinets for us?"

His bushy brows furrowed. "You want new kitchen cabinets all of a sudden?"

"It's not sudden, Jerry." She gestured to the old cabinets across the room. "Those have been here since we first built this home, and they are getting a bit dilapidated, don't you think?"

He gave a quick shrug. "I suppose so, but. . ."

"It would sure be nice to do some updating in the kitchen. After all, I spend a good deal of my time in here, you know."

"Jah, that is true." He sent her a heart-melting smile. "I'll get ahold of Abe and see if one of his crew can come by to take a look at the old cabinets and then you can discuss what kind you'd like to have built that will replace the old ones."

Marlene shook her head. "I don't want just anyone who works for Abe. As I stated previously, I'd like it to be Paul."

The wrinkles around Jerry's blue eyes deepened as he pointed at her. "You wouldn't be trying to get our granddaughter and Abe's nephew together, now would you?"

A warm flush ran up the back of Marlene's neck and spread quickly to her cheeks. After all their years of marriage, Jerry knew her quite well. "It wouldn't hurt to try." Marlene fiddled with her napkin. "I mean. . .how's Lisa going to get to know this newcomer if she doesn't spend some time with him?"

Jerry lifted his gaze toward the ceiling and gave an undignified grunt. "Do I have to remind you that Lisa teaches school all day? You'll be the one who'll get to know him, fraa, not her."

Marlene tapped her knuckles lightly against the tabletop. "Guess I hadn't thought it all the way through."

"So it doesn't matter who comes to build and put in the new cabinets?"

Marlene pressed her lips together as she mulled things over. "No, I'd still like Paul to be the one. If I get acquainted with him, then I'll have a better idea if he could be right for Lisa."

Jerry shook his head slowly and muttered, "Okay, dear wife, I'll see what can be done."

She smiled. Already a plot had formed in her mind. *After all, Dear Caroline did suggest in her reply to my letter that I play matchmaker.*

As Lisa waited on the porch of the schoolhouse for the students to arrive, she thought about the curious expression she'd seen on her grandmother's face this morning when the topic of Paul came up. When Grandma stated that she wondered if Paul might be interested in Lisa, it was all she could do to keep from fleeing the room. *Why would my grandma even suggest such a thing? Is she that desperate to get me married off?*

Another thought hit Lisa that had never occurred to her before—perhaps one or both of her grandparents felt that it was time for her to move out. Maybe they believed they'd taken care of her long enough. Lisa was, after all, twenty-five years old.

Should I bring the subject up—see if they would like me to find someplace else to live? she asked herself. *Or would it be better to wait and see if either of them brings up the topic of Paul being interested in me again?*

Lisa's thoughts scattered when her first two students, Nathan and Nancy, arrived. A few feet behind them plodded a female, midsized dog with floppy ears and a thick coat of curly brown hair that looked like it needed a good brushing. The animal was obviously not a purebred, nor had it been well cared for. Lisa figured it might be a cocker/poodle mixture. One thing was certain: the floppy-eared critter did not belong here at school.

"Is this your dog?" Lisa asked the twins. "Because if it is, you'll need to tell her to go home."

They both shook their heads. "The hund was walkin' along the road and started followin' us when we went by," Nancy replied. "Our brother Simon told it to go home, but it kept walkin' behind us."

"Finally Simon picked up a stick, and the dog took off," Nathan put in. "But then after our bruder held back to wait for some of his friends, that hund showed up again and followed us the rest of the way here."

"Do you know who the dog belongs to?"

"Nope. I bet it's a stray." Nathan approached the dog and reached out as if to pet it.

"Be careful," Lisa cautioned. "The dog may not be friendly, and she could even bite."

"I don't think so, Teacher." Nathan shook his head. "See the way the mutt's tail is waggin'? My daed always says that when a hund wags its tail, it's a sign of friendliness." He grinned up at Lisa. "Ya know how come a dog has a lot of friends?"

"I have no idea."

"Cause it wags his tail 'stead of his tongue." Nathan slapped his knee and laughed, and his sister joined in. "Ain't that *schpassich*, Teacher?"

Lisa chuckled. "Yes, it's funny."

Nancy patted the dog's head and was rewarded with a slurp on her hand. "See, Teacher, the hund don't bite."

"You're right, but let's not encourage her. She might never go home."

"Can we bring her into the schoolhouse with us?" Nathan asked, stepping onto the porch.

Lisa shook her head, remembering the day when a cat got in. She had no doubt that allowing the dog inside would cause a stir among the children, which in turn would mean that lessons would not get done.

She clapped her hands and pointed toward the road. "Go home, doggy! Go back to where you belong!"

The dog released a whimper but didn't budge.

Lisa frowned. "That's just great. Now what am I supposed to do?"

"If the hund's a stray, she ain't got no home to go to." Nathan joined his sister in petting the dog.

"Oh, that's really not a good idea. I wish you—"

Lisa's comment was cut short when Yvonne showed up. "Sorry I'm late. My horse must have thrown a shoe sometime yesterday, so I had to walk this morning."

"It's okay," Lisa said. "Nathan and Nancy are the only students who have shown up so far. Them, and this mangy hund." She pointed to the dog.

"Is it the twins' dog?" Yvonne asked.

"No. Apparently it's a stray, or maybe she belongs to someone locally and wandered off their property, although I've never seen the mutt around before."

Yvonne leaned down and appeared to be scrutinizing the dog. "I don't remember seeing her either."

"Neither have we," the twins said simultaneously.

Lisa pointed at the dog. "I told her to leave, but as you can see, she doesn't listen too well."

"Maybe the dog's lost and can't find her way home." Yvonne gave the animal a few pats. "Is that how it is, girl? Are you confused about where you live?"

The dog tipped her head back and gave a *Woof! Woof!*

"We wanna bring her into the schoolhouse, but Teacher Lisa said no." Nancy's lower lip protruded.

"Your teacher is right," Yvonne said. "It's not a good idea to bring the hund inside, but if the dog's still out here when you go out for recess, you can pet her then."

Lisa resisted the urge to roll her eyes. If the children kept petting and making over the dog, she'd probably never leave.

"Before you head to town to pick up those supplies I asked you to get earlier, can I speak to you for a few minutes?"

"Sure, Uncle Abe." Paul turned at the sound of his uncle's voice and walked back to the woodworking shop. "Is there something else you need me to get?"

"No, just what's on the list I gave you. What I wanted to tell you about is a potential job." Uncle Abe stood in the entrance of his shop. "When I checked for phone messages a few minutes ago, there was one from the harness maker, Jerry Schrock."

There was a pause, and Paul waited silently for his uncle to continue.

"Jerry mentioned that his fraa would like some new cabinets in her kitchen, and he asked if you would come by and talk to her about the project."

"Why me?" Paul asked. "Since you're the boss, and you've known the harness maker awhile, I would think he'd want you to be the one to do the job."

Uncle Abe reached under his straw hat and rubbed a spot on his head just above his right ear. "I don't know the reason, but he made it clear that his wife specifically asked for you."

"Hmm. . ." Paul tipped his head to one side and blinked a couple of times. "But I've never even met Jerry Schrock's fraa."

Uncle Abe shrugged, holding both hands palms up. "I'm not the best at understanding women—not even my own wife. All I know is, it's a potential job, so I'll give you the Schrocks' address and you can drop by there on your way to or from town—whichever time you choose. Okay?"

Paul nodded. What else could he do? He didn't have much choice, since his uncle was also his boss.

"Go away! You can't come with me," Lisa shouted while glancing over her shoulder on the bicycle ride home that afternoon. The determined dog had hung around the schoolyard all day, barking excitedly during the pupils' recess and lapping up all the attention the children gave. Then for some unknown reason, the mutt had decided to follow Lisa home.

Why me? she wondered, pedaling harder to pick up speed. *I could understand if the hund had chosen to follow one of the children as they headed to their house after school. An animal like that needs kinner to play with, not an old maid schoolteacher who has better things to do than care for a pet.*

Yip! Yip! Yip! The strong-willed animal caught up with Lisa and ran alongside her bike.

"Go back! You can't come home with me," Lisa hollered, but the now-panting dog wouldn't let up.

Lisa kept going until her grandparents' house came into view. When she approached the driveway, she put on the brakes and looked down at the dog. "Please go away. I can't take care of you."

The mutt looked up at Lisa and cocked her furry head. Either she didn't understand or wasn't about to back down.

Heaving a hefty sigh, Lisa rode her bike up the driveway and into the yard, where she noticed a horse and market buggy parked at the hitching rail not far from the house. Grandma obviously had company, and Lisa didn't want to interrupt their visit, but she needed to get inside and away from the determined dog.

Lisa parked her bike near the barn and sprinted toward the house. But before she could put one foot on the porch, the pooch leaped up, knocking Lisa off balance and causing her to fall.

Groaning, she tried to get up, but it was an impossible task with the dog lying on top of her, slurping Lisa's face with her icky wet tongue.

"Need some help?" a deep voice called.

"Jah, I sure do." Although the dog was relentless with her slurpy kisses, Lisa managed to roll onto her side. Through half-closed eyelids she could see the man who had asked her the question. *Paul Herschberger? What's he doing here?* she asked herself. *Oh, I'm so embarrassed.*

Chapter 8

"From the way that hund of yours is gifting you with all those kisses, I'd have to say that the pooch must really love you." Paul laughed.

Lisa frowned. "It's not funny, and she's not my dog."

"It's a little funny." He held out his hand toward her. "Looks like you might need some help getting up."

"I'm fine." Lisa pushed the dog aside and scrambled to her feet. "I just hope that silly critter doesn't have any fleas."

Another booming laugh escaped Paul's lips. "Now that was really funny. I mean what dog running around outside doesn't have a problem with fleas? If you're worried about it, maybe you should get her a flea collar."

Choosing not to comment, Lisa looked away from Paul and brushed at the dirt, blades of grass, and loose dog hair that had stuck to her dress. "The hund isn't mine," she said a few seconds later, while forcing herself to turn and look at him. "She followed two of my students to the schoolhouse this morning and hung around there all day. Nobody knows who the dog belongs to."

"So you brought her home with you?"

Lisa shook her head. "She followed me, running alongside my bike most of the way."

Grinning, Paul reached down and petted the dog's head. "Seems like a good-natured hund."

Lisa looked down at the mutt and frowned. "She's a *pescht*."

"Are you gonna keep her, even though she is a pest?"

"No way. I'll try to find out where she belongs."

"I bet she'd make a nice pet."

"If I can't find out where she lives, would you like her?"

Paul shook his head. "There are too many animals at my uncle's place now, and since I don't have a home of my own yet, I can't take on the responsibility of a dog."

"I don't want a dog either." Lisa cringed when the mutt licked her hand.

"Oh, but apparently she wants you." Paul winked.

Feeling less intimidated in his presence, Lisa voiced another question: "What brought you over here today? You obviously came out of the house and not my grossdaadi's harness shop."

"You're correct. I came to talk to your *grossmammi* about some new kitchen cabinets she wants built."

Lisa's eyes widened a bit. "Really? She hasn't said anything to me about remodeling the kitchen."

Paul shook his head. "Not redoing the whole room, just replacing the old cabinets."

"Oh, I see."

Woof! Woof! The floppy-eared dog sauntered up the porch stairs and flopped down with a grunt near the door.

I can't believe that silly mutt is making herself right at home on the porch. Next thing she'll be making me feeling obligated to feed and water her. Lisa was glad for the diversion, because observing the way Paul looked at her right now made her feel squeamish. It was as if he was studying her face.

Lisa was tempted to ask why he had begun staring at her with his lips slightly parted, but she decided it was best not to say anything. All Lisa really wanted to do right now was get into the house.

"Umm. . .it was nice seeing you again, but now, if you'll excuse me, I need to go inside and see about helping my grandma get supper started." She hurried past Paul and up the porch stairs.

"No problem. I'm sure we'll see more of each other once I get started on your grandmother's cabinets. Oh, and good luck with your furry friend," he added with a chuckle.

Lisa grimaced as she skirted around the dog and went into the house. She'd had enough excitement for one day.

"I'm glad you're home," Marlene said when Lisa entered the kitchen. "I have some good news to share."

"If it's about getting new cabinets, I already know." Lisa removed her heavy sweater and hung it on the wall peg across the room. "I spoke to that newcomer, Paul, soon after I came into the yard."

"Oh, I'm glad you were able to visit with him."

"We didn't have much of a visit, Grandma. We only talked about the reason for his visit, and the pesky hund lying on our front porch."

Marlene's brows furrowed. "What dog on the porch? Is it our neighbor's collie that likes to come over here sometimes just to chase our poor *katze*?"

"No, it's an unkempt stray that wandered into the schoolyard today. She looks like a cocker/poodle mix, and I don't know if she likes to chase cats or not."

"Well, for goodness' sakes, why is the dog here if she's a stray?" Marlene headed out of the kitchen and opened the front door. "You're right, there that hund is, just lying on the porch," she called toward the kitchen. "The dog appears to really need a bath and a good brushing too."

"Maybe she'll leave in a while," Lisa hollered from the other room.

The dog looked up at Marlene and wagged its tail. Those big brown eyes of hers seemed to call out to Marlene, and it touched her heart. *The poor thing must be lost, and who knows for how long?* Closing the door, she headed back to where her granddaughter was.

"Let's have a seat at the table and I'll tell you the details about the hund," Lisa said.

"Good idea. I'll fix us some lemon-mint tea to drink while we visit."

"That sounds nice. It's kind of nippy out there this afternoon, and I need something to warm my insides." Lisa got out the teacups while Marlene heated the water. A short time later, they sat at the table with their beverages and a few sugar cookies.

"So you don't have any idea who the dog belongs to?" Marlene asked after Lisa had told her the whole story.

"No, I don't, but I intend to find out, because the pooch sure can't stay here."

"Why not? It sounds as though she's taken to you and would no doubt make a nice pet."

Lisa dunked a cookie into her tea and ate it quickly. "I don't need a pet, Grandma, especially one with a slurpy wet tongue. Besides, I'm sure she belongs somewhere, and there's no doubt some people living in the area who are most likely missing their dog. I'm going to make every effort to find the mutt's owner."

"How will you go about doing it?"

"I'll ask around, put up some posters in various places, and if necessary, take out an ad in our local paper."

Marlene took a sip of tea and dabbed at her lips with a napkin. "That's all well and good, but in the meantime, you can't let the poor pooch stay out on the porch whining." She tipped her head. "Can't you hear her, Lisa? No doubt she's hungry and probably lonely too."

Lisa blew out a noisy breath. "All right, as soon as we're done with our snack, I'll give the hund some cold meat loaf from Saturday night's meal. With your permission, that is."

Marlene reached over and patted her granddaughter's arm. "Of course it's all right. It would probably have gone to waste anyway, since your grossdaadi's not that thrilled about eating leftovers more than one day. And after he and I had meat loaf sandwiches last evening while you were at the singing, he made it clear that he wouldn't want more of the same any other night this week."

Lisa smiled. "That sounds like Grandpa, all right."

"In a few minutes I'll have another look in the refrigerator and see if I can find something else to feed that poor dog." Marlene nibbled on the last cookie she'd set out. *It's been some time since we've had a dog here on the property. It might be nice to have a watchdog, and it could very well be this one, unless Lisa finds its owners in the near future.*

With her elbows on the table, Marlene leaned forward and spoke in a bubbly tone. "I'm ever so excited about having new cabinets made for this old kitchen. I believe Abe's nephew will do a good job, because I'm sure his uncle would not have hired him as an employee unless the young man has talent." Marlene gazed up at her old cabinets with a wide smile. "Yes, even having new doors will give this room a much-needed update, and all new cabinets. . .well I'm sure they will be a huge improvement over these old ones."

"I'm happy for you, Grandma," Lisa said. "You work hard around here and deserve to have a nice kitchen."

"I may not be deserving of it, but some new cabinets will surely be nice." Marlene hoped Lisa would not catch on to the fact that she'd asked Paul to do the job in hopes that it might give him and Lisa a chance to get better acquainted. *And who knows,* she thought, smiling inwardly, *a romance might develop between them.*

When Lisa finished her snack, she tossed her napkin in the garbage can and put her cup and saucer in the sink. "Guess I'll take the meat loaf out to the mutt now."

"Don't forget to give her a bowl of water. She's probably as thirsty as she is *hungerich*."

"Okay, Grandma."

Lisa took the meat loaf from the refrigerator and placed it in an unbreakable dish. Meanwhile, Grandma stood by in the kitchen watching her gather the items needed. "Your grandfather is going to think we want this dog," she commented.

"Not if we tell him we are only taking care of the animal until I find her owners." Lisa got a small bucket from the utility room, rinsed it thoroughly, and filled it with fresh water.

"That's true, unless. . ."

"You think Grandpa might like to have the dog around?"

"Maybe." Grandma shrugged her shoulders and motioned for Lisa to lead the way. "Hopefully that meat loaf will help to fill the dog's stomach, but she is fairly good sized and may need more than that small portion to meet her needs." Grandma opened the front door, and when Lisa stepped outside, she wasn't the least bit surprised to see the vagrant dog lying in the same spot she'd left her.

As soon as Lisa set the plate of food and the water bucket down, the predictable animal jumped up, gave it a couple of sniffs, and wolfed the food right down. After licking the plate clean, the pooch lapped up all the water and sat near the spotless dish, looking pathetically up at them.

"Did you see that?" Grandma asked as she stood by the open door.

Lisa nodded as she watched the process from a chair on the porch where she'd taken a seat. "The poor thing acts like she hasn't eaten or drunk water all day. I wonder how long it's been since she had her last meal."

"One thing's for certain, she hasn't been combed, brushed, or bathed anytime recently." Grandma gestured to the dog. "Just look at all those tangles and her matted hair. And I bet she would appreciate something more to eat. I'll go take another look in the refrigerator and see what else I can find," she commented before going inside and closing the front door.

The dog continued to sit near the clean dish, looking up at Lisa like she wanted more food.

Lisa picked up the empty bucket and stepped into the yard to refill it with cool, fresh water from the spigot. The four-legged animal, however, didn't budge from the porch. Lisa carried the bucket back up to the same spot and set it down. About then Grandma came out with something in a container.

"What did you find for our furry friend?" Lisa tilted her head.

"I found some leftover scrambled eggs from a few mornings ago." Grandma tapped the contents onto the plate and stepped back while Lisa watched.

"There she goes again, inhaling the food." Lisa couldn't keep from rolling her eyes.

"I have to say, this is a nice way to get rid of leftovers. One thing's for sure—the garbage can won't get as full as long as this critter stays here." Grandma took the chair beside Lisa.

Lisa hated to admit it, but she'd already begun to develop a soft spot toward the mutt, which was not a good thing. And it appeared that her grandmother might be feeling the same way about the dog. The only answer to the problem was to find out who owned the dog, and quickly.

On the trip back to his uncle's place, Paul thought about Lisa and how she reminded him of someone he'd once known, but he couldn't think of who she could be or where he might have met her. He wasn't even sure what there was about Lisa that seemed familiar, and it really bothered him.

"Makes no sense," Paul mumbled. "This is my first trip to Ohio since Uncle Abe and Aunt Emma moved here from Indiana, so I couldn't have met Lisa before."

He realized that this young lady had a way of amusing him. And she was nice looking with a pleasing smile, although he hadn't seen her smile that often. Paul had also noticed that Lisa seemed to have some sort of a hard shell around her. She'd acted distant and unfriendly at times, and he wondered why. *I hope I haven't done or said anything to upset her. I'd like to get better acquainted with Lisa, as well as her family.* Paul thumped his forehead. "I need to quit thinking about this, because in the long run it's really not that important. My focus should be on doing a good job as a carpenter and keeping so busy that I'll forget about the pain of my past."

Paul relaxed his grip on the reins and gave Cinnamon the freedom to trot. While the mare hurried toward home, Paul tried to change his train of thought to the mixed-breed dog Lisa had tried to pawn off on him.

Like I need a hund to complicate my life. He shook his head. *But if I were a betting man, I'd lay down a good bet that when I return to the Schrocks' home again, that overzealous animal will still be there. And I'd also bet that Lisa will have given the dog a name and be calling the pooch her own.*

Chapter 9

"That hund of yours sure misses you when you're at the schoolhouse all day." Grandma pointed at the dog sitting next to Lisa's chair at the breakfast table with her head on Lisa's knee.

"She does have you here during the day to keep her company."

"True, but I believe she still favors you, and I think she knows you're about to leave again," Grandpa put in.

Lisa's forehead wrinkled. "She'll like it even less when she's put in the pen you made so she won't be able to follow me to school."

"I'd keep her in the house with me all day," Grandma said, "but Paul will be coming over sometime later to take out the old cabinets, which means either the front or back door could be left open for a while. So if Maggie were to get out, she'd no doubt head straight for the schoolhouse, like she did the other day when I went out to get the mail and forgot to shut the door."

"Jah, the best place for her is in the pen when I'm not here, because she wants to follow me everywhere." Lisa couldn't believe it had been two weeks since Maggie showed up at the schoolhouse with Nancy and Nathan and then followed Lisa home when school let out. She'd tried unsuccessfully to find the dog's owner, even paying for an ad in their local newspaper, but with no response. Lisa hadn't meant to become attached to the pooch, but the determined dog had managed to worm her way into Lisa's heart. So when her grandparents gave their approval, she'd given the lovable pooch a name and decided to keep her.

Lisa glanced at the battery-operated clock on the far wall. "I'd better get going. Today we're having some special guests at the schoolhouse, and I need to make sure that everything's neat and tidy."

"Who are the special guests?" Grandpa questioned.

"I'll tell you both about it when I get home this afternoon."

Grandma smiled. "Jah, we'd like to hear all the details."

Lisa gave Maggie a nudge to remove the dog's silky head from her lap and pushed back her chair so she could leave the table. "Be a good girl while I'm gone, Maggie."

The dog wagged her tail and let out a shrill-sounding *Woof! Woof!*

Grandpa chuckled. "She's a *schmaert* hund, and I bet she understood exactly what you said."

"I agree Maggie is a smart dog." Lisa put her dishes in the sink. She didn't bother to ask if Grandma wanted her to help with the dishes before she left, because she already knew the answer. Whenever she asked that question on a school day, her grandmother always told Lisa to go ahead—that she would take care of the dishes.

"I'll put Maggie in her pen when I head out to my shop," Grandpa said.

"Danki." Lisa gave both her grandparents hugs, patted the top of Maggie's head, and went out the door, carrying her insulated lunch bag inside the tote she took with her to the schoolhouse every day.

The first part of the school day had seemed to drag by as Lisa waited for the English couple to show up. They were friends of someone Yvonne knew and often put on performances for children's birthday parties as well as some other special events. Yvonne's neighbor Gayle would be bringing the couple by about an hour before school ended for the day.

Lisa glanced up at the clock. *It shouldn't be too much longer now. I can't help but feel the children's excitement.*

Five minutes later, a knock sounded on the schoolhouse door, and Yvonne went to answer it. When she returned, a middle-aged man and woman were with her. The woman carried a bright purple suitcase, and the man held a large multicolored canvas tote. The couple stood off to one side, while Yvonne walked up to the front of the room.

"Children, I'd like you to meet Mr. and Mrs. Brown. Mr. Brown is going to show us how he makes twisty animal balloons, and Mrs. Brown will demonstrate how she talks for her puppet without moving her lips."

All eyes were centered on the man and his wife as they joined Yvonne and Lisa up front. Mrs. Brown went first. She placed the suitcase on the floor, opened the lid, and lifted out an oversized, silly-looking puppet with bright red hair. The puppet had been dressed in a pair of faded blue jeans and a shirt nearly the same color as its hair.

Mrs. Brown took a seat in the chair Yvonne had provided and placed the puppet in her lap. "Boys and girls, this is my friend Charlie." She looked at the puppet and said, "Say hello to the boys and girls."

The puppet's mouth opened wide, and in a loud, high-pitched voice, it said, "Hello to the boys and girls."

Mrs. Brown shook her head. "No, Charlie, just say an easy hello."

"An easy hello."

Mrs. Brown gave her head another good shake. "No, no. . .just say hello, Charlie."

"Hello, Charlie."

Lisa, along with Yvonne and most of the students, laughed. Some of the children, however, sat staring at Charlie with eyes open wide, as though they couldn't believe what they were seeing or hearing. Although Lisa knew the puppet wasn't really talking, Mrs. Brown's lips didn't move, so it certainly appeared as if Charlie had spoken.

Lisa continued to watch with full attention as the talented woman finished her routine. When she put Charlie back in his suitcase, Mr. Brown stepped forward.

"How many of you like balloons?" he asked.

All hands shot up.

"Well, that's good. Today I'm going to blow up a balloon and then create some bubbles and twists till it looks like a dog." He opened his tote and withdrew a skinny-looking brown balloon, stretched it several times, and put the opening of the balloon up to his mouth. As Mr. Brown blew, his cheeks puffed out and his whole face turned red. Lisa hoped the man wouldn't pass out. Something like that would no doubt scare the children—and Lisa too, for that matter.

Stop worrying, Lisa told herself. *Just try to relax and enjoy the program.*

Mr. Brown kept blowing until the balloon was inflated. Then his fingers moved swiftly as he made several bubbles, securing them in place. Finally, what looked like a wiener dog appeared. Using a black marking pen, he drew a face on the dog.

The students sat spellbound as Mr. Brown made several more twisty creations that included a poodle, a monkey, a lion, a hummingbird, and even a bouquet of flowers. He kept blowing and twisting until everyone in the class had been given a balloon, including the teachers.

"Would anyone like to try blowing up a balloon?" Mr. Brown asked.

Three of the older boys raised their hands, so Mr. Brown gave them each a balloon.

Lisa watched as the boys, one from her class and two from Yvonne's, stretched their balloons and then tried to blow them up. Their faces turned red as they tried unsuccessfully to inflate the balloons.

"This is too hard," one of the boys said with a frown. "I think these must be trick balloons."

"No, they're not." Mr. Brown shook his head. "It just takes practice and lots of hot air."

Everyone laughed, including Lisa. It felt good to take some time out from teaching and allow the students to have a little unexpected fun.

"Can I try?" Abner, who was in the third grade, raised his hand.

Mr. Brown looked at Lisa, and when she nodded, he handed the boy a balloon.

It was hard for Lisa not to step in and tell her young student that he'd tried long enough as she watched him huff, puff, and turn red in the face.

"Pause for a breath and stretch the balloon a little more," Mr. Brown coached.

Abner did as the instructor said, but when he tried again, the balloon still did not inflate. With a determined expression, the boy continued to blow until he fell out of his chair and onto the floor.

"*Ach,* my. . .I think he's fainted." Lisa rushed forward and so did Yvonne, along with Mr. and Mrs. Brown. They all squatted beside Abner, but before they could say or do anything, his eyes popped open and he sat up. "I'm okay. *Ich is bletzlich umechdich warre.*"

Mrs. Brown looked at Lisa. "What'd he say?"

"Speaking in Pennsylvania Dutch, Abner said that suddenly he fainted," Lisa replied. She helped the boy to his feet. "You'd better sit back down and rest awhile."

"I'm okay," he insisted, holding tightly to the balloon.

"All right, but no more blowing today," Lisa said. "You can take the balloon home and practice if you want, but if you feel like you're going to pass out, you should stop and rest."

"Your teacher is right," Mr. Brown interjected. "You never want to keep blowing if you feel that you might faint."

"Well, boys and girls," Yvonne spoke up, "let's put our hands together and thank Mr. and Mrs. Brown for coming today and entertaining us with Charlie and so many balloons."

The students all clapped and said thank you.

Mrs. Brown took her puppet out of the suitcase again and said, "Say goodbye to the boys and girls, Charlie."

The puppet's mouth opened, and it said loudly: "Goodbye to the boys and girls."

The children clapped again, and Lisa smiled. This had been a good day, and she was eager to go home and tell her grandparents about it.

Walnut Creek

Lois sat at the kitchen table with the letters she'd recently received for her Dear Caroline column, trying to concentrate on the question that had been asked of her in the first letter. It was hard to stay focused on her task when she was worried about Orley as she waited for him to get back from his doctor's appointment. Her dear husband hadn't been feeling up to snuff lately, and she'd prompted him to see their doctor. Orley's appointment had been for three o'clock this afternoon, and they'd closed the antique store early so he could go. Lois had assumed she would go with Orley, but during lunch, he'd informed her that he preferred to go alone. Lois had felt left out and a little bit hurt when he'd made the announcement, but she'd kept quiet. If he preferred that she not be with him when he saw the doctor, she would respect his wishes.

I hope there's nothing seriously wrong with my husband. Lois tapped her pen on the writing tablet before her. She remembered her mother saying when Lois was a young girl, *"Never expect the worst, but if it comes your way, ask God to help you deal with it."*

Tears sprang to Lois's eyes, and she blinked them away. It made her sad to think that her mother had passed away so unexpectedly, just a few weeks before Lois's eighth birthday. A young girl with no siblings and an overly strict father needed her mother.

If Orley and I could have had children, we probably would have made our share of mistakes while raising them, Lois thought. *But we would have done our best to teach them God's ways and raise them in a loving manner, without being harsh and demanding, the way my father was when I lived at home.*

Lois directed her thoughts back to the letter a reader of the Dear Caroline column had written. It was from a woman who had been reunited with her sister who'd run away from home when she was a teenager. The sisters were having a hard time reconnecting, since they hadn't seen each other for thirty years.

Lois rubbed her forehead. *If I had a sister or brother whom I hadn't seen in many years, I'd make every effort to reunite with them. What a joy it would be to get reacquainted.* She jotted down a few comments on her notebook to use when she felt ready to fully answer this letter.

Lois was about to move on to another letter when she heard a vehicle pull into the yard. Hurrying out of the kitchen and to the front door, she was pleased when she opened it and saw Orley getting out of his driver's car.

Lois stepped out and gave the man behind the wheel a wave. "How'd your appointment go?" she asked when Orley joined her on the porch.

"Let's go inside, and I'll tell you about it."

"Okay." Lois led the way to the living room and took a seat on the sofa. Orley had barely seated himself in his recliner when she said, "What did the doctor say when you told him you've been feeling poorly?"

"Well, let's see now. . . . First off, his nurse had me take off my shoes and step onto the scale to see how much I weighed. Then she took my temperature and checked my blood pressure." Orley shifted on his chair. "When the doctor came into the examining room and I told him my symptoms, he felt around on my neck, listened to my heart, and also looked in my mouth, ears, and even my eyes. After that, he asked me a whole bunch of questions."

"Did he give you a diagnosis?"

Orley shook his head. "He had his receptionist schedule me to have a few tests run that'll include blood work. I'll be getting that done tomorrow morning, and I have to go to the lab having fasted for twelve hours."

"You probably shouldn't eat anything after supper tonight, then."

He gave a nod, followed by a noisy yawn. "Right now, though, if you don't mind, I'm going to take a little nap."

"You go right ahead. If you're still sleeping by the time supper's ready, I'll wake you."

"Danki." Orley's eyelids closed, and a short time later, his heavy breathing let Lois know that he'd fallen asleep.

Lois said a silent prayer on behalf of her dear husband and then tiptoed quietly from the room to finish the letters she hadn't yet answered.

Hopefully they would know something soon as to the reason Orley had been so tired and had begun to put on weight lately.

Sugarcreek

Paul was about halfway done removing the old cupboards in Marlene's kitchen when he heard Lisa's dog barking from her pen. He hadn't been the least bit surprised when he'd showed up today and seen the dog. When he'd mentioned it to Marlene, she had explained that when Lisa couldn't find the rightful owner, she'd decided to keep the dog and had named her Maggie.

Yep, I was right all along, Paul told himself as he hauled another load of wood from the old cupboards outside.

When Maggie continued to yap, Paul walked around to the side of the house where the pen had been built and nearly bumped into Lisa. "Oops. . .sorry. I didn't realize you were home." He took a step back from her. "But then I should have figured it out with the way your dog, Maggie, was carrying on."

Lisa's cheeks reddened as she stared up at him. "I—I guess my grandma must have told you that I kept the dog and named her."

"Jah." He looked at the pooch, whose barking had turned to a pathetic whine as she pawed from the inside of her pen at the gate holding her prisoner. "Looks like your hund wants out of there pretty bad." Paul looked back at Lisa while gesturing to the desperate dog.

Lisa gave no response to Paul's statement as she let Maggie out of her pen and headed for the house with the dog prancing right on her heels.

Chuckling to himself, Paul put the pieces of wood on the pile with the rest of the cabinets he'd torn out and then hurried back to the house.

When Paul entered the kitchen, he saw Lisa sitting at the table with her grandma. Maggie lay on the floor, close to Lisa's chair.

"Come join us for a glass of apple cider and some banana bread." Marlene motioned to the chair closest to where Lisa sat. "You've been working hard this afternoon and deserve a break."

There was still a little more that Paul needed to get done, but Marlene's offer was hard to turn down. "Sounds good. But I'd better wash up first. My hands are really dirty."

"No problem. Remember, the bathroom's down the hall and to the left." Marlene smiled. "Lisa was about to tell me about her day at school, but she can wait till you get back."

Paul nodded and headed down the hall. He'd noticed Lisa's pinched expression when her grandma had given him the invitation to join them for some refreshments. Was she annoyed by his intrusion? Maybe Lisa didn't feel comfortable talking about her day at the schoolhouse with Paul present. Whatever the case, she'd have to get over it, because he wasn't going to turn down the tasty snack that had been offered.

Paul stepped inside the bathroom and stood in front of the mirror, washing his hands. *I wonder what Lisa will have to say when she finds out her grandma invited me to stay for supper.*

Chapter 10

While Paul was down the hall washing his hands, Grandma informed Lisa that he would be staying for supper.

I was hoping to relax this evening with only Grandpa and Grandma. Lisa felt her frame stiffen. She felt awkward enough with this fellow on the premises but even more so with him staying for their meal. Lisa remembered how Paul had stared at her so strangely awhile back. She still felt unsettled by him doing that, and she wondered why he had. She'd hoped Paul was done, or at least he'd be leaving soon after being there all day. *I guess Grandma had other ideas for this evening. After all, she's only being hospitable, and she likes to do the right thing for others.*

Lisa refocused her attention to the room. The kitchen was definitely in disorder without the old cabinets in place. The upper ones were absent of their dishes, glassware, spices, and dried food goods, along with the lower cabinets that had also been emptied of all of their contents. Grandma seemed all right about making do with this project that had disrupted her usually orderly kitchen, and apparently having a guest for supper in the midst of this disarray didn't bother her in the least.

Lisa hadn't given any thought to remodeling the kitchen, for to her, it looked fine the way it was. *It will no doubt look a lot nicer and more modern when it's done,* she thought. *It'll be interesting to see how things look when Paul has installed the new cupboards in the next day or two.*

Lisa looked at all the boxes stacked up on one side of the room that contained everything that had been in the cabinets. "But Grandma, our kitchen is torn apart right now," she said. "Do you really think this is a good time to be entertaining?"

Grandma flapped her hand. "Oh, Paul doesn't mind. He seemed more than willing to eat with us when I asked him to stay for supper." She gestured to the stack of boxes. "And of course we'll eat in the dining room so we don't have to look at all this clutter."

"What did you plan for the meal?" Lisa asked.

"I made a chicken-n-stuffing casserole and put it in the refrigerator this morning." Grandma snapped her fingers. "Which reminds me—I need to get that in the oven right now." She got up from her chair and moved quickly across the room. "I'm glad Paul's able to join us for the evening meal. It'll give us all a chance to get to know him better."

Lisa didn't voice her thoughts to Grandma, but she saw no reason to get to know the young man at all. He was here to do a job, plain and simple, not socialize with the family or stay to eat supper with them.

While her grandmother got out the casserole and placed it in the oven, Lisa cleaned out her lunch box and put it away. She'd just finished up when Paul reentered the room.

Lisa's grandma gestured to the table. "Let's have a seat now so we can enjoy our snack. I just put a casserole in the oven, and it'll be an hour or so before we can eat it, so the banana bread will get us by till then."

"Sounds good." Paul pulled out a chair at the table and took a seat.

"Should I go out to the harness shop and see if Grandpa would like to join us?" Lisa asked.

Grandma shook her head. "He went into town to pick up a few things, and he's not back yet."

"Oh." It was hard for Lisa to hide her disappointment. She felt uncomfortable around Paul, and if Grandpa could join them, he would surely engage Paul in conversation. Then Lisa could go to her room for a while to read one of the books she'd picked up at the library recently. She would come down in plenty of time to set the table and help Grandma with any last-minute supper preparations, of course. But as it was, Lisa felt obligated to sit and make small talk, or at the very least smile, nod, and pretend to be interested in whatever conversation Grandma got started with Paul.

Would it be too rude to excuse myself and pass up the banana bread and cider? Lisa wondered. *I could say that I've developed a headache.* Lisa's conscience pricked her, and she flinched. But then, that would be wrong because it'd be a lie.

"So now, tell us about the special visitors you had at school today," Grandma said after she'd taken a seat beside Lisa.

Lisa glanced at Paul then back at her grandmother. *I wish he wasn't a part of this conversation. He came here to work, not sit at Grandma's table, listening to what I have to say.*

Seeing Grandma's expectant expression, Lisa knew she couldn't sit here without sharing what had happened at the schoolhouse this afternoon. She took a quick drink of her apple cider and gave an overview of what had occurred with the woman who'd done ventriloquism and her puppet.

Grandma laughed. "I bet it was fun to watch someone speak without moving their lips and make her voice seem as if it were coming from the puppet's mouth."

"Some people call that 'throwing your voice,'" Paul interjected before Lisa could respond. "Of course, the ventriloquist isn't actually throwing his or her voice," he added. "Because they're talking without moving their lips and speaking in a different sounding voice while moving their puppet's mouth, it appears as if the puppet is talking."

"You seem to know a lot about ventriloquism," Grandma said, pouring more cider into Paul's glass.

He shrugged. "Not really. I just read an article about it in a magazine one day." Paul took an unbuttered slice of banana bread and quickly ate it.

Lisa picked up a piece and spread a thin layer of butter on it before taking a bite. "This is good *brot*."

"I agree this is good bread," Paul chimed in.

Grandma smiled. "I'm glad you both like it. We just need to be careful and not eat too much or it'll spoil our supper."

"No problem there. When I've been workin' hard all day, there's always plenty of room in my belly for food." Paul gave his stomach a few thumps.

Grandma pushed the plate of banana bread closer to Paul. "Then by all means, help yourself to some more."

"Thanks!" This time, Paul took two pieces and slathered them with twice as much butter as Lisa had used. She could hardly keep from lifting her gaze to the ceiling and rolling her eyes.

Doesn't this man have any willpower at all? I'm sure he must have eaten lunch today. Surely Paul can't be that hungry.

Lisa cleared her throat and looked at Grandma again. "Would you like to hear what talent the other guest who came to the schoolhouse shared?"

Grandma smiled. "Of course I would."

"He made animals and flowers out of the different-colored balloons he blew up and twisted in several places."

"Did he blow them by hand or with a pump?" Paul asked.

"By hand," she replied.

"You need a lot of air to do that."

Lisa gave a nod. "The man's face turned pretty red when he was blowing those balloons up. Some of the boys in the class wanted to try blowing up a balloon, and one of the younger ones insisted on trying and ended up passing out."

Grandma's eyes widened. "Oh, dear! I hope he was all right."

"He woke up quickly and was fine—just embarrassed is all."

"I would have been too." Paul finished his banana bread and pushed away from the table. "I'd better get the last of those cabinets taken outside now." He looked over at Grandma and said, "Danki for the snack you provided. Both the cider and banana bread sure hit the spot."

"You are most welcome." She offered him a broad smile. "Since you'll be putting in the cabinets tomorrow or the next day, you should join us for supper that evening too."

Lisa was shocked by Grandma's quick invite. *Why, Grandma? We haven't even had the first meal yet.* She wondered just how the young man would respond to her grandmother's invite. Lisa hoped he would decline the kind offer.

"That's very kind of you, but I wouldn't want to impose," Paul replied.

Grandma shook her head. "It will not be an imposition at all."

"Can I let you know tomorrow? My aunt may be planning something special, and I wouldn't want to disappoint her."

"Of course. You can give me your answer about supper when you get here tomorrow or the next day."

Paul nodded and moved across the room to gather the pieces of another cabinet he'd torn out.

"Lisa, would you please open the back door and hold it for him?" Grandma gave Lisa's arm a little nudge.

"Sure." Lisa got up from the table and did as her grandmother had asked. After Paul went out, she closed the door and returned to the kitchen to remove her glass and plate from the table.

"Paul seems like a nice young man, don't you think?" Grandma looked steadily at Lisa.

Lisa shrugged. "I really can't say. I don't know him well enough."

"Well, there's no better way to get acquainted with someone than while eating a meal." Grandma smiled. "Don't you agree?"

"I suppose." *But who says I want to get to know Paul?*

"This is one tasty casserole." Paul looked over at Jerry. "*Dei fraa is en gudi koch*, and I'm glad she invited me to join you and your family for supper this evening."

"I can't argue with that." Jerry looked over at Marlene and grinned. "My wife is a very good cook. Maybe the best in the whole state of Ohio."

She reached over and poked his arm. "Don't you go exaggerating, now."

"I'm not. In my opinion, you're the best." He helped himself to more casserole.

"I think you're just a little bit prejudiced."

Jerry shook his head. "No, I'm not—just stating facts as I see 'em is all." He let out a resonating chuckle. "Well, maybe I should've said, 'as I taste 'em.'"

Marlene smiled, and when she heard a grunt from across the room, she looked over and saw Maggie reposition herself as she lay sleeping. The dog was well behaved, and as long as there was food in her dish, she rarely begged for scraps from the table. Marlene was glad Lisa had decided to keep the dog. Not only was Maggie a good companion for Lisa when she was at home but she kept Marlene company during the days when Lisa taught school.

Looking away, Marlene glanced over at Lisa, who sat beside her. She seemed kind of sullen this evening and hadn't said more than a few words since they'd sat down at the dining-room table. Of course Jerry had monopolized a good deal of the conversation so far, as he'd asked Paul several questions about the new cabinets he would be installing in the kitchen. They'd also discussed their common interest in fishing and agreed that they might plan a fishing trip with each other sometime before winter set in or perhaps in early spring. Marlene had spoken up and asked if Lisa would like to go along, since she also enjoyed fishing. Lisa's only response had been a mumbled, "We'll see."

Paul seems like such a nice fellow, Marlene thought. *He's polite, friendly, and good looking. I sure hope he takes an interest in my granddaughter, and that once Lisa gets to know him better, the feeling will be mutual. Jerry and I won't be around forever, and Lisa's going to need someone after we're gone.*

Paul glanced over at Lisa and was about to ask her a question when her grandpa posed another one of his own.

"How long have you been doing carpentry work, Paul?" Jerry asked.

"I started working in my daed's furniture shop when I was sixteen. As a young boy I liked to mess around learning the names of the tools; Dad took the time to show me the different types of wood he'd use for jobs, and it seemed after that I always had some kind of project going," Paul replied. "When Dad saw that I had a knack for it, he invited me into his shop and taught me the proper way to use woodworking tools and gave me many good tips on how to build things." Paul laughed. "My mamm said that she always knew where to find me if I wasn't in the house or barn doing chores, because my favorite place to be was in the shop with Dad. Shortly before I moved here, Dad started making and selling rustic-looking pieces of furniture in the store for people who owned cabins in the woods or just wanted a woodsy feel in their homes. I enjoyed working with him in that area of the store too."

Jerry nodded. "That's how it was with me and my daed. I liked the smell of leather and hung out in his harness shop every chance I got. Eventually, we became business partners, and after Dad died, I took over the business."

"It's nice when a business can stay in the family—passed from one generation to the next," Marlene chimed in.

Jerry's forehead wrinkled. "Only I have no one to take over the harness shop when I've passed from this world into the next."

"No sons or sons-in-law to follow in your footsteps?" Paul asked.

Jerry gave a slow shake of his head. "Marlene and I were only blessed with two children: a daughter, Caroline, and a son, Andrew." His normally bright blue eyes had lost their sparkle, and his mouth turned down at the corners. "Both of them are deceased, and so is our son-in-law, Raymond."

"I'm sorry for your loss." Paul could almost feel the depth of the man's pain. Did he dare ask what had taken the lives of this elderly couple's children? Would it be too bold or cause them heartache to talk about it?

"Our son died when he was a boy and got hit by a car while he was riding the new bike we had given him for his ninth birthday," Marlene spoke up. Her voice quivered a bit as she spoke. "And our daughter—Lisa's mother—along with her husband and his parents, were killed when the vehicle they were riding in was hit head-on." Marlene looked at Lisa, who sat without speaking as she stared at her half-eaten meal. "Our granddaughter, their only child, was with them, but by some miracle, Lisa survived the crash with only minor injuries. Soon after her parents' and grandparents' funeral, we brought her here to live with us."

Paul sat in stunned silence for several seconds before extending his condolences. He knew now why Lisa reminded him of someone. She was the same girl he'd gone to school with in Goshen, Indiana. He just hadn't realized it until this minute.

Should I say anything? Paul asked himself. *How would Lisa react if I told her I was the boy who used to walk her home from school and had blurted out on more than one occasion that I planned to marry her someday?* He shifted on his unyielding chair. *Or would it better to keep quiet about this—at least for now?*

Chapter 11

"No! No! No!"

At the sound of her granddaughter's shrill screams, Marlene rushed from her room where she'd just gotten dressed. Holding on to the railing, she made her way swiftly up the stairs. When she entered the room Lisa occupied, she saw the young woman rolling from side to side as she continued to shout, "No! No! No!"

"Lisa, wake up." Marlene placed her hand on her granddaughter's arm and gave it a gentle shake. When Lisa's shouts turned to a deep moan, Marlene shook her arm again, a little more forcibly this time.

Lisa's eyes opened, and she blinked several times as she sat up in bed. Her face and nightgown were soaked with perspiration. "Wh–what's wrong, Grandma?"

"You were shouting in your sleep. I believe you must have been having a nightmare." Marlene took a seat on the edge of the bed. "Do you know what you were dreaming about?" She noticed the protruding tendons on Lisa's neck as her breaths burst in and out. Marlene sat close, waiting for her granddaughter to respond to the question.

"I—I was there, Grandma."

"Where?"

"At the cemetery, watching my mamm, daed, and other *grosseldere* being lowered into their *graewer*."

"You dreamed about your parents and grandparents being lowered into their graves?"

Lisa swept a shaky hand across her forehead before nodding. "I barely remember the event, but I saw it in my *draame* just like it was happening right then."

Marlene leaned closer and gave Lisa a hug. "Sometimes dreams bring us back to a time we barely remember, and other dreams are wild and make no sense at all."

"But why'd I have this draame now? I don't think I've ever dreamed about watching my family's burial before."

"It may have been due to the discussion that went on at the supper table last night, when we told Paul how you'd lost your parents and grandparents and the miracle of your survival." Marlene moved her head slowly up and down. "That might have triggered the memory in your mind, and then it was brought forth in a dream while you were sleeping."

Tears formed in Lisa's eyes, and when she blinked, several escaped and rolled down her cheeks. "I don't want to remember that day. It makes me *bedauerlich*."

"Of course it makes you sad." Marlene patted Lisa's back. "Everyone feels saddened when they lose a loved one. And you lost more than just one family member during the accident, which makes it doubly hard."

"I wish you hadn't talked to Paul about it. He didn't know my family, and it's none of his business." Lisa's lips pressed into a thin white slash as she folded her arms across her chest.

I didn't mean to be insensitive to her feelings. Marlene hesitated as she put her thoughts in order. *But I'd like to express my thoughts on the subject in an honest and caring way.*

"That's true, but his kind words, spoken in a soothing tone of voice, showed the sympathy he felt for you and us."

"I barely even know Paul, and I don't need his sympathy." Lisa pushed the covers aside and got out on the opposite side of the bed from Grandma. "I need to wash up, get dressed, and go downstairs to help you with breakfast." She glanced at the battery-operated clock by her bed and pushed the button on top of it to the OFF position. "Since you woke me before the alarm went off, I should have plenty of time to take a shower and wash my sweaty body. Sure wouldn't want to put clean clothes on the way I am right now and then go off to teach school."

Marlene rose from the bed and moved toward the door. "I'll put the kaffi on and see you downstairs."

Lisa nodded slowly.

I think my granddaughter's put out with me and her grandpa for talking to Paul about the tragic loss of her parents and other grandparents. Lisa still misses them and obviously doesn't want to talk about it, but part of healing is being able to share our hurts with others and accept their sympathy. Marlene clung to the railing as she descended the stairs. *That certainly helped me when our son and daughter both died.*

As Lisa stood at the stove, scrambling eggs in a skillet, she thought about the terrifying dream she'd had. She couldn't remember ever having a nightmare like that before and hoped it would never happen again. Lisa didn't want to remember the details of her family's funeral or burial, and she had blanked out most of her earlier childhood when her parents and paternal grandparents were still alive. Even snippets from the past, which sometimes flitted through her mind, caused Lisa to feel fearful and despondent. She'd convinced herself that the only way she could be happy was to keep her focus on the present and refuse to give in to thoughts of the past. Staying busy so her mind couldn't wander also helped.

Teaching the children has given me a wonderful purpose, just like taking care of Maggie. Lisa smiled as she looked over at her dog lying by the kitchen's back door. *I'd say she's pretty content at this point in time. My life is good here, and I'm happy living with my loving grandparents, so I don't need anyone else.*

Although Lisa's biggest fear was losing her maternal grandparents, there was nothing she could do to prevent people she knew from dying. All she could do was try to keep herself from becoming too emotionally attached to anyone, even her grandparents, whom she loved and respected. That had not been easy, though, since she'd been living with them for so many years, and they had provided for her needs. There'd been a few times when she'd let her guard down and talked to Grandma or Grandpa about her feelings, but then she would pull back into her protective shell. The one thing Lisa could not allow herself to do was fall in love with a man and get married. If she did, it would put her in a vulnerable position of possibly losing her husband or children if some tragic event should occur. It was better to stay single than to risk being hurt again and left all alone.

"Is breakfast ready?" Grandpa's question drove Lisa's thoughts aside. She hadn't realized he'd come inside.

"Uh, almost." She looked down at the eggs she'd been scrambling and frowned. They hadn't even cooked at all. *What's going on with this stove?* That's when Lisa realized that she had not turned on the gas burner. *Boy, I need to get my head on straight. The bad dream from earlier is still bothering me, and it's beginning to affect my normal routine.*

She quickly turned the burner on and began stirring the eggs again.

"Where's your *grossmudder*?" Grandpa asked.

"Grandma's in the dining room setting the table."

"How come we're eating in there? We're not having company for breakfast." Grandpa moved closer to the stove and looked at her over the top of his reading glasses. "Are we?"

She shook her head. "With the kitchen missing its cabinets, Grandma said she didn't enjoy eating in here and looking at the vacant spaces."

He chuckled. "That sounds like my fraa, all right."

"What sounds like your wife?" Grandma asked, stepping into the kitchen, sandal footed.

He slipped his arm around her waist and pulled her close to his side. "Nothin' important. I love everything about you, from your cute little turned-up nose, all the way down to your dainty toes. And you're a good cook too," he added.

Grandma poked his arm. "You're such a charming tease."

"I'm not teasing. You're everything a man could want."

They kissed, and Lisa looked the other way. She was glad that her grandparents loved each other, but she felt like an intruder when they displayed their affection in front of her. Although Lisa would never have admitted it, she envied them a bit, for she would never know a love like theirs.

"While you were out doing your chores, did you think to stop at the phone shed and check for messages, Jerry?" Grandma asked.

"Sure did. There was just one from Paul."

"Oh, what'd he have to say?"

Lisa's ears perked up at the sound of Paul's name. Although the eggs were done, she continued to stir them around in the skillet, waiting to hear what Grandpa said next.

"He wanted to let us know that he'll be over around ten o'clock to install the new cabinets, but he won't be able to join us for supper tonight because his aunt invited some friends to come over to their house this evening, and she wants them to meet Paul. He said he thought it would be good to call now and let us know so you didn't plan a big meal that would include him."

"Oh, that's too bad. Paul's such a nice young man. I was really hoping he could join us again."

Lisa couldn't miss the tone of disappointment in Grandma's voice. She glanced over her shoulder and noticed her grandmother's furrowed brows. She was obviously disappointed, but Lisa felt relieved.

"If you're not too busy, do you have a few minutes to talk with me?" Marlene asked when she stepped into her husband's harness shop soon after Lisa left for the schoolhouse.

"I am never too busy to talk to you, my love." Jerry placed the piece of leather he'd been holding onto his workbench and suggested she pull up a chair.

Marlene sat on the metal folding chair customers sometimes used when they brought a harness or some other leather object in for repairs. More often than not, Jerry would sit and visit with his customers after they'd told him what they needed to have done, so he'd made sure to have a few extra chairs in the shop.

"How's it going out here?" Marlene asked.

"It's goin' fine. I just got some phone calls made to a couple of customers, and I was about to begin my leather work. Everything all right at the house?"

"Jah, things are fine, and it shouldn't be long before Paul shows up to begin his work."

Jerry looked up at the battery-operated clock on the wall. "Yep, he'll be here pretty soon. Did the dog follow you out this morning to the shop? I've got her treat, and you know how much she likes those doggy biscuits I bought."

"She came out the door with me, but then headed out back behind the house. I'm sure she'll come by for a biscuit when she's ready."

He nodded.

I feel like I'm such a worrywart coming out here and venting my feelings about our granddaughter. Marlene fiddled nonstop with the edge of her apron and remained quiet as she sat there.

Jerry smiled, and then his brows crinkled. "Okay, fraa, I'm sure that something is up by your nervous actions."

"I'm concerned about Lisa."

Jerry lifted his hands so his palms faced the ceiling. "You're always worried about our granddaughter. What has she done that concerns you now? Is it because she was quiet and seemed preoccupied during breakfast?"

"Jah, to a point. After what happened earlier this morning, I kind of expected she would be quiet while we ate. Lisa always pulls into her shell when something traumatic happens or if she's having a bad day and doesn't want to talk about it."

Jerry's eyes widened. "What happened this morning that involved Lisa?"

"After you went outside to do your chores, while I was getting dressed, I heard Lisa screaming, 'No! No! No!'" Marlene clasped her hands together. "So I hurried up to her room and found her moaning as she rolled back and forth on the bed."

"Was she feeling *grank*?"

"No, she wasn't sick. Her eyes were closed, so I knew she was asleep."

"Was she having a bad draame?"

"Jah. I woke her, and she told me that she'd been dreaming about the day her parents and other grandparents' bodies had been laid to rest." Marlene reached over and touched his arm. "The poor girl was drenched in sweat and quite shaken."

"Were you able to comfort her?"

"I believe so, but Lisa's such a sensitive young woman, and she rarely opens up and says what she's really feeling. I think she holds too much inside."

"You're probably right, but we can't force the girl to talk about her feelings if she doesn't want to." Jerry rubbed his temples. "I can still picture our granddaughter's face the day of the funeral and graveside service. She pressed her hands against her ears and kept shaking her head, as if in denial." He released a heavy sigh. "Then when the last shovels of dirt had filled in those four graves, the poor child collapsed on the ground with sobs louder than any I've ever heard."

Marlene's chin trembled as she slumped in her chair. "Jah, it was heart wrenching when you carried her screaming all the way to our carriage."

Jerry reached over and clasped Marlene's hand. "We both tried so hard to be supportive of our granddaughter that neither of us really had the chance to grieve properly that day."

"That is true," she agreed, "but I spent plenty of days, and nights too, grieving the loss of our daughter, son-in-law, and even Lisa's other grandparents who we barely knew. Of course, I had to do my grieving when Lisa wasn't in the same room. Many nights back then she had horrible nightmares, but it's been a long time since she had one, and it really shook her up." Marlene looked off across the room. *It's interesting how the strong negative memories can be put away and then, one day, released,* she thought. She reached behind the band of her apron, pulled out the tissue she'd tucked there this morning, and wiped her tears. "I can't help worrying about Lisa. We're not getting any younger, Jerry."

He nodded.

"I am determined to see the granddaughter God gave us to raise happily married so she will have a helpmate and someone to love and care for her when we are gone."

"I understand your reason for wanting Lisa to find a husband, but we cannot make it happen. We can only pray and ask the Lord to find our granddaughter someone, if it's meant to be. Also, if and when the right man comes along, it must be Lisa's decision whether to marry him or not."

"But that's not likely to happen if she continues to keep people at arm's length."

"We just need to remain supportive, and like I just said, remember to pray often for her."

And perhaps, Marlene thought, *if Lisa spends more time with Paul, she will see that he's the one.* Marlene had to admit that she didn't know the young man very well, but from the moment she first met Paul, she had a feeling that he was indeed the right man for their granddaughter. She just needed to figure out a way to get Paul and Lisa together so they could get to know each other well. Sometimes in matters of the heart, people needed a little nudge.

Chapter 12

Walnut Creek

"I'd like to go with you today," Lois said as she and Orley stood together in the kitchen on the morning of his doctor's appointment. "I want to be there when the *dokder* gives you the results of the blood test you had ten days ago."

Orley shook his head. "There's no need for that. I can tell you what the doctor said after I get home."

Lois couldn't help feeling discouraged by his response, but she wasn't too surprised, because he'd said things like this to her before when it came to his health. "But you might leave something important out," she argued. "And what if there are questions I would like to have answered by the doctor, and they're not questions you would think to ask him?"

"Are you saying that my memory is bad?" Orley squinted as he thumped the top of his partially bald head.

That's not what I'm trying to say at all. Why won't you just let me come along with you? Lois pursed her lips as she leaned against the counter and released a frustrated sigh. Orley's driver would be here soon, and if she couldn't get her husband to agree that she should go along to his appointment, then he'd be going there alone, and she'd spend the rest of the morning waiting for his return and trying not to worry about his health.

What if there is something seriously wrong with Orley? Lois asked herself. *Would he open up and give me all the details? Or would my dear husband keep quiet in order to shield me from the truth so I don't fret?*

Orley stepped forward and placed his hand on her arm. "All right, Lois, you can accompany me to the doctor's, but only on one condition."

She tipped her head back and looked directly into his eyes. "And what would that be?"

"You let me ask my questions first, and then if you have any of your own, you can chime right in." Orley lifted his glasses and rubbed the bridge of his nose.

Lois bobbed her head. "Jah, I can do that."

"Good, then you'd better get your jacket, outer bonnet, and purse, because I just heard a vehicle pull into the yard, and it's no doubt our driver."

Lois smiled. She was glad Orley had conceded and agreed to let her go with him today. Knowing her carefree husband, he would no doubt ask very few questions of the doctor. So it was good that she would be there to ask her own set of questions and find out everything they needed to know about Orley's health.

"That was some fine work you did on the Schrocks' cabinets." Paul's uncle gave him a pat on the back. "I had stopped by their place to give them the bill and let them know that if they had any questions not to hesitate to ask. They were happy with the work and even mentioned that they liked having you there during the whole process." His uncle's tone was laced with satisfaction. "Yes indeed, I did a good thing when I invited you to come here to work for me. Sure hope you stay put and don't move back to Indiana."

"No way!" Paul responded to his uncle's statement. "I have no intention of moving back to my hometown. There are too many unpleasant memories for me there, and so far I've been liking it here in Ohio. In fact, this could end up being the place where I decide to put down roots." Paul leaned against the desk in Uncle Abe's office.

"Are the unpleasant memories because of the girlfriend who dropped you for your best friend?"

Paul's mouth nearly fell open. "How'd you know about that?" He had deliberately not said anything about his breakup with Susan because it was his personal life and he'd seen no reason his uncle, aunt, or anyone else in Sugarcreek should know about his friend's betrayal.

"Your daed told me." Uncle Abe took a seat behind his desk. "I'm guessing from your look of displeasure that he wasn't supposed to say anything."

Paul couldn't deny his uncle's words. He guessed that Dad telling Uncle Abe about his personal matter wasn't the end of the world. But with the surprise of the reveal still in the air, Paul stood there with no words to say to his uncle. It was an awkward silence as Paul barely managed to nod.

"Well you know how your daed is. He worries about his kinner, even if they aren't little children anymore." Uncle Abe drummed his fingers along the top of his desk. "My brother's a caring person and always has been. Even when we were kinner, he acted more like a daed than a big bruder to me and the rest of our siblings. If one of us got sick, he felt bad and always asked if there was anything he could do to help us feel better." Paul's uncle chuckled. "I kinda liked it, though, 'cause whenever I got in trouble with my mamm or daed, I could always count on my brother Daniel to offer me sympathy."

Paul smiled. "You're right, my dad is a caring person. I guess it's okay that he told you about me and Susan Lambright breaking up. The whole thing is hard for me to talk about, and I'm glad to be living here where I don't have to see her and Ervin Yoder together anymore."

"What you went through will just be a distant memory when you meet the right woman and fall in love." Uncle Abe's words were spoken in a soothing tone of voice. It kind of reminded Paul of the way his own father often spoke to him—full of sound advice but never pushy or controlling.

Paul thought about his mother and how she could sometimes be a bit overbearing when it came to trying to convince Paul or one of his brothers that she knew what was best for them. When he and his siblings were children, there wasn't much they could do about it, but as adults, sometimes Paul and his brothers had to stand up to their mother and remind her that they were grown men and had the right to make their own decisions. Mom would usually back off and say she was sorry, but there were times when she kept pushing. This was yet another reason Paul liked living here—no one was pressing him to do certain things he didn't want to do or to think the way they thought.

Paul wasn't sure that what Uncle Abe had said about him meeting the right woman and falling in love would ever happen, because he definitely was not looking for love. But if a woman should ever come his way who he believed was the right one, he'd make sure to pray about it and seek confirmation from God before proceeding with a permanent relationship.

For some reason, an image of Lisa's face overtook Paul's thoughts. *Now why am I thinking about her right now? Maybe it's because the last time I saw Lisa, I discovered that we knew each other when we were kinner. Of course,* he reminded himself, *Lisa obviously did not remember me, or she would have said something. I have to wonder if she blocked that part of her life out of her memory by choice; or could the trauma from the accident she and her family were involved in have resulted in partial amnesia?*

Paul felt a warm flush creep across his cheeks as another thought came to mind. *If Lisa's parents hadn't died and she'd continued to live in Goshen, I wonder if I would have ended up dating her. When I was a boy, I did believe I would marry Lisa someday.*

"What's wrong, Paul? Your face is red as a ripe apple, and the sweat on your forehead makes it appear that you might be overheated. Is it too warm for you here in the shop this morning?"

Uncle Abe's questions drew Paul out of his musings, and he moved away from the desk. "Jah, it is a little warm, but I'll be fine once your driver comes and we head out to do that job you had scheduled for today."

"That should be soon," Uncle Abe said. "So while I do some paperwork here in my office, would you please go out to the main part of the shop and make sure that all our supplies are ready?"

"Sure thing. I'll let you know when Herb gets here." Paul made a beeline for the door, eager to do something that would get his mind on something other than Lisa.

When school was over for the day and the children had all gone home, Lisa said goodbye to Yvonne before she stepped out the front door and nearly tripped on the curly-haired dog lying on the porch. "For goodness' sakes, Maggie, what are you doing here?"

The dog looked up at her, whined, and wagged her tail.

"What's going on? Who are you talking to?" Her coworker poked her head outside of the door.

"It looks like my dog missed me today and came to see me home."

"Oh, I heard you talking and thought maybe a student had come back for something they'd forgotten." Yvonne came out from the doorway and gave Maggie a few rubs on her flanks. "Your dog is sure sweet and friendly."

"Danki, and jah, I have to agree. Maggie has a way of warming hearts. It started with me and Grandma, which is why we ended up keeping the mutt." Lisa pointed at Maggie. "Guess I'd better go home with my furry companion now."

"All right, I'll see you tomorrow." Yvonne smiled and went back inside the schoolhouse, no doubt to finish cleaning the blackboard and gather up her things.

Lisa looked down at Maggie again and tapped her chin. *I wonder how you escaped the yard without Grandma knowing.* At this moment Lisa wished her dog could talk. She didn't know whether Maggie had been in her pen and somehow gotten out or if she'd been inside the house with Grandma and snuck outside when the door had been left open. Either way, Maggie should not have been out on the road by herself. She could have gotten hit by a car.

"Come on, girl." Lisa clapped her hands and started down the steps, glancing over her shoulder to see if the dog was coming. She needn't have worried, because Maggie was right on her heels.

When Lisa climbed onto her bicycle, she called to the dog and pointed as she commanded her to stay on the side of her bike farthest from traffic.

Maggie was obedient, and the only thing negative she did along the way toward home was bark at a few cars going in the opposite direction.

Lisa felt relief when they made it home safely without any problems. She shuddered to think of what could have happened when Maggie left her grandparents' yard this afternoon and headed for the schoolhouse with no supervision.

Was she really that desperate to see me? Lisa asked herself. *Maybe my hund has insecurities like I do and wants to be with someone who makes her feel safe.*

When she pedaled her bike up her grandparents' driveway, Lisa spotted her grandmother getting out of one of their driver's vehicles. Lisa parked her bike near the house and waited for Grandma to join her on the porch, where Maggie had already found a comfortable spot to lie down.

"How was your appointment?" Lisa asked, remembering that Grandma had mentioned this morning that she planned to see the chiropractor.

"It went well. My sore shoulder feels much better than it did yesterday." Grandma took a seat in one of the wicker chairs and motioned for Lisa to do the same. "When you came in on your bike, I saw that Maggie was with you and felt relieved. The little *schtinker* slipped out the front door when I went to get the mail shortly before my driver, Ida, picked me up. I called and called but she kept running, and then Ida showed up and I had to either go or be late for my appointment." Grandma looked down at Maggie, who lay with her eyes shut, apparently sleeping. "Did she end up at the schoolhouse?"

"Jah. I discovered her on the porch when I came out after the students had left for home." Lisa drew in some air and released it slowly. "She did well staying with me on the way home, but I shudder to think of what could have happened if she'd wandered out into the road on the way to the schoolhouse when she was by herself." She leaned down and stroked the dog's silky ears. "I've become attached to Maggie, and I want to keep her safe."

Grandma nodded. "Of course you do, and I'll do my best to make sure she doesn't get out again."

"I can't believe you've been diagnosed with hypothyroidism," Lois said after she and Orley left the doctor's office and stood waiting outside the building for their driver to pick them up. "No wonder you've been so tired and have gained some weight you've been unable to lose."

"I've also had some joint pain and noticed my fingernails have become really brittle, not to mention that I have experienced an intolerance to cold. I thought they were just signs of old age creeping in." Orley shrugged. "But at least what I have can be controlled by taking thyroid medicine. I will have to get my blood tested from time to time, though, in case the dosage needs to be adjusted."

"I'm so glad I talked you into seeing the doctor and that it was diagnosed quickly. And as the doctor explained, hypothyroidism develops slowly and may go unnoticed for a long time. I was surprised when he also stated that if left untreated, you could develop other symptoms, such as high cholesterol; a slow heart rate; puffiness in the face, feet, or hands; a loss of balance; hoarseness; or eyebrows that have thinned or completely diminished."

"Too bad there isn't something natural I can do about my sluggish thyroid to make it work better." Orley frowned. "I hate taking pills."

"Tsk, tsk," Lois said. "Don't forget, the doctor also suggested taking iodine supplements because it's an essential mineral for good thyroid function." She touched his arm. "He also talked about making some dietary changes and reminded you of the importance of regular exercise."

Orley stroked his throat and grimaced. "Wish I was a kid again and could be healthy as a horse like I once was."

"Not all horses are healthy, you know."

Orley was about ready to comment when their driver pulled up. "Good," he muttered under his breath. *Now at least we won't have to talk about this anymore. Of course, the subject will probably be brought up again after we get home.*

Chapter 13

Sugarcreek

The first Saturday in November was Paul's day off, so he had decided to make a stop at the Christian bookstore in town to pick up a book his aunt had ordered a few weeks ago. Running errands for Aunt Emma when he was free to go was the least Paul could do, considering that she did his laundry and fed him most meals. When Paul first moved in with his aunt and uncle and started working for Uncle Abe, he'd insisted on paying something for his room and board. But he looked forward to the day when he could rent or buy his own home. He liked the idea of being completely independent.

On his way to the bookstore, he noticed a place for sale. It had a good-sized home on sprawling property and a few outbuildings as well. Paul could see that the place had electricity connected to it, and if he was really interested in buying the home, after he'd made the purchase, the power would have to go. But for now he was only looking and getting a feel for the area. At this point he could easily look farther out from town and see what else was available.

He coaxed his horse to move more quickly by jiggling the reins. *Maybe out of curiosity, I should do some pricing on the homes around the area.*

It wasn't long before the businesses came into view, and Paul watched for the bookstore.

As usual on weekends, a good number of cars and people were in town. He hoped to find a place available at one of the hitching rails to secure his horse and buggy and was pleased when he spotted one. No cars had been parked close, which was good. It wasn't often that a car would try to park near the horse and buggy areas, but there were those rare times.

Paul guided his horse, Chester, to the hitching rail and climbed out of his buggy. He felt at ease riding in his own rig again and had missed it. At least Paul could leave some of his personal things in the carriage and know that they would be at his disposal any time of the day or night. Both Chester and Paul's closed-in buggy had been transported to Sugarcreek a week ago, and he was glad to have them. Paul had missed the well-behaved gelding. Chester also had plenty of get-up-and-go when it was needed, which Paul appreciated. Neither his aunt's nor his uncle's horse, although dependable, had the energy Chester did.

Paul secured the horse and gave him a gentle pat. "You behave yourself while I'm gone now, ya hear?"

Chester's ears pricked up, and he nickered. Paul took that as a sign that his horse had been listening and understood his master's request, although some would say that the average horse would not understand Pennsylvania Dutch or English.

As Paul headed toward the bookstore, he thought about where else he'd like to go while in town. When Paul entered the place of business a few minutes later, he heard soft music playing in the background. Several shoppers mingled among the books and other items displayed around the store. The Mennonite woman up front by the register smiled as Paul approached. "Hello there. If you're looking for anything special, just let me know."

Paul nodded and had just started down an aisle when he spotted Lisa's grandmother looking at some of the gift items.

"Hello, Marlene," Paul spoke in Dutch in a quiet tone as he stepped up beside her, not wanting to disturb the other patrons. "How are you today?"

"I'm doing just fine. Are things going well with you?"

Paul gave a nod. "Have you been enjoying your new kitchen cabinets?"

Wearing an enthusiastic smile, she bobbed her head. "Oh, jah, very much. You do good work, Paul, and I appreciate your efforts in making the cabinets just the way I had wanted."

"I'm glad you're happy with them."

"What brings you into the Christian bookstore this morning?" she questioned.

"Came to get a Bible study book that my aunt ordered."

"I came to buy a few books for my granddaughter, but as you can see, I've been looking at a few gift items as well." Marlene gestured to a variety of religious plaques on the display table. "During Lisa's free time she can often be found reading a book. She especially has a fascination with history and enjoys reading novels or nonfiction books that are set during historical times."

"I see." Paul was tempted to tell Marlene that he knew Lisa when she was a girl and mention how she had liked to read back then too. But he decided it was best not to say anything, at least at this time.

Paul glanced at the rows of books on the shelves. Although he wasn't much of a book reader, he didn't mind looking at magazines like the *Connection* or the woodworking publications.

"I wish Lisa had more of a social life. She's been reserved and has kept to herself a lot ever since she came to live with us after her parents died." Marlene heaved a heavy-sounding sigh. "She needs to spend time with other young people her age. Maybe then she would become more social instead of distancing herself so much."

Paul let what she'd said sink in. *I thought it was me or the things I've said that made her clam up.* "So it's not just me she acts quiet and kind of timid around?"

"Oh no. Lisa is that way with almost everyone. It took several years for her grandpa and me to get her to open up and talk more to us." Marlene shifted the sack she held over to her other hand. "But Jerry and I have kept trying, and some of the barriers have come down—at least between us and our granddaughter. And of course she was able to pursue a teaching career and has done well around the children."

"That's good to hear." Ever since he was a boy, Paul had taken pleasure in fixing things, and at the moment, he wished there was something he could do to fix Lisa so that she would become the happy, carefree young girl he used to know. But was that same person still in there, or had Lisa closed the door on her past?

Maybe if I try to befriend her, I'll succeed, he thought. *I just need to figure out something we can talk about that she might be interested in. I'd like to be the one to help Lisa step out of her comfort zone and become more outgoing. Maybe I could ask her what she likes to do as a hobby, or I could talk to her about Maggie. Guess now isn't the time to be thinking about this, though. I need to get my errands run.*

Paul said goodbye to Marlene and headed for the counter to pick up his aunt's book. Right now his goal was to drop the book off to Aunt Emma after he left the store, and then he'd be heading to Walnut Creek to see if Orley Troyer had gotten any new milk bottles since the last time he'd visited Memory Keepers Antique Store.

Walnut Creek

Lois had gone to the post office to get the mail she'd received from her Dear Caroline column, and when she returned to the antique shop she found Orley sitting behind the front counter with a disgruntled expression.

"What's wrong?" she asked, approaching him.

"I've been going over the mail we received at home this morning and brought to the shop because we were running late and didn't have time to go through it there."

"Is there something in the mail that has you upset?"

"Jah." Orley shook his head as he held up a piece of paper. "It's a note from our bank, letting us know that a check one of our out-of-state customers gave us two weeks ago bounced." He released a puff of air. "Now we're stuck paying the fee."

Lois was about to comment, but Orley rushed on. "In addition to that, we're out the money we thought we'd made when that antique desk the man bought left our store."

"This kind of thing can happen sometimes," Lois said. "We'll need to be more careful and make sure that unless we know the customers personally, we ask for proper identification, as well as a working phone number, whenever we take a check."

Orley nodded. "Jah, and since we aren't set up to take credit card payments and have always expected our customers to pay with cash or a check, we take a chance whenever someone pays by check and we know very little, if anything, about them."

"That's especially true if a customer is from out of town."

"It can be downright frustrating." Orley reached for two pieces of candy from the bowl they kept on the counter for customers to enjoy and popped one into his mouth.

Lois frowned. ""You eat too many *schleckerei*, husband, and the candy won't remove the frustration you're obviously feeling right now."

He shook his head. "I don't eat too many sweets."

Lois pointed to the candy dish. "I've noticed that this bowl of candy has gone down considerably since we first set it out, and I don't recall seeing many of our customers helping themselves to any of it."

Orley gave no response as he averted his gaze.

"I'm not trying to pick on you this morning, but too much sugar is bad for a person's health, and you're already dealing with one health issue due to your hypothyroidism." She paused for a few seconds then continued. "You're doing well so far on the medication the doctor prescribed, but you sure don't need another problem if your blood sugar gets out of control."

Orley put the other piece of candy in his mouth. "I'm fine, so don't worry. A little bit of sugar never hurt anyone." He looked at Lois pointedly. "I hope you don't start hiding candy and other sweets from me like that woman I read about in *The Budget* the other day."

"What woman? What did it say about her?" Lois questioned.

Orley rested his elbows on the countertop. "Apparently her husband was hooked on a certain kind of candy, and so she decided to hide it someplace where she thought he'd never find it."

Lois leaned forward, eager to hear more of this story. "Did she discover such a place?"

"Sure enough. That determined lady placed the candy in a plastic ziplock bag and hid it in the top part of the toilet tank." He scrunched up his nose. "Can you imagine such a thing?"

Lois chuckled. "No, I certainly can't. And don't you worry, because I would never go that far to hide candy from you." She shook her finger at him. "But if you don't behave yourself, I might quit buying it to set out here in the store."

He gave her a pouty little-boy look, with his lower lip protruding. "I won't eat too much candy. I promise."

Lois was about to comment when the bell on the front door jangled and a customer stepped in. This discussion, if it needed to go further, could wait for another time.

Orley smiled at the young man who had entered the shop, and he stepped out from behind the counter. "Guder mariye. It's nice to see you again, Paul."

"Good morning. It's my pleasure to see you too." Paul gave Orley a hearty handshake. "I came in to see if you may have gotten any more milk bottles since the last time I came here."

Orley gave a nod. "A few. I'd planned to call and let you know, but I misplaced your number. Would you like me to show them to you now?"

"Jah, please do."

Orley led the way to the section in the store where a large selection of old bottles and jars was displayed. He gestured to the five new milk bottles. "Are any of those close to what you've been lookin' for?"

"Unfortunately, none of them are like the old bottle that used to belong to my grandma." Paul shook his head. "Sure wish I hadn't accidentally broken hers."

Orley reached under his glasses and rubbed the bridge of his nose. "I sure feel bad about losin' the phone number where you could be reached. If you'll give it to me again, I'll put it in a safe place and give you a call when I get more vintage milk bottles in the store."

"I'd appreciate that." Paul told Orley the number, and Orley wrote it down on the small tablet he'd taken from his trousers pocket along with a pen.

"Have you been keeping busy with your carpentry work?" Orley asked, taking their conversation in another direction.

"Definitely. My uncle's business is growing, and we've been busier than ever lately. If things keep going like they are currently, he may have to hire another carpenter who is able to work full-time."

"How many people does he have working for him now?"

"Just me and my seventeen-year-old cousin Kevin. My uncle is still hands-on with his business, so when he's not out giving bids to prospective customers about work they want done, he's on the job working with me, Kevin, or Gary Yoder, who started working for my uncle a few months before he hired me. Gary has his own business raising goats, so unfortunately he can only work part-time for my uncle."

"It's great that Abe's business is doing so well. Not every business can say the same."

"I understand. I heard that many of the restaurants in the area are short on help so they've had to cut back on the hours they're open for business."

Orley rolled his shoulders, as if his shirt was causing discomfort. "It's a shame that so many young people these days either don't want to work anymore, or they're only looking for high-paid positions. Back when I was still single, I rarely was out of work. Course I wasn't picky and would have done most any job that had been offered to me." He looked right at

Paul. "You strike me as bein' the same way. Am I right about that?"

Before Paul could respond, another customer entered the store. Since Lois had gone to the back room with their mail from both home and the store, Orley excused himself to go wait on the middle-aged English woman. As he approached the front of the store, he noticed that the bowl of candy was missing from the checkout counter. *That fraa of mine—she worries too much about my health, and apparently she doesn't trust me either.*

Although Paul hadn't found what he'd come for, he figured he might as well look around to see if anything else might catch his eye. So after Orley walked away, Paul meandered around the store, checking things out. Orley and his wife had acquired some pretty nice things to sell in their antique shop. One unusual piece in particular that he'd noticed in the old tool section caught Paul's eye. It was an antiquated-looking drill that hadn't been used in a good many years. Paul was tempted to buy it but changed his mind since it wasn't something he would use on the job and would end up being just a novelty piece.

While browsing farther along the other side of the store, Paul noticed several old books that made him think of Lisa. He remembered once again how, when they were children, she had been a bookworm—always reading in her free time. After talking with Lisa's grandmother this morning, Paul believed he may have discovered a topic that he could discuss with Lisa. As soon as he got the chance, he would invite Lisa to come here to Memory Keepers with him and show her the old books they had for sale. He hoped she would be willing to accompany him.

And who knows, Paul thought, feeling a ray of hope, *the topic of books might give Lisa a spark of enthusiasm, and talking about books could even jog her memory.*

Chapter 14

Sugarcreek

A brisk breeze blew in through an open window in Deacon Herschberger's buggy shed where church was being held. Lisa shivered, wishing she had put on something heavier before rushing out the door. She'd noticed that the majority of the congregation had worn heavier clothing today. She felt silly only having her lightweight shawl for warmth. *What was I thinking? I should have gone back into the house before leaving for church and gotten my black jacket to wear under the shawl.*

Lisa rubbed her chilly hands together, hoping to warm them up and wishing someone would close the window on the women's side of the room. There was no doubt about it—the colder weather had arrived, and like it or not, soon winter would be upon them.

Of course, Lisa thought, *despite the frigid weather that will be coming within the next few months, there'll be good times to look forward to. The schoolchildren will enjoy frolicking in the snow during recess. We'll also have sledding, ice-skating, and caroling as we approach the Christmas holiday.* It was fun to take part in some of the outdoor activities—especially when Lisa could do it with her students. But when it came to doing things with other young people her age, Lisa usually turned down most invitations that involved outdoor winter activities. Since she loved to sing, Christmas caroling was the only exception.

When another waft of air blew in, Lisa wrapped her shawl around her shoulders a little tighter, and her attention returned to the sermon being preached on the topic of friendship. The minister quoted from the book of Proverbs, chapter 18, verse 24: "A man that hath friends must shew himself friendly: and there is a friend that sticketh closer than a brother."

Lisa listened as the preacher went on to say that everyone needs good Christian friends for fellowship, for fun times, and to share one another's burdens.

"It's not good for people to close themselves off from others for fear of getting hurt. We are all imperfect and make mistakes, but mistakes can be forgiven." The minister's gaze traveled around the room. "Ecclesiastes 4:9 says: 'Two are better than one; because they have a good reward for their labour.'"

Lisa pressed her body firmly against the unyielding wooden bench she sat upon. It hadn't been as though no one had ever invited her to events in the community. Others might see her as the unfriendly type, but they didn't understand Lisa's need to protect herself from the possibility of having her heart being broken by allowing anyone besides her grandparents to get close to her. Other than Yvonne, Lisa had no friends near her age, and the truth was Lisa and Yvonne didn't see each other much outside of teaching school and attending church every other Sunday.

Am I going against God's Word by not establishing more friendships? Lisa wondered. *Should I attend more young people's gatherings and try to engage in conversation with those I don't know very well? Do I dare take a chance?*

The pounding of hooves in the yard outside the shop brought Lisa's thoughts to a halt. She craned her neck to look out the window. *Oh no! It looks like some of the horses broke free from the hitching line.*

When Paul heard the commotion outside, he knew instinctively what had happened. He also knew that if the horses weren't rounded up quickly, they could leave the yard and end up out on the road.

Without hesitation, he left his seat and followed three other young men out the door. Although it would mean missing part or all of the minister's sermon on friendship, Paul did what he felt was right. Someone had to get the horses secured again, and it would take more than one man to do it.

When Paul stepped into the yard, he quickly held up his arms as one of the five horses approached, tossing its head from side to side. "Whoa, now. Steady, boy." Paul reached out to grab the horse's halter, but a second horse passed by in a flash, followed by two more energetic horses.

Paul continued to wave his arms, as did the other three men who had come outside to help get the horses back where they belonged. Apparently none of the stubborn animals wanted to be caught, for they kept running around the yard, leading the men on a merry chase.

Just then, Aaron Wengerd came out of the shop and joined the pursuit, but the horses kept going at lightning speed. They circled the building where church was still taking place, thundered across the front lawn, and headed in the direction of the barn.

In some ways Paul felt relieved that his horse wasn't among those that had broken free. On the other hand, Chester would have been easy to catch, because all Paul would have had to do was just give a whistle and the gelding would've come right to him. Even Uncle Abe's horse, Cinnamon, would have been easy to catch. These crazy horses, however, weren't familiar with Paul, and he wasn't even sure who owned them.

As luck would have it, or by divine intervention, all the horses went straight into the barn.

"Let's put 'em in the stalls," one of the men hollered. "Then we can go out to the hitching line and make sure all the other horses are still there and secured."

Paul was the last man to enter the barn, and after quickly shutting the door, he joined the others in getting the horses put safely in stalls. Once that was done, they headed out to the area where the horses had been tethered.

Paul felt relief seeing that Chester had remained secure, along with all the others. Apparently only part of the line had broken, which should be easy to fix.

"Let's head back to church now. The horses can remain in the barn, and we can take care of the line after our service and noon meal is over," one of the other men directed. He had the beginning of a beard, which indicated that he was newly married.

Paul gave Chester a few pats, told him to be good, and started back toward the shop. Hopefully they hadn't been gone long enough to miss the rest of the minister's sermon. Paul had enjoyed listening to the scriptures that the preacher had quoted on the topic of friendship. He wondered if Lisa had appreciated them too.

Paul swiped a hand through his damp hair. *There I go thinking about her again. Why can't I get Lisa out of my thoughts?*

Before reentering the buggy shed for church, Paul tucked the ends of his rumpled, sweaty shirt back inside the front of his black trousers and made sure his vest looked okay. It was a miracle that he and the other fellows who'd chased after the horses and done all that waving looked even halfway presentable now.

After the noon meal was over, some people left for home, while others sat or stood around visiting for a while. Paul had helped repair the hitching line and scanned the remaining people to see if he could locate Lisa anywhere. He saw no sign of her talking to any of the women who remained and didn't see her grandparents either. Had they left without him noticing, or could they be in the house talking with the hosts of today's church service?

Paul glanced at the field where the buggies had been parked and saw Lisa walking toward one of the carriages, which he assumed belonged to her grandfather. He rubbed his hands briskly together to warm them from the cold. *This is my chance to talk to Lisa, so I'd better take it now, before she leaves.*

He hurried across the field and reached Lisa before she stepped into the buggy. "Hey, Lisa, can I talk to you for a moment?"

She turned, and a flush of red erupted on her cheeks. "Umm. . . sure."

Paul took a few more steps until he stood beside her. "I stopped by Memory Keepers Antique Store yesterday and noticed that they have quite a few old books." He transferred his weight from one foot to the other. "So I was wondering if you'd like to go there with me this coming Saturday."

"How did you know I like to read?" Lisa looked at him with a curious expression.

"Umm. . ." Paul hesitated, giving a little kick to a clump of weeds. He had wanted to talk to her days ago, in order to get to know her better, but hadn't had the opportunity until now. He felt funny at this point using the information from what Lisa's grandmother had told him about her and then utilizing it to try to convince this young woman into going to the antique store with him.

I'd best be honest with Lisa. "Your grandmother told me the other day that you liked to read historical books. And when I was at Memory Keepers I noticed they had a shelf with a nice amount of old literature there."

"And you thought of me?" Lisa spoke in a soft tone as she tilted her head from side to side, as though trying to decide. Finally, when Paul thought she was not going to answer, she said in a near whisper: "Jah, that would be nice."

Looking straight into her eyes, Paul smiled. "That's great. How about if I come by and pick you up around ten o'clock Saturday morning? Or would you rather leave later than that?"

"Ten is fine."

"Sounds good." Paul couldn't believe Lisa had agreed to go with him, and he hoped she would enjoy visiting the antique store and looking at the old books.

"Are ya ready to go, fraa?" Jerry asked, nudging Marlene's arm as they stood outside of the buggy shed.

She could see her granddaughter standing near their carriage with Paul. *I hope in time a spark of interest will grow between them.*

Marlene looked at Jerry and shook her head. "Not quite. Let's wait till Paul and Lisa are finished talking." She pointed toward their buggy. "And let us keep our voices down so no one hears us talking."

A good many people were still milling about getting ready to go, and some were in the process of leaving on foot or with their horse and buggy. Marlene didn't want her and Jerry's private conversation to be heard by anyone.

The wrinkles in Jerry's forehead deepened. "Why do we have to wait? It's chilly out here, and I'd like to get home. I'm sure Paul and Lisa won't mind if we show up at our buggy while they are talking. I mean, what could they have to say to one another that they wouldn't want us to hear?"

"I'm cold too, but they shouldn't be long." Marlene rolled her eyes. "And seriously, Jerry, can't you remember how it was when you were a young man speaking to a girl you might have an interest in?"

His brows lifted high on his forehead. "Has Paul given you some reason to believe he's taken an interest in our *grossdochder*?"

"He hasn't actually said so, but I've seen the way he looks at her."

"Oh? How's that?"

"Your voice is getting louder." Marlene placed one finger against her lips and made sure she spoke quietly. "You know very well what I'm talking about. Now can we stay here on the porch until Paul moves away from our carriage?"

Jerry gave a quick nod and stuffed his hands inside of his jacket. "I'll wait as long as you say, dear matchmaker. It would be nice if that young man took an interest in our granddaughter."

I agree. Marlene made no comment as they remained on the porch. *I can't help being curious about what he's saying to Lisa.* When she saw Paul move away from their buggy and head toward the line of horses, she touched her husband's arm and said, "Okay, we can go now. Let's not keep our granddaughter waiting."

Now it was Jerry's turn to roll his eyes. "You're so predictable."

Lisa watched as Paul walked away. She couldn't believe she had agreed to go to the antique store in Walnut Creek with him. *What was I thinking?* she asked herself as she climbed into the back of her grandfather's buggy. Lisa looked off toward the road as another buggy pulled out to leave. *Guess I took today's sermon on friendship to heart. When the minister spoke on the subject, I couldn't help feeling as though he was speaking to me.*

Lisa's thoughts refocused as she saw Grandpa head over to the hitching line to get his horse. A few minutes later, Grandma showed up and climbed into the buggy. She turned to look at Lisa and smiled. "Was that Paul I saw you talking to a bit ago?"

"Jah. He mentioned that the antique store in Walnut Creek has some old books for sale, and he asked if I'd like to go with him this Saturday."

Grandma gave Lisa a wide smile. "It was nice of him to think of you. I'm sure you'll have a good time browsing around the antique store—especially if there are old books to look at."

Lisa nodded. She hoped her grandmother wouldn't make a big deal of this. She wasn't going on a date—it was just a friendly trip to look at some vintage books.

"Will Paul be picking you up, or are you supposed to meet him there?"

"He said he'd pick me up around ten o'clock Saturday morning."

"That'll be nice. It will give you two a chance to get to know each other a little better."

"I suppose." Lisa sucked in her lower lip while dropping her gaze to her lap. *Great. Looks like she is going to make something out of this.*

"Aren't you eager to get better acquainted with Paul? Or is there something you don't like about him?" Grandma questioned.

"I have nothing against him, and I don't know Paul well enough yet to decide whether there is something I don't like about him," Lisa answered honestly. "After the message we heard today on friendship, I thought it would be good if I tried to be a little friendlier, so I agreed to go to the antique store with him."

"That's *wunderbaar*, Lisa. You need more friends." There seemed to be a twinkle in Grandma's eyes as she smiled at Lisa.

Lisa wished now that she had never told her grandmother about Paul's invitation. But if she'd kept quiet about this, then when he came to pick her up, she would have to offer her grandparents some sort of explanation.

She felt relieved when Grandpa showed up and got his horse hitched to the buggy. Hopefully now Grandma would take her attention off Lisa and focus on something else, because usually she and Grandpa had plenty to talk about on the way home from anywhere. Most likely today it would be about the horses that broke free from the line and created a ruckus outside the shop where church had been held. In fact, Lisa hoped the topic was brought up as soon as Grandpa got into their carriage. She sure didn't need him to start asking questions about why Paul had been talking to her outside the buggy.

"Everyone set to go?" Grandpa asked, taking up the reins.

"I'm ready," Grandma replied.

"Me too, and I think I'll take a nap on the way home." Lisa leaned against the back of her seat and closed her eyes. At least this way she wouldn't have to answer any questions.

Chapter 15

Paul snapped the reins to get Chester moving faster. He thought about how he'd fussed earlier over which shirt to wear and ended up choosing his new pale purple one. But then he'd spilled some hot chocolate down the front of it before he left to pick up Lisa and had to change into one of his older light blue shirts.

Paul reflected on how his aunt had come into the room before he'd left and said she'd thought he had been wearing a new shirt earlier. Paul's ears had burned with the embarrassment he'd felt when admitting that he'd managed to drip hot chocolate on the shirt. Aunt Emma had put Paul's mind at ease, though, when she'd told him in her usual calm voice not to worry, that she would put something on his new shirt to keep it from staining and would soak it for a while too. She'd also assured Paul that the older shirt he'd changed into looked fine. Then, just before Paul walked out the door, Aunt Emma had said she hoped he would have a nice time visiting the antique store with Lisa.

Paul had sure been surprised when Lisa agreed to go with him to Memory Keepers. He hoped she would find some books she liked and wondered if Lisa would be more talkative today.

I'll have to make it my job to see that she is, he told himself as he urged his horse on.

Paul wondered if Lisa had spoken to her grandmother about him knowing she had a love for reading. He hadn't handled what he'd learned with much thought and didn't want to cause a problem between Lisa and her grandmother.

Paul's plan was to gain Lisa's trust, and if and when she began to open up more, he would tell her that they used to know each other when they were children. If he could get her to remember that, it might bring other things from the past into focus as well.

Paul felt good about the possibility of helping Lisa and wished he had thought to do it sooner—when he'd first realized who she was.

"Better late than never," he said aloud. "But I can't rush into it. I need to wait for the right time to tell her."

Chester's ears twitched, and he let out a whinny.

"That's okay, bud. I wasn't talkin' to you." Paul grinned. Chester had always been attentive to his words, even if the shiny brown horse didn't always understand what had been said.

When the Schrocks' place came into view, Paul slowed Chester and guided him up the driveway. He angled to the right, stopped at the hitching rail, and stepped out of the buggy. Paul had just secured his horse when Lisa came out of the house. She wore a black shawl over an aqua dress, which went well with her blond hair peeking out the front part of her stiff white head covering. Lisa walked with her head held high, but her gaze seemed to be on Chester rather than Paul.

"You have a nice-looking *gaul*," she said. "I like the white blaze on his head."

"Me too." Paul smiled and gave the horse a few pats. "His name is Chester, and he's usually quite friendly, even to strangers."

Lisa reached up and stroked the horse's neck. "Hello, Chester. I'm glad to meet you."

Chester flicked his ears and bobbed his head, as though he'd understood what she had said.

Paul chuckled. "I think he agrees with you."

Lisa looked at Paul, and when she gave a brief smile, he got a glimpse of the Lisa he'd known when she was a girl.

"Shall we head out?" he asked.

"Jah." Lisa climbed in and seated herself on the left side of the buggy, which was where the passenger up front always sat.

Paul released Chester from the rail, climbed in on the right side of the buggy, and took hold of the reins. Then he backed his horse up and headed down the driveway. "Even though it's a little chilly, at least the sun's shining today," Paul commented as he turned his horse and carriage onto the road.

"Jah."

He glanced over at Lisa and saw that her fingers were clutched tightly around her purse straps as she stared straight ahead. Paul wondered if he should try to strike up a conversation at this point or just ride quietly into Walnut Creek.

Guess I'll keep quiet unless she says something to me, he decided. *Maybe we both need to just relax and enjoy the scenery.*

Walnut Creek

When Lisa entered the antique store, where a vintage Welcome sign and the chime of a bell above the door greeted them, her eyes widened. She had never been in this shop before, and she detected the scent of old wood, leather, dust, and a strange musty odor. From where she stood, Lisa's eyes began to study many of the old things that were on display around her. She was fascinated with the uneven texture of chipped paint on a distressed cabinet and the crisp white doilies draped over some of the end tables. Most of the aisles were narrow, with table displays on both sides and shelves and more antique furniture along three of the walls. Lisa was eager to check it all out.

"Let's go up to the checkout counter before we start looking at things," Paul said. "I'd like you to meet the owners of Memory Keepers."

Lisa hesitated, but when Paul gave her arm a tug, she followed him to the front of the store where a middle-aged Amish couple stood.

When they stepped out from behind the counter, Paul greeted them with a handshake, and then he gestured to Lisa. "Orley and Lois, I'd like you to meet my friend Lisa Miller." He turned to face Lisa before gesturing to the Troyers. "These nice folks are Orley and Lois."

Lisa's face warmed as she shook hands with the Amish couple. It had taken her by surprise when Paul referred to her as his friend, since they didn't know each other very well. *But then,* she reasoned, *it would have sounded odd if he'd called me his acquaintance.*

"It's nice to meet you, Lisa," Lois and Orley said at the same time.

Still feeling a bit shy, she gave a quick nod. "Nice to meet you too."

Orley looked at Paul with furrowed brows. "Sorry to say, but I haven't gotten in any new milk bottles since the last time you were here."

"That's okay," Paul responded. "We mostly came by so Lisa could look at your old books. She's a schoolteacher and likes to read."

"We have plenty of books here to look at." Orley pointed to one of the shelves across the room. "Maybe there will be something there to your liking."

"Okay, I'll take a look." Lisa began moving in that direction and paused to glance over her shoulder to see if Paul would join her. Instead of following her, he continued to visit with the Amish couple.

Making her way down one of the aisles, Lisa paused to slide her fingertips over the wood grain of a handmade cheese board. She was fascinated with several old trunks with leather handles, a pitted metal oil lantern, some cigar boxes with polished stone inlays, and an intricate thimble collection. She had never seen so many vintage items all in one place and hadn't even viewed everything.

As Lisa approached the bookshelf, the old wooden floorboards creaked beneath her feet. Even the ceilings and walls of the building had a vintage feel about them.

She reached up to pull one of the books off the shelf and noticed a cloth Amish doll with no face. A doll such as this was no longer played with by most Amish children the way it had been many years ago. Lisa had read once that the dolls were left faceless because everyone was alike in God's eyes and that lack of facial features agreed with the Bible's commandment against graven images. She'd also read that antique Amish dolls made for and used by Amish children from the past were highly collectible and could sell for as much as $1,000. However, the newly made faceless dolls found in many tourist shops in Amish country sold for much less.

Lisa had never owned a doll without a face like the one her grandmother had sitting on a straight-backed chair in her sewing room. When Lisa had first come to live with her grandparents, Grandma had let her play with the doll. Although she'd thought it was strange for the cloth doll to have no face, Lisa had found comfort in holding it. Even now, whenever she saw the faceless doll in Grandma's sewing room, Lisa was tempted to pick it up and give it a hug.

She turned her attention back to the book she held and opened it to the copyright page. It had been written in 1952 and was about two young orphaned sisters who had been sent to a boarding school that was owned by a mean woman who treated the children who lived there badly.

Lisa bit the inside of her cheek. *If it weren't for Grandpa and Grandma taking me in, I'd be an orphan too. I'm ever so thankful that they have always been kind and treated me well.*

She put the book back on the shelf and reached for another, but before she could open it to the first page, Lois stepped up to her.

"Have you found any books that interest you?" she asked.

Lisa shook her head. "Not yet, but then I've only looked at one."

"The book you're holding in your hand?"

"No, this is the second one I've pulled off the shelf, but I haven't really looked at it yet." Lisa held the musty-smelling book against her chest.

"I enjoy reading and writing too," Lois said.

"Are you an author?"

Lois's cheeks colored a bit. "Oh, no, nothing like that. I do enjoy writing letters though."

Lisa wasn't sure how to comment, so she merely offered the older woman what she hoped was a pleasant smile.

"Paul mentioned that he's from Sugarcreek. Is that where you live?" Lois questioned.

"Jah."

"Sugarcreek is a lovely town. Sometimes Orley and I go over there just to eat at the big Dutch Valley Restaurant. Oh, and we always enjoy looking at the giant-sized cuckoo clock in Sugarcreek." Lois grinned as she bobbed her head. "The huge timepiece was built in 1972, and every thirty minutes, Bavarian music is played as a three-foot doll-like couple on tracks dances the polka." Lois grinned. "But then, you probably knew all that."

Lisa nodded. *This woman is so outgoing and friendly,* she thought. *I suppose she has to be since being a business owner means greeting people on a regular basis.*

"Have you always lived in Sugarcreek?" Lois asked.

"No, I came there when I was a young girl, still in school. I lived in Indiana before that."

"That's a lovely state too. What prompted your parents to move to Ohio?"

"My parents died in an accident, so I went to live with my grandparents."

"I'm sorry for your loss." Lois placed her hand on Lisa's arm.

Lisa's fingers flexed around the book she held as her gaze bounced from place to place. She felt uncomfortable talking about this, especially with a person she hadn't met until today.

Lisa placed the book back on the shelf. "I've developed a *koppweh,* so

I'm going to tell Paul that I'd like to go."

"I'm sorry to hear you have a headache. Perhaps the musty aroma from the old books is the cause." Lois's words were spoken in a soothing tone.

"Jah, maybe so." Lisa hurried back to the place where Paul stood talking to Orley. "I think the smells in here have given me a headache," she said. "Take your time if you want to look around. I will wait for you in the buggy, and don't hurry on my account. I'll be fine."

Wincing as though he felt her pain, Paul said, "That's too bad, but you don't have to wait alone. I don't need to look at anything in the store today, so we can head out right now."

Lisa felt all her tension release. Although the musty-smelling books may have been part of the reason the headache had come on, most likely it came about from being put in a position where she had to mention her parents' deaths. Lisa was glad the conversation had ended before Lois could ask her more questions.

After Paul and Lisa left the store, Lois joined Orley up front to go over some paperwork they hadn't gotten done yet this morning.

"Paul's friend seems like a nice young woman," Orley commented as Lois stepped behind the counter with him. "Too bad they couldn't have stayed longer."

"I agree. Lisa did seem nice enough, but I believe she's a troubled young woman."

Orley tipped his head. "Oh? What brought you to that conclusion?"

"When I asked if she'd always lived in Sugarcreek, she said she used to live in Indiana and that she'd moved to Ohio after her parents died in an accident."

Orley's brows furrowed. "That's a shame. Did she give you any details on how the mishap occurred?"

"No, and before I could ask any more questions, Lisa announced that she had a *koppweh*, which was why she and Paul left our store so quickly." Lois pursed her lips. "The young woman couldn't even maintain eye contact with me when she spoke."

"We need to pray for her."

"Jah, and if Paul brings Lisa into our shop again, I'm going to see if I can get her to open up and share more about her past with me."

"Dear Caroline is at it again, huh?" Orley gave Lois a crooked grin.

She bobbed her head. "Only this kind of mentoring will be in person, not in my newspaper column."

Sugarcreek

"How's your koppweh?" Paul asked as they neared Lisa's grandparents' house.

She shrugged her shoulders. "A little better. It's not gone, but at least it's not pounding like it was back at the antique store."

"Glad to hear it. Guess you didn't find any of those musty-smelling books that caused the koppweh to be of much interest to you."

"No, but then I didn't get the chance to look at all of them before the headache came on."

"The next time we go looking for books, maybe we should check out the library or Christian bookstore here in Sugarcreek."

Next time? Is Paul suggesting that we should get together again? Lisa chanced a look at him but then turned her head back to focus on the road. "That'd be nice," she said quietly.

"How about next Saturday? Would you be free to go then?"

"I—I think so, but I'll need to check with Grandma first to see if she will need my help with anything that day."

"Okay. I'll give you a call sometime early next week to see if you'll be free, and if you are, we can talk about what time would work best for both of us to go."

"All right. That sounds good." Lisa didn't want to admit it, not even to herself, but she looked forward to spending time with Paul again. He was easy to talk to and didn't ask her a bunch of questions she wasn't willing to answer.

Maybe I could develop a relationship with Paul, Lisa thought as she fiddled with her purse straps. *But only as a friend—nothing else. I definitely have no romantic interest in him, and I'm sure he has none in me either.*

Chapter 16

"What time did you say Paul is supposed to pick you up?" Marlene asked as she and Lisa did the breakfast dishes the following Saturday.

"Ten o'clock." Lisa glanced at the clock on the far wall. "It's only nine thirty, so we have plenty of time to finish the dishes before he arrives."

Marlene nodded. She was glad the young man had taken an interest in her granddaughter. Lisa needed more friends and a social life. And maybe in time, Paul and Lisa would begin courting, which in turn could lead to marriage. That would put Marlene's mind at ease concerning her granddaughter's future. Marlene hated to think of what Lisa's life would be like if she didn't have a husband and family of her own by the time her grandparents died.

I can't worry about it, she told herself. *I just need to pray that things will work out for Lisa according to God's will.* Marlene smiled as she sloshed the sponge over another dirty dish. *And I guess it wouldn't hurt if I invited Paul to join us for a few more meals, although it can't be today, since I have already made other plans for the noon meal.*

Lisa dried the last clean dish and had put it away in the cupboard when she heard Maggie barking by the back door.

"I bet your excitable hund is letting you know that Paul must be here," Grandma said.

"I wouldn't be surprised, although I didn't hear a horse and buggy enter the yard." Lisa opened the door and looked out. No sign of Paul or his horse and buggy.

"No one is there," she said to Grandma. "I think Maggie must have been barking because she needs to go outside."

"You're probably right. She's only been out once this morning."

"I'll go with her." Lisa opened the door wider, and when Maggie bounded out, she followed. She'd barely stepped off the porch when Paul rounded the corner of the house and they nearly collided.

"Wh–where did you come from?" Lisa asked breathlessly as he reached out and clasped her arms.

"I stopped over at the harness shop to talk to your grandpa and left my horse and carriage at the hitching rail there."

Before Lisa could respond, Maggie darted up to Paul and gave a few barks as she pawed at his pant leg.

Lisa clapped her hands. "Maggie, stop it!"

"It's okay." Paul leaned down and patted the dog's head a few times. "How ya doin', girl? Are you happy to see me?"

Woof! Woof! Woof! Maggie's tail swished back and forth in perfect rhythm.

Paul laughed. "I'm glad to see you too."

"I'll take her out to the pen, and then we can go," Lisa said.

"I don't mind taking her while you get whatever you need for the trip to town."

"Danki. I'll meet you by the harness shop."

"I can get Chester and my carriage, so why don't you wait on the porch for me?'"

"Okay." Lisa gave Maggie a few pats before returning to the house. On her way across the yard, Lisa slowed to watch Paul walk and coax the tail-wagging dog to her pen. *It was nice of him to give me a break from taking care of Maggie so I could go inside to get my things.* Lisa felt a little anxious about going with him again, but maybe spending a few hours with Paul would help relieve some of her tension.

"Is Maggie still outside?" Grandma asked as she squeezed some hand lotion into the palms of her hands and rubbed them together.

"Paul's here, and he's taking her out to the pen while I get my things."

"Well, for goodness' sakes, I didn't even hear his rig come in."

"He stopped by the harness shop to say hello to Grandpa, so he tied his horse to the rail over there." Lisa took her jacket and outer bonnet down from the wall peg where she'd hung them last night and then picked up her purse from one end of the counter. "Paul will be picking me up out front shortly."

"I see." Grandma smiled. "I hope you two have a nice ride to the bookstore and that you'll find some books to your liking. Oh, and you may want to consider going to lunch afterward. Wouldn't that be nice?"

"Maybe, but—"

"I would invite Paul to join us for lunch here when you get back, but your grandpa will be attending an auction today. And I have plans to spend the day with my friend Clara, which will include having lunch together."

"That's fine, Grandma. I hope you and Clara will enjoy your day. If Paul and I don't go out to lunch, I'll fix something for myself after he drops me off." Lisa gave her grandmother a hug and headed for the front door. She didn't have to wait long before Paul pulled up with his horse and buggy.

Lisa couldn't help but notice the way Paul's horse pawed at the ground as though he was eager to go. Paul spoke to Chester in a soothing tone, and the horse calmed right down. She waved at Grandpa when he stepped out of his harness shop, and then Lisa climbed into Paul's carriage. A short time later, they were heading toward town.

It was a lovely fall day—a bit crisp, but the sun had come out, and Lisa felt cozy, wearing her warm jacket. She looked forward to visiting the Gospel Shop Christian Bookstore, because she hadn't been there in quite a while.

When they entered the bookstore a short time later, Paul went to look at the study Bibles, while Lisa browsed the section where Christian fiction was sold. He'd only been looking at the Bibles for a few minutes when one of the store clerks stepped up to him.

"May I help you with something?" she asked.

He shook his head. "I'm just checking to see what you have available."

The clerk smiled. "Okay. I'll be at the register if you decide to make a purchase or have any questions."

Paul continued to peruse the different Bible versions, but undecided, he left that section of the store and moved over to where Lisa stood. "How's it going? Have you found anything to your liking?"

She shrugged her slim shoulders. "There are so many good ones to choose from; it's hard to decide."

"Do you normally buy books or check them out at the library?"

"I do both, and sometimes, if I can part with them, I donate books to the library."

Paul smiled. "That's great. I'm sure they appreciate it."

Lisa nodded.

"Are you lookin' for historical fiction or contemporary?"

"I read both, but I favor historical."

Paul pointed to a book with a covered wagon on the cover. "That one looks interesting."

"Jah, but I already have it. In fact, it's one that I'm keeping to read over and over again."

"That good, huh?"

She bobbed her head. "Would you like to borrow the book? It's filled with a lot of action and gives interesting insight as to what the pioneers dealt with during their trip along the Oregon Trail."

"Sounds like something I'd enjoy reading, all right."

"I'll get the book for you when we get back to my grandparents' home."

Paul hoped he had made a little headway, talking to her on a topic she liked. All he had to do later was to accept the loaned book and give it a good read. *Who knows, maybe I'll get into the story and enjoy it.*

When Lisa smiled at Paul, a deep dimple formed in her right cheek. Now this was the old Lisa he remembered seeing so many times when they were children. Paul hoped he would eventually see more of that joyful side of her in the weeks to come.

"Are you hungerich? Would you like to go out someplace to eat lunch?" Paul asked after they'd left the Christian bookstore with their packages.

Lisa hesitated, remembering her grandmother's suggestion that she and Paul should go out for a bite to eat. Of course, Lisa would never be so bold as to suggest going out to lunch with Paul, but since he'd brought it up, she decided to accept his invitation. "That would be nice. Where would you like to eat?"

"How about Dutch Valley Restaurant on Old Route 39? We can order off their menu or choose from the buffet."

"I'm fine with that." Lisa hoped that if anyone they knew saw them together, they wouldn't think she and Paul were on a date, because they certainly were not. They were just two newly acquainted people who'd decided to eat lunch together, and Lisa definitely planned to pay for her own meal.

When Lisa and Paul entered the restaurant a short time later, the delicious aroma of roasted chicken mingling with other food items greeted them. The place was busy, but then again, it was the Saturday lunch hour. She wondered if they would be seated at a table out in the middle of the restaurant, near a window, or in a booth. Lisa didn't have a real preference, because at the moment, her stomach felt empty and she couldn't wait to eat.

Her mouth watered, just thinking about the food available on the buffet. She hadn't realized how hungry she was until now.

They waited their turn to be seated and a few minutes later were taken to a booth not far from the all-you-can-eat barn-raising buffet. Soon a waitress came and asked if they wanted to order off the menu or serve themselves from the buffet.

"I'd like the buffet." Paul gestured to Lisa. "How about you?"

She looked up at the server. "I will have the same."

The dark-haired young waitress smiled. "Good choice. The buffet includes the salad bar, and for an extra ninety-nine cents, you can also get a cup of soup."

"I'll be fine without the soup," Lisa said.

Paul gave a nod. "Same here."

"Would either of you care for something other than water to drink?"

"Water's fine for me," Lisa said.

"Think I'll have a glass of iced tea. With a slice of lemon, please," Paul added.

"Feel free to go up to the buffet anytime. While you're doing that, I'll get your drinks, and they will be waiting for you when you've returned to the table."

After the waitress left, Paul suggested that they bow their heads for silent prayer before going to get their food.

Lisa closed her eyes and lowered her head. *Bless this food to the strengthening of our bodies, Lord. And please help me to think of some things to say during our meal so Paul doesn't think I'm bored with his company.*

She opened her eyes and waited for him to do the same. Apparently Paul had more that he needed to pray about than Lisa did, for his eyes were still shut.

After Paul finished praying, they left their seats and got in line at the salad bar. When it was her turn and she'd picked up a plate, Lisa filled it with lettuce, shredded carrots, and several other fresh vegetables. After adding poppy-seed dressing, she sprinkled some sunflower seeds on top and returned to their table to put the plate down. Paul was right behind her, and they both went back to the buffet to get chicken, ham, mashed potatoes, gravy, and cooked green beans. Normally Lisa didn't eat this much for lunch, and she hoped she'd be able to finish everything she had taken. No doubt she wouldn't be eating much for supper this evening.

She set the warm plate down on the table and slid inside the booth. Then Lisa began to work on her salad, enjoying the tasty flavors of the fresh vegetables. Paul started with his salad too, but he soon went in for the chicken. Lisa took her time eating and noticed that he ate through his food at a quick pace. *I wonder if he'll be going back up to the buffet for seconds. Maybe Paul would get his money's worth here today.*

They ate in silence for a while, and then Paul engaged Lisa in conversation about the book she had told him about. "Does the historical book you have at home mention what kind of food the pioneers ate along their journey?" he asked.

"Yes, it does," Lisa replied. She went on to list all the food items she had read about.

When she'd finished what she had to say on the topic, Paul looked over at her and smiled. "I think I wouldn't mind another piece of that chicken. It's mighty good."

"They've got plenty, so why not help yourself?"

"While I'm up there, can I get you anything?" Paul waited by the table.

Lisa shook her head. "Thanks for offering, but I'm fine with what I still have here to finish."

"Okay." He left his plate and headed off to get back in the buffet line.

Paul has a good appetite, but the amount of food he eats sure doesn't show on him, Lisa mused.

A different server came by and picked up Paul's empty plate, then moved on to another table.

Paul returned, holding a new plate with a couple of things on it. "I sure like their chicken, and the rolls are good, especially with some apple butter."

Lisa nodded as she picked through her salad, skipping most of the lettuce and going in for the other vegetables. She'd eaten what she wanted from her warm plate, leaving some of it behind as well.

As they neared the end of their meal, the waitress came and asked if either of them would like a slice of pie.

Lisa shook her head as she placed both hands on her stomach. "I'm too full to even think about dessert."

"I can't eat anything more either," Paul said. "Maybe some other time we can come in just to sample some pie." He looked at Lisa, as though waiting for an answer, but she made no comment.

Lisa flinched at the eerie sound of sirens out on the road. No doubt there had been an accident somewhere nearby. Her hand trembled as she grabbed for her water glass and took a drink. At the moment, all Lisa wanted to do was go home and take a nap. She'd had enough excitement for one day.

"What's wrong?" Paul asked, leaning forward with his elbows on the table. "Are you grank?"

"No, I. . ." She held her hands against her ears. "The sound of those sirens just makes me feel. . ." Her voice trailed off. Lisa didn't want to talk about this right now.

Paul gave her an understanding nod and picked up the check. "I'll pay the bill now, and we can be on our way."

"Oh. . .uh. . .that's all right. . .I can pay for my own meal." Lisa's voice quivered as she struggled to keep her scattered thoughts from taking over.

He shook his head. "Nope. I invited you out for lunch, and I'd planned on paying from the start." Paul looked straight into Lisa's eyes. "Are you okay with that?"

"Jah, all right."

Lisa carried her purse, followed him to the register up front, and waited until he'd paid for their meal. Thankfully she could no longer hear any sirens, so that helped her relax a bit. When they got back to her grandparents', she would get the book she'd promised to loan Paul and politely tell him that she was tired and needed to lie down for a while. Maybe after a nap she would feel better and could put aside the fear she'd felt hearing those sirens. Lisa had never told anyone before, but whenever she heard sirens, she remembered that dreadful day when she'd lost her dear family members in the tragic accident that had changed her life forever.

Chapter 17

When Paul entered his uncle's barn, his senses immediately recognized the aroma of nose-tickling straw and sweet-smelling hay. He'd come here to groom his horse before starting work and almost wished he could stay here the rest of the day.

Paul glanced at the wooden ladder leading up to the loft, remembering how he'd enjoyed playing in his father's barn when he was a boy. The sounds of rustling hay, creaking boards, and animal noises had always held an appeal for him. He'd even liked listening from the loft when grain spilled into the horses' troughs and bales of hay thumped to the floor.

Paul stood still for several seconds, taking it all in and thinking about the fun he'd had as a young boy. He could almost hear his father's heavy boots thumping across the floor as he headed into his horse's stall for feeding and grooming.

Moving on, Paul gathered the items to groom his horse from the cabinet where he kept them outside of the stall. The barn could be a place to do some deep thinking about his future. What was the Lord's plan for his life? How would he know for sure? Paul's thoughts went to Lisa and how he'd been doing a lot of praying for her. *I hope that I'll see some change in her life. Lisa is a good person, and I want to see her happy again, the way I remember her when we were children.*

Paul carried a couple of brushes he'd chosen, made his way into Chester's stall, and was greeted by an eager-sounding whinny. As he stood inside the cubicle with the currycomb in his hand, Paul's thoughts returned to Lisa. Throughout the final weeks of November, he had stopped at the Schrocks' to see Lisa at least once a week. Although they'd eaten their Thanksgiving meals with their own families, Paul had gone over to see Lisa that evening. He'd enjoyed a piece of pumpkin pie and worked on a puzzle with Lisa, while her grandparents dozed in their comfortable living-room chairs, with Maggie stretched out on the floor between them. Who could blame the nice couple? After a day of eating too much good food, Paul figured most people had probably been resting or sleeping it off that evening.

The more time that Paul spent with Lisa, the more he enjoyed her company. It had even been fun to discuss the historical book she had loaned him previously. Although they seemed to be getting along okay, Paul had not yet mentioned that he'd known Lisa when she was a girl. He didn't feel that it was the right time yet. Paul had to be sure he had gained her trust before he opened up a sensitive topic. His worst fear was that if Lisa felt betrayed by Paul's knowing her previously and not saying anything, then she might become distant again and revert to her timid turtle-like shell. Would she back away from their established friendship? Paul wasn't sure how he would even know when he should tell her the truth. It was one more thing to pray about.

Paul's folks had been disappointed that he hadn't come home for Thanksgiving, but he wasn't ready to visit and take the risk of running into Susan or the so-called best friend who had stolen his girl. At this point, his gut told him to stay put in Ohio, where his heart could continue to heal from the disappointment and hurt he'd left in Indiana.

During a phone call on Thanksgiving morning, Paul's mother told him that Susan and Ervin were officially engaged to be married. The ceremony would take place next year in early May. Paul felt certain that he wouldn't be invited to the wedding, which was fine with him, because he had no desire to watch Ervin and Susan become husband and wife. That would be like pouring vinegar on an open wound. Paul remembered all too well how he'd once soaked a piece of tissue in vinegar and put it up his nose to stop a nosebleed. It had worked well, but not without the misery of burning and stinging like fire while the blood coagulated.

Chester nickered and stomped a front hoof, driving Paul's distasteful memory aside.

"Okay, boy, I hear ya. Let's get this job done." Paul pulled the currycomb slowly through the longer hair running down his horse's neck. As he fought against tangles in Chester's mane, his thoughts returned to Lisa again. "I wonder how long I should wait to tell her. . . ."

"You talkin' to yourself?"

Paul's face warmed as he whirled around at the sound of his uncle's voice. "No, I. . .uh. . .was just thinking out loud."

Uncle Abe chuckled as he stepped inside the stall. "No need to be embarrassed. I do that sometimes too." He put his hand on Paul's shoulder. "Breakfast is ready, and we need to eat soon so we can go bid a few jobs. Kevin will do some cleaning in the shop while we're gone, and my part-time worker will be off today."

"Okay. I'll put Chester's grooming supplies back where they belong, close up his stall, and be right in to eat."

"All right then. I'll let your aunt know that we'll see you at the table soon."

"I'll hurry so I don't hold things up." Paul glanced at Uncle Abe while brushing a little more with the currycomb.

The older man slowed his steps on the way out and spoke to his horse. "I'll be back to get you ready to go, Cinnamon, so for now, enjoy your breakfast."

When his uncle left the barn, Paul expelled a deep breath. *Sure am glad Uncle Abe didn't ask who I was thinking out loud about. He'd probably make a big deal out of it and begin teasing me, saying that Lisa must be my new girlfriend.*

Lisa had no more than stepped onto the schoolhouse porch when it began to snow. She stood watching the fluffy white snowflakes as they drifted to the ground and quickly covered the grass. For a few seconds she had a mental picture of herself as a young girl, standing next to a fat-looking snowman with a knitted scarf around its neck and a man's straw hat on its head. A young brown-haired boy stood beside Lisa, holding a carrot in his gloved hand.

That's really odd, Lisa thought. *From the time I came to live with Grandpa and Grandma Schrock, I don't remember ever building a snowman in their yard, much less with the help of a boy my mind doesn't recognize. Why did that thought come to mind? Who was the boy with the carrot?*

Lisa felt a feeling of heaviness in her limbs as she struggled to remember. *Could this have occurred before the accident that took my mamm, daed, and grosseldere from me?*

Lisa's pensive thoughts evaporated when a group of five schoolchildren filed into the yard, talking, laughing, and pointing up at the now-swirling snow.

"Teacher, can we build a snowman during recess?" Simon Burkholder asked, joining Lisa on the porch.

"That all depends on if there's enough snow built up on the ground by then," she replied. "It could quit snowing before noontime, you know."

With a single-minded expression, he gave his head a vigorous shake. "I'm pretty sure it'll still be snowin' out here."

Lisa gave his shoulder a pat. "We'll have to see how it goes, Simon."

"But if it keeps comin' down like it is now, can we build a snowman?"

She smiled at the determined set of the boy's jaw. "Yes, anyone who wants to join in can help build a snowman."

Simon turned toward the others who had come into the yard, cupped his hands around his mouth, and hollered, "Teacher Lisa said we can build a snowman during noon recess."

A chorus of cheers went up, and Lisa couldn't help but smile. Sometimes, like now, she wished she was still a child. *But then,* she reminded herself, *I'd have to live through the pain of losing my family all over again.*

Walnut Creek

"Now would ya look at that? Here it is only the first Monday of December, and there's *schnee* comin' down hard out there." Orley pointed out their antique shop's front window.

Lois joined him. "Well, for goodness' sakes. That white stuff sure came out of nowhere. The last two weeks of November were chilly, despite the sunshine we had, but there was no sign of snow until now."

"Well, like it or not, looks like a new weather front's come in, and I kinda hope it sticks around for a while." Orley looked at Lois with a wide grin. "I'm sure lookin' forward to ice-skating and sledding again."

She squeezed his arm. "I'm not one bit surprised. I know how much you enjoy frolicking in the snow."

"Jah." Orley gave his full beard a tug. "I wonder if Jeff Davis will want to join me when our hill at home has enough snow for sledding, like he did last year."

"Don't get your hopes up, Husband. With all the responsibilities at the inn he and Rhonda bought before their baby came, Jeff may be too busy to go traipsing and sliding through the slippery snow with you this winter."

Orley's mouth slackened. He reminded her of a little boy who'd been told he couldn't have a bowl of ice cream before going to bed.

"If Jeff isn't available, I'm sure you can find someone else who'd be willing to go sledding with you—one of our neighbor children perhaps."

Orley's eyes brightened, and he snapped his fingers a couple of times. "I know who I can ask."

Lois tipped her head slightly. "Who would that be?"

"Paul Herschberger. It would be an opportunity for me to spend some one-on-one time with him and talk about his *druwwel*."

"What problem is that?"

"The one concerning his friend Lisa."

Her brows furrowed. "Is there some trouble between them?"

"Not exactly. Paul wants to help Lisa regain the part of her memory she lost from childhood, back when they knew each other."

Lois's eyes widened. "This is the first time I've heard anything about that. How long ago did Paul share this information with you?"

"Last week he came by the store while you were at the post office picking up letters that had been sent to your Dear Caroline column." Orley cleared his throat a few times. "Paul shared it in confidence with me, but he said it'd be okay if I told you about Lisa's lapse of memory. I didn't think to tell you about it until now."

"Is there anything more you can share with me about the situation?"

"Sure, I'll tell you everything I know."

Lois listened quietly as her husband repeated the things Paul had told him concerning the deaths of Lisa's parents and paternal grandparents, and how she'd come to live with her maternal grandparents in Sugarcreek. Of course, Lisa had already told Lois about her parents' deaths, but Lois didn't want to interrupt Orley or remind him of what she already knew.

"It must have been very difficult for a young girl to deal with a tragedy like that," Lois said. "I can't begin to imagine how terrible she must have felt."

"You're right—it had to be quite traumatic." Orley moved his head slowly up and down. "Paul also said that Lisa is kind of an introvert with very few friends. He's been working at establishing a friendship with Lisa and wants to tell her that they used to know each other when they were children. But he is waiting for the right time, when he's gained her trust."

"I see." She paused and tapped her chin. "That day he brought Lisa into the shop and I asked what prompted her folks to move to Ohio, Lisa said her parents died and that her grandparents raised her. It wasn't more than a moment later that she developed a headache. Although Lisa said the cause was the musty odor in the shop, I believe otherwise."

"What are you thinking?" Orley's brows lowered.

"I believe from the way she reacted when talking briefly about her past that Lisa has never fully come to grips with it." Lois folded her hands in a prayer-like gesture. "We should definitely keep her and Paul on our prayer list."

"Amen to that."

Their conversation was interrupted when an English couple entered the store and asked if there were any antique tables for sale.

Orley moved away from the window and went to show them where the vintage furniture was located, and Lois walked up to the front register to wait in case the couple decided to purchase something.

She glanced at a plaque hanging on the left of the room that read: God hath said, "I will never leave thee, nor forsake thee." Hebrews 13:5.

Lois closed her eyes briefly. *Heavenly Father, my prayer is that Lisa will know, if she doesn't already, that even though her parents and one set of grandparents are gone, You will never forsake her.*

Sugarcreek

By noon, the ground in the schoolyard was covered with at least two inches of cold, white flakes, and it continued to snow. Excitement ran high when the schoolchildren finished their lunches and hurried to put on their coats, gloves, and boots before running outside. Lisa and Yvonne joined them to watch and supervise.

In no time at all, the children had made numerous footprints, snow angels here and there, and a few snowmen in the yard. Squeals of laughter could be heard as some of the boys chased after a group of girls, with snowballs flying this way and that. The girls gave it right back to the boys, however, and it didn't take long before everyone was drenched with the heavy, wet snow that continued to fall.

Lisa watched as Linda, one of her youngest students, struggled to get up after she'd slipped and fallen. Sharon, an older girl from Yvonne's class, went over to help the crying child get back on her feet.

Lisa smiled as she thought about a saying she'd heard her grandma repeat on several occasions: *"Kindness is like snow: it beautifies everything it falls upon."*

Being kind to others was the way every Christian should act. The ministers in their church district had preached on that topic many times.

Lisa always tried to be kind and patient with her students, even when they became unruly or defiant. Her grandparents had been good role models, and Lisa appreciated the kindness they showed to her, as well as others.

"It's time for the children to go back inside now," Yvonne said, interrupting Lisa's musings. "While they are hanging up their outer belongings to dry, I'll go down to the basement, light the propane stove, and make a big pot of hot chocolate."

"That will be nice. I'll oversee the scholars while you're gone, and once all the younger ones are seated at their desks, I'll send an older student down to help you bring up the hot chocolate and cups for everyone."

Yvonne nodded. "Thank you."

After her friend hung up her outer garments and headed down the steps to the basement, Lisa put her own coat, gloves, and boots away, and then she directed the students to do the same. She hoped the snow would hang around for a few days so that the children could enjoy playing in it again. Truthfully, Lisa looked forward to doing the same. And when she got home this afternoon, she would let her dog out to romp in the snow too. It would give Maggie some exercise that didn't involve chasing the poor cats.

No doubt, Lisa thought, *playing with Maggie in the snow will make me feel like a kid again. And when we come inside, I bet Grandma will fix something warm for me to drink and serve it with some of those peanut butter cookies that she'd begun making before I left for school this morning.*

Although Lisa enjoyed teaching, she had to admit that coming back to the shelter of her grandparents' home would be the best part of her day.

Chapter 18

"I can't believe it's snowing again." Lisa's grandmother peered out the kitchen window, slowly shaking her head. "I thought when it first began snowing three weeks ago that it would have all melted and we wouldn't see any more for a while."

"Unless the weather pattern changes, it appears that we may get a white Christmas this year," Grandpa commented as he picked up the coffeepot and poured himself a second cup of the steaming brew.

The room felt cozy with the warmth and crackle of the wood-burning stove they used for extra heat. Her grandfather would keep it going most of the time during the winter months, and Lisa appreciated the kind gesture. It was nice to come in from the cold and park oneself near the cozy stove to warm up. And it was a good little dryer for all their wet boots they would place by it on chilly days.

"I hope the cold, snowy weather won't keep people from coming out for the students' Christmas program this evening," Lisa spoke up as she carried her breakfast dishes to the sink. "The kinner have worked long and hard on their parts, and they'd be disappointed if we had to cancel or attendance was low."

"I don't think you'll have to worry about that," Grandpa said. "People don't usually stay home because of a little schnee, and the weather report I saw in the paper yesterday made no mention of any severe storms on the horizon."

Lisa released a small sigh of relief. "That is good news." *All I'll need to do before the program this evening is to go over the younger children's parts with them sometime today. Yvonne will do the same with the older students. Hopefully, everything will go smoothly.*

"What a beautiful picture that makes." Grandma pointed out the window. "Look—four cardinals just came to rest on one of the snow-covered trees in our yard."

Grandpa stepped over by them and looked out. "Those are such beautiful *veggel.* And speaking of birds, when I was outside earlier, I saw a pair of ducks near the barn where I spilled some corn the other day."

"Really, that's not something you see every day." Grandma pursed her lips as though in thought.

"I know, but it's true. I enjoyed watching them eat every bit off the ground and felt disappointed when the pair flew away."

"If there was a small pond outside, I wonder if those ducks would come around regularly." Lisa stepped over to the window and looked out just as one of the male cardinals flew out of the tree and landed on a nearby feeder. "Those redbirds are sure pretty, jah?"

"Most definitely. I can't believe how many birds we have in the yard right now. When it started to snow a few weeks ago, we put more feeders out, and now the bird feed is disappearing so quickly."

"That's how it goes," Lisa said. "One bird tells another, and pretty soon a whole flock swoops in, just like those ducks Grandpa saw."

"True, but I don't mind paying the price for birdseed because they're sure fun to watch." Grandpa sipped on his coffee and set it back down on the counter. "I wonder, Marlene, do you think if we had a place to put a water feature in the yard that we could attract some ducks?"

She flapped her hand. "I think you'd be better off just leaving more corn out for them. You could put it in some type of pan, but only this time a little closer to where we could all see them from the house."

Grandpa smiled. "I could give that a try. I've got plenty of corn, so I'll just need a pan to put it in rather than scatter the seed on the ground."

"I'm sure I can find you a good-sized metal container that would be right for the job," Grandma was quick to say. "Maybe we could set the pan near one of the trees within our view while looking out the kitchen window."

"A flower bed farther out in the yard might work." Lisa pointed toward the window.

"Okay, we can try it your way first, and if nothing happens, then we'll put the corn near one of the small trees."

Just then Maggie let out a robust yawn as she stretched and rose up on all fours. Grandpa reached out and gave the dog some attention. She gave a contented grunt and leaned into his fingers as they scratched her back. "You're a good dog, Maggie, and you can be fun to watch too—just as long as you're not chasin' any birds." He shook his head. "They don't like that, and neither do the cats."

Lisa couldn't argue with what her grandfather had said. She enjoyed watching the various kinds of birds that visited their yard, which was why she would scold her dog whenever she bothered them.

Grandma joined Grandpa at the table, where he sat reading the newspaper. "Why are you wearing such a big grin?" she asked, pointing to the newspaper. "Is something funny written in there?"

He gave a nod and snickered. "I'm reading the Dear Caroline column."

"Is that a fact? And what did Caroline say that you think is so humorous?"

"It's not what she said. It's the question one of her readers asked."

"What did she ask?"

"Oh, it wasn't a woman who wrote the letter. It was a man."

Lisa watched in amusement as Grandma's eyes widened and her brows lifted high on her forehead. "I just assumed most of the letters written to Caroline would be written by women. What did the man have to say that made you laugh?"

Grandpa looked back at the newspaper and read in a clear, booming voice: " 'Dear Caroline, my wife fixes tuna fish casserole every Friday night, even though she knows I don't like it. How can I get her to fix something else?—Powerless Husband.'" Grandpa leaned his head back and chuckled. "Can you imagine that?"

"What—that he doesn't care for tuna fish? Is that what you think is so funny?"

Pulled unexpectedly into their conversation, Lisa waited to hear what her grandpa would say. He quickly responded to Grandma's question.

"I laughed because I think it's *lecherich* that this poor man would have to write a letter to a woman he doesn't even know with such an *eefeldich* question."

"It's not ridiculous, Jerry, and I don't think it's a silly question." Grandma crossed her arms as her chin jutted out.

Holding her hands behind her back, Lisa clenched her fingers into the palms of her hands. *Oh, boy. . . I hope they don't get into a heated argument over this—especially since it's not even important.*

Grandma looked over at Lisa with a hopeful expression. "What do you think? Would you agree that the man asked Caroline a silly question?"

"Please don't pull me into this or ask me to take sides. Don't you think you and Grandpa should just agree to disagree?"

Lowering her arms, Grandma shrugged. "Maybe, but not till he's heard the rest of what I want to say."

Grandpa looked at her and crossed his arms in the same manner she had a few moments ago. "By all means, please give us the rest of your opinion."

Grandma pulled her shoulders back and kept her back very straight. "I can understand fully why the man wrote the letter. He was clearly frustrated because his fraa didn't seem to care that he didn't like tuna and wouldn't fix him something else to eat on Friday nights."

"Be that as it may, would you like to know what Caroline said in response to his letter?"

"Jah, sure."

Grandpa picked up the newspaper and held it close to his face. " 'Dear Powerless Husband: If you have asked nicely, and your wife won't fix you something other than tuna casserole on Friday evenings, why don't you offer to make supper or even take her out to a restaurant to eat? That should take care of the problem.'" Grandpa put down the newspaper and looked at Grandma with a smug expression. "Now wasn't that a good answer?"

Her lips formed a smile as she turned her hands palms up.

Before either of them could say anything more on the subject, Lisa grabbed her outer garments, along with her lunch pail and purse, and moved toward the back door. "I need to go so I won't be late to the schoolhouse this morning. I'll see you both when I get home." She turned back toward them and smiled. "I hope you two will have a nice day." Before either of her grandparents could respond, Lisa slipped quietly out the door. Although Lisa felt sure that her grandparents weren't angry with each other, it bothered her to hear them quarrel—especially over something as silly as some dissatisfied man's letter to Dear Caroline. *But I suppose all married couples disagree sometimes,* she told herself. *I'm just glad Grandma and Grandpa don't do it all the time, like that man and wife who used to live in the house closest to us. It seemed like every time I was outside and they were in their yard, I could hear them arguing about something or other.*

Lisa had a momentary flashback and remembered seeing her parents in the kitchen the morning of the accident. They stood by the kitchen sink with their arms around each other, and a few seconds after their driver pulled into the yard and honked his horn, Lisa's father pulled her mother into his arms and gave her a kiss. Lisa was too young to be embarrassed by it then, but at the moment, her face felt like it was on fire. She stepped into the barn, closed the door, and leaned against the closest wall. It always upset her when she had any kind of a flashback like that, but what really bothered Lisa was the fact that her early memories never came back. She closed her eyes and sucked in a deep breath. *Why can't I remember anything before the day of the tragic accident? Is there some reason I've blocked it all out?* Lisa had thought about discussing the situation with one of her grandparents, but the idea of trying to talk about it was too upsetting. So for now at least, Lisa would keep her thoughts and concerns to herself.

Feeling the need for a short break, and with Uncle Abe's permission, Paul stood near the shop window and watched the snow that seemed to be coming down harder all the time. Hopefully it would slow down before tonight.

"Are you looking forward to seeing Danny do his part in the Christmas program at the schoolhouse this evening?" Paul asked his uncle, who was sanding a nearly finished piece of furniture for an English customer.

Uncle Abe bobbed his head. "I think my youngest boy's a bit naerfich about playing the part of Joseph, though."

"Ah, he has nothin' to be nervous about," Kevin hollered from across the room where he'd been sweeping up some sawdust. "I played the part of Mary's husband once when I was still attending school, and it was as easy as brushin' my teeth." Paul's lanky-looking cousin cocked his blond head to one side. "All I had to do was sit there starin' at the doll that represented the baby Jesus lying in a manger. It was the easiest part in the whole play." Kevin made a kind of snorting sound. "Wanna know what I think, Daed?"

"What's that?" Uncle Abe asked.

"My little bruder worries too much. He'll do fine tonight, and then afterward, I will go right up to him and say, 'See, I told ya so.'"

Uncle Abe stopped what he was doing and pointed at Kevin. "You'd best get back to work on that heap of sawdust and quit making plans to tease your brother."

The teenage boy did as he'd been told, and Paul moved away from the window to resume work on the table leg he had previously been sanding. He looked forward to going to the program tonight and liked the fact that the backdrop of this weather made it feel more like Christmas. It would be fun to watch the kids recite poems, sing songs, and act out the story of baby Jesus being placed in a manger. Paul was also eager to see Lisa in her element as a teacher. *And maybe,* he told himself, *if her grandparents don't mind, I'll ask if I can give her a ride home after the festivities. It'll give us a chance to talk, and if I feel the time is right, I may even surprise Lisa with the fact that I knew her when she was a young girl.*

"All right, boys and girls, we're going to run through everyone's part for the Christmas program one more time before we go outside for our afternoon recess." Yvonne looked over at Lisa. "Why don't you start with the younger ones, since that's how we'll be doing it this evening? While your children practice, I'll sit with my students and watch."

"That's good," Lisa said. "You can let us know if anyone is talking too fast or not loud enough to be heard from the back of the room."

"Yes, and you and your pupils can do the same for us when it's our turn to rehearse." Yvonne took a seat near the back of the room while Lisa got her students in position to say or sing their parts.

Things went along fairly well until Lisa corrected Nancy and Nathan Burkholder after they'd said each other's parts instead of their own. When Lisa asked them to start over, Nancy began to sob. She cried so hard that Lisa wasn't sure she could get her to stop.

"It's okay. It was just an error. We all make mistakes sometimes." Lisa gently patted the girl's back. "Why don't you and Nathan take your seats for now while the others practice their lines? I'll give you an opportunity to try again later."

With her head dipped down, Nancy sniffled all the way back to her desk. Although Nathan didn't cry, his cheeks turned red as he mumbled something under his breath about his sister wanting his part instead of hers. Then the boy shuffled back to his seat and sat down with his arms folded.

Lisa pressed her lips tightly together. She hoped things would go better at the program tonight and that all the children would be able to remember their lines and behave appropriately. Otherwise, there would be some embarrassed parents and other family members in the audience.

Lisa wouldn't be nearly as upset if any of her students messed up as she would be if they gave in to tears or refused to take part in the program.

Two more students said their parts, and Yvonne asked them to speak a little louder. Lisa feared the young girls might cry like Nancy had, but they kept their chins up and spoke their lines loud and clear this time.

As Melanie Beachy stepped forward to take her turn at reciting a Christmas poem, a disturbing memory flashed unexpectedly into Lisa's head. She saw herself as a little girl, standing in front of a roomful of people—many of whom she didn't recognize. But there, near the back, sat her mother and father wearing eager expressions as they waited for her to speak.

"Lisa," her teacher coached, "please share your Christmas poem with us."

Lisa opened her mouth, but the only thing that came out was a pathetic-sounding little squeak. Then, with tears rolling down her hot cheeks, she made a dash for her seat, put her head on the desk, and sobbed.

"Teacher, did I do okay?"

Lisa's mind snapped back to the present. She felt a bit shaken from having remembered something from her past that she'd obviously forgotten, especially when it had involved seeing her parents. *At least I remembered something, even if it did make me feel sad. Could it be that after all these years, I'm starting to get my memory back?*

"Teacher, did I do okay?" Melanie repeated.

"Umm. . .would you mind saying your poem once more?"

Melanie scrunched up her face. "Did I mess up? Is that why I hafta say it again?"

"I'm sure you did fine, but I didn't hear all of the poem, so would you please say it one more time for me?"

"Okay." The young, blue-eyed girl recited the poem in a clear voice, without missing a single line.

"Thank you, Melanie. Your poem was well done."

The child looked up at Lisa and grinned before skipping back to her desk.

As the rest of her students said their lines and sang a song together, Lisa made sure to keep her focus on them and push all thoughts of her scattering past to the back of her mind. If any more memories from long ago found their way into her head, Lisa hoped it would be when she had no distractions and could take the time to sit, think, and let it all sink in.

Lisa really wanted to remember more from her past—just not today, and especially not tonight during the play. She wanted everything to go perfectly and for everyone in attendance to enjoy themselves.

Chapter 19

"This is sure good stew," Paul said as he sat at the supper table with his aunt, his uncle, and their two boys.

Aunt Emma smiled and passed Paul the basket of buttermilk biscuits. "I'm glad you like it. I figured with it being so cold outside, some hot, hearty stew would be a good way to warm our insides before we head to the schoolhouse for the program." She looked over at Danny, who sat beside her, and nudged his arm. "You've barely touched your supper. Aren't you hungry this evening?"

The boy shook his head. "I'm too naerfich to think about food. I was hopin' I'd come down with a bad cold or somethin' so I wouldn't have to go to the Christmas program and do my part."

She gave Danny's shoulder a few pats. "There's no reason to be nervous, Son. You'll do a fine job playing Joseph."

"But what if I mess up and do somethin' stupid?"

"I don't see how you could mess up just sitting in a chair," Kevin interjected. "Unless you fall off it or miss the chair completely when you go to sit down." He chuckled behind his hand.

"It's not funny, and stop teasing your bruder," Uncle Abe spoke up. "Danny needs our encouragement right now and should not be teased."

"Sorry," Kevin mumbled around a piece of biscuit he'd put into his mouth.

Danny sat staring at his bowl of stew.

The tension in the room faded as Uncle Abe and Aunt Emma changed the topic of conversation to fixing the worn-out lock on the back door.

Paul couldn't help feeling sorry for his young cousin. He remembered how it felt when he was a boy and his brothers, Harley, Glen, Mark, and Amos, used to tease him. Sometimes he would think of something to say back to them. Other times Paul would try to ignore their catty comments. That always worked better than talking back or trying to be one up on the pesky brothers. Paul had learned a long time ago that it was better to keep quiet about some things than make a fuss.

Danny remained quiet, but he finally ate some stew and nibbled on his biscuit. The snow fell outside and could be seen through the kitchen window while they all ate their satisfying meal.

Paul was eager for this evening and had looked forward to it all day. Just seeing Lisa tonight would make it worth going. He smiled and envisioned her accepting his invitation to ride home with him after the program. *I hope she says yes.*

Paul buttered one of his aunt's flaky biscuits then enjoyed every tasty, moist morsel as he ate it. Following that, he finished his stew and took a drink of water. Paul had made up his mind that if he had the chance to be alone with Lisa tonight, he would definitely tell her the truth. The secret he'd been keeping weighed heavily on his heart, and no matter how she reacted, it would feel good to finally get the words out and wait for what he hoped would be a positive reaction.

Walnut Creek

"That was one tasty *reeschde*." Orley patted his stomach a few times. "It was so good, I'm tempted to help myself to a few more pieces."

Lois pointed at him and shook her finger. "You've already had several pieces of roast beef, and if you're not careful, you'll be gaining more weight."

His mouth slackened as he gave his belly another thump. "Are you saying I'm *fett*?"

"You're not fat yet, but with the hypothyroid situation, you could become fat if you don't watch your calorie intake."

"I don't have time for calorie countin'." His brows furrowed. "If I'm gonna count anything, I'd like it to be something like money, old marbles, vintage buttons, sheep in my sleep, or. . ."

She held up her hand. "Okay, I get what you're saying, Orley, but have you forgotten what the dokder said about the importance of making good food choices and not overeating?"

"I remember." *How could I forget when you remind me so often?*

"If you're still hungerich, why don't you have a few of these?" Lois gestured to the dish of cut-up veggies in the center of the table.

He wrinkled his nose. "No thanks. I already had some, and I'm full enough."

She shrugged in response.

Orley loved his wife dearly, but she worried too much about his health, and he felt frustrated when she pestered him about it. Didn't Lois understand that he was a grown man and could think for himself?

"What do you plan to do after we finish eating?" Orley asked, seeking a safer topic.

"I have some letters that were sent to the newspaper for my Dear Caroline column that need to be answered."

"Oh, I see. I'd kinda hoped we could make a batch of popcorn and work on a puzzle together."

Her lower lip pulled in. "I don't know, Orley. You know how it goes when we begin working on a puzzle. We get so involved and often sit there for hours."

"How about if we set a timer? That way you can work on the puzzle for as long as you like, and there will still be time for you to answer some of those Dear Caroline letters."

"Okay, but only for an hour or so."

He smiled and reached for a few carrot sticks—just to make his wife happy. Then Orley pushed back his chair, picked up as many empty dishes as he could carry, and made his way across the room. After placing them in the sink and running warm soapy water over them, he looked out the window. It had quit snowing, but beneath the white glow of the moon he saw that their yard was covered in at least two feet of fresh snow. It was strange how the moonlight shining down from the sky to the ground caused the snow to look as though it had taken on a bluish hue. Orley had heard once that during the winter months, moonlight often appeared stronger because of the snow's ability to reflect it.

Orley went to the utility room and opened the back door. He shivered when a blast of cold air hit him in the face with the fierceness of a blizzard wind.

"What are you doing, Orley? Is the back door open?" Lois called from the kitchen. "I can feel some cold air seeping in that wasn't here before."

Orley quickly shut the door and went back to the kitchen. "I opened the door so I could see what the weather is like. It's mighty cold and windy, which means the roads could be icy tonight."

"We have nothing to worry about because we're not going anywhere this evening."

Orley nodded. "But others will be out traveling for schoolhouse Christmas programs and other things taking place. Several of our customers who came into the store today mentioned that they have children or grandchildren involved in plays this evening. And not all of them were from Walnut Creek."

"Jah, the week before Christmas is usually a busy time for Amish schoolhouse programs. Which is why we should remember to pray for everyone's safety." Lois folded her hands, holding them close to her chest, as she often did when preparing to pray.

Orley stood near the kitchen door and bowed his head to join her in prayer. *Lord, please be with those who are traveling on this cold winter-like night, and guide them safely to their destinations.*

Sugarcreek

Lisa watched with satisfaction as Nathan and Nancy said their lines perfectly during their part in the Christmas program. *No mess-up this time,* she told herself. *I'm glad they both did so well and remembered the correct words for their parts.*

When each of the younger pupils had taken a turn, all the children from the class Lisa taught sang a song. Although they were immature compared to the older students, Lisa was pleased with how well these young voices sounded as they sang each verse from "Away in a Manger."

When the song ended, Lisa and her students took a seat to watch the older pupils perform.

Everyone from Yvonne's class did a good job, including Danny, playing the part of Joseph. Originally, he was supposed to stand beside the chair where Barbara Miller, who played Mary, sat looking down at the doll representing the baby Jesus in the manger. But when Danny had told Yvonne that he'd be too nervous to stand and might cave in, she'd agreed to let him sit in a chair next to Barbara. The boys playing shepherds and the girls who had angel parts also did well as they'd gathered around Mary,

Joseph, and the baby to sing "Silent Night."

In Lisa's head, she sang each of the meaningful verses with her sweet students. During a moment like this, all the hard work of cleaning, decorating, and practicing for the program was well worth it. She felt sure that the parents and other family members of the students who had come out tonight appreciated the effort their children, as well as the teachers, had put into this special performance.

Lisa fanned her face with the piece of paper she held in case she'd needed to coach any of her students with their lines. Despite the cold weather outside, with nearly one hundred people inside the schoolhouse, the room had become quite warm and stuffy.

Better too warm than too cold, she thought. *It wouldn't be good for the scholars to be shivering as they said their parts.*

After the last song had been sung and the program was officially over, refreshments were served in the basement. Most of the children had gifts for their teacher or other students in their class, so the excitement ran high during this special time.

Her pupils with their families sat at one of the rows of tables to eat and visit with others. One long table off to the side had been filled with an abundance of cookies and cakes. Each of the desserts had been furnished by many of the women who'd come for the program this evening. The table next to it had a couple of clear punch bowls filled with bright red sparkling juice and cups ready for thirsty guests. The room hummed with conversations going on about upcoming plans for the Christmas holiday. The smiles on the children's faces warmed Lisa's heart. *It was a lot of work in the beginning, but it was worth it in the end,* she decided.

Lisa finished drinking a glass of fruit punch and had tossed the paper cup into the trash can when she saw Paul heading her way. He carried a plate with him, as well as a cup of the punch.

"I see you found the goodies." Lisa gestured to his plate.

"Jah, and there's sure plenty to choose from."

"I agree."

"That was a great program," he said, stepping closer. "Your students did very well, and so did Yvonne's."

She smiled. "The way things went during practice earlier today, I wasn't too sure how it would go this evening."

"That's how it usually goes. I remember during one of the Christmas programs I was involved in when I was a boy. . ." Paul's voice trailed off as he sat down at the closest table.

"What were you going to say?" She sat beside him.

"It wasn't really important. I was just thinking about a time when I forgot my lines and my brothers razzed me about it all the way home." Paul nibbled on a jelly-filled cupcake. "Say, I was wondering if it would be all right if I take you home when you're ready to go."

Lisa answered with no hesitation. "I'd like that, Paul. I'll just need to let my grandparents know. I'm sure they won't mind, because it will give them the opportunity to leave now if they want to, without having to wait on me."

"Great. Just let me know whenever you're ready to go."

"I'll need to help Yvonne clean up, so it could be a while yet."

"No problem. I'll help with the cleanup too."

"That's kind of you. We'll appreciate the extra pair of hands."

Paul finished eating the food on his plate, drank all the punch in his cup, and put the paper products in the trash can.

By the time Paul and Lisa got into his carriage, it had started to snow quite heavily again. He'd turned on the buggy's lights and got back out to clean off the windshield with a scraper. Paul also let Lisa know that a folded blanket lay behind them if she wanted more warmth. Because of scraping off the snow, he now had a good layer of flakes on his coat.

"Look at you," Lisa commented. "It is really coming down hard."

"Jah, and Chester's hair is turning white too. It's becoming a winter wonderland out there." He brushed off most of the snow before closing the door and getting the horse moving.

Paul would need to guide Chester at a slower pace than normal as he watched out for any vehicles on the road. The last thing he needed was a collision between a car or truck and his horse and buggy.

It wasn't long before they were on their way to Lisa's grandparents' place. Paul got his horse going at a steady pace and kept his focus on the road ahead. At least they didn't have too far to travel, but as cold as it was, it would be nice to stop in to warm up before he headed home for the evening, so he hoped Lisa would invite him into her grandparents' house when they arrived.

It's nice being with Lisa, and I hope she enjoys being with me. I wonder if she'd be available to go somewhere with me tomorrow evening. Paul kept a good hold on the reins as he continued to think about the young woman sitting beside him.

Her sweet voice broke into his thoughts. "This is sure some weather we've been having. Just when we think the snow might let up, it starts up again."

"Jah. From the looks of it, my guess is that we're heading into what will probably be a pretty bad winter."

"Oh, I hope not. If it should get too bad, school might be canceled for several days, like it was two years ago during the first week of January. But of course, you weren't here for that," Lisa added.

No, but I wish I had been. If I'd been living here instead of Indiana, I would have never gotten involved with Susan and ended up getting hurt when she dropped me for Ervin.

Paul gripped the reins tighter as a car went past, going faster than he thought it should have, considering the ice and snow on the road. Fortunately, the vehicle stayed in its own lane, and Chester did well too.

I wonder if I should tell Lisa what's on my mind now or wait until we get to her grandparents' house to make my confession.

Paul had made up his mind that it was now time to say something when he saw a car parked along the side of the road with its flashers on. Thinking the driver might be having some sort of problem, he guided Chester over and stopped the carriage. In the headlights of the car, he saw a dog lying by the side of the road. A feeling of dread coursed through Paul's body when he heard Lisa scream, "Oh, no, it's Maggie! I don't know what she was doing out on the road, but she must have been hit by that car!"

Chapter 20

The joy of the evening had been completely wiped out as Lisa got down from Paul's carriage with tears streaming down her face. Unmindful of the cold and icy snow, she dropped to her knees beside Maggie.

"Is she alive?" Paul asked.

"I—I don't know." Lisa, barely aware that Paul had gotten out too and stood beside her holding Chester's bridle, could hardly speak around the burning constriction in her throat. She feared that her dog was in fact dead but couldn't say the words out loud. The tears escaped as Lisa remained by Maggie's lifeless-looking body. The overwhelming scene blurred her vision, and she wiped her eyes with the end of the jacket sleeve, trying to get a better view. *My poor Maggie. She looks so helpless.* Lisa looked up at her friend, hoping for any support from him.

Paul leaned closer to Maggie, and after a few seconds passed, he looked at Lisa. "The dog's right front leg is bleeding pretty badly, and there's a big gash on her head. However, she appears to be breathing. We need to get her some help right away, though."

All Lisa could do was nod in response.

The car that appeared to have been involved in the incident was still there with its flashers running. The woman behind the wheel opened the door and got out.

"Are you all right?" Paul asked.

"I–I'm fine." The woman's widened eyes were turned on Maggie. "Do either of you know the owner of this dog?"

Paul's voice sounded so somber as he pointed at Lisa. "It's her dog."

The woman stepped closer. "I'm so sorry. I didn't mean to hit your dog. As I'm sure you realize, the roads are icy, and I lost control of the car. I didn't even see the dog until it was too late." She paused for a breath. "I guess it must have been walking on the shoulder of the road, and when my car slid that way. . ." Her voice faltered, and Lisa knew that the young English woman was close to tears.

"My cousin Brent is a vet, and his clinic isn't too far from here. I'll call his emergency number right now and see if he can meet us at the clinic."

Lisa nodded slowly. She appreciated the woman's offer, but something deep inside told her that Maggie's injuries might be too bad and nothing could be done to save her.

Just like my mother and father, she thought. *The doctors couldn't save them or Grandpa and Grandma Miller. Why does everyone I love have to die? Doesn't God care about me at all?*

Paul got a blanket from his buggy and wrapped Maggie in it. She opened her eyes for a bit but made no effort to get up. No doubt she was not able to do so.

With every fiber of her being, Lisa wanted to help her dog. She glanced at the woman, now talking on her phone. *I sure hope she can reach her cousin and that he'll be available to take care of Maggie.*

When the woman, who'd introduced herself as Judy, got off her cell phone, she said her cousin had agreed to meet them at the clinic. "I'll drive you and your dog there." She touched Lisa's shoulder as she looked at her with eyebrows drawn together in obvious concern.

Lisa was relieved that Judy had reached the veterinarian and he'd be meeting them soon. She got into the back of Judy's car, and Paul placed Maggie, securely wrapped in the blanket, on the seat next to her.

Lisa slid closer and put Maggie's head in her lap. "Please don't die, girl," she murmured as more tears fell. "We're gonna get you some help real soon."

"I'll go to your grandparents' house and tell them what's happened," Paul said. "Then I will meet you at the vet's office."

All Lisa could do was manage a brief nod. Her thoughts were fully on Maggie, and she barely heard Paul ask Judy for directions to the clinic.

Lisa sat in the back seat of Judy's car, gently stroking Maggie's head. Although it had quit snowing, the roads were slick, and she worried that the vehicle might slide off the road again.

Maggie gave a pathetic whimper and made an attempt to lift her head.

"Stay still, girl. We're going to get the help that you need." Tears seeped out of Lisa's eyes and splashed onto her cheeks. "I'm so sorry, Maggie. I should have made sure the door latch on your pen was fastened securely. If you don't make it, I'll be at fault."

"We'll be there soon," Judy called over her shoulder. "My cousin's clinic is about a mile up ahead."

With the dog becoming more active, it was apparent that the shock had begun to wear off. Also, the wounds poor Maggie had would hurt and make her uncomfortable.

Lisa hoped they would get there in time. Maggie had begun panting, and Lisa felt the dog's saliva on her hands. She also detected something warm, which she assumed was blood from the wound on Maggie's head.

"Don't die, Maggie. Please don't die," Lisa repeated once more as she squeezed her eyes shut. *Dear Lord, please don't let my dog die. I love her so much.*

When Paul knocked on the Schrocks' front door, he was greeted by Lisa's grandmother, holding a battery-operated light in her hand. She smiled then looked past him. "Where's Lisa?"

"She's at the veterinarian clinic with her hund."

Marlene leaned against the doorjamb, as though needing it for support. "Has Maggie been hurt?"

"Jah, she was hit by a car." Paul paused when he heard Marlene's sharp intake of breath.

"Come inside where it's warm and tell us about it."

Paul brushed the snow off his jacket and stomped his feet on the doormat. When he entered the house, he appreciated the warmth it afforded.

"Jerry's in the living room. Let's go in there, and you can give us both the details. We've been concerned ever since we got home and discovered that Maggie was not in her pen."

Paul followed Marlene into the living room where a nice, cozy fire burned in the fireplace, sending plenty of warmth into the room.

Jerry got up from his chair and shook Paul's hand. "I wasn't eavesdropping, but I heard your conversation with my fraa from in here." His brows knitted together. "How badly has Maggie been hurt?"

"We won't know until the vet examines her."

When Marlene suggested that Paul remove his coat and take a seat, he did as she said. Then he cleared his throat and proceeded to give them the details of what all had occurred.

Marlene wiped a few tears from her eyes, and Jerry rubbed the bridge of his nose. "I don't understand how Maggie got out of her pen. I saw Lisa go out there to put the dog in when I was getting my horse and buggy ready to take us to the schoolhouse this evening."

"Maybe she was in a hurry and just thought she had the latch on the door secured," Marlene said. "With everything there was to do because of the program, Lisa mentioned during supper that she'd had a lot on her mind all day."

"I can only imagine." Paul glanced toward the door. "I'd better get going. I'm supposed to meet Lisa at the veterinarian clinic. I'll bring her home as soon as we find out how badly Maggie was hurt and we know what will need to be done for the dog." He looked at Jerry and gave a slow shake of his head. "I hate to say this, but things don't look good for Lisa's hund. Her breathing was shallow, and there was a lot of blood seeping from her wounds."

Marlene stood up from her chair and went to stand in front of Jerry. "I think you and I should go too, because if Maggie doesn't make it, Lisa is going to need all of us there to offer our support."

"You're right," he agreed. "I'll get our outer garments right now."

As Lisa waited in the reception area of the clinic, it was hard not to give in to negative thoughts and despair. Judy sat in the chair next to her and tried to make conversation, but it was all Lisa could do to respond. She looked up at the electric clock on the wall, watching its second hand move steadily over the numbers. Lisa closed her eyes, trying to refocus her thoughts. *My grandparents must know by now what has happened since Paul said he'd go by there to tell them. It would be nice if they decided to come to the clinic with Paul. I'd really like to have them here with me.*

The time dragged on while Lisa waited for information on Maggie's condition. Any noise from the back of the clinic made Lisa look in that direction. Patience was the key right now, but she struggled to hold herself together. Lisa wished she could barge into that examining room and be with Maggie right now. But the doctor had asked her to wait out here and said he would let her know the extent of Maggie's injuries as soon as possible.

Minutes later, a car pulled into the lot, and soon a woman came into the clinic. She removed her coat right away and headed to the room where the doctor had gone.

Judy cleared her throat. "That was one of the doctor's assistants. He must have called her and asked if she could help out."

While Lisa appreciated Judy waiting with her, she didn't want to talk right now. Apparently the young woman must have figured that out, because she picked up one of the magazines lying on a small table nearby and began thumbing through the pages.

Soon after they'd arrived, Lisa had told Judy that she didn't have to stay with her because Paul would be coming here after he'd stopped by her grandparents' house and told them what had happened. But Judy had insisted, saying she wouldn't feel right about leaving and wanted to find out for herself how the dog was doing.

In an effort to keep her mind occupied, Lisa focused on the different things she saw in the reception area. The floor had been covered with blue-gray tile, which went well with the gray walls and light blue chairs. Across the room, several pet supplies had been displayed, consisting of shampoos, leashes, collars, toys, vitamins, and both nail and hair clippers that were all for sale. Looking on the other side of the room, Lisa noticed several posters showing different breeds of dogs and cats had been tacked to the walls.

Lisa tipped her head when she heard muffled voices behind the closed door of the examining room, followed by what sounded like water pouring into a sink. She wished she could be in there with Maggie right now, but it was probably for the best that she'd been asked to remain here. If Maggie had whimpered when the vet examined her, it would have been like a stab to Lisa's heart. She hoped her poor dog would be given something for the pain.

Lisa's nose twitched at the distinct odor of disinfectant, but at least that was better than the smell of blood and wet fur that had filled her senses on the ride to the clinic.

When the front door opened and Paul, along with her grandparents, stepped in, Lisa felt relieved. Grandma came toward her with open arms, and Lisa quickly stood and rushed into them, struggling not to sob.

"How is Maggie?" Grandpa asked in a tone of deep concern. "Is she going to be okay?"

"I—I don't know yet. The doctor and his assistant are still in with her, and I haven't been told a thing." Lisa gestured to the closed door of the examining room.

Paul crossed over to Lisa. "You look *mied*. This has been a difficult thing for you to be faced with tonight."

All Lisa could manage was a nod. Admittedly, she was tired, but her throat was swollen, and it felt like she'd swallowed a wad of cotton. How could such a wonderful evening have turned out so badly?

Everyone found a seat, but they'd only been sitting a short time when the veterinarian came out of the examining room and walked over to Lisa.

"Your dog has some head injuries that will require stitches, plus her right front leg is severely damaged." He paused for a few seconds, and his voice deepened as he spoke his next words. "I'm sorry to have to tell you this, Lisa, but your dog's leg needs to come off."

The doctor's words rang in Lisa's ears like a clanging bell as she sat there, trembling, unable to form any words.

"But she will live, won't she?" The question came from Lisa's grandmother.

"The dog has a good chance of survival, but only if the leg is amputated."

"Will it be expensive?" Judy questioned.

"I can't quote you an exact price at the moment, but it will likely add up to several thousand dollars."

The young woman released a heavy sigh. "Since I'm the one who hit the dog, I feel obligated to pay for the operation, but I don't have that kind of money. All I'd be able to contribute would be a few hundred dollars."

"Is surgery the only option?" Grandpa asked.

"Yes," the doctor replied. "It's either that or put the dog down. She won't make it without proper treatment."

"No, that's not an option!" Lisa cried. "I'll find some way to pay for it." A fresh set of tears streamed down her hot face. *I'm to blame for Maggie's injuries since I was the one who had put her in the pen before we left for the schoolhouse's Christmas program.*

"Don't worry." Grandma gave Lisa a hug. "We'll help with the expenses." She looked at Grandpa. "Right, Jerry?"

"Jah," he said with a firm nod. "We will do whatever we can."

"Same here," Paul interjected. "Maggie's a good dog, and she's worth saving."

Although greatly distressed about her dog's situation, Lisa felt a little better knowing that if Maggie had the surgery, she would likely live. But she couldn't imagine how the poor dog could possibly manage to walk on three legs instead of four. Lisa bit down on her bottom lip until she tasted blood. *My poor Maggie will never be the same.*

Chapter 21

When Paul left the Schrocks' home at two thirty the next morning, he felt a sick feeling in the pit of his stomach. It had been hard enough to see poor Maggie's injuries and think about the pain she must be in, but observing Lisa's reaction to it had really gotten to him.

I wish there was something I could have said or done to make her feel better, Paul thought. The fear he'd seen on Lisa's face when she'd signed the papers giving the veterinarian permission to operate on Maggie had been so obvious—especially after the doctor had explained the risks that went with the surgery and talked about any complications that might arise.

Paul smiled as the buggy rolled along. At the clinic, he'd seen the full extent of the love Jerry and Marlene felt for their granddaughter. They'd spoken of the need to be with Lisa no matter what the outcome would be for her dog and had offered to help with the expense of Maggie's surgery. When Lisa's mother and father died, despite their own grief, this older couple had taken on the role of being her parents in such a heartfelt way.

Maggie's surgical procedure had taken nearly three hours, and Paul thought about how, in addition to fatigue setting in, everyone seemed to have been on edge as they'd struggled to make conversation. The clock on the wall in the waiting room had showed that it was 1:00 a.m. by the time Paul, Lisa, and her grandparents left the clinic, and then they had nearly another hour to get back to the Schrocks' house. Paul had stayed for a short time, and now he had another half hour until he arrived at his aunt and uncle's place. Fortunately because it was Saturday, Paul didn't have to work today, so he could go to bed as soon as he got home and get some much-needed sleep.

Paul took it easy with Chester on the icy roads, and after arriving home, he didn't waste any time putting his horse and buggy away.

Using his flashlight, he made his way to the house and unlocked the back door. Upon entering the dark kitchen, he found the battery-operated light on the counter and clicked it on so he could see the room better. Certain that everyone had gone to bed, Paul quietly removed his coat and boots and put them in the laundry room. He was about to head upstairs when he realized how thirsty he felt. Paul got a glass down from the cupboard and filled it with cool water from the sink. After downing the whole thing, he realized that he hadn't drunk anything since the fruit punch he'd had at the schoolhouse.

He set the glass in the sink and shut off the light. With only the light from his flashlight, Paul headed through the familiar dark spaces to the upstairs.

Once in his room and after getting ready for bed, his mind played through the events of the evening. What a nice time he'd had at the schoolhouse seeing Lisa with the children and observing how attentive she'd been with them. After the program, Paul enjoyed getting to talk to her as he'd helped with the cleanup. On the ride to her grandparents' home, things had been going so well until they'd come upon the scene of the accident. Paul was glad he hadn't said anything to Lisa about having known her before. For now, the topic of their childhood friendship was better left unsaid. She'd been upset enough about Maggie and didn't need anything else to feel anxious about. Paul would wait until her dog's injuries were healed and Lisa could cope with things better before he broached that sensitive subject.

Paul climbed into bed, stretched to get the kinks out, and yawned. He was more tired than he'd realized. *I hope Lisa will be able to get some rest and doesn't lie awake worrying about Maggie.* Paul closed his eyes, whispered a prayer on her behalf, and within minutes gave way to much-needed sleep.

Lisa stared at the teapot sitting on the kitchen table. She'd had two cups of chamomile tea, but the mellow-tasting liquid hadn't made her feel relaxed or even sleepy. Her head was filled with thoughts of Maggie and everything the poor dog had been through and would have to face in the weeks ahead. Before performing the surgery, the vet had assured Lisa that her dog would adjust to having only three legs and, after a while, would be able to walk, run, and climb stairs again. It would take some time, but Maggie would learn to compensate for the missing limb.

Lisa felt some measure of comfort when Grandma stood behind her chair and began to massage her shoulders, neck, and upper back. "Maggie will be all right, Lisa." She spoke in a soothing tone. "Your hund is a determined one, and she will come through this just fine."

"I—I hope so." Lisa swallowed around the constriction in her throat. "Maggie will require a lot of care when she comes home, so I'll need to see if I can get someone to teach my class while I'm here providing for my dog's needs."

"That won't be necessary," Grandma said. "I'll be here all day, and I promise that I will take good care of Maggie."

"Really? You wouldn't mind?"

"Of course not. Maggie's a nice dog, and I know how important she is to you." Grandma continued to rub Lisa's tight muscles.

"Danki. I appreciate that." Tears welled in Lisa's eyes, and she swiped at them with the back of her hand. "I will want to be with her, though—at least for the first few days after she comes home. Maggie will be scared and uncertain about everything at first. She will need lots of love and reassurance."

"That's quite true, and we'll all do our part in helping her recover from the surgery, as we take one day at a time." Grandma ended her massage and stepped out from behind Lisa's chair. "Right now, however, I think the two of us should follow your grandpa's lead and head for *bett*."

Lisa nodded and pushed back her chair. She would go up to her room and get ready for bed, but with her thoughts still on Maggie, it was doubtful that she would get much sleep.

"We never heard you come in last night," Paul's aunt said as she handed him a plate of scrambled eggs. "Did you get home late?"

He let out an uncontrollable yawn and spoke in a groggy voice. "I didn't get back here till after two thirty this morning." Paul helped himself to some eggs and passed the plate on to Danny.

Uncle Abe's eyebrows shot up. "What were you doing out with Lisa at that hour? You took her home after the program, right?"

Paul nodded and cleared his throat a couple of times. "But we didn't get to her grandparents' house until way after midnight, because we were at the vet's with her hund."

Aunt Emma blinked rapidly. "What happened to Maggie?"

"She was hit by a car." Paul paused to pour some ketchup on his eggs and then filled the family in on the whole story.

Aunt Emma's fingers touched her parted lips, Uncle Abe jerked his head back slightly, and Paul's cousins looked at him with their eyes wide open.

"Is the hund gonna be okay?" Danny questioned.

"I believe so," Paul replied, "but losing a limb will be quite an adjustment for Maggie."

"I can only imagine." Aunt Emma heaved a heavy sigh. "Poor Lisa. I bet she was pretty *umgerennt* about the situation."

"You're right. She was very upset." Paul drank some grape juice and looked over at Uncle Abe after he set his glass down. "Unless you have some chores for me to do, I'd like to go over to the Schrocks' and see how Lisa is doing."

"My boys can handle any chores that need to be done. So feel free to go offer Lisa the support she obviously needs."

"Danki." Paul appreciated his uncle's understanding. Lisa had become a good friend, and he wanted to be there for her during this time of need.

As the sun streamed in through a small hole in her bedroom window shade, Lisa's eyelids fluttered and then opened. Looking at the battery-operated alarm clock on the small wooden table beside her bed, she saw that it was ten o'clock in the morning. Although she did not feel refreshed at all, at least she had been able to get a few hours of sleep.

Lisa forced herself to sit up and put her legs over the side of the bed. She wished what had occurred last night had only been a bad dream, but in reality Maggie was at the veterinarian clinic right now, recovering from her emergency surgery.

Lisa rubbed her eyes. *I wonder how my poor dog is doing after the rough ordeal she went through. I hope Maggie is comfortable and not in a lot of pain.*

Hoping the doctor or his assistant might have left a message for her, Lisa got up and hurried to get dressed. She figured her grandparents would probably be up and would already have eaten or at least started their breakfast. So the first place she planned to go was out to the phone shed.

Lifting the window shade, Lisa was glad to see blue skies and sunshine, with no sign of snow on the horizon, although the ground was still white. She hoped the clear skies meant their weather would be taking a turn for the better. If it warmed up and the snow melted, traveling would be easier on bare roads instead of ice and snow, like they'd been faced with last night.

Moving away from the window, Lisa left her room and hurried down the stairs. The door to her grandparents' room was closed, so she figured she must have been mistaken and that they were most likely still in bed.

In the entryway near the front door, Lisa took her outer garments from the clothes tree and put them on, then slipped into her boots. She'd no more than opened the door and stepped onto the porch when she saw Paul's horse and carriage coming up the driveway.

She drew in a deep breath and waited for him to join her on the porch.

"How are you this morning?" Paul asked when he came up the steps a few minutes later.

"I didn't get much sleep after you dropped us off last night, so I'm quite mied."

"It makes sense that you would be tired. I'm feeling that way myself."

"I'm sorry for keeping you up so long."

He shook his head and reached out to touch her arm. "I can do without sleep once in a while, especially when staying awake to help out an old friend."

She tipped her head slightly. "Old friend? I didn't know you saw me as old."

"Oh. . .um. . .it was just a figure of speech." Paul's cheeks reddened. "You definitely do not appear to be old."

Lisa lowered her gaze to the porch before looking up at him again.

"Have you heard anything from the vet this morning about how Maggie fared through the night?" Paul asked.

Lisa was glad for the change of subject. The strange, almost conflicted, way he looked at her right now made her feel something she couldn't explain.

"I was on my way out to the phone shed when you arrived," she said. "I'm hoping there will be a message letting me know how Maggie is doing."

"Mind if I go with you, so we can listen to the message together?" Paul stuffed both hands into his jacket pockets.

"That'd be fine." Lisa managed a smile, even though tears pricked the back of her eyes. She hoped she could keep them from slipping out and dribbling onto her cheeks.

Paul led the way, and Lisa shuffled along through the snow, following in his footprints, which were much larger than hers. When they arrived at the shed, he opened the door and held it so she could go in.

Lisa stepped into the small wooden building and shivered. It felt colder in here than it had outside. She took a seat on the wooden stool, and Paul stood off to one side. The light on the answering machine blinked in rapid succession, letting Lisa know there was at least one message. She clicked the button and listened intently to the message, which to her relief was from the veterinarian.

"Hello, this is Dr. Hughes with a message for Lisa. I wanted you to know that your dog is resting comfortably, thanks to the pain and relaxation medication we've given her. She's also been given an anti-inflammatory to help with swelling. Maggie will be able to leave the clinic once she is able to stand, walk a few steps, eat something, and eliminate on her own. It's not unusual for a pet to remain in the recovery ward longer than a day, especially after major surgery. Please feel free to call my office with any questions you may have. We will let you know when it's time to pick up your dog."

Lisa felt a tightness in her chest as she held her hands tightly together. "I hate that Maggie's going through this, and I wish I could be with her right now."

Paul placed one hand on her shoulder and gave it a gentle squeeze. "She'll be okay, Lisa. You'll see."

"I hope so. I don't know what I'd do if Maggie didn't make it." Lisa's eyes burned with unshed tears, and she squeezed them shut in an effort to keep them from spilling over. "Danki for being my friend, Paul. I appreciate your support and all that you've done."

He patted her shoulder. "I only wish I could do more."

Lisa rose from the stool. "Let's go inside, and I'll fix you a cup of coffee or some hot chocolate. Although it's past our normal breakfast time, I'd also be happy to fix some eggs, toast, or whatever you like."

Paul shook his head. "That's okay. My aunt made the family some breakfast this morning. I would be glad for a cup of hot chocolate, though."

"Okay then, hot chocolate it shall be."

They left the phone shed, and Lisa pulled her jacket up closer to her neck to keep out the chill. Despite the cold, Lisa felt a warm bond with Paul through this experience with her dog.

Lisa's spirits lifted just a bit as she and Paul headed for the house. Until now, she'd never had a friend who seemed to care so much about her.

Chapter 22

Lisa's pulse quickened as she waited with Grandma for their driver to pick them up Tuesday afternoon. After spending four days at the veterinarian's clinic, recovering from her surgery, Maggie was finally ready to be brought home. Lisa hoped what they had come up with for the dog's sleeping arrangement and having foods to camouflage her pain pills would be just right for their patient.

Lisa had taught at the schoolhouse yesterday, and again today, which had helped to keep her mind occupied with something other than Maggie. But now that school was over for the day and they were preparing to pick the dog up, she could only think of one thing. Lisa was eager to bring Maggie home, but the thought of seeing her poor animal with one leg missing, not to mention the incision, swelling, and bruising, made Lisa's stomach feel queasy. The usual time frame for most pets that had an amputation was to remain at the vet's for one to two days. On the second day, however, Lisa had been informed that Maggie had managed to dislodge her drain tube, and some bleeding had occurred. The doctor thought it best to keep the dog and monitor her for a few more days.

Grandma paused from reading the newspaper and nudged Lisa's arm. "Please try to relax. I can see by your furrowed brows that you're apprehensive about picking up your hund."

"You're right," Lisa admitted, "and I am trying to get my mindset in the right place before we head to the clinic. It's a good feeling to know that Maggie is alive, but at the same time it's hard to accept that her life with us will be different from now on."

"Not that different," Grandma said. "Remember what the doctor told us before we left the clinic on the night of Maggie's surgery?"

"He said a lot of things. What are you referring to?"

"The veterinarian stated that animals do better after amputation surgery than humans. In time you will see that Maggie can do many things she did before the accident, and she will become stronger. He also reminded you to keep a positive attitude and said if you do that, your pet will reflect positivity right back at you."

Lisa pushed a strand of wayward hair back under her head covering. "I'll do my best to stay positive and keep a cheerful attitude when I am talking to Maggie."

Her grandmother went back to reading, and they sat there together in the quiet of the living room. It was difficult not to be overwhelmed by all of this. Lisa wished she could be as confident as Grandma in her way of thinking. She tried to refocus by looking out the window and watching the birds as they flew to and from the feeders, keeping a steady stream of movement going. She especially enjoyed seeing the male cardinals with their pronounced red coloring. Outside, the corn sat in a metal pan for the ducks, but so far only the small wild birds had eaten any. Lisa figured Grandpa's sighting of the ducks had only been by happenstance.

She glanced at the battery-operated clock on the far wall. *Our driver should be arriving anytime now.* Lisa folded her arms as she thought about how things had gone in class today. The children had done well taking turns reading aloud from age-appropriate stories Lisa had chosen for them. During lunch break, she'd graded the spelling tests the children had also taken that morning. Many of them had good scores. It was obvious that her students had practiced at home, no doubt with some coaching from their parents or older siblings.

When a horn tooted outside, Lisa and her grandmother both got up from the couch and went to put on their outer garments. Lisa also picked up an old towel and a sheet to put under Maggie on the ride home. She resolved to give herself a pep talk on the way to the clinic, so that when she saw Maggie for the first time since her surgery, she wouldn't give in to tears but would instead respond in a positive way.

When their driver, Herb, pulled into the parking lot of the clinic, Lisa's heart began to pound. *What if Maggie acts different toward me now? What if I can't deal with seeing her incision and the area where her right front leg used to be?*

"I'll wait here in the van," Herb said. "But if you need my help carrying the dog out to the vehicle, come get me."

Perspiration beaded on Lisa's forehead. Until now, she hadn't even thought about how they would get Maggie out to the van. Would she need to be carried, or could she walk by herself? But even if the dog was able to walk on her own, she would need some help getting up into Herb's vehicle. It was just one more thing to stress about, and Lisa certainly didn't need that.

She opened the back door of the passenger van and stepped down, thankful for her boots, because there was still some snow on the ground. Grandma had been sitting up front in the passenger's seat, and she got out as well.

When they entered the clinic, the faint odor of antiseptic made Lisa's stomach churn. It reminded her of the other evening, as they'd waited during Maggie's surgery.

Lisa stepped up to the receptionist's desk and told the young woman her name and that she was here to pick up her dog.

"Please take a seat." The woman smiled. "Your name will be called as soon as your dog is ready to leave."

Lisa hesitated a moment. "Oh, uh. . .what about my bill? Will you be sending it to me in the mail, or would you prefer that I take care of it right now?"

"If you're able to pay today, that would be appreciated."

Lisa reached into her purse and retrieved her checkbook. When the receptionist gave her the bill, Lisa wrote out a check. She was thankful for the substantial amount of money Grandpa and Grandma had given her and for Paul's help as well. Lisa felt blessed by their generosity and the moral support each of them had given her because of all she'd gone through with Maggie so far.

After Lisa received a receipt, she walked over to where Grandma sat and took a seat beside her.

Grandma smiled. "It'll be nice to have your dog back, and in a little while we'll be home getting her all settled in."

Using a light touch, Lisa drummed her fingers on the arm of the chair. *Will I be taken into an examining room to see Maggie, or will they bring her out here?* Lisa had never dealt with anything like this, and she felt quite confused and vulnerable.

Grandma took a magazine and began thumbing through it, but all Lisa could do was think negative thoughts as she picked at a hangnail on her thumb. *So much for trying to keep a positive attitude,* she thought.

Several minutes went by until Lisa was asked to go into one of the examining rooms. Grandma went with her, and Lisa was glad, because she desperately needed the moral support.

The doctor greeted them and then gestured to his assistant who stood by the table where Maggie lay.

Lisa heard a ringing in her ears, and every muscle in her body felt as if it had become frozen. Maggie whimpered, and the pathetic sight of her dear pet lying there with only three limbs nearly broke Lisa's heart.

"I am aware that the incision surgery site is a bit shocking," the doctor said. "It's not easy to see your dog looking so wounded and different, but try to remember that Maggie is happy to see you and wants to go home. So please look her in the eye, and don't focus your attention on the incision. Show that you're happy to see Maggie, because your positive attitude will set the tone for the dog's recovery."

"I—I will do my best." Lisa reached out with a trembling hand and stroked the top of her dog's head, being careful to avoid the stitches.

Maggie whimpered again, and then she nuzzled Lisa's arm with her nose.

Maggie still loves me, and I'm sure she wants to go home as much as I want to take her there. I just hope I can do all the right things for her. Lisa swallowed around the lump in her throat. She had missed her dog so much and hated to see her suffer.

"My assistant has some instructions for you about Maggie's home care. We also have a sling available that you can put around the dog's belly, which will help her with mobility the first few days if needed. An e-collar may also be a good idea. It will prevent Maggie from licking or chewing at her surgical wound."

Lisa nodded, although her head felt like it was spinning with all the dos and don'ts she would be faced with while caring for Maggie.

The doctor's assistant gave Lisa a clear plastic bag, explaining that it had Maggie's pain medication inside, along with the instructions for her care.

"Please let us know if you have any questions or if any problems arise," the doctor said. "With the aid of the sling around Maggie's belly, my assistant will help you take Maggie to your vehicle now. Oh, and I would like to see your dog again by the first of next week, to make sure that everything is healing properly." He offered Lisa a reassuring smile. "I understand you must feel a bit overwhelmed right now, but once you get home and have established a routine, you will feel more relaxed and confident that everything is going to be all right for both you and Maggie."

Lisa looked at her grandmother and felt some encouragement when Grandma smiled at the doctor and said, "I will be helping my granddaughter with Maggie's care, and we'll both make sure that we follow the instructions you're sending home with us."

He nodded. "Good to hear, and please don't hesitate to call if any problems should arise or you have a question that isn't addressed in the list we're giving you. Now let's get Maggie ready to go home."

Walnut Creek

"Where are you going?" Lois asked when Orley entered the kitchen via the hallway entrance, wearing a heavy jacket, stocking cap, gloves, and boots.

"Thought I'd do a little sledding while there's still some schnee on our hill out back." He gave her a wide grin.

"But it won't be long till supper. Besides, even if the snow melts soon, there will almost certainly be more as *winder* sets in."

"We might have a mild winter this year." Orley winked at Lois.

She gestured toward the window. "It's starting to get dark. What are you going to do—hold one of your powerful flashlights out in front of you as you sled down the hill?"

He shrugged. "That could work."

Lois rolled her eyes at him.

"Don't forget that my doctor said I should exercise to help keep my weight in check."

"Sliding down the hill doesn't take much energy."

"No, but trudging back up it sure does."

Lois lifted both hands in defeat. There was no way she could convince her determined husband not to get out his sled. "Okay, Orley, but supper will be on the table in one hour."

"I'll be back in the house by then, no problem." Orley kissed Lois's cheek, and with a whistle, he went out the back door.

Lois lifted her gaze to the ceiling. "For goodness' sakes, will that husband of mine ever grow up?"

She moved over to the refrigerator and took out a package of ground beef for making meatballs. "I guess I should count myself as fortunate to be married to a fun-loving man like Orley. If I had chosen someone else, I might not be so lucky. Some men, like that grouchy customer who came into our store this morning, would certainly be difficult to live with."

Lois got out an onion and the cutting board. "If all I have to complain about is a husband who likes to have a little fun, then shame on me," she scolded herself. "There are lots of people in our world right now facing bigger problems than mine."

Sugarcreek

Lisa knelt on the floor next to where Maggie lay on the comfy bed they had fixed for her. Under normal conditions, it would have been a nice sleeping arrangement. But Lisa wasn't sure her dog could be comfortable in any sleeping or resting arrangement or that lying on a cushioned doggy bed would help relieve the pain the poor animal must feel. Even the position the vet had said Maggie would need to lie in, with the amputation side toward the ceiling, looked uncomfortable.

Lisa had planned to mix Maggie's pain pill in a small amount of turkey-flavored baby food, as the instructions she'd been sent home with suggested. Some other suggestions to stimulate the dog's appetite had also been mentioned, such as offering her some smoked cheese like Gouda. Apparently the stronger smells were supposed to appeal, but so far, Maggie hadn't touched a bite, and she'd only lapped a little water from her elevated bowl. Lisa couldn't help but worry, because even if she had placed a pill in the food dish, Maggie probably would not have eaten it. The poor thing seemed so listless. Lisa felt sure her dog was depressed.

"How's it going in here?" Grandpa asked, stepping into the utility room.

Lisa shook her head. "Not well. I can't get her to eat, and if she doesn't eat, she won't get the medicine I want to put in her food."

"Is it time for her pill?"

Lisa nodded.

"Not to worry. I know of several tricks to get your pooch to take her medicine."

She tipped her head. "Such as?"

"One thing you can do is cut a marshmallow in two and wedge the pill in the middle of it. Then let your dog take a sniff of it, and offer it for her to eat." Grandpa jiggled his brows. "It's an inexpensive, low-calorie treat."

"I suppose it'd be worth a try," Lisa said.

"You could also spoon out a dollop of peanut butter, ball it up, and push a pill into the middle of it. Chunky peanut butter works best, because the peanut chunks disguise the pill inside." He paused and bent down to scratch Maggie behind her ears. "You could also try feeding her some thick, fruit-flavored yogurt with the pill mixed in."

Lisa's eyelashes fluttered. "Wow, Grandpa, how did you learn so much about giving a pill to a hund?"

"That's simple." He lowered himself to his knees. "I had plenty of pets when I was growing up and even in the early days of your grandma's and my marriage."

"Did any of your animals ever lose a limb?"

He shook his head. "But there were times when one of 'em got injured or sick and had to go to the vet's. So because they were my pet, I had the privilege of caring for them when they came home from the veterinary clinic."

Lisa's shoulders relaxed a little. She'd never thought of it as being a privilege to take care of Maggie, but now that she let the idea sink in, it made sense.

Lisa leaned closer to Maggie and gave her head a few gentle pats. "I'm going to the kitchen now, girl, but I'll be back soon with a special marshmallow treat for you."

The dog lifted her head just a bit and made a little grunting sound. *Hopefully she likes that idea,* Lisa thought.

Chapter 23

"Are you sure you can handle things with Maggie while I'm at the schoolhouse today?" Lisa asked her grandmother the following morning.

"Try not to worry. I'm sure we'll do fine." Grandma gestured to where Grandpa sat reading the newspaper at the kitchen table. "If a problem should arise and I'm not sure what to do, I'll go out to the harness shop and get your grandfather."

"Okay, good." Lisa felt better hearing that Grandma would seek Grandpa's help. She still couldn't get over how easily she had gotten Maggie to take her medication last night by taking Grandpa's advice and hiding the pill inside a marshmallow.

Last night Lisa had slept in the downstairs guest room, and with Grandpa's help she'd moved Maggie and her dog bed into that room as well. It was either that or Lisa would have slept on an air mattress in the utility room, because she wasn't about to leave her dog unattended overnight. She hadn't had the most restful sleep during the night. In fact, she'd woken up a few different times. And while Lisa was awake, her number one priority was to check on Maggie to see how things were. Each time she checked on the dog, Lisa had been pleased to find Maggie with her head down and eyes closed. She hoped that her faithful companion would get the sleep she needed to help with the healing process. Taking care of Maggie and doing all she could for the dog had given Lisa a taste of what it would be like to be a mother.

"Are you okay, girl?" Lisa called when she heard Maggie whimper from the utility room, where her doggy bed had been moved back this morning after they'd taken the dog outside to do her business. She tipped her head and listened, but there was no more noise. Lisa figured that the pain medication might have worn off. Or maybe the dog had bumped the tender area in her sleep. Lisa hoped things would go well during the time she'd be away from her dog. Truth was, she still felt apprehensive about leaving Maggie in order to teach school today, but tomorrow Lisa would be home all day, since it was Christmas, and she'd be celebrating the holiday with her grandparents. Paul would also be dropping by sometime on Christmas Day. Lisa had found a message from him this morning when she'd gone to the phone shed to let the veterinarian know how Maggie had fared through the night.

Lisa looked forward to seeing Paul again. This would be the first time she'd seen him since the day after Maggie's accident. He'd been busy working with his uncle, and she'd been busy teaching school. Lisa hadn't seen Paul at church either, because last Sunday had been an off Sunday when their district didn't hold services, so they'd both attended church with their families in other neighboring districts.

"Would you like me to pack your lunch box this morning?"

Grandma's question pulled Lisa's thoughts aside. "Oh, jah, it would be appreciated. And while you're doing that, I'll try to get Maggie to eat something."

"Good idea." Grandpa set his newspaper aside and stood. "I'm going to fix myself another cup of kaffi, but if you need my help coaxing your hund to eat, just give a holler."

"I will, Grandpa. Danki." Lisa left the kitchen and entered the utility room. She was glad to see that Maggie was awake and lapping water from her dish.

Lisa made sure to praise the dog when she drank, took a pill, or ate, hoping to encourage the positive behavior. It would be a tough road ahead for Maggie as she recovered from her surgery and the wound on her head. Lisa felt hopeful when occasionally Maggie's tail would wag in a slow manner after being praised or receiving attention. It made Lisa happy to see her dog trying to respond like she had before the accident.

Lisa placed the food dish in front of her dog. It contained Maggie's favorite kind of canned dog food with her pain pill mixed in.

Maggie sniffed the bowl, ate a few bites, and laid her head back down. Lisa figured the dog must have tasted the pill and didn't care for the bitterness of it.

"Oh, great." Lisa picked up the pill Maggie hadn't touched. Then she went back to the kitchen, got a marshmallow, cut a slice in the middle, and stuffed the pill inside. *I think Maggie has a sweet tooth for marshmallows, but then so do I.* She picked one out for herself and popped it into her mouth.

Returning to the utility room, Lisa squatted down beside her dog. "Here, Maggie. Would you like a tasty marshmallow?"

Maggie snatched the treat and chomped it right down.

Lisa smiled. "Good girl." *Guess if that's what it takes to get my hund to take her pill, then I'll just have to keep feeding her marshmallows.*

She stroked her dog's silky head. "Now you be a good dog for Grandma while I'm gone today. I'll miss you, girl, but I'll be back this afternoon, and tomorrow I'll be here all day."

Goshen, Indiana

"Your Christmas cookies are the best, Mavis." Daniel took a bite and sipped on his steaming cup of coffee.

"I hope you don't get carried away with what I've made and eat too many." Mavis shook a finger at her husband.

He flapped his hand. "It's all good. I'm enjoying these soft sugar cookies with the frosting, and they're sure tasty."

Frowning, she held up a paper. "I need to change topics. This is important."

He took another bite of his cookie. "What's up?"

"Would you look at this and tell me what's wrong with our son?" Mavis handed her husband the letter she'd received in the mail this morning.

"Is Paul sick, or has he been hurt in some way?" Deep wrinkles formed across Daniel's forehead.

"As far as I know our son is fine physically, but he is not coming home for Christmas and didn't even have the courtesy to call and tell us." She grimaced. "No, instead, he chose to convey the news via a letter."

Daniel's face relaxed, and he set the piece of paper on the table. "I don't see what the big deal is. Paul probably figured if he'd talked to you on the phone, you would have pestered him about staying in Ohio for the holiday."

Mavis placed both hands against her hips as she shook her head. "I would not have done that, although I may have asked for a better reason than he gave us in his letter."

"What reason would that be?"

"If you had read all of Paul's letter instead of tossing it on the table, you would know what I'm talking about."

Daniel picked up the paper and slipped on his reading glasses. His lips formed the words as he read Paul's letter. When he finished, he looked at Mavis. "Seems clear enough to me. Our son has an aldi, and he's staying in Sugarcreek so he can spend Christmas with her. I think it's fine that he has found someone new. It shows he's healing from the hurt of the previous young lady."

She released her hands from her hips and took a seat across from him at the table. "Paul never referred to Lisa as his girlfriend. He said she was a friend, plain and simple." Mavis paused. "I have to agree with you, though. It is good to see our son moving on, but I don't see any evidence of a relationship brewing."

He pulled his long fingers through the ends of his thick beard and made a grunting sound. "Come on, now. Who does our son usually talk about whenever he writes a letter or leaves a message on our voice mail?"

She moistened her lips with the tip of her tongue before speaking. "He has mentioned Lisa, of course. After all, they used to know each other when they were kinner. But he talks about other things too—like his job working for Abe, what the weather is like there, and—"

"He talks more about Lisa than he does the weather. And the fact that he wants to spend time with her during the holiday speaks volumes."

"It—it does?"

"Jah. Don't you remember how often I went over to your folks' place to see you when we were courting?"

"Well, yes, but Paul has never told us that he and Lisa are anything more than friends. I doubt that they are courting." Mavis rapped her knuckles on the tabletop. "If he is getting serious about her, and they should end up getting married someday, it would probably mean he'd stay in Sugarcreek. That is, unless he can talk her into moving here."

"I don't think that's likely. Remember, it was here where her parents and paternal grandparents lived. And you know the memory of the accident that took their lives might make it hard for Lisa to live here again." Daniel picked up his coffee cup and took a drink. "Also, in case you've forgotten, Paul left here to live with my bruder Abe and his fraa because his heart was broken when his best friend moved in on Paul's aldi. So in my opinion, our son's not likely to move back here again."

Mavis bit down on her lower lip. *Would it be wrong to hope, and maybe even pray, that Paul and Susan would get back together? That would definitely give our son cause to make Indiana his home again.*

"And while we are on the topic of Christmas," Daniel said, cutting into Mavis's thoughts. "We really can't complain, because we still have our sons Harley, Mark, Amos, and Glen living close by, and we'll be able to spend part of the holiday with each of them and their families."

"Believe me, I appreciate that. It would just be nice if all our sons could be with us for Christmas."

"Maybe next year Paul will come home."

Mavis looked right at Daniel and squinted until her eyelids were nearly shut. "He'd better not wait that long to come see us. I miss our son very much."

Sugarcreek

Excitement ran high in the schoolhouse as the children filed in the door, talking and laughing. Lisa heard several of her pupils say that they couldn't wait for tomorrow to get here so they could open their gifts and eat the delicious food their mothers would fix for Christmas dinner. Lisa wanted to share in their enthusiasm, but all she could think about was her dog and how Maggie would do today in the care of Grandma. She hoped things would go well and that Grandma could get Maggie to eat, drink, and take her pill when it was time for pain medication. Here it was, just the beginning of the school day, and instead of her focus being on teaching, Lisa's thoughts were on her desire for the day to end so she could go home and see Maggie.

If I can't concentrate on my job here and keep my attention on the students, then maybe I'm not cut out for teaching, Lisa told herself. *I do care about these children, though, so I must try to do better.*

She glanced at the clock on the far wall. The day would be over soon enough, and she had a job to do. Lisa turned her attention to the blackboard and the words written near the top: If We Use the Golden Rule at All Times, We Won't Need Any Other Rules.

She reflected on what the Golden Rule, found in Matthew 7:12, said: "Therefore all things whatsoever ye would that men should do to you, do ye even so to them: for this is the law and the prophets."

Although the schoolchildren in all eight grades memorized the Golden Rule in German and English, the most important thing was learning to practice it in their everyday lives. Lisa and Yvonne often stressed to the scholars the importance of using the Golden Rule during playtime and all other situations here at school.

In addition to learning the Golden Rule, Amish children were taught in school to be cooperative; show respect to their teachers, as well as other students; and learn responsibility by helping to keep the classroom clean and orderly, which included keeping their own desk tidy. Another important thing the children needed to learn was obedience. It was the teacher's job to get her students to obey out of love and not merely because it was expected of them. Parental support made a huge difference in teaching the children the basic guidelines and values, because if children had been taught these things at home, they were more likely to comply in a positive way during school hours.

Once everyone had taken their seats, Yvonne read a verse from the Bible, and then it was time for the children to sing a hymn and recite the Lord's Prayer.

What a wonderful way to start each day, Lisa thought as she felt herself begin to relax. Hearing God's Word and singing along with the children had lifted her spirits, and she now felt ready to begin her day of teaching. Although some people who weren't Amish might not understand why an Amish education consisted of only eight grades, Lisa knew that Amish teaching provided a good foundation scholastically, as well as giving the children an emphasis on the value of hard work, community service, and preparation for eventually joining the Amish church.

Walnut Creek

As soon as Paul entered Memory Keepers Antique Store, Orley stepped out from behind the front counter and greeted him with a hearty handshake.

"Happy day before Christmas." The older man offered Paul a pleasant smile. "I haven't seen you in a while. How have you been?"

"I'm fine, but my friend Lisa nearly lost her hund last week," Paul replied. "I came here to see if I could find something she might like for Christmas. Lisa was pretty shook up when her dog, Maggie, got hit by a car, and she could use some cheering up."

Orley's brows furrowed. "I'm sorry to hear that. Is the dog going to be okay?"

"Her right front leg was injured pretty badly, so the vet had to amputate." Paul paused a few seconds. "But if there are no complications, the dog should be okay."

"When I was a boy, a friend of mine had a hund with only three legs," Orley said. "But the dog got along pretty well and was able to do most things that other dogs could do."

Paul pulled off his stocking cap and stuffed it in his jacket pocket. "I'll be seeing Lisa on Christmas Day, and I'm eager to see how Maggie is getting along."

Orley smiled. "So what kind of gift do you have in mind for Lisa?"

"I'm not sure. I'd thought about an old book, but the time I brought Lisa here she seemed to be sensitive to the musty odor of the books." Paul gave his left earlobe a tug. "So I'm kind of at a loss about what to buy for her."

"Let's go ask my fraa." Orley gestured to Lois, who stood across the room, rearranging some items on a table. "I'm sure she'll have some suggestions for what a young woman might like."

They made their way across the room, and when Orley explained to Lois that Paul had come in to find a gift for Lisa, she smiled and said, "That's very thoughtful of you, Paul, and I think I might know just the thing."

Chapter 24

Lois sat on the couch in their living room, looking at the cards she and Orley had received for Christmas this year. One stood out in particular. It was from her father and stepmother, Sarah, who lived in Kentucky. Lois had invited them to come to Walnut Creek for the holiday, but they'd declined, saying Lois's seventy-year-old father had a bad cold and didn't want to expose anyone.

Lois hoped that was actually the reason and that her dad wasn't using it as an excuse to get out of spending Christmas with her and Orley. It wasn't that he had a bad relationship with his son-in-law. It was his relationship with Lois that was strained and had been for a good many years.

Lois released a lingering sigh. The tension between her and Dad was mostly on his part, because she'd forgiven him a long time ago for being so controlling and insensitive to her needs.

Never mind about that, Lois told herself. *Orley and I had a nice dinner early today with his brother Ezra and Ezra's wife, Maryann.* Two of Orley's nephews had been there also, along with their families, and a good time was had by all. But truth was, Lois yearned to have that positive connection with her father and to have from him an unconditional love.

"Would you like a piece of pumpkin pie or something else to eat?" Lois asked Orley.

He set the book down that he'd been reading and smiled. "The pie sounds nice, and some fresh coffee would hit the spot too."

"I have to agree with you. That does sound good. So I will be back shortly." Lois got up and ambled into the kitchen. She got the pot of coffee started before pulling the pie and some whipped cream from the refrigerator. When Lois cut into the pie, its spicy aroma tickled her nose. Then she pulled a spoon from the drawer and dunked it into the heavy white cream she had whipped that morning. Each slice was adorned with a hefty scoop of the fluffy, sweet addition. Lois couldn't resist enjoying the remnant left on the spoon and smiled. She felt like a kid again, enjoying for a moment this fleeting pleasure.

When Lois returned to the living room with two slices of pie, she found her husband standing in front of the window, looking out. She set their plates down on the coffee table and went back for the coffee.

Returning to the living room, Lois was surprised to see that Orley still stood at the window. "What are you looking at, Husband?"

He turned to face her. "Just seeing how much the schnee has receded. With it being warmer today, quite a bit of snow has already melted." His shoulders slumped. "If we don't get more of the white stuff soon, it'll put an end to sledding for me."

"I'm sure we'll have plenty of schnee over the next couple of months, and you'll be able to do lots of sledding and horsing around in the snow." Lois gestured to the cups of steaming coffee and the mouthwatering pie she'd brought out. "Shall we eat it in here or sit at the dining-room table?"

"Here's fine with me, unless you're worried I might spill hot kaffi or drop crumbs from the pie crust on the floor."

"I'm sure you'll be careful, like always." Lois took a seat on the couch, and Orley sat next to her. She watched him take the fork and disperse all the whipped cream over the top of his dessert. Lois couldn't help smiling at her husband's happy expression as he ate the first bite of pie.

"Yummy. . .this is sure *gut karebsekuche*." Orley smacked his lips. "Pumpkin pie is my favorite, especially at Christmas and Thanksgiving."

Lois smiled at her husband's exuberance. "I like it too."

Between bites of pie and sips from their cups, Lois and Orley talked about several things, including Paul Herschberger's visit to the store yesterday afternoon.

"I wonder if Paul's friend Lisa will like what he bought for her," Lois said.

"I don't see why she wouldn't." Orley wiped his mouth on the napkin Lois had provided. "What young woman wouldn't like a pretty teacup?"

Sugarcreek

"That was a mighty good meal you ladies fixed for us. Danki." Grandpa's smile appeared to be directed at Grandma, but then he looked at Lisa. "The only problem is, I ate too much and now I'm too full for dessert."

"There's no hurry. We can have our pie once our stomachs have settled." Grandma pushed away from the dining-room table and picked up several dishes.

Lisa jumped up and helped her, and Grandpa carried some dishes out to the kitchen too. In no time at all the table was fully cleared and the kitchen sink was filled with hot soapy water.

Maggie sat whining at the back door, so Grandpa volunteered to dry the dishes while Grandma washed, allowing Lisa to take the dog outside.

Lisa put on a heavy jacket and a pair of boots, and she got Maggie ready by using the sling she'd gotten from the veterinarian clinic. This made it easier for the dog to go down the porch stairs.

They'd only been outside a few minutes when Paul's horse and carriage entered the yard. Lisa waved, and she watched as he pulled up to the hitching rail and got out.

Paul waved back. After he'd secured his horse, he reached inside the buggy and withdrew a small cardboard box. *"Hallicher Grischtdaag,"* he said as he approached Lisa.

"Merry Christmas to you as well." She was about to ask what he had in the box when he spoke again. "It's great to see Maggie. How's she doing?"

"As well as can be expected, I guess. She still has some pain, but I don't have to give her the medication as often as I did when she first came home."

Paul set the box on the top porch step and went over to pet Maggie. The dog responded by licking his hand.

"It's hard to see her with only three legs," Lisa observed, "but the vet said she will adjust to it."

"I believe she will too."

"Did you have a nice Christmas meal with your aunt and uncle and their family?" Lisa asked.

"I sure did, but we all ate too much."

She laughed. "That's what my grandpa said too, after we finished our meal. The three of us weren't ready for dessert right away, but Grandma will be serving some of her delicious pumpkin and apple pies soon. You will join us for some, I hope."

"Definitely. It'll give me that much more time to spend here with you."

The tender expression she saw on Paul's face caused Lisa to feel a fluttery feeling in her chest. *Does Paul see me as more than a casual friend? Do I want him to?*

She shook the thought aside by focusing on Maggie. "Are you ready to go in now, girl?"

Arf! Arf! The dog wagged her tail.

Lisa felt a sense of hope and calmness. Was it being in Paul's presence or the fact that Maggie seemed to be a little more like her old self? Of course, the dog still had a ways to go in her healing.

"Let's go inside now," Lisa said to Paul. "We can talk better in the warm house."

"Agreed." He looked down and gestured to Maggie. "Do you need help getting her back inside?"

"Thanks for offering, but I can manage. The sling helps a lot."

"Okay." Paul picked up the box, went up the steps, and opened the door. Then he stood off to one side while Lisa and Maggie entered. Once they got the dog situated in her doggy bed, Lisa led the way to the kitchen. When she and Paul entered the room, Lisa was surprised to see that the dishes were done and her grandparents were no longer in the room. She figured she'd either been outside longer than she thought or Grandma and Grandpa had figured out some way to do the dishes really fast.

"You can take off your jacket and stocking cap and hang them over there." Lisa motioned to the wall pegs near the kitchen door. After placing the box on one end of the kitchen counter, Paul used one of the wall pegs for his things, and Lisa used another to hang up her outer garments.

"Would you like to see the trick I use to get Maggie to take her pain pills?" she asked.

"Sure."

Lisa opened a cupboard door and removed a bag of marshmallows. Then she took one out and proceeded to cut a slice in the middle. Next, she opened the medicine bottle, took out a pill, and slipped it inside the slit she'd made on the marshmallow.

She smiled at Paul. "Follow me, and I'll show you how it's done."

"Would you like a yummy treat, Maggie?" Lisa held the marshmallow in front of Maggie's nose.

The dog wagged her tail and let out a couple of noisy barks.

Paul chuckled. "She seems pretty eager to eat the treat you brought her."

"Jah, she is." Lisa held out the marshmallow, and without any prompting, Maggie opened her mouth and snatched the sticky morsel.

"Well, what do ya know?" Paul shook his head in disbelief. "How'd you come up with that idea, Lisa?"

"My grandpa suggested it, and I'm glad it has worked so well." Lisa crinkled her nose. "I was afraid I might have to open Maggie's mouth and put the pill in at the back of her tongue in order to give her the medication."

"That wouldn't have been the most ideal situation, so I'm glad using a marshmallow worked out." He leaned closer to her and smiled. "I mean, who doesn't enjoy eating a sweet treat like that?"

"Exactly. So why don't we go back to the kitchen now? I'll fix us some hot chocolate with a marshmallow on the top."

Paul licked his lips. "That sounds great. And while we're drinking our beverages, you can open the gift I brought you."

Lisa fidgeted and rubbed her hands on the front of her apron. "I wasn't expecting you to bring me a Christmas present, and I feel bad that I don't have anything for you. I've been so preoccupied with Maggie that I—"

"Don't worry about it, Lisa. I didn't expect a gift." Paul offered her a heart-melting smile. "Just being here with you is the only gift I need."

Lisa swallowed hard. She wasn't sure how to respond.

Paul reached into the box and pulled out a smaller box wrapped in green tissue paper and handed it to her. "I hope you like it."

When she tore off the paper and opened the box, Lisa was pleased to discover a delicate bone china cup with a gold rim. Dainty purple violets had been painted on the cup and matching saucer. "Danki, Paul. This teacup is so *schee*, it's almost too beautiful to drink from."

"Well, it's up to you," Paul responded. "You can either use it for drinking tea or sit it up on a shelf to look at and enjoy."

"I may do both."

"It's an old cup. Turn it over and see where it was made."

Lisa did as Paul suggested. The writing on the underside of the cup read Made in Germany.

"I bought it at Orley and Lois Troyer's antique store."

"It's a thoughtful gift, and I appreciate it very much."

Lisa's grandmother entered the room just then. "Hallicher Grischtdaag, Paul." She greeted him with a hug.

"Merry Christmas," he responded.

"I hope you're hungry, because I am going to set out some pies."

Paul gave a nod. "I believe I could manage to eat a piece."

"Would you like pumpkin or apple?"

"I like 'em both so either is fine with me."

Grandma looked at Lisa. "How about you?"

"I'll have the pumpkin, please."

Grandma got out the pumpkin pie and served Lisa and Paul each a piece. "Now, why don't you two young folks sit in here and visit while you eat your pie, and I'll take a piece for me and your grandpa to eat in the other room."

"Don't you want to join us?" Lisa questioned. "I'm sure you would enjoy talking with Paul."

"Of course, but your grandpa and I have a new puzzle started, so we'll keep working on that while you and Paul visit." She looked at Lisa and smiled. "I bet you'd like to talk to Paul about Maggie."

"Well, yes, but. . ."

"Very well then, I'll leave you two alone." Grandma scooped up two plates of pie and quickly left the room.

Paul took a bite of his piece of pie and followed it with a drink of hot chocolate. In the process, he ended up with a blob of melting marshmallow on his upper lip.

Lisa laughed and pointed.

His brows furrowed. "What's so funny?"

"You have marshmallow on your lip."

Paul chuckled and stuck out his tongue to swipe it off. "There, is that better?"

"Jah." Lisa giggled again. It felt nice to be here with Paul this evening, and it was good to find something to laugh about. Things had been too serious around here ever since Maggie's accident.

Marlene smiled when she heard Lisa and Paul's laughter coming from the kitchen. She was glad she had taken Dear Caroline's advice and played matchmaker with Paul and Lisa by asking him to build their kitchen cabinets.

I was even wiser when I invited him to join us for supper soon after that. He and Lisa seemed to be getting along well, and Marlene figured it was just a matter of time before the young couple would begin courting.

"What's that big grin on your face all about?" Jerry asked. "Did you find another puzzle piece when I wasn't looking?"

"No, I did not." She gestured toward the kitchen door.

He blinked a couple of times. "Huh? What about the kitchen?"

"Paul makes our granddaughter laugh," Marlene whispered. "Now isn't that a good thing?"

Jerry bobbed his head and ate some of his pie. "This is as good as always."

Marlene rolled her eyes. *Doesn't that man of mine think of anything but food? Is he completely unaware that Paul and Lisa are attracted to each other and could end up as a couple?* She took a drink from the cup of tea she'd brought in earlier. *I certainly hope that will be the case. I can't think of anyone better suited for Lisa.*

Chapter 25

The first day of January brought more snow, and by Friday of that week, a good twelve inches covered the ground. A lot of shoveling had been done at Uncle Abe's place, but with the snow continuing to fall, it was hard to keep up.

Paul gritted his teeth as he tromped through the slippery snow toward the phone shed. A few minutes ago, he'd checked the outdoor thermometer hanging on the back porch wall. The gauge showed nineteen degrees.

Too cold for me. Paul shivered and tried to pick up speed. There was no doubt about it—winter was not Paul's favorite time of the year.

Wish I was in Florida with Grandma right now. He'd heard that his grandmother had traveled there to get out of the cold and wondered if she knew how lucky she was to be able to spend the winter months in a warm place.

Upon entering the phone shed, Paul saw the light blinking on the answering machine, so he took a seat on the wooden stool and clicked the button to retrieve all the messages.

The first one was from an English customer, checking to see how soon the kitchen cabinets they'd ordered would be coming in. Paul jotted the man's name and phone number down on the notepad by the phone and then waited to hear the next message. He was surprised to hear Orley Troyer's voice and even more astounded when Orley said that he had come across some old milk bottles in a box in the storage room that he'd forgotten was there. Orley also stated that he had bought the box at a flea market last fall and thought it was full of old magazines. He'd had no idea there were any milk bottles at the bottom of the box and was surprised to discover them that morning when he began rummaging through some things in the storage shed at his antique store and opened the box. Orley ended the message by saying that one of the bottles looked like the item Paul had described previously and had been searching for.

"I'll set the box aside for you," Orley said at the end of his message. "When you get the chance to drop by, you can take a look and see what you think."

Paul drummed his feet against the floor. He looked forward to going to Walnut Creek after work to check out those milk bottles. Even if none of them were the one he'd been looking for, it would be nice to talk to Orley and his wife again.

Since there were no other messages on the machine, Paul pulled off the page with the customer information for his uncle and stood. He was about to step out the door when the telephone rang. Since it was so cold inside the small building, Paul was tempted not to answer and to let the voice mail kick in, but he figured a few more minutes of enduring the frigid temperature wouldn't matter. He sat back down and picked up the receiver. "Hello."

"Hey, Paul, it's me, Harley."

"Hey right back to you." Paul gave a quiet chuckle. He couldn't believe his older brother recognized his voice when he'd only uttered a single word.

"I never expected you'd pick up. Thought for sure I'd have to leave a message."

"I came out to check for messages and was about to head back inside when the phone rang, so naturally I picked it up." Paul blew out his breath and watched as the warm puff of air drifted upward.

"I'm glad you did, because there's something I wanted to tell you."

"Oh, what's that? Everyone there is okay, I hope."

"Jah, all in our family are fine, but I figured I'd give you the news in case you haven't heard it already."

"News about what?" Paul leaned forward with his elbows resting on the counter where the phone sat.

"Susan and Ervin are making plans to get married sometime toward the end of May, but I don't know the exact date."

"Yeah, so I heard, and good for them. I hope they'll be happy in their marriage."

"Do you really mean that, or was that a *scheppmeilich* comment?"

Paul drew a stick figure of a horse on the empty page of the notebook. "I was not being sarcastic. I've moved on with my life, and I wish Ervin and Susan well."

"It's great to hear you talking in such an upbeat manner. I'm guessing it might have something to do with the fact that you have a new aldi. Am I right?"

Paul stiffened. "Who told you that?"

"Mom. She said that Lisa was the reason you chose not to come home for Christmas, and when she told Dad about it, he figured it out."

"Spending time with Lisa at Christmas was only part of the reason I stayed in Sugarcreek for the holiday. Oh, and you can let our mamm know that Lisa is not my girlfriend. We are just good friends." Paul drew in a deep breath, released it slowly, and closed his eyes. *But I wish it were more. If I could only be sure how Lisa feels about me, I'd ask her to go steady with me.*

Paul sucked in more frigid air. Even though he had promised himself that he wouldn't fall for another woman, somehow he had. There was something special about Lisa, like the way she cared for her students and even her dog. She seemed sincere and honest, and Paul felt certain that she would never hurt anyone intentionally.

"Umm. . .Harley, it's been nice talking to you, but I need to get out of this cold building and go back to the woodworking shop with a message for Uncle Abe."

"Oh, sure. . . Of course. . . I'll let you go. Take care, little bruder, and come see us soon."

"Maybe some time in early spring."

"Okay, you'd better, or I'll come to Ohio and get you. We all miss seeing your handsome face."

Paul let out a bark of laughter. "Yeah, right." He said goodbye and hung up the phone.

As Paul made his way back to the house, he thought about the news Harley had given him. A few months ago, hearing that Susan and his used-to-be good friend were planning their wedding felt like a stab to the heart. Now it didn't matter at all.

"Where's your brother today?" Lisa asked her student Karen Yoder when she entered the schoolyard after being dropped off by her father.

"After school yesterday, Gabe broke his arm in two places." The little girl blinked rapidly. "He was slidin' down the hill on an inner tube out behind our place and crashed right into a tree."

"I'm sorry to hear that," Lisa said earnestly. "Were you also sledding when it happened?"

Karen shook her head. "He went with our cousin Robert, and Mama said I couldn't go."

Before Lisa could form a response, her young student stomped the snow off her boots and went into the schoolhouse. Normally most of the children played outside until the bell rang, but with it being so cold outside, Lisa understood why Karen would want to get indoors quickly.

She shivered, watching from the porch as several more children came into the yard. Some stopped to make a few snowballs, but most made a beeline for the warmth of indoors.

Lisa was about to ring the bell when Yvonne came out and joined her on the porch. "I hope all this snow melts soon," she said. "Spring is still more than two months away, and I'm already longing for bright sunshine and warmer days."

"Same here. Winter is definitely not my favorite time of the year."

"There are some fun things to do in the winter, though, right?"

"Jah, like sledding on an inner tube and ending up with a broken arm." Lisa grimaced. "You'll never get me on one of those things."

"Sledding can be a lot of fun if one is careful."

"I suppose. Did Karen tell you about her brother's accident?"

Yvonne nodded. "Since he's in my class, I'll have to make a trip to his parents' house and take him some homework to do until he's able to come back to school."

"That makes sense. Otherwise Gabe will fall behind."

"How's Maggie doing these days?" Yvonne asked.

"She's getting around fairly well. Better than I expected. I guess the vet was right when he said that my dog would adjust to having only three legs."

"I'm glad she's doing better." Yvonne pointed to the bell in Lisa's hand. "I think it's about time to bring the rest of the children inside, don't you?"

"Yes, and it's time for a certain teacher to go indoors too. Brr. . .it's sure cold this morning." Lisa rang the bell and stepped aside as their students filed into the building. As the last two children—a boy and a girl—went in, a vivid picture popped into Lisa's head. She saw her six-year-old self, entering the schoolhouse she'd attended on a cold, snowy day. A young boy came in behind her and whispered in Lisa's ear, "I'm gonna marry you someday."

What a silly thought I just had, Lisa told herself as she stepped into the schoolhouse and closed the door. *Did it really happen, or was it only a figment of my imagination? And if it did actually occur, who was that boy?*

Walnut Creek

When Paul entered Memory Keepers that afternoon, he found Orley and Lois moving a small table from one side of the room to the other.

"Can I help you with that?" Paul hurried over to them.

"Danki for offering, but it's not heavy, and we can manage." Once the table was in place, Lois dusted it off while Orley came over and shook Paul's hand. "Good to see you. Did you get my message about the milk bottles?"

"I sure did." Paul glanced over at Lois and smiled when she waved; then he turned his attention to Orley again. "That's why I came by—to take a look at them."

"I wanted you to see the old bottles first, before I set them out to sell, so they're still in the storage room. Let's go there now and you can have a look-see." Orley motioned for Paul to follow him as he headed toward the back of the store.

When they entered the storage room, Orley turned on a couple of battery-operated lights and pointed to a shelf where six milk bottles had been placed.

After Paul stepped up and took a good look, he was pleased to see that one of the bottles looked almost exactly like the one his grandma used to own before he had carelessly broken it. He picked the ornate bottle up and studied it carefully. "This is it." He grinned at Orley. "It's very similar, if not identical, to the one I've been searching for. How much do you want for it?"

Orley quoted a reasonable price, and Paul said, "That sounds fair. Any chance you could gift wrap it for me?"

Orley bobbed his head. "I'm sure my fraa would be glad to accommodate that request."

"I'd sure appreciate it. My grandmother's birthday isn't till the end of April, and she won't be back from her winter vacation in Florida until close to that time." Paul fingered the raised bubbles on the bottle, feeling a sense of eagerness. "So I will wait until then to make a trip to Indiana and surprise Grandma with the old bottle for her birthday."

"I'm sure she'll be even happier to see you than she will be with the milk bottle."

"I hope so. It'll be nice to see her and the rest of my family."

"I bet they miss you."

"Jah, but they're well aware that I like it here and plan to stay."

"Sometimes change is good. A person can gain a new perspective when they start over in a new place."

"I agree with you on that." Paul left the storage room with the bottle and waited at the register to ask Orley's wife if she would be kind enough to gift wrap the milk bottle.

"No problem." Lois stepped behind the counter, pulled out some tissue paper, and began wrapping up the glass item with care. Then she showed Paul some samples of the different kinds of gift wrap available. "Which one would you like to use?"

Paul pointed. "I think she would like the one with the birds and flowers the best."

"You chose wisely." She smiled. "If there is anything else you'd like to look at, feel free to wander around the store. I'll have your gift wrapped by the time you come back to the register."

Paul thanked Lois and went to speak to Orley again. He found him standing near the front window, looking out. "Mind if I ask you a question?"

Orley gave him a wide smile. "I don't mind at all. Ask away."

"How long did it take you to know if Lois was the woman you wanted to date?"

There seemed to be a twinkle in the older man's eyes. "Not long at all. Course I waited awhile, till I was pretty sure she was interested in me too, before I asked."

Paul shifted his weight from one leg to the other. "I'm not sure what I'll do if she says no."

"Is Lisa Miller the 'she' you're referring to?"

Paul felt a rush of heat flood his face as he nodded. "Jah."

"I thought that might be the case." Orley moved closer and placed his hand on Paul's shoulder; then he gave it a couple of pats. "Look at it this way—the worst thing that can happen is she'll say no, and then you'll come to realize that she wasn't the right girl for you."

Paul wasn't sure he wanted to hear that, but Orley was right—he did need to find out where he stood with Lisa. He just hoped he would have the courage to do it soon.

"Oh, before I forget. . ." Orley thumped his forehead. "If you're not doing anything tomorrow afternoon, I'd like to invite you to join me on the hill out behind my home for some seriously fun sledding."

"That does sound interesting, but I don't have a *schlidde*."

"No problem. I have several old sleds in my barn, so if you don't have one, you're more than welcome to use one of those."

"That would be great." Paul hesitated a minute before asking a bold question. "Would you mind very much if I invited my friend Lisa to join me?"

"No problem. The more the merrier." Orley glanced over at Lois, who was still busy wrapping the gift for Paul, and she grinned in their direction. "If Lisa comes with you, I may even be able to talk my fraa into joining us. Normally she prefers to stay inside, but this time she might change her mind and come sledding."

"That would be nice. It will give Lisa someone to talk to in case she gets tired of sledding and decides to stand on the sidelines and watch."

Orley clasped Paul's shoulder. "All right, then, we'll look forward to seeing you tomorrow afternoon." He took a piece of paper and wrote down his home address, then handed it to Paul.

"What time would work best for you?"

"Oh, how about sometime between one and two?"

"Sounds good." Paul headed over to the register to pay for his purchase and wait for Lois to finish gift wrapping the milk bottle. As soon as he left, he planned to head over to see Lisa, and he sure hoped she would say yes.

Chapter 26

Sugarcreek

After Paul left Memory Keepers, he decided to stop by the Schrocks' place and see if Lisa would be interested in going sledding with him Saturday. He hoped she'd be able to, because it would be good for her to get away from the house for a while and have a little fun in the snow. Between teaching school and taking care of her dog, Lisa's life involved more work than play these days.

Paul urged Chester forward until the Schrocks' home came into view, and then he guided the horse up their driveway. Paul set the brake and got out of the buggy. A few minutes later, he had Chester secured at the hitching rail. After a short tromp through the snow, Paul stepped onto the sidewalk that had obviously been shoveled and sprinkled with ice melt sometime earlier today.

Stepping onto the front porch, he heard Maggie bark from inside the house. A few seconds later, Lisa opened the door with the dog by her side.

"Hello, Paul. It's good to see you. Would you like to come in?" She held the door open for him.

"Jah, sure." Paul stepped inside and bent down to pet Maggie. "How ya doin,' girl? Are you getting along better these days?"

The dog wagged her tail while licking Paul's hand.

He looked up at Lisa and smiled. "I think she likes me."

Lisa nodded. "I believe you're right. Maggie likes you a lot."

Do you like me too? Paul kept the thought to himself. It would be too bold to come right out and ask her that question. And it would be embarrassing if her grandfather or grandmother heard him ask that of Lisa. He gave the dog one final pat and stood to his full height.

"May I take your jacket?" Lisa asked. "We can sit in the living room and talk until it's time for me to help my grandma fix supper."

"You're welcome to stay for supper, Paul," Marlene hollered from the kitchen.

Lisa's cheeks colored. "I guess she was listening."

Paul chuckled. "I'd love to stay for supper, but I need to get home. I promised Aunt Emma that I'd pick up a few things for her at the store, and I haven't done that yet." Paul took a step closer to Lisa. "The reason I stopped by is to invite you to go sledding with me tomorrow afternoon. I was at the antique store in Walnut Creek today, and Orley invited me to try out the hill behind his house. He said I could borrow one of his sleds and mentioned that you'd be welcome to come too."

Lisa twirled the ties on her head covering around her index finger. "That sounds like fun, but I should probably be here to take care of Maggie."

Marlene stepped into the hallway. "Your hund's doing fine, and I'll be here to take her outside whenever she needs to go there." She gave Lisa's shoulder a tap. "After a long week of teaching school, you deserve to get out for a while and have some fun."

Come on Lisa. . .please join me tomorrow. Paul stood quietly at her side.

Lisa hesitated but finally nodded. "All right, Paul. What time should I be ready?"

"I'll pick you up around one o'clock. How's that sound? Or would you rather go a little later?"

"I can be ready by one."

"Great. I'll see you tomorrow then." Paul said goodbye to Lisa and her grandma, gave Maggie's head a few pats, and went out the door. When he got to the hitching rail and released his horse, he paused for a moment and stroked Chester's silky neck. "She said yes, boy. Maybe tomorrow, while we're traveling to or from Walnut Creek, I'll get up the nerve to tell Lisa how much I've come to care for her. I sure hope she feels the same about me."

The next day, dressed in a heavy jacket, scarf, gloves, and boots, Lisa stood waiting at the living-room window for Paul to pick her up. She looked forward to spending time with him again but felt bad about leaving Maggie for her grandmother to care for. Grandma had assured her, however, that she didn't mind and reminded Lisa that with the exception of going outside with the dog when needed, there really wasn't much else to do. Maggie was off her pain medication and didn't have to be coaxed to eat or drink anymore. The dog's stitches had come out, and she'd been getting around with little effort while adjusting to her disability. Grandma had also commented that Lisa worried too much.

Lisa reflected on how well she and her dog had bonded when Maggie first came to live with them. She smiled, thinking about how one night a few days after she'd made the decision to keep the dog, she had discovered Maggie upstairs in her bedroom, curled up at the foot of the bed. Another time the dog had found a roll of her grandfather's quarters and managed to tear it open. Grandpa was none too happy when he'd discovered money all over the floor, but Maggie's winning personality won him over, and soon all was forgiven.

Lisa's attention reverted back to the present when she heard a horse's whinny. She shielded her eyes from the glare the sun had cast on the snow in their yard and was pleased to see Paul's horse and carriage enter the yard.

Lisa waited until she heard Paul's boots clomping up the porch steps before she went to open the door. Maggie hobbled into the hall's front entrance and stood beside Lisa.

"No, girl, you can't come with us," Lisa said when the dog whined and pushed her head against Lisa's leg.

"Maybe next year," Paul interjected. "She'll be completely healed and raring to go way before then."

Next year. Lisa smiled. *That must mean Paul is planning to stay and make his home in Ohio.* Lisa hoped that he would, and for the first time ever, she allowed herself to imagine what it would be like if she and Paul got married.

Now where did that thought come from? Lisa wondered. *I've never wanted to get married or establish a close relationship with a man. Besides, I don't know if Paul feels anything toward me but friendship.*

"Ready to go now?" Paul asked.

She nodded. "I'll just go into the kitchen and tell my grandparents goodbye."

"Mind if I go with you?"

"Course not. I'm sure Grandma and Grandpa would like to say hello."

Lisa clapped her hands and called Maggie to follow. The dog went obediently behind her, and when they entered the kitchen, Maggie bedded down on the throw rug near the sink.

Lisa's grandparents sat at the kitchen table finishing the last of their lunch. They both looked at Paul and smiled, and Grandpa got up and shook Paul's hand.

"As always, it's nice to see you," he said.

"It's good to see you folks as well." Paul glanced at the table, then looked at Lisa. "Did I get here too soon? Were you able to get some lunch?"

"Jah, I ate around noon."

"If you'd come by sooner we could have all eaten together," Grandma said in her usual cheery tone.

"That's okay. I ate at home." Paul's cheeks reddened a bit. "What I meant to say is, I ate at my aunt and uncle's home. I sure don't own it."

"Do you think you'll ever settle down and buy a place of your own here in Sugarcreek?" Grandma asked.

The color in Paul's cheeks darkened, and he lifted his shoulders in a brief shrug. "Maybe. . . I hope so. I've priced a few places, but I'm just waiting to see how things go."

Sensing that he seemed uncomfortable with this conversation, Lisa suggested that they get going.

"Jah, we probably should," he agreed. "It'll take us a while to get to Walnut Creek, and I don't want to keep Orley waiting."

"Is it necessary to go all the way over there?" Grandpa questioned. "Aren't there some places around here where you can sled?"

"I'm sure there are, but since Orley invited us to try out his hill and I already said yes, I don't want to go back on my word."

"That makes sense." Grandma gave Paul a wide smile. "I hope you and Lisa will have an enjoyable time."

Lisa and Paul said their goodbyes and hurried toward the front door. Lisa was glad that Maggie had fallen asleep or she'd have probably tried to sneak outside with them.

Paul steadied Lisa by putting his arm gently around her waist as they made their way through the slippery snow to his carriage. Although she couldn't feel the warmth of his hand through her heavy jacket, she felt a sense of pleasure at his touch, and knowing that he cared enough to keep her from slipping and falling in the snow made her feelings for him even stronger. Whether he felt anything more than friendship toward her or not, he certainly was a good friend, and she felt thankful for the comfortable relationship they'd developed.

"Would you like another cup of kaffi before you head out to the harness shop?" Marlene asked her husband.

He shook his head. "I'd better not. Too much caffeine makes me jittery, and I've already had two cups of coffee with lunch, not to mention the one I drank during breakfast." He smiled at her from across the table. "But danki for asking."

She nodded and fingered the napkin next to her plate. "What do you think about Lisa and Paul?"

Jerry shrugged. "What about them?"

"Their relationship, Husband. Where do you think it's going?"

His shoulders lifted again. "I have no idea. Guess time will tell."

Marlene tapped her fingers on the tabletop. "I believe they have gotten really close, and I wouldn't be one bit surprised if Paul asks Lisa to go steady with him." She looked at Jerry and blinked several times. "I think they're in love, and I'm wondering why Paul hasn't asked her already."

"Maybe he has, and our granddaughter has chosen not to say anything to us about it."

"That's lecherich. I see no reason why Lisa would not have mentioned it."

"It's not really ridiculous. She might like to keep her private life private." Jerry pushed away from the table and stood. "Would you like my help with the dishes before I go out to the shop?"

Marlene shook her head. "There are only a few, and I'll take care of them."

"Okay. I'll be back in the house in a few hours." He came over, bent down, and kissed her cheek. "Enjoy the quiet, and try not to concern yourself over Lisa and Paul. If they've decided to go steady or proclaimed their love for each other, I'm sure we'll hear about it when Lisa is ready to share the news."

"I hope so. She often keeps things to herself."

"Yes, most of the time. The fact is, all we can do is commit it to God." Jerry slipped on his jacket and knitted cap; then he went out the back door.

Marlene bowed her head in prayer. *Dear Lord, help me remember not to meddle in this or press Lisa about her relationship with Paul. If it's Your will for their friendship to go deeper, then it will happen in Your time.*

Walnut Creek

"Thanks for the loan of these great sleds," Paul said as he, Orley, and Lisa stood at the top of the Troyers' snow-covered hill.

Orley grinned like a child with a new toy. "No problem. I'm glad you could join me today."

Lois hadn't come out with them because she'd been busy writing some letters. She had, however, extended an invitation for Paul and Lisa to join her and Orley for some hot chocolate and cookies when they either got too cold and needed to warm up or had experienced all the sledding they could stand.

"Would you like to go first, Lisa?" Orley asked.

She shook her head. "Think I'll watch from up here while you two go down, and if nobody falls off their schlidde, I'll get on mine and meet you at the bottom of the hill."

Paul gave Lisa's arm a little poke. "Oh, so you're waiting to see if one of us gets hurt or ends up facedown with a mouthful of schnee?"

She laughed and poked him right back. "Exactly."

"Okay, well, here I go." Paul lay on his belly, grabbed hold of the wooden steering apparatus, and pushed off with one foot.

Lisa watched as he sailed down the hill, hollering at the top of his lungs, "Fun! Fun! Fun!" When his sled came to a stop, he got off, looked up toward them, and waved.

"You want to go next or shall I?" Orley questioned.

"I'll wait till you're at the bottom of the hill." Lisa hadn't been sledding since the first winter after she'd come to live with her grandparents. Although she didn't want to admit it, the thought of speeding rapidly down the snowy slope sent shivers of apprehension up her spine.

"Okay, here I go." Orley paused and gave her a silly-looking grin. "During my youth I was given the nickname 'Big O' because I was a good baseball player. Then when I became known by more and more people as Big O, it became almost like my second name." He gestured to his sled. "So stand back and watch Big O make his way down this snowy hill."

Instead of lying on his stomach the way Paul had done, Orley sat on the sled and took hold of each side of the rope that was connected to the steering apparatus. With a noisy huff, he pushed off with both feet and was soon on his way down the hill.

Lisa was impressed when he made it to the bottom with no problem. For a man in his fifties, Orley had a lot of spunk. She figured Paul would probably be the same way when he reached middle age. Lisa hoped she would still know him by then.

It was her turn now, and with Paul and Orley standing down there watching, she felt a determination to set her fears aside and make it safely to the bottom of the hill. She wasn't sure, however, whether to sit on the sled in the manner Orley had done or lie down on her stomach like Paul. Either way, if Lisa wasn't careful, she could end up crashing into something or simply losing her bearings and falling off the sled into a mountain of snow.

Finally, deciding to go facedown, Lisa positioned herself on the sled. She gritted her teeth. *It would be a lot easier to do this if those two men weren't down there, watching me and waiting.*

At the count of ten, Lisa pushed off. About halfway down, she gained momentum, and although the ride felt exhilarating, she lost control. The next thing Lisa knew, her sled hit a bump, and she bounced off, causing her to land facedown in the snow. She coughed and sputtered as a clump of frigid snow traveled up her nose. Lisa was thoroughly embarrassed, and her face felt like it had been frozen in place. She wasn't even sure if, when she opened her mouth, she'd be able to speak.

"Are you okay, Lisa?" Paul reached out his hand to help her up.

"I—I think so." Once on her feet, she brushed at the snow clinging to her face, scarf, and jacket.

"Maybe you should go inside and warm up for a while," Orley suggested. "You're pretty wet and shivering badly."

Lisa nodded and started walking toward the house, pulling the sled behind her. Although she enjoyed spending time with Paul, getting cold and wet with a face full of snow wasn't her idea of having fun.

Chapter 27

Lois heard a knock on the back door and went to see who it was. She had been engrossed in writing a couple of letters and getting them ready to send. Lois had always been a person who enjoyed crossing things off her to-do list. And for now she'd managed to check off everything and could toss that paper away.

When Lois opened the door, she was surprised to see Lisa on the porch, shivering and quite wet.

"Is—is it okay if I come in for a while?" Lisa's teeth chattered as she spoke.

"Of course. You need to get warm and dried off." Lois led the way to the laundry room where her gas-powered wringer washing machine sat. "You can take off your *schtiffel* and leave them here, and I'll set your jackets, scarf, and gloves near the fireplace."

"Danki." Lisa took off her boots and placed them near the washing machine before removing her other outer garments and handing them to Lois.

"How'd you get so wet?" Lois asked as she led the way to the living room, where the warmth from the fireplace greeted them. "I hope those eager fellows didn't start a snowball fight."

"No, no, they'd didn't." Lisa stood in front of the glowing fire, rubbing her cold, reddened hands together. "On my first and only attempt at sledding down the hill, I hit a bump and fell off the sled." Lisa grimaced. "I landed face first and ended up with snow up my naas."

Lois gave an understanding nod as she hung Lisa's jacket, gloves, and scarf on a wooden rack she had set up near the fireplace. "I've had that happen before too. Sledding used to be fun when I was a girl, but not so much anymore." She gave a quick shake of her head. "Of course, my fun-loving husband doesn't mind getting cold and wet. He will go out to sled or ice-skate on our neighbor's frozen pond whenever he gets the chance."

Lisa laughed. "I think Paul might be like that too. He seemed pretty excited about coming here to go sledding."

Lois's nose wrinkled. "If I had gone out sledding like Orley wanted me to, it probably would have been me who'd fallen off the sled and would be standing here, soaking wet. I've never cared much for activities in cold, snowy weather." She noticed that Lisa had quit rubbing her hands together. Lois bent down and checked the wood in the fireplace. *I wonder if Lisa would like a hot beverage to warm her up more. She'd probably appreciate being able to sit and relax after her unpleasant sledding experience.*

"Let's sit here in the living room where it's nice and toasty." Lois gestured to one of the chairs. "Feel free to take whichever seat you would like. While you're getting comfortable, I'll get us some hot chocolate."

"That sounds good. Is there anything I can do to help?"

"There's not much involved in making it, so just relax and enjoy the warmth from the fireplace."

"All right. Danki for your kindness."

Lois smiled and hurried from the room.

While in the kitchen readying the hot chocolates, she peeked through the frosted window and saw the men walking back up the hill, pulling their wooden sleds. *If it weren't for my husband's long beard, I'd have a harder time distinguishing who is who out there.* Lois stepped over to the pantry to retrieve a bag of marshmallows. *My Orley is like a big kid at times. I can't help wondering if he'll ever start acting his age.* The water heated on the stove, and she began measuring and filling the mugs with her fragrant homemade chocolate powder.

When Lois returned to the living room with two mugs full of hot chocolate, she found Lisa on the couch with her head leaning against the back cushion and her eyes closed. Thinking she might have fallen asleep, Lois set the mugs on the coffee table and took a seat in one of the recliners. At the moment, the room seemed so quiet and peaceful.

A few seconds passed, and then Lisa opened her eyes.

"Sorry if I woke you," Lois apologized.

"It's all right. I really wasn't sleeping—just feeling fully relaxed."

"That's good. Everyone needs to take some time to relax." Lois got up and handed Lisa one of the mugs, taking the other one for herself. "Be careful not to burn your mouth. I'm afraid the hot chocolate might be a little too warm. There are some marshmallows right here too."

"Marshmallows are always so good in hot chocolate," Lisa said, "but did you know that they can be used to disguise a pain pill?"

"I'm not sure what you mean."

"When my dog first came home after losing one of her front legs, she wouldn't cooperate and take her pills."

Lois sipped on her beverage and listened attentively as Lisa explained how she'd used marshmallows to hide her dog's pain medication and was pleased when it worked.

"I'm glad it worked out okay and she cooperated."

Lisa sat quietly, drinking her hot chocolate, and Lois wasn't sure what else to talk about, since she didn't really know the young woman that well. *I could ask her if she and Paul are going steady.* Lois reached for some marshmallows to add to her hot chocolate. *She's a little timid, and that might seem like too bold of a question, so maybe it would be best if I ask more questions about her dog.* "How's your hund doing now?" Lois questioned.

"Much better, but she's not quite back to being her old self yet. The first week after her surgery was pretty rough."

Lois listened again as Lisa shared a few more things about Maggie's recovery and how terrible she'd felt seeing the poor dog in pain.

"I was so worried about her those first few nights that I set up a doggy bed for her on the floor in the downstairs guest room where I had decided to sleep. That way I could check on her frequently." Lisa looked away, then back at Lois. "At first I blamed myself for Maggie's injuries, since I was the one who'd put her away in her pen that evening."

"Do you know how she got out?"

"I suppose that Maggie could have played with the latch enough times to have gotten it open, but I'm not really sure." Lisa sighed. "I was so worried those first few nights, it was hard to sleep."

"You must care for your dog very much."

"Jah, Maggie is very special to me. She's a good companion and is ever so smart."

"I'd like to meet her sometime. Maybe this spring when the weather is nicer, you could bring her by here or our antique store. Or another thought would be for Orley and me to stop by your grandparents' place sometime when we are in Sugarcreek. Your grandfather owns the harness shop there, right?"

"Jah, and it would be nice if you could meet Maggie. She's a friendly hund, and I'm sure she'd warm right up to you." Lisa blew on her hot chocolate and took a sip. "This is really good. Is it a ready-made mix, or did you make it from scratch?"

"It's my own—well, my mother's, actually. I found it in her recipe book several years after she died."

"How old were you when she passed away?"

"I was still a young girl—just eight years old."

"Did your daed remarry?"

"Jah, he married a widow lady from our community in Mifflin County, Pennsylvania, a year after Mama died, but that marriage only lasted a few years. Selma got cancer and didn't survive. It was hard to deal with because my siblings and I had grown fond of her." Lois swallowed hard in an attempt to push the lump in her throat down. Even after all these years, she still felt sad talking about her first stepmother's death.

"Did he find a third wife or stay single after that?"

"He chose a single lady who had never been married, but that wasn't till I was grown and had moved here. My daed is still married to Sarah, but they live in Kentucky and I don't see them very often."

Lisa took another drink from her mug, then set it back down on the coffee table. "Life is unfair, and there are so many uncertainties."

Lois drank some of her hot chocolate before speaking, which gave her a few seconds to think about how she should respond. "What you said is true, Lisa, but it's how we choose to deal with the unexpected happenings that occur. Some of them are tragic, to be sure, but we need to pray and have the faith to believe that the Lord will see us through."

Lisa pressed her elbows into her sides. "I try, but sometimes it's so hard. Ever since I lost my parents and paternal grandparents, I've feared that the worst will happen."

"In Second Timothy 1:7 we read, 'For God hath not given us the spirit of fear; but of power, and of love, and of a sound mind,'" Lois quoted. "Whenever I feel overwhelmed by fear, I try to remember that scripture."

"It is a good verse," Lisa said. "I'll try to focus on that whenever I'm full of doubts and fears."

When the men came inside an hour later, Lois removed Lisa's dried things, putting her jacket and scarf, along with her gloves, on the wall peg by the front door. Then she returned to hang the men's jackets, gloves, and stocking caps by the fire.

Lisa couldn't help but notice how red Orley's and Paul's noses were. Was it just from the cold, or had they both fallen off their sleds into the frigid snow? Before she had a chance to ask, Lois asked the men if they would like some hot chocolate.

"You bet we would." Orley looked at Paul. "Right?"

Paul bobbed his head. "Drinking something warm might help the inside of my body to feel warmer, and the cozy blaze in your fireplace will no doubt take away the chill my body feels. It sure has gotten really cold out there."

"I think it may have something to do with the fact that you and Orley both got so wet," Lois commented.

"That's true," Orley admitted. "Paul and I did fall off our sleds a few times. But don't worry, we never got hurt."

Lois gave a small laugh. "I figured as much." She turned toward the kitchen. "I'll be back soon with your beverages and some kichlin."

Lisa stood up. "I'll help you with that." She followed Lois into the other room. "What would you like me to do?"

"Would you mind going back to the living room to get our mugs? I'd like to have some more hot chocolate, wouldn't you?"

"Jah, I would."

"I'll slice some gingerbread while you're gone, and I'll get out some chocolate chip cookies I made this morning."

"Both sound yummy." Lisa left the kitchen and was almost to the door of the living room when she heard Orley mention her name. "How are things going between you and your aldi?"

Lisa tipped her head and waited for Paul's response.

"Lisa isn't officially my girlfriend, but I'm hoping she will be soon. When I take her home, I'm planning to ask if she'll go steady with me."

Paul had spoken quietly, but Lisa heard every word he'd said. She leaned against the wall, holding her hands against her chest as she pulled in a few deep breaths. *Paul wants me to be his girlfriend. When he asks me to go steady with him, what should I say? Should I give Paul my answer right away or say that I need to think about it?*

Sugarcreek

Paul's thoughts had been so scattered he'd barely been able to think of anything to talk to Lisa about on the drive back to Sugarcreek. But here they were, pulling into her grandparents' yard, and he still hadn't told Lisa how he felt about her or mentioned going steady.

She'd been quiet too, staring straight ahead most of the way and picking at the material on her gloves. *Is she still embarrassed about falling off her sled? Could she be upset because we didn't have much time to be alone with each other today?* Paul clamped his teeth together so hard his jaw ached. *When Lisa quit sledding and went into the Troyers' house, maybe I should have put away the sled I borrowed from Orley and gone in with her, or maybe we should have headed back to Sugarcreek.*

Neither Lisa nor Paul made an effort to get out of the buggy. They both sat staring out the front window at the backside of his horse.

What are you waiting for? he asked himself. *You can't put this off any longer.*

"Would you like to come inside for a while?" Lisa asked.

"Umm. . .jah, but there's something I'd like to say to you first."

She turned her head in his direction. "What is it, Paul?"

He moistened his parched lips with the tip of his tongue before clearing his throat. "As I'm sure you must realize, I enjoy spending time with you."

"I like being with you too."

"I'm glad, and, umm. . .well, the thing is. . ." Paul paused and took in some air. "I've come to care for you, Lisa. In fact I haven't cared about anyone the way I do you since my girlfriend back home and I broke up." He waited a few seconds to see if Lisa would say anything, but when she just sat there looking at him, he continued. "So I was wondering if you would go steady with me." There, it was out, and Paul felt a little better, but now he had to wait for her answer, and he didn't know what he would say if she said no.

"I have feelings for you too." Lisa's voice was barely above a whisper. "And jah, I would like to go steady."

Releasing the breath he'd been holding while waiting for her answer, Paul reached across the seat and took hold of Lisa's hand. He would rather have kissed her but didn't want to move too fast. Paul felt it best to take it slow and easy with Lisa, just as he'd done so far.

"Why don't you come inside, and we can tell my grandparents what we've decided," Lisa suggested.

"Jah, that'd be great. I hope they will approve."

"I don't think you have to worry about that. Grandma and Grandpa have said many times that they think you are a fine young man."

"Okay then, just let me get Chester secured at the rail."

Paul got out of the buggy, and as he went around to his horse, he reminded himself that he still hadn't told Lisa that they used to know each other. But he'd convinced himself that it could wait awhile longer. Maybe in another month or two, when their relationship had grown stronger, he would drum up the courage to tell her. For now, Paul would simply enjoy their courtship, and someday, if everything went well between them, he might even propose marriage.

Chapter 28

"Winter. . .winter. . .winter. . . Will spring ever get here? It seems like all we've had these first few weeks of February is ice and snow," Marlene complained to Jerry as they sat in the kitchen having a cup of coffee together before he headed out to his shop. "I can't believe our weather was so bad last week that school had to be canceled for two days. Although Lisa enjoyed being at home and spending time with Maggie, I think she missed teaching school on those days."

"It was pretty severe weather," her husband agreed, "but at least we have no blizzard-like conditions this week."

"Jah. Since today is Valentine's Day, and Lisa and Yvonne planned something special for their students, everyone would have been disappointed if there was no school today."

"What do they have planned?"

"In addition to a few of the parents bringing in hot lunches, Lisa took cherry-vanilla cupcakes to share with the children. As a special touch, she put a heart-shaped candy on the top of each one." Marlene paused to drink the rest of her coffee and set the cup down. "Before Lisa left for the schoolhouse this morning, she mentioned that Yvonne would be bringing two kinds of cookies."

Jerry chuckled. "Guess the kids will go home on a sugar high today. I bet their parents will love that."

She poked his arm. "Since it's Valentine's Day, I'm sure the children's parents will know what to expect."

"No doubt about that." Jerry started to get up, but then he sat back down. "Did I tell you what I heard about our bishop's son Eric the other day?"

"No, I don't believe you did."

"Es is ihm aartlich schlecht gange."

"In what way did things go badly for him?" Marlene questioned.

"After school yesterday, he went sledding with some of his friends. The boy wasn't gone very long before he came running into the house hollering like crazy, and with his mouth open and tongue sticking out."

Her eyes widened. "Oh, dear, what happened?"

"Well, the bishop said that Eric's *zung* had come in contact with the cold sled, and when it froze there, he just jerked his head back and pulled his tongue right off the sled."

"Oh, dear, I can't imagine how badly that must have hurt. It will probably take a while for the boy's injury to heal up."

Jerry bobbed his head. "I did some stupid things when I was a boy, but never anything like that. Makes me wonder what the young fellow was thinking."

"Maybe one of his friends dared him to do it. Or perhaps when Eric slid down the hill, in the excitement, he opened his mouth to scream and his tongue came out of its own accord and got stuck."

"Jah, either of those things could have been the reason."

Marlene pushed the plate of lunch meat closer to her husband. "Would you like me to make you another sandwich before you head back to work?"

Jerry gave his belly a few thumps. "No thanks, I'm full enough. I will have a few more chips though, and then I need to head out."

Marlene waited until he'd helped himself to a handful of potato chips before she spoke again. "Have you noticed the change in our granddaughter since she and Paul began going steady? I'd have to say Lisa seems like a different person since Paul came into her life, and that makes me so happy." She pursed her lips. "I'm also glad Aaron Wengerd has finally given up his quest to win our granddaughter's hand."

Jerry nodded. "I agree. I don't think Aaron would have been the best choice for Lisa."

"I hope the weather stays as it is right now so Lisa and Paul don't have to change their plans to go out for supper this evening."

"According to the weather report I read in this morning's paper, it's not likely to get worse. But even if it should, I'm betting Paul will put on some snowshoes and make his way over here just to be with Lisa."

Marlene smiled as she pictured Lisa's boyfriend blazing a trail through the heavy snow from his aunt and uncle's place to here. Every time Marlene saw the big smiles on Paul's and Lisa's faces when they were together, it brought tears to her eyes. If anyone deserved to be happy, it was Lisa.

Maggie got up from the braided rug she'd been sleeping on and gave a few loud barks.

"I know, girl," Marlene said. "You want to go out. Guess I'd better put my jacket on so I can keep a close eye on you out there." Even though Lisa's dog was doing so well, Marlene always went out with her. She couldn't take the chance that Maggie might leave the yard and try to make it to the schoolhouse in search of Lisa—especially after what had happened the night of the schoolchildren's Christmas program.

Marlene started to rise from her chair, but Jerry told her to sit back down and relax. "Since I have to get bundled up against the cold anyway, I'll take the hund out and bring her back in before I head to the harness shop."

"Danki, Jerry. Oh, and by the way—our granddaughter was thoughtful enough to leave us both a cherry-vanilla cupcake to celebrate Valentine's Day." Marlene gestured to the plastic container on the kitchen counter.

"It was nice of her to share. I'll get one after I bring Maggie back in and take it out to the shop with me." He turned to the dog and slapped his knee. "Come on, Maggie, let's go out."

Marlene watched them head to the door. Although her dear husband had never been the romantic type, he was a kind, generous man, and she'd never regretted marrying him. She hoped if Lisa and Paul got married that Lisa would feel thankful she'd chosen the right mate. Marlene casually anchored a hand against one hip. *And if I have anything to say about it, that marriage will happen.*

Lisa smiled as she watched her students give out their Valentine cards to each other. She and Yvonne received several too. The scholars had been served a hot lunch at noon and spent some time playing in the snow, and after a few more lessons, the party had begun.

Once the cards had been passed out, Lisa and Yvonne set out the treats they'd brought, along with some fruit punch left over from lunch. The kids ate the cupcakes and cookies, talking and laughing the whole while. Lisa was pleased that nearly all of them had said thank you. It was only right that the children were being taught proper manners at home as well as at school.

"Do you have any special plans for this evening?" Yvonne asked, stepping up to Lisa.

"Jah. Paul is taking me out for supper."

Her friend smiled. "You two make a really nice couple. I'm happy you've found someone special, Lisa."

"You'll find the right someone when the time is right."

A rosy glow erupted on Yvonne's cheeks. "I—I think I may already have."

"Oh? Is it someone I know?"

Yvonne nodded. "Aaron Wengerd has come over to see me several times in the last few weeks. And he invited me to join his family for his sister's birthday supper tonight. So that's how I'll be spending my Valentine's Day evening."

"That's wonderful, Yvonne. I hope things work out for you and Aaron." Lisa didn't voice her thoughts, but she was glad Aaron had quit trying to see her socially and found someone else.

As far as Lisa was concerned, there was no one better suited to her than Paul Herschberger.

"Are you excited about your supper date with Paul this evening?" Grandma asked as Lisa stood in front of the hall mirror adjusting her white head covering.

"Jah. Today was a busy day at school, and I'm looking forward to spending the next few hours relaxing and enjoying a nice meal at the restaurant he's chosen." Lisa's brows drew together as she looked at Maggie when she came in with her unique walk and sat down at Lisa's feet. "I wish it was springtime and Paul and I were going on a picnic. Then we could take Maggie with us." She leaned over and stroked the dog's ears. "You miss me when I'm gone, don't you, girl?"

Maggie whined and turned her head so she could lick Lisa's hand.

"Once school is out in a few months, I'll be here more, and we can spend a lot of time together."

As if she'd understood what Lisa had said, Maggie barked three times.

Grandma laughed. "That hund is too schmaert for her own good. Sometimes I think she can read my mind and knows what I'm going to say before the words come out of my mouth."

Lisa laughed too. *If I'm this devoted to my dog, I wonder how I would be if I had children someday. I can't believe how my life seems to be changing, because I never thought I would even be thinking about getting married and having children.*

A horse whinnied outside, and Lisa let her thoughts drift away. No doubt Paul had arrived, and she was eager to go. Even so, Lisa didn't want to appear too anxious, so she waited until he knocked on the door to open it.

Paul had barely stepped inside when Maggie began barking again and wagging her tail.

He bent to pet her. "Are ya happy to see me, Maggie girl?"

Woof! Woof! Woof!

Paul gave the dog a little more affection, then stood to his full height and handed Lisa a bright red gift bag. "Happy Valentine's Day."

Her cheeks warmed. "You didn't have to give me anything. Going out to supper with you would be gift enough."

"I wanted to do something a little extra special. Go ahead and open it."

Lisa reached into the bag and pulled out a book.

"It's a historical novel I found at the Christian bookstore," Paul explained. "It's set during the California gold rush days, and I thought you might find it interesting."

She turned the book over and read a short blurb that told a little about the story. "This looks quite interesting. I'll be eager to begin reading it. Danki, Paul."

"You're welcome." He offered her a wide smile. "I'd hoped you would like it."

Lisa's grandmother stepped into the front entrance, and Lisa showed her the book. "See what Paul gave me?"

"It certainly does seem like an interesting book." Grandma greeted Paul with a hug. "I hope you two will have a lovely evening."

"Where's Grandpa?" Lisa asked. "I'm sure Paul would like to say hello, and I want to say goodbye to both of you before we go."

"He went down the hall to get a new puzzle from the closet." Grandma looked in that direction. "Oh, here he comes now."

Grandpa appeared a few seconds later, holding a box with a picture of a covered bridge on it. Lisa figured he and Grandma would start to work on it as soon as she and her date left.

"*Guder owed,* Paul." Holding on to the puzzle box with his left hand, Lisa's grandfather extended his right hand.

With an eager expression, Paul shook Grandpa's hand. "Good evening.

How have you been?"

"Right as *regge*." Grandpa put a sly little smile on his face. "Or maybe it would be more reasonable to say, 'right as snow,' since we haven't seen any rain in a good long while."

"That's true, but March is only a month away, so maybe the schnee will melt soon, and we'll get some rain clouds."

"If I had to pick between the two," Grandma chimed in, "I'd choose rain over snow any day." She sniffed deeply. "I've always enjoyed the clean, damp smell after we've been blessed with a good hard rain."

"Same here," Lisa agreed. "But I'd rather have plenty of sunshine, especially on days during the school year when I walk or ride my bike to the schoolhouse."

The four of them chatted a few more minutes, and then Paul looked at Lisa and said, "I don't know about you, but I'm getting hungry, so are you ready to go?"

"Most definitely." Lisa slipped into her outer garments, hugged her grandparents while saying goodbye, and gave Maggie a few pats on the head. "You be good now, ya hear?"

The dog cocked her head to one side and wagged her tail.

Paul opened the door, and the two of them stepped out onto the porch.

Once Lisa was situated in the passenger's seat of Paul's buggy, Paul undid the horse and climbed in.

Although it was a chilly night, Lisa didn't mind. With the carriage robe in Paul's buggy draped over the lower half of her body, she felt pleasantly warm. Besides, they would soon be sitting inside a cozy restaurant and wouldn't have to deal with the cold at all.

As Paul and Lisa headed back to her grandparents' house that evening after a delicious meal at Dutch Valley Restaurant, once again he considered telling Lisa that he used to know her when he was a boy. Something held him back as he looked over at Lisa. *Maybe now isn't the best time. If she were to get upset hearing this news, it would ruin the nice evening we've had.*

When Paul looked out the front window and saw white flakes on Chester's back, he realized it had begun snowing again. Fortunately there was not a strong wind, so it didn't look like they'd be faced with another blizzard like the one they'd had last week. On those days Paul and Uncle Abe had been able to get some work done in his shop, but neither of them had ventured out onto the roads.

"I can't believe it's snowing again," Lisa said, breaking into Paul's thoughts. "I want spring to come so bad, I can almost taste it."

"I hear what you're saying. It's a lot easier to get around when the weather is nice."

"It'll be better for Maggie too. She's able to walk easier now in the house, but all the snow in the yard makes it harder for her when she's outside."

"Makes sense to me. Even on my two good legs it's hard to get around in the snow. If I'm not struggling in snow up to my knees, I am slipping and sliding around on the paths that have been cleared."

"This colder weather isn't good for doing the wash either," Lisa put in. "My grandma doesn't like to hang her laundry outside where it freezes on the line, so she usually hangs everything that's been washed in the basement on a couple of drying racks. Sometimes, when we need things dried faster, she will set the drying racks in the living room in front of the fireplace." Lisa snickered. "Of course, that can prove to be embarrassing if those racks are full of wet clothes and someone drops by unexpectedly. That happened two weeks ago when one of our neighbors came over."

Paul laughed. It was nice to see how easily Lisa engaged him in conversation these days. It was a pleasant change from the quiet, shy young woman he'd met when he first arrived in Ohio. Paul liked to think that he'd had a little influence on her in that regard, but whatever the reason, it was good to see the outgoing Lisa he remembered from childhood resurfacing.

Paul saw the Schrocks' place come into view, and soon he guided Chester up the driveway. He hated to see his pleasant evening with Lisa end, but it had gotten late, and with both of them having jobs to go to tomorrow, it was time for them to say good night.

After Paul had Chester at the hitching rail, he did something he'd wanted to do for a long time. Paul pulled Lisa gently into his arms and kissed her lips. Warmth spread throughout his chest when Lisa didn't resist but responded to his kiss by putting her hands on the back of his neck. The nearness of her made Paul feel possessive. He wanted to take Lisa as his wife. But it was too soon for a marriage proposal, so instead of saying the words on his heart, Paul kissed her again.

Chapter 29

Winter moved on, and by the middle of March, spring had sprung. Flowering bulbs had begun creeping through the soil, robins were nesting, many lawns had turned green because of the rain, and sleds had been traded in for bicycles.

"What a beautiful day we've had so far," Lois commented as she and Orley entered the town of Sugarcreek with their horse and buggy. "It's almost warm enough that we could have taken our open carriage on the road today."

"That'll happen soon enough." Orley glanced to the left as they passed a well-kept farmhouse. "It's always nice to see bright green leaves filling out the trees and people outside working in their yards."

"Jah," she agreed. "And I always love the earthy smell when gardens are turned over in preparation for planting."

"At least our garden is tilled and ready for seeds and prestarted plants."

Lois gave a brief nod. "I have some ideas of what seeds I would like to put in this year. Since we didn't have enough small cucumbers for pickling last year, I'd like to get more of those plants too. Also some dill weed would be nice."

He smacked his lips. "Your bread-and-butter pickles are sure tasty, especially during those hot, sticky months that lie ahead. Yep, they're good, alone or on a burger."

"I'm glad you like them so much. Another thing I like to do after I make pickles is give them as gifts to friends and family." She shifted on the soft, cushioned buggy seat.

They conversed more about their garden, until Orley pointed up ahead and announced that the Schrocks' harness shop was coming into view.

"I hope Lisa is home from teaching at the schoolhouse by now," Lois said. "I'd sure like to see that hund of hers."

"Me too, but I'm also wanting to pay Jerry Schrock a visit at his harness shop. I'm hoping he can fix that old bridle I got the other day, which I'd like to sell in our store."

"Should we pull up to the rail by the harness shop first?" Lois questioned as they entered the Schrocks' property.

Orley shook his head. "There's no point in you sitting in the carriage waiting while I talk to Jerry. How about if we stop at the house first, and if Lisa is at home, you can visit with her while I take care of business in the harness shop. When I'm done, I'll come back and join you. How's that sound?"

Lois hesitated a few seconds as she mulled things over. "I guess that would be okay, but I would feel uncomfortable if Lisa isn't home yet, and I would need to explain my presence to her grandmother."

Orley had opened his mouth as if to comment when Lisa rode into the yard on her bike. She stopped near the house, got off, and came over to Orley and Lois's carriage. "Well, hello. Did you come by to meet Maggie?"

"Our mission is twofold." Orley held up one finger. "We came to see your hund." A second finger came up. "And I have a harness that I hope your grandfather can repair."

Lisa smiled. "Maggie's not in her pen, so I'm sure she's in the house with my grandma. Come on in, and I'll introduce you to both of them."

"Grandma, we have company," Lisa called when she entered the house with the Troyers.

A few moments later, her grandmother came out of the kitchen and joined them in the entryway.

Lisa made the introductions, explaining that Orley and Lois owned an antique store in Walnut Creek.

"It's nice to meet you." Grandma gestured to the living room. "Let's go in there, where we can sit and visit." She led the way, and they all took a seat. "My husband's working in his harness shop right now." She looked at Lisa. "If he doesn't have a customer at the moment, why don't you go get him?"

"That's all right. There's no need to bother him," Orley was quick to say. "I brought something with me for your husband to repair, so I'll be going out to the harness shop soon anyway."

"Oh, okay. In the meantime though, would either of you care for some coffee, tea, or something cold to drink? I also have a loaf of banana bread that I made this morning." Grandma smiled. "Lisa and I usually have a snack when she gets home from teaching school."

"A glass of cold *wasser* would be nice," Lois spoke up.

"Water would be fine for me too," Orley added as he scooched over on the couch closer to Lois.

"Would you like my help?" Lisa asked her grandmother.

Grandma shook her head. "No need for that. I'll put the beverage glasses on a tray and carry it in."

Soon after Grandma left the room, Lisa's dog came in with her new tripod way of walking. "This is Maggie," Lisa announced. "She's quite friendly, so if you like dogs, don't be afraid to pet her."

Orley didn't have to be asked twice. He patted his leg and called Maggie over to him. The dog came without any further coaxing and laid her head on Orley's knee.

Lisa snickered as Maggie made a little grunting sound as she soaked up the attention. "She's always been a big baby, but even more so since her operation."

"With everything this poor hund's been through, she deserves a lot of attention." Lois leaned closer to Orley and reached over to stroke Maggie's ear.

"She's doing quite well now and has adjusted to her disability better than I thought she would. She's still playful and sometimes gets into things like she did before the accident." Lisa's nose wrinkled. "The other day I entered the kitchen and caught her ripping up a roll of paper towels that had been left on one of the chairs when we emptied the grocery sacks."

Orley chuckled. "When I was a boy, I had a dog that used to stick his snout in the trash can. He liked to pull out used napkins and wrappers." Orley slapped his hand against his leg and laughed. "That hund looked so silly when I came into the kitchen one day and found him with a paper bag over his head. I had a horrible time getting him to hold still so I could take it off."

"Do you have any dogs now?" Lisa asked.

Orley shook his head. "With our busy schedule we don't have time to take care of a pet." He looked at his wife as she scratched behind Maggie's ears. "Isn't that right, Lois?"

"Jah."

Lisa glanced toward the kitchen door. "I wonder what's taking my grandma so long. I should probably go see if she needs my help." She stood and was almost to the door when Grandma stepped into the room, red faced and carrying a tray full of water glasses.

"Sorry for taking so long," she apologized. "I was cutting some pieces of banana bread, and the next thing I knew, the whole loaf slipped off the counter and ended up on the floor in pieces." She set the tray on the coffee table. "It took me a while to clean up the mess, and I'm sorry that I don't have anything else to serve you all now."

"It's okay," Lois spoke up. "We don't need anything to go with our water."

"My fraa is right." Orley picked up one of the glasses and drank the water right down; then he rose to his feet. "Think I'll walk on out to the harness shop now." He smiled at Lisa's grandmother. "It was nice meeting you, as well as Lisa's hund. Oh, and danki for the water."

"You're welcome. Feel free to drop by anytime when you're in the area."

"We certainly will." Orley said goodbye and headed out the door. A few seconds later he popped back in. "I almost forgot, Lois—I'll come back here to get you when I'm through with my business at the harness shop."

She gave him a thumbs-up.

Lisa couldn't help but smile. It was nice to see how well this sweet Amish couple interacted with each other. Of course, her grandparents were the same way, and Lisa couldn't help but envy them. The nagging fear she'd felt for so many years had lessened some, but sometimes the thought of being alone when they died sent shivers of apprehension up her spine.

She looked down at her dog, now lying at her feet. Even the thought of how close she came to losing Maggie caused Lisa to feel tense.

Do not fear, Lisa told herself. *Remember to pray and trust God for all your needs.*

Paul gripped the reins tightly as he headed toward the Schrocks' place with Chester pulling his buggy at a good clip. He'd been invited to their house for supper this evening, and this was the night he planned to tell Lisa that he'd known her when they were children. In fact, Paul felt it was almost imperative, because he'd put it off longer than he had planned.

Lisa seemed to be doing better now and had become more open to him, so Paul felt confident that she would accept the information he had to share. He hoped it might even bring them closer and could possibly jog Lisa's memory.

"I'll know soon enough," Paul said aloud. "Because I plan to talk to her after supper when we have a chance to be alone."

He let go of the reins with one hand and stroked his chin. *Or would it be better if I bring the topic up while her grandparents are in the room? At least that way, if Lisa should become upset, Jerry and Marlene would be there to help calm her down.*

Paul fought the urge not to tell her at all. *Would it really be so bad if she never found out?* He gave the side of his head a good thump. *No, it wouldn't be good to keep this secret from her forever. I'll tell her this evening, no matter what the consequences.*

"This sure is a good meal," Paul commented as he sat around the kitchen table with Lisa and her grandparents.

"I can't take any credit for it." Grandma gestured to Lisa. "My granddaughter made the pizza as well as the salad."

"You're a good cook." Paul smiled at Lisa, and her cheeks warmed.

"Danki." Lisa kept her gaze on her plate. She felt better when she changed the topic of conversation to something else.

"Orley and Lois Troyer came by this afternoon." Lisa directed her comment to Paul. "They wanted to meet Maggie and my grandparents."

"That's great. I bet they were surprised to see how well the dog is doing."

Lisa nodded.

"After Orley went out to the harness shop to speak with Lisa's grandpa, Maggie decided to put on a little show for Lois," Grandma said.

Paul reached for another slice of pizza and put it on his plate. "What did the dog do?"

"She disappeared for a while, and when she came back to the living room, Maggie had one of my husband's dirty *schtrimp* in her mouth, and she shook it like a rag doll." Grandma's brows lowered and then pinched together. "I tried to get the sock from her, but the stubborn hund did her tripod hop all around the room, and then she disappeared down the hall. Lois thought it was humorous, but Lisa and I were embarrassed."

Lisa nodded in agreement. "After the Troyers went home, Maggie came out of hiding and dropped the *schtrump* at Grandma's feet."

Paul chuckled. "Guess that's a good sign that the dog's feeling like her old self again."

"Jah, one never knows what that hund's gonna do next." Grandpa looked over at Grandma and winked. "Isn't that right, Marlene?"

"For sure. Maggie keeps life interesting around here."

When they'd finished their meal, Lisa helped her grandmother clear the table and do the dishes, while Grandpa and Paul retired to the living room to visit. It had been decided that they would have their dessert in about an hour, after their pizza had time to settle in their stomachs.

Maggie lay on the rug not far from where Lisa stood drying the dishes. Every once in a while the dog would make a grunting sound as she changed to a different position.

After all the dishes were dried and put away, Lisa hung the damp towel on a rack to dry. "Should we take kaffi in to the men now, or wait till we're ready to serve the cake you made?"

"Let's wait on the coffee for a while," Grandma replied.

"Okay. Guess I'll go see what Grandpa and Paul are up to now."

Lisa left the kitchen and was almost to the living room when she heard Paul mention her name. Although it wasn't right to eavesdrop, she didn't want to barge into the room and interrupt the men's conversation. She stood quietly near the door, planning to wait there until Paul stopped talking before entering the room.

"I need your advice on something, Jerry," Paul said. "It concerns Lisa."

"What about my granddaughter?"

Lisa's ears perked up, and she inched her way a bit closer to the door, being careful not to be seen.

Paul cleared his throat. "The thing is. . . Well, I used to know Lisa when she was a girl."

"Oh? You mean here or back when she lived in Indiana?"

"It was in Indiana. Our families lived in the same church district, and Lisa and I attended the same school." There was a pause, and then Paul continued. "I used to tease her back then, saying that I was going to marry her someday."

"Is Lisa aware of this, Paul?"

"No, not yet. I was planning to tell her tonight."

"Why'd you wait so long? Did you want it to be a surprise?"

"Not really. I. . .uh. . .was afraid of how she might react, since she doesn't remember much of her past before the accident. I also know it's difficult for her to talk about certain things, but I figure she has the right to know that the two of us used to be friends."

Lisa blinked rapidly as her mind tried to process what she'd just heard. She had no knowledge of having known Paul until he moved to Sugarcreek. She shook her head in denial. *No, what he said couldn't be true. Surely I would have remembered if I'd known Paul before.*

She flexed her fingers as she stood there trying to decide what to do. Finally, when Lisa could stand it no longer, she dashed into the room and stood directly in front of Paul's chair. "If it's true that we knew each other when we were kinner, then you should have told me right away." Lisa pointed a shaky finger at him. "I don't appreciate you keeping the truth from me, which means you can't be trusted. I—I never want to see you again." Lisa turned and fled the room.

Chapter 30

After climbing the stairs and pausing for a quick prayer, Marlene knocked on Lisa's bedroom door. When there was no response, she turned the knob and peeked in through the crack so she could see into the room. "Lisa, are you awake?" When her granddaughter gave no reply, Marlene opened the door wider and stood silently as she viewed Lisa lying on top of the quilted covering on her bed. With the room illuminated only by the small battery-operated light on the table beside the bed, Marlene saw that her granddaughter's gaze appeared to be focused on the ceiling. *I hope Lisa will listen to me and that she'll rethink her rash statement to Paul. The way that poor young man explained the situation to Jerry and me downstairs just now, I'm certain that he did not want to hurt her.*

Marlene stepped inside, shut the door, and went over to the bed, where she took a seat at the end near Lisa's bare feet. "I understand that you're upset right now, but you were rude to Paul, and I think you overreacted to what you heard him say to your grossdaadi."

Lisa sat up and folded her arms. "He lied to me, Grandma. Paul pretended to be my friend, all the while keeping a secret that he should have told me when we first met and he realized who I was." Her voice quivered, and she released a heavy, lingering sigh.

She is really upset, and I'm not sure if I can reason with her. Marlene shook her head. "He didn't lie. Paul was afraid to tell you for fear of your reaction. He's still downstairs in the living room, talking to your grandpa." She placed her hand on Lisa's leg. "Don't you think you should go talk to him about this—give him a chance to explain why he chose not to mention until now that he used to know you?"

"No, I don't want to talk to him." Lisa sat with rounded shoulders and a downcast expression. "I thought he was sincere and honest, but I know now that Paul can't be trusted."

Marlene felt bad hearing the pain in her granddaughter's voice, but for the moment, nothing she could say would convince Lisa that her anger toward Paul was unjustified.

I suppose I'll have to tell Paul that I've tried to reason with her, but she's just too upset at this point to want to listen to anything he has to say. She gave her granddaughter's leg a few pats, stood up, and quietly left the room.

Downstairs, Marlene still felt heaviness in the air from Lisa's response to Paul before she ran from the room. Marlene found Jerry and Paul sitting in chairs next to each other, engaged in a solemn conversation about Lisa.

Marlene dreaded letting Paul know that Lisa was done with him. It was obvious that the young man wanted to talk to her, but at this point, Marlene couldn't make Lisa do what she thought was the right thing. *My granddaughter can be timid, but I'm also seeing a streak of stubbornness too. She needs to listen to what Paul has to say and forgive.*

As she approached the men, Paul stopped talking and looked at her. "Is Lisa all right? Is she willing to let me explain and apologize to her?"

Marlene shook her head. "She's quite upset. Hopefully in a few days she'll be ready to talk, but unfortunately, not at this time. Lisa needs the chance to sort things out. Perhaps as she does, she will remember more of her past and be willing to talk about it."

Paul swiped a hand across his forehead. "I'm afraid I've messed things up real bad between me and Lisa. I should have either told her right away or said nothing at all."

"I don't see it that way," Jerry said with a slow shake of his head. "If you'd kept silent about having known Lisa when you were children, and she had remembered it on her own, she'd have probably been even more upset, wondering why you didn't speak up."

"Maybe so." Paul lowered his gaze. "I'm afraid I've ruined my friendship with her."

"Please give Lisa some time. I'm sure she'll come around." Marlene hoped her words sounded reassuring. Truth was, she was not certain that her granddaughter would keep a relationship going with Paul now that she knew the truth. Above all, Marlene hoped that Lisa would not pull back into her protective shell again.

As Paul guided Chester in the direction of his aunt and uncle's home, he continued to berate himself for bringing up the topic to Jerry about having known Lisa when she was a girl. He let go of the reins with one hand and reached up to rub the back of his neck where a painful knot had formed. *It might have gone better if she'd heard it directly from me rather than hearing it secondhand,* he thought with regret. *She probably thinks I can't be trusted now.*

"Shoulda, coulda, woulda," Paul muttered. "Guess I'm not so good at fixing things after all, no matter how hard I might try." His jaw clenched. "Maybe Lisa doesn't want to be fixed. She may not wish to remember the past and prefers to live a guarded life, trying to keep a protective hedge around herself for the rest of her days."

He continued to replay the whole mess in his head, and all it seemed to do was add pain. Speaking with Marlene after she'd come downstairs with the bad news that Lisa didn't want to talk to him had only added to his frustration.

Paul figured when he arrived home that he would have to tell his aunt and uncle that his relationship with Lisa appeared to be over. He would have to retell the whole painful story again. "Good job!" he shouted into the night sky. "I've sure made a mess of things."

Chester's ears perked up, and Paul realized that his loud voice had frightened the poor horse. "Sorry, boy, I'm upset, but it's nothing for you to worry about."

As he approached his aunt and uncle's home, a realization came to him. *What I need to do more than anything else right now is to pray for Lisa and ask God to show me how I can restore my relationship with her. I'm also going to drop by Memory Keepers soon and have a talk with Orley. Maybe he can help me figure a way out of the mess I created. At the very least, I'm sure Orley will be understanding and sympathetic.*

Walnut Creek

Upon hearing the wind howling outside the bedroom window, Orley woke up and discovered that Lois was not on her side of the bed. *Could she be up late working on more letters to those who write to her Dear Caroline column?* He frowned. *I wish sometimes that Lois would give up that newspaper column.*

It takes up too much of her time, and I think she would do better if she stuck to mentoring folks one-on-one like I do when troubled people come into our store.

Orley pulled himself to a sitting position, got out of bed, and put on his robe and slippers. Grabbing a battery-operated light, he padded down the hall toward the kitchen. Upon entering the dark room, however, he saw no sign of his wife. *That's strange. I wonder where Lois could be.* He paused and looked out the window. Even though it was dark outside, he could hear the wind pushing at the trees and, under the moonlight, see the branches being swished about. Orley hoped that things like their roofing would hold firm until morning.

As Orley made his way through the rest of the house and saw that each room he'd entered was dark, he began to worry. *Where could my fraa be? Surely she wouldn't have gone outside.*

Continuing on his trek, Orley went back down the hall. This time he stopped in the living room. With the light held in front of him, it didn't take long for Orley to spot Lois sitting on the sofa with her head bowed close to her chest. *Has she fallen asleep in that position or could Lois be in prayer?* He hated to disturb her, but the hour was late, and she really should be in bed.

When Lois had something on her mind to pray about, she didn't argue with God. It was like the Lord had prompted her to pray right now, and she figured it was good to follow her heart. The wind howled outside, and the homemade chime by the front door clanged loudly. When she'd first taken a seat here, the moon had cast a gentle glow through the windows and into the room, but now it was dark.

Lois had been sitting in the dark living room, devoid of light, with her head bowed for nearly an hour when she heard footsteps. She opened her eyes and saw Orley enter the room with a battery-operated light in one hand.

"I thought you'd gone to bed," she said when her husband approached.

"I did, but I was expecting you to join me, and I fell asleep soon after my head hit the pillow. So when I woke up and discovered you were not on your side of the bed, I became concerned."

"Sorry if I caused you to worry, but there was no need for concern."

Orley took a seat on the sofa beside her. "Did you fall asleep in here? Is that why your head was bent forward?"

"No." Lois shook her head. "I knew if I came to bed when you did, I wouldn't be able to sleep, so I came in here instead."

"How come? Has my snoring been too loud lately? Is that why you couldn't stay in the room with me? Or were you worried that I might fall out of bed again and wake you up like I've done several times in the past?"

"No, it was neither of those things."

He tipped his head. "What, then?"

"I don't know why, but I've been thinking about Paul's friend Lisa all evening and felt led to sit here in the quietness of night and pray for her."

"I see. Is there anything specific you believe she needs prayer for?"

"Not really. I just have this feeling that she's dealing with something unsettling right now and needs the Lord's intervention." Lois placed one hand against her chest.

Orley reached over, took hold of Lois's hand, and bowed his head. "If that's the case, then I'll join you in prayer."

"Danki, dear husband," Lois said in a near whisper. "I appreciate your willingness to pray with me." She leaned her head close to his and prayed a heartfelt silent prayer: *Heavenly Father: Please be with Lisa tonight, and if there is something troubling the young woman, I ask that You give her a sense of peace. May Your will be revealed to Lisa in the days ahead, and may she seek Your approval in all that she says and does. Please give my husband and me an understanding heart and wisdom to know what to do and say if either Lisa or Paul reaches out to us again.*

Sugarcreek

Lisa lay on her bed, eyes closed and tears streaming down her hot cheeks. She hadn't even gone downstairs to say good night to her grandparents or to see how Maggie was doing or if the dog needed anything. *She's probably fine. Grandpa will take her outside before going to bed,* she told herself. *And Grandma will make sure a bowl of water is near the place where my dog sleeps at night.*

It had been at least an hour since Paul left for home. Lisa had heard his horse and buggy leave the yard and felt relieved. *I'm sure he's upset with me, but no more than I am with him. I still can't believe how he deceived me.*

Lisa's head ached as she tried to force herself to remember having known Paul when they were children, but nothing came to mind. It frustrated her to be unable to regain her memory, and it frightened her too. What if she never regained any memory about her life prior to her parents' deaths?

She pulled in a deep breath. If Lisa was being totally honest with herself, she would have to admit that part of her did not want to remember the past. In fact, just thinking about it caused her to feel terrified that something bad would happen if she opened herself up to remember the details of the life she used to know before the tragic accident.

Maybe I'm losing my mind, she told herself. *A normal person should not be thinking such things.*

Although Lisa had never spoken the words out loud, she felt guilty and unworthy for being the only survivor the day her parents and paternal grandparents died. After all, what right did she have to be alive when their lives had been snuffed out that fateful day? Lisa had battled with this issue many times, trying to make sense of it all. It seemed when she became upset about something it tended to bring these feelings she didn't understand right back to the surface. And since she'd felt betrayed and angered by Paul this evening, all the old emotions came back again. But the one obvious thing she had to think about was that the Lord had allowed her to survive for a reason. Even so, Lisa hadn't figured out what it was.

I still can't believe I let Paul gain my trust. Why would he wait so long to confess that he already knew who I was? She squeezed her eyes shut. *All I want to do is stay here in my room and not see anyone right now—least of all Paul.*

Lisa pulled her fingers tightly into the palms of her hands until she felt the pain of her nails dig into her flesh. *I wish I had never met Paul. It would have been better for me and him if he'd remained in Indiana instead of moving here.*

Lisa wondered what other secrets Paul had been hiding from her. Had he known she'd moved here after her parents died and then come to Sugarcreek to try to jog her memory? Lisa realized she wouldn't know the answers to her questions unless she asked Paul. But could she question him about it? Did she have the nerve?

Chapter 31

Lisa sat at the kitchen table, massaging her forehead. The morning light warmed the room, but its intense glow made her feel the need to squint her eyes.

Oh, dear. . .I hope I'm not working on a migraine, she thought. A bad headache that could end up making her stomach sick would not be a good thing since Lisa had a full day ahead with her students. She'd slept poorly last night and had awakened with her head throbbing. Lisa had no idea how she could make it through a day of teaching school, but she felt that she had no other choice. She had a to-do list in her purse to go through today, not to mention starting new books with her young scholars. Lisa had stored those new books away in the back room and was the only one who knew exactly where she'd put them. It was too late to see about getting a substitute, and it wouldn't be fair to ask Yvonne to teach all eight grades today. So with a determination she didn't feel, Lisa made up her mind that she would power through no matter how bad she felt. The pulsating pain made her realize it would probably increase if she rode her bike this morning, but on the other hand, it took more work to get the horse and buggy ready to go.

"Are you okay, Lisa?" Grandma's wrinkled brows and anxious tone of voice revealed her obvious concern.

Lisa cringed. *Does it look that obvious that I'm not feeling well?* "I woke up with a koppweh," she replied.

"Have you taken anything for the headache?" Grandpa asked.

She shook her head. "I'd hoped it would go away on its own."

Grandma rose from the table and opened the cupboard door where she kept all her medications and natural remedies. She returned with a bottle of aspirin and handed it to Lisa. "Here you go. Take two of these, and it should help."

"Danki." Lisa opened the lid, took out two pills, and swallowed them with the grape juice in her glass. She couldn't help thinking about last night when she and Paul had their falling-out. *I really don't want to discuss yesterday right now, especially feeling like I do, so I hope Grandpa and Grandma don't bring the topic up.* Lisa squirmed under her grandmother's scrutiny. She suspected there might be some questions about Paul forthcoming.

Grandma opened her mouth as if to say something, but to Lisa's relief, Grandpa spoke first, asking Grandma a question.

"Is there any more kaffi, or should I make another pot?"

She gave him a quizzical look. "There's still plenty of coffee, Husband, so feel free to help yourself."

"Oh, okay."

Lisa figured Grandpa would jump right up and pour himself another cup, but he remained in his seat and started another conversation—this time in regard to the work frolic that would be held at a neighbor's place in a few weeks to put a new roof on their home.

Lisa listened as her grandfather went on and on about the details of the upcoming event. Since she'd just taken the pill for pain, the homemade sticky buns in front of her called out, so Lisa helped herself to a small one from the platter. It didn't take long to nibble through the tasty sweet roll. Grandma's recipe was really good, so Lisa picked out a second bun and put it on her plate. She was tempted to have more but decided to stop at two.

"I'm glad you're able to eat, even with your head not feeling well." Grandpa smiled and reached over to pat Lisa's arm.

"It's hard to pass up Grandma's delicious sticky buns."

He bobbed his head. "I have to agree."

Lisa had to wonder if Grandpa might be deliberately trying to keep Grandma from bringing up the topic of Paul and what had transpired last night. If that was the case, she felt grateful, because the last thing she wanted to talk about this morning was the betrayal she still felt. It would be a struggle for Lisa until the pain relief fully kicked in. She hoped once she'd arrived at school that her head would feel better—it would be a good start to her day at least. Lisa figured that Yvonne would want to chat about this past weekend, and no doubt the subject of her and Paul could come up. Lisa hoped it wouldn't, though, because she didn't want to have to skirt around the topic or have to explain what had taken place.

Lisa looked at the clock on the far wall and drank the rest of her juice. It was time to put her dishes in the sink and head off to school.

"You look mied this morning, Paul. Did you not get enough sleep last night?" Aunt Emma asked.

"I am tired," he admitted before reaching for his cup of coffee. "Things didn't go well last night at the Schrocks' place, and I had a hard time falling asleep when I got home."

"Anything you'd like to talk about?" Uncle Abe questioned from across the breakfast table.

When Paul's cousins looked over at him with curious expressions, he realized that he should have kept quiet. *What was I thinking, blurting that out? If I'd wanted to open up about what occurred last night, I should have waited until I could speak to my uncle and aunt alone.* No way would he deliberately say anything about his personal problems in front of Kevin or Danny. They were both talkers and could end up blabbing whatever he said all over town.

"It's nothing I can talk about right now," Paul responded to his uncle's question. "I'm sure it'll work itself out in time." He fiddled with the fork beside his plate of poached eggs. *At least I hope it will work out. Truth be told, I'm not sure Lisa will ever speak to me again.*

Paul's uncle gave him a quizzical look. It seemed to him that his uncle might not be buying into his last comment. For the moment, the room had fallen silent, and Paul couldn't help but squirm in his chair. He felt relieved when the conversation at the table turned to other things and no one questioned him further.

"What's our first order of business going to be today?" Paul asked his uncle as he resumed eating his morning meal. "Will we be working in the shop all day or someplace else?" He grabbed a piece of toast and took a bite.

"Some things need to be done in the shop this morning, but I also have a few jobs I'll need to bid outside of Sugarcreek this afternoon." Uncle Abe sprinkled quite a bit of salt on his eggs, apparently unmindful of his wife's raised eyebrows.

Paul was surprised that his health-conscious aunt didn't come right out and say something, as she often did when her husband overused the saltshaker. *"A little salt goes a long way,"* Aunt Emma would often say with a shake of her finger. Today, however, she'd chosen to remain quiet.

Paul's nephews continued to eat like the growing boys they were. He couldn't help noticing how fast they could put away their mom's tasty home cooking, yet they were both skinny as rails.

Paul looked at his aunt. "I have an errand I need to run in Walnut Creek when I get off work today, so don't hold supper on my account. I may stop for a bite to eat on the way home."

She nodded. "No problem. If you change your mind and come home without having had supper, I can always heat something up for you."

Paul smiled. "Danki."

"I'm worried about our granddaughter," Marlene said as she and Jerry drank a final cup of coffee before he headed out to the harness shop.

"She'll be fine. I'm sure the aspirin you gave her will take away her koppweh," he responded.

"I'm not talking about her headache. I was referring to Lisa's emotional state." Marlene drew in a quick breath and released it with a huff. "I wanted to talk to her about it this morning, but you kept changing the subject."

"Remember last night, when you told Paul that he needed to give Lisa some time?"

"Jah."

"Well, your good advice was meant for us too. What Lisa needs now is the opportunity to think things through and reach her own conclusions rather than being told what she should do or how she ought to feel."

Marlene pursed her lips. "You're right, but I'm worried that she will use what she heard Paul say to you as an excuse to revert to her introverted ways. Her denial to face or even talk about the past is not a good thing, Jerry. She'll never fully recover from the trauma of losing her family until she faces her fears head-on." Marlene paused to finish her coffee and then rushed on. "We will not be around forever to shield and protect our granddaughter. Sooner or later she will have to deal with her future and accept the good and bad that goes with life. I believe it's our job to prepare her for that. Don't you agree?"

Jerry nodded with a sober expression. "But we can't force Lisa to come to grips with her past or find the courage to trust Paul or anyone else who has hurt her. Our granddaughter needs a spiritual awakening that will strengthen her faith, which can only come from God."

"So what are we supposed to do—just sit back and do nothing?"

He shook his head. "We can pray and be ready to listen when Lisa is ready to talk."

Marlene hated to admit it, but her husband was right. No matter how difficult it might be, she would take a step back and allow the Lord to work in Lisa's life.

Walnut Creek

At the end of his workday, Paul headed for Memory Keepers, where he hoped to speak with Orley. From what he'd been able to tell, the kindly Amish man was full of wisdom, and Paul certainly needed some sound advice concerning Lisa.

Upon entering the antique store, Paul spotted Orley down on his knees on one side of the room, emptying a box of vintage signs that advertised some products from the 1940s. Curious to get a better look, he crossed the room and knelt beside Orley.

"Well, hello there." Orley grinned at Paul. "It's good to see you again."

"Same here." Paul gestured to the box of signs. "Those look quite interesting. I especially like that one with a picture of an old soda pop bottle on it."

Orley nodded. "It's one of my favorites too. Now I just need to find the best place to hang these old signs where they'll get the most attention."

"How about there?" Paul pointed to a mostly bare wall near the front of the store.

"Jah, danki for the suggestion." Orley clambered to his feet. "What brings you into the store today? Are you lookin' for another vintage milk bottle?"

Paul stood too. "No, I. . .uh. . .need your opinion on something."

"Oh?" Orley tipped his head. "What can I help you with?"

Paul was quick to tell Orley what had transpired the night before and how Lisa had responded when she'd come into her grandparents' living room after hearing what he'd said to her grandfather. "She was really upset with me, and I don't know what to do to make things right between us."

"Did you try to explain your reasons for not telling her sooner that you used to know each other?"

"She wouldn't let me explain. Just ran out of the room after saying she never wanted to see me again." Paul clenched his teeth. "I realize now that I waited too long. I should have told Lisa right away that I knew her when we were children."

Orley placed his hand on Paul's shoulder and gave it a reassuring squeeze. "I'm sorry, Paul. Perhaps you should try talking to her again."

"How long should I wait to do that?"

"Well, that all depends."

"On what?"

"On how much time you think she needs."

Paul gave his earlobe a tug. "I'm not sure. I could wait a few days or maybe a week, but then what should I do if Lisa still won't listen to me? I'll be leaving for Indiana in a few weeks, and I'd sure like to get things resolved with Lisa before I go."

Orley's brows lifted. "You're moving back to your home state?"

"No, no, it's nothing like that. I'll be going there for my grandma's birthday celebration, and that's when I plan to give her the old milk bottle I bought from you."

"Oh, I see. Well, it might be good if you could resolve things with Lisa before you go, then."

Paul gave a nod. "Any idea what I should say, other than I'm truly sorry?"

"I have a suggestion," Lois spoke up from across the room.

Paul hadn't even noticed her until now. He waited until she approached them before asking for her suggestion.

"I didn't mean to eavesdrop." Lois looked at Paul. "But I was on the floor behind the front counter looking for something I had dropped this morning, and I couldn't help hearing what you said to Orley." She paused a moment, glanced at her husband, and then looked back at Paul. "Last night before going to bed, I felt a strong need to pray for Lisa, which I told Orley about. So we both prayed for her, even though we had no idea what the extent of her need was. Now I realize why God laid that upon my heart, and I see that we should have been praying for you as well, Paul."

"It's not too late," he said. "I could use your prayers and your advice to help me figure out what I should say when I see Lisa again and how long I should wait to make that happen." Paul pinched the bridge of his nose. "Do I wait a few weeks, till I get back from seeing my family in Indiana, or do I try to talk with Lisa before I go?"

"It's your decision, of course," Lois replied, "but I think it might help if you write Lisa a note of apology soon, and then say that you would like to talk to her in a few weeks, after you have returned from Indiana. That would give Lisa more time to think things over, and it would also give me the opportunity to speak with her."

"You'd be willing to do that?"

"Definitely."

Paul tilted his head from side to side as he weighed his choices. Giving Lisa more time might be the best thing, and writing her a letter rather than talking to her directly was a good idea too. He just hoped that when the time came for them to meet face-to-face, she would be willing to talk to him, and they could work things out.

Chapter 32

Sugarcreek

A sky filled with pretty shades of pink and orange greeted Lisa when she went to the kitchen window and lifted the shade. She watched for several seconds and squinted against the bright ball of orange rising up on the horizon. Lisa hoped that the weather wouldn't turn bad and thought of the old sailors' rhyme that said, "Pink sky in the morning, sailors take warning." But that was superstitious, and a beautiful sunrise should not be taken as a warning.

Lisa opened the window a crack, listening as the silence gave way to the sound of chirping birds swooping from tree to tree in search of food from the carefully placed feeders.

She felt thankful that today was Saturday and she didn't have to get up early to teach school. Yet here she was, up at the crack of dawn. Well, at least it was by her own choice and not because she had to fulfill a duty.

The past week had been difficult, as she'd struggled not to think about Paul's admittance to having known her when she was a girl. She didn't understand why he couldn't have been honest with her in the first place. Lisa was glad he had not tried to talk to her since then. She wasn't ready to discuss it with Paul, or anyone else for that matter. So far her grandparents hadn't pressured her about this either. She appreciated them allowing her to do what she wanted about the situation. Fortunately, Lisa's coworker hadn't brought up the topic of Paul lately either. Yvonne seemed to be absorbed in her blossoming relationship with Aaron.

Maybe my prayers have helped, Lisa concluded. *I did ask to be left alone to ponder things for myself.*

Pushing her thoughts to the back of her mind, Lisa glanced at the clock, surprised that Maggie hadn't heard her and come into the kitchen, begging to go outside. Apparently even her dog had decided to sleep in this morning. Maybe Lisa, Grandma, Grandpa, and even Maggie all had a touch of spring fever.

At least I got out of bed of my own accord and not because I'd set a blaring alarm to wake me up, Lisa mused. *But I'm glad I woke up when I did so I could fix a nice breakfast for my grandparents.*

Lisa's grandmother had been so kind the last few days, staying away from the topic of Paul and fixing Lisa's favorite meals. Grandpa had been pleasant and upbeat too, also refraining from saying anything about Lisa's relationship with Paul. It was the least she could do to let her grandparents sleep in this morning and have breakfast waiting when they got up.

She moved away from the window and took a loaf of raisin bread from the refrigerator. Grandma liked to store her homemade bread there to keep it fresh longer. *I wouldn't mind some french toast. It appeals to my urge to have something a little sweet this morning.*

She got out a carton of eggs and cracked two large ones into a deep-dish ceramic pan. To the egg mixture she added some milk, honey, and a bit of salt, then mixed the ingredients thoroughly. Next Lisa heated butter in a skillet on the stove. When it was ready, she dipped the bread slices into the honey mixture and fried both sides over medium heat until golden brown. When the slices were done, she placed them in an ovenproof baking pan and repeated the process with two more pieces of bread. Once six slices had been cooked, Lisa placed them in the oven to keep warm until it was time to eat breakfast.

She'd finished the last piece of bread and had put the pan in the oven when Maggie ambled into the room using her new gait. She paused in front of Lisa, lifted her snout, and gave a few barks.

"Smells pretty good, doesn't it, girl?" Lisa leaned over and rubbed the dog's ears. "I bet you'd like a taste, huh?"

Arf! Arf!

Lisa snickered and moved over to the sink to wash her hands. "Okay, but first, let's take a walk outside." Although the dog was housebroken, Lisa didn't want to risk Maggie getting too excited and piddling on the kitchen floor. Before readying her dog, she made sure the oven was on low so the french toast would stay warm.

Following that, Lisa got out the dog's purple harness, and a few minutes later they were in the backyard. Maggie loved being outside, and today she pulled on the lead to roam around the shrubs. Lisa thought it was neat to see the animal acting more like she did before the accident.

The sun was fully up, and birds were chirping everywhere. Lisa didn't know how the little creatures could always sound so cheerful. It seemed as though they didn't have a care in the world, despite the dangers all around. Predators such as cats and larger birds could be a threat, but the cardinals, sparrows, and other songbirds warbled on as they continued their hunt for food or rested on tree branches from above.

Woof! Woof!

Lisa turned to look at Maggie. "All done with your business and ready to go back inside?"

The dog let out a few more noisy barks.

Lisa put a finger against her lips. "Shh. . . Keep that up and you'll wake Grandma and Grandpa." She guided Maggie up the porch steps and into the house.

In the utility room, Lisa poured dog food into Maggie's dish and gave her a bowl of fresh water. From there, she returned to the kitchen, where to her surprise, she found Grandpa sitting at the table.

"Somethin' smells mighty good in here." He grinned at her. "Did you fix your special honey-raisin-bread french toast for breakfast?"

"You guessed correctly." She pointed to the oven. "I've been keeping it warm for you and Grandma. Is she up yet?"

"Jah. She's puttin' her hair in a bun and should be here shortly." Grandpa glanced at the clock on the far wall. "We both slept later than usual today. Guess we should have had our alarm set. I'd likely still be asleep if I hadn't heard your hund barking from outside."

"Sorry she woke you."

"No, it's okay. There's plenty I have to get done today, so I needed to get up and at 'em."

Lisa began to set the table with plates and silverware. "It's okay, Grandpa. You and Grandma deserve to sleep in once in a while. That's why I got up early to fix breakfast."

Grandma entered the kitchen just then, smiling from ear to ear. "What's that delicious aroma in here? I could smell it all the way to the bedroom."

"Lisa made breakfast for us, Marlene." Grandpa gestured to the oven door. "And she deliberately let us sleep in."

"Well, for goodness' sakes." Grandma opened the oven and peeked in. "Yum, yum. You're spoiling us this morning, Lisa."

"You deserve to be spoiled once in a while."

Grandma flapped her hand. "I don't know about that, but it sure is nice to be treated to breakfast."

"Please take a seat and I'll put the french toast on the table." Lisa grabbed two pot holders and moved toward the stove.

"Oh, my. . .this looks so delicious." Marlene's stomach growled in anticipation when Lisa set the platter of french toast on the table.

"And I'm sure it'll taste as good as it looks," Jerry added, smacking his lips.

Lisa set a jar of honey on the table, along with some apple butter and a bottle of amber-colored pure maple syrup. "Would either of you like a glass of *millich* with your meal, or would you prefer kaffi instead?"

"Milk sounds good for a change," Marlene said. "I'll wait till the end of the meal to drink my coffee."

When Lisa looked at her grandpa, he nodded and said, "I'll have what your grossmammi is having. And I wouldn't mind some grape jelly to put on mine."

"I'll grab the jelly and set it by your plate." Lisa did that first then got out three glasses and set them on the table, along with a bottle of milk. After she'd taken her seat, they all bowed their heads.

Heavenly Father, Marlene prayed, *thank You for the wonderful breakfast our granddaughter so graciously prepared. Please bless, guide, and direct her life in the days ahead. And bless Paul too,* she added before opening her eyes.

As they ate, Lisa brought up the topic of the garden she planned to help Marlene plant after breakfast.

"I'll appreciate your help as much as I do you making this tasty meal." Marlene poked her fork into a piece of french toast and swirled it around in the amber-colored honey oozing off the edges.

"You're a good cook," Jerry interjected. "You'll make some lucky man a fine wife someday."

Lisa's cheeks colored, but she said nothing as she reached for her glass of milk.

Jerry liked grape jelly and had put a good amount on his first piece. Following that, he'd poured on the maple syrup. "Now this is the way to have tasty french toast."

Marlene wrinkled her nose. "I'm not sure how you can have so much sweetness on top of yours. It would make my teeth tingle with all of that sugar added."

"Nonsense. It tastes good, and this is how I've liked my french toast, and even pancakes, since I was a little boy."

Marlene rolled her eyes in disgust. "I doubt that even Maggie would eat a piece of french toast with all that sweet stuff on it."

"Bet she would." Jerry looked at Lisa. "Would ya mind if I gave the dog a taste of my french toast?"

Lisa shrugged. "I guess a small piece wouldn't hurt."

Jerry cut a piece from one of his, called Maggie over to the table, and fed it to her. "Here, girl, see if you like this."

The dog gave a quick sniff then consumed the morsel and appeared to be waiting for piece number two.

With a smug expression, Jerry announced, "See, I was sure Maggie would like it."

Marlene couldn't hold back her laughter, and neither could Lisa. The dog seemed eager to have another piece, but Jerry refrained from giving her one. He finally told Maggie to go lie down, and she obeyed his command. They chatted a little longer while they ate and enjoyed their breakfast together.

They were getting close to being done when Jerry snapped his fingers and pushed back his chair. "Forgetful me—I almost forgot about the mail I brought in yesterday after I quit working for the day." He made his way across the room and lifted a stack of envelopes from the rolltop desk. "There's a letter from your cousin Sara." He handed it to Marlene. "Oh, and here's one for you too, Lisa." He laid the envelope next to her plate.

Marlene couldn't help but notice that the crimson color in her granddaughter's cheeks was deepening as she stared at the letter.

"Who's it from?" Marlene questioned. "Did my cousin send you a letter too?"

Lisa slowly shook her head. "It–it's from Paul. His name is on the return address." She made no effort to open the envelope.

"Aren't you going to see what he has to say?" Marlene's curiosity was about to get the best of her.

"I—I guess so." A muscle in Lisa's jaw quivered as she tore open the envelope.

Marlene watched with mounting curiosity as Lisa read the letter silently. She fought the urge to ask, "What'd he say?" but pressed her lips together and kept silent.

Several seconds went by, and then Lisa set the letter aside and shifted in her chair. "Paul wrote to let me know that he'll be leaving for Indiana soon, where he'll attend his grandma's birthday celebration." She paused and swallowed a couple of times. "He didn't say how long he'd be gone, but he wants to talk to me after he returns to Ohio."

"Will you be willing to listen to him?" Marlene dared to ask.

Lisa lowered her gaze and gave a brief shrug. "I don't know yet. I'll need to think about it."

Marlene was on the verge of saying something more but stopped herself when Jerry cleared his throat and gave a quick shake of his head. She knew her husband well enough to realize that he thought it was best if Marlene didn't say anything more, so she honored his request. Marlene would, however, be praying that by the time Paul returned from Indiana, Lisa would listen to what he had to say and be willing to forgive.

"Would you like another helping of baked oatmeal?" Aunt Emma asked, moving the dish closer to Paul.

He thumped his belly. "No thanks. It was sure tasty, but I've had plenty. If I eat any more, I may not be able to get any work done today."

Uncle Abe chuckled. "Now that would be the day. I've never known a young man who could work as hard as you do, even on a full stomach."

"What about me, Daed?" Danny puffed out his chest. "I can eat a lot and still work hard, right?"

Uncle Abe smiled. "Jah, Son, you're a hard worker too." He looked across the table at Kevin. "You and your brother are both able to get a lot of work done."

The teenage boy shrugged and said, "On that note, can I be excused so I can get out to the barn and finish my chores?"

Uncle Abe nodded. "Of course, but please clear your dishes first."

Kevin picked up his plate and silverware and carried them to the kitchen sink. His younger brother did the same.

"While you boys are out there, would one of you run to the phone shed and check for messages?" Aunt Emma asked.

"Sure, Mom, I'll do it," Danny replied. "If you want, I'll check for messages first, before I start my chores."

Aunt Emma looked at her husband, and he nodded. "Danki, Danny," she said. "If there are any messages, please be sure to write them down and bring the piece of paper from the notepad into the house before you head out to the barn."

Danny gave her a thumbs-up and strolled out the door.

Paul smiled. His cousins were good kids and respectful to their parents. He hoped if he ever had children that he could raise them to be that way. *Of course, I'd have to get married first,* Paul thought. *And unless Lisa changes her mind about me, she and I will never be husband and wife.*

Paul thought about the letter he'd sent to Lisa three days ago and wondered if she'd received it by now. He leaned both elbows on the table and massaged his forehead. *If so, will she be willing to listen to me when I get back from Indiana?*

Chapter 33

Goshen

After paying for his ride and saying goodbye to his driver, Bob, Paul stepped out of the van and went around to remove his canvas satchel and the box with his grandmother's gift inside. Paul turned then and looked up at the house. It was hard to believe he'd been gone from here for eight months, because for the most part, everything looked the same. His parents' three-story white farmhouse still stood tall and stately, with pots of colorful flowers scattered around the porch and a neatly mowed lawn.

Paul's gaze went to the two hickory rockers situated between a two-seater wooden glider. Flashing back to the past, Paul thought about all the times he and Susan had sat upon that glider, holding hands and talking about their future after enjoying one of his mother's delicious meals.

Paul's fingers clenched around the handles of the satchel he held in one hand, while he gripped the thin piece of rope tied around the box in the other. He'd tried to fight those feelings that he'd felt sure had gone away. But being back home seemed to bring out his painful memories. *Susan and I would most likely be married by now, and maybe even starting a family, if Ervin hadn't stolen my girl. And now I've found someone I love even more, but it doesn't look like that relationship is going to work out either. Lisa has closed herself off from me, hiding behind a past that she's tried so hard to forget, and she may never open herself up emotionally to me again.* He gripped his satchel tighter. *What am I doing? I started with thinking of Susan, and now I've bounced to Lisa.*

Paul's thoughts were halted when the front door swung open, and with open arms, his mother dashed out to greet him. "Oh, Paul, it's so good to see you. It's been too long since you've been home, and we've all missed you so much."

"I've missed you too," Paul answered honestly. *I just haven't missed the unpleasant memory of Susan breaking up with me for the man I'd thought was my best friend.*

Paul resituated his belongings so he was able to slip one arm around his mother's slender waist as they entered the house. Her petite frame made it hard to believe that she'd ever given birth to five hefty boys.

"Where's Dad? Is he working today?" Paul asked.

She nodded. "He's had more orders than usual for rustic furniture, so he's been working sometimes six days a week at his store to try to keep up." She peered at him over the top of her glasses. "He really misses your help in the shop."

No pressure, please. I really don't want to come back here and work again. Paul's brows furrowed. "Hasn't Dad found a replacement for me? I thought he hired a man from Shipshewana."

"He did, but after a few months things didn't work out."

Feeling a little guilty, Paul figured he should follow up carefully on the topic.

"Really? I had no idea. How come Dad never said anything to me about it?"

"Guess he didn't want you to worry or feel guilty for leaving." Mom moved toward the kitchen. "If you haven't had lunch yet, would you like me to fix you a roast beef sandwich?"

"No thanks. My driver and I stopped at a place about an hour from here and had a bite to eat." Paul set the box with Grandma's gift in it on the counter. "If you don't mind me setting this here for now, the box is a gift for Grandma."

"No problem, it should be fine there." His mother smiled.

"Think I'll go upstairs to my old room and hang my clothes up so they don't get too wrinkled. I wanna look presentable for Grandma's birthday party tomorrow evening. It's being held here, right?"

"Jah, but if you have some shirts or trousers that are wrinkled, I'd be happy to iron them for you."

"I think they'll be fine once they're hung up, but I'll let you know if they're not."

"Okay. While you're doing that, I'll fix something cold for us to drink. Would a glass of apple juice appeal to you?"

"Jah, sure. Thanks, Mom." Paul hurried up the stairs to his room.

When Paul walked into his old bedroom, everything looked basically the way he'd left it. He noticed that the window was open, letting in a nice soft breeze. After he'd hung his clothes in the closet and put some other things in one of the dresser drawers, he headed back down the stairs.

When Paul entered the kitchen, he spotted two glasses of apple juice on the table. Looking at his mom, he picked one up and took a drink. "Ah, that sure hits the spot."

Paul's mother gestured to a chair and suggested that he take a seat. "It's been a while since we've talked, and I was hoping we could get caught up."

Paul could hardly say no to his mother's request, but he hoped she wouldn't ask about Lisa or start pressuring him to move back to Indiana and help with his dad's business. Paul pulled out a chair and sat down.

"Would you like some banana bread?"

"No thanks. I'm fine with the juice. Besides, I wouldn't want to spoil my appetite for supper later."

"Okay. Let me know if you change your mind." She took a seat across from him. "How is your daed's brother and his family these days?"

"Everyone's doin' okay. Uncle Abe's business is going real well, and we're keepin' plenty busy."

"That's good to hear." She sipped some of her juice and leaned forward, looking straight into his eyes. "How are things with Lisa? Are you two still going steady?"

I had a feeling she'd want to know about Lisa. Now that I've messed up my relationship with her, it's kind of embarrassing to talk about.

Paul moistened his lips with the tip of his tongue. "Well, uh. . . I'm not sure."

"What do you mean?"

Paul gave a brief explanation, ending it by saying that he would know more after he returned to Ohio and had spoken to Lisa. "That's if she's willing to talk to me," he added.

"I'm sure you're hoping things will work out, but have you ever thought that maybe Lisa isn't the right girl for you?"

Mom, you've never met Lisa as an adult—only when she was a child. Paul's stomach muscles knotted, and he felt sure that if he didn't leave the room, he was likely to say something his mother wouldn't like. He pushed back his chair and stood. "Is it all right if I borrow your horse and buggy, Mom?"

Her forehead creased. "Right now?"

"Jah."

"How come?"

"Thought I'd take a little ride into Shipshe and say hi to Dad. While I'm in town, I should buy a birthday card to go with Grandma's gift. But don't worry, I'll be back in time for supper," he quickly added.

She sat quietly for several seconds and finally nodded. "Sure, Son, you're welcome to use my horse, Holly, but before you go, I think you ought to know that—"

"Great! Danki, Mom. I'll see you in a few hours." Without bothering to finish his juice, Paul grabbed his straw hat and raced out the back door. He hadn't wanted to be rude, but he wasn't up to a lengthy conversation about Lisa with his mother right now.

On the way to the barn, Paul passed the chicken coop. The weathered wood framing and chicken wire created a safe yard enclosure for his mother's collection of ten fluffy hens and one noisy rooster. A few weeds poked up through the dirt around a dusting of wood shavings that had been scattered on the ground.

Paul glanced into the coop where the board rose on a slant and led to a raised area and the coop door. Bits of straw spilled over onto the exit platform—probably knocked out by the chickens from their nesting boxes. Cleaning the coop used to be Paul's job. He figured the responsibility fell on his mother now, since none of his brothers lived at home anymore. For the few eggs his parents would need, Paul wondered why Mom bothered with chickens at all. It would be a lot easier to buy them at the store or from some neighboring farm. *Maybe she likes having the freshest of eggs.* He reached under the brim of his hat and scratched his head. *Who knows—Mom might actually enjoy raising chickens.*

Paul moved on until he came to the tall double doors of his father's barn. When he opened them, he saw rough wooden walls with hooks made to hold various kinds of tack and equipment like shovels, rope, pitchforks, and brooms. Paul spotted Holly's harness and lifted it off the hook where her gear rested. The old barn was a welcome sight with its sweet-smelling hay. In the past, this place had often been his little getaway from life's problems—a quiet spot to think things through for a better perspective.

As he headed toward the horses' stalls, Paul glanced up, and his gaze came to rest on the wooden ladder leading to the loft overhead. He remembered fondly how he and his brothers had played up there during their boyhood. Since Harley was the oldest, he'd often played tricks on Paul, Mark, Amos, and Glen. Paul remembered one time when he and Amos had taken a nap in the loft and had been spooked by Harley, who'd dragged a large fake spider across their noses, awakening them both. Amos had screamed like he'd been stuck with a pin, but Paul had gotten mad and threatened to tell their dad. He hadn't done so, however, because he didn't want to be labeled a tattletale. Instead, Paul had gotten even with his older brother by hiding his good shoes one Sunday morning when it was almost time to depart for church. Harley had gotten a stern lecture from Mom about the need to keep better track of his things, and Dad had been none too happy because they'd almost been late for worship service that day while everyone waited for Harley to locate his shoes. It had been a dirty trick to pull, and Paul had apologized to his brother later on, but he'd learned a good lesson that morning when Preacher John delivered a message on doing to others as we would want them to do to us.

The huffing of a horse's breath brought Paul's musings to a halt. He stepped into Holly's stall and was greeted by the mare's gentle whinny as she leaned her chestnut head against his shoulder. "Ready to take me to Shipshe?" Paul reached for the horse's bridle. "If you get me there in good time, I'll have a treat for ya when we get back."

Holly pawed a couple of times with her right front hoof and bobbed her head as though she understood.

Paul chuckled. "Okay, girl, I'm glad you comprehended what I said."

Shipshewana, Indiana

Paul decided to make a quick stop at Esh's to get a birthday card for his grandmother before going to Dad's shop to say hello. He'd only been inside the store a few minutes and had just begun looking at the cards when someone tapped his shoulder. Paul whirled around, surprised to see Susan Lambright. *You have got to be kidding! Out of all the people to see here on my first day back.*

"It's nice to see you, Paul." Susan's velvety eyelashes accentuated her dark irises as she offered him a dimpled smile. "You've been gone a long time. Are you here visiting your family, or have you decided to move back home?"

He moistened his dry lips with the tip of his tongue. "I. . .uh. . .just got here today. Came to help celebrate my grandmother's birthday, which will be at our place tomorrow evening."

"Jah, since my mamm and yours are friends, I heard about the celebration. Just didn't realize you would be here for it."

Why not? I guess you really didn't get to know me that well when we were dating. "Yep, and I brought her a special gift. It's a fancy old milk bottle almost identical to one she used to own before I carelessly broke it."

"I'm sure she'll be happy to have you at the party."

"I'm glad I can be here." Feeling a bit uneasy standing so close to his old girlfriend, Paul swallowed a couple of times. "How are things with you? I guess you've been real busy getting a lot of last-minute things done for your upcoming wedding."

"There won't be a wedding," she murmured with a slow shake of her head. "Ervin and I broke up a few weeks ago, so we won't be getting married next month after all."

Paul stared at her in disbelief and blinked several times. "Seriously?"

"Of course I'm serious. I have no reason to make up such a thing. Your mamm knows about the breakup. I'm surprised she didn't tell you."

Paul shook his head. He was hesitant to ask the next question but decided to go for it anyway, because he felt he had the right to know. "What went wrong? I thought you two were head over heels in love? Isn't that what you said when you broke up with me? Didn't you even say that you believed God had brought you and Ervin together?"

Susan's gaze dropped to the floor, and her voice lowered to a near whisper. "I—I did think that until he. . ." She stopped talking and folded her arms.

"Until what?" Paul prompted.

She lifted her face toward his. "Until Ervin found someone he liked better."

Paul's mouth nearly fell open. "Are you kidding?"

She gave a solemn shake of her head. "He used to go with Ava Miller when we were all running around together, remember?"

"Sure, I remember, but then her folks moved to Oklahoma and Ervin and Ava lost touch with each other."

"Jah, but now she's back, and all it took was one look at her, and Ervin practically fell into her arms." Tears welled in Susan's eyes. "I was never his first choice, but I'd convinced myself that I was. I think Ervin only wanted me because I was your girlfriend and he wanted what was yours. He always did try to be one up on you—even when we were kinner."

Paul stood almost frozen, trying to take all of this in. He'd been hurt terribly when Susan dropped him for Ervin, and now here he was, feeling sorry for her because she'd had her heart broken by his so-called friend. Some people might have gloated over the fact that the person who had hurt them was now facing the same kind of rejection and pain. Truth was, Paul felt sorry for Susan. She'd been taken in by Ervin's charms, only to be left with a broken heart.

Paul stepped aside when an elderly woman came up to the rack of greeting cards. Getting a card for his grandma could wait. All Paul could think about at the moment was offering Susan some needed support. He motioned for her to move over to the next aisle with him and said, "Should we go somewhere for a cup of coffee so we can talk about this more?"

Susan tipped her head back for a moment and briefly closed her eyes. "Jah, Paul, I would like that very much."

Chapter 34

Walnut Creek

Lois stepped up to Orley and nudged his arm. "Ever since Paul came by and told us about his situation with Lisa, I've had her on my mind. So I was wondering what you would think about going to Sugarcreek to pay Lisa a visit after we close the store this afternoon."

Orley stopped cleaning the front window and turned to face her. "That's a nice idea, but what reason would we offer for being there? Lisa would probably be upset if she knew Paul had told us what transpired when she overheard him telling her grandpa that he used to know her."

"You're right; we certainly can't blurt that out." Lois tapped her chin. "What if we make plans to eat supper at one of the restaurants in Sugarcreek, and we invite Lisa to join us?"

Orley gave his beard a tug, like he often did when he was thinking. "That could work, I suppose, but what if she has other plans for supper?"

"This is a weekday, and she's no doubt teaching school, so it's doubtful she'd be eating out." Lois poked her tongue against the inside of her cheek. "Of course, it would be rude to invite Lisa to join us for supper and not include her grandparents."

Orley's head moved slowly up and down. "Do you think she would open up and talk to us if her grandparents were there?"

"I don't know. It could be a problem—maybe even awkward in a way, I suppose." Lois placed her hand on his arm. "What do you think we should do?"

He sprayed more window cleaner and began to scrub the glass again. "I think we should go over to see Lisa and invite her and the grandparents to go out to supper with us. But it would not be a good idea to bring up the subject of Paul at a restaurant, so if they agree to go out with us, we'll wait till we take them home to bring up the topic of Paul."

Lois smiled. "Good idea, Orley. How thankful I am that I married such a schmaert man."

He chuckled and stepped back from his work. "How does this window look now? Have I got all the smudges and fingerprints wiped off?"

Moving forward and looking intently at Orley's hard work, Lois gave a nod. "You've done a good job. I don't think you could get that window any cleaner than it is." She patted his shoulder. "You're not only smart but a handy husband."

Shipshewana

"Are you hungerich? Would you like something besides kaffi?" Paul asked after he and Susan had taken seats at a small table inside the Corn Crib Café.

She shook her head. "I'm fine with the coffee we ordered. But if you're hungry, feel free to order whatever you like. Their sweet potato waffle fries are always good, and it'll be my treat." Susan offered Paul a smile that used to make him feel weak in the knees. Now Paul wasn't sure what he felt. Compassion for sure, because Susan had been hurt by Ervin, but he didn't think he felt anything other than that. He hoped not, at least, because Paul was in love with Lisa. Not that Susan wasn't a pretty young lady and a nice person at that. He figured in time she'd find someone new and would start fresh.

Paul had some reservations about the day he'd be speaking to Lisa after he returned to Sugarcreek. He fiddled with the menu their waitress had left on the table. *What if Lisa never forgives me and won't listen to what I have to say when I go back to Sugarcreek? Will there be any point in staying there if she rejects me?*

Paul glanced down at the menu but not because he was hungry. He just needed something else to focus on. *If Lisa and I don't get back together, I may as well return to Indiana and work for my daed. Mom made it pretty clear that he needs my help.*

"A dollar for your thoughts." Susan's shoe bumped the toe of Paul's boot under the table.

"Oh, sorry. I was just thinking about something is all."

"From the way you were frowning, they must have been some pretty heavy thoughts."

Paul gave no response. Instead he picked up the cup of hot coffee their waitress had just brought them, blew on it, and took a careful sip.

"Your mamm mentioned that you've been dating a girl from Sugarcreek." Susan looked at Paul, and her lips parted slightly. "Is it true?"

Boy, my mom and her mom sure must do a lot of talking to one another. I wonder just how much Susan knows about my private life. Paul drank some more coffee and swallowed hard, wondering how much he should tell her. Throwing caution to the wind, Paul blurted, "Her name is Lisa Miller. I knew her when she was a young girl. That was before you and your family moved here."

"I see." Susan fiddled with the napkin beside her cup. "So I assume at some point she moved to Sugarcreek with her family?"

"No, it was only Lisa who moved there." *Apparently Susan doesn't know everything.*

The next thing Paul knew, he'd told her the whole story of how Lisa had been the only survivor of the horrible accident that had killed her parents, paternal grandparents, and their driver.

After Susan offered some sympathetic comments, Paul continued by telling her that he hadn't realized who Lisa was when he'd first moved to Sugarcreek. "Then one day it dawned on me."

"Did she recognize you?"

Paul shook his head. "Apparently, the tragedy of the accident caused Lisa to forget most of her childhood before the deaths of her relatives. So until recently, she had no idea that she'd known me before." Paul finished the story by telling Susan how Lisa had overheard him telling her grandfather the truth.

"I bet she was surprised."

"Jah, but more than that, she was angry at me for keeping the truth from her all this time." Paul lowered his gaze. "I really messed things up between me and Lisa, and I'm not sure how to make them right, or if it's even possible." He looked away, wishing that the perfect answer would fall right into his lap, one that could fix all of this for good.

Paul continued to mull things over. *I miss Lisa so much, but I'm worried that we won't ever be together as a couple again.*

"We humans sure know how to make a mess of things, don't we?" Susan pointed to herself. "I know that better than anyone."

Paul sat quietly for a while. He was about to say something when Susan spoke again.

"I'm really sorry for hurting you, Paul. If I hadn't been swayed by Ervin's charms, you and I would probably be married by now."

He nodded slowly.

"But then, that would mean you wouldn't have reconnected with Lisa." Susan's words were spoken in a soothing tone. "I can see how much you love her. Your face seems to light up when you say her name."

As much as Paul wanted to deny it, he couldn't. Sitting here with Susan and telling her all of this had made him keenly aware of just how much he longed to be with the little girl, now a grown-up, he'd once promised to marry.

"I realize there's no chance of you and me getting back together," Susan said quietly, "but would you like a piece of advice?"

"Jah, sure. It couldn't hurt."

Susan leaned a little closer to Paul's side of the table and placed her hand on his. "If you care deeply for Lisa, then the day after your grandma's party, you should head straight back to Sugarcreek, Ohio, and declare your love for that girl. And if you really love her, Paul, don't take no for an answer."

Sugarcreek

Lisa was about to take Maggie outside when she heard a horse and buggy come into the yard. When she opened the door, she was surprised to see that the rig belonged to Lois and Orley Troyer.

Holding on to her dog's harness, Lisa stepped into the yard and waved. She figured the friendly couple had probably come by again to see how Maggie was doing.

By the time Maggie had finished her business, Orley had secured his horse, and he and Lois were headed Lisa's way. When they approached, Orley shook Lisa's hand and Lois gave her a hug.

"It's nice to see you." Lois pointed at Maggie. "It appears that your dog has made a lot of progress since we were last here."

Lisa nodded. "Maggie has adjusted quite well, and her disability doesn't hold her back from doing most of the things she used to do before the amputation."

"It's amazing how well an animal will adjust to something like that," Orley said. "We humans don't always deal well with physical challenges." He thumped his stomach and grimaced. "Take me, for example. I take medicine for my hypothyroid condition, yet I still have to watch what I eat in order to keep from gaining too much weight. I'll admit that I get frustrated sometimes."

Lisa, having never dealt with a thyroid issue or a problem with her weight, couldn't relate to Orley's situation. However, in Lisa's mind, her partial loss of memory was a disability, and it frustrated her to no end.

"Speaking of eating," Lois said, "my husband and I were wondering if you and your grandparents would like to go out for supper with us to one of the restaurants here in Sugarcreek."

"Maybe Dutch Valley," Orley put in. "A person can get filled up on their soup and tasty salad bar alone."

"That's kind of you, but I believe my grandma may have already started our supper."

"Indeed I have, and the Troyers are invited to stay and eat supper here with us this evening," Grandma called through the open screen door. She stepped out and gestured for them to join her on the porch.

"That's a gracious offer, but we wouldn't want to impose," Lois said after she and Orley had greeted Lisa's grandma properly.

"It's no imposition whatsoever. I have scalloped potatoes with ham in the oven, and there's more than enough to go around." Marlene smiled at Lois. "Please say you'll join us. It would be nice to have extra time to visit, and it will be much easier to talk in our dining room than at a noisy restaurant."

Lois looked at Orley, and when he gave a nod, she said, "Danki, Marlene. We would love to join you for supper."

"That was some delicious meal. Danki for inviting us to eat here with you." Orley patted his stomach before pushing away from the table. "Everything was so good, it was hard not to overeat."

"Jah," Lois agreed, "we appreciate the tasty food as well as your warm hospitality."

"It was our pleasure," Lisa's grandma replied.

Lisa's grandfather bobbed his head and grinned at Orley. "One of these days I may drop by your antique store. It would be fun to see some of the vintage items you have available."

"Feel free to come by anytime you like. We're open five days a week."

"Which five days?"

"Normally it's Tuesday through Saturday, but sometimes we'll close the store on a Saturday to go hunting for old things at yard sales, swap meets, or auctions."

Jerry got up from the table. "How'd ya like to join me in the living room for a game of checkers?" His question was directed at Orley.

"Sounds good to me, but I have to warn you, I haven't played checkers in a long while, so I may not be a competitive player."

Jerry winked at him. "No problem there. As I'm winnin' the game, I'll teach you my strategy."

Orley chuckled. "Game on."

"Have you heard anything from Paul lately?" Lois asked as she and Lisa did the dishes and Marlene put things away.

Lisa shook her head. "I assume he's in Indiana, where he was going to celebrate his grandmother's birthday." She grabbed another dish to dry.

"Jah, that was my understanding too. He came by Memory Keepers before he left and told us he'd be leaving."

Lisa stared straight ahead.

Lois cleared her throat. "Umm. . .I hope I'm not speaking out of turn here, but there is something I'd like to discuss with you, Lisa. In fact, it's been on my mind for several days."

"Oh, what's that?" Lisa barely glanced Lois's way.

Does she know what I'm about to say? Is that why Lisa won't look at me? Since Marlene had stepped out of the kitchen to use the restroom, Lois decided to plunge ahead, as it might be her only chance to speak with Lisa alone. "Paul mentioned that the two of you had a falling-out."

"I guess it could be called that. I suppose he told you that I walked in on him telling my grandpa that he used to know me when we were kinner."

Lois nodded. "He also said you refused to discuss it with him and said you never wanted to see him again."

"It's true." Lisa picked up some silverware to dry. "Paul sent me a letter before he left for Indiana, asking if I would be willing to talk with him when he returns."

"Are you willing, Lisa?"

"I—I don't know. Paul kept something very important from me—something that may have helped my memory return—and I'm not sure I can trust him now."

"Don't you think he deserves a chance to explain himself?"

"I suppose."

"If he apologizes, would you be willing to forgive?"

"I should, but it's hard for me to trust." Lisa's chin trembled. "I'm afraid of getting hurt—afraid of being alone—and fearful that I might never get my memory fully back."

Lois dried her hands on a towel and went across the room to get her purse, which she'd hung on a wall peg soon after she and Orley had arrived. She removed a writing tablet—one she often used when responding to letters she'd received in her Dear Caroline column—and brought it, along with a pen, over to the table. "I'm going to write down some Bible verses that came to me last night. Would you sit with me while I share them?"

"Jah." Lisa set her drying towel aside and took a seat in the chair beside Lois.

Lois wrote down three passages of scripture on the topic of fear and handed the paper to Lisa. "There have been times during the course of my life when I've felt fearful, and one or more of these Bible verses helped me get through whatever trial I had to face. I hope the same will be true for you, Lisa."

Lisa's chin dipped slightly as she studied the list. "I'll look these up tonight before going to bed."

Lois clasped Lisa's hand. "Please give me a call if you have any questions or would like to talk about this more. In the meantime, I'll be praying for both you and Paul."

Chapter 35

Lisa sat on the living-room floor with her back against the front of the couch, staring at the glowing embers in the fireplace. She was alone and had time to think and do some reading in pure quietness. Lisa wanted to take advantage of this time to reflect on some things. Grandpa and Grandma had gone to their closest neighbor's house for an evening of games and snacks. They'd invited Lisa, but she'd declined, saying she had some things she wanted to get done.

Lisa's day at school with the children had been busier than usual, and she'd been tired when she got home. Now she sat with her sleeping furry companion by her side. Maggie brought a soothing comfort and a sense of protection for Lisa, especially at times like now, when she was the only adult in the house.

Last night, after the Troyers went home, Lisa had spent some time reading the Bible passages Lois had written down for her. But she hadn't yet read the little self-help booklet Lois had given her right before the Troyers climbed into their buggy and left for home. Lois had shown Lisa such kindness, and her husband was supportive too in the words he'd spoken before they'd left.

Orley and Lois are truly a special couple. I'm glad God brought them into my life. Lisa smiled. *The Lord knows each of us very well. He also knows what needs to happen for each of us at the proper time.*

The house was quiet, except for Maggie's snores from where she lay beside Lisa, so this was a good time to get some more reading done. Before settling down, she had grabbed a few cookies and some lemonade from the kitchen to enjoy while doing her reading.

I can't wait to try the chocolate chip cookies, since Grandma added pecans to them. Lisa took a bite of her first one and enjoyed its flavor. "This is sure tasty. Grandma knows how much I like pecans, so this was a nice surprise." Lisa ate the rest of it and sipped on some lemonade before wiping her hands on a napkin from the wooden tray she'd placed on the other side of her.

She opened the book to a page Lois had marked with a strip of paper. The words "Why me? Why wasn't I taken too?" seemed to jump off the page, and Lisa drew in a sharp intake of breath. *That's me. Whoever wrote this book must have been writing about me.*

Lisa rubbed her forehead as a sense of reality set in. She had never met the author before and didn't recognize the woman's name, so there was no way she could know Lisa or have any knowledge of her situation. Apparently others out there had lost family members and suffered with survivor's guilt. Those people may have been dealing with a similar type of problem as Lisa, and they needed help to deal with their fears and insecurities.

Tears sprang to Lisa's eyes, and soon after, they ran down her hot cheeks. Lisa knew this much—she had never fully come to grips with her parents' and grandparents' deaths and had always wondered, but never voiced out loud, why her life had been spared.

"I wasn't more important than the others in that van," Lisa murmured, barely able to get out the words. "Did God save me for some special reason?"

Lisa read on. "Love hurts, but we cannot avoid pain. Retreating into ourselves is not the solution." She paused to stroke Maggie's silky head before continuing to read.

"Fear doesn't stop death; it stops life. And worrying doesn't take away tomorrow's troubles; it takes away today's peace. Although we cannot understand why God does what He does, we can find comfort in knowing that He responds to us with love, comfort, and peace. Our heavenly Father is everywhere, and He knows everything about us. When we go through deep waters and feel that we are all alone, that's when it's time to remember that He will never leave us or forsake us. So if you're hurting from the loss of a loved one, or someone you know has let you down, your faith in God can be restored by trusting in Him."

Lisa closed her eyes and bowed her head. *Dear Lord,* she silently prayed, *please remind me daily that I am not to blame for the deaths of my family members, and I shouldn't feel guilty because I survived the accident. Help me to take one day at a time, trusting You and without fearing the unknown.*

Goshen

"It's so good to see you again, Paul. Danki for being here to help me and the rest of my dear family celebrate my seventy-fifth birthday." Paul's grandmother's blue eyes sparkled through the clear lenses of her glasses, and she gave him a hug.

"I wouldn't have missed it for the world," he responded, gently patting the slender woman's back.

She guided him off to one side of the living room, where no one else sat at the moment. "Your mamm said you have an aldi in Sugarcreek. Would you like to tell me about her?"

Paul looked away. *I had a feeling if Grandma found out about Lisa that she'd want to know all about it.* Being within close proximity of the others made it harder not to be heard by someone other than his grandmother. All Paul could do was try to keep his voice down and hope that his grandma could hear him okay. As Paul searched for the right words, he felt the heat of embarrassment creep up the back of his neck and spread to his face. "Well, I. . .uh. . ."

"Has this girlfriend of yours filled an empty void in your life?"

"Jah or at least she did before I messed things up between us. But I'm hoping when I see Lisa again that she'll forgive me for being so stupid and saying something important to the wrong person rather than telling her."

Grandma gave his arm a tender squeeze. "I'll be praying for that."

"Come on, everyone. Let's gather around," Paul's dad called through his cupped hands. "Let us pause for silent prayer, and then we'll let my dear mother-in-law go through the haystack line first and help herself."

Paul felt relieved to hear his father's announcement, letting everyone know that supper was ready. That concluded the conversation between Grandma and himself about his situation with Lisa. Now he could enjoy the rest of the birthday celebration with his family.

Paul, along with the rest of the family, bowed his head. He prayed for his grandma, that she would remain healthy and live to serve God a good many more years. He thanked the Lord for his aunt, Mary Sue, who had taken Grandma into her home after Grandpa passed away five years ago. Paul also said a prayer on Lisa's behalf, asking God to pave the way before he spoke to her again. Even with his resolve to think positive thoughts, feelings of doubt had crept in off and on during the day as the time drew nearer to seeing her. Paul couldn't help fretting over this matter, which he felt sure was because things had not been resolved yet between him and Lisa. The last thing Paul wanted was to mess up and say or do the wrong thing when he saw her again.

After the meal, when everyone had gathered around to sing, Mavis smiled as she watched Paul play his guitar, while his four brothers accompanied him with their harmonicas. They all seemed to be having a wonderful time, and it felt good to see the whole family having fun as they spent precious time together again.

Mavis wondered if Paul would take his guitar with him to Ohio this time. When he'd left it in his room after leaving Indiana, it had given her a sense of hope that her son didn't plan to stay in Sugarcreek permanently. Now, however, with him having fallen in love with Lisa Miller, it looked doubtful that he would ever move back home on a permanent basis.

Mavis slid her tongue across her teeth and mulled things over. *Unless, of course, Paul returns to Ohio in a few days and Lisa still won't talk to him. Maybe then our son will consider coming back to Indiana for good.*

After playing and singing until his vocal chords felt strained and his fingers ached from chording and strumming the guitar, Paul set his instrument aside and went to the kitchen to get his grandmother's present. He found the box on the desk his mother used when she paid bills and wrote letters.

When Paul returned to the dining room, he handed the guest of honor the box. "Here you go, Grandma. Happy birthday!"

She smiled up at him and blinked several times. "You didn't have to get me anything, Paul."

"Yes, I did. And you'll know why when you see what it is."

"Oh, now you have me feeling quite curious." Grandma tore open the box and gave a little gasp when she pulled out the old, unusual-looking bottle. "Well, for goodness' sakes—this looks almost exactly like my old milk bottle. The one you broke and said you would replace someday."

Paul smiled. "Jah, Grandma, I've looked and looked for a bottle like that and finally found this one at an antique store in Walnut Creek, Ohio. The Amish man and his wife are the nicest couple, and Orley kept me informed whenever he got new milk bottles into the store."

Tears appeared in Grandma's eyes as she held the bottle close to her chest. "Danki, Paul. Although this is not the exact same milk bottle your grossdaadi gave me many years ago, it's very similar, and I will most certainly put it with my other vintage bottles."

Paul leaned down and gave her a kiss on the cheek. "I'm glad you like it."

"Jah, very much." Her voice choked up. "I'm sure if your grandpa was still alive that he would say it's a great bottle too—definitely worthy of being in my collection."

Paul felt good about bringing Grandma this special gift. Not only had it brought a smile to the dear woman's lips but it had released the feelings of guilt he'd carried around for having broken the one that Grandpa had given her.

Grandma opened a few other gifts then, which included a pretty vase with fresh flowers, a devotional book, a basket of yarn, a book with colored pictures of the birds that were native to their area, and a new daily journal.

Paul wondered how many pages and how many journals his grandmother had already filled up by now. His mother had told him once that her mother had been journaling since she was a teenager right out of school. Paul figured there must be plenty of stories in those journals—maybe enough to write several books if someone had a mind to.

It sure won't be me, Paul told himself. *I've never been good with words when it comes to letter writing. I'd sure never be able to write an entire book. Maybe someday, after my grandmother is gone, my mamm will try to get Grandma's journals published.*

"Should we have some cake and ice cream now that the gifts have been opened?" Paul's mother rose from her seat. "And when we're done with dessert, Amos has something special he wants to do for the kinner who are here this evening."

Paul glanced at his brother, wondering what he planned to do, but Amos's placid expression gave no indication as to what it could be. Of course, even when they were kids, Amos had always been able to get that composed expression on his face, giving no indication of what he was thinking or planning. It used to drive Paul batty, but now he was merely curious.

Harley's wife, Katie, along with Glen's wife, Sharon, went out to the kitchen with Mom, and everyone else gathered around the dining-room table again. A short time later, a delicious-looking chocolate cake with white icing, along with cartons of vanilla, chocolate, and strawberry ice cream, had been placed on the table, in addition to bowls, spoons, and forks. It had been a long time since Paul had eaten this much in one sitting, but he enjoyed every morsel of cake and each lick off his spoon of the cold strawberry ice cream he'd chosen.

After everyone finished their dessert, Amos set a chair in the middle of the living room and called his children, along with all of his nieces and nephews, to take a seat on the floor in front of him. Obviously curious about what Amos planned to do, all the adults found seats and sat looking at him too.

Paul couldn't help wondering what was in the cloth satchel Amos had now placed on his lap.

"You all ready?" Amos gave a wide grin as he looked at the children. When they nodded, he stood the cloth bag upright, reached inside with both hands, and pulled out two furry-looking critters. One resembled a sheepdog, and the other looked like a black-and-white long-haired cat. When Amos stuck his hand inside the critters' heads, Paul realized they were puppets. He bit back a chuckle. He'd never seen his brother play with puppets before—not even when they were children. He figured this must be something new Amos had decided to try in order to keep his five active children entertained.

"These are my new pets," Amos announced. He then gestured with his head toward the cat. "This is Patches, and my other friend here is Beau. They're not friends with each other by nature, but they've learned to get along, just like we humans should do."

The room got very quiet, and Paul noticed the wide-eyed expression on several of the children's faces when Amos made the cat say *meow* and the dog go *woof, woof*! Following that, Paul's brother launched into a full routine with the puppets, which included a silly song called "I Can Do Anything Better Than You Can." The most amazing part of the act was the fact that Amos had spoken and sung in both the cat's and dog's voices without moving his lips. This reminded Paul of the time Lisa had mentioned that a man and his wife had visited the schoolhouse, and the woman had used a puppet to entertain the children with ventriloquism.

When did my brother learn to be a ventriloquist, and how long has he been doing it? Paul asked himself. *Boy, a lot sure has happened in the time I've been gone. Think I should have kept in better touch with my family through phone calls and letters.* He gave his earlobe a tug. *If I stay in Sugarcreek, which I hope will be the case, then I must reach out to my family here in Indiana more often.*

Chapter 36

Saturday morning, when Paul came into the kitchen with his guitar and satchel, he found his mother at the sink, filling the teakettle with water. As he approached, she turned and smiled. "Guder mariye, Son."

"Morning, Mom."

"What would you like for breakfast—maybe some eggs? I can make them poached, fried, soft boiled, or scrambled—whatever you like. Oh, and I have a slab of bacon to go with the eggs." She placed the teakettle on the stove and turned on the propane burner.

"Thanks anyway, Mom, but I don't have time for a big breakfast." He glanced at the clock. "My driver will be here shortly."

"What?" Her mouth opened slightly. "You've only been here a few days. Why are you leaving so soon?"

"I told you last night, after everyone left. Weren't you listening?"

"Jah. You said you were eager to get back to Ohio so you could speak to Lisa, but I didn't think you'd be leaving today."

Paul felt bad hearing the disappointment in his mother's voice, but he distinctly remembered telling her last night that he'd talked to his driver, who'd been staying in LaGrange with some friends, and that he planned to leave this morning. He figured Mom either had been too tired to retain what he'd said or had hoped he would change his mind.

"Morning, Paul," Dad said as he strolled into the room. "Are you packed up and ready to go?"

Mom looked at Dad and frowned. "You knew our son was leaving today?"

Dad bobbed his head. "He told us last night—right here in this kitchen, as a matter of fact. Don't you remember, Mavis?"

"I heard him say he'd be leaving soon. I just didn't think it would be today." Mom's brows pulled inward. "We haven't seen Paul for a good many months, and I was hoping for a longer visit with him."

"I promise to stay in touch better than I have, and I will try to make my next visit here with you both last a little longer," Paul said. "I really feel the need to go home now so I can talk to Lisa."

"It seems strange to hear you call Ohio your home."

I'm sure, Mom, that you'd rather have me living in Indiana and not too far from your house either. If things don't work out between me and Lisa, you may get your wish. I'll probably end up coming right back here and begin working for Dad again, since he could use another person in the shop. Paul contemplated the best response to give his mother, but a horn tooted from outside. He peered out the window. "My driver's here."

"Why don't you invite him in to join us for breakfast?" Mom suggested.

Paul shook his head. "We need to get on the road before traffic gets bad." He gestured to the bowl of fruit in the center of the table. "Would you mind, Mom, if I take some fruit for the road?"

"Of course not, but I wish you could take the time to eat a bigger breakfast."

"I'll be fine, Mom." Paul gave her a hug, and his dad stepped forward and embraced Paul too.

"I hope things work out and you're able to find someone to work in your shop soon," Paul said. "I feel bad that I can't stay and help, but—"

Dad held up one hand. "Don't you worry about me. I've put an ad in the local newspaper as well as *The Budget,* so I feel confident that the right person will see that ad and respond to the request soon." Looking directly at Paul, Dad squeezed Paul's shoulders. "After all, I can't expect you to stay here just to help me when you've established a new life in Sugarcreek. None of your brothers have shown an interest in woodworking—especially the rustic kind. And I don't expect any of them to give up the jobs they like in order to help me either."

"Thanks, Dad. It means a lot to hear you say that." Paul heaved a sigh of relief. He was ever so thankful for his father's encouraging words.

When Paul's driver honked the horn a second time, Paul grabbed two apples and stuffed them in his pockets. Then he picked up his guitar and satchel, said goodbye to his parents, and went out the door. *Just think,* he told himself, *if everything goes well, before this day is out I'll be talking to Lisa.* The muscles in his jaw tightened as he put his stuff in the back of Bob's van. *At least I hope she'll be willing to hear me out. If she's not interested in what I have to say, I don't know what I'll do. Guess I could always get down on my knees and beg, but that might not be the best idea.*

Linsey, Ohio

It was about 320 miles from Goshen, Indiana, to Sugarcreek, Ohio, and they were at the halfway point in Linsey. Since they'd left Goshen a few minutes after six that morning, and it took about five hours, plus some extra time for any necessary stops, to get there, Paul figured they should arrive in Sugarcreek around noon.

He leaned his head against the headrest and tried to tune out the country and western CD his driver was playing. Paul didn't mind this type of music, but not with the volume way up. He wondered if Bob just liked it that way, or maybe he needed the loud music in order to keep himself from falling asleep at the wheel.

If Paul wasn't a member of the Amish church and was still going through his Rumspringa, he'd have a car of his own and wouldn't have to listen to any music if he didn't want to. Although Paul wouldn't trade being Amish for living a more modern, English life, he did miss a few things about owning a car. He'd thought for a while, when he had first put his vehicle up for sale before taking classes to join the church, that he'd really miss it, but he hadn't missed it as much as he'd expected. Normally, Paul was content to call upon a driver whenever it was needed and he couldn't travel with his trusted horse and buggy. But at the moment, he felt like a horse chomping at the bit to go.

"Did ya hear that loud boom?" Bob shouted against the blaring music, as the van slowed down as though of its own accord and then veered to the right.

Feeling a jolt when his driver accelerated slightly, Paul grabbed his armrest to steady himself.

"I think one of my back tires blew." A vein on the side of Bob's neck bulged as he let up on the gas pedal, turned on his emergency lights, and pulled the van off the highway and onto the shoulder of the road where it was safe. They both got out of the van and went around to check on the damage to the tire. Sure enough, it had blown, and now they had to put on the spare and hope it got them to the nearest place where Bob could buy a new tire. At this rate they'd never make it to Sugarcreek by noon, but at least the van was okay and neither Paul nor his driver had been injured.

"Whew!" Sweat beaded on Bob's forehead. "I'm glad there were no other vehicles close to my van when that happened. We could have ended up in an accident."

"That's for sure," Paul agreed. "God was watching over us."

Bob didn't respond, but then he rarely did whenever Paul brought up the topic of divine intervention or prayer. Bob had never professed to be a Christian and rarely spoke of religion, but he never seemed to mind whenever Paul brought God or the Bible into their conversation. Hopefully someday Bob would find a personal relationship with Jesus Christ.

Sugarcreek

"Well, we made it." Bob parked his van in front of Paul's aunt and uncle's home; then he looked over at Paul and grinned. "You glad to be back?"

Paul nodded quickly. The trip had taken longer than expected, but at least they'd made it safely back to Sugarcreek in time for him to see Lisa.

Paul paid Bob and told him goodbye; then he went around to get his guitar and satchel from the back. With a wave in his driver's direction, Paul headed for the house. He would say hello to whoever was at home this afternoon, wash up, and put on a clean shirt. Then he'd get on his bike, since it would be faster than getting the horse and buggy out, and head for the Schrocks' place.

Paul had no more than stepped onto the porch when his youngest cousin, bellowing like a wounded calf, ran around the side of the house, nearly bumping into Paul.

"What's going on, Danny?" Paul questioned. "What are you hollering about?"

The boy pointed to a blue Frisbee up on the roof.

Paul groaned. "For goodness' sakes, that's nothing to shout about. Just go get a ladder; then climb up there and get it down."

Beads of sweat appeared above the boy's upper lip as he pressed his arms tightly against his sides. "No way! I'm scared of heights, and I ain't goin' up there."

Paul was on the verge of telling his cousin that if he didn't have the courage to climb a ladder, then the Frisbee would have to stay where it was until a strong gust of wind blew it down. He changed his mind, however, when Danny moved closer and clasped his arm. "Would ya go up there and get it for me. . .please? I'll take care of feedin', waterin', and groomin' your horse every day next week if you get the Frisbee down for me."

Paul was aware that everyone had a fear of something, and apparently climbing a tall ladder was one of his cousin's greatest fears. "Okay, Danny, if you bring the ladder out of the barn, I'll go up and get your toy."

"Danki, Paul." Danny offered him a grateful-looking smile before he turned and hurried toward the barn.

"Where are you headed, Lisa?" Grandma asked when Lisa put on her black sweater and dark outer bonnet.

"I'm going to bike over to Paul's aunt and uncle's house and see if they've heard from him and know when he plans to return to Ohio."

"Can't you just call and leave them a message? I'm sure someone would get back to you later today."

"Grandma, I've been patient for days waiting to hear something from Paul, and I've reached my limit." Lisa shook her head. "I'd rather talk to one of his relatives in person than leave a phone message that might not get answered until Monday."

Grandma nodded. "I understand."

"So if you don't need me for anything, I'm going to get my bike and head over to the Herschbergers' now."

"That's fine, Lisa. We're having spaghetti and meatballs this evening. It will be an easy meal, since the sauce we canned months ago is setting there on the counter, and the frozen meatballs are thawing. Everything is set to go, even our canned green beans. The only other work that'll need to be done is warming the french bread in the oven and cutting up some fresh veggies to have with our meal. I won't need any help until it's time to start supper, which is still a few hours away."

"Okay, that sounds good. Thanks, Grandma. I'll make sure to be back in plenty of time to help with our evening meal."

I really hope when I get together with Paul that things will go all right. Lisa's stomach knotted as she gripped her handlebars and pedaled down the road in the direction of the Herschbergers' place. It would be great if Paul was there already, but there was a chance that he'd decided to stay in Goshen a few more days.

Or maybe Paul will stay there for good, since I'm almost sure he believes that things are over between him and me. Lisa clenched her teeth so hard her jaw ached. *I really messed up where Paul is concerned. I should have given him a chance to explain himself. At least in Paul's letter he said he wanted to talk to me. Grandma said this morning that I should take it as a good sign.*

Lisa glanced at a barking dog on the other side of a white picket fence and thought of her own pet she'd left at home. *I bet Maggie would miss Paul if we broke up for good and he moved away, but not nearly as much as I would.* Tears stung the back of her eyes, and she blinked, hoping to keep them from seeping out. *I can't start thinking negative thoughts or worrying about the what-ifs,* Lisa reminded herself. *I just need to have faith and remain calm.*

The closer Lisa got to his uncle and aunt's place, the more she hoped Paul was there. Her heart beat like a drum with the workout of pedaling as fast as she could manage. *I hope I don't break out in a sweat. That wouldn't be an impressive way to greet Paul or any of his family who might be at home.*

A short time later, Lisa drove her bike into the Herschbergers' yard. She stopped along one side of the driveway. Lisa was surprised to see Paul's cousin Danny standing off to one side of a ladder that was leaning against the house, and even more surprised to see Paul up on the roof holding a Frisbee. If Paul saw her, he gave no indication as he flipped the Frisbee into the air.

Lisa hopped off her bike and set the kickstand. While standing there, she couldn't take her eyes off Paul. Lisa watched as the object drifted to the ground, but she barely noticed when Danny picked it up. Her gaze was on Paul again, as he maneuvered himself toward the edge of the roof.

Lisa held her breath, and her body stiffened as he put first one foot, and then the other, on the top rung of the ladder. It appeared that Paul was about to step on the rung below it when a black crow swept down from nowhere, nearly hitting the top of Paul's head.

Paul leaned to the right, and then to the left, as the crow made another pass at him. Lisa wanted to call out to him, but fearful that he might lose his balance, she just stood there, continuing to hold her breath.

Suddenly, as though in slow motion, Paul lost his grip and tumbled downward.

Lisa and Danny screamed at the same time, as Paul's body hit the ground with a sickening thud. He lay there, unmoving, and Lisa rushed forward, shouting, "Paul! Paul!" She closed her eyes briefly. *Oh, please, Lord, let him live.*

Chapter 37

Lisa's heart thumped in her chest as she dropped to the ground on her knees beside Paul. Blood oozed from a gash on his head, and his left leg lay at an odd angle. She felt overwhelmed. Lisa didn't have a strong stomach when it came to seeing a good amount of blood, in addition to a leg not in its usual position. It was a lot to take in, but soon Lisa managed to open her eyes again and look at him. Paul was breathing, but his eyes remained closed, and he was unresponsive when she called his name.

Tears welled in Lisa's eyes as she laid a hand on Paul's swollen wrist. It felt pretty warm, and she noticed some discoloration–a good indication of a possible bruise. Lisa had no idea how badly Paul had been hurt. She just knew they needed to get some help, and soon.

Lisa looked up at Danny, who stood a few feet away with eyes wide and body shaking like a leaf being blown about the yard on a windy day. *I'll need Danny's help. I'm staying with Paul until the paramedics get here.*

"Danny, go in the house and get your mom or dad. Someone needs to go out to the phone shed and call for help. I don't want to leave your cousin here alone."

Danny stepped closer and looked at Paul for a moment; then he turned toward Lisa with a wrinkled forehead. "Is—is he dead?" The boy's voice quivered as he stared at his cousin.

"He's still breathing." Lisa gave her head a vigorous shake. "Go, Danny! Go get your parents right now!"

Within minutes of Danny's departure, the boy's mom and dad rushed out of the house. Emma held a towel, which she wrapped around Paul's head, and Abe instructed her to stay with Paul while he went to the phone shed to call 911. "And if Paul wakes up while I'm gone," he called over his shoulder, "don't let him move. I'm sure his leg is broken, and he may have a concussion or some internal injuries we don't know about."

"I won't leave his side," she called to Abe, and then knelt on the opposite side of Paul. "I hope we won't have to wait long for the ambulance to arrive."

With a trembling lip, Emma looked at Lisa. "It's hard to see him lying there so helpless, and it's frustrating not knowing how to treat his injuries as we wait here for help to arrive." Her eyes filled with tears.

As Lisa continued to wait with Paul's aunt, she explained how the accident had happened, giving an account of everything she'd witnessed from the ground below.

"He should have left the Frisbee on the roof." Emma's brows wrinkled. "But that's how Paul is—he's always been one to help out whenever he thinks there's a need." Her voice faltered. "When Danny came into the house with the news that his cousin had fallen, he followed me into the kitchen as I quickly grabbed a towel to bring out with me." Emma looked toward the house while speaking. "Danny admitted that he'd been the one who asked Paul to go up on the roof, and now he blames himself for what happened. He's sitting on the couch right now, in tears."

"People often have a tendency to blame themselves when something goes wrong." Lisa hoped her words gave Emma some comfort. Truth was, they were spoken as much for Lisa as for Paul's aunt. In addition to feeling guilty and unworthy because she'd been the only person who'd survived the accident that had taken her family, Lisa had often blamed herself for other events, even while teaching school, that logically were not her fault. It had been easy to blame herself and be miserable instead of enjoying her life the way she should. Lisa hoped those times of feeling guilty were behind her now and she could move forward with the Lord's help to a more positive attitude.

Lisa looked at Paul's pale face and grimaced. In this case, he could have said no to his cousin's request, but Paul chose to do what he felt was right. Truthfully, Paul probably would have gone up to get the Frisbee even if he hadn't been asked.

She breathed a sigh of relief when Abe showed up and said the call had been made and that help was on the way. Even so, the look of worry on Abe's and Emma's faces was unmistakable, and Lisa couldn't help feeling the same way. *My worrying won't help Paul's situation or me wishing I could've helped prevent the accident. The only thing left to do now is pray.*

Dover, Ohio

Lisa sat in the hospital waiting room between Paul's aunt and uncle. Kevin had been hiking with some friends when the accident happened, and Danny had remained at home to let his brother know when he got home. Paul's parents had been notified, and Lisa felt sure that once they received the message, one or both of them would come to the hospital. Lisa had also let her grandparents know about Paul's accident and explained in her message that she would be going to the hospital with Paul's aunt and uncle when their driver arrived but would try to keep them informed when she knew more. That had been three hours ago, and they still hadn't gotten word of Paul's condition.

Lisa glanced at the clock on the far wall. It seemed to be taking forever for them to hear the results of tests being done that would determine how badly Paul had been hurt. She felt helpless sitting here waiting, but she had spent this time praying and focusing on verses of scripture she'd committed to memory. Second Timothy 1:7 stuck out in her mind: "For God hath not given us the spirit of fear; but of power, and of love, and of a sound mind." How thankful Lisa was for the reminder found in God's Word that she should not be fearful.

Lisa thought about Lois and Orley and wondered if she should let them know that Paul was in the hospital. Since she didn't have anything specific to tell them about his condition, however, she decided it would be best to wait until she, Abe, and Emma learned something.

"I can hardly stand this waiting." Emma got up and began pacing.

Abe looked at his wife and shook his head. "Walking back and forth is not going to do you or Paul one bit of good, Emma. If you must walk about, why don't you go down the hall and get a cup of kaffi?"

She stopped pacing and turned to face him. "I don't need any coffee, and I'm feeling too anxious to sit still any longer." She sighed. "I just wish we would hear something."

"I want that too, but we won't hear anything one minute sooner with you walkin' the floor." Abe motioned to the chair she had left empty. "Please sit down and try to relax."

"I don't see how I'm supposed to do that." Emma sniffed deeply.

"Prayer," Lisa spoke up. "I've discovered lately that praying helps me relax and stop worrying."

Emma came back over and took her seat. "You're right, Lisa. I should be praying for my nephew, not fretting over something that is out of my control." She bowed her head and closed her eyes. Abe did the same, along with Lisa.

A few minutes later, Lisa heard footsteps approach. She opened her eyes and saw a middle-aged man dressed in hospital scrubs standing near their row of chairs. "Are you Paul's relatives?" he asked, looking at Abe then Emma.

They both nodded.

"We've finished examining Paul and have done several necessary tests, and. . ." He paused and reached under his glasses to rub the bridge of his nose. "I am happy to report that Paul's injuries are much less than they could have been from a fall like he took. Besides a slight concussion, his left leg is broken, and he sprained his right wrist. The leg break is pretty bad, so we'll need to do surgery and put a few pins in it, but he should be able to go home in a few days."

Lisa slumped against her chair and reached over to clasp Emma's hand. *Thank You, Lord, for keeping Your hand on Paul. His accident could have been so much worse.*

Since Paul's surgery wouldn't be until the next day and he was sleeping due to the pain medicine he'd been given, Lisa, along with his aunt and uncle, decided it would be all right for them to go home. Abe said he would leave a message at the nurse's desk for Paul's parents, letting them know the details and that they should plan on staying at his and Emma's house for as long as they wanted during Paul's convalescence.

It was difficult for Lisa to leave the hospital without talking to Paul, but what she had to say could wait until tomorrow, or even longer if necessary. The most important thing was that after a time of healing, Paul would be okay.

Sugarcreek

Lisa waited until Paul came home from the hospital to go to his aunt and uncle's house, hoping to talk with him about their situation. She wanted to make sure that he felt well enough to discuss things with her and was glad she had written Paul a note and left it on the nightstand in his hospital room, letting him know that she'd been there and would be over to see him soon after he got home.

With Paul's parents still there and his aunt Emma no doubt in the house, it might be difficult to speak with Paul alone. Even so, Lisa was determined that today would be the day she told Paul how she felt about him. She only hoped that, after all that had transpired between them, he felt the same way about her.

After parking her bike near the barn, Lisa hurried across the yard and up the steps to the front porch. She was about to knock on the door when it opened and a slender, brown-haired Amish woman stepped out.

"Are you Lisa?" the woman asked.

Lisa bobbed her head.

"I'm Mavis, Paul's mamm. I knew you when you were a little girl living in Goshen with your family, but you may not remember me."

"You're right, I don't, but there's a lot about my childhood I haven't been able to remember yet." Lisa gave Mavis a brief hug. "I'm glad you could be here, and I'm sure you must be thanking God that your son's injuries weren't life threatening."

Paul's mother gave a nod as she pressed a palm against her chest. "The moment I found out about my son's accident, I began to pray, and I couldn't stop doing so as we traveled in our driver's vehicle from Goshen to the hospital in Dover." She gave Lisa's arm a gentle pat. "I'm going out for a short walk, but why don't you go inside now and talk to Paul? I'm sure he'll be happy to see you."

"Okay." Lisa rubbed her sweaty hands down the front of her apron. She hoped she'd be able to talk to Paul alone, even if it were just for a few minutes. She needed to ask his forgiveness and let him know how she truly felt.

When Lisa entered the living room, she was surprised to see that Paul was the only one in the room. He lay stretched out on the couch, with his broken leg encased in a cast and propped up on a pillow.

He turned his head and smiled as Lisa approached. "I'm glad you're here, because there are some things I need to say to you."

"Jah, I've been wanting to talk to you too." She glanced around. "Where is everyone? Are we alone?"

"We are for the moment. Aunt Emma's out back hanging laundry. My daed and Uncle Abe headed out to the woodworking shop a while ago, and my mamm went for a walk."

"I know. I met her on the front porch before I came into the house."

"I hope you can stay awhile. I'd like you to get to know my folks."

"That would be nice."

Paul pointed to a folding chair that had been placed near the couch. "Please take a seat."

Lisa did as he suggested. She was about to say something, but he spoke first.

"I'm really sorry for keeping the truth from you for so long about us knowing each other when we were kinner. I should have been up front with you about it as soon as I realized who you were." He reached out his arm. "Will you forgive me, Lisa?"

She clasped his hand. "Jah, and will you forgive me for running out of the room the evening I heard you telling my grandpa the truth? I should have stayed and listened to your explanation."

"It's okay. It's in the past now, and we need to move forward."

"I agree. That's what I decided to do after Lois Troyer had a heart-to-heart talk with me. Would you like to hear about it?"

Paul nodded. "Most definitely."

Uncertain of how much time she and Paul would have to be alone, Lisa made short order of telling him about her conversation with Lois. "The things she said, along with the verses of scripture she mentioned, have helped me so much, Paul. I wish I had opened up to Lois sooner and talked about my feelings."

"You know what they say—it's never too late—and maybe it was the perfect time for you to hear what Lois had to say."

"You're probably right. I may not have been open to hearing what she said if it had happened earlier."

"There's something else I need to tell you." Paul stroked Lisa's fingers as he continued to hold her hand.

"What is it?"

"Before Susan dropped me for the man I thought was my best friend,

I believed I was in love with her. But I've realized since then that I've never loved another woman the way I love you."

Lisa's pulse raced as she gazed deeply into his eyes. "I love you too. Very much, in fact."

Paul brought Lisa's hand up to his lips, and he grazed her knuckles with feathery kisses. "When I've healed from my injuries and the time is right, would you consider becoming my wife?"

Lisa couldn't keep the tears that had filled her eyes from falling over as she whispered, "Jah, I would be honored to marry you, Paul."

Lisa leaned closer to Paul, and he caressed her cheek with the back of his thumb. "I'm gonna hold you to that promise."

"Oh, I hope so," she murmured.

Epilogue

Seven months later

With a feeling of contentment, Paul sat beside his new bride at their corner table during the meal following the church service where they'd become man and wife a short time ago. The wedding had taken place at the nearby home of Grandpa and Grandma's Amish friend, and the noon meal was hosted right here at her grandparents' place.

Maggie was in her outside pen, letting out barks and watching the people coming in for the event. Paul couldn't help but smile every time he heard another yip, yap, or woof.

Looking out at all the other tables that had been set up for guests in this thoroughly cleaned barn, Paul's heart overflowed with happiness beyond belief. He could hardly comprehend that the girl he'd chosen back when he was a boy had actually become his partner for life.

Paul felt thankful that his entire family, including dear Grandma, could be here to help him and Lisa celebrate their special day. Lisa's grandparents were there too of course, smiling and laughing as they conversed with other guests. Although Paul had not gone fishing with Jerry yet, due to their busy work schedules, he looked forward to doing so sometime in the near future.

Paul smiled and nodded at Orley and Lois, who sat at one of the nearby tables along with several other visiting friends. Paul felt blessed to have met the nice Amish couple, and he appreciated the guidance he and Lisa had both received from the Troyers. Lois and Orley cared about people, and it showed.

Paul leaned close to Lisa and whispered, "Aren't you glad the Troyers could be here for our special day?"

Lisa nodded. "I hope by the time we're their age that we'll also have been able to mentor many people the way they do."

"If we're open to God's will and His leading, I'm sure there will be plenty of opportunities for us to help others. And who knows," Paul said with a grin, "we could end up with a whole houseful of kinner who will need our guidance."

"That could be, but only God knows what plans He has for our future." Lisa smiled and squeezed his hand under the table. "I am ever so thankful that we have put our lives in God's hands."

LISA'S HONEY-RAISIN-BREAD FRENCH TOAST

2 large eggs, well beaten
¼ cup milk
¼ cup honey
¼ teaspoon salt
6 to 8 slices raisin bread
Butter

Set oven to warm. Combine eggs, milk, honey, and salt with whisk or eggbeater. Dip bread slices into egg mixture. Melt butter in skillet over medium heat. Fry bread on both sides until golden brown. Place first finished slices in ovenproof dish and put in warm oven. Repeat with remainder of bread, two slices at a time. Keep french toast in oven until ready to serve.

GRANDMA'S CHICKEN-N-STUFFING CASSEROLE

STUFFING:

6 cups bread crumbs, browned
¼ cup diced celery
1 tablespoon chopped onion
1 tablespoon parsley flakes
2 eggs
¼ cup butter
Salt and pepper to taste

Mix all ingredients in a bowl and add enough hot water to moisten. Place in greased 9x13-inch baking pan.

CHICKEN:

¼ cup butter
4 tablespoons flour
1 cup chicken broth
1 can cream of chicken soup
15 ounces milk
1 whole chicken, cooked and cut up
Salt and pepper to taste

In a kettle, melt butter. Stir in flour to make paste. Add broth, soup, and milk. Cook until thick gravy forms. Add cooked chicken pieces and season with salt and pepper. Pour over stuffing. Bake at 350 degrees for 40 to 45 minutes until bubbly.

Discussion Questions

1. Lisa faced a terrible tragedy at the age of seven, when her parents, paternal grandparents, and their driver were killed. Lisa was the only survivor of the accident, and the emotional trauma left Lisa with a partial memory loss. Why do you think Lisa blocked out her childhood memories from before the accident?

2. Due to the accident and having been sent to live with her maternal grandparents, whom she didn't know very well at that time, Lisa became an introvert and feared the unknown. It was difficult for her to form a bond with anyone, anxious that something might happen to them. Do you think that was a normal reaction? Have you or someone you know ever been in a similar situation when you've gone through a tragedy? If so, how did you cope?

3. Lisa's maternal grandparents did all they could to help Lisa and give her a loving, stable upbringing, and she'd become quite attached to them. How wonderful it is when a relative steps forward to care for an orphaned child. Have you ever raised a child who was not your own? Did it strengthen the bond between you?

4. Lisa became an Amish schoolteacher, which filled a void in her life. She had no plans to get married and hoped she'd be able to teach for many years. Do you believe Lisa succeeded at filling that void in her life through teaching? Why do you think she would want to do that?

5. When Paul met Lisa during his first few days in Ohio, he had a feeling he'd known her before. He didn't know why, but he was drawn to Lisa and wanted to get to know her better. Have you ever felt that way after meeting someone for the first time?

6. Lois and Orley Troyer were open to God's leading whenever someone they felt needed mentoring came into their antique store. Have you ever known anyone like this Amish couple? Were you

helped in some way by them, or have you ever been the one doing the mentoring?

7. Once Paul realized that he used to know Lisa when they were children, did he do the correct thing by not telling her right away? Did Lisa have a legitimate reason to be upset with Paul? Do you think she responded correctly, or would there have been a better way for her to deal with it?

8. Paul, a carpenter, had always enjoyed fixing things. Aware that Lisa dealt with some emotional things, he hoped that he could fix her problems by being her friend. Can friendship alone help someone who is dealing with something from their past that is affecting their current behavior? What are some ways we can help someone cope with a past trauma that still affects them?

9. Did Paul's mother expect too much by wanting him to live in Indiana, where he'd grown up? Do you think grown children should be allowed the freedom to move away from their parents without having pressure put on them or being made to feel guilty? Is there ever a time when parents should expect their adult child to live close to them?

10. How did Paul's broken relationship with a young woman from Indiana affect his relationship with Lisa? When Susan hurt Paul, he promised himself not to fall in love again. Was it too soon after the breakup with Susan for Paul to begin dating Lisa?

11. Taking in a stray dog, Maggie, was one of the first things Lisa did that helped her deal with her insecurities. Caring for Maggie gave Lisa a sense of purpose. How did Lisa handle it when Maggie lost a leg? Did it make her a stronger person, or did Lisa's fear of losing someone she loved escalate?

12. What helped Lisa the most in dealing with her fears and anxiety? How do you deal with these emotions when faced with a frightening ordeal?

13. How can we help ourselves or someone we know who struggles with worry, fear, or anxiety? Do you have some favorite verses from the Bible about these topics?

14. Who were your favorite characters in this book? What stood out about the characters that made them special to you?

15. Did you learn anything new about the Amish way of life by reading this book?

16. Have you ever been to Amish country in Ohio? If so, what were some of your favorite places to visit there?

17. Did you learn anything specific from reading this story that helped to strengthen your faith in God? Were there any Bible verses that particularly spoke to you? In what way can you incorporate them into your life today?

CREEKTOWN DISCOVERIES

VOL THREE

The Apple Creek Announcement

Dedication

To Pastor Dan and Robyn: Thank you for your ministry that touches so many people's lives.

This is the confidence that we have in [God],
that, if we ask anything according to his will, he heareth us.
1 JOHN 5:14

Prologue

Walnut Creek, Ohio

"Would ya look at this old chair? I think it's a beauty, don't you?" From his kneeling position, Orley Troyer pointed to the vintage oak office chair he'd purchased at a family-run estate sale he and his wife had visited earlier in the day.

"I'd say so, and it appears to be in quite good condition. Not only that, but you got the chair for a fair price," Lois responded. She held up an old washboard she had found at the sale. "But this is one of my favorite items. I don't know if you noticed, but the lettering on the backside of the board looks pretty clear."

Orley nodded. "Now we need to put these items on display in our store."

"I'll place the washboard with the kitchen items, and you can move the chair over with the furniture."

"No problem." Orley stood up and rubbed the small of his back, where a knot had begun to form. "Although business has been strong this spring and hopefully will continue to grow now that it's summer, it has been a while since anyone has come into Memory Keepers with some sort of problem they wanted to talk about." His eyes squinted as he pulled his fingers slowly through the end of his long, full beard. "I miss mentoring folks one-on-one."

"I do too," Lois agreed, "but I'm glad for the opportunity to advise people who contact me via the Dear Caroline column in the local newspaper."

"*Jah*, that must be a good feeling all right." Orley couldn't help feeling a bit envious that his wife had such a unique opportunity to help others. Even so, there were days when he wished Lois would quit the job and spend more time with him. He looked over at her and said, "Maybe the newspaper would be interested in hiring a man to write a Dear Samuel column just for men. Then we'd both be too busy to make popcorn and work on puzzles in the evenings." He jiggled his brows and gave her arm a playful poke. "What do you think, *Fraa*? Would it be a good idea if I went to the newspaper and suggested that they hire me for that job?"

Lois snickered as she rolled her eyes at him. "I think you'd better stick to selling antiques and stay ready for the day when the Lord sends another person into our store who needs some counseling from you."

Orley smiled. "You're right, and I hope that day will come soon."

Chapter 1

Apple Creek, Ohio

Click. . .click. . .click. . . Andrea cringed as her newest piano student's fingers hit the keys while she played the piece of music she'd been given last week. For some piano teachers, the sound of nails clicking on the keys was exasperating. Andrea was one of those teachers.

She waited until the fourteen-year-old girl had finished playing before speaking to her. "Peggy, you hit all the right notes, and your timing was good, but your fingernails are much too long, and I'd like you to cut them before your next lesson."

"But Miss Wagner, the teacher I had before my folks and I moved to Apple Creek never said anything about my nails." Peggy held out her hands. "I like 'em this way, and they don't look as pretty when they're short."

"Having shorter nails will help you maintain a relaxed, curved hand position," Andrea explained.

"Why do my fingers have to be curved?"

"By doing so, you will make them close to the same length, giving each finger equal playing ability. I'm sure your previous teacher must have told you that." Andrea paused to be sure that she had her student's full attention, but the girl merely sat with a glum expression.

Being able to feel the keys with the pads of your fingers will give you a better touch on the keyboard, which in turn will allow you to play with greater control," Andrea continued. "You'll also have greater speed, because long nails could get in the way and might even cause you to make mistakes.

And have you noticed how when your nails hit the keyboard they make clicking sounds?" Andrea placed her hand on the girl's shoulder. "During a recital, would you want the only thing your audience remembers from your performance to be the sound of your nails?"

Peggy lifted her shoulders in a brief shrug. "I guess not."

Believing she had gained a little headway, Andrea added one more thing. "Not only can long fingernails affect a pianist's performance, but they can also increase your chances of getting injured."

"What do you mean?"

"It may seem hard to imagine, but when I was a girl taking lessons, my teacher told me about one of her students who had refused to trim her fingernails and ended up catching one of them between keys, which caused the end of the nail to break and bleed."

Peggy's eyes widened. "Ouch!"

"I agree, but if the student had willingly trimmed her nails, the breakage could have been avoided." She looked directly at Peggy and spoke kindly but firmly. "So what do you say—are you willing to trim your fingernails before your next lesson?"

To Andrea's surprise, the girl shook her head. "After today's lesson is done, I'm goin' home and tell Mom and Dad that I want 'em to find another teacher who isn't picky about my nails. Either that or I'm gonna quit taking piano lessons."

"It's up to you, Peggy, but your folks might not be happy about it—especially since they've paid me in advance for your next eight lessons."

"Okay, whatever. I'll wait and see what Mom and Dad have to say." The girl lifted her chin in a defiant pose. "'Cause I don't think cutting my nails will make me play one bit better."

"You don't have to cut them really short, just short enough so you can easily feel the keys with the entire fleshy part of your fingers."

"All right, I'll do it—but only if my mother won't look for another teacher."

Andrea's toes curled inside her shoes. At a moment like this, she wondered why she had decided to teach private piano lessons when she could be painting pictures full-time. Of course, her artwork didn't sell on a regular basis, making it difficult to pay the bills with what her father had often referred to as "a nice hobby."

With cautious hope, Andrea moistened her lips using the tip of her tongue. *Maybe tomorrow at the open-air market, several of my paintings will sell.*

Andrea pulled her minivan into the parking area, noticing several horses and buggies at the hitching rails on the other side of the lot. Andrea wished she could set up her easel right now and paint the appealing scene set before her, but there was no time for that. She'd arrived at the Farmstead Vintage Market, located on the Pine Hill Farm, later than she'd planned and needed to get to her open-air booth so she could display her paintings before the crowds poured in.

Andrea looked in the rearview mirror to check her hair. She'd showered this morning, but with trying to hurry out the door, she hadn't done much to style her chin-length auburn bob. Andrea pulled out a lip color from her small cross-body bag and applied it with care. Grabbing her purse, she got out of the minivan.

Andrea had no more than opened the back hatch of her van when her best friend, Colleen Jones, showed up. "Oh good, you're just in time." She hugged Colleen and gestured to the items inside her vehicle. "I was afraid I'd have to lug all this stuff over to the booth by myself."

Colleen shook her head. "Promised I'd be here, didn't I?"

"Yes, but I wasn't sure if you'd be able to find a sitter for Tyler."

Colleen offered Andrea one of her usual easygoing smiles. "My mother was more than willing to watch him for me this morning. Of course," she quickly added, "by the time I pick up my active two-year-old, he will no doubt be ready for a nap, and so will Mom."

"I hope if I ever have any children that my mother will be willing to watch them." Andrea reached inside the van and slid out the folding table she'd brought to display some of her smaller paintings.

"I'm sure she'd be willing, and if that good-looking veterinarian you've been dating for two years would get down on one knee and ask you to marry him, there might be a few kids in your future." Colleen grabbed the other end of the table.

"Maybe." Andrea started walking in the direction of the market. Truthfully, she wasn't sure Brandon Prentice would ever propose. If he was as committed to her as he was to his profession, he would have proposed by now. Brandon was a popular vet in their area, and his business was expanding, which meant longer hours for him. He worked at the clinic

Monday through Friday, and sometimes on Saturdays when there was an emergency. Brandon also doctored large animals such as horses and livestock outside of the clinic. Andrea had heard from many sources that his animal patients and their owners liked Dr. Prentice, and it wasn't hard to realize that he liked them too. Brandon's kindness and gentle ways were two of the things that had drawn her to him, as well as his six-foot stature and those piercing blue eyes. *I have to agree with Colleen—my boyfriend is good-looking.*

The tantalizing aroma and sounds of caramel-flavored popcorn being made near the entrance of the market drove Andrea's dreamy thoughts aside. The sweet and salty treat was almost addictive, and she felt tempted to stop and buy some right now. But it would have to wait, at least until she'd set up her booth. And it was definitely time to quit thinking about the man she'd fallen in love with and hoped to marry, because she needed to focus on the day ahead.

After they'd found Andrea's booth space and set up the table, she glanced down the aisle where several other vendors were busy setting their items out. Wind chimes tinkled in the gentle breeze, drawing attention to displays of baked goods, honey, homemade candles and soaps, pottery, jewelry, birdhouses, and various other rustic gifts. So much to look at but no time to do it now. Andrea wished she had time to browse and maybe buy a few items, but she needed to get the rest of her things out of the van and finish setting up.

"It sure would be nice to do some shopping here today," Andrea commented as she and Colleen made their way back to the parking area. "But I guess that's the price I must pay for renting a space to hopefully sell some of my paintings."

"I'll stay with your booth whenever you feel like browsing," Colleen responded. "I want to do some shopping too, so we can take turns."

Andrea put her hand in the small of her friend's back and gave it a few tender pats. "That's nice of you, but I didn't think you'd be staying very long today. Figured you came just to help me unload and set up."

Colleen shook her head. "Nope. I'm here for the duration or until you kick me out."

"Not a chance of that." Andrea opened the van's hatch and reached inside to grab a box filled with some of her larger paintings. "I appreciate the time you're giving up to help me when you could be spending the day with your family."

"I don't mind." Colleen tucked one of her blond curls behind her ear. "It's good for Tyler to bond with his grandparents, and my husband needs a day off to spend with his golfing buddies."

"Guess it worked out well for everyone." Andrea waited until Colleen had picked up a second box, and then they started back toward the market. They hadn't gone very far when she noticed two more Amish buggies pull into the parking lot.

"I wonder what it'd be like to be Amish," she whispered to her friend.

"I don't know, but I can't imagine giving up my car for a horse and black carriage."

Andrea chuckled. "It would be pretty hard to imagine either of us dressed in Amish clothes, not to mention having long hair pulled up in a bun or being seen in public with no makeup to hide our imperfections."

Colleen shook her head. "Nope, not for me. I'm a city gal, even if I do live in a rural community."

At noon, Andrea left her booth in the capable hands of her friend. She would check out a few of the booths on the other side of the market and stop by the food truck to get them something to eat. Of course, she wouldn't go back to her booth without picking up two large bags of kettle corn.

Andrea was pleased that she'd sold two paintings this morning—both images from Amish country. The larger one was of a black buggy parked near a red barn. The second painting featured a clothesline with several Amish quilts flapping in the breeze. That had been one of Andrea's favorites, and she'd hated to part with it, but the money she'd earned had made it worth the sacrifice. Besides, living so close to an Amish community made it easy for her to paint more pictures of quilts and other Amish backgrounds that appealed to her. Rural scenes, especially anything depicting the Plain people's way of life, were Andrea's favorite subjects. Those seemed to be the ones that sold quickly and for more money.

Andrea wandered up and down a few aisles, stopping to smell some lavender-fragranced products. She'd also been invited to sample some mild-tasting herbal tea and had even paused to try a bit of salsa—although it had proven to be a bit too spicy for her taste.

I bet Brandon would have liked it, Andrea thought as she approached the next stand. An assortment of items, most of them appearing to be secondhand or of vintage quality had been spread out on two large tables.

She felt the urge to check out the display.

Andrea had picked through a few of the items when her gaze came to rest on an old quilt that looked like it had seen better days. Something about the faded quilt drew Andrea. She pursed her lips. *Perhaps this would be an interesting piece to drape over a quilt rack and hang in my house so I could paint a picture of it.* She fingered a fraying patch on the quilt.

Andrea noticed a small piece of paper pinned to one corner of the quilt and blinked when she saw the price. *Twenty-five dollars? Could that be right?*

Andrea picked up the quilt and headed over to where a teenage girl, her arms crossed, sat in a metal chair behind a small table that held the cash box.

"Excuse me, but is this the right price?" She pointed to the place where the square piece of paper had been pinned.

The girl nodded. "Yep. My aunt Nicki—she's the one who rented this booth—said everything had been priced."

"Where is your aunt now? Could I talk to her?"

The girl shook her head. "She had to go home 'cause her baby got sick, so she left me in charge. Aunt Nicki said she'd send my uncle to come help me. He should be showing up here pretty soon, so if you have any questions about the quilt, he might be able to help you."

"I can't wait around because I have my own booth and need to get back there soon. Do you know anything about this quilt—how old it is or who it used to belong to?" Andrea questioned.

"Nope."

Continuing to hold the item, Andrea couldn't help feeling the lure of the soft fabric in her hands. "And you're sure it's only twenty-five dollars?"

The girl bobbed her head. "If I remember right, my aunt said she found it at a yard sale a few years ago, and she only paid five dollars for it. She was hoping to make a profit, so if you're interested. . ."

"Yes, I'm definitely interested." Andrea reached into her purse and took out her wallet. After she'd paid for the quilt, the girl put it in a cardboard box and handed it to Andrea. "I don't know what you're gonna do with that old thing, but it's the first sale I've made since Aunt Nicki left, so thank you."

Andrea smiled. "You're welcome." *I'm glad I stopped by this booth. I can't wait to get this quilt home and set out for display.*

Andrea had blanked out all thoughts of getting lunch or even grabbing a couple sacks of the tasty kettle corn she'd been craving all morning. She headed straight back to her booth, feeling like a child who'd opened a favored gift on Christmas morning.

Chapter 2

When Andrea returned to her booth and saw Colleen on her cell phone, she set the cardboard box with the quilt inside under the table and waited near the entrance of her vendor's stand.

"Is everything all right?" Andrea asked when her friend ended the phone call and looked at her with a pinched expression.

"That was my mom, and it's nothing serious," Colleen replied. "She's having a hard time getting Tyler to eat his lunch. He's kind of a picky eater." She patted her stomach. "And speaking of food. . .what took you so long? I'm hungry."

"Sorry," Andrea apologized. "One of the vendors had an old quilt for sale, which I ended up buying." She gestured to the box under the table. "So I set getting lunch aside and hurried back here with the quilt. If you don't mind keeping an eye on things here a little longer, I can get us something to eat right now."

"Maybe it would be better if I go to the food truck," Colleen said. "That way you'll be here to answer any customers' questions. You might have lost a few sales while I was in charge, because a couple of people came by and wanted to know if you would lower the price on some of your paintings."

Andrea groaned. "Oh great. I really hadn't planned on lowering any prices."

"Not to worry—if the potential customers come back, you can let them know that your prices are firm."

"Yeah, I suppose, but I have already lowered the prices a bit on some of the paintings so I can't go too much lower. Did anything sell in my absence?"

"Just one small painting of Lady sleeping on top of your piano."

"Guess that's better than nothing." Andrea smiled. "It was a cute cat pose."

"I agree, but I'm surprised she stayed there long enough for you to paint her portrait."

"Lady's good at sleeping in obscure places, and she usually remains in one position for quite a while."

Colleen smiled and reached for her purse. "I'd better head out to get us some lunch, or the food truck won't have anything left to offer."

"Let me give you the cash to buy my food." Andrea opened her bag. "Here you go. It's much easier to use cash at these places or write a check than try to pay with a card."

"That's true. Some of the vendors are old-school." Colleen slipped the money into her purse.

"Oh, before you go, would you like to see the quilt I purchased? I'd like your opinion."

"Sure, let's see it."

Andrea pulled the box out and removed the quilt. "What do you think?"

Colleen stepped closer and looked it over, rubbing her fingers slowly against the fabric. "Looks like an old one, but it's not in the best condition. I hope you didn't pay much for it."

"It was only twenty-five dollars."

"That was a bargain, even with it being old and not in the best condition. What are you planning to do with the quilt?"

Andrea shrugged. "I'm not sure yet. I'll probably see about getting it repaired, and then I might display it in my house somewhere."

Colleen chuckled. "Here I thought I was the one interested in antiques."

"Normally I'm not, but this quilt is different. I'm curious to know how old it is and find out what it's worth."

"You could take it to one of the quilt shops in our area."

"Would they do an appraisal?"

"Maybe. Or you could take it to an antique store." Colleen looked down at the quilt and snapped her fingers. "Hey, I think I know just the one too. There's an antique store called Memory Keepers in Walnut Creek, and it's owned by an Amish couple. I've been there a few times and was impressed with the variety of vintage things in their store. And who better to ask about an Amish quilt than a member of the Plain community?"

"Would you be willing to go with me—maybe one day next week?"

"Sure. How about Monday? We could have lunch at Boyd and Wurthmann's either before or after we visit the antique shop."

Andrea smiled. "I don't have any piano lessons to teach on Monday, so that'd be great."

"I'll see if Mom can watch Tyler again, because taking a two-year-old into an antique store would not be a good thing." Colleen spoke rapidly. "Even eating out at a restaurant with my active little boy can be a challenge."

"Speaking of eating," Andrea interjected, "the two of us still have not had any lunch."

"Right." Colleen lifted her purse straps over one shoulder. "I'll take care of that problem right now."

Walnut Creek

Lois sat behind the checkout counter, watching Orley across the room, talking with an Amish man from their church district. She couldn't hear what they were saying and wondered if their discussion pertained to antiques or some other topic. For all she knew, they could be talking about the hot, humid weather they'd been having so far this summer. Or maybe this man had a problem he wanted to discuss with Orley.

I'm sure my husband would like that, Lois thought. It wasn't that Orley wanted people to be faced with problems. Certainly not. But he, like Lois, felt blessed whenever they were given the opportunity to minister to someone who was hurting emotionally or needed advice. It seemed that God had given Orley and Lois the desire to help others, along with the gift of knowing what to say and which scriptures to share.

Lois thought about a recent letter that had been sent to her Dear Caroline column. The woman who'd written had stated that she and her husband were having marital problems. It reminded Lois of Jeff and Rhonda Davis, whom she and Orley had mentored almost two years ago. The couple had a little girl now, and they were doing quite well with the inn they'd bought in the area. The answer to Jeff and Rhonda's marriage problems had been finding a personal relationship with the

Lord. That's what Lois hoped for anyone who hadn't accepted Jesus as their personal Savior.

Her thoughts turned inward as she reflected on the day she'd asked God to forgive her sins and had acknowledged His Son as her Lord and Savior. She also remembered the feeling of peace and joy she'd felt as she stood with several other young people her age to acknowledge Christ, receive baptism, and join the church. She'd gone home that afternoon with a spring in her step and the determination to remain firm in her faith. Lois had also resolved to try and set a good example and minister to anyone she met whom she felt had a spiritual or emotional need, although there were times when she felt inadequate.

The bell above the front door jingled, pushing Lois's musings aside. The Amish man Orley had been talking to left the store a few seconds before Paul and Lisa Herschberger stepped in.

Lois left her place behind the counter to greet them, and Orley hurried across the room. Handshakes were shared between the men, and the women hugged each other.

"It's wonderful to see you both. How have you been?" Lois questioned.

"Real well," Paul replied. "We just came from a celebration lunch and wanted to stop by here to give you and Orley our good news."

"We're always open to good news." Orley looked at Lois and grinned. "Isn't that right, Fraa?"

She nodded and turned her attention to the happy-looking couple. "What's your good news?"

Lisa placed both hands against her stomach. "We're expecting a baby."

"That's right. He or she will arrive sometime in early February," Paul added.

"Congratulations." Lois gave them both a hug, and Orley followed suit.

Lois would never have let on, but she couldn't help feeling a bit of sadness because she and Orley had never been blessed with a child. She certainly would not want to dampen Paul and Lisa's joy or hurt Orley's feelings because of his inability to father a child. Although Lois loved her husband dearly and would not allow herself to dwell on being childless, there were moments, like now, when she had to be mindful not to let envy take over. Instead, Lois would continue to thank the Lord for the loving husband she had married.

Apple Creek

Andrea curled up on the sofa, petting Lady's soft white fur as the cat stretched out in her lap. Her cat's soothing purr always helped Andrea to relax after a long or stressful day. She hadn't taken time to unload her vehicle yet because she was tired and decided it could wait until she'd fixed something to eat and rested awhile. At the end of a busy or hectic day, she liked to sit quietly in a darkened room and let her mind go blank.

When the bell rang, Andrea lifted Lady off her lap, turned on a light, and went to see who it was. Upon opening the door, she was surprised to see Brandon on the porch with a smile on his face and a pizza box in his hands.

"I brought supper." He leaned in to give her a sweet, gentle kiss.

Had it not been for the box between them, she would have melted into his arms. "Oh, thank you so much. I'm exhausted and dreaded having to fix anything for supper." She stepped back so Brandon could enter.

"I was thinking about you and thought you might have had an exhausting day at the market. Should I put this on the dining room table or in the kitchen?" he asked.

"Let's eat in the dining room. I'll turn some music on, and we can pretend we're on a dinner date."

He kissed her forehead. "We are. We're just not going out to a crowded, noisy restaurant. By eating here, I'll have you all to myself and won't have to shout to be heard."

She nodded. "Good point. I'll go to the kitchen and get some paper plates and napkins. Oh, and what would you like to drink? I have iced tea, lemonade, and grape juice."

"Iced tea is fine for me."

While Brandon headed for the dining room, Andrea went to the kitchen. A short while later, they were both seated at the table with the Italian-style cheese and pepperoni pizza between them. After saying grace, Brandon pushed the pizza toward Andrea and told her to dig in.

"I should make a tossed green salad to go with this, but I'm hungry and don't want to take the time," she said, reaching for a piece of pizza and putting it on her plate.

"That's okay." Brandon smiled. "This is a family-style pizza, so there's more than enough for us to eat, and I'm sure you'll have leftovers."

"Maybe you'd like to take them home."

He shook his head. "This is my treat, and whatever's left will be yours."

Andrea didn't argue; she just smiled and said, "Thank you." She figured with Brandon's hearty appetite, there might not be anything left.

"How'd your day at the open-air market go?" he asked.

"Not too bad. I sold a few of my smaller paintings, and I appreciated Colleen being there to help me load and unload things as well as set up my booth."

"I wish it could have been me who had helped you, but I had an emergency at the clinic this morning and several farm stops to care for people's horses and livestock." Brandon paused to drink some iced tea. "It was a tiring day, but yours probably was too."

"Yes, especially toward the end of the day as the crowds thinned out. By then there wasn't much left to do except wait for four o'clock, when we could start packing things up."

"If you didn't sell much, do you feel like it was worth your effort and the money you spent to rent a booth?"

"I did hand out several of my business cards, so it's possible that I'll get a few calls from interested buyers." Andrea picked a piece of pepperoni off her slice of pizza and ate it. "I probably missed a few sales when I left Colleen at my booth to go get us some lunch. When I got back—without any food—she said a few people had stopped by the booth and were interested but wanted to offer less for the paintings. I may have taken their offers if they hadn't been too much less than what I was asking."

"Sorry you didn't make many sales. I'm curious, though—how come you returned to your booth without anything for lunch? Did the food truck run out of food?"

"No, it was my fault. I stopped by one of the vendor's stands and ended up buying an old quilt that I'm quite sure is Amish. I was so excited and wanted to get it back to my booth, so I kind of forgot about getting lunch."

"Where is this old quilt that you chose over eating?"

"It's in the back of my van, along with the table I took to the market and all my paintings that didn't sell."

"I'll help you take everything out when we finish eating."

"Thanks. When I first got home, I was too tired to bring everything in." Andrea glanced at her cat, lying on the floor a few feet from the table. "Besides, Lady missed me while I was gone, and she needed some attention."

Brandon chuckled. "I know how that is. When I got home this

afternoon, Duke was so eager to see me that he tried climbing his way out of the pen."

"Pets are great, but they're a lot of work, and they demand plenty of attention from their owners."

"My dog is worth it, though, and I'm sure you feel the same way about your cat."

"Most definitely."

"It's too bad Duke's scared to death of Lady. That might cause a problem when we get married."

Andrea nearly choked on the piece of pizza she'd put in her mouth. "Are—are you asking me to marry you?"

Brandon's eyes appeared even bluer than usual as he looked deeply into Andrea's eyes. "I realize this isn't the most romantic setting, and I probably should be down on one knee right now, but the answer is yes, I am asking you to be my wife."

Andrea felt a sense of weightlessness as she moved her head up and down. "Yes, Brandon, a thousand times, yes. I will marry you."

He left the table so quickly that his chair nearly toppled over and was swiftly at her side. Andrea stood, and they sealed their commitment to each other with a kiss that took Andrea's breath away. She wanted to ask what had taken him so long but figured that question was best left unspoken. The last thing she wanted to do was say anything that might ruin this special moment between them.

Chapter 3

Berlin, Ohio

Andrea glanced at her gold-toned watch. It was one thirty, and she'd been sitting at a table inside Boyd and Wurthmann Restaurant for half an hour, waiting for Colleen. At least she had her guest list to work on and at times would take little breaks, browsing on her phone at different sights of interest. The restaurant was active with the steady hum of conversations going on around her, and the waitresses worked busily, seeing to their customers.

Andrea kept looking toward the entrance for Colleen, but so far only strangers were coming in to sit down for a nice meal.

She picked up her water glass and took a drink. *I wonder what's taking her so long.* It wasn't like her friend to be late for anything. In fact, Colleen prided herself on being punctual, and she usually was.

Maybe they got behind at the dental clinic and she didn't get off at noon like she normally does on Mondays. Brandon's father was a dentist, and Colleen, along with one other dental hygienist, worked for him. Colleen had been working part-time: half days on Mondays and Fridays and full days on Tuesdays and Thursdays. The schedule gave her more time to be at home with Tyler.

Andrea stared down at the paper and thought back to the day at the market and all the Plain people there. It amazed her how they could continue to live such a simple lifestyle and not have electricity.

They're a unique kind of people in the way they dress and their old-fashioned mode of transportation, she thought. *And the Pennsylvania Dutch language they speak to their children and to each other seems strange to me.*

Andrea mulled over how much work it would take to be a Plain person. Without electricity and many modern conveniences, it would be difficult at best. Andrea couldn't imagine doing without her dishwasher, computer, and even the heated styling tools she used on her hair. *How do the Amish function without all the nice comforts I'm used to? I can't help feeling intrigued and wondering why they choose their way of life.*

Andrea looked up from the list she'd been creating and glanced toward the door. Colleen was just entering the restaurant. She wore a soft pink blouse and a pair of gray slacks, which was the style she'd said she liked to work in. On the days she wasn't working, Colleen usually pulled on a T-shirt and blue jeans.

When Andrea noticed Colleen's pinched, tension-filled expression, she wondered if something had gone wrong.

"Sorry I'm late." Colleen paused and swiped a hand across her forehead before taking a seat across from Andrea. "I got off work on time, but the traffic was crazy, plus I needed to stop and fill my gas tank."

"It's okay. I had plenty of time to work on my guest list."

"Are you planning a party?"

Andrea shook her head. "Not exactly. It's my wedding guest list."

Colleen blinked rapidly as she stared at Andrea with her mouth slightly open. "Brandon finally proposed?"

"Yes. Saturday evening he came by my place with pizza, and during our meal he asked me to marry him." Feeling somewhat breathless herself, Andrea picked up the menu in front of her and fanned her face, unable to hide the excitement she felt.

Colleen gave her two thumbs-up. "Well, congratulations, and it's about time. When's the wedding going to be?"

"We haven't set a date yet."

Colleen pointed to Andrea's left hand. "Apparently your future groom didn't give you an engagement ring either."

"We're going to pick it out together one night this week."

"Have you both told your parents?"

Andrea shook her head. "Not yet. We thought it would be nice to take the four of them out to dinner this weekend and share the good news." She put a finger to her lips. "So if you should see my folks or Brandon's mother anytime this week, please don't say anything—especially to

Brandon's dad, since you work for him."

Colleen drew a finger across her mouth. "My lips are sealed."

"Thank you. Now are you ready to take a look at the menu so we can order? I'm starving."

"Same here." Colleen picked up her menu and looked it over. When a waitress came to the table, they placed their orders.

"Did you bring the quilt with you?" Colleen asked after their server walked away.

"I sure did, and I'm anxious to see if we can find out anything about the time period it was made, as well as the value of it now."

"After lunch we can head over to Helping Hands quilt shop and see if they can give you any information." Colleen smiled. "If we don't find out what you want to know there, we'll head for Memory Keepers in Walnut Creek."

When Andrea entered the quilt shop with Colleen, she sucked in a quick breath as her eyes feasted on the amazing array of quilted items. Numerous long table runners had been stacked on display tables, along with lovely coverings of several shapes and colors for smaller tables. On the opposite side of the room, a huge collection of quilted bed coverings had been draped over wooden racks. The walls were adorned with a variety of wall hangings in so many different patterns it nearly made Andrea's head spin. The quilt she'd brought inside the cardboard box she held looked inferior to all these newly made quilted items. Even so, Andrea had already developed a fondness for her old quilt, and it wasn't fair to compare old to new.

"Wow! Did you ever see such a variety of quilts? This place is amazing." Colleen made a sweeping gesture with her hand.

"Haven't you been in this quilt shop before?" Andrea shifted the box in her hands.

Colleen shook her head. "I've known about it for some time but have never come in until today."

A young woman dressed in conservative Mennonite attire stepped up to Andrea and Colleen. "May I help either of you with something?"

"I bought an old quilt recently, and I'm wondering about the age of it as well as the pattern and current price." Andrea set the box on the floor and reached in to retrieve the quilt.

The woman spread the quilt out on an empty table and looked it over. "It's in pretty rough shape, isn't it?"

Andrea nodded. "Do you know the name of the pattern?"

"Yes, it's a Fan quilt."

"How much is it worth?" Colleen interjected.

The young woman shrugged. "I'm not sure how old it is or what the current value would be. If you're interested in having the quilt restored, I know someone who does that kind of thing. Would you like her phone number?"

Andrea tilted her head as she weighed her choices. "Maybe, but I'd like to find out more about the quilt before I have anything done to it. Right now I mainly want to find out the age and value of the quilt."

"Perhaps you should take it to an antique dealer," the clerk suggested.

"Yes, our next stop is Memory Keepers antique store in Walnut Creek." Andrea refolded the quilt and put it back in the box. "Thanks for your time. If I decide to get it restored, I'll call your store for the number."

"You're welcome. I'm sorry I couldn't give you more information. The other woman who works here is on her lunch break, but we're both new, and I doubt she would know much more than I do regarding the value." She shrugged her slender shoulders. "If I gave you a number, I'd only be guessing."

Andrea smiled. "No problem. I'm just glad to know the name of the quilt pattern."

After Andrea and Colleen left the store, she looked over at her friend and said, "Since I've never been to Memory Keepers and you have, you can lead the way and I'll follow in my car."

Walnut Creek

There were no customers in the store, so Lois left Orley up front and went to the office near the back of their building. Unless they got busy, she would spend the next hour or so getting caught up on some paperwork and reading a few of the letters addressed to Dear Caroline she'd picked up at the post office this morning.

Lois had only been sitting at her desk a few minutes when Orley entered the room. "Two English women just came in, asking about an old Amish quilt," he announced.

Lois touched the base of her neck and lowered her brows. "Didn't you tell them that we don't have any old quilts for sale in the store at this time?"

"I did, but the one lady said she wasn't looking to buy a quilt. She brought one in and would like information on the age and value of the quilt." He moved closer and placed a hand on the desk. "My knowledge of old quilts is limited. That's your area of expertise."

Lois nodded slowly. "All right then, please let them know that I'll be right out."

"Will do." Orley kissed her cheek and hurried from the room.

Lois arranged the letters she'd received, checked to make sure her head covering wasn't askew, and left the office. When she approached the front of the store, she saw two women—one with auburn hair and the other a blond—talking to Orley near the checkout counter.

"Hello, I'm Lois Troyer," she said. "My husband, Orley, informed me that you brought in an old quilt for appraisal."

The young woman with auburn hair bobbed her head. "My name is Andrea Wagner, and this is my friend, Colleen Jones. We're from Apple Creek."

"It's nice to meet you both."

"How much would you charge to look at the quilt and give me an estimate of its age and value?" Andrea asked.

"There'll be no charge for that." Lois smiled. "I'd be happy to take a look at your quilt and offer my opinion."

"Oh, thank you so much." Andrea bent down and lifted an older-looking quilt from the box at her feet. "Is there a table where I can lay it out so you can have a better look?"

"All our tables are filled with antiques right now," Lois replied. "But there's a quilt rack in our storage room that we can drape it over." She looked at Orley. "Would you mind getting it for me?"

"Not at all." He headed off in the opposite direction.

Andrea glanced around the antique store as she and Colleen waited for the man's return. Although there were no quilts for sale, she saw plenty of vintage items.

It would be fun to set a few of the old kitchen items on an antique table and paint a picture of them, she thought. *Maybe I'll come back sometime and buy a couple of things.* Her gaze came to rest on a small vintage office chair that appeared to be made of oak. *That would look good somewhere in my home. It'd be a real conversation piece.*

Andrea was on the verge of going over to take a seat in the old chair, when Orley returned with the quilt rack. In no time, he had it set up, and Lois helped Andrea drape it over the wooden rails. Holding the corners of the bed covering, she inspected it carefully. "This is a vintage Fan quilt, probably made in the early 1950s. The design was also quite popular in colonial days."

"It's a simple pattern yet quite intricate." Andrea pointed to the stitching on one of the fans decorating the quilt. "Is there anything you can tell us about how a hand-stitched covering like this would be made?" she asked the Amish woman.

"Why yes. The fan patches are sometimes placed with each of them sitting the same way. It is a simple design that resembles plants tilting toward the sun." Lois gestured to the quilt. "The fans might also be placed against each other in a variety of different ways, which creates rolling lines or colorful circles."

"You certainly seem to know a lot about quilts," Andrea commented. "Are you a quilter?"

"No, but one of my aunts certainly was. I stayed with her for a while when I was a teenager. During that time, she taught me a lot about quilts, but I never tried making one myself." Lois had a far-off look in her eyes as she stood for several seconds with her arms crossed.

"How much would a quilt like this sell for in today's market?" The question came from Colleen.

"Since it's not in the best condition, the bed covering isn't worth anywhere near what a new quilt of this size and pattern would be," Lois responded.

The bell over the door tinkled. When another customer came in, Lois looked that way. "If you have any questions, sir, my husband over there can help you," she called before pointing in the direction where Orley stood.

"Thanks." The man headed in the direction of Lois's husband.

"If Andrea wanted to sell the quilt, how much do you think it would go for?" Colleen questioned.

Lois shifted her stance. "Probably not more than three hundred dollars."

Colleen looked at Andrea with her head slightly tipped. "That's not even close to the high price of newer Amish quilts."

"Three hundred dollars is still quite a bit more than I paid for it."

Andrea fingered one corner of the aging quilt.

"Are you going to sell it?" Colleen gave Andrea's arm a little nudge.

"I don't think so. For some reason, I feel drawn to this quilt." Andrea lifted the item off the rack and put it back in the box. "I may drop by some other time," she said, looking at Lois. "I'd like to browse a bit and see what all you have for sale."

"That would be nice." Lois offered her a friendly smile. "I hope you do stop by."

Andrea glanced at the office chair. *If that's still here when I return and isn't too expensive, I may take it home.*

Chapter 4

Lois watched Orley from across the supper table, wondering why he'd barely touched her baked chicken and mashed potatoes, having eaten only a few bites. Even the pickled beets went untouched. Normally, her husband would have finished them and asked for seconds by now. Of course, she would have encouraged him to be satisfied with only one helping so he wouldn't start gaining weight, which was a concern due to his hypothyroidism. But it bothered her to see Orley pushing food around his plate instead of eating.

"Is something wrong with your appetite this evening, Husband?" Lois asked. "Or is the *hinkel* not baked to your liking or the *gemaeschde grummbiere* not creamy enough?"

Orley looked up and shook his head. "There's nothing wrong with the chicken or the mashed potatoes. My mind's been filled with questions this evening."

"Is it something you'd like to talk about?" Lois took a delicate bite from the serving of potatoes on her plate. She noticed his brow lines deepening before he spoke again.

"I'm still disappointed that no one has come into our store for a good many months with a problem they wanted to share." His shoulders slumped. "Am I getting too old? Maybe God doesn't want to use me as a mentor anymore."

"I can't imagine where you got such a notion." She gave a slow shake of her head. "According to the Bible, the good Lord wants every believer to minister to others in need. No matter how old we are, as long as we're able and willing to serve Him, He will allow us to be His servants. Although lately God hasn't sent anyone who has a need we can help with, I'm confident that at the correct time, the right person will walk into our store and share something that will let us know they need a bit of counseling."

Orley sat silently for a time, as though considering her words. He stroked the salt-and-pepper hairs in his beard before he spoke again.

"I suppose you're right, but I can't help feeling a bit envious of you getting to reach out to people through your Dear Caroline column."

Lois liked how open her husband was, but hearing that he felt envy over her newspaper column wasn't easy. *I hope what I say next will be helpful and make my dear husband feel better.*

"Remember, Orley, I never meet the people who write me letters, so I don't know whether they take my advice or not. It's a lot different than mentoring people one-on-one the way we have done when they come into our store and we sense there's a need." Lois lifted her shoulders in a brief shrug. "For all I know, the ones who write to me might choose to ignore my suggestions."

"I can't argue with that." He pulled a finger down the side of his nose. "Guess there must be some reason the opportunity to mentor someone again hasn't happened yet." Orley picked up his fork and took a bite of the chicken. He looked at Lois. "Maybe the Lord is trying to teach me to have more *geduld*."

"Learning patience can be difficult, but at times we all need to be taught that lesson."

Wooster, Ohio

"Dinner's on me tonight," Brandon said after he, Andrea, and their parents were seated at the City Square Steakhouse. Several years ago, this upscale restaurant had been located inside the historic Germania Hall building, which was built in 1878. Back in its day, it had been known as the "skyscraper." The charming establishment had even been recognized as one of the "Top 100 Steakhouses in America."

Brandon looked at his folks and then at Andrea's parents. *I wonder if I'll be the one telling them the good news about our engagement or if my fiancée will want to do the honors.* Brandon was fine with whatever Andrea wanted to do. And he hoped this evening would go smoothly for him and the sweet woman he looked forward to making his wife.

"Paying for our meals is very generous," Andrea's mother, Evelyn, said. She smiled and gestured to the linen cloth and napkins on their table. "This is such a lovely place to eat."

"I agree," Brandon's mother, Jennifer, said. "And even though the inside of the restaurant is nice, I've always enjoyed eating out here on the covered patio."

The weather was just right for their little evening celebration. The outside dining area had been nicely decorated, and pots brimmed with colorful summer foliage. The view from their table was pleasant.

A waiter arrived at the table and asked if anyone would like an appetizer.

"How about the baked spinach artichoke dip with crispy pita chips?" Brandon's gaze went to each person at the table. "I can get an order for each couple. How's that sound?"

"Sounds good to me," his dad was quick to respond. "Is everyone else okay with that?"

When they all nodded, Brandon looked at the waiter and said: "Three orders of baked spinach artichoke dip, please."

Everyone placed their beverage orders, and then the well-groomed waiter said he would be back with their drinks and appetizers, at which time everyone could order their entrées if they were ready.

After the young man left the table, Brandon's father, Larry, spoke up. "Did you invite us here for some special occasion, or was it simply because it's been a while since we've all gotten together for a meal?"

"Both." Brandon leaned close to Andrea and whispered, "Should we share our good news now or wait till after our meal?"

"I think we should make the announcement now," she murmured quietly.

"Okay. Do you want to tell them, or shall I?"

"Why don't you go ahead?"

"What's all the whispering about?" Andrea's father, Ray, questioned. "Are you two sharing a secret?"

"It is now, but it won't be in a few seconds." Brandon's gaze took them all in. "Andrea and I have an announcement to make." After a brief pause, he continued. "I asked her to marry me, and she said yes."

Both sets of parents applauded and said, "Congratulations." Everyone began talking at once.

"Have you set the date?"

"I don't see an engagement ring on Andrea's finger."

"Where will the wedding be held?"

"Have you made plans for a honeymoon yet?"

Brandon held up his hand. "Andrea and I will be happy to answer all of your questions, but please, just one at a time."

"I'm surprised you're not wearing an engagement ring." A flush of red erupted on Evelyn's cheeks as she looked at her daughter. "Sorry, honey. It's really none of my business."

"After Brandon left his clinic Thursday evening, we went to the House of Silva Jewelry store here in Wooster to pick out our rings," Andrea said. "We found the perfect set, but they needed resizing, so I won't have my beautiful diamond, yellow-gold engagement ring until sometime next week."

Her mother nodded. "That makes perfect sense."

"Have you set a date for the wedding?" Brandon's mother asked.

He shook his head. "Not yet, but we'll let you all know as soon as we do."

Andrea's mother, Evelyn, smiled. "That's good, because we'll have a lot of planning to do, and that will take time."

"I'd like to keep things simple," Andrea said. "Just a nice church wedding with our close friends and relatives will be fine."

"And we'll have a reception in the church fellowship hall afterward," Brandon interjected.

"What?" Jennifer's brown eyes widened. "I understand the church wedding, but our fellowship hall is rather small and kind of plain. Wouldn't you rather have the reception someplace where you can invite more people and celebrate in style?"

"I—I don't know. Brandon and I just got engaged, and we haven't had time to count the number of people we want to invite." Andrea looked at Brandon as though for confirmation.

He gave a decisive nod. "My future wife is right, Mom. We've really made no plans at all."

"Say, I have an idea," Brandon's father put in. "Why don't you have the wedding at Peacock Ridge in North Lawrence? You could make it an all-day event. The grounds are secluded, in the middle of rolling hills with beautiful views. My friend Randy's daughter, Nicole, got married there." He looked over at Brandon's mother. "Remember, Jennifer, how much you raved about that outdoor wedding held by the pond?"

"Oh yes, Larry. And the two geese swimming in the pond gave it such a special touch. Not only that, but the barn, where the reception was held, had been decorated so beautifully with thousands of lights, draped ceilings, and some unique custom-looking chandeliers." She spoke rapidly, with obvious enthusiasm. "There were so many wonderful places for photos to be taken too."

Leaning slightly forward, Andrea opened her mouth like she was about to say something, but Brandon's mother cut her off.

"There's also the lovely Pineview Acres in Massilon." She reached up and touched the bun at the back of her head, as if worried that a hair might be out of place. "I've heard that's a lovely setting for both indoor and outdoor weddings and receptions."

"And don't forget about the Barn at the Meadows in Orrville. The historic barn dates back to the 1820s," Andrea's father spoke up. "That one is closer to home, so there'd be less of a commute, and it even has a hay wagon." He nudged his wife's arm. "Now how fun is that?"

"I suppose it would be, Ray," she responded, "but I wonder how expensive it would be."

"Well, let's keep in mind that Andrea is our only daughter, and we love her very much, so we won't worry about the cost."

"You're right," Evelyn said. "I think we can all agree that we want Andrea and Brandon's wedding to be a day they'll always remember."

Andrea's chin trembled, and Brandon figured she might be close to tears. It was time to call a halt to this whole pre-wedding planning discussion.

And just in time too, he thought, when their waiter came to the table with their orders of baked spinach artichoke dip and crispy pita chips.

Andrea swallowed against the constriction that had formed in her throat. Even though she had twin center-cut filet mignon medallions on her plate, along with rice pilaf and asparagus, she had no appetite. How could she, when it had become obvious that Brandon's parents, as well as her own, wanted to plan her and Brandon's wedding? Even now, as they all ate their meal, the conversation continued to be centered on Andrea and Brandon's upcoming wedding. Didn't any of them realize that the decision as to where and when the ceremony and reception would be held was up to the bride and groom? Didn't she and Brandon have the right to choose? It wasn't that Andrea did not want their parents' help. She just didn't like the idea of allowing any of them to choose the wedding venue.

Andrea felt certain that Brandon's parents would host a lavish rehearsal dinner and no doubt want to pay for all the flowers. Her parents would most likely want to foot the bill for the wedding venue, photographer, catering service, bride's gown, and wedding invitations. Andrea would not feel right asking them to dip into their savings and put out a large sum of money for the use of a wedding venue that they really couldn't afford. Besides, she wanted to get married in their church and felt sure that Brandon did too. Perhaps if they got married during one of the warm weather months, they could have their reception in Brandon's parents' lovely, well-appointed backyard. It was definitely large enough to accommodate their guests.

Andrea made a mental note to speak to Brandon about the possibility. In fact, there were a lot of wedding details they needed to discuss. And they ought to do it soon, before their parents completely took over. Andrea had read once that planning a wedding could be stressful, and now she knew it was true. By simply making the announcement to their parents, her stomach already felt like it was tied in knots. Was it any wonder she had no appetite?

Take a deep breath and remember to pray, she told herself. *Maybe someday I'll look back on this evening and think it was silly to feel so stressed out over a few suggestions about the wedding venue.*

"I'm sorry our meal this evening didn't go better." Brandon reached across the seat in his SUV and took Andrea's hand.

"The atmosphere and food were good," she murmured.

"I can't imagine that you'd know how the food tasted. You didn't even finish your meal."

Andrea looked down at the box filled with her leftover food. "I didn't have much of an appetite."

"And for good reason. When we decided to tell our folks about our engagement, I expected they'd be happy for us and offer congratulations, but I wasn't prepared for them trying to take over and make our plans." Brandon paused to turn on the wipers as rain began to fall. "I realized right away that you were upset, and even though I tried several times to steer our conversation in another direction, someone always brought it back to the wedding plans."

"I know." She sniffed, trying to hold back tears. "At some point, we may have to be firm and let our parents know that this is our wedding, and we need to be the ones to choose where and when we get married."

"Agreed. And speaking of that. . . We still need to choose a date for the wedding. Any thoughts?"

"We do need several months to make plans and take care of all the arrangements. How about February? Maybe we could get married on Valentine's Day."

"Hearts and flowers for the decorations?"

"Yes. And I definitely want to be married in our church, with Pastor Rawlings officiating."

"I want that too." Brandon took hold of her hand again. "Let's get together one night next week and start making plans. Why don't you come over to my place Friday evening, and I'll barbecue some bison burgers."

"Sounds good. By then my appetite should be back, so you may have to fix me two."

He chuckled. "That can be arranged."

Andrea smiled. How thankful she felt for the relationship she and Brandon had. He was always so kind and supportive. She looked forward to becoming his wife and hoped the next seven months would go by in a hurry.

Chapter 5

Apple Creek

Andrea was about to step out the door when her cell phone rang. Checking the caller ID, she saw that it was her mother. Here it was Friday, and Mom had called nearly every day this week. Each time she'd brought up the wedding, asking questions and making suggestions. She wanted her mother to listen to what she desired to do and to have Mom's total support throughout the entire planning of the wedding. In all of her thirty-two years, Andrea had never known her mother to be pushy or controlling.

So why now? she wondered. *Is Mom that eager to see me get married? Or could she be trying to make up for the extravagant, fancy wedding that she and Dad never had?*

Andrea had tried to be patient and polite, but with each conversation, she'd become more frustrated. Andrea considered letting Mom's call go to voice mail but decided it was best to answer.

"Hi, Mom. I've only got a minute, so unless this is important, I'll have to call you back later."

"Are you teaching a piano lesson this late in the day?"

"No, I'll be on my way to Brandon's place soon, and I don't want to keep him waiting."

"I remember the last time we talked you mentioned that the two of you would be making some wedding plans this evening. Is that the reason you're going there?"

"Yes. . .that and to enjoy a meal together. He's planning to grill some bison burgers."

"That sounds good." There was a short pause, then Andrea's mother spoke again. "The reason I called is to tell you that I spoke with Brandon's mother this morning, and Jennifer said she had talked to her husband about them paying half the cost for one of those wedding venues we'd talked about at the restaurant last week."

"Oh well, Mom—"

"We'll need to get one of the places reserved as soon as possible because well-appointed venues like that book up quickly."

Andrea's jaw clenched. "An outdoor wedding would not be good in the middle of February."

"I thought you and Brandon hadn't set a date yet."

"When he drove me home from the City Square Steakhouse last week, we decided on February fourteenth."

"Valentine's Day?"

"Yes, but we've made no plans beyond setting the date and deciding that the wedding will be held in our church's sanctuary."

"Oh, but Andrea—"

"I really have to leave now, Mom. Brandon will be worried if I'm late. Once he and I have made some definite plans, I'll fill you in, and then we can talk about who would like to do what. I'm sure to need your help with many things."

"I hope so, because your father and I want to do everything we can to make yours and Brandon's wedding day special."

"I know, Mom, and I'll talk to you soon."

"Okay, hon. I hope you and Brandon have a good evening."

"You too. Bye for now." When Andrea clicked off her phone and headed out the door, she breathed a sigh of relief. *Hopefully Mom has accepted the fact that Brandon and I will be getting married at church, and she won't bring up any of those venues again.*

"Yum." Andrea smacked her lips. "This bison burger is delicious. Did you buy the meat somewhere locally?"

Brandon shook his head. "I got it via the internet from a business in Nebraska. I ordered several boxes, and they came frozen, packed well with dry ice. I was pleased to see that none of the meat had thawed, so it went right into my freezer."

Arf! Arf! Arf!

Andrea looked down at Brandon's rusty-colored Brittany spaniel, Duke. The dog had inched his way to the table and sat looking up at them as though desperate for food. "I think Duke's hoping we might share some of our burgers with him."

Brandon laughed. "Yeah. He started begging the minute I put the patties on the grill." His face sobered. "In addition to wedding planning, we need to talk about the situation between my dog and your cat and how we are going to work things out once we're married."

Andrea blotted her lips with a napkin. "Oh, you mean the fact that Duke is scared of Lady?"

"Yeah. He's a good dog, and I don't want to get rid of him. I'm sure you feel the same way about Lady."

"You're right about that, but we can't let those two come between us or put a damper on our marriage. Maybe you can figure out some way to teach Duke not to be so intimidated by my cat's presence." Andrea paused to add another scoop of potato salad to her plate. "And I'll work on the problem of getting Lady to approach Duke in such a way that he won't be afraid."

"Sounds like a plan. I hope we can make it work. Otherwise, my poor pooch will spend most of his time in hiding once we are married." Brandon reached over and placed his hand on Andrea's arm, giving it a few tender pats. "We'll work it out. Lady's not a mean cat. Duke's just a big baby. I remember the day you first came to my clinic when Lady had a nasty thorn in her paw. Even though the poor thing was hurting, she remained calm and didn't try to scratch or bite me."

Andrea smiled. "That's because she sensed your gentle, caring spirit, just as I did."

"I sensed that about you too, sweetie." He finished what was on his plate and pushed back his chair. "How about we clear these dishes, and then we can go into the living room and make some plans for our wedding."

"Sounds good to me."

Brandon took a seat on the couch beside Andrea and kissed her cheek. "Ready to talk about our wedding?"

She held up the notebook in her hand. "Definitely. I just hope my mother is still speaking to me when I tell her whatever decisions we've made." Andrea tapped her pen against the notebook. "She called me before I came over here and said she had talked to your mom this morning. I believe they both want us to get married at one of the venues that were brought up during our meal at the restaurant in Wooster last week."

"I know they do." Brandon frowned. "I'd barely gotten home this evening and was about to heat up the grill, when my mom called. I told her I was expecting you soon, but she went on and on about the one venue with peacocks and swans, and I could barely get a word in edgewise." Brandon's brows lowered. "I don't want to hurt their feelings, but we're going to have to be firm and let them know that it's our wedding we're planning and it's our right to make all the final decisions."

"I agree." Andrea held her pen against the notebook. "So let's begin at the beginning."

Walnut Creek

The following day, Andrea decided to visit Memory Keepers again to see if the vintage oak desk chair was still there.

I should have bought it the day Colleen and I went to the antique store, Andrea thought as she searched for a parking spot near the store. *If it's gone, I'll have no one to blame but myself.*

Sometimes, like when Andrea had bought the old quilt, she made hasty decisions. Other times, such as last night at Brandon's, Andrea couldn't decide what she wanted. She and Brandon had worked on their wedding plans for several hours, going over the pros and cons of each detail. They'd definitely decided that their wedding ceremony would be held at the church, but to make their parents happy, they'd agreed that it might be nice to have the reception at one of the venues they'd talked about. Andrea would ask her father to take care of the arrangements. That way he could choose the one he felt would fit his budget. Brandon had said his parents would no doubt be willing to help with the cost too. Andrea would ask Colleen to be her maid of honor, and Brandon wanted his brother, Joe, to be his best man.

When someone pulled out of the parking spot in front of the antique store, Andrea pulled her minivan in. It was time to set wedding plans aside and see if that old chair was still available.

Lois had been washing a streak off the front window when she spotted the auburn-haired woman who had visited the store previously asking about an old quilt she'd bought. When the young woman entered the store, Lois set her cleaning supplies aside and went to greet her.

"Well, hello. . . It's Andrea, right?"

"Yes, I'm surprised you remembered."

"My wife has a great memory—especially for people's names," Orley called from across the room, where he'd been hanging a few vintage signs he'd picked up at a yard sale that week. "It's a lot of work to pick through other people's things, but we nearly always find some old item, and it feels like we've unearthed a piece of history."

Andrea looked at Lois and smiled. "I came by to see if you still had that old oak desk chair for sale. I looked at it when I was here the last time and wished I'd bought it."

"Yes, we still have it. The chair is over there by that old desk." Lois pointed.

"I'll take another look," Andrea said, "but I'm almost certain that I still want it."

Lois led the way. When they stood next to the chair, Andrea bent down and rubbed her hand across the seat. It was then that Lois noticed a sparkly diamond ring on the young woman's left hand. She did not recall seeing it the last time Andrea was here. *But then*, she reasoned, *my concentration was on the vintage quilt not Andrea's hand.* Although Lois and other Amish church members did not wear jewelry, she knew that when a single English woman wore a diamond ring on her left hand, it meant she was engaged to be married. A second ring—a wedding band—would mean she was already married.

"This is really a nice chair, and I'll take it." Andrea stood and reached into her purse. "Will you accept a credit card for payment?"

Lois gave a slow shake of her head. "I'm sorry, but we're not set up for that. We only take cash or checks."

Andrea's cheeks turned rosy as she rubbed the bridge of her nose. "Oh, that's right. I noticed your sign by the cash register when I was here before. Sorry, I'm a bit stressed out right now, and my brain feels kind of fuzzy."

With no other customers in the store, Lois felt it was safe to speak to her openly. "I'm sorry to hear that. Is it anything you'd like to talk about?

My husband and I are pretty good listeners."

"And sometimes we offer advice," Orley added after he'd gotten down from the ladder and walked over to them.

Lois couldn't believe he had blurted that out. To Andrea, it might seem as though he was sticking his nose in her business.

She briefly closed her eyes and said a little prayer inwardly before she spoke. "We don't wish to pry, and if you'd rather not talk about whatever is bothering you, that's fine."

Andrea leaned against another desk that sat behind her and released a lingering sigh. "It might actually feel good to talk about it with someone who isn't biased. So if you have the time, I'll tell you what's been happening since my boyfriend, Brandon, and I told our parents that we were engaged."

For the next twenty minutes or so, Lois and Orley listened while Andrea told them about hers and Brandon's parents—especially their mothers, who seemed to want to take charge of the wedding plans. "So now you know why I'm feeling so stressed out."

Orley spoke first. "Planning for a wedding, whether it be English or Amish, can be a hectic time for any engaged couple, so it's important to remain calm and avoid conflict as much as possible." He stopped talking long enough to give his earlobe a tug. "Sometimes parents may feel insecure due to the fact that they're losing a child. They want to feel important and appreciated."

Using her fingertips, Andrea made little circles across her forehead. "I hadn't thought of that. Since I'm an only child, Mom and Dad probably feel a sense of loss even though I've been living out on my own in a small rented home for some time."

"Your parents might feel neglected if they are not involved in your wedding plans, which is not to say that you and your fiancé shouldn't be the ones to decide where and when you'll get married," Lois interjected. "I think it would be helpful if you stay in communication with your parents about each aspect of the wedding."

"Asking for their help and communicating your ideas to them would be good, in addition to updating them on any decisions you and your groom-to-be make," Orley added.

Lois placed a hand on Andrea's arm and gave it a pat. "Your wedding should be a joyous occasion, without the added stress of tension between family members, so try to be patient with them and understanding."

"Thank you for your kind words and sound advice. It helped to talk about this with someone who isn't involved, and the things you've said make good sense." Andrea reached up and wiped away a few tears that had slipped down her cheeks. "I feel better already."

"We're glad we could help, and feel free to come by anytime if other things regarding your wedding plans come up and you need to talk more about them." Orley picked up the oak chair. "Should I take this to the front of the store for you?"

"Yes, thank you."

A short time later, Andrea left with the chair, and Orley turned to Lois with a wide smile. "Well, that was her."

She tipped her head and looked at him with eyes squinted. "What do you mean?"

"I believe God sent that young woman with the pretty auburn hair into our store today so we could mentor her." He slipped his arm around Lois's waist. "Aren't you excited? He's using our willingness to serve Him again. And maybe this won't be the end of it either. Andrea might come back here again, and if she does, we need to be ready to listen and offer more sound advice."

Lois nodded and smiled. It was nice to see her husband's enthusiastic grin. If by some chance Andrea did return to Memory Keepers, she hoped they would have the opportunity to share Jesus with her, because at this point, they really didn't know where she stood spiritually.

Chapter 6

Before heading out on her drive home from Walnut Creek, Andrea took out her cell phone and called Brandon's number. All she got was his voice mail, so she left him a message: "Hi, Brandon. It's Andrea. I'm in Walnut Creek, and I visited Memory Keepers antique store where I'd taken my vintage quilt for an estimate. I went there to look at an old oak desk chair that I'd seen on my first visit to the Troyers' store. The chair was still there, so I bought it." Andrea shifted the phone to her other ear. "The real reason I'm calling, though, is to tell you that I shared with the Amish couple who own the store a couple of things about the situation we've had with our parents wanting to take over our wedding plans, and they offered some good advice. I'll be heading back to Apple Creek soon and plan to stop at my folks' house to bring them up to date on the wedding plans you and I made last night. I also want them to know that any help they'd like to give us will be appreciated. If I don't talk to you this evening, I'll see you at church tomorrow. Love you. Bye for now."

Andrea put her phone away and pulled out into traffic. As she drove in the direction of Apple Creek, she reflected on all the things Lois and Orley had said to her. Andrea felt guilty for being short with her mother yesterday and needed to apologize. Since her parents would be paying for a good portion of the wedding, they needed to be involved in many areas of the planning. Even so, the final decisions, especially where the wedding and reception should take place, ought to be up to Andrea and her groom.

Glancing in the rearview mirror, Andrea spoke out loud. "I need to express that to my parents in a better way." She tapped the steering wheel. "I hope they'll both be home when I get there so we can work things out."

Apple Creek

"I need to ask you something, Ray." Evelyn stepped up to her husband's reclining chair and nudged his arm, but with him focused on the newspaper in his hands, he barely acknowledged her presence.

Evelyn frowned. Ray loved his hobbies, and golf was a big one. He indulged in it at least once a week, weather permitting. Another guilty pleasure of his was being an avid reader of books and the daily news. It wasn't hard for him to become engrossed in either one. If the material was good, Ray's eyes appeared locked on whatever he read, and when that happened, he was determined to finish it. Other times, when news items were deficient to him, Ray would scan through the paper or even fall asleep. Either way, it could be difficult to get or keep his attention.

She nudged him again. "Ray, did you hear what I said?"

He set aside the newspaper and looked up at her. "Umm. . .no, sorry, guess I didn't because I was focused on the newspaper."

"I would have never guessed." She placed both hands firmly against her hips. "When I talked to our daughter yesterday, even though she spoke kindly to me, I felt a bit of an undercurrent when we discussed her wedding plans."

"Could you be making a mountain out of a molehill?"

Evelyn was well aware that her husband was a bit disgruntled because she'd interrupted his reading. Ray's unenthused tone about her concern seemed to say it all. Basically, he didn't want to be bothered right now.

She sometimes felt that her opinion didn't matter to him. *Why can't my husband be more supportive of my feelings? Is it too much to ask?* She looked at him, wishing he'd get a clue, but unfortunately, Ray obviously lacked interest in the topic at hand.

"Maybe you should back off and let Andrea make her own wedding plans." Ray's unexpected comment caused Evelyn to bristle.

"What are you talking about, Ray? You were in on the discussion we all had at the restaurant in Wooster. As I recall, you were in favor of the wedding being held at one of the venues that was mentioned."

"I was, but I've thought it through since then, and I have come to the conclusion that since it's not our wedding being planned, Andrea and Brandon have the right to choose their own venue along with many other things that will be involved in their wedding."

"I agree." Evelyn took a seat in the chair beside him and heaved an audible sigh just as her fox terrier, Frisky, leaped up and tried to squeeze in beside her. "I just don't understand why they want to get married in the dead of winter," she said, moving over a bit so the dog could lie down. "If the weather is bad, some people they've invited might not be able to attend. And of course, an outdoor reception would be out of the question."

Ray's facial features softened, along with his tone, as he reached over and patted her arm. "Let's allow the bride and groom to worry about all those things, okay?"

Maybe my husband is right. I might be making a mountain out of a molehill. Slowly, she nodded. "I just hope—"

The melodic chiming of their doorbell interrupted Evelyn's sentence, and she rose from her seat. "Guess I'd better go see who that is."

When the front door opened, Andrea stepped in and greeted her mother with a hug. Mom smelled of her favorite cologne, and not one light brown hair was out of place from where it had been pulled back into a smooth ponytail. Mom's terrier stood by her feet.

"This is a pleasant surprise. Your dad's in the living room, and we were just talking about you."

"Uh-oh. Should my ears have been ringing?"

Mom shook her head. "It was nothing bad. Now let's go into the living room so you can say hello to your father."

Andrea followed her mother and found her dad sitting in his easy chair, holding the newspaper. "Hey, Dad. Did you make it to the golf course this morning?"

He grinned up at her. "Sure did. I played a pretty good game too."

Andrea smiled in response. "That must have felt good."

"Yep." He gestured to the chair beside him, which was where Andrea's mother usually sat. "Take a seat."

She glanced at her mother, and when Mom gave a nod and took a seat on the couch, Andrea seated herself in the comfortable chair. She'd barely sat down when Mom's terrier darted into the room, leaped onto her lap, and began slurping Andrea's cheeks.

"For goodness' sakes, Frisky, get down! I'm sure Andrea doesn't want your kisses." Mom clapped her hands. "Come here, you naughty little boy."

"You've got it right. That mutt is always getting into some kind of trouble." Dad's brows drew together, and he pointed at Frisky, who had settled down in Andrea's lap instead of obeying Mom's command. "This morning, before I left to play golf, I found him digging in the yard again." He grimaced. "That sure didn't set well with me. I've gone to a lot of trouble to find a reliable lawn care business here in Apple Creek. Those fellows have done an excellent job keeping the yard looking as neat as the greens at the local golf course."

"He didn't dig up any of our plants though, did he?" Mom asked.

"No, but he could have if I hadn't caught him in time." He looked at Mom over the top of his reading glasses. "You oughta put that dog in obedience school."

Mom shrugged. "I'm working with him on my own, and I believe we're making some progress."

"Really? My suggestion is that you need to buy a book on how to train that mutt to behave."

Andrea couldn't miss Dad's sarcastic tone, and she figured it was time for a topic change, so she gave Frisky's head a brief pat and said, "The reason I stopped by is to tell you about the wedding plans Brandon and I made last night."

Mom and Dad turned their heads in her direction.

"I've already told your father that you plan to be married next year, on Valentine's Day," Mom responded.

Andrea nodded. "And we want our ceremony to be at the church."

"We understand," Dad interjected. "You had also previously stated that you wanted the reception to be held there as well."

"We've changed our minds about that. Brandon and I think having the reception at one of the venues you and Brandon's parents mentioned the other day might be a good idea." Andrea paused to give Frisky another pat. "If you feel it won't put a strain on your budget, that is."

"I think we can manage." Dad looked at Mom. "Right, Evelyn?"

"Yes, of course. Andrea, do you have any particular venue in mind?"

"Not really, but we'd be happy with the least expensive one that has adequate indoor seating. There's no point putting out a large sum of money for a few hours of celebration."

"You're so very special to us, and we want you to have a memorable wedding and reception." Mom's voice faltered on the last word.

"I appreciate that," Andrea responded. "And I don't want you and Dad to feel left out, so we'll leave most of the reception planning in your capable hands. For other things pertaining to the wedding, Brandon and I will also keep you, as well as his parents, in the loop and ask for help as needed."

Mom smiled and wiped a few tears from her cheeks. Dad reached over and placed his hand on Andrea's arm, which caused Frisky to jump down to the floor and give a few loud barks. Everyone laughed.

Andrea let her head fall back against the chair. She felt a sense of peace about things now and was hopeful that, from this point on, all the wedding plans would go smoothly.

Walnut Creek

Lois stood at the living room window, watching her husband make his way down their driveway.

The neighbor's dog met Orley, wagging its tail, and he reached down, giving the friendly yellow Lab a few pets. Then the animal walked alongside her husband as though they were the best of friends. She couldn't help but notice the spring in Orley's step as he and the dog headed out to the phone shack, where Orley would make a few phone calls and check for any messages that may have come in while they'd been at their store.

Orley had been full of enthusiasm ever since the young auburn-haired woman had come into the store and shared with them about the situation she'd been having with her parents concerning her upcoming wedding. Lois had to admit that being able to offer some advice had given both her and Orley a sense of satisfaction. She hoped, however, that Orley wouldn't be too disappointed if Andrea never returned to the store or sought their counsel. Surely, in God's time, some other person would show up who needed guidance—perhaps of a spiritual nature, which would be the most rewarding, like it had been in the past with several other people Orley and Lois had mentored. Sometimes the ones they'd helped would move on and wouldn't be seen again. There were some, though, who continued to stop by their antique store to catch up and visit, just like family.

Lois smiled as she reflected on this. *It does my heart good to see the positive outcomes of the Lord's work when we were obedient to His call upon our lives.*

She moved away from the window and headed for the kitchen to start supper. Her first thought was to heat some frozen broccoli and creamy cheddar soup, but it might take a while. Lois wasn't in the mood to cook a big meal this evening and hoped Orley would be okay with a tossed green salad and a bowl of egg drop soup, which was a favorite of hers and easy to make.

Lois opened the refrigerator and took out the ingredients for the salad as well as a carton of eggs, some green onions, and a bottle of soy sauce. Next, she removed a large can of chicken broth, salt, and garlic powder from the cupboard. She'd just taken out a kettle for the soup when Orley came in through the back door with downturned facial features. "I'm sorry to have to tell you this, but I have some bad news," he announced.

"What's wrong?" Lois's chest tightened as she held her breath, waiting for his response.

"There was a message from your stepmother, letting us know that your *daed* had a heart attack this afternoon and is in the hospital. She sounded quite upset and said that his heart is very weak and it doesn't look good." Orley moved toward Lois and placed his arm around her waist.

She set the kettle down and stood with one arm holding the other at the elbow. "We need to go to Kentucky, Orley. If my dad should die before I've had a chance to make things right between us, I'll never forgive myself."

"I understand. I will go back out to the phone shack and call one of our drivers. Hopefully, we can head out within the next few hours, so I think you should go ahead and put whatever we'll need in our suitcase."

"Wh–what about supper?" Lois gestured to all the items she'd put on the counter.

"You may as well put everything away. We can stop somewhere along the road to eat." Orley gave her a comforting hug before going hastily out the back door.

Truth was, she had lost her appetite after hearing the news about Dad. Lois worried about her father's condition. With every fiber of her being, she hoped he would receive the best of care. Time was truly of the essence if she was to get to the hospital, which was many hours from here.

Lois hurried to put all the food items away. She leaned against the counter and closed her eyes. *Dear Lord, if it is Your will to take my father, please don't do it until I've had a chance to see him and make sure he knows that I love him.* Tears coursed down Lois's cheeks as she finished her prayer. *Dad needs to know that even though I still feel that some of the things he did and said when I was a girl were wrong, with Your help, I have forgiven him.*

Turning toward the door, Lois left the kitchen and made her way down the hall to their room, continuing to pray with each step she took. It would take them at least nine hours, allowing for stops, to reach Hopkinsville, Kentucky. She could only hope and pray that they would make it in time.

Chapter 7

Hopkinsville, Kentucky

At three o'clock the next morning, Lois sat in a chair beside her father's hospital bed, holding his wrinkled hand. His wife, Sarah, sat in another chair next to her, and Orley stood off to one side. Lois's sisters, Rebekah and Elizabeth, lived in Wisconsin, and her half-brothers, Benjamin and Jacob, had settled in Oklahoma, so none of them had arrived yet. It didn't look good for their father, and Lois hoped the rest of the family would make it to the hospital in time to say their last goodbyes.

Because she'd been up for almost twenty-four hours, Lois was having a hard time staying awake. Orley also showed signs of fatigue with his stifled yawns and tired eyes. She couldn't help feeling sorry for keeping him here, but Orley wouldn't be anywhere else when he felt needed by her, and she knew it.

Lois looked through blurring eyes at her father. *Besides being here with you and praying, I wish there was something else I could do for you, Dad.* "Has he opened his eyes or said anything to you?" Lois looked over at Sarah.

The silver-haired woman shook her head. "Not since a few minutes before he collapsed at home. I could see that he wasn't feeling well, and when I asked him what was wrong, he said his chest pained him and he felt kind of dizzy." Sarah drew in a shuddering breath. "The next thing I knew, your daed collapsed onto the floor. His breathing was shallow, and when I couldn't rouse him, I made a beeline for the phone shack we share with our closest neighbors."

Unable to speak around the lump in her throat, Lois let go of her father's hand and reached over to clasp Sarah's trembling hand.

At the same time, Orley moved closer and put both of his hands on the women's shoulders. "You must have been terribly frightened, Sarah."

"*Jah*, very much so, and I still am. I don't think my dear husband is going to make it. The doctors said Jeremiah's heart is very weak—too much so for any kind of surgery." Sarah drew in another breath and released it slowly. "Guess that's what happens when old age creeps in."

"We need to pray," Lois murmured. "We can ask God for a miracle."

Apple Creek

The shrill sound of the alarm clock ringing near her head pulled Andrea out of a deep sleep. She rolled over, clicked it off, and sat up on the edge of her bed. Once the cobwebs of sleep cleared, she reached for her cell phone to check for messages. Brandon hadn't returned her call last night before she'd gone to bed, and there were no new messages from him. A sense of dread welled in her chest. It wasn't like him not to call. They talked to each other nearly every day. Could he have been involved in an accident, become ill, or been too busy to check his phone for messages? If it was the latter, that wasn't like him either. Brandon had always been good about returning her calls. Something had to be wrong.

Andrea rose and cleared her throat. She took a drink from the glass of water sitting on the nightstand, closed her eyes, and prayed that Brandon was all right. Afterward, Andrea tried his number in hopes of reaching him and hearing that things were okay, but Brandon's phone rang until it went into voice mail again. She left him another message, asking that he call her back as soon as possible and telling him she loved him before hanging up. *I hope he's okay.* She picked up her phone again. *I'll try his parents. Maybe they've heard from him.*

Andrea punched in his folks' number and felt relieved when his mother answered. "Sorry to bother you, Jennifer, but I can't get ahold of Brandon. Have you talked to him lately?"

"You sound worried, but I think he's okay." Her soothing tone came through clearly. "He called and left a message yesterday shortly before 8 a.m., saying he had a full schedule at the clinic, along with a couple of rural calls, and that he wouldn't have time to join his dad and me for supper, like we had hoped. He also said he would see us at church this morning and that maybe the four of us could go out for dinner after the service."

"I called Brandon yesterday afternoon and left a message, but he never returned my call." Andrea pulled her fingers through the ends of her hair. "A few minutes ago, I tried calling again, but all I got was his voice mail. I'm worried something might be wrong."

"I'm sure it's nothing to be concerned about. Maybe he's in the shower and didn't hear the phone ring." Jennifer's tone sounded hopeful, but Andrea wasn't convinced. She could not believe how unconcerned his mother seemed. Andrea had a sick feeling in the pit of her stomach that something was wrong.

Brandon woke up to the sound of his alarm and padded over to the window to look out. He pulled up the blinds and smiled when he saw the sunshine and blue skies. *What a nice Sunday morning greeting*, he thought. Then, remembering to look for his cell phone, which he had carelessly left someplace at home yesterday and been too tired to search for last night, Brandon put on a T-shirt and a pair of jeans and went looking. *There's still plenty of time before church, and it shouldn't take me long to find it.*

After searching through every pair of pants in his closet and coming up empty-handed, he ambled out of the room and headed for the kitchen to look around. Brandon frowned. *This is strange. Where on earth did I leave it?*

He searched every nook and cranny and even looked in the refrigerator, but there was no sign of his phone. Brandon paused to rub his forehead and think. *When and where did I last use my cell?* He felt frustrated with himself for not keeping better track of the device, but with his hectic lifestyle, Brandon was glad he didn't have to go through this kind of issue often. He always tried to keep all his ducks in a row to avoid forgetting things. Yesterday had been pretty crazy, and he hadn't had time to make a trip back home to look for his phone. At the clinic, it wasn't a problem because there was a landline. But out on the road, heading to the farms he'd been called to, Brandon needed his cell phone and would normally have had it with him.

His brain raced with other ideas as to where the phone could be. He was so desperate at the end of looking in the kitchen that he opened the cookie jar and peered in. All he found were a few stale-looking cookies that had been in there too long. *I think I've checked out this room long enough.*

Brandon moved into the living room and looked under the couch, behind the cushions, on the coffee table and each of the end tables, but there was no sign of his phone. He couldn't take too much more time looking or he'd be late for church.

I hope Andrea's not worried about me. I bet she's tried calling several times. He sat down and thumped the arm of his favorite chair. *Guess I could just go on over to Andrea's place and pick her up for church, but I'd rather call first, if I can find my phone.*

Brandon leaned his head back and closed his eyes as he tried to visually retrace his steps from yesterday morning. *Let's see now. . . . I fixed a cup of coffee and was about to step outside to get the newspaper when my cell phone rang. It was Mom, but I couldn't talk long, so I said I'd see her and Dad tomorrow and hung up. Then with my phone still in my hand, I let Duke out and went to the paper box. After I grabbed the paper, Duke started barking and ran out of the yard. I hollered at him, but he wouldn't come back.*

Brandon's eyes came open and he sat up straight. *Oh brother! I remember putting the phone inside the newspaper box and chasing after my disobedient dog. Sure hope it's still there.*

Brandon made a dash for the front door, and Duke was right behind him. Once outside, he picked up a stick and threw it across the yard, figuring that would keep the dog occupied while he went out the front gate and checked the box.

When Brandon reached his hand inside the box and touched his cell phone, he heaved a sigh of relief. Now he could take it inside, make sure it was charged, and give Andrea a call.

Hopkinsville

Lois had been sitting for several hours beside her father's bed, leaving only once to use the restroom. Orley had stayed by her side, giving all the support she needed. During the wee hours before daybreak, she and Orley had managed to get short catnaps while lounging in their chairs. Lois was concerned for her father and wanted to support Sarah with all the energy she could muster.

Toward daybreak, Rebekah and Elizabeth entered the room. They exchanged tearful hugs and greetings before going over to Dad's bedside. It was a bittersweet moment for Lois. They talked and cried as they remained near their father's bed.

Sometime later, Orley asked if anyone was hungry and volunteered to find food. Sarah informed him that the cafeteria wouldn't be open for another two hours, but she volunteered to go with Rebekah and Elizabeth down the hall for coffee or juice and some kind of a snack from the vending machine.

Orley sprang into action, retrieving some money from his wallet to give the women.

Soon after they left the room, Lois looked at her husband, who sat in the chair beside her. "Would you mind leaving me alone with my daed for a few minutes? I don't think he's going to make it, and I'd like the chance to say a private goodbye."

"Okay." Orley rose to his feet. "I'll join the others. Is there something you'd like me to bring back for you to eat or drink?"

She shook her head. "I'll get something later if I'm hungry."

He gave Lois's shoulder a gentle squeeze and left the room.

She scooted her chair a bit closer to her father's bed. "I forgive you, *Daadi*, for being so harsh with me when I was a girl," she whispered. "I know that I disappointed you many times, and I'm sorry I could never measure up—was not the kind of daughter you wanted me to be." She blinked as hot tears rolled down her cheeks. "I've told God that I'm sorry too, Daadi. I'm sure He's forgiven me. Will you do the same?"

Lois's father opened his eyes briefly, murmured a few words she couldn't understand, and then his breathing stopped. Lois had no idea whether her dad had heard anything she'd said to him or not, but even in her sadness, a sense of peace settled over her like a soft blanket. She felt God's presence, whispering in her ear, *"My grace is sufficient for thee."*

Chapter 8

As the warm August sun beat down on her head, Lois teared up while she stood with her family and other mourners, watching her father's casket be lowered into the ground. Although she and her father had never been close, she'd felt a great loss since his passing three days ago. From the solemn expressions on her four siblings' faces, Lois knew they did as well.

She glanced at her stepmother, shoulders hunched and eyes staring at the ground. When she looked up briefly, Lois saw the wrinkles around the elderly woman's mouth and eyes sag. Although she couldn't comprehend losing a spouse, Lois understood the loss of her father. At moments, the wave of missing him would hit, and Lois's heart ached for what she wished she could've had. *If only my dad and I could have had a closer bond in this life. But for reasons beyond my understanding, it didn't happen.*

Lois's father had been widowed twice, and Sarah was his third wife. He'd met her five years ago while visiting an Amish community in Colorado. After getting married, they'd remained in Colorado two years; then Dad had gotten the notion that they should move to Kentucky. Lois had never understood why he'd chosen that state, since he'd had no family or close friends there, but she'd been glad he wasn't living alone and had Sarah by his side. Lois figured with Dad gone now, Sarah would most likely return to Colorado to live with her oldest son, Henry. He and his wife, Caroline, had hired a driver to bring them to Hopkinsville for the funeral. It was good that Sarah had some of her immediate family's support today, although Lois felt sure Sarah appreciated her stepdaughters and sons being with her as well.

And why wouldn't we be? Lois thought. *Even though we were all married and out on our own by the time Dad married Sarah, she's still our stepmother and we care about her welfare.*

Lois was ever so grateful for Orley's moral support as they stood shoulder to shoulder while the coffin was buried and the minister read the Lord's Prayer.

She glanced over at Sarah, dabbing her eyes. *I can't imagine how much her life will change.* Lois tried to hold it together as she shifted her stance and turned to look at Orley. Their eyes connected for a moment, and he gave her a tender, consoling smile. She couldn't comprehend what her life would be like without her dear husband by her side. Lois hoped that when it was their time to go, the Lord would take them both together.

It tore at Orley's heartstrings to see how hard Lois was taking her father's death. Although she was trying to be strong, the way her lips pressed together and her body trembled indicated the extent of Lois's grief. He wanted to give his wife all the support needed during her time of sorrow. Orley had mentioned to Lois that if she wanted to linger for a few days beyond what they'd intended, he was fine with that. It was obvious to him that his wife and siblings needed this time together, as they shared things about the past—sometimes laughing and at other times shedding more tears. It was a shame Jeremiah hadn't been able to say a proper goodbye to his children. As far as Orley knew, the dying man hadn't opened his eyes or uttered a single word to his wife or daughters. And by the time Benjamin and Jacob had arrived, their father had passed from this world into another.

Once the graveside service was over, Orley put his hand against the small of Lois's back as they walked solemnly with the others toward the waiting horses and buggies. After leaving the Amish cemetery, they would go to Sarah's house for a light meal provided by some of the women in her church district. Once they finished eating, Orley hoped Lois might be able to lie down for a while. She'd only slept a few hours last night and was exhausted. Lois and her sisters had helped Sarah with the preparations for the funeral. Orley had noticed that his wife's appetite had declined, but whose wouldn't under these circumstances? He assumed that being in unfamiliar territory, sleeping in a strange bed, and eating meals at unusual times contributed to his wife's behavior.

Hopefully, she would feel better once they returned to Ohio and opened their store for business again.

Apple Creek

Andrea smiled as she stood in an empty field across from an Amish farm, painting a picture of the barn and a black buggy. The weather was lovely, and the temperature felt pleasant to her. Andrea had driven by this place before, and it had inspired her to return. Of all the rural settings where she often set up her easel and canvas, anything that depicted the Amish lifestyle was her favorite thing to paint. Sometimes she became so absorbed in the scene, she almost felt as if she were Amish.

I wonder if other non-Amish people ever feel like that, she thought. Andrea didn't know anyone personally who had left their English world and joined the Amish faith, but she'd read about a few who had made the transition.

Andrea pursed her lips as she dabbed white paint on the barn in her picture. *That must have been difficult. I might be able to dress plainly, go without makeup, and let my hair grow long, but I can't imagine having to give up my car, cell phone, laptop, or anything that needs electricity. Although their life seems unique and interesting, I am glad I wasn't born Amish, because then I'd have no choice in the matter, unless I left my Amish home and upbringing and became part of the modern world.*

In an attempt to refocus, Andrea stopped painting and glanced across the road once more. Setting down the paintbrush for a moment, she reached for her water bottle nearby and took some sips. *It's so peaceful out here. This open country, fresh air, and beautiful scenery has a way of calming my nerves.*

As Andrea set her water aside, she spotted two teenage girls dressed in Plain clothes, walking toward the Amish carriage by the barn. A few minutes later, an Amish man wearing a straw hat came out of the barn, leading a beautiful, dark-colored horse up to the buggy. Andrea didn't want them to see her staring, so she quickly picked up her brush and turned back to face the canvas.

Her thoughts went to Brandon and how things had gone when he showed up at her home Sunday morning. She'd been relieved, seeing that he was okay and learning why he hadn't returned her calls the day before.

She smiled. The dinner with Brandon's parents after church had gone well too. Jennifer and Larry had obviously been relieved when Brandon announced that he and Andrea had made some definite plans and wanted both sets of parents to be included in various aspects of the wedding preparations.

So everything is back on track. Andrea added a little more color to the barn in her painting. *Now we can move forward with the details for the wedding, knowing our parents are happy and nobody feels left out.*

At the *clip-clop, clip-clop* sound of a horse's hooves, Andrea's thoughts were pulled aside once more. She turned to watch the proud-looking horse pulling the buggy, and she lifted her hand when the Amish girls smiled and waved. *That looks like fun, and I bet it's a peaceful mode of transportation. Wish I had the opportunity to ride in an Amish buggy. I'll have to try to make that happen someday.* She dabbed her brush into the paint again. *Right now, though, I have plenty of other things to think about.*

Hopkinsville

"I checked on Sarah, and she's resting in her room." Lois's sister Rebekah took a seat on the dilapidated couch next to Lois. Even the two overstuffed chairs in the living room looked like they had seen better days.

While Orley and the spouses of Jeremiah's children had gone to the kitchen to put away the leftovers from their recent meal, Lois and her siblings had gathered in this sparsely decorated living room to visit. Lois, Elizabeth, and Rebekah sat on the couch, and their half-brothers had taken the two chairs.

Lois gave a nod in response to Rebekah's declaration that Sarah was resting. "That's good. She needs to get caught up on her rest. When Dad was in the hospital, Sarah stayed by his bed much of the time and got very little sleep. With the funeral and graveside service, today has been a long day for her. I'm sure she must be exhausted." Truthfully, Lois had felt like taking a nap too, but being with her siblings was more important than sleep right now. She would go to bed early tonight if necessary.

For a few minutes, Lois sat silently, reflecting on how she had kept quiet about Dad murmuring something when she was alone in his hospital room. Since she hadn't been able to understand what he'd said, she saw no reason to mention it to anyone.

"I think we're all tired and feeling the effects of the day," Elizabeth said, stifling a yawn with the palm of her hand.

Everyone nodded.

"We need to talk about Sarah and what's going to happen to her now that our daed is gone," Benjamin, the oldest half-brother, spoke up. "I thought her son and his fraa would take her in, but as far as I know, they have not extended an invitation."

Shifting on the faded couch and feeling the need to defend Sarah's son and his wife, Lois spoke up. "I'm sure they will want Sarah to move back to Colorado and live with them. It would certainly not be good for her to stay here all alone."

"I agree," Elizabeth said. "I don't believe she would want to remain here, where she has no family and lives in a house that is quite primitive compared to what the rest of us have. Not to mention how isolated she is out here with no close neighbors."

"Maybe Sarah likes Kentucky," Jacob, who was thirty-eight and the youngest of Lois's half-brothers, commented. "I know Dad sure did."

"That may be true, and it might be hard for Sarah to leave this area since she's lived here for a while with Dad. Even so, it wouldn't be good for her to be left alone." Lois looked at each of her siblings.

"There are enough of us here who I'm sure would be willing to take Sarah in, but whatever she does, it will have to be her decision." Rebekah readjusted her head covering that was slightly askew.

Everyone nodded.

"It's nice for us to all be together like this, discussing things in person, but it's too bad we're all so busy and live in different states. Unfortunately, we only see each other on rare occasions like weddings and funerals," Rebekah observed.

"That is so true." Benjamin looked at them with a sober expression. "We need to make an effort to get together more often."

"Jah," Lois agreed. "Letters and phone calls are fine, but it's more personal when we're in the same room, spending time together like this."

A few minutes of silence passed, interrupted when Sarah entered the room with a cardboard box. She placed it on the coffee table and lifted the flaps. "I have some things that belonged to your daed in here, and I'd like each of you to have one." She reached inside and handed Benjamin his father's gold-plated pocket watch. "Since you are his oldest son, I'm sure your daed would want you to have this."

"Danki." Benjamin choked up, and it took him several seconds to say anything more. "Receiving this item that Dad carried on him most of the time means a lot to me."

Sarah reached into the box again. This time she removed a wooden case that Lois recognized as her father's set of woodcarving tools. She gave it to Jacob.

Sagging against the chair he sat on, Jacob stared at the item with his lips slightly parted. "I—I will put this to good use, and someday I'll hand it down to one of my sons."

Sarah nodded before pulling the next item from the box. "This is for you, Elizabeth." She placed Dad's harmonica on Lois's youngest sister's lap. "Your daed knew how much you enjoyed music, so I'm sure he would want you to have it."

"Danki. I will treasure this and remember Daed when I play it." Elizabeth's hand trembled a bit as she picked up the mouth harp their father had played many evenings after supper when Lois and her siblings were growing up. She held it close to her mouth without playing it.

Sarah took two Bibles from the box. One she handed to Rebekah, stating that it was her father's. The other she gave to Lois. "This was your mother's *Biewel.* Even though she's been gone a good many years, your daed had fond memories of her, which is why I'm sure he kept her Bible."

Rebekah and Lois said danki. Lois held her dear mother's Bible close to her chest. Although it was not one of her father's personal possessions, knowing that it was her mother's and Dad had kept it all this time made it more special.

Tears seeped from Lois's eyes and ran down her warm cheeks. *Oh, Mama, even after all these years, I still miss you. If you hadn't died when I was eight years old, maybe Daadi would have been kinder to me when I did things that were wrong and displeased him.* Lois's throat tightened so that she could barely swallow. *If I could go back and change the past, I would try to be a better daughter so he would not be disappointed. Maybe then Daadi would have loved me as much as he did my siblings.*

Chapter 9

Walnut Creek

"It's good to be back home and open for business again," Orley said after he'd put up the OPEN sign in their antique store's front window. "It seems like we've been gone for a lot longer than two weeks." He looked over at Lois, surprised to see her standing in front of the checkout counter with a blank expression. Orley hoped his wife wouldn't feel as troubled being in familiar territory now. *I suppose we can't leave our troubles behind*, he thought. *I'll need to continue to help Lois through this and offer all the support my dear wife needs.*

Orley walked across the room to stand beside her. "Are you all right?" He slipped his arm around her waist. "Is it too soon for you to come back to work? If so, I'm sure I can manage the store on my own until you feel ready."

She gave a slow shake of her head. "It's not that. Keeping busy will be good for me. I'm just thinking about Sarah and wishing she would have accepted her son's invitation to live with him and his wife in Colorado. At her age, she shouldn't be living by herself with no family close by."

"I agree. She turned down all the other offers too, including ours. But if Sarah doesn't want to leave Kentucky, it wouldn't do for anyone to make her go. And remember, she does have friends in the Hopkinsville area." Orley rubbed Lois's back with the same arm he had put around her waist.

"I'm aware, but living near friends is not the same as being close to family."

Orley finished the rub and rested his hand on the countertop. "I'm sure Sarah will relocate when she feels the need."

"I hope so." Lois released a deep sigh and moved away from the counter. "Guess I should get busy and do something constructive. There's some dusting that needs to be done and a box of vintage clothes in the back room that needs to be gone through. Then when we get home this evening, I have some Dear Caroline letters that need answering." With shoulders slumped, she shuffled off to the back of the store as though the weight of the world rested upon her shoulders.

Orley gave his beard a tug as he mulled things over. *I know my fraa is concerned about her stepmother, but I think her melancholy mood has more to do with losing her daed.* Lois hadn't told Orley much about her childhood other than that her mother had died at a young age, and her father had been overly strict and often critical. This, he assumed, was the reason Lois had not been close to her father all these years.

Orley went around to the other side of the counter and took a seat on the stool. *Perhaps when the time is right, my dear wife will share more about her childhood and Jeremiah. I just can't relate to what she is going through right now, but the Lord knows.*

Orley leaned closer to the counter with his right hand on his knee. *I need to help Lois deal with this and be more sensitive to her needs.* Orley closed his eyes and prayed, *Lord, please help Lois through her time of grieving. She needs Your comfort and strength right now. And show me how I can help my dear wife get through this difficult time.*

Lois knelt in front of the box, pulling out each piece of the vintage clothes and inspecting them for wear and tear. They had been fortunate to find the clothing at a rummage sale a few days before they'd gotten news of her father's heart attack, so this was the first chance she'd had to go through them. Most of the items were from the early 1900s, but a few had been worn during the late 1800s. It wasn't hard to see how modest the period clothing looked at that time. The fabrics had heft, they weren't see-through, and the dresses went to the floor.

She smiled. *I can't help thinking how similar this fashion is to our Plain dresses.* Lois laid the dark brown dress she held on top of one that was deep blue. Some of the pieces would need to be mended, but other than a musty odor, most were in surprisingly good condition. She sniffed deeply and grimaced. A few of the blouses smelled of perfume, so Lois would spray those lightly with a white vinegar solution, which should lift the odor from the material, leveling out the perfume. Lois knew that the pungent vinegar smell would dissipate in a short time, so she wouldn't need to worry about the clothes smelling like salad dressing.

Lois's mind switched gears as an image of her father came to mind. She cringed at the thought of seeing him lying in that hospital bed and not being sure if he'd heard anything she'd said. The emotion of the memory surged through her soul. Oh, how she wished she could have understood the words he had mumbled before succumbing to death. Had he known she was beside his bed and tried to respond to what she'd said? She felt powerless over the past, present, and future. *I'm not even sure about my father's salvation.* Lois looked away from the clothing. *If only I had thought to ask Sarah.* The idea hadn't crossed her mind while everything was going on. *Does this really matter, since my father is gone now?*

Lois's chin trembled as she resigned herself to the fact that she would never know what her dad had said or where he stood spiritually before his death.

She glanced back at the stack of old clothes and whispered, "I need to quit thinking about this and stay busy with the project before me until it's done."

Apple Creek

Brandon sucked in some air through his nose and blew out a long breath from his mouth as he started his rig, eager to head for home. Things had been busier and more hectic than usual at the clinic, and he looked forward to relaxing and spending the evening with Andrea over a nice home-cooked supper. His first stop, though, would be his home to take a shower and change. Then he and his faithful dog would head over to Andrea's place in the hope of getting Duke to accept Lady and not cower and whine whenever the cat came near him. Brandon hoped things would go well this time because he and Andrea's wedding would take place in six months, and the problem needed to be resolved by then.

Brandon gripped the steering wheel as he pulled out of the clinic's parking lot and onto the road. *I can't imagine what life will be like for me and my future wife if we can't get Lady and Duke to get along. I sure hope my dog and her cat won't cause a conflict between us. I can't imagine us breaking up over something like this or feeling forced to get rid of our well-liked pets.*

When Andrea heard a horn honk outside, she looked out the front window and saw Brandon pull his SUV in front of her rental. She turned to Lady, draped over the back of the couch, and stroked the cat's silky head. "Our company is here, and you'd better be nice and not tease my fiancé's dog. We need Duke to accept you."

Lady responded with a quiet *meow* and burrowed her head between her dainty white paws.

Andrea gave the cat's head a couple of gentle pats. "Of course you'll be nice, you pretty little thing. You're the best cat I've ever had."

When Lady closed her eyes and began to purr, Andrea smiled. "How can Brandon's dog be afraid of you? I bet you wouldn't harm a mouse if one got into the house."

She'd had other cats while growing up but hadn't bonded with any of them the way she had with Lady. They were usually outdoor cats that were good at keeping mice away and weren't spoiled or fussed over much.

A knock sounded on the door, and Andrea went to open it. A few seconds later, Brandon entered, leading Duke on a leash.

Brandon hugged Andrea and gave her a kiss. "Well, here we are. Now let's hope things go well this evening between your cat and my dog."

Andrea bent down and gave Duke's head a few pats. "Let's go into the living room. Lady's sleeping right now, so that might help. We can sit and visit awhile before it's time to eat supper."

"Okay, but I'm going to keep Duke on his leash just in case the cat wakes up and he catches sight of her."

When they entered the living room, the wavy-coated spaniel put his nose to the floor and started sniffing as he tugged against the restraint. Brandon allowed the dog to take the lead and followed as Duke made his way around the entire room. As they neared the couch, Lady woke up and jumped down, just missing Duke's back.

Waiting for the dog to react, Andrea held her breath. She figured Duke might growl and chase after the cat. Instead, the frightened animal, cowering against Brandon's leg, alternated between whining and panting.

Brandon rolled his eyes and gave a disgusted-sounding grunt. "I can't believe what a wimp my dog turns into whenever he's around Lady. And don't take it personally, Andrea," he added. "Duke freaks out every time he sees any cat, making it hard sometimes when we go beyond my yard for walks." He pressed his free hand against his chest and frowned. "This type of behavior might be common for some dog breeds, but until I got Duke, I'd never heard of it happening with a Brittany spaniel."

Lady, seemingly oblivious to the fearful dog, pranced back and forth across the room with her tail in the air, which only brought more whimpering noises from Brandon's poor trembling dog. Was she deliberately taunting him or just letting Duke know that this home was her territory?

Andrea made a dash and scooped Lady into her arms. "I think we'd better separate these two," she said, looking at Brandon.

He nodded. "Either that or Duke and I are gonna have to go home."

Andrea shook her head. "Please don't do that. I have a chicken in the oven for our supper, and I fixed that tangy potato salad you like so much."

"Okay, then I'll put Duke in your backyard till it's time for us to leave. Since it's fully fenced at least there's no worry of him getting out."

"That's probably for the best all right. Sorry I can't put Lady outside, but she's an indoor cat and would most likely run off."

"Duke will be fine. He's used to roaming around in my yard." Brandon picked his dog up and turned to face Andrea. "Next time we try getting our pets together, maybe it should be at my place. Since that's Duke's territory, he might not be so intimidated by Lady."

"That's a good idea," Andrea agreed. "I just hope my cat doesn't react negatively to being in strange surroundings."

Chapter 10

Apple Creek

Brandon took a seat in his favorite leather recliner and picked up the magazine he had noticed in his clinic's waiting room before he'd left for home. It had been lying there, wide open on one of the small tables, but he'd never noticed it before and didn't know where it had come from. Brandon assumed his receptionist, Connie, must have brought it in. She was good about putting new reading material in place for people while they waited. This magazine was focused on the unusual habits of dogs and cats. One article discussed what a person should do if they owned a cat and dog who didn't get along. Brandon hoped the article would include an answer to fixing Duke's cowardliness around cats. He felt bad for his faithful companion and wondered if there were other dog owners dealing with a similar issue. Brandon needed to find a way to get his dog to have courage and friendliness around his future wife's cat.

He opened the magazine and thumbed his way to the right page. *I can't help feeling that Duke is just a big baby when it comes to cats, but on the other hand, he's always been fine around children.*

Last week, Andrea had brought Lady over to Brandon's house to see if it would make a difference in the way Duke reacted. It hadn't. In fact, as soon as Duke caught sight of Lady, he'd made a beeline for the primary bedroom, jumped on the bed, and refused to come out. So much for thinking it would make a difference if his and Andrea's pets met in Duke's territory. Poor Lady had spent that evening in her cage, while

Andrea and Brandon shared a pizza, both feeling very discouraged but agreeing to try again soon.

Now, as Brandon read the magazine article, a bit of hope welled in his chest.

"If your dog has been socialized with a cat, he won't have a fearful response," he read out loud. "But if he hasn't spent time with cats, he will either chase or fear them."

Brandon looked down at Duke, sleeping on the floor near his chair. "That would be you, little buddy. You're scared to death of Andrea's cat, and I hope there's something we can do about it, because it's not good for you to be quaking and quivering like a cat afraid of water every time Lady's around."

Brandon read on, noting that all dogs can experience and exhibit signs of fear over specific things. *Some dogs are afraid of thunder, children, fireworks, or going to a vet.* Brandon had witnessed many times in his practice when a frightened dog or cat shivered, howled, and sometimes became combative in a desperate attempt to escape what they feared. He remembered the bite he'd received from a frightened poodle when he'd let his guard down. Although the wound was deep and hurt a lot, it hadn't been bad enough for stitches.

Brandon put his concentration back on the article and continued to read. *Rather than consoling your dog, it's best to teach him to remain calm in the presence of a cat. This can be done through a combination of counterconditioning and desensitization. The ultimate goal is to decrease your dog's reaction to the cat to enable him to be around the feline.*

Brandon looked at Duke again, thankful that he was still sleeping and didn't demand his attention. He then turned his focus back to the article.

To desensitize your dog, he must be exposed to the cat several times in a controlled environment.

"Yeah, right—we've tried that already, and it didn't make a bit of difference." Brandon's jaw clenched. "Guess I'd better finish the article before I give up on Duke and Lady becoming friends, or at least Duke being able to be in the same space with her without whimpering, whining, or racing out of the room."

The last part of the article listed a few other suggestions, such as training the dog to sit beside you or lie at your feet when the cat is in the room. As a reward, a treat should be given, which would countercondition the dog to perform a positive behavior in place of fear. The article ended by saying that if none of the above worked, it would be best to find an experienced trainer skilled at working with pets that exhibited fears.

Brandon closed the magazine and tossed it on the coffee table near the couch. "If I'd known this would be such a problem, I never would have gotten a dog. Maybe I'll buy a child's stuffed kitten and introduce it to Duke. If he can adjust to that, maybe there'll be some hope for him to accept Andrea's cat." He frowned. "Of course, a stuffed animal wouldn't smell or act like a real cat."

This situation needed to be dealt with, but for now, after a hectic day, Brandon's eyes felt heavy. He brought up the leg rest of his recliner and felt the tension in his muscles begin to release.

Andrea had said goodbye to one of her piano students and shut the front door when her cell phone rang. She figured it might be Brandon, but it turned out to be Colleen.

"Hey, good friend and future maid of honor, how are you doing?" Andrea took a seat on the couch, and a few seconds later, Lady jumped into her lap.

"I'm good. How 'bout you? Still busy making plans for your wedding?"

Andrea stroked her hand gently over Lady's back and felt a bit of tension release in her shoulders when the cat began to purr. "Yes, but Brandon and I have run into a little snag."

"What's wrong? The church is still available on Valentine's Day, I hope."

"Yes, and we're still planning to have the ceremony there. It's after the wedding that I'm worried about."

"You mean the honeymoon?"

"No, we haven't made any definite plans for that yet. The problem we're faced with is Brandon's dog and my cat. The way things are now, they could never live in the same house together."

"Is Lady freaked out by Duke?"

"It's the other way around." Andrea continued to stroke her cat's head as the tension in her shoulders had returned. "We've tried getting them together a few times, and Duke either hides or sits close to Brandon, trembling and whining the whole time. Meanwhile, Lady acts aloof, like she doesn't know or even care that he's there."

"Did the meeting take place at your house or Brandon's?"

"We've tried both, but it made no difference." Andrea sighed deeply.

"If we can't figure out a way for Lady and Duke to get along, one of us will have to get rid of our pet. Either that, or we won't be able to get married."

"Oh, don't say that. Don't even think about the possibility." Colleen spoke with conviction. "There has to be way to train Duke so he's not afraid of your cat."

Andrea sat quietly, feeling the vibration of Lady's body as her purring grew louder. "Brandon did mention that he might have to hire a dog trainer to help with the problem. But there's no guarantee it would work."

"Have you done an internet search on the topic of a dog being afraid of a cat?"

"No, I never thought about that."

"It's worth a try, don't you think? Maybe someone else who has dealt with the same problem and been successful in solving it has posted ideas on a blog or some special web page."

"That's a great idea. Don't know why I didn't think of it myself. I'll boot up my laptop and start searching for answers as soon as we hang up."

"I should probably let you go now so you can begin. I'm sure you'd like to get this situation resolved ASAP, and for sure before you and Brandon get married."

Andrea's hand moved to the back of her neck, where a knot had formed. "I agree. It could be a real problem for us."

"I can hear the concern in your voice," Colleen said. "Are you worried that Brandon might break off your engagement if Duke won't accept Lady?"

Andrea sucked in her lower lip. "I hope not, but I suppose it could come to that if neither of us is willing to get rid of our pet."

"That would be terrible. You and Brandon are in love, and I'm sure you'll figure out an answer or at least a compromise concerning your pets."

Andrea wished she felt as confident as her friend sounded. Unless she could find something helpful on the internet and it worked for Duke, giving up Lady might be her only recourse, because she couldn't stand the thought of breaking up with the man she loved.

Andrea sat in front of her computer, reading the second article she'd pulled up. This one had some suggestions she thought might work, so she wrote the ideas on a piece of paper to share with Brandon. The one suggestion she thought might work best was to allow the cat and dog to smell some item that belonged to the other while keeping the animals separated.

Once the two animals appeared to be relaxed in the same room, the dog's leash could be dropped. Another suggestion was to feed both pets at the same time but on opposite sides of a closed door. The cat and dog would be able to smell each other while eating and begin to associate the smell with food. One final suggestion was to let the cat roam around several rooms of the house while the dog was outside in the yard. Then when the dog came back in, the cat should be put in its carrier behind a closed door, which would allow the dog the freedom to roam around to explore and smell the scent of the cat. When the dog seemed more comfortable, the cat carrier should be brought in, and if things were going well, the carrier door should be opened to allow the cat to come out. Once the dog showed no signs of fear, he could be let off the leash.

Andrea wrote down each idea and reached for her phone to call Brandon. It was time to schedule another meeting so they could try some of these ideas.

Walnut Creek

Lois was wearing one of her older work frocks and had tied a black scarf on her head to do her chores. Earlier that morning, she had done a few loads of laundry and hung all the wet clothing outside on the line to dry. Then she had come back inside to dust in the living room. She liked to keep her home clean and orderly.

Lois worked steadily until all the surfaces had been wiped off and everything looked spotless. Keeping busy was good for her. She welcomed the minor distractions that kept her from thinking about her father's death.

Feeling ready to switch gears from cleaning to answering letters from readers with problems, she put the dustrag away. Lois first heated up some water for a cup of tea to enjoy while tackling the letters.

A short time later, Lois sat at the kitchen table, reading the recent letters she'd received for her Dear Caroline page.

After having been in Kentucky for two weeks, she'd gotten behind on her work for the newspaper. Fortunately, Lois had turned in enough copy so that the paper had plenty to publish in the last two issues, but it was definitely time to do a little catching up.

The first letter she opened had been written by a widowed woman whose children wanted her to sell the home she'd lived in for forty years and relocate to another state to be close to family. The woman stated that while she knew she would enjoy living near her grown children and their families, it would be difficult to leave her friends, knowing she may never see any of them again. The letter was signed "Wondering What to Do."

Lois tapped her pen against the writing tablet, contemplating her response. It was a challenge to think of anything right now, when her mind kept replaying the scene in the hospital when she'd said her final words to Dad before he died. It was hard not to dwell on this when she should be focusing on other things.

Lois said a quick prayer and began to write on her tablet:

> *Dear Wondering What to Do:*
>
> *Moving from one place to another can be stressful, and leaving friends behind makes a person feel sad. But if you keep your focus on the family you'll be living near, it will make the move easier. You can keep in touch with friends through letters and phone calls and maybe visit them on occasion. Or perhaps some of your friends will come to see you. It should be comforting to know that your family wants you to move close to them.*

Lois swallowed hard as tears formed in her eyes. *Maybe if my daed had been living closer to Orley and me, our relationship could have been restored before he died.*

"Your shoulders are shaking. Are you crying, Lois?"

Lois felt her husband's strong hands on her shoulders. All she could do was nod.

"What's wrong? Does it have something to do with one of the Dear Caroline letters you've been reading?" he questioned.

She shook her head and pushed her chair away from the table. "It's hard for me to concentrate on answering these letters. All I can think about is my daed."

Orley pulled Lois gently to her feet and wrapped his strong, comforting arms around her. "It's always difficult when we lose someone we love, but the pain will lessen with the passage of time."

She listened and stayed in his reassuring embrace. *I missed so many years of trying to reconcile with Dad. I shouldn't have waited so near to the end of his life to openly forgive him.*

Lois wasn't sure if she regretted the timing of bearing her heart to

Dad or if she wished she knew if his heart had changed and he wanted to make things right between them. Each day since he died had been a challenge for Lois, and she was ever so grateful for Orley and his comforting hugs.

Lois leaned her head against her dear husband and let the tears flow freely. The truth was, she hadn't realized how much she loved her father until it was too late. Now her heart ached for all that she'd lost, and she wasn't sure it would ever completely heal.

Chapter 11

Apple Creek

Andrea pulled her car up the driveway in front of Brandon's house and turned off the ignition. She sat there a moment, looking forward. It had been a week since she and Brandon had met at his place in hopes of getting their pets together without Duke being fearful of Lady. They'd talked on the phone a few times, going over the things they had both learned since their last meeting and deciding which ones they might want to try. Now it was time to see how one of those ideas might work.

Andrea hoped something would change, because this problem with their pets was exasperating and took some of the excitement out of wedding planning. It would be nice if Duke could at least learn to tolerate Lady.

Andrea got out of the car and opened the back door to retrieve Lady in her carrier. The cat let out a couple of noisy meows as Andrea gathered her things from the back seat and made her way up to the house. Lady had never been fond of being cooped up in her carrier for long.

"It's okay, pretty Lady. You're going to see Duke again, and you'd better be on your best behavior, because we really need him to accept you this time."

Andrea glanced at the freshly mowed lawn and beautiful flowering shrubs in Brandon's yard. She looked forward to living in this house and spending time in the lovely yard after they were married. Due to Brandon's work schedule, he was too busy to keep the yard up, but he'd hired a landscaping service in the area, which was the reason it looked so nice.

Once her feet touched the welcome mat, Andrea fumbled for the doorbell button as Lady bumped around inside of her cage. "Settle down, pretty kitty."

When Brandon opened the door to let her in, she heard Duke barking but saw no sign of him. "Where's your dog?" Andrea asked after she'd set Lady's carrier down and Brandon had greeted her with a kiss.

"He's in the kitchen with the door shut, waiting to be fed."

She set down her purse and a brown paper bag she'd brought in with the items needed to try out their experiment. "Should I leave Lady in the carrier or take her out?" Andrea noticed her cat pawing at the bars of the cage.

He gave her a thumbs up and a comforting smile. "You can let her out when we try feeding them while they're on opposite sides of the kitchen door. But first, you'd better give me a few minutes to get into the kitchen, put food in Duke's bowl, and set it by the door."

"Okay." Andrea waited until Brandon had gone to the kitchen and let her know that Duke was eating from his bowl. Then she poured some dry cat food into the small dish she'd brought along in the paper bag. As soon as Lady's carrier door opened, the cat sprang from her cage and began chomping on the food. Andrea didn't know if the cat and dog could smell each other or the other pet's food with the closed door between them, but she heard Brandon say that Duke was doing fine with no apparent fear.

At least it's a start, she thought. *But things might change as soon as Brandon opens the kitchen door.*

Brandon stood off to one side, watching his hungry dog chow down on the crunchy food. If Duke had any awareness of Lady's presence on the other side of the door, he gave no indication.

"One small step for mankind." Brandon chuckled. "Sure hope the next step goes as well."

When Duke had finished his meal, Brandon clipped the leash to the dog's collar in preparation for taking Duke outside to do his business.

"I'm taking Duke out back for a few minutes," Brandon called through the door. "I'll bring his favorite ball in with me for your cat to sniff. While she's doing that, Duke can take a whiff of whatever toy you brought of Lady's."

"Sounds good," Andrea responded. "I'll have it out of the paper sack and ready for Duke's sniffing pleasure."

When Brandon came back into the kitchen with Duke, he told the dog to lie down, then he opened the door to the living room just wide enough to hand Andrea Duke's well-used tennis ball. In turn, she gave him a fuzzy, gray stuffed mouse.

Brandon was tempted to give Andrea a kiss, but he didn't want to take the chance of the cat getting into the kitchen, where his dog lay calm and unsuspecting. "Let's give our pets ten or fifteen minutes to get acquainted with each other's toys before we proceed to the next step," he said.

"Okay. I sure hope this works," Andrea responded.

"Same here." Brandon shut the door between them and dropped the stuffed mouse on the floor, close to Duke's nose. Instead of sniffing the item, like Brandon had hoped, his dog pounced on the toy and quickly tore it to shreds.

Brandon groaned. In addition to the fact that no sniffing had been done, he would now have to buy Lady a new toy mouse.

After Andrea put Lady's food dish away, she rolled Duke's ball across the floor and waited to see what would happen. Lady meandered over to it, took a few dainty sniffs, and walked away. Apparently, the old tennis ball held no interest for her.

Andrea gave the ball a gentle kick and watched as it rolled in another direction. This time the cat pranced across the room, heading toward the small round object. Although Lady didn't sniff the ball, she gave it a good whack with her paw, sending it into the dining room and under the table. Andrea expected the cat would go after it, but Lady went and sat next to her carrier instead.

Andrea released an exasperated breath. *When I let her out to eat, I'd hoped she would be more interested in the dog's toy, but I sure didn't expect her to just sit there—especially since she's usually eager to get out and explore.*

"Come on, Lady," Andrea coaxed. "Come and play with the tennis ball, or at least act like you're curious enough to smell the item real good." She picked up the ball and placed it in front of the cat's nose.

Lady gave it a couple of sniffs and curled up with her nose between her paws.

Andrea lifted her gaze toward the ceiling. *At least she showed enough interest this time to check out the odor of the dog's ball.*

"We're coming in now," Brandon called. A few seconds later, the kitchen door opened, and he entered the living room with his dog on a leash.

"How'd it go in there?" Andrea asked. "Did Duke get a good whiff of Lady's toy mouse?"

Brandon's brows furrowed as he glared at the dog. "I'm not really sure how much he actually smelled, but he went a little crazy and chewed up Lady's toy."

"What?" Andrea's mouth dropped open. "Oh my!"

"Unfortunately, this is all that's left." He showed her the item. "Sorry about that. I'll buy a new one to replace it. In fact, I think we still have some cat toys at the clinic. I'll check on it when I go to work tomorrow morning." Brandon took a step closer to Andrea, giving a tug on Duke's leash. The dog whimpered, dropped to the floor, and rolled over. Meanwhile, Lady remained in the same position, with her eyes closed and purring like a motorboat.

"Didn't Lady respond to Duke's tennis ball?" Brandon asked with lowered brows.

"She batted it around a few times and then headed over to her carrier. I put the ball in front of her nose, and she took a few sniffs, but then she closed her eyes and fell asleep." Andrea sighed. "I don't think we've accomplished much here this evening. Maybe I should take Lady home and call it a night."

Brandon's gaze darted from her cat to his dog, then back to Andrea. "You're not giving up on our quest to get our pets to accept each other, I hope."

She gave a noncommittal shrug. Truth was, Andrea figured it might be a hopeless situation. She worried that their wedding may not take place. What if their animals could not get along? Andrea wasn't ready to give Lady away, and Brandon liked Duke as well. She looked at her cat and heaved a sigh. *What are we going to do?*

Brandon stuffed what was left of Lady's mouse in his pocket and placed his hand on Andrea's shoulder. "We can do this, Andrea. There has to be a way. We just need to keep working at it and be willing to try some new things." He gave her shoulder a tender squeeze. "This is an important issue, and I refuse to give up. In the meantime, let's concentrate on our wedding plans and try not to worry about Duke's reaction to Lady, because I'm sure it'll work out."

Andrea rubbed her forehead and gave a slow nod. "Not tonight, though. I've developed a headache, so I'd better go home and sleep it off."

"Okay, sweetie. I hope you feel better soon." Brandon gave her a gentle kiss.

Andrea put Lady in her carrier, closed the door, and picked it up by the handle. "I'll talk to you sometime tomorrow, Brandon."

"Sounds good. I hope you sleep well tonight."

I'd sleep a lot better if my head wasn't pounding and I wasn't worried about the problem we have with our pets, Andrea thought as she went out his front door. She had a sick feeling in the pit of her stomach that if Duke didn't get over his fear of her cat, Brandon might ask her to find another home for Lady.

Walnut Creek

After tossing and turning for a few hours and not being able to sleep, Lois slipped quietly out of bed, being careful not to wake Orley. Maybe a cup of herbal tea would help her relax and allow her to sleep.

Downstairs in the kitchen, she filled the tea kettle with water, and while she waited for it to heat, she sat at the table with her mother's Bible. The feel of the soft leather beneath her fingers gave Lois an unexpected sense of peace. She opened the Bible to a page that had been marked with a pale blue ribbon and was surprised to see that one of the verses had been underlined: "Humble yourselves in the sight of the Lord, and he shall lift you up" (James 4:10).

That's a good verse, Lois thought. Although she had known her mother for only eight years and her early childhood was a distant memory, she still recalled how sweet and humble Mama was and how she could often be found sitting in her wooden rocking chair, reading God's Word or with her eyes closed in prayer.

Lois turned to another section that had been marked in her mother's Bible with a ribbon—this one was green. "Thy word is a lamp unto my feet, and a light unto my path" (Psalm 119:105). *Another good reminder from God's Holy Bible,* she thought.

A bit later, a page had been marked with a yellow ribbon. "I wait for the Lord, my soul doth wait, and in his word do I hope" (Psalm 130:5).

A red ribbon revealed another verse her mother had underlined. "This is the confidence that we have in [God], that, if we ask anything according to his will, he heareth us" (1 John 5:14). The last verse spoke to Lois's heart. "Whatever I pray for needs to be according to God's will, not mine," she whispered. "Because He knows what is best for me and every believer."

Lois tipped her head back and closed her eyes, feeling a sense of gratitude well in her soul. It was a wonderful gesture for Sarah to have given her this special Bible. It gave Lois a small connection to her mother, knowing Mama's fingers had touched the same pages as she was doing now, and reading the special verses that had been underlined in her mother's Bible. For the moment, the peace of God prevailed, and Lois knew that she could rest in Him. *I'm so glad to have the honor of possessing Mama's Bible.*

The silence in the room was interrupted by the whistle of the tea kettle. Lois opened her eyes and got up to fix a cup of chamomile tea. Returning to the table, she searched through the Bible for more ribbons and underlined verses.

On a page marked with a white ribbon, Lois found this verse underlined: "And as ye would that men should do to you, do ye also to them likewise" (Luke 6:31).

Lois wiped tears from her cheeks. Oh, how she wished she had gotten to know her mother better, but now, as she continued reading verses from this special Bible, Lois felt as if Mama was right there beside her, offering encouragement, wisdom, and comfort. Lois determined that she would keep Mama's Bible where it could be seen and wouldn't let a day pass without reading a few passages of scripture from it.

Chapter 12

Apple Creek

The next Saturday night, Brandon let Duke outside before getting ready for bed. The dog had been kind of hyper all evening, running through the house and barking a lot, which had tried Brandon's patience. He'd had another hectic day making farm animal calls and looked forward to getting a good night's sleep.

Brandon had made himself a frozen pizza for supper and needed to put away the leftovers, which only amounted to a few slices that he placed in a plastic container and set inside the refrigerator.

He grabbed the sponge and wiped down the counters and table. Content with the results, he thought about having more to drink.

After filling a glass with ice and water, Brandon took a seat at the kitchen table to wait for Duke to scratch at the door to come back in. He sat there thinking about how nice it would be to have all of the wedding details planned. The day when he and Andrea would be married was always at the forefront of his mind. He loved Andrea so much and couldn't imagine spending the rest of his life with anyone but her.

He drank some of his water, then closed his eyes. *I can't wait for the day I get to introduce her as Mrs. Brandon Prentice. It has a nice ring to it.* Brandon's eyes opened, and he couldn't help but smile. After they were married, they'd be living together here. Brandon was well aware that his bachelor pad would go through some changes. No doubt Andrea would want to add some of the furniture from her rental, and his closet space would shrink with the addition of her clothing.

Brandon looked around his kitchen, wondering what changes she might make to this space. *I'm not into decorating, and it does look a little barren in here. I'm sure in time Andrea will make some changes, and it will probably look much nicer.*

His thoughts scattered when he heard several shrill *yip-yips* coming from the backyard. Brandon left his seat in a hurry and went to see what was up with his dog.

When Brandon opened the door and turned on the porch light, he saw no sign of Duke. He cupped his hands around his mouth and hollered, "Where are ya, Duke? Come here, boy!"

A whimper came forth, and a few seconds later, the dog came out from behind a bush, whining and limping toward the porch steps. Brandon's adrenaline flowed as he looked in expectation about the yard. Could there be another animal around that might have provoked this situation? He didn't see anything out of the ordinary. All was quiet except when his dog let out another pathetic whine.

Filled with concern, Brandon picked up Duke and carried him up the stairs and into the house. Once inside, he put the dog down and looked him over thoroughly, touching and pressing on certain points to see if they were warm, swollen, or out of place. Each time Duke tried to walk, he would limp and yip. Brandon had no idea what the dog may have done to injure himself, but he figured Duke must have somehow sprained or strained his left front leg. He wouldn't know for sure until he'd taken an X-ray, which was important in order to rule out a broken bone. Despite the lateness of the hour, Brandon decided it would be best to take Duke to his clinic right away.

By the time Brandon returned from his veterinary clinic with Duke, it was well past midnight. This wasn't the peaceful evening he'd planned for himself. Brandon's idea was that after his pizza, he'd relax in his easy chair, maybe fix some popcorn to munch on, and watch a good movie, featuring one of his favorite actors. Now it was late, and he'd run out of steam to do anything but call it a night.

After a thorough examination and X-ray of Duke's leg while at the clinic, Brandon had determined that his dog's leg had been sprained, but thankfully, there were no broken bones or dislocations. He'd given Duke a nonsteroidal anti-inflammatory drug to ease the inflammation and applied an ice pack for the drive home. Now Brandon needed to make sure the dog rested and didn't jump or run. When he took Duke outside, he'd need to be on a leash and walk slowly. If Duke continued to limp and whine, Brandon would use a brace or some other support to hold the dog's muscle in place. He would also gently massage the injured area and make sure Duke didn't eat too much, which might cause him to gain weight. Since it could take several weeks for the sprain to heal, Brandon would not leave the dog alone in his pen outside or even in the house. He planned to ask his mother to sit with Duke while he was at work next week because he couldn't take the chance of the dog reinjuring himself when no one was at home.

The drug he'd given Duke seemed to make his faithful companion more comfortable. Duke sat on an area rug in the living room while Brandon gathered a couple of things for the dog. He couldn't wait to get Duke and himself settled in after such a long day.

Brandon placed Duke's doggie bed next to the couch, and then he flopped onto the soft cushions, thankful for his training as a veterinarian, which gave him the knowledge of what to do for his dog in a situation such as this. At the moment, Brandon was too tired to go down the hall and get ready for bed, so he figured he may as well sleep on the couch. He wouldn't bother to set an alarm because he'd have to skip church in the morning to take care of Duke. He would explain things to Andrea when she came over in the afternoon, like they'd planned, and would leave a message on her cell phone saying he wouldn't be at church.

With one arm dangling over the edge of the couch, Brandon stroked his dog's silky head. "Goodnight, Duke." He gave in to a noisy yawn. "Sleep well, and I hope you feel better in the morning."

The dog gave a quiet whimper and put his head between his paws. Brandon closed his eyes and succumbed to sleep.

Andrea loaded Lady into her carrier and carried it out to the car. She had listened to Brandon's voice mail this morning, saying he wouldn't make it to church and would explain things later. Since they'd agreed upon sharing a meal this afternoon and getting their pets together again, she assumed that was still in the plans. If it wasn't, surely Brandon would have said so in his message.

Lady let out a pathetic *meow* and scratched at the front of the cage when Andrea set the carrier on the back seat. "Hush, sweet kitty; you won't be cooped up long because we don't have far to go."

She shut the back door, took her place in the driver's seat, and turned on the ignition. When Lady continued to carry on, Andrea put a CD in and turned up the volume so she could drown out the cat's noise and listen to one of her favorite Christian artists.

A short time later, she pulled into Brandon's driveway and turned off the engine, pleased that her cat had finally settled down. It was short-lived, however, because as soon as Andrea carried Lady's carrier up the sidewalk and stepped onto the porch, the boisterous meowing began again.

Andrea glanced at the living room window and noticed that the drapes were drawn. Her forehead wrinkled. *That's odd. Why would Brandon have the curtains closed in the middle of the day?*

She rang the doorbell and waited, trying to hush her determined cat. Several minutes passed before the door opened. She was surprised to see Brandon looking at her through half-closed eyes. His clothes were wrinkled like he'd slept in them, and the top of his hair stood straight up. "Were you sleeping?" she asked.

He gave a nod. "Duke kept me up half the night, and the couch I slept on was not nearly as comfortable as my bed would have been."

"What do you mean? What happened that kept you up and caused you to sleep on the couch?"

She set Lady's cage on the floor and listened while Brandon explained what had transpired the night before.

"I'm sorry to hear about Duke's leg." To be heard, Andrea spoke loudly, above Lady's incessant meows.

"You can let her out if you want to," Brandon said. "I'll close the door to the living room, where Duke's lying on his doggie bed."

Andrea looked down at the carrier and back at Brandon. "It might be best if I take Lady and go home. This is obviously not a good time to try and get our pets together in a friendly manner."

"You're right, but I'd like to spend some time with you today, and I did promise to fix something for our Sunday dinner."

Andrea shook her head. "If anyone's going to cook dinner, it should be me." She reached up and smoothed his rumpled hair. "What were you planning to have?"

"Grilled sausages, sauerkraut, three-bean salad, and potato salad. The makings for most of it is in the refrigerator, including some boiled eggs." He gave her a sheepish-looking grin. "Of course, the potatoes would need to be cooked."

"No problem. I'll get started on it right now. I know how much you like my tangy potato salad."

He gave her a hug. "You've got that right. It's one of my favorites."

While Andrea made a potato salad and set the table, Brandon went out back to grill the sausages. He felt bad that he'd missed sitting beside Andrea during church today, but at least they could enjoy a nice meal together this afternoon.

When the sausages were fully cooked, he put them in a pan and carried it inside. "Should we eat in the kitchen or dining room?" he asked, seeing that Andrea had the potato salad almost done.

"How about the dining room? That's where I left Lady after I let her out of the carrier." Andrea laughed. "She quickly found a spot under the table to take a nap."

Brandon placed the pan of meat on the table. "Speaking of pets. . . I'd better go check on Duke. He may be awake by now and need to go outside."

"Okay. While you're doing that, I'll finish up the potato salad and bring the food into the dining room."

Brandon passed through the dining room and was surprised to see that the door to the living room was slightly ajar. He thought he had shut it when he'd left his sleeping dog to answer the front door.

Brandon took a few steps toward Duke's doggie bed and halted. There lay Andrea's cat right next to Duke, with her head nestled close to his. Their eyes were closed, and Duke breathed in and out, while soft purring came from Lady. Brandon could hardly believe the scene set before him. It seemed as though Lady might be offering comfort to Duke, and the amazing thing was, Duke had apparently accepted her sympathetic gesture. Maybe something good had come from Duke's accident. Perhaps the animals could be friends after all.

Brandon went back to the kitchen. "You'll never guess what's going on in the living room."

She turned away from her job at the counter. "What is it?"

"Your cat and my dog are sleeping next to each other." Brandon swiped a hand through the back of his thick hair. "I could hardly believe my eyes."

Andrea's brows lifted. "They're both in the living room?"

"Yeah."

"How did Lady get in there?"

"The door was slightly open, so I must not have closed it tightly when I left Duke to answer the door when you arrived." He took hold of Andrea's hand. "Come on. You need to see this for yourself."

When they entered the living room, Brandon pointed at the sleeping duo. "What do you think of that?" he whispered.

Her lips parted slightly as she stared at their contented-looking pets. "I think it's a miracle. A definite answer to prayer."

He nodded and slipped his arm around Andrea's waist. "Wouldn't it be great if these two actually became friends?"

"It sure would, but I wonder what prompted Lady to approach Duke and lie down beside him."

"I'm thinking she might have detected that he'd been hurt and needed comforting. Some animals have a sixth sense about things like that."

"That could be, but why would Duke have tolerated Lady lying down beside him when he's been so frightened of her?"

"I can't be sure, but with the need for sympathy, he must have set his fears aside."

"Well, whatever the case, let's go eat and not disturb their peaceful sleep."

"Sounds good to me. I'm eager to sink my teeth into the sausages I grilled, not to mention eat your tangy potato salad."

The two of them quietly left the room, and Brandon left the door open slightly so that if Lady and Duke woke up, he could hear if there were any problems.

Before they ate their meal, Brandon prayed, asking God to bless the food, as well as his and Andrea's relationship. He ended the prayer by giving thanks for what he and Andrea had witnessed with their pets in the next room.

When they'd both finished eating, Andrea suggested that they take a peek to see if anything had changed between Duke and Lady. She was pleasantly surprised to find them both awake and even more pleased to see that her cat was now licking the dog's injured leg while Duke laid there calmly, as though enjoying the attention.

Brandon smiled. "Looks like my dog has gotten over his fear of your cat. I sure never expected to see this, did you?"

"No, but as I said earlier, it's an answer to prayer." She clasped his arm. "Now that we don't have to worry about either of us feeling the need to get rid of our pet, there's nothing standing in the way of us getting married."

"That's right," he agreed. "It's going to be clear sailing from here on."

Chapter 13

Walnut Creek

"I can't believe it's the middle of October already." Orley eyed the perpetual calendar sitting on the kitchen windowsill.

Lois nodded as she filled the sink with warm water and detergent. "Time marches on, that's for sure."

"Indeed it does." Orley moved to stand beside her. "How about if I dry the dishes while you wash this morning?"

Lois looked over at him and smiled. "Danki, I'd appreciate that." She glanced out the window. "I'm surprised that fellow you talked to the other day hasn't come by like he said to give us a bid on taking down the old dying maple tree in our backyard."

Orley picked up the dish towel and dried the first dish Lois had washed. "He said he would be here by eight o'clock Monday morning, and here it is nine thirty already. Something must have happened to detain him."

"I hope he didn't forget—especially since we took today off from working at the store to see what it would cost to take down the tree." She gestured to the back door. "Maybe you should go out to the phone shed and call the man to see if he's on his way."

Orley set the dish towel aside. "Good idea. I'll do it now and finish drying the dishes when I get back to the house." He grabbed his hat and went out the door.

Upon entering the phone shed, Orley saw the blinking light on the answering machine, indicating that one or more messages had come in.

He took a seat on the stool and punched the correct button to listen.

"Hey, Mr. Troyer—it's Eddie Bunker here. I hate to tell ya this, but I'm stuck out on the main highway, and thanks to the broken gauge, my truck's outta gas. Could ya bring me some?"

Orley scratched behind one ear, then gave his earlobe a tug. The only thing he used gasoline for was his lawnmower, and he had used the last of that Saturday evening when he'd mowed the lawn. He had plans to get the gas can filled sometime this week, but that was no help at the moment.

Even if I did have any gas, he thought, *I'd have to take it to him by horse and buggy or hire a driver to pick me up, which could take hours if none of our regular drivers are available.*

Orley shut off the answering machine and dialed the man's number, which went to voice mail. He left a short message explaining that he had no gas to bring the English man. Orley had just hung up when the phone rang.

"Hey, Mr. Troyer, it's Eddie Bunker. I called one of the guys who works for me, and he's bringing me some gas, so I should be there in the next half hour or so." There was a pause, then he added, "One of these days, I'm gonna get the gas gauge on my truck replaced."

Orley figured it might be a while before Eddie made it to his house. He was tempted to tell the man not to bother coming but figured he may as well hear his bid, so he responded with "Okay." At three o'clock, another man would be coming to look at the tree. Once that was done, Orley and Lois would make the decision on whose bid to choose.

After Lois finished washing the dishes, she gathered up some scraps to take out to the compost. Orley had come in ten minutes ago and told her about the message he'd received from the man giving them a bid on their tree. After he'd finished drying the dishes, Orley had gone outside to wait for Eddie Bunker, who was already two hours late.

Lois slipped into a pair of old sneakers, and since she was in a hurry to get busy answering some Dear Caroline letters, she didn't bother to tie the laces, just hurried out the back door. She noticed the man had finally arrived as she plodded across the slippery grass, still wet from yesterday's rains, and sidestepped a few mud puddles on her way to the compost pile. Lois was almost there when her shoestrings tangled, causing her to wobble in several directions before making a crash landing.

Lois's face heated as she scrambled to her feet and glanced around, hoping Orley and the man hadn't seen her fall and scatter all the scraps on the ground. They continued talking while looking at the pathetic old tree and didn't give a glance her way.

At least they didn't see me make a fool of myself, Lois thought as she brushed some dried mud and food scraps off her dress. *Guess that's what I get for not taking the time to tie my shoes. Sure won't make that mistake again.*

Once she had tied her shoes properly, Lois eyed their pumpkin patch. The bold, orange squashes poked out between the big green leaves. *I think some of those pumpkins would look nice on the front porch.* Lois stepped up to them and selected the ones she liked best. She carried two of the medium-sized pumpkins across the yard and placed them on the porch. After two more trips from the garden and back, she had enough pumpkins for her liking.

After Lois finished arranging them, she noticed quite a bit of mud from the garden had been tracked all over the porch from her grimy shoes. With a sigh, she went to get the outdoor broom they kept in the barn. The tree guy and Orley were over by the picnic table, and she noticed the man writing something on a piece of paper, which he handed to Orley.

Back on the porch, Lois used the broom to brush the caked mud from her sneakers. Then she swept the porch and even went after the cobwebs. She stepped down into the yard again and looked back at her finished work. *I think all those pumpkins look kind of cute. I wonder if Orley will notice and say something to me when he's done outside.*

Eager to get back into the warmth of the house, Lois hurried up the porch steps, leaving the broom propped near the door.

Apple Creek

Brandon entered his office at the veterinarian clinic and took a seat at his desk. He'd been busy all morning, and now it was time to take a brief lunch break. He had considered hiring another vet to help with the workload because at times his schedule was so tight, he had to work right through his lunch hour. He knew of other veterinary clinics that had more staff, and it probably made things easier. *I sure wouldn't mind being able to take vacations, sick leave, and even have the ability to come into work late or leave early when needed.*

He opened his insulated lunch bag and took out the ham and cheese sandwich he'd put together. He said a silent prayer before taking his first bite, thanking God for the meal set before him. He also asked the Lord's blessings on his family and friends. Brandon ended the prayer, thanking God for the sweet Christian woman who had come into his life. He looked forward to Andrea becoming his wife in four months. Things were going well with the wedding plans, and he felt relieved that Duke had accepted Lady. Now that the dog's leg injury was fully healed, Brandon felt comfortable leaving Duke at home without supervision while he was at the clinic. Of course, Brandon kept his pooch barricaded in the laundry room so he couldn't roam the house and potentially get into trouble. About a year ago, he had made the mistake of giving Duke free run of the house unattended, and he'd come home to a couple of messes. Not only had the dog gone to the bathroom where he shouldn't have, but Duke had gnawed a hole in one of Brandon's bedroom slippers, which he'd left on the floor by his recliner. Those things were nothing, though, compared to what one pet owner who'd come to the clinic had told Brandon. The owner's dog was blind in one eye and had been born deaf. Training the animal had been a challenge, and on one occasion after leaving the dog alone in the house for a few hours, the man and his wife had returned home to find the cushions on their couch torn to shreds. The couch looked so bad, the man had hauled it outside until he could dispose of it. Needless to say, his wife had been quite upset, especially since they'd had the couch only a little over a year.

Focusing once again on his lunch, Brandon tore open the bag of potato chips and ate a few. Not too long after, he heard a couple of raps on his office door. "Come in," he called.

His assistant, Fran, entered. "We have someone on the phone whose dog has quills from a porcupine and needs to have them removed." She paused. "Do you think we can squeeze the poor animal in to be seen today?"

"I believe so. We'll just need to work it into the schedule."

"All right, I'll let the caller know and let you go back to your lunch. Thank you, Dr. Prentice."

"You're welcome." He watched the door shut behind her and continued to eat his lunch. It would be a busy afternoon, and he'd possibly end up going home later than normal, but that was just part of the job.

I hope Duke's doing okay today. It was good of my mom to volunteer to come over to the house and check on him while I'm here at work. Brandon had always been able to count on his mother when he needed help, and this situation was no exception. He picked up his bottle of water and took a drink. Brandon was glad he'd become a vet, even though it had taken four years of undergrad school and an additional four years of veterinary school. He'd had a way with animals since he was a boy and cared about the welfare of people's pets. It was always difficult when a person had a pet with an incurable illness that needed to be put down. But being a vet had many benefits, such as seeing a dog, cat, or some other animal recover from an illness or injury, and those were the things Brandon liked to focus on.

Andrea closed the door behind her last piano student of the day and sank onto the couch with a groan. There were days when things went really well with her students and other times, like today, when everyone seemed to think they should play the piano their own way. Peggy still wasn't keeping her nails trimmed as short as they should be, but at least her parents hadn't found another teacher for her. Another girl, Anna, played with flat hands instead of curving her fingers as Andrea had asked. Then there was Todd, her only boy student, who played by ear and didn't want to learn the notes. Even her adult student, Kara, who had taken a few lessons as a child, could be a challenge because she lacked self-confidence. There were times, such as now, when Andrea wished she could quit teaching piano and concentrate fully on her artwork.

"Maybe after Brandon and I are married, I can do that."

Lady leaped into Andrea's lap and began to purr.

"Did you think I was talking to you, pretty Lady? Did you believe I was inviting you up?" Andrea gently rubbed the cat's back, which brought on more vibrations.

She smiled at the contented cat while thinking about the last few weeks and how well Lady and Duke had been getting along during their scheduled visits. It was a relief, knowing that neither she nor Brandon would have to part with their pet when they got married.

Andrea sighed. *Things are back on track and going well again. All I need to do now is concentrate on making all the final plans for Brandon's and my wedding. I can hardly wait for the big day.*

Andrea's cell phone rang from across the room, where she'd left it on an end table, so she moved a disgruntled Lady to the sofa cushion and went to see who was calling. Her mother's number showed on the screen, so Andrea quickly responded to the call.

"Hi, Mom. How's your day been so far?"

"Not well, Andrea." Mom's voice faltered, and Andrea heard a muffled sob.

"What's wrong? Has something bad happened?"

"Yes. I—I just got a call from your cousin, Vincent, saying his dad had been killed in a motorcycle accident around noon today. His mother was too upset to let anyone know. Vincent said Karen passed out when she got the news." Mom paused and sniffed deeply. "Oh, Andrea, I can hardly believe my brother is gone. I wish he and his family lived closer and we could have seen them more often. With them living out west in Idaho, our visits have been few and far between, and because of it, you never got to know your uncle Dave or any of his family very well."

Andrea sat quietly, breathing in and out. The pain she heard in her mother's voice brought tears to Andrea's eyes. "When is Uncle Dave's funeral service?"

"The family hasn't made any final arrangements yet, but Vincent said he would let us know." There was a short pause. "Will you be able to go with me and your dad? It would mean a lot to me if you could."

Andrea didn't hesitate to answer. "Of course I will go with you. Let me know as soon as you find out when the service will be, and I'll rearrange my teaching schedule."

"Thank you, sweet daughter. I don't think I could get through this without your support, and, of course, I'll have your father's also."

"Absolutely."

When Andrea hung up the phone a few minutes later, she returned to the couch where Lady lay curled into a ball as if she didn't have a care in the world.

Oh, the life of a cat, Andrea mused. *No schedules to keep or funerals to attend—all they have to worry about is where their next meal will be coming from.*

She leaned her head against the back of the couch and closed her eyes. Even though she didn't know her uncle Dave very well, Andrea felt bad to hear of the unexpected tragedy that had taken his life so suddenly. Life was full of ups and downs, and it could throw a curve when least expected. How thankful she was for her Christian faith and the confidence that the Lord would be with her every day, guiding, directing, and offering encouragement through His written Word. Looking to the future and all of its uncertainties was much easier to do when a person had a personal relationship with Jesus Christ as their Lord and Savior. Andrea fully expected that if she and Brandon were blessed with children someday, they would bring them up in a home filled with love and the knowledge of the Lord. For now, though, she would concentrate on attending her uncle's funeral and being there to help Mom deal with the pain of losing her only brother.

Chapter 14

Walnut Creek

Orley guided his horse and buggy to the hitching rail at an Amish house on the other end of town. "I think when we're done looking at yard sales, we should grab a bite to eat before heading home."

"That sounds like a good idea." Lois dabbed her nose with a tissue. "I'm still hoping to find what I'm looking for at one of the sales."

Her husband set the brake and grabbed the thermos that sat in a box behind his seat. "Thank you for providing us with hot coffee to drink."

"No problem. With the temperature down the way it is, we need to keep warm."

Orley poured some coffee into his and Lois's mugs before putting the thermos back. "Most of the yard sales have been busy today. It's too bad we've come away from each of them without buying something."

"I agree, and I wish the weather was warmer. The older I get, the less my old bones like this chill." She sipped her hot beverage, feeling warm and toasty on the inside as she watched a woman carrying her purchase of a wooden chair over to her car. The lady opened the back door and tried to wrangle it into a spot, but from what Lois could see, it wasn't working too well.

"If that poor woman didn't already have so many other things piled up in the back, she would have more room," Orley commented. "I'll get out and secure my horse and then see if I can help her." He handed Lois his mug, got out, and secured the horse.

Lois smiled. It wasn't unusual for her husband to do a good deed for people he knew or perfect strangers. She drank the rest of her coffee, put their mugs away, and climbed down from the carriage. As she followed Orley to the English woman's car, she heard him ask if he could be of assistance.

"No, thanks. I'll manage," the woman replied. "I'm used to doing things on my own."

"Do you think she'll get that chair into her car?" Lois asked, keeping her voice low.

Orley shrugged. "I'm not sure, but she seems determined enough. I'd say she'll win out and get it in there eventually."

The woman paused a few minutes, set the chair on the ground, and then climbed back into her vehicle, where she tried to rearrange the stuff already packed inside.

Lois continued to watch, wishing the bedraggled woman would have accepted Orley's help.

Finally, the woman pulled a table lamp from the back of the car and, with some effort, put it up front by the driver's seat. Then she closed the door and picked up the chair. With a little more work, it finally went in.

Orley looked at Lois and winked. "Are ya ready to see what this yard sale might have for us? It could be something exciting."

"Oh, I'm ready all right." Lois followed Orley, walking quickly to keep up with his strides.

"I hope we find something interesting here," Orley said as he and Lois entered the sale on this chilly Monday morning.

"It's too cold to be out here looking for vintage items, when we really should be at our store." Lois pulled her heavy sweater a little tighter around her neck and shivered. "I'm surprised there are so many yard sales going on this time of the year."

Orley nodded. "At least it's not raining."

"Or snowing," she added. "This frigid air makes me think it won't be long before we see some heavy white flakes falling from the sky."

"That could be. Some years we have had *schnee* as early as October."

"I know, and I wasn't ready for it."

Orley chuckled. "Are we ever ready for things we don't like?"

"I suppose not."

They walked farther into the yard sale where several people milled around by two long tables full of kitchen utensils and some decorator items.

Lois had spotted an old teacup she wanted to look at, but her attention was turned toward a loud voice coming from the aisle across from them. She turned to see who was shouting and was surprised to see a middle-aged English woman shaking her finger at the tall man who stood beside her.

"That tool you're holding is too expensive," the woman said, her voice rising higher with each word. "We can't afford to spend money foolishly, Ted."

The man's brows furrowed. "It's not foolish. I've been looking for a tool like this, and you can be sure that I'll put it to good use making some gifts to give out at Christmas."

The woman, who Lois assumed to be his wife, folded her arms and shook her head forcibly.

Lois glanced over at Orley to see his reaction. She wasn't surprised to see the wrinkles in his forehead deepen as the couple continued to argue.

Lois fought the urge to say something to the woman, who was doing most of the shouting, but she didn't feel it was her place to intervene—especially since these people were strangers. If they'd come into Memory Keepers and began quarreling, Lois was quite sure that Orley would have said something. And if he hadn't, she certainly would have.

The arguing couple made Lois think about Jeff and Rhonda Davis and the marital problems they'd had before they'd given their lives fully to the Lord. Both Orley and Lois had mentored the couple and prayed for them often. Although it was best to remain quiet right now, Lois would definitely remember to pray for the man and woman here at the sale. She felt relief when they stopped arguing and walked away—without the tool the man had wanted so badly.

Heavenly Father, Lois prayed, *please show that woman a better way of talking to her husband than yelling at him to make her point known. And if they are having serious marriage problems, please guide and direct them to the right person who can offer good counsel.*

Apple Creek

"No, Mrs. Allen, it's not typically dangerous for your dog to eat grass. In fact, it's fairly common," Brandon patiently explained.

The elderly woman gestured to her cream-colored miniature

poodle and frowned. "It's a nasty habit, in my opinion, just like digging holes in the yard."

"Most dogs do like to dig." Brandon stroked her dog's silky head. "Most of the time it's for play, to create a cool dirt bowl on a hot day or because they're bored."

Mrs. Allen blinked rapidly. "My Dixie's never bored. When she isn't sleeping, she keeps herself busy playing with her toys or following me around the house or yard."

Brandon smiled. "Dixie seems to be in good condition, and her weight is where it should be. I think you'll have her around for a good many years."

"I'm glad to hear it." The older woman picked up her dog and moved toward the door. "I hope she doesn't outlive me, though, because I have no one to leave her with after I'm gone."

"What about your daughter? Wouldn't she take Dixie in?"

"No, Karen's allergic to dogs—and cats too."

"I'm certain that your daughter will find Dixie a good home if it becomes necessary." Brandon hoped his words sounded reassuring. He hated to send Mrs. Allen home from his clinic with a sense of hopelessness.

She nodded slowly. "Thank you, Dr. Prentice."

"You're welcome."

After the woman left the examining room, Brandon made a few notes on Dixie's chart and looked at his watch. *Andrea and her parents should be boarding the plane about now.* He closed his eyes to offer a prayer. *Please be with them, Lord, and keep the Wagners safe as they travel to Idaho. Offer comfort over the loss of Andrea's uncle to all of his family at the funeral tomorrow.*

Cleveland, Ohio

Andrea took her aisle seat in the second row of the first-class cabin, directly across from her parents. Andrea's father had accumulated quite a few air miles and used them to pay for their upgraded seats. Since there would be two stops along the way—one in Minneapolis and one in Seattle—the trip to Boise would take a little over ten hours, and they wouldn't arrive until nine forty-five tonight. The comfortable seats in first class would make the long trip a little more bearable.

Andrea stretched out, appreciative of the extra legroom, and put her neck pillow in place, hoping she might be able to get a good nap on the first leg of this flight. She hadn't slept well last night, worrying about Lady and how she would do at Colleen's place during her absence. Andrea had also thought about Brandon and wished he could have come with her on this trip. But his schedule at the clinic was full, and he had obligations to fulfill. She hoped he would be able to take at least a week off after their wedding for a honeymoon. Maybe by then he would have found another veterinarian to work with him in the clinic, which would ease the pressure he was under.

Andrea yawned and was on the verge of dozing off when an elderly woman with silver-gray hair stopped at her seat. "I'm sorry for the inconvenience, but would you mind stepping into the aisle so Serena and I can take our seat by the window?" The woman gestured to the carrier she held.

Andrea knew right away from the long, plaintive *meowww*, that Serena must be the cat in the carrier. She quickly stood up and stepped into the aisle, moving close to her mother's seat.

Mom looked up and gave Andrea a sweet smile, then she mouthed the word *Meow*.

Andrea nodded. One thing was for sure: if the cat's owner was the conversational type, Andrea, with her love of cats, would have plenty to talk about.

After she took her seat again, the older woman looked over at her and said, "My name is Darlene, and the noisy one in the carrier is Serena."

Andrea smiled. "It's nice to meet you. I'm Andrea."

"Where are you headed?" Darlene asked.

"Our first plane change will be in Minneapolis, and then it's on to Seattle. Our final destination is Boise, Idaho. Those are my parents sitting across the aisle from us. We'll be attending a funeral in the town of Caldwell."

"That's too bad. Funerals are always so sad. Was the deceased a friend or family member of yours?"

"The funeral is for my uncle. What's your destination?" Andrea asked, quickly changing the topic.

"I'll be getting off in Minneapolis. My daughter, Sandra, lives there with her husband and two teenage girls. Sandra's invited me to move in with them, so I thought it best to check things out before committing to anything permanent."

Andrea was about to comment when Darlene spoke again. "My husband passed away a year ago, and we only have one daughter. I do have a good many friends in Cleveland, and I'd miss seeing them if I moved away." With downturned facial features, she looked at her cat's carrier, where squeaky chirrups could be heard. "My other concern is that Serena might not be able to adjust to new surroundings. She's used to a quiet life in my home, with just the two of us now."

Andrea placed her hand gently on the woman's arm. "I understand. My fiancé is a veterinarian, and he's mentioned how everyone's pet is different. While some may adjust easily to new surroundings, others have a difficult time."

Darlene released a heavy sigh. "Guess I won't know till we get there and have spent a few weeks living in the basement apartment my son-in-law has fixed up for me and Serena."

"I have a cat too. Her name is Lady," Andrea said. "She has quite a unique personality."

Darlene tipped her head to one side. "In what way?"

"Somehow she managed to befriend my fiancé's dog, who up until recently was afraid of cats."

"That's remarkable. How did she accomplish it?"

Andrea explained the situation and ended it by saying, "Needless to say, Brandon and I are relieved that our pets are finally getting along. We'll be getting married in February, and we would have been faced with the decision of one of us needing to part with their pet if Lady and Duke couldn't even be in the same house with each other."

Darlene's eyes widened. "Oh my! I can't imagine being forced to give up my cat." She leaned over and put her hand against the carrier, which caused Serena's chirrups to turn to loud purrs.

Andrea smiled. It was nice to see the love this woman had for her pet. She hoped if Darlene decided to move in with her daughter and family that everything would work out well for both the sweet lady and her cat.

The plane had only been in the air thirty minutes when Evelyn glanced over and saw that her husband was engrossed in some movie. Flying had never bothered Ray as much as it did her. Unless food was being offered, he either slept or watched whatever movie caught his interest. Not Evelyn. She'd never cared for watching movies or much of anything at home on the

TV. She enjoyed going out to lunch with her friend Fiona and managing their church library, and she felt thankful that Fiona had agreed to take care of Frisky while they were gone.

Evelyn thought about the things she did enjoy—she liked to knit, cross-stitch, spend time in her garden during warmer weather, and tend to her indoor plants year round. Some evenings she sat in the living room with Ray while he watched TV, but Evelyn's concentration was usually on whatever knitting or cross-stitch project she'd begun. It was difficult to sit here on the plane with nothing constructive to do.

Guess I should have brought a book along to read, she thought. *It would give me something to do that would help take my mind off the funeral service we'll be attending tomorrow morning.* Evelyn squeezed her eyes tightly shut. *I wish I could have talked to my brother one last time before he died. There's so much I would have said to him.* Tears seeped out from her lashes and trickled down her cheeks. Her brother had become a Christian in his late teens, so at least she had the confidence that Dave had gone to heaven when he died.

Evelyn opened her eyes and dabbed at her face with the tissue she'd put in her pocket before they boarded the plane. *I need to get ahold of myself so I can be strong for Dave's family when we get there. The last thing Karen or Vincent needs to deal with is me falling apart.*

She glanced across the aisle to where Andrea sat talking to the gray-haired woman beside her. With the noise of the plane, Evelyn couldn't make out every word they were saying, but she figured their conversation was most likely centered around the topic of cats.

She looked over at Ray again, clearly engrossed in what looked like an action/adventure movie. *I may as well join him. It's either that or try to sleep*. Evelyn slipped her earbuds in and touched the screen to see what her options were. Maybe one of the movies would be good enough to hold her attention. If not, she would watch the flight tracker on the monitor. At least that would keep her in the know about how far they were from Minneapolis, where they'd board their next flight. Evelyn hoped that when they arrived in Boise, someone from Dave's family would be there to pick them up.

Chapter 15

Apple Creek

Brandon had just finished eating supper when his cell phone rang. He picked it up quickly and was pleased to see that the caller was Andrea. "Hey, sweetie, it's sure good to hear from you. Are you in Boise?" Brandon stood and carried his dirty dishes to the sink.

"Yes, we just landed and will soon be pulling up to the Jetway."

"Glad to hear. Were all the flights good?"

"For the most part. We had some turbulence on the flight from Minneapolis to Seattle, but it wasn't too bad."

"I've been praying for you, and I'm glad you made it there okay. I will be praying for you and your family tomorrow too, when you attend your uncle's funeral service."

"Thanks. Prayers are always appreciated." There was a brief pause. "I'd better go, Brandon. We're pulling up to the Jetway now."

"Okay. Take care, and remember how much I love you."

"Love you too. Bye for now."

When Brandon ended the call, he sat quietly at the table, thanking God for giving Andrea and her parents a safe trip. He missed her already and looked forward to seeing his beautiful, sweet fiancée in a few days. He was glad to be marrying a good person who cared deeply for her family.

Woof! Woof! Woof!

Brandon opened his eyes and looked down at his dog, staring up at him with his head cocked to one side. "That's one way to cut short a person's prayer time."

The dog barked again, a little louder this time, and raced over to the back door.

"What are you after, Duke? Do ya want some attention, or do you need to go outside?"

Arf! Arf!

"All righty then. I know exactly what you want now." Brandon got up from his chair and opened the back door. Duke zipped right out and into the yard. Brandon stood on the porch and leaned against the railing as he watched the dog. Duke occasionally got what some people called the *zoomies*, when he would run around excitedly for no obvious reason. Brandon figured Duke's sudden burst of energy might be his way of expressing how happy he was. Sometimes Duke would exhibit his zoomie behavior at certain times of the day, like after he'd eaten or been given a bath. The last thing Brandon needed was for his dog to reinjure his leg, so he watched him closely.

Duke made two circles around the backyard, sniffing the ground. He finally went to the area where there was no grass, which Brandon had taught the dog to use as his personal bathroom. A short time later, Duke was back up on the porch.

"Ready to go inside now, boy?"

Duke wagged his tail and let out a few arfs!

"Okay, you can keep me company while I do the dishes." Brandon opened the door and waited for Duke to go inside, then entered behind him.

Brandon went to the sink to rinse the dishes before putting them in the dishwasher. He'd attempted to make himself spaghetti, which hadn't turned out so well. Now Brandon had some tough cleanup to do. Since he'd overheated the sauce and scorched it, cleaning the pan would be a chore.

Guess that's what I get for leaving the sauce simmering on the stove and looking in on that movie on the television. If Andrea had been here for supper this evening, she would've kept a closer eye on the things cooking, and I wouldn't be working so hard right now to clean up this pan.

Duke stood beside him, pressing up against the lower part of Brandon's leg. From his knowledge of dogs and their body language, Brandon knew this behavior was one of the signs that his dog loved him. There were other things too that Duke did to show love, such as curling up close to Brandon when he was resting on the couch, jumping up in excitement whenever he walked in the door, rolling around on his back to get his belly scratched, resting his head on Brandon's lap, and licking Brandon's face and hands.

Brandon looked down at Duke and smiled. "You're a good dog, and I'm glad that you've accepted Lady and will be able to adapt when Andrea and her cat move into this house after we're married." He left the partially cleaned pan in the sink to soak some more in the warm soapy water. Then Brandon rinsed off the suds that clung to him and dried his hands. "I could use a little break from putting dishes in the dishwasher."

Duke's response was a little grunt as he dropped to the floor and rolled over with all four feet in the air.

Brandon laughed and rubbed Duke's belly with the toe of his sneaker. *The only thing that could make this evening nicer would be if Andrea was here beside me right now.*

Caldwell, Idaho

Clutching her mother's arm, with Dad on the other side doing the same, Andrea entered the chapel inside the funeral home. If ever there was a time that Mom needed her support, it was now. The poor thing was taking her brother's death pretty hard. Last night when they'd arrived, Vincent had picked them up at the airport in Boise. He'd looked tired but seemed to be handling things well. It was another story for Vincent's mother, whom they hadn't seen until they got to the house. Aunt Karen had sobbed when she'd talked to them about her husband's untimely death. While the grieving widow sat in the front row of the chapel now, her shoulders shook. It was hard to watch Aunt Karen bearing through the pain of her loss. Andrea wished there was something to ease all the suffering she felt and help with her mother's sadness too.

Before the service began, Andrea prayed for Aunt Karen, her mom, and the rest of the family gathered there. While praying, she heard weeping from her aunt nearby. Mom also started crying again. Andrea opened her eyes and saw Dad's arm come around her mother's waist as he gave a needed hug. She looked about the room. A mixture of fresh, neatly arranged flowers up front softened the area near the casket.

Andrea's heart went out to Vincent as he sat with both hands resting against his forehead. Although she hadn't known her uncle well, she felt the heavy loss her cousin obviously felt.

An usher had seated Andrea and her parents in the front row, reserved for family members of the deceased. Since Uncle Dave's parents were no longer living and his only sibling was Andrea's mother, it was just Vincent, Aunt Karen, Andrea, and her parents sitting in the first row.

Andrea glanced at her cousin again, sitting right beside her, and drew in a slow breath. She couldn't help noticing the spicy aroma of Vincent's aftershave. It reminded her of Brandon and how nice he always smelled when they were together. It had only been two days since Andrea had seen Brandon, and already she missed him. She wondered what her future husband was doing right now while she sat here waiting for the service to get started. Andrea figured he'd most likely be at work taking care of someone's dog or cat.

It wasn't long before Andrea heard someone speaking in a low, soothing tone. Her attention was drawn to the front of the room, where a man wearing a black suit, who she assumed was the pastor, stood at a podium not far from the closed casket.

Several minutes passed, and then Andrea glanced over her shoulder. Nearly every chair in the room had been filled. Apparently Uncle Dave had been well known and liked by several in the community and his circle of friends.

An unexpected thought popped into Andrea's head. *When I'm gone someday, I wonder how many people will attend my funeral. Since I have no brothers or sisters, no nieces or nephews, and just one cousin, if my parents are no longer living by the time I die, it may only be a few friends, some church people, maybe a few piano students, and of course the dear man I will soon marry.*

Then another thought overtook her, so emotionally gripping that she had to choke back a sob. *What if Brandon should go before me?* The idea of becoming a widow, whether in the prime of her life or as a senior citizen, caused a deep ache to penetrate Andrea's soul. She loved Brandon so much and couldn't imagine her life without him. Their bond was strong, and Andrea felt sure that nothing short of death could ever keep them apart.

As the eulogy was read, Evelyn reached over and clasped her sister-in-law's trembling hand. *Poor Karen.* It was a good thing her son, Vincent, still lived at home and would be available to help her get through the lonely days ahead. Of course, friends and people from church would be near, but Evelyn felt that having a family member close by would offer the most comfort for Dave's widow.

Ray sat on the other side of Evelyn, and she looked over at him briefly. His expression was stoic, and she wondered if he might be having the same thoughts. *How would I feel if it were me sitting here today, after having lost my spouse?*

Death held a certain finality, yet for a believer in Christ, when a person's soul left the body, it was not the end. It was a comfort to know that when a Christian died, they became absent from the body but present with the Lord.

As the minister preached a message on the very things she'd been thinking, Evelyn reminded herself to stay in touch with Karen through notes of encouragement and phone calls. It was the least she could do, since once they returned home, she couldn't be here in person to offer comfort.

In need of a breath of fresh air, Andrea stepped out of her aunt's home and into the yard. A meal provided by some of the women from Karen's church had been served at the house after the funeral and graveside service. Most of the people who had come to eat and visit with the bereaved had gone home, but a few people still lingered inside.

The chilly autumn air blew leaves from the trees, and Andrea buttoned her jacket all the way up. It was surprisingly much colder here in Idaho than it had been when they'd left home in Ohio, and she half expected to see snow falling from the sky any minute. She looked up but saw only a star-studded sky on this clear moonlit evening.

"Mind if I join you, or would you rather be alone?"

Andrea turned at the sound of Vincent's deep voice. "I don't mind your company. I just needed to get out of the house for a while and enjoy the quiet and breathe in some fresh air."

"I know what you mean. That's why I came outside too." He leaned against the trunk of a stately pine tree. "So catch me up with what's new in your life."

"You may have heard that I'll be getting married in February."

"Yeah, my mom mentioned that. Guess your mother told my dad the last time they talked, and she passed the information along to me." Vincent took a step closer. "Congratulations. It's great that you've found someone you want to spend the rest of your life with." He dropped his gaze to the ground. "Wish I could say the same."

"There's no special woman in your life?"

"Not right now, but that's okay. I keep busy with other things." He rubbed the bridge of his nose. "Besides, my mom's gonna need me more than ever now."

Slowly Andrea nodded. "Yes, she will, but you need your own life too."

"I have a job, my music, and a hobby of carving duck decoys that keeps me busy."

"You manage a hardware store, right?"

"Yeah."

"What kind of music do you like?"

"Mostly country. That's what I play with my guitar, but I also enjoy gospel music."

"I teach piano lessons to several students, and I also earn some money selling some of my paintings." She smiled. "Since we're both musical, it seems like we have a few things in common."

"You're right, and since we're both adopted, we have that in common too."

Her brows furrowed. "Adopted?"

"Yeah, both of us, when we were babies."

"Who told you that? Where'd you get such an idea?" Andrea felt sure that Vincent had made this up. But the question was—why?

"My folks told me I was adopted as soon as I was able to understand. Didn't your parents tell you too?"

A wave of heat cascaded over Andrea's body, driving away the cold. "No, they did not, and it can't be true." She pointed a shaky finger at him. "Why would you say such a thing to me? If my parents had adopted me, surely they would have said so."

He cleared his throat. "Well, uh. . .maybe. . ."

Andrea placed both hands behind her back, gripping one wrist tightly with the other hand. "Why would they have kept such a thing from me all these years?" She heard the tension in her own voice.

"I—I don't know. Maybe you should ask them since they're the ones who kept the truth from you for so long." Vincent shook his head. "Unbelievable. It is unbelievable."

Andrea bit the inside of her cheek. She had no choice but to confront them and find out the truth, but here, in the center of all this grief, might not be the best time. She would wait to talk to her parents until they were back in Ohio. If what her cousin had told her was the truth, then she would at least have the support of her fiancé to help her deal with this unexpected, shocking revelation.

Chapter 16

"Aren't you going to eat something for breakfast?" Evelyn asked her daughter after everyone had gathered around the table the following morning.

Avoiding eye contact, Andrea shook her head. "I'm not hungry, so I'll just have a cup of coffee."

Evelyn took a seat, wondering what was up with her daughter. *Did I or someone else in the house say something to make Andrea upset? Maybe she's not feeling well this morning and is keeping it to herself, but I will try again, because I'd like to know what's going on.*

"You really should have something to eat. Coffee alone might make you jittery, and a little protein or even some carbs will do the opposite." Evelyn gestured to the stack of toast she had put on the table along with some boiled eggs.

"I'll be fine with coffee, and I'll take it outside." Andrea kept her gaze on the table.

The sharp tone in Andrea's voice and her lack of eye contact were good indications that she was upset about something. She sat watching her daughter and thinking.

"But it's cold out there," Aunt Karen spoke up. "Wouldn't you rather stay in here and visit with us where it's nice and warm?"

Andrea's lips might be pursed, but at least she looked directly at her aunt, unlike her avoidance of me. Evelyn cringed. *Have I said or done something to irritate her? Could it be my comment about Andrea needing to eat something for breakfast?*

Before Evelyn had the chance to say anything more, Andrea pushed back her chair and got up from the table. "I appreciate everyone's concerns, but I only want coffee, and I'd prefer to drink it outside." She rushed out of the room before anyone could respond.

At the moment, Evelyn wished that she could also leave the room, but that would be impolite. She was embarrassed by her daughter's abrupt and strange behavior. *What caused Andrea to act that way?* Evelyn wondered. *I can't believe she would be so rude.*

Evelyn looked over at Karen and placed a hand on her arm. "I apologize for my daughter's abruptness. She's not normally like this, and I can't imagine what has come over Andrea this morning."

"It's okay," Karen responded. "Yesterday took a toll on all of us, and I think everyone's on edge."

"I'll talk to her." Vincent grabbed a piece of toast and quickly departed the room.

Evelyn hoped Andrea's cousin could help out in some way. Ray had stepped out to use the restroom, so he'd missed all the action. She wondered what his thoughts would be on this.

Andrea took a seat on the front porch, holding her steaming cup of coffee in both hands for the warmth. Aunt Karen had been right, it was a cold day. Even with her jacket on and buttoned all the way up, Andrea felt the frigid temperature seeping in. But worse than the cold air were the unanswered questions. *Am I really adopted? But why would my birth parents, if this is true, hand me off to complete strangers?*

She'd only been sitting there a few seconds when Vincent showed up. "Mind if I join you?" he asked in a muffled tone around the piece of toast as he ate.

Still upset, she looked over at him and mimicked his full mouth as she said: "What did you say?"

He blinked as though in surprise. "I'm sorry. Where are my manners? I said, 'Mind if I join you?'"

"No. Actually, I should be the one apologizing. I'm upset with my mom and took it out on you. I'm sorry, Vincent."

"It's okay. Yesterday was rough—especially for my mom, and my dad's funeral affected each of us in some way."

"I owe your mother an apology for dashing out of the house like I did."

"I'm sure she wasn't offended. Mom's emotions are so raw, she may not have even noticed what you said or did."

"Whether she noticed or not, I still need to tell her I'm sorry." Andrea shivered despite being bundled in a fleeced jacket. "It's pretty cold out here. You might want to put a jacket on."

He rubbed the arms of his red-and-black checked flannel shirt. "Naw, I'm fine. Truth is, I like this brisk kind of weather. It's a pleasant change from the dry hot days we often get during the summer months."

"Do you get much rain in this part of Idaho?" she asked.

"Some but not a lot. Nothing like they get on the west side of Oregon and Washington." He cleared his throat a couple of times. "Listen, about last night. . . I'm sorry for what I blurted out, but I really thought you knew that you'd been adopted."

The sound of the word *adopted* didn't sit well with Andrea. Not to mention that dealing with the shocking news had made her night miserable. While sleep had eluded her, she hadn't known what to think—one moment believing what Vincent had said and the next denying the words of her cousin and clinging to the hope that he was wrong.

Andrea gripped her mug a little tighter. "I had no idea, and I still can't believe it's true."

"Well, it must be. Like I said last night, I've heard my folks talk about it."

Andrea sat perfectly still, staring up at the gray-colored sky. Until she heard it from her parents' lips, she could not allow herself to believe what Vincent told her was factual. It just didn't seem possible.

"Have you talked yet to your mom or dad about what I said?"

She shook her head. "I thought it might be best to wait until we get back to Ohio, but maybe that's a mistake."

Vincent placed his hand on her shoulder and gave it a tender squeeze. "I agree. I think it would be best to get this out in the open once and for all. Otherwise, you'll probably be fretting about it all the way home tomorrow."

Andrea contemplated his words and stood. "You're right, Vincent. I'm going back in the kitchen right now and confront my parents about this matter. If I was adopted, they have some explaining to do."

When Andrea entered the warm kitchen, where the odor of coffee, toast, and eggs greeted her, she found Mom, Dad, and Aunt Karen still at the table. From the looks of the bowl of boiled eggs and plate full of toast, it didn't appear as if much had been eaten. Perhaps the grief they felt over losing Uncle Dave had diminished their appetites.

Andrea figured it wouldn't be good to blurt out the question she'd come here to ask in front of her aunt, so after she apologized to Aunt Karen for her abrupt departure, she looked at her father and asked, "Could I talk to you and Mom alone for a few minutes?"

He glanced at Andrea's mother, and when she nodded, Dad looked back at Andrea. "Certainly. Should we go to the living room?"

"That's fine." Andrea led the way but not before she gave a quick look in Aunt Karen's direction. The poor woman's eyes were red from crying so much the day before, and her lips were pressed firmly together as though she was trying to hold it together. The last thing the grieving woman needed was to witness their discussion, which could end up with some heated words.

In the living room, Andrea took a seat in the rocking chair, and her parents sat next to each other on the couch.

"There's no easy way to ask this question," she said, leaning slightly forward. "So I may as well spit it right out."

Mom sat up a little straighter. "What do you want to ask?"

"Was I adopted?"

With jerky motions, Andrea's father rubbed the back of his neck, and her mother drew in a series of short breaths as though she needed more oxygen.

"Was I adopted or not?" Her voice had risen, but it was too late to lower it now.

"Yes, you were." Dad's face turned as red as a springtime radish.

Andrea bit her lip until she tasted blood. "Then Vincent was right when he told me last night that something we had in common was the fact that we both had been adopted."

Mom's cheeks had become flushed too, and the skin around her eyes had tightened. "You were just a day old when we got you."

Andrea got up from her chair and moved over to stand in front of them. "Why did you keep this from me? Didn't you think I had the right to know?" It became increasingly difficult for her not to shout.

"Of course we did," Mom said tearfully. "We just could never find the right time or the right words to tell you about it." She lifted her hands and then let them fall into her lap.

"That's right." Dad's eyes darkened. "The longer we waited, the harder it became."

"So you allowed me to believe your deceptions because there was never a good time to tell me the truth?" Andrea's jaw clenched as she folded her arms firmly across her chest in an attempt to control the anger she felt bubbling in her soul. In all her thirty-two years, she'd never felt this frustrated with the parents who had raised her. *But they aren't my biological parents*, she thought with regret. Andrea lowered her gaze. *How could they have done this to me?*

"Please hear us out." Her mother's chin quivered as she laid a hand across her breastbone. "We'd like the opportunity to explain the situation more fully."

"I believe I've heard enough for now." Andrea turned and started for the front door.

"Where are you going?" Dad called out.

"I need to make a phone call, and then I'm going to pack. It's time for me to go home."

"Right now?" Mom's question was barely a squeak.

"Yes, if I can get a flight." Andrea turned and raced out the front door.

On the porch, she took a seat and pulled her cell phone from her jacket pocket. Although it was a weekday and Brandon would no doubt be at the clinic, she took a chance and called his number anyway. When he didn't pick up, Andrea left a message. "Hi, Brandon, it's me. If I can get a flight, I'll be coming home later today. If none are available, then it will be the day after tomorrow, as I'd told you before. Something's happened that has me pretty upset, and I need to be with you as soon as possible. I'll call you again and let you know if I was able to get an earlier flight. Otherwise, I'll see you two days from now as planned." Andrea's voice cracked. "I—I love you, Brandon. That's the only thing I'm sure of right now."

Apple Creek

At noon, when Brandon took his lunch break, he checked phone messages and found one from Andrea. After listening to what she'd said, Brandon put down his cell phone and leaned forward, resting both arms on his desk. *I hope she's okay. She sounded upset. I wish Andrea had explained why she wants to come home two days sooner than planned. I should give her a call right now.*

Brandon glanced at his phone and noticed that he'd received a text from

Andrea, which had come in half an hour ago. He clicked on it and read her message: COULDN'T GET A FLIGHT TODAY. NO NEED TO CALL. I'LL SEE YOU AT THE AIRPORT WHEN YOU PICK US UP THE DAY AFTER TOMORROW.

That's odd. Why wouldn't she want me to call her back? And what happened that made Andrea want to come home today? I hope it's nothing serious.

Tap! Tap! Tap! A knock sounded on Brandon's office door. "Come in," he called.

"I'm sorry to interrupt your lunch, Dr. Prentice, but a man just came in with a dog that needs immediate attention." Fran, his assistant, frowned. "Apparently, the poor animal got in a fight with another dog, and it looks like he's lost a lot of blood. The dog and his owner are in the first examining room."

Brandon snapped his lunch box shut and stood. "I'll be right there." For the time being, he needed to set his concerns for Andrea aside and concentrate on the emergency at hand. When he picked Andrea and her parents up at the airport at the expected time, he would find out what was going on.

Caldwell

Evelyn had watched their daughter walk straight out the door, and she could do nothing to stop her. "Oh, Ray, we've made a big mistake by not telling Andrea that she was adopted. She was really upset, and I'm afraid she might never forgive us for withholding the truth about her adoption." Evelyn grasped her husband's arm.

"I've often wondered when or if this might all come out. To tell you the truth, I'm glad the matter of Andrea's adoption is no longer hidden."

"Seriously? Even with the way she's acting toward us?"

He reached over and took hold of her hand. "She won't stay mad, Evelyn. Our daughter has a forgiving spirit, and once she's had time to deal with the information, she'll calm down and realize how much we love her. She's bound to know that we did what we felt was best and certainly didn't mean to hurt her."

"I hope you're right. To be honest, it is good to have the burden of the secret we've kept far too long finally lifted." Evelyn sniffed deeply. "I hope you are right, Ray, because if you're not, I fear the wonderful relationship we've established with Andrea might be over."

He shook his head. "I think you're worried about nothing, dear. Our daughter loves us, and she'd never turn her back on the parents who raised her."

A lump formed in Evelyn's throat, making it difficult to swallow. "I'm not so sure about that. Didn't you see the look of betrayal on our daughter's face when we admitted that she was adopted?"

"I saw her expression, but I think it revealed more confusion and hurt than betrayal." Ray gave her fingers a gentle squeeze. "Everything will be fine. You'll see. We just need to pray and ask God to work this all out."

Evelyn felt helpless and was unsure of how to fix the mess they'd created by putting off being honest with their daughter. She tried to put herself in Andrea's shoes. *If my folks had done something like this to me, I'd be pretty upset—especially when you count on your parents to be honest and trustworthy.* Evelyn dabbed at her eyes. *I will pray, but it won't stop me from being concerned. If we lose our daughter over this, I'll never forgive myself.*

Chapter 17

Boise

After a tearful goodbye with Aunt Karen and Vincent, Andrea followed her parents through the TSA line and placed her carry-on items on the conveyor belt. She was exhausted, and her throat hurt from crying so much. It still didn't seem possible that she'd been adopted. Andrea had felt disoriented ever since her parents had admitted the truth. It was as though she didn't know who she was anymore.

It had been difficult to engage in conversation with Mom and Dad since learning that she'd been adopted. Even now, as Andrea sat across from her parents waiting to board their plane for Seattle, Andrea chose to remain quiet. She needed time to think it all through before asking them more questions that had been floating through her mind. What city and state was she born in? Did they know who her biological parents were or where they lived?

Do I even want to know the answers to those questions? Andrea asked herself. *If I learn who the woman who gave birth to me is, should I try to contact her?* Andrea massaged her throbbing forehead. *I wonder if Vincent has tried to contact his biological parents. I should have thought to ask.*

She pulled out her cell phone, and sent her cousin a text message. A few minutes later, he responded. NO, I'VE NEVER FELT THE NEED TO SEEK OUT MY BIOLOGICAL MOTHER OR FATHER. I'VE ALWAYS FELT THAT THE PARENTS WHO RAISED ME WERE MY REAL MOM AND DAD, AND THAT'S BEEN ENOUGH FOR ME.

Andrea wasn't sure how to respond to that, so she texted him back with a few simple words: Take care, Vincent. We'll let you know when we get home. She paused and added one more thing: I'll keep you and your mother in my prayers as you deal with the loss of your dad.

Vincent's text was a thank-you, followed by: I'm praying for you and your folks too. I feel bad that I gave you the news of your adoption. Please give yourself some time before deciding on whether to search for your biological parents or not.

She swallowed around the thickness in her throat. Part of Andrea wanted to know who had given birth to her, but the thought of finding out was frightening too. Besides, at this point she didn't even know where to begin.

"We will begin boarding at this time, starting with those passengers who need a little extra time getting down the Jetway, followed by first class." The voice behind the loudspeaker drove Andrea's thoughts aside.

She told Vincent goodbye, and after all the preboarders had shown their boarding passes and started down the Jetway, Andrea boarded the plane behind her parents. They were in the bulkhead seats on the right side of the plane this time, but Andrea's seat was two rows back, on the left side. She would be sitting next to a stranger again, but that didn't matter. She would watch a movie and, with any luck, drown out all thoughts about her adoption.

Walnut Creek

"Today was a good day, jah?" Orley asked after he'd joined Lois on the back seat of their driver's van.

She smiled and nodded in response.

"Weren't you surprised at how many people came into our store?"

"We did have more than usual, but that's probably because of all the activities going on in our area right now. Fall is always a busy time of the year." Lois shifted on the seat and reached around to rub a sore spot on her back.

"Are you hurting?" Orley reached over to touch her arm.

"It's nothing serious. As you know, my back always tightens up if I'm on my feet too long."

"Jah, mine too," Orley responded. "But I can't complain. We sold a lot of merchandise today, and I was able to talk to that one English man who'd been struggling with his faith in God since his wife died."

"It was good he came in during a time when there were no other customers. Otherwise, you wouldn't have been able to talk privately with him."

"True."

"I'm sure a lot of business at our store will be for gift giving, since Christmas is on its way," Lois responded.

"You're right about that," their driver, Todd, spoke up. "Seems like this year Christmas decorations were up in other stores before Halloween was even over. What's up with that?"

"I have no idea," Orley said. "It's funny, though, how some folks want to move on so fast instead of enjoying the time that is right before them."

"I suppose it might be that some people are just too impatient," Lois interjected.

"It's true," Orley agreed. "A lot of people are in a hurry and are quite unhappy, especially when they have to wait for anything. For example: driving behind our buggies seems to bring out some impatient drivers, and some end up doing something foolhardy as they hurry down the road. In my opinion, our slow mode of transportation is nice and can help a person to unwind, refocus, and enjoy living more simply."

"I have to agree." Todd glanced over his shoulder briefly, then looked back toward the road. A few minutes later, he drove the van up Orley and Lois's driveway and shut off the engine.

"I'll go in the house and get supper started while you're paying for our ride," Lois said when she and Orley stepped out of the vehicle.

"Okay. Since we're both tired, let's keep things simple and have leftover soup and sandwiches."

"Good idea. *Danki* for the suggestion."

Lois made her way toward the house but stopped short when she reached the front lawn, where several letters and magazines had been scattered. "For goodness' sakes!" Although her back hurt more than it had on the ride home, she bent down and picked up each of the items. *I wonder why this stuff was not put in our mailbox, and how did it end up in the yard? We must have had some strong winds here today to blow it all over like that.*

Lois stepped onto the front porch and was surprised to see a few more pieces of mail along with a package. She entered the house and placed the mail that she had picked up on the entry table, then went back out to get the package and rest of the mail on the porch.

When she reentered the house, Lois gathered up the package and all of the mail and placed everything on the kitchen table. Preparing to open the package first, she looked at the return address and realized it was from her sister Rebekah. Curious as to what could be inside, Lois quickly opened the package. Inside, she discovered several handmade dish towels, two jars of apple butter that had been protected with bubble wrap, and a business-sized white envelope with a sticky note attached to the outside. It read: *I found this envelope inside our daed's Biewel, and since it had your name on it, I figured I should send it to you right away.*

I wonder why Dad would write my name on an envelope and put it inside his Bible. Lois took a seat at the table and tore the envelope open. Tears welled in her eyes as she read out loud what her father had written:

> *Dear Lois,*
>
> *Someday when I'm gone, I hope you will find this letter inside my Bible and have a better understanding of my actions toward you during the time you lived under my roof. After your mamm died, I put more responsibility on you as the oldest daughter. In addition to needing your help, I expected you to behave a certain way, but you were often rebellious. I spoke to you harshly sometimes, which I'm sure put a distance between us that has remained to this day. I want you to know that I'm sorry for not being the kind of father you needed, and I hope you will find it in your heart to forgive me for every poor decision I made in regard to you. Please know that I have always loved you, even though I didn't show it in the best way.*
>
> *With all sincerity,*
> *Dad*

Lois blinked as tears escaped her lashes and rolled down her hot cheeks. *Oh, Dad, I wish you were still alive so I could say to your face that I have forgiven you. The past is in the past, and it can't be changed, and even though I didn't agree with some of the decisions you made, I have always loved you. Oh, how I wish that I could tell you that. If only I'd had the chance to be with you prior to your heart attack, but unfortunately, I waited too long. You may not have even heard the words I spoke to you before your death.*

She sat several minutes, holding her father's letter, until the tears finally stopped. It was time to dry her eyes and take yesterday's soup from the refrigerator so it would be heated by the time Orley came inside.

Cleveland

Brandon stood in the baggage claim area, waiting for Andrea and her parents to arrive. He knew their plane had landed because she'd texted him a few minutes ago. He was excited to see her and still curious as to why she'd wanted to fly home the day after her uncle's funeral. *I wonder if her folks had also wanted to leave Idaho a day early. Guess I'll know soon enough.*

Brandon kept watch for passengers beginning to enter the baggage claim. No luggage had shown up on the conveyer belt yet, but it usually took anywhere from fifteen to twenty minutes for the luggage to arrive. Some travelers who'd been waiting near a different conveyor belt nearby hustled to grab their bags from a previous flight. Brandon glanced at them as his anticipation mounted for his future family to appear.

He was on the verge of pacing when several people pulling their carry-on bags entered the area. With heart pounding, he stood watching until Andrea and her parents came into view. Andrea walked ahead, while Ray and Evelyn, moving slowly, lagged behind. No doubt they were tired from the long day of travel, not to mention the stress and sorrow of attending Andrea's uncle's funeral, and the two days afterward.

As Andrea drew closer, Brandon smiled and waved.

Releasing what sounded like an uncontrolled sob, she ran and practically threw herself into his arms. As her sobs increased, he rubbed the small of her back. "What's wrong, Andrea? Surely you're not crying because you missed me so much after only being gone a few days."

"I—I did miss you, but my tears are for a different reason, which I can't talk about right now," Andrea whispered as she glanced over her shoulder in the direction of her parents.

"All right then, we can talk on the way to your house after I drop your mom and dad off at their place."

Andrea nodded, and as her parents approached, she moved over to the conveyor belt where the luggage had started to come down.

Brandon greeted Evelyn and Ray and said he would get their luggage.

"We just have one suitcase between us," Ray responded. "I can get that while you fetch Andrea's."

"Okay." Brandon looked at Evelyn and saw that her eyes were red. No doubt, she too had been crying. Was it because of her brother's death, or had something else caused Evelyn and Andrea's tears?

Apple Creek

After Brandon dropped Andrea's parents off at their home, Andrea pushed hard against the back of her seat and released a heavy sigh. It would be a relief to get home to her own place, where she wouldn't feel obligated to make idle conversation with her parents or fight the need to ask for more information about her adoption. She still hadn't decided what the best approach to this whole situation should be and needed more time to think about it.

As he pulled out of her parents' driveway and onto the road, Brandon reached across the seat and placed his hand on Andrea's arm. "Are you going to tell me what's going on now? Have you and your parents had some sort of falling out?"

"I guess you could call it that." Andrea clutched her purse straps so tight that it caused her fingers to ache. "The evening of my uncle's funeral, my cousin, Vincent, informed me that I had been adopted."

"Seriously? And you had no prior knowledge of that?"

"None whatsoever. I grew up believing the people I have called Mom and Dad were my biological parents." Andrea released her purse straps and locked her hands into fists. "You can imagine how shocked I was to learn that all these years my parents have been lying to me."

"Did you tell them that your cousin told you about it?" he asked.

"Yes, but I waited until the next morning to confront them, and I believe they were equally shocked to learn that I knew the truth about their deception." She paused and drew a few short breaths in through her mouth. "Not only was it a shock to learn that I was adopted, but my parents' deception has caused me not to trust them now. I mean, if they would withhold the truth about my adoption, what else haven't they told me?"

"Did they offer an explanation as to why they had kept your adoption a secret?"

"Mom said they couldn't find the right time or words to tell me. My dad said the longer they waited, the harder it became." Andrea groaned.

"What lame excuses. They had plenty of time and opportunities."

"Maybe when you were a child they felt like you weren't ready to hear that you'd been adopted."

"Are you defending them now?"

"No, of course not. I'm just thinking maybe you should try to understand."

"I understand all right. Two people I have loved and trusted since I was a baby didn't care enough about me to tell the truth. My cousin said he's known that he was adopted since he was a child."

"It would probably have been better if they'd told you sooner, but—"

"Can we not talk about this anymore? I just want to go home and get a good night's sleep so I can get up early tomorrow and go over to Colleen's to pick up Lady. I'm sure she's missed me while I've been gone."

"Okay, I understand. I'll drop you off, and we can talk again tomorrow." He touched her arm again. "Andrea?"

"Yeah?"

"Please remember that I love you very much, and I'm here for you when you're ready to talk more about this."

Andrea sagged against her seat. "Thanks, I appreciate that." It was good to know that she had her future husband's support, and tomorrow, when she told Colleen about her adoption, she felt sure that she would have her support as well.

She closed her eyes tightly, trying to keep tears from falling. *Now I just need to decide what my next step regarding all of this should be.*

Chapter 18

The following day, Andrea was up bright and early, eager to head for Colleen's to pick up Lady. Andrea hoped that getting back into her routine of painting, teaching piano lessons, and taking care of her house and cat would help get her mind off the fact that she had been adopted and was never told about it by her adoptive parents. If it weren't for Vincent, she would still be living in total unawareness of the truth. She had to wonder whether Dad and Mom would have waited indefinitely to confess the matter if the truth hadn't come out unexpectedly. Most likely, her folks would've said nothing and continued to live as though Andrea's adoption had never taken place.

She picked up her coffee cup and took a couple sips. *When I put myself in my mother's shoes, I feel certain that I would have told my child the truth. It's not fair to be my age and find out that I'm not really their biological daughter.* The whole thing hung over Andrea like a dark cloud about to burst open. If she had been informed of this when she was a child, she would have come to grips with it by now and might even have contacted her biological parents.

Andrea stared at her unappealing, mushy bowl of cereal and plucked a few frozen blueberries out of the bowl. *Maybe Colleen will have an idea about what I should do. She's not close to the situation, so her thinking will be much clearer than mine is right now. I'm sure that Colleen will be understanding and give me total support concerning my frustrating situation.* Andrea drank a few more swallows of coffee. *I'll need to do more praying, asking the Lord to give me wisdom in mending my relationship with my parents—especially since I'm hardly speaking to them at this point.*

Andrea's cell phone vibrated, and she picked it up to see who had called or sent her a text. Seeing that it was a text from Vincent, asking if she and her parents had gotten home okay, she slapped a hand against her forehead. *Oh great. I can't believe I forgot to let him know last night. It may have been late here, but Idaho is two hours behind Ohio, so I wouldn't have disturbed him by calling or sending a text.* The fact was Andrea's fatigue, coupled with the stress she felt, was the reason she'd forgotten to let him know. Hopefully, her mother had contacted Aunt Karen. *But if she did, then why is Vincent texting me now?*

Andrea responded to him: WE MADE IT BACK SAFELY, BUT IT WAS LATE WHEN WE GOT HOME. SORRY, I SHOULD HAVE LET YOU KNOW SOONER.

Another message came back: GLAD TO HEAR IT. TAKE CARE, AND LET'S STAY IN TOUCH.

YES, DEFINITELY. PLEASE LET AUNT KAREN KNOW WE MADE IT HOME TOO.

WILL DO.

After Vincent's last message, Andrea slipped the phone into her purse and cleared her dishes. She flushed the cereal down the disposal, but she managed to drink the rest of her lukewarm coffee before heading out the door.

"How was your trip?" Colleen asked after Andrea had entered her house and given her friend a hug.

"Sad, tiresome, and emotionally draining." Andrea poked her tongue against the inside of her cheek while exhaling.

"That makes sense. The death of a loved one is always difficult, not to mention the fatigue of traveling that far with a two-hour time change. You must be exhausted."

"Yeah."

Colleen gestured to the living room. "Let's go in there and take a seat. Hopefully, we'll have a few minutes to visit before my rambunctious two-year-old gets up."

Andrea followed her friend into the other room and collapsed on the couch. "Where's Lady? Is she hiding out somewhere?"

Colleen shook her head. "The last time I looked, she was asleep on Tyler's bed."

Andrea rolled her eyes. "That figures. I leave my cat for just a few days and already she's forgotten about me and has become your son's best friend."

"Oh, she missed you all right. The first twenty-four hours you were gone, Lady hid under Tyler's bed. I tried coaxing her out with food, and so did Shawn, but all we got out of her was a fierce-sounding *meow*. It took our little boy crawling under the bed with Lady to get her out." Colleen laughed. "They've been best buddies ever since."

Andrea smiled. "When I take Lady home, you may have to get a cat of your own so Tyler won't miss her so much."

"Maybe when he's a bit older and can help take care of a pet." Colleen brushed an unruly strand of hair away from her face. "I pretty much took care of all your cat's needs."

"Thank you for that." Andrea looked down at her hands, clasped tightly in her lap. "I need to tell you something." She lifted her gaze. "Needless to say, I was totally shocked when I found out this news."

"You look so serious. Is anything wrong?"

Andrea nodded. "The night of my uncle's funeral, I found out that I'd been adopted. My cousin, Vincent, let the cat out of the bag."

Colleen's eyes widened. "Are you serious?"

"Couldn't be more. I confronted my parents about it the next morning, and they admitted that they'd adopted me when I was a baby."

A little gasp came out of Colleen's mouth. "And this was the first time you knew anything about it?"

"That's right. They've been lying to me all these years." With both arms held firmly across her stomach, Andrea leaned forward. "You can only imagine how shocked I was—and still am, for that matter."

"I'm sorry, Andrea." Colleen patted her back and then spoke in a much-needed sympathetic tone. "Did your folks explain why they'd never told you about the adoption?"

"Their excuse was that they'd never found the right time or words to say it, and the longer they waited, the harder it became." Andrea looked upward, despairingly shaking her head. "I feel as though my identity has been taken from me, and I don't really know who I am anymore." Her eyes stung with unshed tears. "I can't help feeling betrayed by the parents who raised me. I'm upset by the fact that they kept something so important from me."

"I'm so sorry you've had to deal with this." Colleen's words were spoken in a gentle, soothing tone.

A few tears rolled down Andrea's cheeks. "How could so-called loving parents keep such a secret for so long from someone they claimed to love? Isn't love supposed to be based on respect, honesty, and trust?"

"Yes, but sometimes well-meaning people do things without thinking it through properly. Your parents may have thought they were doing you a favor by keeping your adoption from you."

Andrea's toes curled inside of her shoes. "Humph! It was no favor to me. How could it be, Colleen? In addition to feeling betrayed, I don't know who I am anymore."

"What are you going to do now? Will you try to find your biological parents?"

"I—I don't know. I haven't had time to think it through."

Colleen opened her mouth as if to say something more, when Tyler plodded into the room with Lady in his arms. When the cat spotted Andrea, it jumped down and leaped onto her lap. After a thorough licking of Andrea's hands, arms, and chin, Lady pushed against her and began to purr.

"You missed me, didn't you, girl?" Andrea stroked the cat's silky head. "I missed you too."

The fluffy animal finally settled down in her lap while continuing to purr. Andrea felt loved by her cat's affection, and it made her situation feel a bit more bearable.

Tyler plodded over to the couch and climbed up beside Andrea. Then he reached over and ran his hand down Lady's back. "Kitty cat."

She smiled and nodded. "It's nice to see you, little man. I hear that you liked having my cat around."

Tyler grinned before leaning his head against Andrea's arm and continuing to pet Lady.

"Let me get Tyler some breakfast, and then I'll be back so we can talk some more," Colleen said as she fussed with the barrette in her curly blond hair. "I have some coffee made. Would you like a cup?"

"That would be nice, but I really need to get home. I have a piano lesson to teach at noon and a few other things to get done before Brandon comes by this evening."

"I understand. Maybe we can have lunch together someday soon. You choose the place, and I'll buy."

"That'd be nice. I'll call you tomorrow, and we can set up a day." Andrea picked Lady up and stood. "I'll follow you to the kitchen to get Lady's carrier and food, and then I'll be on my way."

They all headed for the kitchen. After Andrea put Lady in her carrier, Colleen snapped her fingers and said, "Say, I have an idea."

Andrea tipped her head. "What's that?"

"Since you're struggling with this whole adoption thing, why don't you write a letter to the Dear Caroline newspaper column? Whoever the author is, she seems to have some pretty good advice."

Andrea gave a small laugh. "You really think I want to talk to some stranger about this?"

"You wouldn't be talking to her. It's just a letter, signed anonymously."

"Yeah, maybe. I'll think about it." Andrea moved toward the door. "Again, thanks for watching Lady. Whenever you need a sitter for Tyler, I'll return the favor."

Colleen's eyes brightened. "I might take you up on that offer."

Andrea grinned and headed out the door. At least some things in her life hadn't changed, such as the moral support and encouragement she'd received from her good friend.

Evelyn picked up the phone and dialed her sister-in-law's number. Karen answered on the second ring.

"Good morning, Karen. I hope I didn't wake you."

"No, I've been up for hours, looking for things to keep me busy. If my hands are occupied, then my brain doesn't have to work so hard."

"I understand." Evelyn paused and drank some of her mint-flavored herbal tea. "The reason I called is twofold. One, to let you know that we made it home okay, and two—to find out how you are doing."

"Yes, I heard from Vincent that you made it safely home. I guess he and Andrea had texted each other earlier this morning. And to respond to your second reason for calling—I'm doing as well as can be expected under the circumstances."

"I can't pretend to know what you're going through because I haven't lost my husband. However, I can relate to your pain in that I'm grieving the loss of my brother."

"Yes, I understand you two were quite close when you were children."

"We were, but we kind of grew apart after he left home and moved to Idaho."

"It's difficult to be away from family when you are miles apart, but I'm glad we can keep in touch via phone calls and visits in person whenever possible."

"True." Evelyn toyed with the idea of bringing up the situation with Andrea finding out about her adoption but figured Karen had enough to deal with right now and didn't need to hear her frustrations over the way Andrea had responded to her and Ray since she had learned the truth. This, in addition to the sadness Evelyn felt over losing Dave, was almost too much to bear. But with God's help and Ray's support, she would somehow get through it. All Evelyn could do at this point was pray for Andrea and hope that she would forgive them. Her desire was that their relationship could be restored and ultimately become stronger. If not, Evelyn didn't know what she would do, because she loved Andrea so much and couldn't imagine being estranged from her indefinitely.

Brandon glanced over at Duke sitting on the seat next to him and smiled. They were on their way to Andrea's place, and Brandon had picked up some burgers and fries for supper. Although it wasn't the healthiest meal, he looked forward to spending the evening with his future wife and hoped that his dog would get along with her cat. Since the animals hadn't been together for several days, it was possible that Duke might revert to being skittish around the cat.

"We'll know soon enough, buddy." Brandon reached across the seat and gave his dog's head a pat. Duke responded with a loud *Woof!*

A short time later, Brandon pulled his rig onto Andrea's driveway, turned off the engine, got out, and reached in the back seat for the takeout bag. Duke bounded out after him and made a dash for the front porch, barking all the way. Brandon took it as a good sign that the dog was eager to be here. The question was, had the excitement been about seeing Andrea or was it regarding her cat?

Brandon was about to knock when Andrea opened the door. "Ah, so that's the barking I heard." She pointed to his dog. "I see you brought Duke along."

"Yeah. Besides the fact that he started carrying on as soon as he saw me getting ready to leave the house, I figured it would be good to see if Duke and Lady will still get along."

"Good idea."

He stepped inside the house and handed her the sack. "Should we eat these burgers while they're still warm?"

"Of course."

Brandon noticed Andrea's quieter-than-normal demeanor. She hadn't even given him her usual welcoming smile. Was she still upset over her uncle's passing, or did it have more to do with the news she had received about having been adopted?

As Andrea and Brandon ate the burgers, fries, and cut-up veggies she'd contributed to the meal, she watched Duke and Lady lying side by side across the room. What a difference from the days when the poor dog trembled and hid at the mere sight of her cat. It seemed like a miracle that the cat and dog had not only been getting along but seemed like good friends.

"How did your day go?" Brandon asked. "Did you have any piano lessons to teach?"

"Just one, and it went okay." Andrea drank some of her cold apple cider.

"That's good. Did you talk to either of your parents?"

"No, and frankly, I dread seeing them at church this Sunday because I don't even know what to say."

Brandon reached for a few more fries and a couple of sliced cucumbers and carrots. "I assume you're still upset because they kept your adoption a secret from you."

"Of course I'm upset. If you were in my place, wouldn't you be?"

"I suppose, but—"

"When I went over to pick up Lady at Colleen's today, she gave me some food for thought."

"What was that?"

"Since I can't make up my mind what to do about all of this, Colleen suggested that I write a letter to Dear Caroline."

Brandon's forehead wrinkled. "Who's that? Don't think you've ever mentioned anyone by that name before."

"I doubt that it's her real name, but she uses it for the newspaper column she writes."

"Newspaper column?"

"Yes, people write to her with their problems, and she offers them advice."

He lifted his gaze to the ceiling. "I hope you're not actually considering that."

She shrugged. "I don't see how it could hurt. Maybe Dear Caroline will have some words of wisdom for me."

Brandon's neck bent forward, then stiffened back up. "You can do whatever you want, Andrea, but I think it's a dumb idea."

Andrea made no comment, but she wasn't about to admit to Brandon that tomorrow morning she planned to pen a letter to Dear Caroline regardless of what he thought.

Chapter 19

Walnut Creek

Lois stepped into the living room, where Orley sat reading the newspaper. "Sorry to interrupt, but I forgot to remind you about the errands we need to run tomorrow before heading to Memory Keepers, so we'll need to get an earlier start."

He looked up from the paper and smiled. "No problem. I remembered, and I'll make sure to set the alarm by my side of the bed so we can be up early, eat breakfast, and be ready in plenty of time before our driver gets here."

She pursed her lips. "I wish we had a place for the horse behind our store so we could take the horse and buggy instead of paying a driver to take us to work when it's too cold to ride our bikes."

"That would be nice, but there's no room for a barn there, and we can't leave the poor animal tied to a hitching post all day."

"True." Sometimes Lois wished their place of business was closer to home or even on the same property so that getting to and from work wasn't an issue.

"Do you think you'll have time on our day off this week to fix that leaking gutter near our front door?" Lois asked, changing the subject. It frustrated her when it rained and she sometimes got soaked by the stream of water that poured from that spot.

"Yep, but I think I'm going to need a part from the hardware store, unless I've got what I need in the barn to fix it. I'll check in the morning."

"Danki." Lois smiled. "I need to answer a couple of letters for my column now, so I'll let you get back to reading the paper."

"All righty then."

Lois returned to the kitchen and sat down at the table to read the letters she'd recently received for her Dear Caroline column. Some were about problems encountered with friends, relatives, or neighbors. One in particular had caught Lois's attention because, as she read the letter out loud, she could almost feel the frustration of the person from the words they had used:

> *Dear Caroline:*
>
> *I just discovered as an adult that I was adopted when I was a baby, and it's quite overwhelming. How do I cope with this unsettling news, and how can I ever trust my adoptive parents again, who should have told me this when I was a child?*
>
> *—Late Discovery*

Lois's lips pressed together as she tapped her pen against the tabletop, contemplating the best way to respond to this letter. When nothing came to her, she closed her eyes and prayed about it, asking God to give her the right words. At times like this, she felt inadequate to be offering advice, especially to people she had never met and didn't know personally. It made it even harder when they asked her questions about serious topics, like this one from someone who'd been adopted. What if she gave the wrong answer? What if the person who wrote the letter took her advice and things got worse?

After more contemplation and prayer, Lois opened her eyes and spoke the words as she wrote on a separate piece of paper:

> *Dear Late Discovery:*
>
> *No two people are the same. What's best for you will depend on your needs and circumstances. You may want to reach out to friends or family members for understanding and support. Since you are having trouble trusting your folks, hopefully you can find someone to speak to about this who would be objective. It's important that you decide what is comfortable and best for you.*

Lois held the pen above the paper. *Is that enough, or should I say anything more? This one seems harder than normal for me because I don't want to give a wrong answer about something so important.*

Orley entered the room, and Lois's thoughts came to a halt. "Are you still working on those letters?" he asked.

She nodded.

"I thought you'd be ready for *bett* by now." He pointed to the clock on the kitchen wall.

"I just have a few more to do," she responded. "Why don't you go on ahead to bed?"

"I'd rather wait for you." He pulled out a chair on the opposite side of the table and took a seat. "Is there anything I can help you with?"

"No, not really." She patted the two envelopes she'd placed on her left side. "As soon as I answer these, I'll be done for the night."

"Do you enjoy writing the Dear Caroline column?"

"Most of the time, but there are moments when I wonder if the advice I give is what people need to hear." She sighed deeply. "I feel inadequate to be telling others what I think they should do."

"You pray about it, don't you—asking God to give you the right words?"

Lois bobbed her head.

"If you write what you believe God has directed you to say, then your words are not inadequate."

She smiled. "Danki for reminding me of that."

"You're welcome." Orley pushed away from the table and stood. "I'll go brush my teeth and get ready for bed while you finish up here. Hopefully, you won't be too long. Tomorrow's a big day at the store since it'll be the first of November and we're having our 25 percent off everything sale."

"I haven't forgotten, and I'll join you shortly."

Orley came around to her side of the table, bent down, and gave Lois a kiss on the cheek. "See you soon."

Lois felt blessed to have such a loving, caring husband as Orley. After he left the room, she picked up her pen again to reply to the next letter addressed to Dear Caroline.

Apple Creek

The shrill, desperate-sounding cry of a baby woke Andrea. She sat straight up in bed and looked around, realizing that she was in her own room and must have been dreaming.

But it seemed so real. Andrea rubbed the corners of her eyes. *I saw a baby crying for its mother, but no one would pick it up.* She had never dreamed about a baby before. *Why now?* she wondered. *Could it have something to do with me having been adopted?*

Andrea's head jerked back when Lady jumped up on the bed and began meowing while licking her face.

"Okay, girl, I get the hint. You want to be fed, don't you?" She gently pushed the cat aside and climbed out of bed.

Lady jumped down too and continued meowing as she moved back and forth, rubbing Andrea's legs.

"You're sure persistent, aren't you? Well, just give me a few minutes." Andrea slipped her robe on and stepped into the slippers near her bed. She went over to the window to look out. Pulling back the curtain, she was surprised to see white flakes falling from the sky. "An early snowfall," Andrea murmured. "I wonder if that's an indication of a cold, snowy winter ahead."

She rubbed her arms briskly. "I hope not, and this snow had better not keep me from meeting Colleen for lunch later today."

Andrea thought about her and Brandon's wedding, which was now just three and a half months away. No doubt the weather would be cold and the ground white on Valentine's Day. The plan was for them to go to sunny Florida for their honeymoon, which would be nice. Andrea looked forward to being someplace where the weather was much warmer than Ohio.

The cat meowed and bumped against her leg while Andrea wondered how Brandon would do driving to work if the snow kept falling. The winter weather didn't seem to make a difference to him since he had a four-wheel-drive vehicle. Andrea wished she could look at the snow with no reservations, but it made her nervous at times—especially thinking of how bad the upcoming winter conditions could get.

She glanced down at Lady, who was now making circles around her legs. "Okay, you persistent little thing. Let's go to the kitchen."

A short time later, Lady lapped up her food while Andrea sat at the table, eating a piece of toast spread with chunky peanut butter and perusing the newspaper.

She sought out the Dear Caroline column, hoping there might be an answer to the letter she'd written. It had only been a little over a week since she'd mailed it, so Andrea wasn't surprised that there had been no reply. Besides, if Dear Caroline received a lot of letters, she might not have time or space in the paper to respond to all of them. Andrea figured some may even get tossed.

"Oh well," she said aloud, "I'll keep looking, and if I don't hear something within the next few weeks, I'll give up on Dear Caroline and go with plan B." She gave a quick shake of her head. "Whatever that is." Truth was, Andrea had no plan B. For the last two Sundays, she'd made excuses not to get together with her parents and hadn't even sat on the same pew with them during church. She needed to ask some important questions but wasn't ready to ask them just yet. Andrea wanted a little more time to think of everything she needed to know, and she'd been so stressed out that she'd barely begun to make a list.

Brandon had no more than pulled up to the veterinary clinic when his cell phone rang. He turned off the ignition and answered the call.

"Good morning, Son. I hope I didn't interrupt anything."

"No, Mom. I just got to work and haven't gone inside yet." He glanced at his watch and then at the snow as it stuck to the front windshield. "I have a few minutes now, or I can call you back during my lunch break if you want to talk longer."

"I don't want to bother you while you're eating. I just called to tell you that I ran into Andrea's mother at the store yesterday. She was pretty upset because Andrea has barely said more than a few words to her and Ray since they got home after attending the funeral of Evelyn's brother." There was a brief pause. "I felt so bad seeing the sadness in her eyes, and when I asked her what was wrong, she quickly changed the subject."

"I guess she didn't want to talk about whatever was bothering her." Brandon suspected Evelyn's sadness might be because of Andrea's recent and unexpected adoption discovery, but he didn't think it was his place to reveal this information to his mother.

He looked to his left when a car pulled in with its wipers going at fast speed. *Because of the weather, I wonder if the clinic won't be as busy today.* The snowflakes that had begun falling earlier this morning had thickened, and a couple of inches of snow covered the ground already.

"Sorry, Mom, but I need to cut this conversation short and get inside. Someone just pulled up to the building, and they're getting out of their vehicle."

"Oh, okay. I'll call you sometime this evening. Goodbye for now, Son."

"Bye, Mom." Brandon felt relieved when his mother hung up. He was fairly certain that she'd called hoping he would try to persuade Andrea to make amends with her parents. *But that's not my place, and Mom needs to let the Lord work things out*, he told himself. *If I start pressuring her to talk to her folks when she's not ready, she might pull away from me.* Brandon pushed his shoulders straight back as he opened the door and stepped out of his SUV. *If there's one thing I know for certain, I need to stay neutral in the situation with Andrea and her parents and, above all else, make sure that my future wife knows she has my love and support.*

Walnut Creek

"I'm sure glad the snow has let up," Andrea commented as she and Colleen sat at a table inside Rebecca's Bistro, where they had met for lunch. "This is one of my favorite restaurants, and I didn't relish the idea of canceling our plans."

Her friend nodded. "Me neither. The white stuff is pretty, but it can cause an awful mess on the roads and make driving hazardous."

"I know. If it had kept up the way it was when I first got up this morning, I probably would have called you and canceled our lunch date."

"I understand how nervous you get this time of year when the roads start to get slick." Colleen smiled and gestured to her apple, pecan, blue cheese salad with poppy-seed dressing. "I'm glad we didn't have to cancel, because this is so good. You should have ordered one too."

Andrea twirled her spoon around in the bowl of tomato basil soup setting on her place mat. "Your salad looks good, but I'm fine with a bowl of warm soup." She gazed out the window, then looked back at Colleen. "I haven't had much of an appetite lately."

"Because you're still fretting about the fact that you're adopted?"

"Yes. If I'd been told straight up when I was a child that my parents had adopted me, I could have accepted the idea. It's the fact that they kept it a secret that bothers me so much. My cousin was told when he was a child, which was why he assumed that I already knew about being adopted. He seemed surprised that I had no idea I'd been adopted all those years ago." Andrea blew on her soup and tasted it. The sweet and savory flavors balanced perfectly. "I've never felt so emotionally crushed—especially by the two people I love so dearly. I don't understand how parents who go to church every Sunday and call themselves Christians could lie to their only child."

Colleen leaned forward, resting one arm on the table. "They didn't really lie, my friend. Your parents simply chose not to mention that you'd been adopted."

Andrea's face tightened. "Which was wrong."

"Yes, it was," Colleen agreed, "but they apologized for that, right?"

Andrea nodded before releasing a sigh. "Even so, I'm still having trouble dealing with all of this, and I have so many unanswered questions."

"Have you met with your parents to ask those questions?"

"Not yet." Andrea paused for another bite of soup. "I have started a list, and I also took your advice and wrote a letter to the Dear Caroline newspaper column."

Colleen looked at Andrea and blinked several times. "Really? Did she respond?"

"Not yet, but I hope she will soon and that her words might give me a sense of direction." Andrea heaved another sigh. "Right now, I don't know which way to turn. I keep asking myself if I should try to find my biological parents or if that would be a mistake."

"What would keep you from searching for them? Is it because you don't want to hurt the parents who raised you?"

Andrea squeezed her eyes shut as she rubbed the bridge of her nose. "That's part of it, but there's something else to consider."

"Such as?"

"What if I did find the woman who brought me into this world, and she wanted nothing to do with me?" Andrea's chin quivered. "I don't think I could deal with the rejection."

"Try not to worry about that, and remember to keep praying about your situation."

"That's all I can do for now, but in the meantime, I'm struggling with the fact that I don't know who I really am, where I came from, or who my biological parents are."

Colleen offered her a playful smile. "You're my good friend, Andrea Wagner, who will soon be Mrs. Brandon Prentice."

"You don't understand. Since I found out I was adopted, part of me feels homesick for a place I've been but don't remember." Andrea took a drink and blotted her lips on the napkin. "When I look in the mirror, I don't recognize myself anymore."

Colleen lifted her gaze to the ceiling. "You're still the same person you always were."

"I guess so, but I can't help wondering why my birth mother gave me up. How could she have turned me over to complete strangers? If I had a child, I wouldn't give her up for anything in the world."

"There may have been extenuating circumstances. She may not have had any choice."

Andrea's gaze dropped to the table. "I have to know the reason, and I need to pursue this, no matter what."

Chapter 20

Apple Creek

A week later, as Andrea sat down to eat a cold sandwich for supper, she picked up the newspaper to read the Dear Caroline column. To her surprise, her question had been answered.

> *Dear Late Discovery:*
>
> *No two people are the same. What's best for you will depend on your needs and circumstances. You may want to reach out to friends or family members for understanding and support. Since you are having trouble trusting your folks, hopefully you can find someone to speak to about this who would be objective. It's important that you decide what is comfortable and best for you.*

Andrea sat quietly, mulling over Dear Caroline's response and trying to decide what she should do.

It's probably time for me to talk to my folks. I need to have some questions answered. Yesterday Andrea had finished her handwritten list. It was filled with what she thought was important to ask them about her birth mother. *I hope my parents will freely give me all the information that I am desperate to know. I'm also hoping they'll be honest with me now, because I truly want things to be better between us.* It was harder to trust them now, but Andrea wanted to give her folks a second chance.

She finished eating her meal and went to get the phone. If her mom and dad were home, she would go over there now.

Andrea's heart pounded as she made her way up the porch steps of her parents' house. She had called earlier to see if she could come by this evening. Mom had sounded pleased until Andrea mentioned that she wanted to talk about her adoption. Then her mother had cooled off a bit and seemed hesitant until Andrea pushed the issue. Now that she was here, she hoped it would go well, because she had considered the risks and weighed all the pros and cons and had come to the place that she felt almost desperate to know the circumstances of her adoption. It was time to get started on this new and important venture.

Andrea's father answered the door after she knocked. He stood tall and welcomed her with a hug. "Come on in. Your mother will join us in the living room in a few minutes. She's getting some brownies ready to serve that she baked when she heard you were coming over."

"Okay." Andrea followed him into the other room and seated herself on the couch. Her mother knew she loved brownies, and Andrea wondered if she'd made them as some sort of peace offering to show how sorry she was for keeping the truth from her all these years.

As Dad took a seat in his favorite chair, Andrea opened her purse and got out the list she'd created. *I really want to learn something about my birth mother today and have a better understanding of why she gave me up for adoption.*

Mom entered the room, carrying a plate of perfectly shaped brownies. Her parents' home was warm and cozy, which felt inviting, but tonight that feeling was reinforced by the fragrance of freshly brewed coffee and just-baked chocolate permeating the air.

"Hello, Andrea. It's so nice to see you." Mom smiled and placed the plate on the coffee table in front of Andrea, along with three napkins. "Please, help yourself."

I hope you're not going to try and butter me up with something sweet to eat. "Maybe later, after we've talked awhile," she mumbled.

"Oh, okay." Her mother took a seat in the rocking chair and folded her hands. She glanced briefly at Andrea's father and then back at her. "I see you have a piece of paper. Would that be a list of questions you want to ask us?"

Andrea nodded.

"Well, fire away," Dad spoke up. "We'll answer all your questions to the best of our knowledge." He looked at Mom. "Right, Evelyn?"

She gave an affirming nod. "Of course."

Andrea lifted the paper she held and cleared her throat. "I'd like to start by asking if you know or have at least met my biological mother and father."

"I'm sorry, but we never met either of your birth parents." Andrea's father shifted in his chair as though trying to find a more comfortable position. "It was a closed adoption, so we don't even know the name of the woman who gave birth to you."

Andrea's shoulders drooped as she lowered her head. "I just thought..." Her voice trailed off. If it was a closed adoption, and they didn't know the woman's name, how was she ever going to find out who had put her up for adoption?

Andrea looked down at her paper, realizing that most of her other questions would not get an answer. *This isn't going so well—not at all like I had hoped it would.*

Lifting her head, Andrea posed the next question. "Where were you living when you adopted me?"

"Right here in Ohio," her mother replied. "We went to Pennsylvania to pick you up at the hospital."

"Wasn't my birth mother there too?"

"If she was, we were never introduced to her," Dad responded. "A woman from the adoption agency was there, and once we signed the official paperwork, we took you home with us."

I wonder if my biological mother is from Pennsylvania. If so, maybe she's still living there. "So my biological mother could have still been at the hospital when they gave me over to you?" Andrea pressed a hand against her abdomen.

"Well, I. . .umm. . .suppose, but if she was, no one said so." A pink flush appeared on Mom's face and neck. Was she hiding something or just flustered from talking about this?

"So you have no other information to give me?" Andrea's ribs grew tight, restricting her breath.

"No, not really," Dad spoke up. "It was pretty much cut and dried."

She blinked several times, trying to process this. *Why wouldn't they have asked my birth mother's name—maybe even asked to meet her? I would think they would have wanted to know as much about her as possible. What if she was a criminal, a drug addict, or both?* Andrea's scattered thoughts danced in her head as she stared at her list. *My parents make it seem as though they want to help me, but I'm not feeling helped at all.*

Andrea's frustration mounted as she looked at her mother again. "Surely you must know something about the woman who brought me into this world but chose not to raise me. I can't believe you would have adopted a child without knowing anything about the infant's background or parents."

"We only know that it was a young, unwed mother who was not in a position to raise a child." This answer came from Andrea's father.

"Seriously? That's all you can tell me?" Andrea heard the tension in her own voice. *I'm not gaining anything at all.*

"Please stop pushing, Andrea. We've told you all that we know." Tears gathered in Andrea's mother's eyes and dribbled down her crimson cheeks.

At least you know who your real parents are. Andrea shoved the piece of paper back in her purse and stood. "Fine then. I'll find out what I need to know on my own." *I can't believe I let myself get my hopes up for this.*

"Where are you going? Don't you want to have a brownie and talk with us some more?" Although Mom's pleading voice would have normally prevented Andrea from leaving, she headed for the front door, calling over her shoulder: "I can't talk about this right now."

When Andrea got into her car a few minutes later, she let her head fall forward and sobbed. This meeting with her parents hadn't gone well, and not one thing had been resolved. Andrea knew as little about her biological mother now as she had when she'd walked through her parents' front door. She didn't know how or where to begin, but Andrea made up her mind that no matter how long it took, she would find out who her birth parents were.

"Andrea doesn't believe us," Evelyn sobbed from where she still sat in her rocking chair with Frisky in her lap. "If we'd only prayed about this and trusted the Lord to help us to tell our daughter the truth years ago. We made a horrible mistake by not telling Andrea when she was a child, and now we've lost her and may never get her back."

"I must admit there have been times through the years when my faith hasn't been the strongest. And I should've been a better spiritual leader in our home. I think it's time for both of us to draw closer to the Lord. There are times when I feel like we're basically warming a pew on Sundays and giving a small tithe. That isn't enough." Ray got up from his chair and walked across the room. Then he picked up the dog, set him on the floor, and pulled Evelyn to her feet. "We haven't lost her. She's just upset and frustrated because we did not have the answers she sought."

"But you saw her reaction. She walked out of the house without saying goodbye or even eating one of my brownies."

He gently patted her back and spoke to her like one would to a distraught child. "Eating a brownie would not have changed anything, dear."

Evelyn sniffed. "Yes, it would. It would have given me the reassurance that she's not mad at me."

"I don't believe she's angry—just disappointed and hurt. We need to give her more time and be supportive."

Evelyn pulled back and swallowed hard as she looked up at Ray. "How much time?"

"As long as it takes."

"How can we be supportive if she won't talk to us? Our daughter would barely look at us while she was here."

"I'm aware of that."

"So what are we supposed to do—sit here and twiddle our thumbs while we wait for her to forgive us?"

Ray shook his head. "We can pray and help Andrea search for her birth mother."

Evelyn's eyes opened wide, and her mouth dropped open. "Are you kidding?"

"No, I'm not. It's our duty to try and help her." He paused. "We need to trust the Lord that this will all work out."

"I'll try." Evelyn's voice trembled as she sank into her chair. "If she connects with the woman who bore her, we might lose Andrea for good."

"That's negative thinking. We raised Andrea. She can't erase all the years we've spent together and all of the things we've done with and for her." Ray spoke in such a tone of assurance that Evelyn almost believed him. Even so, her heart was filled with doubts. If they lost their only child because they hadn't told the truth in the first place, Evelyn would never forgive herself.

I'm glad my husband was honest about his lack of faith, and I need to be too. Another thought popped into her head. *If Ray and I could find Andrea's biological parents, would she be grateful and forgive us then?*

Brandon was on the verge of dozing off in his recliner when Duke started barking and ran for the front door. He sat up and rubbed his gritty eyes, wondering what all the commotion was about.

"What's the matter, boy? You need to go out?"

Arf! Arf! Arf!

"Okay, okay. . .I'm coming." Brandon got up, yawning, shuffled toward the front door, and turned on the porch light. He had put in a long day at the clinic and was more tired than usual this evening. And he couldn't help being irritated, because he'd let Duke out half an hour ago, yet here the dog was asking to go outside again. *Maybe he drank more water than he should have.*

When Brandon opened the door, nearly tripping over Duke, he was surprised to see Andrea standing on the porch. Her face looked puffy, and the whites of her eyes were red.

"What's wrong, sweetie? Have you been in an accident? Are you hurt?"

She shook her head and gulped on a sob.

"Come in. Get out of the cold." Brandon took Andrea's hand and guided her into the house. Once inside, he led her to the living room, and they sat together on the couch. Duke, who obviously had no need to go outside, sat in front of the couch with his tail wagging.

Brandon gave Andrea a few minutes to compose herself before he asked her again what was wrong.

"I. . .I just came from seeing my folks. I went there to ask if they knew who my biological parents were, and they said no." She paused and drew a shaky breath. "They said it was a closed adoption and that they'd never met my birth mother and don't know her name."

"I'm sorry, Andrea." He reached over and clasped her cold hand.

"I'd really hoped that when I went over there today, they'd be able to answer most of the questions I'd brought with me." She looked over at him and squinted her eyes. "I think they might have lied to me about that."

"For what reason?"

"They're afraid if I know who she is I will make contact with her."

"Would that be so bad?"

"They might think I'd like her better than them. I don't know." Andrea shrugged. "Maybe. I suppose knowing who she is could turn out bad for me."

"How so?"

"My birth mother no doubt has made a life for herself. She could be married and have children that she didn't choose to adopt out." Tears rolled down Andrea's puffy cheeks. "She obviously didn't love me, or she wouldn't have given me to strangers."

"It's hard to say." Brandon spoke softly and chose his next words carefully. "There are many reasons why a mother might give up her baby—one being that she may have been young and single, unable to care financially or physically for a child."

Andrea lowered her head. "It's too late for me to go back to my mom and dad's place tonight, but I do need to talk to them again soon and apologize for leaving in a huff and not even bothering to say goodbye." She looked at Brandon again. "When I left their house, I made a decision."

"Oh? What was it?" he asked.

"Even if the parents who raised me don't want me to, I'm going to search for my birth mother." Andrea swiped a hand across her face. "If I'm able to locate her and she doesn't want to see me or make me a part of her life, at least I won't spend the rest of my life wondering who she is and what she's like. The truth is, I have a lot of questions for her that I'd like to ask."

Chapter 21

Walnut Creek

"I think it's time for me to buy a new coin purse. This is no good anymore." Lois held hers up.

Orley glanced over at her from the driver's seat of their carriage. "What's wrong with it?"

"The clasp is broken, and I lost some of my money."

"When did that happen?"

She shrugged her shoulders. "I'm not sure. I first noticed it after supper when I was going to leave a tip for our waitress at the restaurant in Berlin. It was after you left the table to use the restroom."

"I'm confused. Why would you feel the need to leave a tip when I had already left one?"

A warm flush crept across Lois's cheeks as her chin dipped down. "I didn't think it was enough."

"Oh, so now you think your husband is a cheapskate, huh?"

"Not at all. The young woman waiting on our table was so attentive to our needs, and I thought she deserved a little extra."

"I see. Did you have enough in your coin purse?"

"There was a five dollar bill, which I gave her, but that's all I had. Apparently, the rest of my bills, plus the coins, must have fallen out sometime today; maybe when I went to the post office for stamps."

"It was nice of you to give the extra tip to our waitress." Orley reached over and patted her arm. "I'll give you some money tomorrow so you can buy a new coin purse."

She smiled. "Danki. You're such a kind, thoughtful man. I did well when I married you."

"I'm the one who did well. I couldn't ask for a better fraa." Orley spoke in such a sincere tone it caused Lois to tear up. There were times when she didn't feel deserving of his love.

Apple Creek

After Brandon brought Duke in from his nightly walk, he took a seat in his recliner and picked up his cell phone to make a few calls. The first would be to his mother in response to the message she'd left him earlier today when he'd been at the clinic. If it had been an emergency, he would have called sooner, but the message she'd left had been about the rehearsal dinner, which was still nearly three months away.

"But that's my mom." Brandon chuckled. "She's a stickler for details and always ahead of the game."

Duke's ears perked up, and he gave out an *Arf!*

Brandon rolled his eyes. "I wasn't talking to you, buddy, but that's all right."

The dog cocked his head to one side before leaping onto his owner's lap.

"You always want my attention, don't ya, boy?" Brandon scratched behind Duke's ears and smiled when the dog burrowed against his hand.

"If you were a cat, I bet you'd be purring real nice right now." Brandon continued to scratch Duke's ears, alternating with a few pats on the animal's head. It wasn't long before Duke's eyes closed, and he conked out on Brandon's lap.

Brandon reached into his shirt pocket and pulled out his cell phone. It was time to call Mom. He wasn't surprised when she answered on the first ring. Apparently, she'd been waiting for him to return her call.

"Hey, Mom. How's it going?"

"It's going fine here. I've been working on my list for the rehearsal dinner and needed to ask you a few questions. But before we get into that, I wanted to tell you something."

"Sure, Mom. What's up?"

"I ran into Andrea's mother today at the styling salon. I was totally surprised by what she told me."

"Oh? What did Evelyn have to say?"

"She said that she and Ray adopted Andrea when she was a baby and that Andrea found out about it while attending her uncle's funeral. Did you know about this, Son?"

"Andrea told me after she and her folks got home from Idaho."

"How come you didn't mention it to me or your dad? Why the big secret since the news was out?"

Brandon cringed. He felt like a young boy getting a reprimand from one of his parents.

"It wasn't my place to tell. I figured if Andrea or her parents wanted others to know, they would do the telling."

"I suppose that makes sense." His mother's tone was a little softer now. "Evelyn said Andrea is quite upset and doesn't understand the way her parents feel about this."

"Andrea's hurting too, Mom. Learning that she'd been adopted was a real shock. She's trying to work through it and deal with her emotion, but it's difficult."

"I understand that, but I would think that Andrea could be more understanding of Evelyn and Ray's feelings."

"I would think her parents could be more understanding as well, since they should've been honest with her from the beginning."

"Of course, you're right, but still. . ."

Brandon yawned. "I put in a long day today, Mom. Can we drop this topic and talk about the rehearsal dinner some other time?"

"All right, but let's not put it off too long. It's important to get all the details ironed out before the big day arrives."

"I know. I'll call you in a few days."

"All right then. Good night, Son."

"Night, Mom. Tell Dad I said hello."

"I will."

After Brandon ended the conversation with his mother, he wanted to see how Andrea was doing, so he punched in her number.

"Hi, sweetie," he said after she picked up. "Just wondered how your day went and if you're doing okay."

"No lessons to give today, and I didn't do any painting either, but I did call my mom and apologized for last night," she replied.

"That's good. I'm sure it must have made you both feel better about things."

"I felt better for clearing the air with her but not better about learning that I was adopted." Andrea paused, and he heard her draw in a deep breath. "I think I'm having an identity crisis. It's like I don't know who I am anymore."

"I know exactly who you are, Andrea. You're the woman I love and am planning to marry in a few short months. That hasn't changed, and neither have you. You're the same person now as you were when we first met."

"I know, but. . ." Her voice trailed off. "It's hard to explain, and unless you had also been adopted, I wouldn't expect you to understand. It's hard not to focus on the differences between me and my adoptive parents."

"There aren't that many differences, Andrea. All three of you are Christians who enjoy many of the same things."

"True, but I'm musical, and neither of my parents plays any kind of an instrument."

Brandon was about to comment when Andrea spoke again. "And think about it. . . I don't look anything like either of them. My hair is auburn, and Mom's is light brown. Dad's hair is blond with a little gray mixed in. Our eye color doesn't match either. Mine are brown, and theirs are both blue. I never thought much about it till I discovered that I was adopted, but the evidence has been right there in front of me the whole time."

"Lots of children don't have the same hair or eye color as their parents. Those characteristics can be passed down from grandparents, aunts, uncles, or—"

"Not in my case, though. I don't look like my parents because I have none of their blood flowing through my veins."

Brandon wanted to tell Andrea that she had been fixating on all of the unimportant details, but he thought better of it. No point in giving her something more to be upset about. Instead, he said, "Despite the differences between you and your adoptive parents, the one thing that has always rung true to me is their undying love for their daughter. You know that, right?"

"Yes, but they didn't love me enough to tell me the truth."

"I can't begin to understand all their reasons for that, but we all make mistakes that we wish we could undo. I'm sure keeping your adoption from you was one of the things they deeply regret."

"I believe you're right." She released a yawn. "Sorry about that. I didn't get much sleep last night, and I spent most of today cleaning and organizing some things around here, so I'm pretty tired."

"That's understandable, and on that note, I think I will say goodnight and let you go. We'll talk again soon, though."

"Okay. Thanks for calling and for your support. I love you, Brandon."

"Love you too. Sleep well."

"You also. Bye for now."

When Brandon clicked off his phone, he closed his eyes and said a prayer for his bride-to-be. *Dear Lord, please give Andrea a sense of calm, and help her to remember to focus on the people in her life who love her so much.*

"You seem much calmer this evening than you were last night after Andrea left in a huff," Ray commented when he carried his supper dishes over to the sink where Evelyn stood, rinsing her own dishes.

"I've felt a little better since Andrea called me this morning to apologize for her abruptness last night."

Ray handed Evelyn his dishes and placed both hands on her shoulders. His gentle touch made her relax. "I believe Andrea still loves us, Ray."

"Of course she does. From the time we brought her home from the hospital, we've nurtured our daughter and showered her with our love and attention." He began massaging her shoulders. "Remember how excited we got when Andrea took her first few baby steps?"

"Our daughter was unwavering, even when she fell." Evelyn smiled. "I can still picture Andrea pulling herself up in front of the couch and taking a few more steps with a determined look on her pretty little face."

"Yeah." Ray took a few dishes from the sink and placed them in the dishwasher. "Whenever Andrea has wanted something, she's always gone after it until she accomplished her goal."

"And now she has a new goal—to find her birth parents." Evelyn's shoulders sagged. "Truthfully, I can't say that I'm excited about her newest goal."

"Are you afraid we're going to lose her?"

She shrugged. "I hope not. Our bond has always been strong. My biggest concern is that if she's not able to locate her biological parents, she'll feel a sense of emptiness and defeat." Evelyn sidestepped Frisky and added a few more dishes to the dishwasher. "My other concern is that Andrea may find her birth parents and discover that they want nothing to do with her. I believe that would upset her as much, or more, as learning that she was adopted."

Ray waited until Evelyn had filled the dispenser with the dishwasher liquid, then shut the dishwasher door and turned on the machine. "It will be a risk for Andrea to take, but we'll be here to help her deal with whatever the outcome will be."

Evelyn nodded. "Yes, and I intend to assist our daughter in her endeavors to locate the woman who chose to give her away nearly thirty-three years ago."

He looked at her pointedly. "How exactly do you plan to go about that?"

"I'm not sure yet, but the first thing I plan to do is tell Andrea the name of the adoption agency we used."

"Let's hope the place is still in business. Remember, it's been almost thirty-three years."

Evelyn blinked. "Oh dear... I hadn't even thought of that possibility. I'll do some investigating in the morning."

It was well past her usual bedtime, and Andrea had been lying under the covers for over an hour, listening to her cat's gentle purring from the foot of her bed, while trying to relax. She'd muted her cell phone so she wouldn't be interrupted, but the quiet of the evening had not evaporated Andrea's scattered thoughts. She'd felt a bit better after talking to Brandon earlier, but now the doubts she'd felt before had crept back in.

Another twenty minutes went by, and when sleep still wouldn't come, Andrea got up and plodded out to the kitchen to fix a cup of calming herbal tea. Once it was brewed, she took her cup and went to her art studio, which she also used as a home office. Taking a seat in front of her desk, Andrea booted up her computer.

A short time later, she was online, looking at a website on how to find a person's birth parents. Since Andrea had called her mother this morning and apologized for leaving so abruptly and being curt with them last night, she now felt ready to start a new chapter in her life as she began the search for her biological parents.

The first article Andrea found described how to find birth parents involved in either an open or closed adoption. An open adoption would obviously make it easier, but Andrea was not without hope—not yet, anyway. *Leave no stone unturned*, she reminded herself. *I won't quit until I've done everything I can to find my biological parents.*

Andrea scrolled until she came to the closed adoption information.

Right off the bat was a reminder that a person looking for his or her birth parents needed to be prepared for both a good or a disappointing outcome.

Andrea paused to ponder that fact. *If I located my biological mother, how would I respond? Would I have the courage to contact her, and if so, what if she didn't want to meet me?*

She pivoted her chair and reached for the cup of lavender-mint tea she'd brewed thirty minutes ago. One sip and she frowned. It was barely lukewarm.

Andrea got up and went to the kitchen to heat the tea in the microwave. While it heated, she grabbed two peanut butter cookies and a napkin. Once the tea was the desired temperature, Andrea returned to the desk in her art studio. Continuing to read from the website she'd found, she focused once again on the information about closed adoptions.

"Step one," Andrea said aloud. "Collect information." She scratched her head. "How am I supposed to do that? I don't have any information."

She scrolled a little farther and read some questions to answer. "What is the year, month, and date of your birth?" That was easy enough since Andrea knew she'd been born on March 21 and would be turning thirty-three in a few months. She also knew, according to what her parents had said the other night, that the adoption had taken place in Pennsylvania. *But what city and which adoption agency?* Those were questions she had forgotten to ask. Andrea wrote them down on the notepad next to her computer. "Okay, what's next?"

"Step two: Use a mutual consent adoption registry." After reading that the site mentioned was a common format for adoptees, birth parents, and siblings to register their information in the hope that it would match with another searcher, Andrea jotted down the name of the website.

She paused for a drink of tea and went on to read the third step, which was DNA matching. To go this route would mean that Andrea would need to order a DNA kit from one of the major DNA services like MyHeritage, AncestryDNA, FamilyTreeDNA, or 23andMe. She wrote the names of those sites down as well.

Step four: Hire an adoption detective.

"I'll bet a detective would be expensive." Andrea frowned, but she wrote it down anyway, marking it as a last resort.

She leaned back in her chair and breathed a lingering sigh. *I can see that searching for my biological parents could take a lot of my time and energy. How am I going to do all those things listed and continue with my plans for a wedding?*

Chapter 22

As Thanksgiving Day approached, Andrea found herself wondering what her biological parents might be doing to celebrate the holiday. *Do they live in Pennsylvania, where I was born? Are they married? Do they have other children?*

To take her mind off things, Andrea decided to work on making up the dessert for tomorrow's holiday meal. The recipe she enjoyed using was foolproof, always tasted good, and was not that difficult to make.

She pulled out the apples from the refrigerator and noticed Lady coming into the kitchen. "Hello, pretty kitty."

The cat swished her tail as she strolled over to her water dish and began to drink.

Andrea got out the rest of the items needed to prepare the apple pie. It wasn't long before Lady was underfoot and meowing up at her. "What's up, pretty kitty? Are you hungry?" Andrea looked at the time and realized that it had been a while since the cat's last feeding. "Okay, okay, I'll take care of you first."

Andrea picked up the cat's empty dish and filled it with the proper amount of dry cat food. Lady stayed right by Andrea's feet. "You act as though you haven't eaten all day, but we both know that you ate this morning." She set the bowl next to Lady's water dish. "Now I need to get back to making the pie."

Andrea peeled and sliced all the apples she had bought the other day. The fruit looked so good, she ate a couple slices before mixing in the rest of the pie-filling ingredients. When that was finished, she went to the refrigerator and got the chilled pie dough to roll out. Once the pastry, filling, and the last shell were in place, Andrea's creative side kicked in, and she enjoyed fluting the edges of the crust to look fancy.

Living at home as a child, Andrea had been intrigued with the pictures in her mother's cookbooks and had learned to cook well by the time she was a teenager.

Andrea put the chilled ball of dough on the floured surface and used the rolling pin to smooth out the crust and make it the correct thickness. She wanted this pie to be just right for Thanksgiving.

Andrea's mom and dad had also been invited to join her and Brandon at his parents' house for Thanksgiving. It would be the first time they'd all been together for a meal since their dinner out, when she and Brandon had announced their engagement.

Andrea wondered if the topic of her adoption would come up and if Brandon's parents even knew about it. Most likely he had told them, or maybe Mom had said something since she and Jennifer were friends.

She placed the evenly rolled dough inside the pie pan and poured the sliced apples that had been mixed with cinnamon, sugar, and butter on top. *Perhaps Brandon hasn't mentioned my adoption to his folks. He may think it's my place to do the telling if I choose to.* Her lips compressed. *I hope he hasn't said anything, because I'd like to get through Thanksgiving without any additional stress.* Thinking about the need to find her biological parents was one thing, but talking about it brought Andrea's feelings to the surface. The last thing she wanted to do was break down and cry in front of her future in-laws. If that should occur, Andrea's mother would probably do some crying of her own, which would make it even more embarrassing.

I'd better take my lavender-scented roller bottle with me tomorrow, Andrea reminded herself. *I may need it in order to stay calm if any stressful topic is brought up.*

Forcing herself to focus on the task at hand, Andrea covered the apple filling with a second neatly rolled crust, fluted the edges, and placed it in the oven, closed the door, and set the timer. Soon the kitchen would be filled with a wonderful aroma, which would make it difficult not to try a piece once the pie was done and had cooled sufficiently. But Andrea would restrain herself and satisfy her sweet tooth with a pumpkin-flavored protein snack bar and a cup of apple-cinnamon tea. Following that, she had some more adoption research to do.

Walnut Creek

"Business has been rather *langsam* today," Orley commented as he and Lois worked together, opening four boxes they'd taken from the storage room. Each one was filled with some newly found items they hoped to sell. Now that yard sales were few and far between because cold weather had set in, there wasn't a lot left in the storage area to pull out and add to their displays in the store.

"Things may be slow right now, but it'll be a different story on Friday when many people will be out doing their Christmas shopping," Lois responded.

"Good point." Orley held an antique washboard in his hands. "I wonder if this might be of interest to somebody."

Lois tilted her head from side to side as she studied the object. "I suppose it could lend a nostalgic touch to someone's washroom, but I doubt anyone would be inclined to use it." She smiled. "I'm certainly grateful for my diesel-generated ringer washing machine. It gets our clothes much cleaner and is easier on a person's back than bending over a galvanized tub, scrubbing clothes against a washboard like our ancestors used in the past."

"Do you wish you had a machine that would dry our clothes, like most English people use?" he questioned.

"I don't mind hanging things out to dry—especially during nice weather. When I bring them back inside after they're dry, everything smells so nice and fresh."

"That it does, and I always appreciate climbing into bed with clean-smelling sheets."

The bell above the front door jingled. Lois glanced toward the front and was surprised to see Jeff Davis enter the store.

Orley must have seen him too, for he stood up and hurried forward to greet him.

Lois clambered to her feet as well and joined them.

"It's sure good to see you, Jeff." Orley shook the young man's hand.

"It's great seeing you two as well." Jeff gave Lois a hug. "How have you both been?"

"Getting along just fine," Orley replied, and Lois nodded.

"Glad to hear it. Your names come up in Rhonda's and my conversations quite often."

"We talk about you as well." Orley gave Jeff's back a couple of thumps. "So how are things with you, Rhonda, and your little girl these days?"

"Good." Jeff's eyes brightened. "Our daughter is getting quite spoiled, what with all the attention Emily gets from the people who stay at our inn."

"We'll have to drop by and see her again one of these days," Lois interjected.

"How about tomorrow?" Jeff gave a broad smile. "I know it's a last-minute invitation, but if you don't have other plans, Rhonda and I would like to have you join us for Thanksgiving dinner."

"Orley and I were going to have a quiet dinner, just the two of us, but being part of your celebration would be lovely," Lois was quick to say. "We wouldn't want to intrude on your family gathering, however. I'm sure you'll have a full house."

Jeff shook his head. "Not really. My dad and Rhonda's mom will be there, but her siblings and mine all have other plans."

"What about guests at the inn?" The question came from Orley.

Jeff turned his palms upward. "Only two couples are staying with us right now, and they both have plans to spend tomorrow with family members in the area." He looked steadily at Orley and Lois. "Please say yes. We'd really enjoy having you as our guests."

Orley looked at Lois, and when she nodded, he smiled and said, "Name the time, and we'll be there."

"We'll eat at two, but feel free to come anytime after noon."

"We shall definitely come a bit early," Lois said. "That way I can help Rhonda with whatever needs to be done in preparation for the meal. I'd also like to bring something. Perhaps a green bean casserole or a pumpkin pie?"

"Either one, or both, is fine." Jeff winked at Lois. "You're such a good cook, and I'm certain we'll enjoy whatever you bring."

Her face warmed at the compliment. "Please tell your dear wife that I shall bring the casserole as well as a pie."

"Sounds great. Rhonda will be glad to know that you're coming." Jeff turned toward the door. "I'd better get going. I promised to pick up a few things at the store before going home."

"We'll see you tomorrow." Orley shook Jeff's hand again, and Lois gave another hug. The thought of spending Thanksgiving with the Davises had put a spark of joy into her day and wiped away the fatigue she'd felt earlier. Lois looked forward to visiting with the adults tomorrow, but more than that, she could hardly wait to see sweet little Emily again.

When Orley guided their horse and buggy up to the hitching rail outside the Davises' beautiful country inn, a sense of joy swelled in Lois's soul. Jeff and Rhonda had come a long way since she and Orley had first met the couple, who'd been struggling in their marriage. So much had happened since then—the Davises had committed their lives to the Lord, their marriage had been restored, they'd purchased this inn, and Rhonda had given birth to a sweet baby girl. It almost seemed like the couple now lived the perfect life.

But that can't be true, Lois reminded herself. *No one's life while living on this earth is perfect. There will always be some sort of trouble to face.* Lois wondered how those who did not have a personal relationship with Christ dealt with the unpleasant and sometimes tragic situations they had to face. At least those who were Christians could go to God in prayer during difficult times and seek spiritual and emotional counsel through others who were like-minded and had put their trust in Jesus. Lois didn't know what she would have done while going through various trials and disappointments over the years without her faith in God and the ability to give her troubles to Him through prayer and Bible reading.

"Sure is nice that Jeff had a hitching rail put on their property soon after they purchased this place." Orley's comment drove Lois's thoughts aside.

"Jah," she agreed. "It's helpful for people like us who come here to visit and also for Amish folks in the area who want to stay at the inn for a night or two to experience a kind of mini-vacation."

Orley nodded and handed Lois the reins. Then he stepped down from the buggy and secured Biscuit to the rail. While he was doing that, Lois got out and reached into the buggy to retrieve the container that held the pumpkin pie and green bean casserole she was contributing to the Thanksgiving meal.

When Lois and Orley stepped onto the porch that encompassed almost the entire front of the inn, Orley rang the bell. Within a few seconds, the door opened, and Jeff greeted them with a wide smile and welcoming hug. "Welcome, friends, and Happy Thanksgiving!"

"*Hallich Dankfescht*," Orley responded.

Jeff grinned. "You said, 'Happy Thanksgiving' in Pennsylvania Dutch. Jah?"

"That's right." Orley nodded. "Have you been studying our language?"

"I've picked up a few words here and there." Jeff took the container Lois held. "I'm guessing this goes in the kitchen?"

Lois smiled. "That's right. The green bean casserole is my contribution to dinner, and the pie's for dessert."

"I'll take it to the kitchen and let Rhonda know you're here. Her mom and my dad haven't arrived yet, but they should be here soon, I expect." Jeff gestured to the coatrack in the entryway. "You can hang your jackets there, and feel free to take a seat in our living room down the hall." Jeff looked at them. "You know the way to our living quarters here at the inn, right?"

"Jah, but if we get lost and can't find it, I'll give a holler so you can send out a search party for us." Orley winked at Jeff before the young man headed off toward the kitchen, shaking his head.

After they took off their outer garments and hung them up, Lois bumped Orley's arm with her elbow. "You were just teasing about getting lost, I hope. This isn't the first time we've been here, you know."

Orley wiggled his brows as he looked at her with a smug expression. "Of course I was only kidding."

With a quick roll of her eyes, Lois followed him down the hall. When they entered the living room, Lois stopped short. Sweet little Emily sat on the floor, surrounded by several toys. The child looked so angelic, it was all Lois could do to keep from swooping the little girl up and giving her a big hug. She held herself in check, though, because Emily didn't know them that well, and she didn't want to frighten the child. To avoid doing anything that might cause Emily to cry, Lois quietly took a seat in the rocking chair across from where Orley had seated himself in one of the two recliners.

When the little girl looked their way, Lois gave a little wave and watched Emily pick up the baby doll lying beside her and give it a hug. The tender scene brought tears to Lois's eyes. She glanced at Orley and noticed that he seemed to be watching Emily too. *Is my husband thinking the same thoughts I am?* she wondered. *Does Orley wish we could have had a child of our own? If we had, we could likely be grandparents by now.*

Lois was glad when Rhonda entered the room with Jeff, ending her musings. It wasn't good for a person to dwell on things that were not meant to be or feel sorry for oneself.

Lois and Orley stood, and each gave Rhonda a hug.

"Thank you for inviting us to join you today," Lois said. "Is there something I can do in the kitchen to help you right now?"

Rhonda shook her head. "Everything is pretty much ready. As soon as our newlywed parents get here, you can help me put things on the table."

Jeff slipped his arm around his wife's waist. "They've been married to each other for almost two years now, honey, so they've gone beyond being called newlyweds."

"Compared to us, they are." Rhonda smiled. "Who would ever have thought that my mother and Jeff's father would end up getting married?"

"That's right," Jeff agreed. "And it just goes to show that with God all things are possible." He gestured toward his daughter. "What do you think of our Emily? Hasn't she grown since the last time you saw her?"

"For sure," Orley responded. "And she's a beautiful little girl, just like her mother." He gestured to Rhonda, who smiled in return.

"Oh, I don't know about that," Jeff interjected. "I kinda think our little girl looks a bit like her father. Even if she doesn't," he added, "I bet our son will take after me."

"Your son?" Lois turned to look at Rhonda, whose cheeks had turned rosy. "Are you expecting another baby?"

Rhonda nodded. "The last ultrasound I had let us know that we are having a boy this time."

Happy tears sprang to Lois's eyes. "Congratulations. I am so pleased for you."

"I am as well." Orley looked at Jeff and gave him a big grin. "Maybe you'll be right, and your son will look like you, but no matter who he resembles, one thing I'm sure of is that, just like Emily, your boy will be loved."

The doorbell rang, and Jeff said, "That must be my father and mother-in-law. I'll go let them in, and shortly after we can all eat until we're too full to get up from the table."

Apple Creek

"You sure outdid yourself with this tasty meal," Andrea's father said to their hostess as he took another slice of succulent turkey and put it on his plate.

Jennifer smiled while gesturing to Andrea and her mother. "I can't take all the credit. Your wife and daughter contributed with the two different salads they brought. They also helped me serve everything up after you all arrived."

"And don't forget about the pies both women brought," Andrea's dad put in. "My heartfelt thanks goes out to each of you dear ladies, but I may not be as thankful when I'm so full of food that I can't push away from the table." He chuckled and patted his stomach. "When it's time for dessert, I'm sure I'll find room for that too."

Andrea fought the urge to roll her eyes or say something about his ability to exaggerate when he thought it was humorous, but she kept silent. So far the day had been going well, and she wasn't about to say something that might disrupt that pattern.

"You know, Ray, you could just learn to say no to second helpings," Brandon's dad, Larry, put in.

"Good point." Andrea's father held up his thumb. "But it's hard to say no when there's so much good food available."

"Too bad Joe and his family had other plans and couldn't join us today," Brandon interjected. "I'm sure my brother would have eaten enough for two people." He looked over at Andrea's father and grinned. "That would have saved you from feeling the need to eat so much, because with him at the table, there might not have been enough food for seconds."

Everyone laughed, including Andrea. It felt good to laugh and relax around the dinner table with Brandon's parents and hers. Being here today had helped to take her mind off the need to find her biological parents and focus instead on how thankful she felt for the parents who had raised her. Andrea had been fairly calm since she and Brandon had arrived at his folks' house, and she hadn't needed to use the lavender rollerball she'd put in her purse.

She looked across the table at Brandon's mother and father, now chatting with her folks about the light dusting of snow still on the ground. *I'm thankful for Larry and Jennifer too*, she thought. *I could not ask for a nicer couple to have as my future in-laws.* She glanced at Brandon sitting beside her. *And I'm ever so thankful for my soon-to-be groom.*

Brandon reached for her free hand and gave it a gentle squeeze. She wondered if he was having similar thoughts about being thankful.

Walnut Creek

"You're awfully quiet," Orley said as they headed home from Jeff and Rhonda's place that evening. "Did you eat too much food and end up with a *bauchweh*?"

Lois reached across the buggy seat and bumped his arm. "I did eat more than my share, but I don't have a stomachache. I am just tired and pleasantly full."

"Same here."

Lois had no intention of admitting to her husband that she felt a bit sorry for herself because they had no children or grandchildren. She didn't want to hurt Orley's feelings or remind him that he was unable to give them children. After they'd first learned of his condition, they had decided not to adopt. Lois had been fine with it at first and never complained. But as time went on and she observed other people with their children, Lois fought moments of envy and had to pray about it. Keeping busy helped, but at times like today, after enjoying the Davis family, deep regrets set in.

I need to stop this negative thinking before self-pity takes over, Lois told herself. *I can't let Orley know what I've been feeling. It would hurt him deeply.*

"It was a full day for us." Orley's statement pushed Lois's thoughts aside. "I can understand why you'd be tired."

She yawned as he snapped the reins, which got his horse moving a bit faster. "It was a *gut* day, though, jah?"

"Yes, the food was good, and so was the time we spent visiting with the Davises and their parents."

"That little girl of theirs sure took a shine to you," Lois said.

"That's probably because I gave her so much attention."

"Emily's a sweet child. Jeff and Rhonda are blessed to have her—especially after they waited so many years for Rhonda to conceive. The good Lord gave them a miracle with the birth of that child."

"He certainly did."

Lois held both hands firmly in her lap as she closed her eyes and offered a prayer. *Heavenly Father, please help me to learn to be content and appreciative for all that I have. Continue to use me and Orley whenever You open the doors for us to minister to others who are hurting and in need of spiritual guidance. Help me to be the kind of wife Orley needs, for he certainly has been a good husband to me.*

Chapter 23

By the first week of December, enough snow had fallen that children had begun to bring out their sleds. Lois chuckled, watching from the window as her husband pulled his well-used sled up the hill out behind their house. He'd invited her to join him, but Lois had declined. She had received more letters sent to her Dear Caroline column and needed to answer them this morning, on their day off from the store. Christmas cookies waited to be baked, and she'd already rolled out four cookie sheets full of them. She'd added crushed peppermint candies to half of the dough. These cookies were some of Orley's favorites and went well with hot chocolate. She'd slid in sheets of vanilla-flavored sugar cookies. Like a child, she couldn't wait to sample the first of this year's delights.

The timer sat ticking as Lois paused to stir hot cocoa in a kettle on the stove. The warmth from the copper-bottomed pan and the heat from the oven made the room feel cozy. As the fragrance of the peppermint began to fill the room, her mouth watered in expectation of having her hot beverage with a soft, warm sugar cookie.

When the buzzer sounded, Lois grabbed two pot holders, retrieved the baking sheets from the oven, and placed them on cooling racks. *When Orley comes in from outside, he'll surely want one.*

Lois had put two more sheets of cookies in the oven, when the kitchen door swung open and in walked her husband. A chill of air followed him, and she watched as he shook some snow off his pant legs.

"It feels good here in the house." His eyes seemed to brighten as he sniffed the air. "And somethin' sure smells mighty nice."

Lois set the timer again. "I have hot chocolate on the stove and some fresh-baked sugar cookies to enjoy."

"I came in for a drink of water, but what you've suggested sounds much better." He stepped over to the sink and washed his hands.

She got out a mug, poured his hot cocoa, and set two cookies on a napkin. "Did you want to sit down at the table?"

"No, I'll just stand while I eat these." He took a sip of his drink and ate a cookie.

"How does it taste?"

"Very good. Your *kichlin* are always tasty."

"Danki." Lois took a freezer container from the cupboard. "I'll put the cookies in this when they've cooled and then pop them into the freezer. When it gets closer to Christmas, I can add some frosting to them."

He held the second cookie in his hand. "This tastes fine just the way it is."

"Thank you, and eating them with less sugar is probably better for us."

He nodded. "When I'm done here, I'm going back outside to do more sledding. It's nice out there, and it feels like we could get more snow. Are you sure you don't want to join me?"

"I need to get some of those letters answered and a few Christmas cards made out as well." Lois pointed to the mail on the table. "It would be nice if I could answer all of them today, but it does take time to come up with what I hope will be the right answers."

"I'm sure the people needing advice from Dear Caroline would appreciate an answer pretty soon," Orley commented.

"Yes, and some of the letters aren't too difficult to answer, but other times I'm not sure if I have an answer."

"If you need my help, let me know." Orley popped the last bite of cookie into his mouth and carried his cup to the back door.

"Are you leaving already?"

"Yep. I'll take what's left in my mug and head outside."

"Okay, have fun out there." Lois watched him go out the door. She grabbed the container and put the cooled cookies inside.

Not long after, the timer went off, and she removed another batch of cookies from the oven. She wanted to keep baking, but those letters needed to be answered. Lois turned the oven off and placed the dirty dishes in the sink. She wrapped the remaining cookie dough up tight in waxed paper and placed it in the refrigerator.

Lois glanced toward the window and saw that snow was coming down again. It looked mesmerizing as it drifted in sparkly flakes to the ground. She imagined how a decorated snowman would look out in the yard, greeting people passing by on foot or riding in their vehicles. *If it weren't so cold outside, I wouldn't mind making a snowman, and I'm sure I've got some notions in my sewing room to give it a face.* Lois heaved a sigh. *But I'm afraid that will have to wait for another time when I'm not so busy and it's not quite so cold.*

Lois poured herself a cup of hot cocoa and picked out one plain and one peppermint cookie from the baking sheet. She then brought her treats over to the kitchen table and took a seat. Her first bite of the soft, warm sugar cookie tasted so good as it melted in her mouth. After a sip of cocoa, she set the mug down and read the Christmas card they'd received from her stepmother. Sarah had included a letter, wishing them a Merry Christmas and stating that she planned to visit her son in Colorado for the holidays. Lois had hoped that her father's widow might decide to move there to be close to her family, but Sarah kept insisting that she was happy living in Kentucky.

Lois sighed. *It's Sarah's choice, so all I can do is pray that she continues to do well and reaches out to others in her community for help and companionship if she needs it.*

Setting the Christmas card aside, Lois picked up one of the letters that had been sent to her Dear Caroline column. After reading it, a smile covered her face.

> *Dear Caroline,*
>
> *I'm having a problem with my neighbor who doesn't like the color of my house. Apparently, the elderly lady doesn't like yellow. She says it's too bright and informed me that she wears sunglasses when she walks past, even if the sun is not shining. I want to be a good neighbor, but I like the color of my house and don't want to change it. Is there an answer to this problem?*
>
> *—Yellow Makes Me Happy*

Lois took another sip of hot chocolate and shook her head. *Now how am I supposed to answer that one? Should I ignore this letter? Tell the person to change the color of their home?*

She set her mug down and reached up to massage her forehead. *Maybe*

I should put all this away and go sledding with Orley. Lois rubbed her arms. *Dealing with the cold weather and climbing back up the hill might be easier than trying to come up with answers to people's problems.*

Lois left her chair and got out a bag of mini-marshmallows. After putting several in her cup of hot chocolate, she picked up the mug and left the room.

Maybe I ought to quit the Dear Caroline column, Lois told herself as she wandered into the living room. *When Orley and I mentor people, we talk face-to-face and have a better chance of knowing whether they took our advice.* The problem with the Dear Caroline column, aside from it taking up a lot of time, was that she never found out whether the things she'd suggested helped anyone.

Lois took a seat in her rocking chair and set the mug on the small table beside her. *Pray, Lois. You need to pray,* her inner voice commanded.

Without hesitation, she bowed her head. *Dear Lord, please give me a sense of direction concerning the Dear Caroline column. If I'm supposed to continue writing it, please give me a sign—something that will let me know if my responses are helpful or not.* Lois continued with her prayer by thanking God for the many blessings He had bestowed upon her and Orley, including the antique business and their marriage.

Lois ended her prayer with a heartfelt request: *Lord, please keep my husband safe while he's out there in the cold, taking chances on that old sled of his.*

Orley's boots crunched as he tromped through the snow. Being outside with white flakes coming down was exhilarating and made him feel like a kid again. But of course it would be more fun if he had someone to share it with. *Too bad my fraa doesn't like being out in cold weather. She'd probably like it if we lived in one of the southern states where it's warm most of the year.*

Orley trudged up the hill, pulling his sled by the rope attached to the handles. His feet almost went out from under him once, but he regained his balance in time and kept on going.

"Next time I go sledding, I'm gonna invite one of our neighbor kids to join me," he mumbled. "It'd be a lot more fun than trompin' up the hill and sledding down by myself. At least there would be someone for me to laugh with when we both took tumbles or did something really stupid."

When Orley reached the top, he positioned himself face-down on the sled and pushed off. The ride down the hill was exhilarating, and when he reached the bottom, he didn't even mind when a little snow went up his nose.

He thought about Lois again, wishing she'd come out here to cheer him on and watch. Although it could just be his imagination, Orley thought his wife had seemed a little down lately. Could it be that she'd been thinking about her father's death? The Christmas holiday fast approaching could be a harsh reminder that loved ones who had passed on would not be here to celebrate what should be a cheery, festive season.

Of course, Orley reasoned, as he made another trip back up the hill, *Lois and her father hadn't been close, and he'd never come here for Christmas. Even so, it was quite possible that she was still grieving.*

Maybe I should do something special for my fraa for Christmas, Orley told himself. *I just need to think of what she might like.*

Apple Creek

Brandon stepped out of the first examining room and glanced at his watch. Things had been busy at the clinic all morning, and he was more than ready to eat lunch. He'd dealt with everything from a dog that had eaten its flea collar to a finicky cat that wouldn't eat anything except a certain kind of expensive cat food. Both pet owners had been concerned about their animal's eating habits—especially the one who had a German shorthaired pointer that preferred his own flea collar to a rawhide chew stick or a beef-flavored doggie treat. Fortunately, the flea collar hadn't appeared to make the dog sick, but if the dog ate enough of them, eventually there might be a serious problem.

Brandon's advice to the finicky cat owner was to keep trying some other foods in the hope that Snowball would eventually find one she liked. To the collar-eating dog owner, he suggested that he quit buying flea collars and protect the dog by other means, such as a flea bath, powder, or special pill.

Brandon entered his office and took a seat at his desk. He had a few phone calls to make before he ate lunch—the first one would be to Andrea.

He picked up his phone and brought up her number. A few seconds later, she answered.

"Hello." Andrea's voice sounded groggy, like she'd just woken up.

"Hi, sweetie. You weren't sleeping, I hope."

"Uh, no." He heard a noisy yawn. "I am tired, though. I was up late last night trying to finish a painting that someone ordered for Christmas. I have two more to complete for someone else, and then I'm done," she added after a second yawn.

"That's cutting it pretty close to Christmas," he commented.

"I suppose so, but I have fallen behind because I've been spending a lot of time on some of the internet sites for people who are searching for their biological parents."

Brandon stiffened. He was tempted to ask Andrea if that's all she cared about anymore. It sure seemed like it, which caused him some concern. Their wedding was only two months away, and they still had some details to work out. At the rate things were going, they'd never be ready on time.

"Umm, listen, the reason I called is to invite you for supper this evening." The phone was quiet on Andrea's end as he sat waiting for her response. "Andrea, did you hear what I said?"

"Yes, I did, but I got distracted by a text message that just came in."

"Was it important?"

"I'd say so. It was one of my adult piano students, letting me know that she won't be at the piano recital I have scheduled for next week because she broke her arm in a sledding accident, which means she can't play."

"That's too bad. Hopefully, all your other students can be there."

"Yes, because I've gone to a lot of trouble planning this recital, and I'm hoping for a good turnout."

Brandon paused a few seconds and took a drink from his bottle of water. It wasn't cold, the way he liked it, but his thirst was quenched, and that was all that mattered. "Now back to the reason I called. Will you be free to go out to supper with me this evening?"

"Not tonight, Brandon. I have more work to do on the paintings, and after that, I want to spend some time on the computer."

"More adoption stuff?" Brandon tried not to let his irritation show, but he was pretty sure she could hear it in his voice. This was not the first time Andrea had turned down an invitation to spend the evening with him. She'd passed up the opportunity for them to spend time together twice last week.

"I'm planning to do a DNA test soon," she said. "And I want to make sure of all the details and that I'm doing it right."

Is it really that important for you to locate your birth mother? Brandon thought, but he didn't voice the words that he felt sure Andrea would take offense to. "I hope it goes well." The words nearly stuck in his throat. It would have been right to say something encouraging, but those words wouldn't come out of his mouth.

"Sorry, Brandon, but I'm getting another call. I'll talk to you soon, okay?"

"Yeah, sure. Have a good rest of your day."

After they'd ended the conversation, Brandon sat with his lips pressed together and his arms folded. He wanted to talk to someone unbiased about this situation. The question was, who?

He scratched his head and gave it some thought. *Maybe I'll give my dad a call tonight and see what he has to say.*

Brandon didn't seem very understanding, Andrea thought after she'd set her cell phone aside. *Doesn't he realize how important it is for me to find my birth mother and learn about my heritage? I've always been accepting whenever he's been busy with work and can't spend time with me. Why is this any different?*

Releasing a sigh of frustration, she got up from the couch and headed for her art studio. As desperately as Andrea wanted to be on the computer right now, she was determined to finish the paintings so she could get paid. Normally, by this time in December, Andrea had all her Christmas shopping done. But that wasn't the case this year because in addition to earning a living, her top priority was finding her birth mother.

"But what if I never locate her?" Andrea spoke out loud. "Can I go through the rest of my life not knowing who she is or why she gave me up for adoption?" She shook her head. "I don't think so. I need to keep digging until I find answers, and I won't let anything or anyone get in the way."

Chapter 24

"Do you have a minute, Dad?" Brandon asked the following evening when his father answered the phone.

"Sure, Son. I always have time for you."

"Is that Brandon?"

Brandon heard the excited tone in his mother's voice. It sounded as though she was close to Dad's phone.

Brandon's fingers clenched around his phone. *Oh great. Dad obviously has his speaker mode on.*

"Yes, Jennifer. It's our son. He called to talk to me."

"Oh, I see." Mom's tone had changed to what Brandon recognized as one of disappointment.

It wasn't that Brandon didn't want to talk to his mother—just not now. He needed a private talk with Dad. Mom was the emotional one in the family and would no doubt offer advice that could end up getting him in trouble with Andrea, which would only make things worse. It had gotten harder for him to deal with his fiancée's seemingly fanatical mindset to find her real parents. Andrea's preoccupation had caused her to neglect their wedding plans and any quality time for them to spend together, which didn't set well with Brandon. His forehead creased. *My sweet Andrea seems to have morphed into someone I don't know. I need some advice before things get any worse.*

"Listen, Dad," Brandon said, "would it be possible for us to meet someplace for lunch tomorrow? I need to discuss a few things with you that could affect my future." He grimaced and nearly bit his tongue. If

Mom was still listening, which no doubt she was, she might assume that he and Andrea were having some kind of problem and try to fix it. While his mother was good at fixing little things that had broken around their house and was helpful in many ways, she often made things worse when she tried to meddle in affairs of the heart. Brandon remembered when he was dating a girl named Nadine in high school. They had disagreed about something, and when Mom got into the act, giving her thoughts on the topic to Nadine, the girl broke up with Brandon. Although their relationship probably wouldn't have lasted, Brandon blamed his mother for the split and wished she had kept out of it. He'd seen her interfere in a few other people's lives over the years, and her actions usually spelled disaster. He felt sure that his mom always meant well, but he would not give her the chance to mess things up between him and the woman he planned to marry.

"Brandon, did you hear what I said?"

"Umm. . .no, Dad, sorry. I was thinking."

"About where we should go to eat?"

"No, something else." Brandon moistened his dry, chapped lips. "Are you free to meet for lunch tomorrow?"

"Yes, I am. Should we eat at Lem's Pizza at noon?"

"Sounds good, Dad. I'll see you then. Say hi to Mom for me too, okay?"

"She's standing right here. Why don't you tell her yourself?"

Brandon shifted in his chair to look at Duke, standing by the front door. "Hi, Mom. Say, I have to cut this short because my dog needs to go out. I'll see you at church, Sunday, okay?"

"Sure, Son. Have a good rest of your evening."

"Bye, Dad. Bye, Mom." Brandon clicked off, slipped on a jacket, and went to take care of Duke. This was one time when he was glad for the inconvenience of going out into the cold.

Jennifer stepped away from Larry and folded her arms. "I can't believe our son did not want to talk to me."

"Didn't you hear what Brandon said? He had to let his dog out."

She took a seat on the couch. "That may be true, but he didn't include me in your lunch plans."

"I guess Brandon wants a little father-son time. Is there anything wrong with that?"

"Well no, but he said that he wanted to talk about his future, which involves Andrea, no doubt."

Larry picked up the remote and pointed it at the TV from his recliner.

"Please don't turn that on right now. We are in the middle of a discussion."

Larry looked at her pointedly. "There isn't much to discuss, and I don't believe there's any need for you to be concerned. Brandon probably wants to discuss some financial matters with me, and since I'm a bank manager..."

She fiddled with the gold bracelet on her right wrist. "What makes you think it's a financial issue? He might be having a problem that involves Andrea. She hasn't been acting like herself since she found out she was adopted, and maybe it's affecting their relationship."

He waved the remote in her direction. "You worry too much when you should be praying."

Jennifer shook her head vigorously. "That is not true, and you know it. I do plenty of praying. When our son shuts me out, I feel like he doesn't want me to be part of his life."

"Brandon is his own person, Jen, and if you pray like I keep reminding you to do and give it to the Lord, you won't worry so much—especially when we aren't even sure what it's about." His forehead creased. "And even if you did know what's going on in Brandon's life right now, it would be out of your control."

"I'm not trying to control anything. It would just be helpful if I knew what to pray about."

"For now, you can pray that my lunch with our son goes well tomorrow, and if it's anything you need to know, I'll say so." Larry pointed the remote at the TV again. "Can we please not talk about this anymore? I'd like to catch the news before it's time for bed."

"Okay, but I'm not interested in watching the news. It reminds me of all the horrible things going on in our world right now." She rose from the couch. "I'm going to our room and get ready for bed." Jennifer moved across the room. "Oh, and I will definitely pray for our son and his bride-to-be after I get into bed." She rushed out of the room before he could say anything more. Jennifer felt incredibly frustrated when she was left out of things.

She turned on the hall light so Larry could see when he came to bed. *I wish Brandon had invited me to join them for lunch too, but hopefully Larry will tell me whatever our son says when he gets home from work tomorrow evening.*

Andrea squinted as she rubbed the bridge of her nose. She'd been sitting in front of her computer for nearly three hours, looking at various sites for people who had been adopted and taking notes. There was so much information out there, it made her head swim.

"If I had my original birth certificate, it would make things easier," she muttered. "At least then I would know my biological parents' names." The birth certificate Andrea's parents had gotten when they adopted her was legal and included their names, as well as the one they had chosen for her, but it did not give Andrea the information she needed to locate her biological parents.

"Why did they agree to a closed adoption?" Her jaw ached as she clenched her top and bottom teeth, and she reached for her rollerball filled with lavender essential oil. "Apparently, they didn't want me to know who had given birth to me."

Andrea paused to roll some of the essential oil on her wrists, neck, and forehead before leaving the website where she'd been reading about the difference between closed and open adoptions and clicked on AncestryDNA. She'd looked at similar sites, but this one had very large databases, so she decided to open an account and purchase a DNA kit online. She'd receive a prepaid envelope and a test tube, which she'd need to fill with a saliva sample and return to the company through the mail.

Andrea's heartbeat quickened as she read that Ancestry relied on a large online database that might include relatives who had done similar testing in the past. If this had occurred, she would not only discover her ethnic background but also any relatives who had tested as well.

Without hesitation, Andrea purchased the DNA kit. "There, that's done. Now all I have to do is wait for it to arrive, and the rest will be up to me."

Lady stirred from where she lay curled in Andrea's lap and let out a quiet *meow*.

"Sorry, girl, I didn't mean to wake you." Andrea glanced at the computer clock at the bottom of her screen. "Twelve thirty already? Where did the time go, my sweet little Lady? I need to shut this computer down so we can go to bed."

Andrea turned it off, picked up Lady, and headed down the hall to her room. Tomorrow would be another long day, filled with teaching piano lessons and putting the final touches on some paintings she'd been hired to do. Even so, she would squeeze in some time to look at more adoption sites because, to her, that was most important.

Walnut Creek

"Are you ready for bett?" Orley called from the living room where he'd been reading a magazine article about identifying certain kinds of old bottles.

"I'll be there soon," Lois responded. "I have a few more letters to answer."

He grimaced. *Again? Is there no end to those letters that keep pouring in?* As much as Orley didn't want to admit it, he figured a lot of people must enjoy Lois's Dear Caroline column.

Feeling a bit put out, Orley told Lois goodnight and left the room. *Am I envious of her?* Orley asked himself as he plodded down the hall. *Lois is reaching a lot more people through that column than I ever could in our store.*

He paused to scratch an itch behind his left ear. *It's been a long time since anyone's come in with a problem and asked my advice. Maybe I should start a column of my own and offer it to the newspaper. I could call it Dear Amos, and it could be a column for men. He clunked the side of his head. No, that's a* dumm *idea. I'm good with words when talking to someone one-on-one but not with the written word. My grammar would be off, and I'd be so rattled trying to think of the right answers, I would be a nervous wreck.* Orley shook his head. *No, I don't think I could express myself right unless I was talking directly to a person. So I'd better scratch that idea and stick to what I do best.*

Orley reached the bedroom and got a drink of water from their bathroom sink. That way his wife could keep working undisturbed at the kitchen table.

He smiled to himself, thinking about yesterday when he and Lois had made a snowman together in their front yard with the sun shining against the glistening snow. Although his wife had a lot on her plate these days, it was good when she took time out to do something fun.

Apple Creek

"Coming here to Lem's Pizza was a good idea, but I think I'm gonna opt for a sub sandwich," Brandon said. "They make some pretty good ones."

"Agreed," his dad said. "Think I might have one of those too."

The place was busy, but that wasn't unusual. Brandon studied the menu before ordering a turkey and provolone full-size sub with lettuce, tomatoes, green peppers, pickles, and onion, along with a cup of coffee. His father placed an order for the same sandwich, only he asked for swiss cheese, mushrooms, and green olives to be added to his.

"It's interesting that this place was opened by a man named Mark Lemon, whose nickname was Lem," Dad commented as he sat across the table from Brandon.

Staring into his cup of coffee, Brandon nodded.

"This restaurant sure has some neat local memorabilia on the walls, both historical and current."

"Uh-huh."

"Son, you're not really listening to me, are you?"

When Dad snapped his fingers, Brandon blinked and looked up. "Umm. . .no, guess I wasn't. I have other things on my mind."

"That's the reason you wanted to meet with me, correct? It was something about your future you needed to discuss."

"Yeah, Dad. I'm worried about my relationship with Andrea."

Dad's brow furrowed a bit. "What about it? Things are okay between you two, aren't they? You're still planning to be married in February, right?"

Brandon shrugged. "I'm not sure."

"She hasn't called off your engagement, I hope." Dad's gaze flitted around the room, and he looked back at Brandon with furrowed brows. "Your mother has made a lot of plans regarding the rehearsal dinner, and she'd be pretty upset if—"

Brandon held up his hand. "As far as I know, the wedding is still on, but the thing is. . .she's so caught up in trying to find her biological parents that she doesn't have time for me anymore."

"Seriously? Did Andrea tell you that?"

"No, but she's turned me down several times when I've wanted to get together for a meal."

"Did she state the reason?"

Brandon's neck bent forward, and his shoulders slumped. "She's either too busy teaching piano, painting pictures, or researching on the internet for ways to locate her birth parents."

"Haven't there been times when you've been too busy to get together with her?"

"Yeah, of course, but it's not just her busyness that bothers me. When we are together, which isn't as often as before, all she talks about is her need to locate her birth mother. We don't discuss much else."

"Have you been supportive of Andrea's desire to know about and possibly meet her biological family?"

"I've tried to be, but it seems like it's becoming an obsession with her, and I don't want that to be all we talk about."

"It's understandable."

"What if Andrea hasn't found her birth mother by the time we get married?" Brandon rubbed a twitching eyelid. "I want my future wife's full attention when I talk to her about something, and after we're married, it'll be even more important."

"Have you discussed this with Andrea—told her how you feel?"

Brandon shook his head before taking a sip from his cup. "If I say too much, she might think I'm not being supportive enough, and that would only make things worse." He looked directly at his father. "What do you think I should do?"

Dad rubbed his clean-shaven chin. "If I were you, I'd take a chance and discuss your feelings with her. Andrea may be so caught up in her quest to find the woman who gave birth to her that she's unaware of the fact that she is shutting you out."

Brandon gave a brief nod. "Could be."

Just then their sandwiches arrived, and they paused to pray. When Brandon opened his eyes, he bit into the sub, and his dad did the same.

"I'll give what you said some serious thought." Brandon drank some more coffee. "Thanks for taking the time to meet with me today. I really appreciate it."

"No problem. That's what dads are for."

Brandon ate more of his sandwich, then paused to ask another question. "Would you mind keeping our conversation to yourself? I'd rather not let Mom know what's going on between me and Andrea. She would only fret about it and maybe try to intervene on my behalf." His brows furrowed. "I'm sure that wouldn't go over well with Andrea, because then she would know that I've been talking about it to someone other than her."

"No problem," Dad said. "I won't say anything to your mother or anyone else."

Brandon felt relieved about that much at least. Now if he could only decide how and when to tell Andrea the way he'd been feeling. Maybe it would go better than he thought. Andrea might understand and make more time to spend with him while spending less time on a quest that could end up at a dead end with no other place to go.

Chapter 25

Saturday afternoon when Andrea entered the church she and her parents had attended since she was a child, she was greeted by the custodian, Arnie Smith.

"The building is plenty warm, and lights are on in the sanctuary as well as the fellowship hall. Everything's ready for you and your students." The elderly but still active man gave Andrea a pleasant smile.

"Thank you, Arnie. I appreciate being able to use the church for my students' piano recital." She returned his smile with one of her own. "And I am grateful for all that you've done in preparation for my event."

"It's part of my job. But I enjoy what I do here at the church, and I'm thankful to be employed." He gestured toward the sanctuary. "Is there anything else you need me to do at this time?"

"No, I think we're all set. I'll take the refreshments I brought to the fellowship hall, and then all that's left is waiting for my students and their families to arrive."

Arnie gave a nod. "All right then. I'll be back in a couple hours to clean and close up the church."

"Thanks. Have a good afternoon."

"And you as well. I hope everything goes real good here today."

Andrea smiled. She hoped it would too.

Andrea sat on the front pew, watching and prompting her piano students when necessary as they took turns playing their pieces. So far, everyone had done well, and it was nice to hear the appreciative applause from those in the audience. Andrea's parents had come to cheer her on, but she was a bit disappointed that Brandon hadn't made it, although she understood why. He had called her shortly before the recital started to let her know that he was needed at a farm to deliver a calf whose mother was having a difficult labor.

And so goes the life of a veterinarian, she thought. *I'd better get used to it if I'm going to marry him, just like he needs to realize that I lead a busy life too. Even so, I do wish Brandon could be a little more understanding when it comes to my decision to search for my biological parents. I've been supportive of him and have tried to be understanding when he can't always attend events that are important to me, such as this one recital.*

Andrea refocused when her last and only adult piano student finished playing her piece and everyone applauded. She felt pleased with how well the recital had gone and was proud of her students. Even Peggy, who had previously said she wanted her parents to find a different teacher, had done a good job, although she still hadn't trimmed her fingernails adequately. Since Peggy's parents had insisted on keeping Andrea as their daughter's teacher, the teenager had become easier to teach and, for the most part, did as she was told.

Andrea left her seat and stood on the platform, holding a microphone. "Thank you all for coming here today. I am pleased with how well all of my students did, and I have every hope that they will continue to learn and improve in the weeks and months ahead. Now, before you return to your homes, I hope you will all join me in the fellowship hall, where refreshments are waiting."

Everyone clapped again and rose from their seats. As they began filing out of the sanctuary, Andrea's mother came up and gave her a hug. "Your students are progressing nicely, and your father and I are so proud of your accomplishments as both a pianist and an artist."

"Thank you, Mom. I enjoy what I do, and it's a good feeling when my students do well at their recital."

Andrea's father joined them and gave Andrea a hug too. "That was a great recital. Your mom and I enjoyed it very much, and now I'm ready to go see what you brought for refreshments."

Andrea laughed. Dad was a man of few words, unless it came to food.

Berlin

After Brandon left the farm call in Mt. Hope, where he had helped a struggling cow give birth, he'd decided to visit some of the stores in Berlin. He wanted to give Andrea a special gift for Christmas and hoped he would find something in one of the shops. He had tried talking to her last night about their relationship, but he'd made no progress whatsoever. She had made light of his concerns and said it was just a busy time for her right now and that once she found her birth mother, things would be better all the way around. As they'd continued to talk, their conversation had turned into a near-argument, so Brandon had dropped the subject.

"Yeah, right," Brandon mumbled after he left one of the gift stores and got into his vehicle. He could feel Andrea pulling away from him a little more each day and couldn't help worrying. What if she never found the woman who'd given birth to her? Would Andrea push him further away until they had no relationship at all?

Maybe if I give her something really nice for Christmas, it'll smooth things over with her for not being able to attend her students' recital today and for the heated words we had last night. Brandon put the key in the ignition. *She likes vintage items. I wonder if I should pay a visit to that antique store in Walnut Creek she told me about. I bet they might have something she would like.*

Walnut Creek

Earlier today, Lois and her husband had gone through several boxes of antiques in the back room that they'd received from an English woman whose mother had passed away. The woman said she didn't have time to sort through all the old things or run an ad to try and sell them, so Orley had paid her what he felt was a fair price. He'd told Lois that he figured somc or all of the items might have value. Yesterday and again this morning, Lois had helped Orley clean and price an old table lamp, some jewelry, a variety of books, several pieces of clothing, and a few other vintage items.

"I'll be able to put some of these items out now." Orley ran his thumb up and down one of his black suspenders as he looked at Lois.

"I was surprised that we received so many items from her, and it's all a little different from what we have in our shop." Lois held up an old washboard. "This one is bigger than the one we have out front on display."

"I agree, and this old oil brand sign is in nice shape for its age too." Orley gestured to it. "Not to mention there are some old tools, gardening reaping hooks, oil cans, and other vintage items."

"We will definitely have more things to put out on the floor before Christmas." Lois smiled as she picked up a small box with a few indistinguishable items inside. "I'll find places to put these, but I'd like to get your opinion first."

Orley followed her from the back of the store, carrying the sign that needed to be displayed on the wall for prospective buyers. They'd no more than approached the register when the phone rang. Lois placed the box on the counter and answered their business line, which they'd recently received permission from their church leaders to have in the store. "Hello, Memory Keepers."

The person on the other end asked about their hours and wondered if they had any antique jewelry. Lois said they did have some and told the man that he was welcome to come by for a look. Then she hung up with the customer and waited, wanting to show her husband what was inside the box she held.

Meanwhile, Orley had leaned the sign against the wall he'd chosen for its display. "I think it will go well right here. What do you think, Lois?" he asked.

"It's a good spot and blends well with the others that are hanging there already." Lois gestured to the small box on the counter. "Would you care to see what I have here?"

"Sure thing." He came up by the register. "Whatcha got?"

"I picked these up a while back and forgot about them." She unwrapped each one from the tissue paper. "I'd like your thoughts on these."

He leaned closer as she placed three small Amish dolls on the counter.

"What do you think?" Lois asked.

He pushed his glasses up to the bridge of his nose and picked up the first doll. "This boy doll is made of plastic, so it's probably not worth much," he stated. "But the girl doll made of wood and the other one made from cast iron would probably go for more."

Lois nodded. "That's what I was thinking. I'll set them out next to the other vintage dolls we have on display. Since it's so close to Christmas, someone might come into Memory Keepers and buy one or more of the dolls we have for sale."

Orley pointed to the doll made of wood. "Do you think someone would buy an old doll like this for their little *maedel*?"

Lois shrugged. "Could be. I had one when I was a girl. In fact, this *bopp* looks quite similar to mine." Her brows knitted together as she stared intently at the doll. "But, of course, it's not the same."

"What'd you do with your wooden doll?" Orley asked.

"My sister Elizabeth ended up with it." Lois had a faraway look in her eyes as she stared across the room. "I had other dolls too."

"What happened to all your dolls? Do you have them tucked away somewhere and never bothered to show them to me? Were you worried I might want to sell them?"

She shook her head. "I gave most of them away when I grew too old to play with dolls anymore." Ending their conversation, Lois picked up the dolls and made her way across the room, where she placed them on the shelf with the other dolls that hadn't yet sold.

Orley gave his head a quick shake. He seriously doubted that any young girl, English or Amish, would want a rigid-looking doll that they couldn't cuddle. More than likely, if any of the dolls here sold, it would be to a doll collector.

He looked back at the wall where he'd left the metal sign. *I'll try to get that hung at some point today if it doesn't get too busy in here.* Orley grabbed a piece of candy from the small plastic bowl sitting by the register for their customers to enjoy. Lois usually filled it with peppermint candy, but for Christmas she'd added some cinnamon candies too, which made the red and green colors look festive.

"I'm returning to the storage room to see what else we might have to put out on display," Lois called to him before she headed off in that direction.

"Okay, but don't get too involved looking. Anyway, the oil lamp and that washboard can be brought out to sell."

"I'll get them first."

"If things start to get busy, like they were earlier this morning, I may need your help out here," he reminded her.

"If that should happen, please come and get me," Lois responded before she disappeared into the storage room.

My wife sure seemed to be in a hurry to leave this room, Orley thought. *I wonder if she has more of those Dear Caroline letters to write and is afraid I might say something about it.*

Lois came back a short time later with the items he'd spoken of and rearranged the places where she'd chosen to set them. Orley couldn't help but smile. His wife had always liked things a certain way both at home and here in the store.

After Lois returned to the storage room, Orley's thoughts shifted gear. *I hope my dear wife will like the gift I got her for Christmas.* He bent down to tie a loose shoelace. He'd almost finished tying it when he heard the bell above the front door jingle. *Oh good—sounds like a prospective customer.*

When Brandon entered the antique store, a combination of odors wafted up to his nose. This small building smelled like wood, leather, and musty cloth with a few other scents he couldn't identify mixed in.

He glanced around the building but saw no one in sight. Brandon cupped his hands around his mouth. "Hello! Anyone here?" Surely the shop owners wouldn't leave their business unattended—especially with so many valuable vintage items displayed. And this place was full of old things. In every direction, he saw things like antique furniture pieces, old dishes, iconic business signs, vintage clocks, a shelf full of books, and many other items that looked and smelled old.

Brandon was getting ready to take a stroll around the room when a middle-aged Amish man with a full beard popped up from behind the front counter where an antiquated cash register was located.

"Good afternoon," the man said. "My name is Orley Troyer, and I don't believe we've met before. Are you new around here?"

"Not new to the area, but this is my first time in your store. My name is Brandon Prentice, and I live in Apple Creek. My veterinarian clinic is there too."

"Oh, so you're an animal doctor?"

"Yes, I am. And since I was in Walnut Creek today, I decided to stop here to see if I could find a nice Christmas gift for my fiancée."

"Are you looking for anything in particular?"

Brandon shrugged. "I'm not sure. She likes antiques, so I'm hoping if I can find something to her liking, she might pay more attention to me and spend less time doing research on her computer." A knot formed in Brandon's stomach. *Now what made me say something like that to a man I've never met before? I can only imagine what he must think of me.* "Sorry, I shouldn't have blurted that out. I'm feeling a little stressed right now and not thinking as clearly as I should be."

Orley stepped forward and placed a hand on Brandon's shoulder. "Are you and your future wife having some problems right now?"

"Truthfully, yes. She recently found out that she was adopted as a baby, and now she's so busy trying to find her biological parents that she doesn't have time to spend with me or even finalize the plans we've been making for our upcoming wedding." Brandon didn't know why, but strangely enough, he felt comfortable talking about this with the Amish man. Maybe it was the look of concern on Orley's face, or perhaps it was being able to speak with someone who was completely removed from the situation.

"I'm a pretty good listener," Orley said. "I've also been known to hand out a little advice to people who choose to share their problems with me."

"I see." Brandon thought over the man's statement for a few seconds, and then, throwing caution to the wind, he said, "What would you do if the woman you were engaged to marry became so involved with the quest to find her birth mother that she had no time for you anymore?"

Orley's lips pressed together, and he tipped his head to one side as though contemplating the question. A few seconds passed, and then he looked directly at Brandon and said matter-of-factly, "I would sit down and have a talk with her about it. I'd mention that I feel left out of her life and miss spending time with her."

Brandon nodded. "I did that the other night, but I think my comments fell on deaf ears."

"She didn't say anything in response?"

"Oh, a response came from her all right, but it was one I didn't like." Brandon shifted his stance. "She said I should be more understanding and stated quite firmly that after she finds out who gave birth to her, she'll have more time to spend with me."

"That could be a difficult, time-consuming process. What if she never finds out?"

"Exactly." Brandon frowned. "I don't like the way things are headed, but at least she's agreed to spend Christmas with me. Of course, we'll spend part of it with her folks and mine, but I'm sure there will be some time when we're alone and can hopefully discuss our wedding plans." Brandon glanced across the room, then back at Orley. "Speaking of Christmas... Is there anything here you think my fiancée might like?"

"Let's see now..." Orley started across the room, and Brandon followed him over to a large bookcase. "Does she like to read old novels?"

Brandon shook his head. "She keeps busy teaching piano lessons and is also an artist, so she doesn't have much time for reading."

"Here's something interesting she might like." Orley moved over to another shelf where some old dishes had been placed and picked up an ornate dome-shaped item. "This is a very old butter dish that was made in England a good many years ago."

Brandon leaned forward and studied the piece. It appeared to be quite fragile and would no doubt break easily if bumped or knocked over. He could see the disaster that would follow if Andrea's cat, who sometimes hopped up on things, brushed against the vintage butter dish and it toppled to the floor. *Goodbye Christmas present, and hello upset wife-to-be. No, not a good gift for Andrea.*

"Think I'd better find something that's not so easy to break." Brandon moved to the area where some furniture had been displayed and leaned down to place his hand on top of an antique coffee table that was in good shape. "This might be nice. Yeah, I think my bride-to-be would like this, and it won't clash with any of my furniture when she moves into my home after we're married." He looked at the price tag attached to the table and smiled at the bearded Amish man. "I'll take it." *And if I know Andrea as well as I think I do, I believe she'll like this vintage coffee table.*

"Let's go up to the checkout counter, and you can pay for it there," Orley said. "Then I'll help you take it out to your vehicle."

"I appreciate the offer, but I should be able to manage it on my own." Brandon followed Orley to the front of the store. "Thanks for allowing me to share my problems and also for taking the time to offer your advice."

Orley nodded. "It was my privilege to do so. If you're ever in the area again, feel free to stop by, even if it's just to talk."

Brandon smiled. "I might take you up on that offer. I can tell that you're a man who cares about people."

"Yes, I do, but God cares about folks even more."

"That's true. I've been a believer since I was a young boy, and I don't know what I'd do without the Lord in my life."

"Me either." Orley spoke with a certainty in his voice. "On that note, I'll just say that God knows about whatever problems we may have to face in this life, so the best thing to do when dealing with any kind of situation beyond our control is to pray about it and let the Lord work things out."

"Good advice," Brandon agreed. "And thanks for the reminder, because

I'm the kind of guy who often tries to figure things out on his own. When it doesn't work out and nothing gets resolved, that's when I remember that I should have taken it to the Lord in prayer right away and let Him help me with the problem."

Orley nodded. "I'm guilty of that too, so the words I just spoke were to myself as well as to you."

Brandon reached into his pocket for his wallet to pay for the coffee table. He was glad he'd come by here today. Meeting Orley Troyer and talking about his troubles had been good for him and brought things into a better perspective. Quite likely in the days ahead he would find an excuse to drop by Memory Keepers Antique Store again.

Chapter 26

"*En hallicher Grischtdaag*!" Orley said when he entered the kitchen where Lois was busy getting their breakfast ready to put on the table.

"A Merry Christmas to you too." She smiled and went to give him a hug.

"Have you been to your sewing room this morning?" he asked.

She gestured to the pancake batter she was about to pour on the griddle. "The only place I've been is right here, preparing our Christmas breakfast, and I certainly don't have any time to sew."

Orley chuckled. "I wasn't asking you to. I just wanted to know if you had been to that room."

She shook her head. "No, and I probably won't go there until sometime next week when I do some much-needed mending."

"Well, please turn off the burner and let's go there right now."

Lois looked puzzled. "What's gotten into you, Orley? Aren't you *hungerich* this morning?"

"Jah, I'm hungry, but eating breakfast can wait till you've opened your Christmas present from me."

Lois figured that if her gift was in the sewing room, Orley must have gotten her a new sewing machine. She didn't really need one—hers was fine—but if that was what he'd bought, she would be appreciative.

Lois turned off the stove and removed the griddle from the burner. "All right, my dear husband, please lead the way."

When they entered the sewing room, Lois was surprised to see what looked like it could be a piece of furniture covered with one of Orley's tarps. From the size of it, she was sure the item was not a sewing machine.

"Go ahead and open your present." Orley pointed to the large object.

Lois stepped up to it and pulled one corner of the drop cloth aside, and as she continued pulling, her mouth opened wide. "*Ach*, my! This oak desk is *brechdich*!"

Orley grinned. "I think it's pretty magnificent too." He moved closer to her. "I'm glad you like it."

"I do—very much so in fact. Danki." She gave him a hug.

"You're welcome. I thought this would be better for you to sit at while you answer your Dear Caroline letters than being seated at the kitchen table. And I think there's enough room for it to be kept right here in your sewing room, which is why I asked our neighbor, Harvey Miller, to help me bring it into the house last night after you'd gone to bed."

"You're a sneaky one." She poked his arm playfully. "And I agree about keeping the desk here—just not in the middle of the room."

"Course not. You choose where you want the desk, and I'll move it there."

"How about up against the wall by my sewing machine? With two windows on that wall, I'll have plenty of light when I'm sitting at the desk during daylight hours."

"Good point. I'll move it there right now."

"Here, let me help you."

"No, that's okay. I can do it." Orley positioned himself near the center of the desk and pushed. He'd barely gotten it against the wall, when he put both hands against the small of his back and let out a yelp.

"What's wrong?" Lois's pulse quickened as she rushed to his side.

"My back spasmed. It really hurts. Think I'd better sit down." Bent over at the waist, he made his way slowly over to the chair in front of Lois's sewing table. Orley winced as he lowered himself into it.

"I think you should lie down before the pain gets worse," Lois said. "I'll help you to the couch and get an ice pack to put against your back."

"No, I'll be all right. Just help me to the kitchen so I can eat."

She placed her arm gently around his waist and guided him in that direction. When they reached the table, Orley gritted his teeth and lowered himself into a chair. Lois hoped he'd be able to get out of it after he finished eating breakfast—all because her stubborn husband wouldn't accept her help when it came to moving the desk.

Lois felt bad that she hadn't been able to give Orley the gift she'd bought for him before his back went into spasm, but that could wait until they'd eaten breakfast and he'd made it to the couch to rest with an ice pack on his back.

Lois didn't voice her thoughts to Orley, but if his back pain didn't improve by noon, they wouldn't be going to his brother's house for dinner. She pulled her fingers into the palms of her hands. *What a way to begin our Christmas. I hope it gets better as the day goes along.*

Orley lay face-up on the couch with a cold ice pack under his back. Lois had talked him out of going to Samuel and Esther's, which meant his sweet wife had to come up with something to fix for their afternoon meal. Orley wished he hadn't been too stubborn to let Lois help him move that desk. Now he was paying the price for not swallowing his pride and trying to prove how strong he was. He'd asked his neighbor for help getting the desk into the house. He should have let Lois help him move it.

"I have something that might cheer you up." Lois came over to the couch with a green gift bag in her hand. "Merry Christmas, Orley." She placed the bag on his belly.

"You didn't have to get me anything."

"Of course I did." She smiled. "Now reach inside and see what it is."

Orley tipped the bag over, put his hand in, and pulled out a nice-sized Mississippi harmonica. Tears welled in his eyes. "Danki, Lois. This looks like the harmonica my grandpa Troyer used to play for me and my brothers when we were boys." He looked up at Lois and smiled. "Where did you find this mouth harp?"

"At the thrift store near Berlin. Do you like it?"

"Jah, I sure do. It was a thoughtful gift."

Lois took a seat in the rocking chair near the couch. "Do you feel up to playing something—maybe a Christmas song?"

"I can try, but it's been a good many years since I've had a harmonica between my lips."

"I bet it's just like riding a bike," she said. "Once you learn how, you never forget."

Orley rolled over onto his side and pulled himself to a sitting position. Placing the ice pack behind his back, he held the harmonica up to his mouth and blew a couple of notes. Then, like it was yesterday, Orley played "Silent Night" followed by "Away in a Manger." He looked at Lois and grinned, despite the continued throbbing in his back. "This gift has made my Christmas a little brighter, and I thank you for that."

She left her seat and came over to give him a kiss on the cheek. "Your Christmas present made me happy as well." Lois patted his knee. "If it doesn't hurt too bad to keep sitting up, why don't you continue to play while I go to the kitchen to fix our Christmas dinner."

"I believe I can do that."

As soon as Lois left the room, Orley began playing the mouth harp again. Being able to fill the room, and maybe the whole house, with music helped to take Orley's mind off his sore back. His thoughts were on Jesus and how thankful he felt for God's precious gift to the world.

Apple Creek

Andrea had spent Christmas morning on the computer while she nibbled on a piece of toast with peanut butter. It wasn't much of a breakfast, but she'd have plenty to eat when she and Brandon went to his parents' house for Christmas dinner. Brandon would be by to pick her up around twelve thirty, but that was an hour from now, so she could continue browsing the internet for a while yet.

Andrea had clicked on a page about adoption that she hadn't been to before, when her cell phone rang. She recognized Colleen's number and answered right away.

"Merry Christmas, my good friend." Colleen's voice had an upbeat tone.

"Merry Christmas to you too. Have you opened your presents yet?"

"We just finished, and now there's wrapping paper and bows scattered around the living room." Colleen chuckled. "You should have seen Tyler tear into his gifts. He was one excited little two-year-old."

"I can imagine."

"Shawn and I waited till Tyler had opened all his gifts and was busy playing with his new toys until we opened our presents. And that leads me to one of the reasons I called. I wanted to thank you for the beautiful painting you gave me of an Amish home with a horse and buggy going by."

"Do you like it?"

"It's beautiful. Sure wish I had your ability to paint. You are one talented lady."

"Thank you, and I'm glad you like the painting. When I dropped the gift by your house two days ago, I figured you might open it then."

"I admit I was tempted, but it's so much fun to wait and open presents on Christmas Day, I decided to wait."

"I understand." Andrea shifted on her chair when Lady leaped into her lap. She rubbed the cat's ears as she continued her conversation with Colleen.

"I haven't opened your gift yet either. It's still under the little tree I set up in the living room."

"Why don't you open it now? I'd like to know whether you like it or not."

"Sure, I can do that. Hang on while I get to the tree." Andrea lifted Lady off her lap and put her on the floor. Then she headed for the living room and picked up Colleen's gift. Although her friend had chosen to wait until Christmas Day to open her gift, Andrea had not committed to doing the same. She'd planned to open it last night, after Brandon brought her home from Christmas caroling with a group of single adults from their church, but she'd been too tired. Andrea had stayed up late nearly every night since she'd learned of her adoption and pushed herself each day to get all the necessary things done. Now she was on the brink of exhaustion.

Andrea put the phone in speaker mode and placed it on the couch beside her so she could keep talking while opening the gift.

"Okay, I have the gift, and I'm going to open it now." Andrea spoke loudly with her head turned in the direction of the phone.

"Great. Let me know what you think."

Andrea tore the wrapping paper off, lifted the lid on the box, and withdrew a square glass container with a beautiful red cardinal painted on it. "Oh, Colleen, it's beautiful!"

"You like it?"

"Of course I do. You know how excited I get whenever I see a cardinal."

"Yes, I do, and I gave it to you for another reason as well."

Andrea set the container on the end table near the couch and picked up the phone. "What's the other reason?"

"Since you love to paint and are such a talented artist, I thought you might want to consider painting some things on glass jars, bottles, or. . ."

"Oh, I don't know, Colleen. I'm really too busy right now to start any new projects."

"Of course, because of your wedding plans, right?"

"Umm. . .yeah. . .that and trying to locate my birth mother."

"Have you found anything out so far?"

"No, and I'm pretty discouraged. I ordered my DNA kit a few weeks ago and still have not received it." Andrea sighed. "I figured the kit would have been here by now."

"With the holiday season, the mail's probably slow. I'm sure it will arrive soon—maybe after the first of the year."

"I hope so. I'll take the test as soon as it gets here and send it back right away."

"Have you considered waiting until after you and Brandon are married to pursue your quest to find your biological parents?"

"No way! This is too important to me, and I can't wait that long."

"Okay. Like I've said to you before, let me know if I can be of any help."

"I will. Thanks, Colleen—for the painted cardinal and your friendship."

"You're welcome. I appreciate your friendship too."

The doorbell rang, and Andrea got up from the couch. "I'd better go. I think Brandon's here to pick me up to go to his parents' house for dinner. I'll talk to you again soon, okay?"

"For sure, and please let me know if there's anything I can do to help with either your wedding plans or the search for your birth mother."

"I will. Have a good rest of your day, and please tell your hubby I said, 'Merry Christmas.'"

"Will do, my friend."

After Andrea clicked off, she headed for the front door, nearly tripping over Lady, who'd found the wrapping paper from the box Colleen's gift had been in and was joyfully batting at it with her front paws.

When Andrea opened the front door, Brandon stepped inside, out of the cold, blustery day. "Merry Christmas, my beautiful wife-to-be."

"Merry Christmas, Brandon."

He enveloped her in a hug. "I have your gift in my vehicle. Should I bring it in?"

Andrea couldn't miss the gleam in his eyes. Whatever the gift was, she knew he was excited to present it to her. "That would be fine," she responded. "Unless you'd rather give it to me at your parents' house."

He shook his head. "The gift belongs here in your house—for now at least. Once we're married, I'm sure you'll want to bring it to my place when you move in with me."

She tipped her head then glanced at his SUV parked in the driveway. "Yes, please bring it in. You've aroused my curiosity."

"Okay. Take a seat in the living room, and I'll bring it right in."

After scooping Lady into her arms, Andrea did as he asked and seated herself on the couch. Brandon had left the front door open, and the last thing she needed was for her cat to make the great escape into the snowy front yard.

Several minutes went by before she heard the front door close, and then Brandon entered the room, carrying a beautiful vintage coffee table. "I hope you like it," he said, placing the table in front of the couch.

She let go of Lady, who promptly resumed playing with the wrapping paper, and placed both hands against her cheeks. "Oh my. . . It's so beautiful! Where did you get this old piece of furniture that's in such good condition?"

"I bought it at the same place you went to have that old quilt you bought this summer appraised."

"Memory Keepers in Walnut Creek?"

"Yes. The man who co-owns the shop was sure friendly and talkative."

"His wife was too. Did you meet her as well?"

Brandon shook his head. "Just Orley." He gestured to the table. "Do you like it?"

"Yes, very much. Thank you, Brandon. It's a thoughtful gift."

He offered her a wide smile and sat down beside her to give her a tender kiss. "I can't wait to make you my wife. February can't come soon enough."

Andrea swallowed hard and pulled her tongue across her lips. "About that. . . I'm wondering if it would be best to postpone the wedding."

Deep wrinkles formed across Brandon's forehead, making him look older than his thirty-five years. "Are you saying that you don't want to marry me?"

She shook her head vigorously. "No, no, I'm not saying that at all. I just think Valentine's Day is too soon."

His eyes narrowed as though in confusion. "Too soon for what? That's the day we both chose, and we'll be sending out wedding invitations next month, so we can't change the date." His voice had risen, and a sheen of sweat covered his forehead. Brandon was clearly shaken by her suggestion, but she needed to explain.

"The invitations haven't been sent to the printer yet, so there's still time to change the date."

"I don't want to change the date, and I can't believe that you apparently do." He stared at her. "What's the problem, Andrea? Do you not love me anymore?"

She clasped his arm. "Of course I love you. It's just that I'm so busy right now trying to find my biological parents, and it's taking longer than I'd hoped."

"I get that, but it's a concern to me that you would want to set our marriage plans aside in order to keep searching for someone who may not even want to be found."

Andrea's jaw tightened as she folded her arms across her chest. "I don't need that reminder, and I wish you'd be more understanding of the way I feel about finding my birth mother and knowing my true heritage."

Her words had apparently cut like a knife, and Brandon was quick to retaliate. "I've tried to be understanding, but you're so caught up in your search that you're not making time for us anymore."

She drew in a sharp intake of breath. "That's not true. We were together last evening, and I'm with you right now."

"Yes, but last night was the first time in a couple of weeks." A vein on the side of Brandon's neck bulged, the way it always did when he was upset.

Andrea was upset too. *He should be more understanding*, she thought. *And this is Christmas, so we should not be arguing.* She wished now that she hadn't brought up the topic of postponing the wedding. If they kept up with this conversation, they might end up canceling it altogether.

Chapter 27

"Let's table this discussion until later, okay?" Andrea left the couch and went over to stand by the Christmas tree. Did she know how upset he was, and was that why she felt the need to put some distance between them?

Brandon sat silently, unable to respond. The way he saw it, she cared more about finding her biological parents than becoming his wife. The fact that she'd even suggested postponing their wedding was like a punch in the gut.

Andrea has the right to look for her blood family but not at the expense of her relationship with me. Brandon closed his eyes and leaned his head against the back of the couch. *If Andrea had known about her adoption when she was a child and had found her birth parents by now, this would not be happening to us.*

"Brandon, did you hear what I said?"

His eyes snapped open.

"I have something for you." She handed him a silver-colored gift bag. "It's not nearly as nice as the gift you gave me, but I got you something that you'd said you needed."

Brandon took the gift and reached inside. The black wallet he took out was made of leather and provided plenty of space for credit cards, driver's license, and even a few business cards. "Thanks, Andrea. The wallet is great, and I appreciate your thoughtfulness."

"I'm glad you like it." She offered him a pleasant smile, then glanced at her watch. "It's about time we headed to your folks' house, don't you think?"

"Without finishing our conversation that involves you wanting to cancel our wedding plans?" With forced restraint, Brandon spoke through his teeth.

She shook her head. "I said postpone, not cancel. After things settle down in my life, we can sit down together and set a new date for our wedding."

I believe she's already made up her mind to do what she wants, no matter how this hurts me. "What if I don't want to postpone the wedding? Shouldn't I have some say in this?"

"Well, of course, but. . ." Andrea looked at her watch again. "We're gonna be late if we don't leave now, and I would prefer to discuss this some other time."

This bad news has spoiled my holiday cheer. And next we'll be going to my parents' place to ruin theirs and Andrea's parents' too. Brandon's spirits sank like a stone that had been tossed into a well. Unable to look at Andrea, he folded his arms and stared straight ahead. "I'd like to resolve it now. You either want to marry me or you don't."

"I do want to marry you, Brandon. Just not in February. As I stated before, I think it's too soon."

"No, it's not. We've been planning this for months already. My parents have made plans for the rehearsal dinner, and your folks have secured a venue for the reception."

"I'm sure they could get their money back or have it applied to a different date once we've decided when that will be."

"Maybe, but places like that are difficult to secure, and since you haven't suggested an alternate date for our wedding, there might not be time to get the nice venue for our reception that your parents want."

"I can't give you a specific date because I have no way of knowing when I might find my biological parents."

Brandon pulled his fingers through the back of his hair. "So let me get this straight. . . . You're not planning to marry me until you locate the woman who gave birth to you. Is that what you're saying?"

She fingered the hem of her dark green velveteen dress. "Not exactly."

"What are you saying?"

"I'm in the early stages of all this and don't even know the name of my birth mother. There's plenty more I still need to do, and it's going to take some time."

"I get that, but you can continue your search after we're married."

"I'd rather resolve this first so that after we're married, we can concentrate fully on each other."

Brandon's chin jutted out as he tapped one foot against the carpeted floor. This conversation was going nowhere, but he had one more thing to say, and he'd better say it quick, before he lost his nerve. "I love you, Andrea, but I am not going to take a back seat to your determination to find someone who may not even want to be found."

She pulled back as though she'd been slapped. "Are you saying that if I don't marry you in February, there will be no wedding at all?"

Is that what I'm saying? Brandon asked himself. *Am I willing to give up the woman I love because I don't want to wait indefinitely?*

Brandon cleared his throat a couple of times as he tried to make sense of everything. Endless moments passed. He turned to Andrea and said, "Okay, for now we can postpone the wedding. I'll give it a few months and see how it goes." Brandon leaned in, hand on one knee. "And while we're at my folks, eating our so-called merry Christmas dinner, you can be the one to tell both sets of our parents."

Andrea sat stiffly in the passenger's seat of Brandon's SUV as they headed for his parents' house. It had begun to snow again, and she kept her gaze on the road rather than looking at or conversing with Brandon.

Brandon remained quiet too. No doubt he was unhappy with her.

Andrea couldn't believe that he expected her to make the announcement to both sets of parents that they'd decided to postpone their wedding. *Maybe he's hoping they'll be upset over my decision and try to talk me out of pursuing my search.* She rolled her shoulders. *Or maybe they'll understand my situation. I guess Brandon wants them to know it was my idea and not his.* She fiddled with her purse straps. *In all honesty, it is, but I had hoped he might help me tell them. Maybe Brandon will back me up when I give the news. That's the least he should do since he agreed to my suggestion about postponing the wedding, although his disappointment was evident.*

She had hoped Brandon would be more understanding about the urgent need she felt to locate her biological parents and learn her true heritage. Apparently, that wasn't important to him. It bothered Andrea to realize that the man she planned to marry had so little understanding of what was driving her. If Brandon were in her place, wouldn't he want to know who had given him up for adoption and why they had done it?

Brandon turned right and drove up his parents' circular driveway, bringing Andrea's contemplations to a halt. Her father's car was parked near the garage, and Brandon pulled his vehicle next to it and turned off the ignition. She thought he might say something to her, but he just got out, opened the back door, and took out the box with the gifts they had brought along for their parents.

Andrea glanced at her reflection in the visor mirror and got out. She reached inside to get the plastic container holding the two desserts she'd brought along. She would need to force a smile on her face before going into the house and pray that everyone would understand when she told them about the wedding being postponed.

Walnut Creek

"I sure enjoyed your tasty egg drop soup." Orley tipped his mug and drank the last bit before setting it down. Even though they hadn't eaten a big Christmas meal today, he'd gotten stuffed with cheeseballs, crackers, and his wife's delicious soup.

"I'm glad you liked it." From across the table, Lois smiled at him. "I'm also happy that your back is feeling a bit better."

"Me too. The way it was hurting earlier, I wasn't sure I'd be able to leave the couch at all today." He grinned back at her. "I'm sure it was the cold ice packs and liniment you rubbed on my back that made it feel better."

"I'm glad it helped, but you should probably go lie down again while I clear the table and do the dishes." Lois gazed at him with sympathy in her eyes. "When you hurt, I do as well, and I want to make sure you take it easy for the rest of the day."

"I appreciate your concern, and I will heed your advice." He pushed slowly away from the table and stood. "When you're ready for dessert, can we eat it in the living room?"

"Of course. I'll bring it in after I finish the dishes. In the meantime, why don't you get comfortable on the couch and play some more Christmas songs on your harmonica? Or maybe you'd rather take a nap."

"No, I dozed long enough this morning, and if I keep napping, I won't sleep tonight when we're in bed."

Lois took an ice pack from the freezer section in their refrigerator and handed it to him. "You might want to take this with you."

"Danki. You're such a thoughtful fraa."

She waved his compliment aside. "Go on with you, now, and take it slow and easy."

"I will." Orley made his way out of the kitchen and ambled into the living room. Although his back didn't throb like it had earlier, he could still feel a strain, so it would feel good to sit or lie down on the comfortable couch again.

After he'd taken a seat and positioned the ice pack behind him, he picked up the mouth harp and played "The First Noel."

What a nice gift my wife gave me, he thought. *I'll always be thankful for the day I met her and even more thankful that she agreed to become my fraa.*

Apple Creek

When Andrea and Brandon entered the house, they were greeted by his parents. After they exchanged hugs, Jennifer took the container Andrea had brought and excused herself to return to the kitchen, while Larry said he was going back to the living room. Andrea's parents came from the back of the house just then.

"You look lovely in that velveteen dress," Andrea's mother commented after she gave Andrea a hug.

Andrea forced a smile. "Thanks. You look nice too."

"You do look pretty," her father agreed, "but your droopy eyelids make me think you may not have been getting enough sleep lately."

Andrea stiffened. *Since when is Dad worried about how much sleep I get?*

"Honey, don't you know it's rude to tell someone they look tired?" Mom nudged Dad's arm.

"Sorry. I was just stating a fact, and as a father, it's my right to worry about my daughter." He turned to Brandon, gave him a hearty handshake, and said, "You'll find that out someday, when you and Andrea have children."

"Yeah, I suppose." Brandon threw Andrea a glance, and then he looked back at her father. "Shall we join my dad in the living room to visit and watch TV till dinner is ready?"

"Sounds like a plan. That's what Larry and I were doing before you and Andrea arrived."

Brandon bent down and picked up the box with the gifts he and Andrea had brought. After giving Andrea one more quick glance, he followed her dad to the living room.

"Jennifer and I have things pretty well under control in the kitchen." Andrea's mother gave Andrea's arm a pat. "If you'd like to relax in the living room with the men, that's fine with me."

Andrea shook her head. "I'm sure there must be something in the kitchen for me to do."

"Yes, dear, I suppose there is, but as your dad pointed out, you do look a bit tired, so I thought maybe. . ."

"I'm fine, Mom, and I'm going to the kitchen with you." Andrea couldn't believe that her mother had brought up the topic of her looking tired, when a few moments ago she'd told Andrea's dad that it had been rude of him to comment on her tired appearance.

Mom gave Andrea's arm another pat. "Okay, dear, if you don't want to rest, we'll find something for you to do."

"You've outdone yourself this year," Brandon said, looking at his mother as he held up a piece of turkey. "This is a really tender piece of meat, and it's not a bit dry either."

His mother smiled. "Thanks, Son. I'm glad you like it. I bought an organic turkey this year and cooked it in one of those baking bags."

"It's very good," Andrea spoke up. It was the first thing she'd said since they had all taken their seats around the dining room table. Brandon wondered if his parents and hers felt the tension growing stronger between them with each passing minute.

Is she ever going to bring up the topic of our wedding? he asked himself. *I hope Andrea's not waiting for me to do it—especially since I made it clear that since the change of plans was her idea, she'd need to be the one to make the announcement.*

"Every bit of food on the table is delicious," Evelyn spoke up. "Even the green bean casserole I brought." Her cheeks colored. "I don't mean that in a bragging sort of way. I just followed the recipe I found in a magazine not long ago."

"It's okay," Andrea's dad said, leaning close to her. "The casserole, like all the food you ladies served, is real tasty. You and Jennifer have every right to brag. And I'm eager to try some of the pumpkin bread and apple pie Andrea brought for dessert," he added. "She takes after her mother when it comes to her baking skills."

Andrea dropped her gaze to the table.

The conversation moved from raving over the food to discussing the weather.

"I'm glad it has finally stopped snowing," Jennifer commented. "A white Christmas is beautiful and really sets the mood, but I'm already looking forward to when spring comes and brings warmer weather."

Everyone nodded except Andrea. She stared at her half-eaten meal while pushing a green bean slowly around on her plate.

Talk about the weather continued, and then it changed a few more times when someone brought up a new topic. Still Andrea had not said anything about their wedding plans.

Finally, when Brandon thought he couldn't stand it anymore, he gave Andrea's foot a little nudge under the table. She looked over at him with furrowed brows but made no comment.

Several more minutes passed, and after clearing her throat a few times, Andrea finally said, "There's something Brandon and I need you all to know."

"What would that be?" her father asked.

She looked at Brandon as though hoping he might say something, but he didn't budge.

Without looking at anyone in particular, she proclaimed, "We've decided to postpone our wedding."

"Wh–what?" Andrea's mother gasped. "You're not getting married?"

Andrea shook her head vigorously. "Oh no, I didn't say that. It just won't be in February."

"Why not?" The question came from Brandon's mother, who spoke in a disbelieving voice. "So many plans have already been made. I can't imagine why you'd need to change them—especially at this late date."

"That's right," his dad put in. "It makes no sense to cancel when you're this far along with your plans."

The only parent who had not spoken up was Andrea's dad. He just sat there, slowly shaking his head. Finally, he looked over at Brandon and said, "Have you and my daughter had a falling out? Is that the reason you want to postpone the wedding?"

"No, no, Dad. . .that's not it." Andrea's chin trembled, and Brandon knew it was time for him to speak up on his own behalf.

"I still love Andrea very much, and it wasn't my idea to delay our wedding."

"Why then?" her mother asked, looking at Andrea again.

"As all of you know, I have been in the process of searching for my biological parents." Andrea paused and sucked in a quick breath. "The process is taking some time and could take even longer. If I were to marry Brandon in February, as we had originally planned, I may still be looking for my birth parents." She stopped talking and took in another breath. "The extra time I will need to spend wouldn't be good for a new marriage, and I will not do that to Brandon." She gave a slow shake of her head. "It wouldn't be fair."

Brandon's mother looked at Andrea with a watery gaze. "What if you never find your birth mother? You can't expect our son to wait for you indefinitely."

Brandon's muscles became rigid. "Mother, please! This is between me and Andrea, and we will work things out."

She blinked rapidly. "Of course. I'm just concerned about both of you."

"So am I," Evelyn put in. "I don't think putting your marriage off is the answer."

"What is the answer, Mom?" Andrea asked.

"I don't know, dear, but this is something we all need to pray about." She looked over at Ray. "Don't you agree?"

"Yes, I do," he responded, "but in the end, it's Andrea and Brandon's decision."

"I concur," Brandon's dad spoke up. "We all need to pray and then let the bride- and groom-to-be decide what's best for them."

Brandon reached for his glass of water and took a drink. He'd thought he had known what was best for him and Andrea until she'd brought up the topic of putting their marriage on hold. Now he wasn't sure about anything.

Chapter 28

Jennifer sat at the kitchen table, massaging the back of her neck. "Our poor son. I can't believe Andrea wants to postpone their wedding. Didn't you see the hurt expression on his face when she made the announcement? He still appeared to be upset when they left here a short time ago."

"Yes, I'm aware." Larry got up and went around to stand behind Jennifer and take over her neck rub. "Try not to worry so much, Jen. Brandon is a grown man, and we can't shield him from situations that are not in our control."

"I realize that, but he needs our full support right now. What Andrea is putting him through is just not fair." Jennifer grimaced as Larry hit a tender spot on her neck. "If she's more interested in finding her birth mother than marrying Brandon, then I think he should break up with her."

"You're kidding, right?"

"No, I'm not. I am still dazed about Andrea wanting to postpone their wedding in February, and I don't understand why she couldn't give us a new date. Andrea can't expect Brandon to wait forever."

"Maybe she'll find out something soon in regard to her adoption. Evelyn did mention before Andrea and Brandon got here today that Andrea had sent away for a DNA test. That could be the ticket to learning who her biological parents are."

"You can stop massaging my neck now. It feels better," Jennifer said, making no comment regarding her husband's last statement. Even if Andrea found her birth mother tomorrow, it didn't change the fact that the young woman had postponed her wedding to a man she was supposed to love. Brandon deserved better than that—if not with Andrea then with some sweet woman more deserving of him. *And maybe,* Jennifer thought, *if this whole thing with the search for her blood parents goes on much longer, Brandon might decide she's not the right woman for him and find someone else.*

"Ray, would you please slow down? The roads might be icy." Evelyn glanced nervously out the front window of their car as they headed home.

"It's warmed up, and I seriously doubt we'll find any patches of ice."

"Well, go a little slower anyway, please. I'm really on edge tonight." She could see the speedometer and felt relieved when her husband slowed their vehicle.

"I'm not surprised you're feeling anxious. When Andrea told us that she and Brandon had postponed their wedding, from that point on, you were wound up tighter than a clock."

Evelyn tried to calm herself on the ride home by looking out the passenger's side window at homes decorated with colored lights and yard displays for Christmas. But the views did nothing to relieve her anxious thoughts. *I had hoped my daughter could juggle the adoption business and still prioritize things for her and Brandon's future. I don't believe she's thought this through.* Evelyn shifted in her seat, letting out a deep sigh.

"I can't help feeling wound up," she stated, glancing in Ray's direction. "All these months we've been planning for the wedding, and now we have to cancel everything, including the use of our church." Evelyn twisted the ties attached to her coat collar around her fingers and frowned. "What are we supposed to tell everyone now? There are so many people who know about the wedding plans."

"We will tell them the truth—that the wedding's been postponed until a later date. Nobody has to know the reason."

Evelyn drew a deep breath and released it with a huff. "I wish Andrea's well-meaning cousin had never said anything to her about being adopted. Nothing has been the same for anyone in this family since she found out, and now it's affected her relationship with Brandon."

"I don't think you have anything to worry about, dear. Andrea and Brandon love each other, and they'll work things out."

I can't help having regrets about what the past is doing to us now. If only Ray and I had been honest with our daughter when she was a child, things might be different right now. She glanced at some more Christmas decorations as they went past. *If we'd been up front with her a long time ago, Andrea might not have chosen to look for her birth parents at all, or she might already know who they are and that would be it.*

Evelyn thought about the promise she'd made to herself to help Andrea find out who her birth mother was. She'd been so busy with other things that she hadn't done much of anything to help her daughter find out what she deserved to know. *I need to get busy on that*, she told herself. *My first order of business will be to find out if the state of Pennsylvania has altered their law about not releasing original birth certificates in closed adoptions. If the law is still in place, then maybe the adoption agency Ray and I used will be able to help.*

The ride back to Andrea's house Christmas evening was quiet. She couldn't think of anything nice to say because she felt like Brandon had thrown her under the bus by insisting that she be the one to tell their folks about the decision to postpone the wedding. From the moment Andrea had announced it, the atmosphere in the room changed. At first it seemed as though everyone was in shock, and then came the questions and concerns raised by Brandon's parents and hers. Andrea was fairly certain that no one understood her reasons nor did they seem to care whether she found her biological parents. *I had hoped someone would understand my situation and back me up 100 percent. I thought family was supposed to be there for you—especially at a time like this.*

Andrea rubbed her throbbing forehead. She'd felt a nagging headache coming on soon after they'd eaten their meal, but she had toughed it out until they'd eaten their dessert a few hours later. Finally, when the throbbing increased, she'd told Brandon that she had a headache and needed to go home. After he'd agreed to her request, she'd said a hasty goodbye to everyone, put on her coat, and hurried out the door, forgetting about the gifts she'd received from his parents and hers. Brandon hadn't forgotten, though, for he'd hauled the box full of gifts out to his SUV and put it in the back.

Andrea was thankful that the temperature had warmed up some and the roads were wet, not icy. That was one thing she didn't have to worry about as they continued driving.

When they approached her house, Brandon put the blinker on and pulled his rig onto the driveway. "I'll get the box from the back and carry it into the house for you." It was the first thing he had said to Andrea since they'd left his parents' house.

"Okay," she responded. "I'll take the gifts out that are mine, and you can take the box with your gifts to your house."

Brandon just got out of the vehicle and went to the back to get the box.

Andrea got out too and hurried up the front porch steps to open the door. She stepped into the hall and noticed that Brandon was right behind her. "You can take the box into the living room," she said. "I'll take my gifts out there and place them under the tree for now." Putting their open presents under the tree for a day or so after they'd received them was something Andrea's parents had done ever since she could remember. Her mother had said many times over the years that it was fun to look at what they'd received for a while until it was time to take down the tree and put everything away.

Brandon did as Andrea had asked, and after she'd removed her presents and placed them under the tree, he turned to her and said, "We need to talk."

Andrea grimaced. "Brandon, you know I have a headache."

"I'm aware, but you took two aspirin before leaving my folks' house, and what I have to say is important, so I'd appreciate it if you would hear me out."

"All right." She gestured to the couch. "Let's have a seat."

They'd no sooner sat down when Lady darted into the room and leaped onto Andrea's lap. The cat's soothing purr and the feel of her sandpapery tongue as she licked Andrea's hand helped her feel a bit more relaxed.

"What do you want to talk about?" She turned her head to look at Brandon.

"You. Me. Our relationship that seems to be on pretty shaky ground."

Andrea couldn't miss the hurt in his eyes. "It doesn't have to be if we just give it some time."

"How much time?"

She shrugged. "I—I'm not sure. At least until—"

"Oh, there we go again. I'm supposed to wait patiently until you find the woman who gave birth to you. Right?"

"I've explained this to you before. I need to find out about my true heritage." Andrea stroked Lady's ears, hoping the feel of the cat's silky hair might make her feel calmer.

"How about concentrating on us for a change?"

The tension she heard in Brandon's voice let Andrea know how frustrated he felt.

She forced herself to look at him. "You're not being fair."

A muscle in his jaw twitched. "I'm the one not being fair? You said you loved me, and you were eagerly planning our wedding until your cousin revealed your family's secret that you were adopted."

"I still love you, Brandon," Andrea murmured. "I just can't commit to marriage right now. It wouldn't be fair to either of us."

"Speak for yourself." He heaved a sigh and pulled his fingers through the back of his hair. "I love you, Andrea, and I want you to be my wife, but I get the feeling that you think finding your birth mother is more important than me or anything else right now." He paused and then stood. "I think it would be better if we didn't see each other anymore."

Her eyes widened. "Are. . .are you breaking up with me?"

"Yeah, guess I am." His expression was as solemn as an unyielding mask. "If you ever change your mind about us, let me know."

She blinked slowly, trying to let his words set in. "I haven't changed my mind. I just. . ."

He held up his hand. "I can't deal with this anymore, Andrea. It's not fair to expect me to sit around waiting for you to find what you're looking for, knowing it might not happen at all. You may spend the rest of your life searching for something you'll never find. I'm sorry, but if I'm not at the top of your list, then I'd rather not be on the list at all." He picked up the box with his gifts and headed for the front door.

The words "Brandon, wait!" were on the tip of Andrea's tongue, but he went out the door before she could speak them.

"Maybe he's right," Andrea murmured, as her tears dripped onto Lady's back. "He's better off without me since I don't know what my future holds." She touched the engagement ring on her left hand. *I'll need to see that he gets this back. Maybe Colleen would be willing to return it for me.*

The phone rang the next morning, pulling Andrea out of a deep sleep. She looked at the clock beside her bed and realized that she'd slept until 10 a.m.

"Oh boy." She rubbed her eyes and reached for her cell phone. "Hello," she rasped, barely able to find her voice.

"Hey, friend. How'd your Christmas go? Did you have a nice dinner at Brandon's parents?"

"The food was good, but that's about all." Andrea sat up and dangled her feet over the edge of her bed.

"What do you mean?" Colleen asked. "Did something upsetting happen yesterday?"

"You could say that, and it didn't end at the dinner table."

"Sorry to hear it. Can you fill me in?"

Andrea spent the next several minutes telling Colleen how she'd announced to her parents and Brandon's parents that she and Brandon had decided to postpone their wedding."

"You're kidding."

"No, I'm not."

"What made you and Brandon do that?"

"It was my idea. I'm really tied up right now with trying to search for my birth mother, and I didn't think getting married in February would be a good idea since there's a good chance I won't have the answers I seek by then."

"I guess that makes sense, but I bet everyone was disappointed."

"Yes—especially Brandon. He's not supportive of my endeavors to find my biological parents, and if I married him before I found answers and kept on with my search, it would be bound to affect our marriage."

"You might be right, but you both love each other, and I'm sure Brandon would help with your search if you asked him to."

"I would never ask him to do that. He's too busy with his clinic." Andrea's eyes filled with tears, and she grabbed a tissue to blow her nose. "You haven't even heard the worst of it yet."

"You mean there's more?"

"Yeah. When Brandon brought me home last night, we broke up."

"What?" Colleen's voice was practically a screech. "Why would you do that?"

"It was his choice. He's convinced that I care about the quest to find my birth mother more than I do him, so he basically said we should call it quits." Andrea swallowed around the constriction in her throat. "I still love him, but maybe breaking things off is best for both of us."

"You can't mean that. Surely, there's some way you two can work things out."

"I don't know what it could be, short of me giving up the search that involves my adoption." Andrea paused to reach for another tissue. "I have a big favor to ask of you."

"Anything. Just name it."

"Would you be willing to return my engagement ring to Brandon? I should have done it while he was here, but I was flustered. I didn't think about giving the ring back to him."

"Don't you think that's something you should do yourself?"

"I can't. It would hurt too much. Please, Colleen. It's really important to me."

Her friend was quiet. Finally, she said, "Okay. I'll come by later today and get the ring."

"Thank you."

"I only agreed to do it because you're my best friend, but it doesn't mean I agree with your decision, because I think you're making a mistake."

Andrea didn't respond to that. Instead, she posed another question. "If I do find my birth mother, do you think Brandon would take me back?"

"I don't know. It might be too late by then." Andrea heard the sound of Colleen's finger snap. "Say, I have an idea. Why don't you write another letter to the Dear Caroline column? She gave you good advice before, and maybe she will again."

"I'll give it some thought." Andrea glanced at the clock. "In the meantime, I'd better get dressed and try to get something done today. I went to bed with a splitting headache last night and slept much longer than I'd planned."

"Okay, I'll come by around two o'clock. Would that work for you?"

"Yes, and thanks again for agreeing to take the ring to Brandon."

"As a good friend, I don't see I have any other choice. I'll see you later, Andrea. Bye for now."

Andrea clicked off the phone and went to the window to look out. No snow on the horizon, but the ground was still white from what had fallen before. She reflected on what a day she'd had yesterday. It still bothered her that neither his folks nor hers had said they understood and supported her need to keep searching until she found her birth parents. Worse yet, at the end of an already difficult evening, her fiancé had broken their engagement.

I'm glad Colleen is in my corner, even if she doesn't think Brandon and I should have broken up. At least she cares about me and supports my decision. Andrea felt the familiar bumping of a tail about knee height as she continued to stare out at the snow, trying to ignore her determined cat. It was a new day, and Andrea was free to do whatever she needed to get done. But having Brandon out of her life was not what she wanted or intended to have happen. Her chin trembled. *I thought he loved me as much as I love him.*

She looked down at Lady, who continued rubbing against Andrea's legs. "Okay, girl, I'm coming. I know you want to be fed."

Andrea put on her slippers and robe, then plodded out of the room. She felt an uncomfortable heaviness in her chest and limbs. *Why can't things be different right now? I wish I'd never found out that I was adopted. After I've had some breakfast, I'm going to take Colleen's advice and write another letter to Dear Caroline.*

Chapter 29

Brandon left the first examining room and headed down the hall for room 2 with a sense of determination. It had been nearly a week since his breakup with Andrea, and he dreaded tomorrow evening and spending New Year's Eve alone.

Of course, he reasoned, *I could always go over to my folks' place and join the little gathering they have planned with my brother Joe and his family. Mom did invite me, after all.* He pursed his lips. *I think she felt sorry for me and wanted to cheer me up after I told her and Dad that Andrea and I broke up.*

He paused in the hallway to let his thoughts sink in. It was hard for Brandon to concentrate on his animal patients when all he could think about was his broken engagement with Andrea. Despondency clung to him like a wet garment, only he couldn't take it off. Had he done the right thing? Could they ever get back together? Maybe, if she either found her birth mother or gave up the search. But that was doubtful since she seemed so determined to proceed. *And what about my dog and her cat? Now that Andrea and I aren't seeing each other, Duke won't be spending time with Lady anymore.* He frowned. *What good did it do for Andrea and me to work so hard at getting our pets to like each other?*

A dog's bark coming from the second examining room reminded Brandon to keep walking in that direction. No matter what happened in the future, Brandon's clinic was his responsibility and a job he enjoyed. He owed it to his animal patients and their owners to give them the best care possible, so that's what he would do.

Andrea had said goodbye to one of her younger piano students when the mailman stepped onto the porch.

"Here you go." He handed her a stack of mail along with a larger, padded envelope. "I hope not too many of them are bills. You know how it is. . . . Before Christmas it's lots of ads, and after the holiday, the bills come in."

"Thank you." She forced a smile, gave a brief nod, and stepped back inside.

After placing the mail on the table inside the entryway, Andrea discovered that the padded envelope was from AncestryDNA.

"Oh good, it's finally here!" Her pulse quickened. "I'll take this right away, then send it back in the mail. Hopefully, I'll know something soon." Andrea wanted to find out everything possible about her lineage. She hoped the test would bring to light her nationality and shed some light on who her birth parents were.

Andrea was about to go through the rest of the mail when her cell phone rang. She'd left it in the kitchen while she taught piano lessons this morning, so she hurried to grab it before it went to voice mail.

"Hi, Mom." Andrea recognized her mother's number right away. "Guess what? I have good news."

"Are you and Brandon getting back together?"

"No, it's not that."

"I'm sorry to hear it. When you called the day after Christmas and said Brandon had broken things off with you, I really felt bad. You two are a special couple, and I'd really hoped that—"

"Mom, my DNA test kit came in the mail today. I'm excited to take it and can't wait for the results to see if there might be a match."

"That's wonderful, dear, and I have some good news too."

"What is it?"

"I did some checking on an adoption website for the state of Pennsylvania and discovered that a law they'd previously made had been changed back in 2017. Sure wish I would have had knowledge of that sooner."

"What law was that?"

"The one that said birth certificates from closed adoptions could not be available to anyone. Under the new law, adoptees over the age of eighteen can apply for their original birth records for the first time in thirty-three years."

Andrea's thoughts were scattered. "Let me get this straight—you said the law's been changed. Does that actually mean I can gain access to my original birth certificate now?"

"Yes, Andrea. You can apply to the state Department of Health for a copy of it. There is a twenty-five-dollar filing fee, and applications are expected to take about forty-five days to be processed."

Andrea's senses heightened. "Oh Mom, that is such good news. I don't know why I didn't think to check on that myself. It should have been one of the first things I did in my quest to search for the woman who gave birth to me. I just thought since it was a closed adoption that there would be no way I could acquire a copy of my original certificate."

"And now you can." There was a brief pause. "I'm happy for you, Andrea, and I hope that once you discover the name of the woman who gave birth to you, you'll be able to locate her."

"Thank you, Mom." Andrea felt good knowing that her adoptive mother had been helpful in the endeavor to discover her true heritage.

Walnut Creek

Lois shivered and went to the living room to stoke the fire in their free-standing woodstove. They'd had a cold snap two days ago, and the frigid temperatures had frozen their neighbor's pond. So as soon as school let out for the day, several children from their neighborhood had gotten out their ice skates and headed for the ice. Orley, with all the exuberance of a teenager, had found his old skates and informed Lois not to start supper too soon because he'd probably be gone a few hours.

She opened the stove door and saw that the fire had burned up most of the wood. She picked out a couple nice-sized logs and carefully added one at a time to the hot embers. She moved the logs in farther with the metal poker that rested nearby and then closed the door. The heat she longed for wouldn't take long to begin warming the room. *I'm thinking by the time Orley comes in from frolicking on the ice, this front room should be warm and inviting.*

Lois took a seat in one of the recliners. She couldn't believe that her husband, who had recently recovered from a sore back, would risk reinjuring it while skating—and in such cold weather, no less.

"But I shouldn't be surprised," Lois murmured. "Even when Orley's body is hurting, he never stays down very long. He's been a go-getter all the time I've known him." She could only imagine what her enthusiastic husband must have been like as a child. Probably not much different than he was right now, only Orley had been able to do a lot more foolhardy things back then.

For supper, Lois had put a small ham in the oven an hour ago, and she would serve it along with some boiled potatoes and peas. While the ham baked at a low temperature and she waited for Orley to come home, she would try to get some Dear Caroline letters read.

Lois felt the room beginning to warm up, along with the inviting popping and crackling coming from the wood-burning stove. She had always liked the warmth of a real fire and the heat it gave. Not that electric heat wasn't good, like in her English neighbor's place, but a good wood fire seemed to warm a person clear to the bones. Lois had placed a manila envelope full of letters on the small table beside her chair, so she picked it up and pulled out the first letter.

> *Dear Caroline,*
>
> *I've written to you before, after learning that I was adopted, and I'm currently in the process of trying to find my biological parents. The man I was planning to marry doesn't understand why this is so important to me. When I told him I wanted to postpone our wedding, he was upset, and last week he broke up with me. What can I do to get him to be more understanding and take me back? Do I need to stop the search for my birth mother, or am I better off without a man who doesn't support my endeavor?*
>
> *—Brokenhearted*

Lois held the letter against her chest while closing her eyes in prayer. *Dear Lord, please give me the right words to share with this distraught woman. I can only imagine how much she is hurting. May my words be Your words when I respond to her desperate-sounding letter.*

As Orley limped home from the neighbor's place, he thought about what Lois would say when she heard that he'd fallen several times, leaving him with two very sore knees. No doubt she would say something like "You're getting too old for ice-skating. You should leave that kind of sport to the younger ones who have better balance."

"You're only as young as you feel," Orley muttered. "Course, right now I don't feel so young."

When Orley reached his home, he grabbed hold of the handrail and made his way slowly up the stairs. Upon entering the house via the back door, he was greeted with the tantalizing aroma of baked ham. It would feel good to eat but even better to get out of his cold, wet clothes and put something soothing on his sore knees.

Maybe I can sneak into the bathroom and take a shower before Lois sees me, Orley told himself as he hobbled down the hallway, gritting his teeth.

No such luck, however. His wife must have heard him come in, for she stepped into the hallway from the living room as he was going by. "I'm glad you're back, but why are you limping so badly?" Her brows drew together.

He turned to face her. "I fell on the ice. More than once, I might add." Orley pointed to his knees. "I didn't break any bones, but I think my *gnie* must be bruised. On top of that, I'm so cold, my teeth are chattering."

She placed her hands against her hips. "You'd best get a warm shower and put some of that arnica cream on your sore knees. It's on the second shelf in the medicine cabinet."

He looked at her through half-closed eyes. "Aren't ya gonna say, 'I told you so'?"

Lois shook her head. "What would be the point? You've no doubt figured out that you should have stayed home where it's nice and warm and let the young people take their chances on the ice."

"Jah, but you know me—once my knees feel better, I'll probably grab my skates again and head right back out to that frozen pond."

Lois moved closer to him and reached up to stroke his cold cheek. "I guess some things never change."

Exhausted and hungry, Brandon entered his kitchen to fix something to eat. He wasn't in the mood to cook and wished now that he'd stopped at Lem's to get a pizza to bring home, but he was here now and may as well make the best of it.

Before checking the refrigerator for something easy to fix, Brandon poured dog food into Duke's dish.

The Brittany spaniel looked up at him and barked.

"Go ahead, buddy, eat your supper. After we've both finished eating, I'll take you out for a walk. I'll look at the neighbors' Christmas lights that haven't been taken down yet while you pull on the leash and sniff your way along, wagging your tail."

Duke ran over to the door and barked again, a little louder this time.

Brandon thumped the side of his head. "Oh, right. . .you want to go out right now. Well, that means no walk outside of the yard till after supper, but I will let you roam free in the yard."

Woof! Woof!

Since Brandon hadn't removed his jacket yet, he opened the door and stepped out onto the front porch. Duke zipped between his legs, raced down the steps, and into the yard.

Brandon shook his head. *Wish I had half as much energy as my dog does tonight.* He leaned on the porch railing and watched as Duke made his way around the yard a couple of times. Although the front of Brandon's property was fenced in, he'd forgotten to shut the gate. So rather than close it now, he would remain on the porch and watch until the dog was ready to come back inside. Duke never left the yard as long as Brandon was nearby, keeping a close watch on him.

Brandon observed his own breath as he blew out several puffs of air. As he continued to wait for Duke to do his business, he let his thoughts wander.

I wonder what Andrea is doing this evening. Does she miss me as much as I miss her, or is she so engrossed in searching for her birth mother that she hasn't even given me a thought today? I wonder if she's made any plans for New Year's Eve. Last year they'd gotten together with some other unmarried couples from church for an evening of games and refreshments. This year Brandon had made no plans. He'd probably veg out in front of the TV with a movie, his dog, and a bowl of buttery popcorn.

Woof! Woof!

Brandon looked down, surprised to see Duke sitting at his feet looking up at him. He hadn't even realized the dog had come onto the porch.

"Ready to go inside?"

Woof! Duke made a beeline for the door.

Brandon had to smile despite his melancholy mood. It was a pleasure to own a dog like Duke—always eager to please and wanting to be near his owner.

Back in the kitchen, Duke went to work on his dog food while

Brandon hung up his jacket and took out the ingredients to make a ham and cheese sandwich. He had just taken a seat at the table when the doorbell rang. His heart beat a few extra beats. *Could that be Andrea?* He shook his head. *It's not likely that she'd be coming to see me, but I guess I'd better go see who rang the bell.*

When Brandon opened the front door, he was surprised to see Colleen on his porch.

"Sorry to show up unannounced, but I figured I'd probably find you at home around this time. I hope I'm not interrupting your supper."

"It's okay, I haven't eaten yet. Come on in out of the cold." Brandon held the door open wider and waited until Andrea's friend came fully into the house before asking the question on the tip of his tongue.

"What brings you by here on this cold night?"

"I came to see how you're doing and to deliver this." Colleen reached into her purse and withdrew a small green velvet box. "Andrea asked if I would return this to you."

Brandon didn't have to open the box to know what was inside. It was the beautiful engagement ring he'd carefully picked out for her. He took the box and set it on the entryway table. "I'm guessing she didn't have the courage to give it to me herself."

"Right." Colleen touched Brandon's arm. "I was sorry to hear about your breakup with Andrea. You have to know how much she loves you."

"Yeah, right. Andrea loves me so much that she has put finding her birth mother ahead of marrying me." He looked down and gave the green box a tap. "She's the one who called off our wedding, you know."

Colleen shook her head. "She didn't call off the wedding, just decided it would be best to postpone it until—"

"I'm aware." Brandon couldn't keep the disillusionment he felt out of his voice. "Andrea cares more about that than she does me."

"So you ended your relationship with her." Colleen's words were not posed as a question. She'd stated a fact.

"Yes, I did," he admitted. "Under the circumstances, it seemed like the only sensible thing to do."

Colleen's brows furrowed as she looked up at him. "So you're not willing to wait until Andrea finds the answers she's seeking?"

He shook his head. "She might be searching indefinitely and never find closure, which would mean that marrying me would never happen."

"Does that mean you'll be looking for someone to replace my dear friend?" At the end of her sentence, Colleen's lips pressed together.

His muscles tensed, and he gave a huff. "I am in no hurry to find a replacement for Andrea. I'm still in love with her, but I can't be expected to wait forever, and if she really loves me as much as she says, then I should come first, not a biological parent she's never even met. A woman who may not want to be found," he added with emphasis.

"I understand why you would feel that way, but I'm bothered by the fact that you aren't more understanding of how Andrea feels. If you really love her, shouldn't you stand beside her in all this and maybe even take part in the search for her mother?"

Brandon stood with his hands clasped tightly together. "I'm not an insensitive man. As I'm sure you must know, my veterinary practice keeps me very busy, so I really don't have time to begin a hunt for Andrea's blood relatives."

"No one's asking you to, but you could have been more supportive of Andrea in all this. The fact that you broke up with her was like a slap in the face. She's deeply hurt and misses you very much."

"Did Andrea tell you that?"

"Yes." She placed her hand on his arm again. "Did you pray about this matter, or did you break up with Andrea because you were angry?"

"Not angry but hurt that I seem to be the last item on her list these days." He pressed one hand against his chest. "You're right about one thing, though. I have not prayed about this, so thanks for pointing that out."

"I hope you will spend some time in prayer." Colleen turned toward the door. "I'll let you get back to whatever you had planned this evening. I need to head for home. Shawn graciously agreed to fix supper for us this evening so I could come over here. I'm sure the meal is about ready by now, and I don't want to keep my family waiting."

Brandon opened the door for her. "Thanks for sharing your thoughts with me. I know you have Andrea's best interest at heart. She's fortunate to have a good friend like you."

"I have your interest at heart too, and I'm praying for both of you," she said before going out the door.

Brandon watched until Colleen had gotten into her car and pulled out of the driveway. Then he shut the door and returned to the kitchen, where he sank into a chair at the table. *I do need to pray about this. I need to seek the Lord's will and ask for His wisdom in deciding what is best for my life as well as Andrea's.*

Chapter 30

Walnut Creek

Orley wandered around Memory Keepers with a clipboard and paper in one hand and a pencil in the other. It was that time of the year when he and Lois did inventory of the stock on hand for tax purposes and also to determine what else they would need to acquire for the new year. Lois had been helping him this morning and had already finished one side of the store, but she had letters to mail, so Orley said he would finish the job while she went to the post office.

His thoughts went to how he and Lois seemed to have an eye for finding the right objects to sell in their business. Orley liked to see the happy faces of customers who found special treasures in their store. The other day a married couple had come in looking for nostalgic old advertising signs. They'd seemed pleased when they discovered one hanging on the store wall that featured an old soda pop product.

Orley moved on to one of the other shelves and counted the crystal pieces, making note of them on his clipboard. *I know a couple of these have sold lately and a few brass items as well.*

Orley paused from his work to look out the front window. He had heard from one of the customers earlier that the weatherman said Walnut Creek might see more snow this evening—maybe up to a few inches. Orley had not noticed any sign of it so far and wondered if their driver would be coming to pick them up for the trip home before any snow fell. He'd only seen a few people out shopping today, but they were two weeks into the new year already, and it wasn't unusual for people to do less shopping after the holidays. Besides, the weather in this part of Ohio was still plenty cold.

Normally, Orley would have enjoyed the lower temperatures, but he had not taken advantage of the colder temperatures to go ice-skating again or even taken his sled out on the hill. Since he'd bruised both knees so badly, Orley had temporarily lost interest in all outdoor games that could cause some sort of an injury. He'd been content to spend his free time with Lois, putting puzzles together, playing board games, or blowing on the mouth harp she'd given him for Christmas. Although he enjoyed outdoor fun, he was not about to risk getting hurt again. Next time he fell, it could be something more serious, like breaking a bone or falling through a section of thin ice.

Orley thought about an entry in *The Budget* last week, where one of the scribes from Wisconsin had written about a young boy from their community who had fallen through the ice and drowned. *How sad*, Orley thought. *My heart goes out to that child's parents. I wonder if the boy had gone skating alone or if there were others around who had witnessed the accident. I'm sure if there had been other people at the pond, they would have done all they could to try and save him.*

Continuing to gaze out the window and forcing aside his sad thoughts, Orley spotted the veterinarian who had visited the shop before Christmas and noticed that the young man seemed to be heading this way. Sure enough, a few minutes later the bell above the front door jingled and the man stepped inside the store.

"Well, hello there." Orley extended his hand. "It's Brandon, right?"

"Yes. I was here a few weeks ago." He gave Orley a hearty but cold handshake.

"I remember. You bought a vintage coffee table for your fiancée."

Brandon gave a nod. "Only we're not getting married after all."

"That's too bad. I hope it didn't have anything to do with the gift you gave her." Orley moved toward the front counter and placed the clipboard and pencil on it.

"No, she liked the coffee table. It's me she doesn't like very much anymore." Brandon dropped his gaze to the floor for a few seconds and then lifted his head and looked back at Orley with a grim expression. "She's in the process of trying to find her biological parents and said she wanted to postpone our February wedding because she's so wrapped up in her quest."

"Did you agree to that?"

"No, not really, but she insisted. I tried to reason with her, stating that we could still get married and she could keep looking for her real mother. Andrea refused, saying that as soon as things settled down in her life that we could sit down together and set a new date for our wedding. I was hurt that she had made up her mind on this and that my feelings didn't seem to hold much weight in this final decision. Then later, on Christmas Day, while we were eating dinner at my parents' house, Andrea told them that we had decided to wait to get married." A film of sweat erupted on Brandon's forehead, and he reached in his pocket for a hanky, which he used to wipe it off. "Of course, that's partly my fault, because when she first brought up the topic of postponing our plans to get married, I said that she should be the one to tell both sets of our parents."

"I see."

"The more I thought about Andrea putting the search for her mother ahead of marrying me, the more upset I became. So after I brought her home that evening, I told Andrea that we should go our separate ways."

Orley gave his beard a tug. "You broke up with her?"

"Yeah, and she gave me the engagement ring back. Well, she didn't have the courtesy to do it herself. Instead, Andrea asked her friend to bring it to me, which I also found upsetting."

"How come?"

"Because she should have given it to me herself."

"How do you feel about the decision you made to break up?"

"Terrible, but I can't be expected to wait around forever while she goes on a hunt for parents she may never find."

"Have you prayed about this matter?" Orley questioned.

"Yes, I have, but nothing has come clear to me yet."

"Do you want my advice?"

"I would appreciate it. That's why I came in here today. I could tell from my last visit that you're the kind of person who cares about people and has good advice to offer."

"I do my best, but I can't take the credit for my suggestions."

"Oh, why's that?"

Orley pointed upward. "Everything I say that is worth anything comes from what God lays on my heart."

"That makes sense." Brandon leaned one arm on the counter. "So what is God asking you to tell me now?"

Orley placed one hand on Brandon's shoulder. "If I were in your situation, I'd ask myself one very important question."

"What would that be?"

"How much do I love the woman I was engaged to marry? Can I picture myself spending the rest of my life without her being a part of it?"

"And if I can't see myself without Andrea in my life?"

"Then get down on one knee, if that's what it takes, and ask her to marry you again."

Brandon shifted his stance. "I'll give it some thought."

"And prayer?"

"Yeah, that too. I was alone on New Year's Eve except for my dog, and I tried to keep occupied by watching TV until midnight, but all I could think about was Andrea and how much I missed her."

"That says a lot, and it might be your answer."

"Could be, but I still have some doubts."

Orley was on the verge of saying more, but two customers came into the store, which interrupted their conversation.

"I'd better go and let you take care of business." Brandon shook Orley's hand. "Thanks for taking the time to listen and also for your advice."

"No problem. Anytime you need a listening ear, you know where to find me."

"Thanks, I appreciate that."

As Brandon left the store, Orley turned to the English couple who had come in. "May I help you?"

Lois hurried toward Memory Keepers, adjusting the scarf that her sister Rebekah had knitted and sent to her for Christmas. One of their customers had said they'd be in for a few more inches of snow this evening, and she thought they might be right.

Lois looked up at the thick gray clouds hovering overhead, but so far there wasn't any sign of flakes. She couldn't help longing for warmer weather, but the cold was likely here to stay until winter ended. Even though the post office was only a few blocks away, it had been a chilly walk to and from, and she looked forward to the warmth of their store.

Inside the cloth bag Lois carried were more letters she'd received for her Dear Caroline column. Sometimes she wished she could take a break from answering all the letters that came in on a regular basis. At other times it gave her a good feeling to know she might be helping people with the answers she gave. Of course, unless Lois met someone in person who had written to her and she revealed her true identity, she would never know for sure if anything she'd said had made a difference in anyone's life. Even so, she planned to keep writing under the name of Dear Caroline until, and unless, God directed her to stop.

"How'd it go while I was gone?" Lois asked when she entered the store and joined Orley where he stood with his clipboard near a shelf full of old canning jars.

"A few people came into the store, which is why I haven't finished inventorying this side of the building." He gestured to the old jars.

"Did you make any sales?"

"The English woman who came in with her husband bought a few pieces of vintage jewelry." Orley chuckled. "She said it was a late Christmas gift from her to her."

Lois smiled. "I'm glad she found something she liked. Was she the only one who purchased something?"

"Her husband seemed interested in one of the old tools, but I think he was just looking while his wife checked out the jewelry." Orley paused and made a notation on his clipboard. "Oh, and Brandon Prentice came by."

She tipped her head in question. "Who?"

"He's the veterinarian who came in before Christmas and bought that nice old coffee table for his fiancée." Orley frowned. "Only she's not his future bride anymore."

"How come?"

Lois listened as Orley shared with her what Brandon had said during his visit.

"That's a shame."

"It sure is."

"Did you offer him any advice?"

Orley nodded. "I suggested that he get down on one knee and ask her to marry him again, because it sounded to me like he still loves the girl. Oh, and of course I also said he should be praying about the situation, which is the most important thing anyone should do when faced with a serious decision."

"You're absolutely right." Lois's brows pulled downward in concentration. Hearing the things her husband had shared reminded Lois of the Dear Caroline letter she'd received from a woman whose fiancé had recently broken their engagement. She wondered if Brandon might be that man and thought about her response to that letter. Lois pursed her lips. *I hope what I said to the woman may have helped.*

Apple Creek

When her stomach rumbled, reminding Andrea that she hadn't eaten lunch yet, she left the piano, where she'd been playing one of her favorite hymns, and went to the kitchen. There she found Lady rolling around on the floor with her new Christmas toy filled with catnip.

"Okay, little Lady, you've had enough of that for now." Andrea bent down and took the toy.

The cat looked up at her and gave a loud *meow*!

"I know you want to keep playing with it, but more than fifteen minutes is not good for you, and it's been that long at least." Brandon had given Andrea this information when she'd first gotten Lady and asked about letting the cat play with catnip. He'd also stated that failure to take the catnip-filled toys away after a few minutes of playtime would likely cause her cat to become bored. Additionally, Brandon had mentioned that if a feline exceeded the recommended amount of catnip consumed, they could experience some mild adverse effects, like nausea or vomiting. Andrea certainly didn't want that to occur.

Reflecting on Brandon's instructions caused Andrea to feel sad. She missed him, and it had been especially lonely on New Year's Eve when she sat home alone with Lady, thinking about how she and Brandon would have spent a wonderful evening together if their relationship hadn't gone sour. No doubt he would have brought Duke along so that he and Lady could enjoy each other's company.

She reflected on last New Year's Eve, when she and Brandon had spent the evening with some other couples from church. It was fun playing board games and chatting with others their age. At least Andrea had those happy memories to look back on and soothe the sadness she felt right now. *At that time, things were normal to me since I was still under the impression that Ray and Evelyn were my biological parents. I was happy in my relationship with Brandon, and my focus was on having a future with him. But now everything's drastically changed.*

"Maybe it's not God's will for us to be together," Andrea mumbled as she opened the refrigerator and perused the contents. She saw a cheeseball her mother had brought by the day before New Year's, when she'd invited Andrea to join her and Dad at their house for open-faced sandwiches that evening. Andrea had politely explained that she appreciated the invitation but felt tired and preferred to stay home and rest. She figured her mom must have thought Andrea would turn down the invitation. Why else had she brought the cheeseball along?

Andrea took the cheeseball out and retrieved a package of crackers from the cupboard. It would not be a filling lunch, but she didn't feel like going to the trouble of making a sandwich or even heating a can of soup. Her appetite had suffered ever since she and Brandon had broken up. At least she hadn't been the one to push for them to end their engagement. After all, he could've been more understanding to her needs and not given up on them. *I've always appreciated the fact that the man I still love is a devoted Christian, but apparently he's not devoted to me.*

Andrea's eyes burned with unshed tears, and she blinked a couple of times to keep them from spilling over. *I will not give in to more tears.* She'd already spent enough time crying, and where had that gotten her? Tears hadn't brought Brandon to her front door to apologize and say that he'd been wrong. Tears wouldn't change the fact that he obviously didn't care whether she found her birth mother or not. In the years she had known Brandon, Andrea had never thought of him as the insensitive type. He'd certainly shown compassion where his animal patients were concerned. Up until Andrea had learned of her adoption, Brandon had been loving and supportive of her endeavors to paint and teach piano lessons. Why couldn't he have done the same when it came to Andrea's need to spend time on the internet in search of her biological parents?

She grabbed a knife and dipped it into the cheeseball, then slathered some on a cracker. *Guess I'd better get something to drink.* Andrea found some eggnog in the refrigerator that was due to expire in two days, so she figured she ought to drink the rest of it. After filling a glass to the rim and putting more crackers and cheeseball on a plate, she took them into her studio and sat down at the desk, where she had turned on her computer before deciding to play some hymns on the piano.

As always, Andrea went first to her email box to see if she'd received any word from Ancestry. She scanned through the junk mail and deleted all that she didn't want. Hope welled in her chest when she found the message she'd been watching for in regard to her DNA test. The email stated that Andrea's DNA sample had been received, but unfortunately no matches were found in their data base.

Andrea frowned. *That's sure odd. Surely at least one of my blood relatives, either on my mother's or father's side, must have had a DNA test done at some time or another. This makes no sense.*

She sat stoically, staring at the computer screen. *If there is no match, which seems unlikely to me, what am I supposed to do next? I can't give up.*

Another thought flashed into Andrea's head. *I'm not at the end of the line at all, because as soon as the birth certificate I sent for arrives, I'll know my birth mother's name. Then all I will have to do is find out where she lives. Since she gave birth to me in Pennsylvania and may still live in that state, I'll start there.*

Excitement, mixed with a bit of trepidation, welled in Andrea's soul as she contemplated what might lie ahead. If she found her mother and made contact with her, would she be welcomed or would her birth mother prefer to have no contact with Andrea at all?

She leaned forward so that her head nearly touched the computer screen. *Since my mother gave me away, it must mean that she didn't want to raise me, but I need to know why.* Tears rolled down her cheeks. Even though it was likely that she and Brandon would never get married, if necessary, she would spend the rest of her life trying to uncover the truth that surrounded her birth. It was that important to her.

Chapter 31

After supper one evening toward the end of January, Andrea picked up the newspaper and took a seat on the living room couch. As she had done every night for the past three weeks, the first thing she looked at was the Dear Caroline column. She'd begun to think that her latest letter either hadn't been read or was not going to be answered due to lack of space in the column. There had to be some letters that Dear Caroline would never see or chose not to respond to at all. Tonight, however, Andrea was pleased to discover the letter she'd written as well as Dear Caroline's answer, which she read out loud.

> *"Dear Brokenhearted:*
>
> *When a couple breaks up, it can be difficult for one or both of them. It would be especially hard to accept when a person is on the brink of marriage. If you feel passionate about finding your birth mother, don't let anything stop you from pursuing that goal. If your fiancé really loves you, he should be more understanding and offer his support and help in locating your mother. There's really nothing you can do to make him more supportive. He needs to come to that realization himself. You might express to him, if you haven't already, that although you love him, you are not willing to give up the search for your biological mother."*

Andrea placed the newspaper on the couch beside her and pondered Dear Caroline's suggestions. *I have already told Brandon that I love him.*

Would he be receptive if I said it again? Her mouth felt dry, and she poured herself a glass of water and took a drink. *If I did talk to Brandon again, I would have to let him know that I can't give up the search for my biological parents even if we do get back together, and that's where the problem is.*

She bowed her head, and with her eyes closed tightly, Andrea prayed out loud. "Dear Lord, please guide and direct my life, and if it's meant for Brandon and me to be together, let us both know it and show us the way."

When he heard an odd clicking sound, Brandon glanced up from the newspaper he'd been reading while eating a late soup-and-sandwich supper. He was surprised to see Duke prance across the kitchen floor, walking backward.

Brandon chuckled. "You crazy little mutt. You sure know how to keep me guessing what kind of silly thing you'll do next." Last week Brandon had walked into the living room one evening and found Duke's back end on the couch with his head resting on one of the end tables.

Brandon watched in fascination as Duke went full circle around the kitchen, still walking backward, and then, with an undignified grunt, plopped down on the throw rug in front of the sink.

Maybe now I can read in peace. Brandon put his concentration back on the newspaper. After reading the local news, sports, and a few ads, he noticed the Dear Caroline column, which he normally skipped. One of the letters caught Brandon's eye, however. "Dear Caroline," he read aloud, "I've written to you before, after learning that I was adopted, and I'm currently in the process of trying to find my biological parents. The man I was planning to marry doesn't understand why this is so important to me. When I told him that I wanted to postpone our wedding, he was upset, and last week, he broke up with me."

Brandon took a deep breath. *I'm almost sure Andrea wrote that letter. She has to be talking about me, and I guess she doesn't care about keeping our relationship private. Anyone who knows us and reads this column is bound to figure out that the letter to Dear Caroline was written by my ex-fiancée.* Brandon's jaw clenched. *Why doesn't she just contact the local radio and TV stations too? She could run an ad that would let the whole world know about our breakup.*

He folded the newspaper and slapped it against the table without even bothering to read Dear Caroline's response. Brandon couldn't help feeling a sense of betrayal on Andrea's part. *If Andrea loves me as much as she has said in the past, then she should have come to me and tried to work things out instead of contacting a perfect stranger who writes for a newspaper column that I am certain many people who live in our area must read.* Warmth crept up the back of Brandon's neck and traveled around to his face. *I don't see how anything can ever be resolved between me and Andrea now.*

Brandon sat a while longer, staring at Duke, who slept peacefully on the rug, emitting doggie snores. "That dog of mine doesn't have a care in the world," he muttered. "He knows I'll take care of his needs and doesn't have to worry about whether I'll feed him or not."

Brandon finished the rest of his nearly cold soup and ate the last half of his sandwich. He felt stunned by Andrea's written comments and wished she hadn't done it. "I would never have written or sent a letter like that to the newspaper! What was she thinking? I would have gone to our pastor for advice first. At least that's confidential."

Duke's eyes popped open, and he looked toward his owner. Apparently, Brandon's ranting must have awakened the dog.

Brandon rose from the table, and after sidestepping Duke, he put his dishes in the sink and stormed out of the room. This whole thing bugged him to the core—especially after realizing how much the situation had escalated. "It all started with Andrea's cousin revealing the truth, and now it's all about her finding her birth parents, with nothing for me."

After taking a seat in his recliner, Brandon reflected on what Orley Troyer had said to him a few weeks ago. *I need to pray*, he told himself. *It's not good to get so worked up that anger and resentment sweep in, and it is certainly not very Christlike.*

He leaned his head back and closed his eyes. *Lord, what should I do? I need some kind of a sign to let me know if I should approach Andrea again. Do I tell her that I read the letter I believe she wrote to Dear Caroline? Should I apologize and say that I was wrong to break up with her?*

If I offered to help Andrea in the search for her biological parents, Brandon asked himself, *would that make a difference*?

The following morning, Andrea bundled up and went outside to get the mail. Seeing a manila envelope postmarked from Lancaster County, Pennsylvania, a sense of excitement welled in her soul. She felt sure the envelope contained her original birth certificate.

Back in the house, Andrea hung up her jacket and scarf. Then she went to the kitchen table to open the mail. As suspected, inside the manila envelope, she discovered her birth certificate. Her fingers trembled as she held it in her hands and read the most important parts out loud. "County of Birth: Lancaster. Name: Ruth Ann Miller. Sex: Female. Father's Name: Unknown. Mother's Name: Mary L. Miller."

Andrea's forehead creased as she continued to study the certificate. *The name Miller sounds kind of Amish to me, but then there's a family from our church whose name is Miller, and they aren't Amish.* Her fingers twitched as she held the document. *Since my father's name is listed as not known, it indicates that my mother must have been unwed. And there's no way for me to know who he was unless I'm able to contact my birth mother and get that information from her, because she must know who fathered her baby.*

She sucked in a quick breath and covered her mouth. *My birth mother named me Ruth Ann. Did my adoptive parents know that I had already been given that name when they got me? If so, why didn't they keep Ruth Ann as my name? Another question for me to ask Mom and Dad. Oh boy. . . I can hardly wait to tell them that the birth certificate issued when I was a newborn arrived in my mailbox today. I hope they will share in my joy over this and be willing to answer more questions.*

Something else popped into her head. *How do I go about finding Mary Miller? If she was single when she gave birth to me and has since married, which seems likely, then her last name would no longer be Miller. I am thankful to have my original birth certificate now, but am I any further along in the search for my mother than I was before?*

Walnut Creek

"This is sure a lot of work, but it'll be well worth it when we dig a big spoon into your tasty vanilla ice cream." Orley leaned closer and kept cranking the handle on their old-fashioned ice-cream freezer, which they had set up in the barn. Whenever they made homemade ice cream during the summer months, he usually set it up and did his cranking on the front or back porch. But it was too cold for that, and he didn't want to bring it inside the house, where spilled rock salt or ice could make a mess on his wife's clean floors.

Lois smiled at him from a wooden bench nearby and winked. "You're right, Big O. The ice cream will be a nice treat for us. I thawed some strawberries to put on top, and there's also some chocolate syrup in the cupboard I can open if you like."

Orley licked his lips in anticipation. "Sounds good. I can hardly wait." He looked over at her and grinned. "I kinda like it when you call me by the nickname I acquired when I was a teenager."

She winked again. "I know you do."

"Say, I just remembered to tell you about a message I found on our answering machine when I went out to the phone shed while you were mixing the ice-cream ingredients."

"Who was the message from?" Lois questioned.

"Paul Herschberger. He called to let us know that Lisa gave birth to a baby boy early this morning."

"Oh my!" Lois's eyes opened wide. "I thought she wasn't due for a few more weeks. Is she okay? Is the baby all right?"

"Paul said in his message that Lisa and the little guy they named Andrew Paul are both doing fine."

"I'm so glad. How happy they must be." Lois glanced away, then looked back at Orley. "Were there any other messages?"

He shook his head. "Not on our answering machine, but one of the customers who came into our store this morning asked if I heard about the accident our bishop and his fraa had yesterday," Orley said, taking their conversation in a more serious direction.

Her brows furrowed. "What happened?"

"They'd left the home of an elderly woman from outside our church district who has been laid up with a broken leg. On the way back to their home, the horse pulling their carriage somehow managed to get its tail under the lines. The buggy ended up tipping over."

"Oh dear! Were either of them seriously hurt?"

Orley shook his head. "The bishop's wife got a bump on the head, and he had a few bruises, but they're both okay. The Lord was watching out for them, because it could have been much worse. Either one of them could have been killed in the accident."

"You're right about that," she agreed. "So often when a buggy topples over, the occupants end up with serious injuries."

"On a different topic," Orley said, switching arms to do the cranking. "I read your Dear Caroline column this evening while you were mixing the ingredients for our ice cream."

"Oh?" She tilted her head to one side. "What did you think of it?"

"I was interested in the letter from the woman whose boyfriend broke things off with her because she's been too busy trying to find her biological parents. It made me think about Brandon Prentice. In fact, I have to wonder if it was Brandon's ex-girlfriend who wrote the letter."

"I suppose that's possible." Lois rubbed the bridge of her nose. "Did you think the answer I gave her was all right?"

He bobbed his head. "You always give good answers."

"I hope so. I pray about each of the letters I receive before writing my response to their questions."

"Jah, prayer is always a good thing. That's what I told Brandon when he came into our shop a few weeks ago." Orley stopped cranking. "I do believe this is done. It won't crank anymore, so I'm sure it's as frozen as it's gonna get."

"Good, and as cold as it is, there's probably no need to let it set for a while with ice over the top of the container, like we often do during the warm summer months."

"Right."

"Would you like me to carry the container into the house?"

"No, that's okay. I'll do it."

"All right then, I'll go ahead and get our bowls set out along with the berries and chocolate syrup." She rose from the bench and left the barn.

Orley knocked some ice off the top of the container, and with his gloved hands, he lifted the container out and headed to the house.

As he made his way, his boot hit a patch of ice. The next thing he knew, he was lying in a pile of snow. The impact had caused the lid on the container to come off, and some of the ice cream oozed out. Although not hurt, Orley was embarrassed by his fall. He looked about the yard and to the street, hoping no one was outside and had seen him take a tumble. He didn't feel much like Big O at the moment, but he was relieved that this incident had gone unnoticed. About that time, two of their bigger barn cats ran out of the barn and began lapping up the ice cream that had escaped from the can. Orley quickly put the lid back on, scrambled to his feet, and headed toward the house, this time walking carefully with each step he took. He was glad slipping on the ice and landing on the ground hadn't injured him. He thanked the Lord for sparing him from injuring his back again—or any other parts of his body, for that matter.

When Orley entered the kitchen a few minutes later, he set the container in the sink and told Lois what had happened.

"Oh dear. . .I hope you weren't hurt."

"No, I'm fine, and don't worry, there's still plenty of ice cream in the container." He laughed. "I was glad when the *katze* came along 'cause at least the ice cream that ended up in the snow didn't go to waste."

Lois shook her head. "Sometimes, I can't believe you, dear husband. Only you could make a joke out of falling in the snow."

"But you still love me, right?"

She kissed his cold cheek. "Absolutely."

Their dessert was tasty, and Lois enjoyed each bite of the creamy delight. She had added some berries and a bit of chocolate syrup into the vanilla in her bowl and blended it all together. "Mmm. . . this is so good."

"Did you want a second helping before I put the rest of the ice cream in the freezer?" Orley called from the kitchen.

"I still have plenty in my bowl, but thank you for asking," she replied.

A couple of minutes passed before Orley returned to the living room with his second helping. "You know me—I can never be satisfied with just one bowl of delicious ice cream. The berries you froze from our garden add a nice touch too."

"I'm glad we had a big crop to freeze and make jelly."

"Jah, and eating those berries makes me long for spring."

"I hear you," Lois replied. "This cold weather gets tiresome, but the warm season will return before we know it." She placed her spoon in the empty bowl. "I wish we could take a trip to someplace warm and sunny, like some of our friends do this time of the year."

He smiled. "Maybe you and I should plan a vacation. We just need to figure out where we'd like to go."

Lois tapped her chin. "There are lots of places I'd like to visit. I've heard some interesting things about California, Texas, and Florida, but they are all quite a ways from here, which would mean we'd probably need to be gone a few weeks."

"Those states you mentioned are a lot warmer this time of the year, and a couple of them are tropical."

"The only problem is, what would we do with our business if we took an extended vacation? Could we find someone to fill in for us, or would it be best to close Memory Keepers while we're gone?" Lois picked up her spoon and licked the little bit of ice cream that remained.

"That's a good question, and we should do the best thing."

"What's that?"

"Pray about it, and see what the Lord guides us to do."

"I agree," Lois said, "but meanwhile we're stuck dealing with this cold, sometimes icy, winter weather."

"True, but if we can figure out where to go and a way to keep the antique store open while we're gone, we can travel like you want to, away from this chilly place."

Lois nodded. "It would be nice to be somewhere warm right now. And it would be fun to see some unusual places, but unless the good Lord opens the door for us to go, we'll need to be content to stay put."

"Jah." He put another spoonful of ice cream in his mouth.

Lois figured with the good amount he'd eaten already, when her husband finished this second bowl, he'd probably close his eyes and take a nap. It had been nice talking about taking a trip together, but right now it seemed unlikely.

Soon after Orley had set his empty bowl on the coffee table, he fell asleep in his favorite chair as she'd predicted.

Lois scooped up their bowls and took them to the kitchen. After washing and drying the dishes, she headed for the desk in her sewing room. She needed to read and hopefully answer more letters that had been sent to her Dear Caroline column, but for some reason, she wasn't in the mood.

Although they were nearly a full month into the new year already, Lois began to reflect on the previous year, and she asked herself a few questions. *What did I do during the past twelve months that was of value in God's eyes? Have I done enough when it comes to helping others who need food, clothing, or financial assistance?* While Lois and Orley often attended benefit auctions and the like, and they always made a contribution, she sometimes felt that it wasn't enough.

Lois leaned forward with both arms resting on her new desk. *And what about my newspaper column? Have the words I shared helped anyone to make a change for the better? Have I prayed when I should have? Read my Bible often enough? Told others about the love of Jesus our Redeemer when I was given the opportunity? Orley and I have been so blessed—with our business, our health, and the precious moments we've had together and with friends. To list all of our blessings would be impossible.*

Lois paused and took a sip of the apple-cinnamon tea she'd brought into the room with her. She had lost her father this past year, and that had been difficult. But at least she'd been with him when he died, and the letter he'd written to her, which had been found in his Bible, had helped to heal a lot of Lois's emotional wounds from her childhood.

"God's will be done," she murmured, then closed her eyes. *Help me and Orley to be thankful every day of this new year for our many blessings. And please show us when and what to say whenever You bring a hurting soul our way.*

Chapter 32

Apple Creek

"How are things going with the search for your birth parents?" Colleen asked when she stopped by Andrea's house the following day.

"In some ways, good. In other ways, not so much," Andrea replied as Colleen removed her outer garments and did the same for her son, Tyler.

"What do you mean?"

Andrea gestured for her friend to take a seat in the living room. Colleen sat on the couch and tried to coax Tyler to join her, but the rambunctious two-year-old took off after Andrea's cat.

"Tyler, come back here." Colleen cupped her hands around her mouth.

"It's okay. Lady will find a place to hide if he bothers her too much." Andrea took a seat beside Colleen. "Would you like a cup of coffee or some tea?"

"Maybe later. Right now I'm more interested in hearing how your adoption search has been going."

"My original birth certificate came in the mail yesterday. Would you like to see it?"

"Yes, of course. You must be excited about that."

"Yes, and I'll be right back." Andrea left the room. She was almost to her bedroom when she heard a crash coming from within. Upon entering the room, Andrea saw that her nightstand lamp wasn't where it should be. Tyler stood near the bed with his eyes wide open and tears on his cheeks. The lamp was on the floor, and the bulb had broken. Meanwhile, Lady, who'd been under the bed, darted out the door in a blur. Andrea did not want Tyler to go near the shards of glass, so she took his hand, led him out of the room, and shut the door behind them. "How about you play with the kitty out here?"

The little boy looked up at her and nodded.

"I'll be right with you. I have a little cleaning up to do in my bedroom," Andrea called to Colleen from the kitchen a few minutes later.

It wasn't long before her friend came in. "What's going on?"

"The bedroom lamp got knocked over, and there's broken glass from the lightbulb on the floor." She removed the broom from the storage closet. "There's a spare bulb in here, which I'll take care of putting in the lamp later on."

Colleen looked down at Tyler, who had followed Andrea and her cat into the kitchen. "I'm guessing my son was responsible for knocking over your lamp?"

Andrea shrugged. "I believe Tyler went into my room, chasing after Lady, but he may not have been responsible for the lamp toppling off the nightstand. Lady could have knocked it over trying to escape."

"I'm sorry it happened. My son should not have been chasing the cat or gone into your room." She reached for Tyler's hand. "Please settle down and stay close to Mommy."

"It's okay. It was just the bulb. The lamp is fine." Andrea went to her room to clean up the broken glass. Afterward, she unplugged the lamp and carefully removed the guts of the bulb. *Tyler's a cute little guy, but I think I've gotten a taste of what it would be like to have a child. I have to say, they do keep things lively, and you can't let them out of your sight for long.* Andrea heaved a sigh. *If only Brandon and I could work things out, then one day we might have a child.* She pushed that thought aside and opened her top dresser drawer to get the birth certificate.

Andrea put the broom away and then went to the living room, where Colleen sat with Tyler on the couch. Andrea removed the certificate from the manila envelope and handed it to her friend. "I'm eager to know what you think."

Colleen studied the document before handing it back to Andrea. "So your biological father is unknown, and all you have is your birth mother's name, which was most likely her maiden name. That's not much information, but it's better than nothing. So now where do you go?"

Andrea shrugged. "I'm not sure. I talked to my folks yesterday, and

Mom suggested that I should visit a website called Spokeo that she'd discovered. She said it's a place where a person can confidentially search more than fourteen billion publicly available records and other information. She also mentioned that from the basic search, you can discover locations, age, and relatives." Andrea's words were rushed. "So I may try that."

Colleen smiled. "I hope it works out for you. I'm sure this must all be pretty stressful."

"It is—especially since my desire to locate my birth mother caused Brandon to end our relationship, which was something I never thought would happen. He's always seemed so devoted to me."

"Have you heard from him lately?"

"No, and I doubt that I will."

"Have you considered making the first move in an effort to get back together?"

"Yes, and I've prayed about it too. The trouble is, I'm afraid nothing I could say, except that I'd be willing to give up my search, would satisfy him." Andrea shook her head forcibly. "I can't do that. Finding my birth mother is too important to me."

"I would have to say that you've had more time to focus on locating your birth mother since you've parted ways. Just look at what you have done already. Little by little, you are getting closer to your goal." Colleen glanced at Tyler. He'd gotten off the couch and now lay on the floor with Lady sleeping beside him.

"Do you really think I'm getting closer?" Andrea questioned. "It hasn't been easy turning over every stone I can think of, but there seems to be a driving force that is propelling me on." She took a seat on the couch beside Colleen. "I still love Brandon, and I wish things could be different, but at this point, it seems doubtful."

Colleen leaned close and gave Andrea a hug. "Guess if I was in your shoes, I would feel the same way. Even so, I wish you and Brandon could get back together. You always seemed like such a happy, well-suited couple."

Andrea sniffed, trying to hold back tears. "We were—until I found out that I'd been adopted. Then everything changed."

Evelyn sat quietly at the kitchen table, eating the taco salad she'd fixed for lunch. Since Ray was at work and she'd be eating alone, it was a good opportunity to enjoy some of her favorite hot sauce, which her husband didn't like. In fact, Ray didn't care for anything spicy. Whenever he indulged in spicy food, he'd end up with heartburn.

We may not always have the same taste in foods, she thought, *but Ray and I agree on so many other, more important things.* They had both agreed that they should support Andrea's decision to search for her birth mother. It had nearly broken Evelyn's heart to witness their daughter's reaction when she'd first learned of her adoption. Since then, with Andrea postponing her wedding and then Brandon breaking things off, Evelyn had been quite distressed. She hoped that if Andrea could locate her birth mother soon, she and Brandon might get back together. But with her daughter being so focused on locating the woman who'd given birth to her, Evelyn couldn't help worrying that this could drag on for a while. The thought of seeing her daughter lose a nice fellow like Brandon saddened Evelyn. And she felt odd—like she wasn't as important to Andrea anymore and could be replaced by the biological mother. It was hard not to feel a little jealous.

Evelyn thought about her husband. She figured with Andrea's biological father's name having been left off the birth certificate, Ray wouldn't feel any concern about the possibility of another man taking his place in their daughter's life. *Of course*, she mentally added, *for all we know, Andrea's birth mother may not be living anymore.*

Evelyn finished the last of her salad and placed her dishes in the dishwasher. *What I need to do now is haul the last of the boxes full of Christmas decorations up to the attic*, she told herself. *None of them are heavy, and I've put this off long enough.*

Evelyn left the kitchen and went to the spare bedroom at the end of the hall, where she had temporarily put the decorations. She picked up the first box and headed upstairs, being careful not to trip and fall. As she passed Andrea's old bedroom on the second floor, a lump formed in her throat. *I miss the days when our daughter lived here and life seemed so simple and joyous.* Andrea had always been a pleasant child, never disrespectful or defiant like some kids could be. Evelyn wondered if their daughter would have been any different as a child if she'd known about her adoption. *Would she have been just as happy and content, or would knowing the truth at a young age have caused her to feel insecure—not sure where she belonged?*

I need to stop dwelling on this and focus on the here and now. Evelyn shifted the box to her hip and opened the attic door with her free hand. Taking her time and being careful with each step, she made her way up to the third floor. When Evelyn reached the top and entered the dark, dusty attic, she clicked on the overhead light and set the box down on the squeaky floor. Instead of going back down for another box, Evelyn paused to look around. The first thing she spotted was Andrea's old toy box, filled with many of the things she had played with during the early part of her childhood. Dust particles danced in the shaft of light coming in through one of the small windows. Some old board games, a rolled-up rug, and a number of picture frames had been stacked against one wall. Several storage tubs filled with outdated clothing adorned another wall. So many memories and keepsakes were stored up here. Evelyn wished she had time to comb through each one and dwell for a while on the past.

She rubbed her chilled arms while standing in the middle of the room. The winter chill seeping in was not comfortable. *I should have thought to put on a sweater before coming up here.* She moved back near the attic entrance, where she felt some warmth coming in from the heat rising through the house.

Her gaze traveled to the opposite side of the unfinished room, where her grandmother's old trunk sat. Over the years, Evelyn had put some family heirlooms in there. *I think I'll just open it and take a peek. It won't take long, and then I'll go back downstairs for the next box of decorations.*

Evelyn knelt on the floor in front of the vintage trunk and opened the lid. Peering inside, she spotted Ray's old uniform from when he'd served in the military before they were married. She also discovered a box of letters he had written to her when they'd been dating. He'd always said that he could put down on paper the way he felt about her easier than saying it to her face.

Evelyn smiled. *That husband of mine is such a romantic. I wonder if he truly realized how much those letters meant to me.* Evelyn was tempted to sit in the old rocking chair nearby and read some of Ray's love letters, but if she got started, it would probably be time to start supper when she got back downstairs. *I'll look through a few more things and then go after the next box to bring up.*

Half an hour later, she reached down to the bottom of the trunk and felt something soft. She grasped the item between her fingers and pulled it out. "Oh my, I can't believe I forgot all about this until now."

Evelyn held the cloth doll against her chest as the memory of the day she'd been given it filled her mind. When she and Ray had gone to the hospital to get their adopted daughter, a nurse had handed Evelyn the doll and said, "This belonged to the baby's birth mother. She wanted her little girl to have it."

Forgetting about the rest of the boxes downstairs still needing to be brought up, Evelyn closed the trunk lid and got up from the floor. *I am going over to see Andrea right now. She needs to see this doll.*

Andrea had been so involved in painting a picture of the adorable Amish child she had seen during a shopping trip the other day that she had lost track of time. It wasn't until her stomach rumbled that she looked at the clock and realized it was almost time to start supper.

I'll finish working on the little girl's hair and then go make myself something to eat.

Andrea was surprised when she heard the doorbell ring. She didn't have any piano students today and wasn't expecting company.

She set her paintbrush down and left the studio to answer the door. When Andrea opened it and saw her mother on the porch, she felt concern. Mom rarely came by without calling first to see if Andrea was home or in the middle of a lesson. To drop by unannounced and so close to supper must mean that something was wrong.

"Mom, are you all right?" Andrea reached out and touched her mother's arm.

"I'm fine. Why would you ask? Do I appear to be sick?"

"No, not at all, but since you rarely come by without calling first, I thought something might be wrong."

"No, I'm fine, and so is your dad."

"Oh good. I'm glad."

Andrea opened the door wider. "Come on in out of the cold. Would you like something warm to drink?"

"Maybe later. First, we need to talk." Her mother stepped in, and Andrea hung her coat on the coat tree in the entryway.

"So to what do I owe this pleasant surprise?"

"Not what but who." Mom moistened her lips with the tip of her tongue. "Can we go in the living room and sit down?"

"Of course." Andrea led the way. Once they were both seated on the couch, she leaned closer to her mother and asked, "Who do I owe this visit to?"

"Your birth mother."

Andrea's eyes widened, and her mouth dropped slightly open. "You know where she is? Have you spoken to her?" The mere thought of it seemed too good to be true.

Mom shook her head. "It's nothing like that, but I found something in the attic today that she wanted you to have."

"Seriously? What is it?"

"This." Mom reached into her oversized handbag and withdrew a small cloth doll with no face dressed in Amish girl's attire.

Andrea's ribs tightened, and her lips quivered when she spoke. "How do you know it was her doll and that she wanted me to have it?"

"Because when your dad and I went to the hospital to pick you up, a social worker, along with a nurse, brought you out of the maternity ward to us. The nurse said the woman who gave birth to you wanted you to have the doll. She said it had been her own doll when she was a child."

Andrea's hand shook as she reached out and took hold of the doll with no face. "It's an Amish doll; I've seen others similar to this in some of the gift stores in our area as well as those in Holmes County." She pursed her lips. "So my birth mother's last name, Miller, must be Amish, which means that—"

"That the woman who gave birth to you was Amish." Mom finished Andrea's sentence.

Andrea's head moved slowly up and down while she tried to digest everything. They sat staring at each other as Andrea struggled not to give in to the sob rising in her throat. *No wonder I've always been so intrigued with the Amish way of life. And that's the reason I've chosen so many Amish buggies, houses, barns, and children to paint.*

"If you've had the doll since I was a baby, why'd you wait so long to give it to me?" Andrea looked directly at her mother.

"When we came home with you, I put the doll in my grandmother's trunk, along with other mementoes," her mother replied. "I had intended to give it to you when we felt you were old enough to be told about your adoption, but. . ." Tears gathered in the corners of Mom's eyes.

"But then you and Dad decided not to tell me, so you just left the doll there, believing I would never find it and ask where it had come from?" Andrea couldn't keep the resentment she felt from her tone of voice. She'd thought she had forgiven her parents for keeping the truth from her all those years, but now a feeling of bitterness was creeping in, and she had to do something to stop it before it took hold.

"I didn't leave it there on purpose, Andrea." Mom spoke quietly but in a sincere tone. "Your dad and I were caught up in the joy of raising you, and we really did forget the doll was in the trunk."

"Okay." Andrea placed the doll in her lap and lowered her head. A strange feeling came over her as she gazed at the faceless doll. It was hard to believe that she could actually be holding a doll that her biological mother wanted her to have. While the feeling was exhilarating, it didn't answer the big question on Andrea's heart, mind, and soul. *Where is this Amish woman who gave birth to me nearly thirty-three years ago?*

She leaned her head heavily against the back of the couch and closed her eyes. *Dear Lord, how am I ever going to find the woman who gave birth to me? Since I was born in Lancaster, Pennsylvania, would a trip there be the best place to start?*

Chapter 33

I hope Memory Keepers is open today and that Orley Troyer is in the store, Brandon thought after he left his clinic and headed across the parking lot to his vehicle. *I need to speak with Orley before I make any contact with Andrea. I've gotta be sure I say and do the right things and don't let my emotions get in the way of good judgment.* Brandon regretted that he had broken things off with Andrea. Doing it hadn't helped him feel any better—in fact, he felt worse. He kept asking himself if it would have hurt to have supported Andrea instead of thinking only of himself. Now the road to getting back with his girl seemed long and humbling. Brandon was amazed by how one wrong decision could have such consequences in a person's life. He wasn't happy and felt lonelier than ever. Brandon grimaced. *Why did I let my pride lead me to break things off with her?*

For the past few weeks, Brandon had been praying about his relationship with Andrea as Orley had suggested. He'd finally reached the point where he thought he could talk to her but needed some reassurance before he plunged ahead.

As Brandon stepped through patches of snow approaching his SUV, he noticed that the parking lights were on. "Oh great," he mumbled. "I hope it didn't drain my battery." He touched the button of his key fob, and the door unlocked for him. *Maybe my rig will start.*

Brandon climbed into his cold vehicle, closed the door, and turned on the ignition. He frowned when it didn't start. "What's up with this?" He tried again. Still nothing. He made a couple more attempts and finally gave up. He hoped it was just a dead battery and nothing more serious.

Brandon pulled his cell phone from his jacket pocket to call for roadside assistance, which was one of the benefits included with his insurance policy. After speaking with the person on the other end, he was told that someone would be out to assist him within the hour.

That's just great. By the time I get to Walnut Creek, the antique store will probably be closed. Brandon massaged his temples. There was nothing he could do except wait, but it was too cold to sit in his vehicle. He got out and went back to the clinic where he could at least stay warm.

Both Brandon's receptionist and his assistant had already gone home, so the clinic was dark and quiet. He flipped on the light in the waiting room and took a seat. It seemed strange to be sitting where the owners of his animal patients usually sat.

He glanced around the room, wondering if the things set out in this room were pleasant enough and offered the people who came here a comfortable, relaxing place to wait. The posters of various breeds of dogs and cats were interesting. Pet supplies displayed on one side of the room and ready for purchase made it easy for people to see what was available at Brandon's clinic.

As he sat there, Andrea came to mind. *I sure miss her pretty face and being able to spend time together like we used to.*

In an effort to clear his head, Brandon glanced at the clock on the wall. It was close to dinnertime, and his stomach gurgled at the thought. *I'm getting hungry, and there's nothing here to eat unless you're a dog or cat.* He looked over at the reading materials on the end table. *I should've put an extra bag of chips in my lunch box today, but how was I to know this would happen? Oh well, maybe I can find something interesting to read in one of the magazines here on the table.*

He picked up a pet-centered magazine and thumbed through it, stopping when he came to an article titled "How to Tell If Your Dog Loves You." Brandon chuckled. *I have no doubt whatsoever that Duke loves me. He wags his tail and barks when I get home and likes to curl up beside me on the couch or drape himself on my lap when I'm in my recliner. He also follows me around the house and paws at my leg to get my attention. Yep—my dog loves me a lot, and I love him.* Brandon thumped his head. "Course, not nearly as much as I love Andrea. I just wish that she—"

A horn honked out in the parking lot, jolting Brandon out of his musings. He put the magazine down and went to open the door. Roadside assistance had arrived, to his relief. If they couldn't get his vehicle started, though, he'd need to have it towed to the nearest mechanic.

Andrea held the faceless doll in her hands as she carried on a phone conversation with Colleen. Just seconds ago, she had told her friend about the doll.

"Wow, that's amazing." Colleen gave a little whistle. "I can only imagine the excitement you must have felt when your mom presented you with it and said your biological mother had wanted you to have it."

"It was quite a shock, and at first I was a little peeved that Mom hadn't given it to me sooner, but then she explained she'd forgotten the doll was in that old trunk in the attic."

"Know what I would do if I were you?"

"What?"

"I'd take that old doll to the antique store in Walnut Creek to get an appraisal."

"How come?" Andrea asked. "You should know that I'm not going to sell it. This doll is precious to me. It's all I have from the woman who gave birth to me."

"I wasn't suggesting that you sell it, Andrea. I thought you might think it was interesting to find out how much the doll is worth, and in the process of asking, maybe the Amish couple who own the store could shed some light on what Amish community the doll might be from."

Andrea's fingers traced over the doll's empty face. "I doubt that a doll such as this would be any different from one community to another. Except for the fact that my doll looks well-used, she's not much different than the ones I have seen for sale at some of the gift shops in our area."

"Maybe you're right, but I still think it'd be a good idea to take it in for an appraisal. You never know, you might have been given something quite valuable."

"I doubt it, but maybe I will take it in. I'll do it tomorrow since I'm going to be in Holmes County anyway."

"How come?"

"There's a Christian bookstore in Berlin, and I want to get something for my mom there. Would you like to come along?"

"Normally, I would, but I have a dental appointment tomorrow, and since my mother will be watching Tyler, I promised to take both of them to lunch afterward. I'll call you tomorrow evening, though. I'd like to hear what you found out about the old doll."

"Okay, I'll talk to you soon. Have a good evening."

"You too."

When Andrea ended the call, she took the doll into her studio and placed it on the desk next to the computer. *I wonder if my birth mother made this doll.* The longer she studied the cloth memento, the more Andrea wondered what her mother was like. Since the faceless doll had come into her life, Andrea almost felt like a little girl again. No matter what room she was in, she brought the doll with her so she could see it. Every time she looked at the doll, Andrea tried to imagine what her birth mother looked like. Does she have auburn hair like me, or do I take after my biological father? So many unanswered questions swam in Andrea's head it almost made her feel dizzy. One thing was sure: as soon as the weather improved, she was going to make a trip to Pennsylvania with the hope of finding some answers.

Walnut Creek

Since Brandon had no farm calls to make on this cold Saturday afternoon, he was on his way to Memory Keepers Antique Store to speak with Orley. Thankfully, he hadn't needed a new battery yesterday. The jump start had been sufficient, but by the time the man had taken care of the problem, it was too late to make it to Walnut Creek before the antique store closed. That was okay, though. Going there earlier in the day gave Brandon more time to speak with Orley if he wasn't busy with other customers.

Brandon found a parking spot close to the store and made sure his lights had been turned off before he got out. Although no new snow was in sight, the wind had picked up, hitting Brandon's face with a blast of cold air. He hurried toward the store and quickly opened the door, causing the little bell overhead to announce his arrival.

Brandon glanced around and was pleased to see Orley behind the front counter next to Lois.

"Nice to see you again!" Orley smiled and motioned for Brandon to come over.

He didn't hesitate and greeted the bearded man and his soft-spoken wife with hearty handshakes.

"If you're not too busy, I was wondering if I could talk to you for a few minutes." Brandon directed his question to Orley.

"Of course. Lois and I were just going over our inventory list, but I think we're about done with it, so I have time to talk." Orley pointed toward the back of the store. "Why don't we go into the office? That way we won't be disturbed if a customer comes in."

Brandon hesitated before nodding. He hoped Orley's wife didn't feel like they were leaving her out. *But then*, he reasoned, *someone has to stay up front to greet any customers who might come in.*

Brandon followed Orley to a small room at the back of the building. Besides a vintage-looking desk and two chairs, the only other things in the room were two tall filing cabinets and an old manual typewriter sitting on a metal cart. Brandon wondered how they got by without a computer, but from the little he knew about the Amish, he figured most of them were probably old-school when it came to the way they lived and worked.

"Please take a seat." Orley gestured to the chair sitting near the desk. Brandon sat down, and Orley took a seat on the other side of the desk. "How are things going with you?" the kindly Amish man asked. "Has anything changed between you and the woman you'd planned to marry?"

Brandon shook his head. "I've been praying about it, and I do want to get back with her, but nothing has come clear to me yet. If only God would give me a sign."

"Sometimes when I've prayed about something, I didn't receive any specific kind of sign." Orley placed both hands on the desk and leaned slightly forward. "What I did receive, however, was a deep sense of peace once I made up my mind to do something. I took that to mean that it must be God's will, so I moved forward with what I thought I should do."

"Guess my trouble is that I'm full of self-doubts where my relationship with Andrea is concerned."

"What are you feeling doubtful about?"

"I'm afraid that I hurt Andrea so deeply when I broke things off that even if I went to her now and apologized, she would not take me back."

Orley's glasses had slipped down almost to the middle of his nose, and he pushed them back in place before responding. "I can only say this: if you want to resume your relationship with Andrea, then you should go to her and say what's on your heart. The fact is, you won't know unless you try, and if it's meant to be, then you will feel God's peace."

Brandon sat quietly, letting Orley's words sink in. Then he offered a quick, silent prayer. *Lord, whatever way it goes between Andrea and me, please grant me Your peace.*

When Andrea drove her car into the town of Walnut Creek, she began to have second thoughts about going to Memory Keepers. As she had told Colleen when they talked on the phone, there was no valid reason to find out how much the faceless doll might be worth since she had no intention of selling it. Furthermore, it was highly doubtful that the Amish couple who owned the antique store would know what Amish community it had come from.

But I'm here now, Andrea told herself as she pulled up to the curb in front of the store. *So I may as well go inside and show them my doll.*

Lois put the inventory list away and was about to open a box Orley had brought in from the storage room earlier, when the bell above the front door jingled. She turned to see who'd come in and was surprised to see the auburn-haired woman who had been in the shop several months ago. As Lois recalled, her name was Andrea. Lois assumed the young woman might have brought something in that she wanted to sell or leave on consignment, for she held a small box in her hands.

"Welcome back." Lois greeted the young woman near the door. "May I help you with something today?" Lois had hoped she would have an opportunity like this to find out where Andrea stood spiritually.

Andrea gave a slow shake of her head. "I. . .uh. . .have an old doll in this box, and I was hoping you'd have the time to take a look at it."

"Certainly. Are you wanting to sell the doll?"

Andrea shook her head again. "I'm wondering what it might be worth and whether you would have any idea of where it may have come from—like what Amish community, perhaps."

"If you'll bring it on up to the counter, I'll take a look." Lois headed in that direction and Andrea followed.

When Lois set the box on the counter and opened the lid, she squinted over the top of her smudged glasses. "It's a faceless doll—an old one at that, from the looks of the faded dress and yellowed skin-colored material.

"Do you mind if I have a closer look?"

"Please, help yourself."

Lois picked the doll up and continued to squint as she studied its arms, legs, and face.

"I'm guessing the doll's not worth much, right?"

Lois gave no response. Instead, she turned the doll over and pulled the snaps off the backside of the faded blue dress. She studied it, and her mouth quivered a bit. "Where did you get this doll? Did you find it or buy it somewhere locally?"

"No, it was a gift." Andrea paused, wondering how much she should share with this woman she barely knew. After a few seconds' deliberation, she said, "I was adopted as a baby, and my adoptive mother found the doll recently in an old trunk in her attic." Andrea stopped talking and reached out to stroke the doll's arm. "She said it had belonged to my birth mother, and that when she and my dad came to the hospital to get me, a nurse gave them the doll and said the woman who'd given birth to me wanted me to have it." Andrea paused once more and looked at Lois. She was surprised to see that the Amish woman's face had turned paler than the snow outside. The next thing Andrea knew, Lois gasped, and then she collapsed onto the floor.

Andrea's heartbeat quickened, and she had the sensation of things moving too quickly to process. She took a few deep breaths to calm herself and thought about what she'd learned when she'd taken a CPR class. Andrea didn't know for sure, but she thought the poor woman could have had a heart attack. Should she call 911 for help, try to revive Lois herself, or see if Lois's husband was somewhere in the store?

Andrea's sensibility kicked in, and she rushed to where Lois had fallen and dropped to her knees. She called out Lois's name, and when there was no response, Andrea clasped the woman's cold wrist and took her pulse. It didn't seem irregular, but Lois's eyes were still closed. Andrea remembered from the class she had taken that she should have a person who has fainted lie down with their feet elevated. This would make more blood flow to the brain, causing most people to recover quickly after fainting.

Before Andrea had a chance to look for something to put under the woman's feet, Lois opened her eyes. She looked at Andrea, and in a voice barely above a whisper, Lois said, "*Dochder.*"

Chapter 34

Andrea turned when she heard footsteps. Orley and Brandon were heading toward them. *Brandon? What's he doing here?*

Lois moaned, and Andrea turned her attention back to the poor woman, who was attempting to sit up.

"Please, you must lie still," Andrea instructed.

Orley rushed forward and dropped to his knees. "Lois, what happened? Did you slip on something and fall?" Andrea heard the depth of Orley's concern as he leaned close to his wife and touched her face. "Lie still while I get you some water to drink and a wet paper towel to put on your forehead." He looked at Andrea. "Please keep an eye on her while I run into my office for some water and paper towel."

She nodded.

When Orley returned a short time later, he knelt beside Lois again. After placing a dampened folded towel beneath her head, he gave her a few sips of water. "What happened that caused my wife to fall?" Orley directed his question to Andrea.

"I was telling her about the doll my mother found in her attic and explained that it had belonged to my birth mother, and she wanted me to have it. When she looked at the doll, she had a strange expression, and then after looking at the back of the doll, under its dress, she fainted." Andrea's words were rushed and spoken before Lois had a chance to respond to her husband's question. "After she came to a few minutes ago, Lois whispered some word that I didn't understand."

"I said *daughter*." Lois sat up and looked at Andrea with eyes wide, and then she gave a disbelieving shake of her head. "I—I don't know how this could be possible, but that doll was mine when I was a girl. I gave it to a nurse at the hospital to give to my baby girl before she was given to strangers."

Andrea listened to all that was being said, letting it slowly sink in. Even though her ex-fiancé was there with them in the room, she focused on what Lois was saying. It wasn't that she intentionally excluded him, but she had been searching for news of her birth mother for months.

Orley looked up at Andrea with eyebrows squished together. "I think my wife must be delusional. We have no daughter—no children at all."

Andrea wondered why the woman would say *daughter* if she didn't have one.

Lois pointed at Andrea with a shaky hand. "I—I believe that you are my daughter."

Before Andrea could form a response, Orley spoke again. "You're not thinking straight, Lois. We do not have a daughter."

She pointed at Andrea again. "I am almost certain that Andrea is the daughter I was forced to give up nearly thirty-three years ago."

"What?" Orley looked at his wife with a dazed expression. "I have no idea what you are talking about. I believe when you fell and bumped your head, it messed up your thinking."

Brandon stepped forward and pulled his cell phone from his jacket pocket. "Should I call 911? Lois could have a concussion and need to be examined." He looked at Andrea. "Wouldn't you agree?"

Unable to think clearly or form a response, Andrea bit down on her bottom lip. She wanted to know what Brandon was doing here, but now was not the time to ask. The one thing Andrea needed right now was answers to questions she had for Lois.

Lois released her stiff white head covering and reached up to finger the bun at the back of her head, where some of her auburn-colored hair had come loose. "I'm fine; there are no lumps or pain, and I can see clearly. I was so stunned when I saw the doll and heard Andrea's story, that everything started closing in on me and I passed out." She looked over at Brandon and shook her head. "I'm fine, and I won't be needing any medical help."

"Okay." He glanced at Orley and returned his cell phone to his pocket.

"Let's get you up and into a chair." Orley helped Lois to her feet and over to one of the antique rockers that was for sale. Once she was seated, he situated her head covering, then pulled up a straight-backed chair and sat beside her. Lois smoothed the wrinkles in the skirt of her olive green dress and glanced back toward the counter.

Andrea wasn't sure what to do, so she stood off to one side with her arms crossed and heart pounding. Brandon joined her but said nothing.

"Now what's all this talk about Andrea being your daughter?" Orley looked at his wife with concern. "Were you thinking what it would be like if we had a daughter who looked like her?"

Lois shook her head. "No, I was thinking, as I am now, how much she looks like me when I was her age. She has the same auburn hair and brown eyes I do."

Andrea had never thought about it until now, but she and Lois did share those similarities. Even so. . .

"I suppose if she was dressed in Amish clothes and had long hair pulled up into a bun, she would resemble you in some ways."

Andrea could tell by the gentle way Orley spoke to his wife that he didn't believe what she had told him and was merely going along with it to keep Lois from becoming upset. The truth was, Andrea didn't believe Lois either. How could she? It would be too much of a coincidence if Lois was truly her birth mother. Besides, Andrea was born in Pennsylvania, and Lois lived here in Ohio.

"Where's the doll? What happened to it?" Lois tried to leave her chair, but Orley reached out and placed his hands on her knees. "You need to stay seated, Lois. At least till your head is clear and you can think straight again." He looked up at Brandon as though seeking his help. "I'm still thinking that my wife should see a doctor."

Before Brandon had the chance to retrieve his cell phone again, Lois shouted, "Could someone please find the doll and bring it to me?"

"It's over there behind the counter. You dropped it when you fell." Andrea hurried over and picked up the doll. In her concern for Lois, she hadn't thought about the faceless doll until now. She walked to where Lois sat and handed it to her. "I was telling you how I recently learned that a nurse at the hospital where I was born had given this doll to my adoptive parents, saying that my birth mother wanted me to have it."

Tears pooled in Lois's eyes and ran down her cheeks. "Look here." She pointed to a place on the doll's back, where the name Mary L. Miller had been written in black ink.

"Mary L. Miller is the name of my birth mother," Andrea said. "It says so on my original birth certificate, which I also recently acquired."

Lois placed a hand against her chest. "I am Mary L. Miller. That doll used to be mine, and I'm the one who gave it to the nurse and asked her to give it to my daughter."

The shock of what Lois had said surged straight through Andrea, making her dizzy. Brandon must have seen that she was shaky on her feet, for he quickly grabbed another chair and instructed her to take a seat.

"But. . .but isn't your name Lois?" Andrea could barely get the question out as she spoke through trembling lips.

"My given name was Mary Lois, but everyone called me Lois because one of my cousins was also named Mary and my mother didn't want there to be any confusion." Lois touched the spot on the doll's back where the writing was located. "I wrote here what had been written on my baby's birth certificate."

"Oh my!" Andrea clasped both hands over her mouth. "Is it really possible that you could be my birth mother?"

"Yes, I am certain of it."

"But I was born in Lancaster, Pennsylvania, and you live here."

"I didn't always live in Ohio. I grew up in Mifflin County, Pennsylvania, and when my father found out I had gotten pregnant out of wedlock, he sent me to live with my aunt, whose home was in the village of Bird-in-Hand, which is just outside of Lancaster." Lois paused and drew in a shaky breath. "No one knew about my pregnancy except for my father and aunt. It was kept a secret because Dad was embarrassed by what I'd done, and he didn't want to bring shame on our family."

Andrea felt the comfort of Brandon's warm hands on her shoulder. Did he understand the way she felt? Did Brandon realize how overwhelming this was for her?

Orley sat in stunned silence as Lois continued to talk with Andrea about her past. *Doesn't my wife realize what a shock this is for me to hear? Why has Lois never mentioned any of this to me? It makes no sense at all.*

Slowly, Orley pulled his fingers through the ends of his beard as he tried to process everything that had been said. It was hard to fathom that during all these years of being married to Lois she had kept such a shocking secret from him.

Orley's muscles tensed as he thought about her deception. Apparently, his wife must be the kind of person who tried to keep things hidden from him. Lois had done it previously, when she'd been quiet about her job for the paper writing the Dear Caroline column. He'd had no idea she'd been involved in that until she confessed it later on. But Lois had apologized, and they'd worked it out. Some time ago, Orley had forgiven her for keeping him in the dark.

He looked at his trembling wife again. *I need to say a quick prayer about how I should address this topic concerning Andrea to my fraa.* He wanted to confront her about this right now, but not in front of two people they barely knew. The issue was between him and Lois, and they needed to talk about it privately.

Orley cleared his throat. "Umm. . .there are some things my wife and I need to discuss." He looked at Andrea, then Brandon. "Would you two mind leaving us alone for a while? Perhaps you could come by our house later this evening." This statement he directed to Andrea. "It will give you a chance to ask Lois more questions and get better acquainted."

Tearfully, Andrea nodded her head. "I would like that very much."

Orley got up and went over to the counter, where he wrote his and Lois's address on a piece of paper. He came back to where Andrea sat and handed it to her. "Would seven o'clock be too late?"

"No, that'll be fine." Andrea smiled at Lois and clasped her hand. "Finding you has been an answer to my prayers. I am eager to know more about you and look forward to talking with you later this evening. I'd like to find out about my biological father, who was listed on my birth certificate as 'unknown.'"

"I will tell you all that I can." More tears filled Lois's eyes and dripped onto her flushed cheeks. "For a good many years, I too have prayed, and now, at long last, God has answered that prayer."

"I'll see you later then. Goodbye for now." Andrea rose from her chair and looked down at the doll Lois still held in her lap. "Would you mind if I take the doll with me?"

"Of course not. It's yours and was always intended for you." Lois handed it to Andrea.

"Thank you."

"You're welcome."

Brandon was at a loss for words, but if he was going to speak, it had better be now. He couldn't believe he'd just witnessed the woman he loved finding out who her birth mother was. And Brandon couldn't have been more shocked to learn that it was Lois Troyer. He said a hasty goodbye to Orley and Lois, then hurried past Andrea and opened the door, holding it for her to walk out.

"Thanks."

"You're welcome." He walked beside Andrea as she headed for her car. It felt so good to see her again. He had missed that pretty smile of hers and so many other things. Though it was quite chilly outside, with ice dotting the walkway, Brandon thought he could melt like a snowman in warm weather while he was in Andrea's presence. "I was wondering if you'd like to grab a bite to eat with me," he questioned.

"Right now?"

"Yeah."

"I'm not hungry at the moment, and I'd rather not go to a restaurant with my eyes all red from crying." She reached her vehicle and was about to open the door on the driver's side when Brandon stepped in front of it. "Besides, I'm going over to my parents' house to tell them that I found my birth mother."

"We need to talk, Andrea." His tone had become solemn.

She tipped her head back and looked up at him. "You think so?"

"Definitely." Brandon struggled with the urge to take Andrea into his arms and kiss her soundly, but it might not be appreciated since they hadn't worked things out. Right now, Brandon wanted to resume their engagement, but he would have to be the one to fix things since he was the one who'd ended their engagement. But what if he'd blown it and she didn't want to reestablish their relationship?

"How about this—you can go see your folks before going home, and around five o'clock I'll stop by Lem's and get a pizza to go. Then I'll pick up Duke and come over to your place. I'm sure he'd like to see Lady again, and the two of them can get reacquainted while we talk and eat. Would that be okay with you?"

Her forehead wrinkled and she dropped her gaze. Brandon felt sure she was going to say no.

"I. . .I guess it would be all right. I think Lady's missed hanging out with Duke."

Not nearly as much as I've missed you. Fearful that Andrea might change her mind, Brandon didn't say the words on his heart. He didn't deserve a second chance with her, but oh how he longed for one.

He gave Andrea's arm a little tap and stepped away from the car. "I'll see you at your place in a few hours."

"Okay. Bye for now."

As he headed for his SUV, Brandon prayed. *Lord, please pave the way, and give me the right words to say when I get to Andrea's house. I'm truly sorry for not offering her the support and encouragement I should have when she was searching for her mother.*

Chapter 35

Orley left his seat, walked over to the front window, and flipped the OPEN sign over so it said CLOSED. Then he shut the blinds and locked the front door.

"What are you doing? It's not time to go home yet," Lois said, looking toward the battery-operated clock on the wall. "Our driver won't be here for at least another hour."

"I'm well aware, but it's time for us to have a serious discussion." Orley moved the chair he'd been sitting in so that it faced Lois and sat down. "I'd like to know more about this secret you've been keeping from me all these years and why you've kept this very important information to yourself."

Lois shed a few more tears and dabbed at them with a tissue she'd pulled from inside the band on her apron. "I'm so sorry, Orley. I was wrong not to tell you, but there were two reasons I never said anything about the baby I had out of wedlock."

Orley leaned slightly forward. "I'm listening."

She held up one finger. "I was ashamed of what I'd done and thought you would think less of me if you knew, like my father did." Her chin trembled. "He was very upset when he found out that I was pregnant, and he would have done just about anything to keep those in our church district from finding out."

"What's the second reason?" Orley questioned.

"I knew how badly you felt about not being able to have any children of our own, and I thought if you knew I had given birth to a child and then gave her up for adoption, it would have caused you even more emotional pain."

Orley's lips pressed together in a slight grimace. "I thought you knew me better than that. I love you, Lois, and I've always believed our relationship was strong enough that you would feel free to tell me anything. But now that the truth has come out, I want to understand your thinking and try to help mend this emotional wound for both of us." He paused briefly as though trying to gather his thoughts. "So now I will listen carefully as you explain everything to me."

"My father was very upset and angry with me when he discovered I was expecting a baby. He couldn't deal with his daughter's mistake and feared that those in our community would look down on him as well as his wayward daughter."

"May I ask who the father of your baby was?" Orley leaned closer to Lois. "I need to know."

"His name was William Hostettler, and we were just a couple of lovesick teenagers when it happened."

"Why wasn't his name on Andrea's birth certificate?"

"Because I never told him I was pregnant, and while I was living with my aunt Eva in Bird-in-Hand, Pennsylvania, I read in *The Budget* that William and his entire family had been in a tragic van accident and everyone died, including their driver." Lois paused and sucked in a deep breath. "No one except for my daed and Aunt Eva, who as you know, are both deceased, knew about my pregnancy. I was instructed not to tell anyone else. Dad contacted an adoption agency in Pennsylvania, and they set things up with an English couple who wanted to adopt a baby." Lois lowered her head and let the tears flow freely. "It's been difficult to keep this secret buried in my heart all this time." She sniffed and blew her nose on the tissue Orley had handed her. "I've lived with my guilt every day, wondering if I should have told you the truth and trying my best to help others who were hurting."

"Helping others is a fine thing, Lois." Orley put his hand under her chin so she was looking directly at him again. "But you can't find true peace in your heart by helping others when you should be seeking your own inner peace, which has apparently been lacking. I believe you have tried to hide the pain of your past by doing good things and trying to help people with their problems."

"I. . .I thought I had succeeded in putting the past behind me until

Andrea revealed who she was by showing me her doll. I never would have known where my daughter was if it hadn't been for that." Lois swallowed against the pain in the back of her throat. "Instead, all I've managed to do is make a mess of things, and now I've lost your love and respect." She blinked several times. "I wouldn't blame you if you asked me to leave your home."

Orley gave a brisk shake of his head. "That will never happen. We've worked too long and hard for our relationship to end that easily. When we got married, it was for life, and my home is your home, plain and simple." His features softened as he clasped both of her hands and gave them a tender squeeze. "Although I am disappointed that you didn't feel you could share your secret with me, I'm thankful that it's finally out in the open and pleased that you have been reunited with your dochder." His eyes glistened with tears of his own while he spoke in a gentle voice. "It looks like our little family has just grown, and now we both have a daughter."

Struggling to find the right words to convey her gratitude, Lois murmured, "Danki, my dear husband. I love you so much."

"And I love you."

Apple Creek

"Come on, boy!" Brandon slapped his leg. "Wanna go for a ride with me to see Andrea and your furry friend Lady?"

Arf! Arf! Duke ran for the front door with his tail wagging, and he looked up at his owner as if to say, "Hurry up, let's go."

Brandon chuckled. "Hang on. Let me get your leash."

He felt really good about seeing Andrea again. It was great that she had discovered who her birth mother was, but it had been a shock to find out that it was Lois Troyer. Brandon liked Lois and Orley, and from what he could tell, they were a caring couple. Andrea couldn't have picked a nicer woman than Lois to be her biological mother.

Brandon had spent some time praying after arriving home from Memory Keepers. He had thanked the Lord for working things out for Andrea and for creating an opportunity for the two of them to talk this evening. He'd changed clothes, brushed his teeth, and combed his hair, and then he inspected himself in the mirror to make sure he looked presentable. Things needed to be perfect for this evening, when he hoped to win Andrea back into his life.

Brandon moved away from the mirror and went to get his dog's leash. After clipping it to Duke's collar, he and his little buddy went out the door.

A short time later, they were in Brandon's vehicle, heading for the pizza place to pick up the order he'd called in. From there, it would be on to Andrea's, where he would apologize. Brandon hoped then they could start with a clean slate. He patted his jacket pocket and sent up a prayer.

Chapter 36

As she finished setting out paper plates and napkins, Andrea hummed one of her favorite choruses that they often sang at church. Soon after arriving home from her parents' house, she had freshened up and changed into a new top. Today had been good but quite emotional. She was glad to have found her biological mother. It would be the start of a new chapter in her life.

She'd taken out the glasses when the doorbell rang. *That must be Brandon.* She looked around for Lady and saw the cat sleeping in one corner of the room. Andrea hoped this evening would go well between her and Brandon. Several weeks had passed since they'd exchanged any words, and she was worried that things might be too awkward.

Andrea left the kitchen and went to the front door. The minute she opened it, Duke darted in, pulling against the leash in Brandon's gloved hands.

"I think he's as eager to see your cat as I am to see you."

"Lady's asleep in the kitchen right now, but you can let Duke loose if you want to." Andrea made no reference to Brandon's statement about being eager to see her.

"Here's the pizza I got at Lem's." Brandon lifted the box he held. "Where would you like me to put it?"

"I'll take it to the kitchen while you release Duke's leash from his collar. You can hang your jacket on the coat tree here in the hallway."

"Okay." Brandon leaned down, and the minute his dog was free, Duke took off down the hall and nearly ran into the wall as he rounded the corner and disappeared into the kitchen.

Brandon rolled his eyes. "I told you he was eager to come over here."

Andrea couldn't resist smiling. In fact, smiling had come easy to her since she'd left Memory Keepers earlier today. When Andrea had stopped by her folks' house, Dad was still at work, but she'd been glad to find her mother at home. Andrea could still see the look of surprise on Mom's face when she'd told her what had taken place at the antique store and about the miracle of finding her birth mother in such an unexpected way. Mom had hugged Andrea and said she was happy for her. She'd even said she would like to meet Lois sometime soon to get acquainted and share pictures of Andrea taken when she was a child.

Andrea's father had called her after he'd left the bank and heard the news from her mother. He too said it would be nice to meet Andrea's biological mother and fill her in on some of Andrea's childhood experiences.

Redirecting her thoughts, Andrea entered the kitchen and placed the pizza box on the table. The mouthwatering smell that escaped from the box made her appetite grow. Duke was in the same room, wagging his tail near the cat's food dish. She wasn't surprised to see that Lady was not only awake but sharing her bowl of water with Duke.

"Those two were meant to be together, don't you think?" Brandon asked when he came into the room.

"Well, I'd have to say they think so." She shook her head. "One would never know that Duke used to be afraid of Lady."

Brandon laughed. "Yeah, my dog was sure a big chicken when it came to your cat."

"I think she has him buffaloed."

Brandon took a few steps toward Andrea. "I want you to know how sorry I am for not being there when you needed me the most. I should have realized how desperate you were to find your birth mother and been more understanding."

"I'm sorry too," she said. "I was not considerate of your needs either."

"I love you, Andrea, and I will do everything I can to prove it." He moved closer and dropped down on one knee, then opened his hand. "Will you marry me, please?"

Her eyes filled with joyful tears as she gazed at the beautiful engagement ring she had foolishly sent back to him, which was now cradled in his hand. "Yes, Brandon, I will marry you, and this time there will be no postponing or canceling the wedding."

"Agreed. We will, however, have to choose another wedding date, because February 14th is just a week away." He slipped the ring on Andrea's finger and stood. Gathering her into his arms, Brandon kissed her so tenderly that Andrea didn't want it to end. She'd had many happy times in her life, but nothing as joyous as today. In addition to the thrill of meeting her biological mother, she and Brandon were together again.

"After we finish eating, would you like to go over to the Troyers' house with me?" Andrea asked, stroking her fiancé's cheek.

"Most definitely. If I'm going to become part of your family soon, then I'd like to get better acquainted with your birth mother and stepfather, Orley, who has also been a big help to me."

"Really? How's that?"

"I'll tell you while we eat our pizza." Brandon gave Andrea another kiss and pulled out a chair for her.

Before they took slices of pizza, they held hands and Brandon prayed. "Heavenly Father, thank You for the food we are about to eat, and bless the hands that prepared it. We are thankful for all that You have done in our lives and are especially thankful for Lois Troyer and the wonderful announcement she made today." He squeezed Andrea's fingers as they both said, "Amen."

During this special moment, Andrea's mind emptied of all concerns as a warm tingle infused her body. She quietly thanked God for answered prayer.

When Andrea opened her eyes and looked at Brandon, a wide smile spread across her face. "I just thought of something."

"What is it?" he asked.

"When I sent my DNA sample in and got the results, the only thing I learned was that I'm of German descent. Now I know why." She spoke in a bubbly voice. "I believe that the reason I've always had an interest in the Amish way of life and painted so many pictures of horses and buggies, barns, and Amish children and was so excited by that old Amish quilt is because of my true heritage." She placed one hand against her chest. "Somewhere deep inside, I must have known that I had been born to Amish parents. And if they had raised me, I'd most likely be wearing Plain clothes and driving a horse and buggy myself."

Brandon gave her a tender smile. "But then, since I am not of Amish descent, you would never have met or agreed to marry me, which in my opinion would not be a good thing."

"You're right, but it didn't happen that way, and I believe that God worked it all out according to His plan."

Walnut Creek

"You were sure out there in the phone shed for a while," Orley said when Lois entered the kitchen and took a seat at the table across from him. "What took so long?"

"I called my sisters and half-brothers and left them all messages. I decided that it was time for Elizabeth, Rebekah, Benjamin, and Jacob to hear that they have a niece none of them have known anything about."

"Did you explain the circumstances of your pregnancy?"

She nodded. "I can't deny that I was not married when my baby was born, and in the messages I left on their answering machines, I gave them the details and told how I was miraculously reunited with my daughter today."

"Do you think they will understand and not judge you the way your daed did?" Orley asked.

"Although I'm sure they won't approve of my actions as a teenager, I believe they will not condemn me."

"I doubt that any of them have lived perfect lives, because we are all born into sin and make mistakes."

Lois swallowed against the lump in her throat. "I asked my heavenly Father to forgive me a long time ago, and I believe He did."

"Of course. Psalm 86:5 says: 'Thou, Lord, art good, and ready to forgive; and plenteous in mercy unto all them that call upon thee.'"

"I am thankful that God loved the world so much that He sent His only Son, Jesus, to the earth as a baby. And I'm even more appreciative that Jesus, after He became a man, bore the sins of the world when He died on the cross."

"Jah," Orley agreed, "and all people have to do is ask His forgiveness and accept Him as their Lord and Savior."

"Absolutely." Lois smiled in spite of the tears she felt behind her eyes that at any moment could spill over.

Lois took out a loaf of bread and placed it on the table. Then she opened the refrigerator and removed a package of lunchmeat and cheese, along with some mustard, mayonnaise, and pickles. "If you don't mind,

Orley, I'd like to keep this evening's supper simple so we can eat it before Andrea and Brandon get here. I'm almost certain he will be with her."

"That's fine with me."

Andrea's stomach tightened when Brandon pulled in front of an older-looking but well-built farmhouse. "According to my GPS, this is the Troyers' place," he announced.

"I'm suddenly nervous," she said. "I am about to see my birth mother's home for the first time, and I'm not sure how to act."

"Just be yourself. Amish folks aren't really that different from you or me. They just live a distinctive lifestyle."

"Yes, one that doesn't involve all the modern conveniences we English people have, such as electricity in their homes, which means no televisions, computers, dishwashers, or electric lights."

"I've visited a few Amish homes around Apple Creek when I've been called to treat a sick or injured animal." Brandon set the brake and turned off the ignition. "Some homes were very simple, with the barest of necessities, while others had a more progressive feel but without all the modern things we are used to." He reached across the seat and took hold of Andrea's hand. "Try to relax and enjoy this evening as you get to know Lois and Orley. And be sure to take the opportunity to ask any questions you may have."

Andrea smiled. "Thank you for coming with me. I really appreciate your support."

He gave her fingers a tender squeeze. "I should have been more supportive from the beginning, when you first told me you wanted to search for your biological parents."

"It's in the past," she said. "Let's just focus on the future we're going to have together."

"Yes," he murmured with his mouth close to her ear. "And we will make sure that Lois and her husband are a special part of our lives. I think it would be good if we introduced the Troyers to both of our families so they can get to know them too."

Feeling content and quite hopeful, Andrea leaned her head on his strong shoulder. "I love you, Brandon."

He put his hand on her forehead and lifted her bangs. "I love you, too, and here's the proof." Brandon pulled Andrea into his arms and gave her forehead and both cheeks feathery kisses. Then his lips captured hers in a tender but firm kiss. "Ready to go knock on the door now?" he asked when the kiss ended.

"Yes, I am." Andrea got out of his SUV, and when he joined her, they walked up the porch steps together. Andrea reached out her hand to knock, but the door opened before her knuckles made contact with the wood.

"Come in. Come in. . . ." Orley greeted them both with a warm handshake and took their jackets. "Lois is in the kitchen, taking a pan of brownies from the oven. We can either join her there or wait for her in the living room."

"I'm fine with going to the kitchen," Andrea was quick to say.

"Alrighty then, you can follow me." Orley led them halfway down the narrow hall, turned left, and entered a warm, cozy kitchen.

Lois quickly set a pan of brownies on a cooling rack that had been placed on a counter near the sink. "I'm so happy to see you again," she said, giving Andrea a welcoming hug. Following that, she shook hands with Brandon. "Did you have any trouble finding our home?"

"Not a bit." He smiled. "I just typed the address Orley gave Andrea this afternoon into the driving directions on my phone, and it brought us right here."

"Oh good." Lois gestured to the brownies. "These need to cool a bit, but while we are waiting, let's go into the living room, where it's more comfortable and we can visit."

Andrea and Brandon followed the Troyers across the hall to a living room that was larger than Andrea had expected. It was furnished with a good-sized couch, two leather recliners, a wooden rocker, and two straight-backed chairs. Lois suggested that she and Andrea sit on the couch, and the men could have the recliners.

Once seated, Andrea noticed two battery-operated lights hanging on hooks from the ceiling. Their brightness illuminated the entire room.

"Have either of you ever been in an Amish home before?" Orley asked.

"I've been in a few, when I made calls to treat some Amish people's animals," Brandon spoke up.

"And you?" Orley looked at Andrea.

She shook her head. "This is my first time."

Lois reached across the space between them. "I hope you will visit here and at Memory Keepers many times in the years to come. I want us to take every opportunity to get to know each other well."

Tears welled in Lois's eyes, which put Andrea on the brink of tears too. "I'd like that," she said with feeling.

"Would you like to know a little bit about my family?"

"So you have no other children?" Andrea asked.

Lois shook her head. "No, we don't, but I do have four siblings, although none of them live in Ohio. Someday, if we can work it all out, I'd like you to meet them and their families."

Andrea glanced at Brandon, engrossed in a conversation with Orley that involved the weather; then she looked back at Lois and smiled. "I would like that very much. Having grown up as an only child and only having one cousin, I've never known what it was like to be part of a large family. Not that I'm complaining," she quickly added. "My parents and I have always been close, and we've done many fun things together."

"I'm sure you have." Lois twirled one finger around the narrow ties of her head covering. "I look forward to meeting your mother and father someday."

"I stopped by their house after leaving your antique store today and told my mother how we found each other and I came to realize that you were the woman who gave birth to me in Lancaster, Pennsylvania, almost thirty-three years ago."

"Was she surprised?"

"Yes, and Mom said she was happy for me. Dad called me when he got home, and he seemed pleased too." Andrea scooched down on the couch so she was a little closer to Lois. "They want to meet you and Orley, so maybe we can pick you up some evening or weekend when you are free, and we'll eat supper at my folks' place."

"You'd all be welcome to come here if you like," Lois said. "I would be pleased for the opportunity to cook a meal for you and your parents." She looked over at Brandon. "You're invited too, of course."

He grinned. "That's good, because I proposed marriage to Andrea before we came here, and since she said yes, I will soon be part of the family."

Orley got up from his chair and went over to give Brandon a few thumps on his back. "That's good news. I knew everything would work out for you two."

Andrea assumed from his remark that Brandon must have told Orley about the problems they'd had. But she didn't mind. Everyone needed someone to talk to when they were going through a troubled situation. She'd shared things with Colleen and had even written a few letters to Dear

Caroline, which gave her the assurance someone cared and wanted to help.

"Would you mind if I asked you a personal question?" Lois asked, leaning a bit closer to Andrea.

"No, not at all."

"When you and Brandon were going through a difficult time, did you by chance write a letter to the Dear Caroline newspaper column?"

Andrea blinked several times. "Why yes, I did. I'm confused though—what made you ask me that question?"

A crimson flush crept across Lois's cheeks. "Since we are telling the truth while sitting here on this sofa, I must admit to you that I am Dear Caroline."

"Really?" Andrea's mouth dropped open. "Wow, that is a surprise, and no wonder you gave such good advice. Now may I ask you a question?"

Lois bobbed her head. "Anything, Andrea. Anything at all."

"How do the Amish say *mother* in Pennsylvania Dutch?"

"Well, there's *mudder* for mother. Or *mamm* for mom."

"Some children call their mothers *mammi* or *memm*," Orley interjected.

Andrea let those words roll around in her head for a minute. Then she looked at Lois and said, "Would it be all right if I called you Memm?"

Tears filled Lois's eyes and dribbled down her cheeks. "Oh, I would like that very much."

Andrea nodded. "And so would I, my dear memm." Her gaze went to Brandon again, and she was pleased when he grinned at her and held up both thumbs. Through all the days of worry and searching the internet for answers, in her wildest dreams, Andrea never could have imagined that she would end up with two very special mothers.

Epilogue

Three months later

"You look radiant, Andrea, but you need to stop fidgeting so I can make sure your veil is on straight."

"Sorry, Mom, but this is my wedding day, and I can't help feeling nervous." Andrea turned to look at her mother. "Weren't you nervous when you and Dad got married?"

"Of course, dear, and I'm sure your groom is as nervous as your father was on our wedding day. Marriage is a huge milestone in a person's life, and you want everything to go perfectly."

"Yes, but life's not perfect, and I know there will be bumps in the road."

"You've got that right—especially when you start having kids," Colleen interjected as she looked at her reflection in the full-length mirror Andrea had brought from home. They'd been told that the bridal party could use any of the Sunday school classrooms to get ready for the wedding, but the room lacked mirrors.

Andrea smiled as she looked at her stunning matron of honor wearing a lovely rose-colored dress. "Even if there are days when we're faced with challenges, I'm excited today about becoming Brandon's wife, and I look forward to whatever time God gives us here on earth as husband and wife."

A rap sounded on the door. "Are you ready in there, ladies?" Dad called. "It's about time for my wife to be seated and for me to walk my daughter down the aisle."

Andrea's mother opened the door. "Come in, Ray, and see how lovely the bride looks in the satin dress I wore on our wedding day."

Andrea's father entered the room, and when he walked over to Andrea, tears pooled in his eyes. "You're as beautiful in that dress as your mother was the day she became my bride." He leaned close and kissed her cheek. "This is probably the most important day of your life, and your mother and I are pleased that you chose Brandon to be your mate for life. He will not only be a good provider, but he's a kind and generous man."

"I agree," Mom said, slipping her arm around Andrea's waist.

"Do either of you have any advice for me before I take that walk down the aisle?" Andrea asked.

"Just be loving, kind, and honest," Dad said. "And remember to keep God at the center of your marriage. Pray about everything, and seek the Lord's will concerning every aspect of your life."

Mom nodded. "I'm in complete agreement with what your father just said."

"Same here." Colleen stepped forward and handed Andrea her delicate white rose bridal bouquet. "Now it's time for us to leave this room because there's a church full of family and friends who are as eager to see you and Brandon get married as I am on this beautiful sunny day in May."

Moments later, following Colleen, Andrea walked down the aisle with her hand in the crook of Dad's arm. As they approached the front of the sanctuary, she spotted her birth mother's white head covering and smiled. Orley stood beside Lois, looking quite dapper in his Amish-styled suit. How wonderful it was that Andrea's new family could be there to witness her marriage to Brandon.

Andrea's gaze went to her groom, dressed in a black tuxedo and standing beside his brother, Joe, whom Brandon had chosen to be the best man. Andrea had a feeling of weightlessness as the minister asked, "Who gives this woman to be wed?" and her father replied, "Her mother and I do."

A comforting warmth radiated throughout Andrea's body as she slipped her hand from the crook of Dad's arm and sought the hand of her groom. It felt as if she'd been waiting for this special moment all of her life.

Tears, like silver, glistened in the corners of Brandon's eyes. Andrea felt moisture in her eyes as well. *Dear Lord, thank You for the blessings I've received in the last few months—for bringing my birth mother and me together and for helping me realize how important Brandon is to me. Please guide and direct us both as we begin our new life*, Andrea silently prayed as she and the handsome, smiling man who would soon be her husband turned to face the minister in preparation for saying their vows.

"Did you ever see a sweeter-looking bride?" Lois whispered to Orley from their front-row seat, where they sat next to Andrea's adoptive parents.

He smiled and gave a brief nod.

Lois's heart swelled with joy as she watched her newly found daughter recite vows to her groom in this church full of people. Although it would have given her the greatest pleasure to have raised Andrea herself, Lois felt thankful that her daughter had been brought up in a Christian home with parents who loved her and had provided for Andrea's needs. Rather than feeling bitter because she'd been robbed of the right to watch her daughter grow up, Lois felt grateful that God had provided a miracle and brought Andrea back into her life. Since that day in their antique store, when Lois realized who Andrea was, she and Orley had been given the opportunity to meet and get to know Evelyn and Ray Wagner. From their first meeting, which had taken place a few days later, Lois had known her daughter was loved and cherished by the man and woman she'd grown up to call Dad and Mom.

Although this was quite different from a traditional Amish wedding, Lois found herself enjoying each moment. When the minister prayed for Andrea and Brandon, read some passages of scripture, and spoke about the importance of good communication and remembering to speak the truth to one another, Lois felt a twinge of guilt creep back in. *Even before we were married, I should have told Orley about my pregnancy and the adoption of my baby. I did us both a disservice by keeping the birth of my child a secret.* But Orley had forgiven Lois, and for that, she also felt thankful.

Looking ahead to the future, she anticipated being included in her daughter and son-in-law's lives. If they were blessed with children someday, Lois would have the privilege of being a grandmother.

Lois shifted on the pew. She had to admit that the padded benches with backs were more comfortable than the backless wooden benches that were used in Amish church services. Even so, Lois wouldn't trade her way of life to become part of the English world.

A smile played upon Lois's lips as she thought about the vacation she and Orley would be taking next week. While Andrea and Brandon spent their honeymoon in Hawaii, Lois and Orley would be getting plenty of sun in Sarasota, Florida. They had heard that the month of May was a good time to go there because the people the Floridians referred to as snowbirds would have returned to their northern homes by then. This meant that the Sarasota beaches and other places would be less crowded. Lois hadn't been to the beach in a good many years, and she looked forward to walking barefoot in the sand, looking for unusual shells.

Lois's thoughts were redirected when the minister told the groom that he could kiss his bride. Although this was definitely not something one would witness at an Amish wedding, Lois found it to be quite endearing. Following the kiss, the minister looked out at those in the audience and said in a loud, clear voice: "I would like to introduce to you Mr. and Mrs. Brandon Prentice." Harmonious organ music filled the room as Andrea put her hand in the crook of her husband's arm and they stepped off the platform. When they walked past the pew where Lois, Orley, Evelyn, and Ray sat, Andrea looked over at them and smiled.

Smiling in return, Lois wiped tears from her cheeks. This was one of the happiest moments of her life. She closed her eyes and prayed: *Heavenly Father, once again I thank You for the miracle that You provided and for this opportunity to witness my daughter's marriage. Please bless the happy couple in the days ahead, and continue to guide and direct Orley's and my life. Remind us daily to set a good example to those we meet, and if it be Your will, send more people into Memory Keepers who need a touch from above as we speak the words that You will place upon our hearts.*

LOIS'S EGG DROP SOUP

Ingredients:

2 cups chicken broth

2 teaspoons soy sauce

2 large eggs

Pinch of salt

Pinch of garlic powder

1 large green onion, chopped

Heat broth and soy sauce in saucepan. While broth is heating, whisk eggs with salt and garlic powder in a bowl or larger measuring cup. When broth starts to boil, use a wooden spoon to stir the soup. Slowly drip egg mixture into broth, stirring continually in the same direction. As soon as egg mixture has been poured in, remove soup from heat. Pour into soup bowls, garnish with chopped onion, and serve. Makes two servings.

ANDREA'S TANGY POTATO SALAD

Ingredients:

4 potatoes, cooked until tender and diced

4 hard-boiled eggs, chopped

¼ cup diced onions

¼ cup dill pickles, cut into small pieces

½ cup mayonnaise or salad dressing

¼ cup brown mustard

1 tablespoon apple cider vinegar or pickle juice

Salt & pepper to taste

Cook potatoes and boil eggs in separate saucepans. When they are done, transfer to a bowl of cold water until both are cooled. Dice potatoes and eggs and place in large bowl. Mix onion and pickles into potato-egg mixture. Stir in mayonnaise, mustard, vinegar, and salt and pepper. Mix gently until evenly coated. Refrigerate for fifteen minutes to half an hour before serving.

Discussion Questions

1. Lois and Orley Troyer felt called to mentor people who came into their antique store with problems. Like this Amish couple, how can we mentor others who are hurting or need guidance and counsel?

2. What problems have you faced recently? How has God provided for you? Did you find guidance from reading the Bible, talking to a friend, listening to a pastor's message during church, or in some other way?

3. Ray and Evelyn had not told Andrea the truth about her adoption, which created a problem when she found out accidentally. Was it wrong for them to keep their daughter's adoption from her for over thirty years? Why do you think they chose not to say anything? Is there ever a good reason for an adoptive parent to keep a child's adoption from them?

4. Andrea was quite upset after her cousin informed her that she'd been adopted. She felt betrayed by her adoptive parents, and it put a wedge between them for a while. Have you ever been in a similar situation where you felt betrayed by someone you had trusted? How did you work through those feelings?

5. Andrea's adoptive father, Ray, trusted God and reassured his wife that their daughter would come around and forgive them for not telling her that she'd been adopted as a baby. What should a person do if someone they hurt is not willing to forgive?

6. Andrea's adoptive mother, Evelyn, was concerned that if Andrea found out who her birth mother was, she might bond with her, and the relationship Evelyn had established with her adopted daughter could suffer. Have you or someone you know ever been in a situation similar to this and worried about how things would turn out? What could Andrea have done to assure her adoptive

mother that their relationship wouldn't change if she located her birth mother?

7. When Andrea began a search for her biological parents, her fiancé, Brandon, felt left out because she had less time to spend with him, and when they were together, all she talked about was her need to find out who had given her up for adoption. When Andrea suggested that they postpone their marriage, Brandon was so upset that he broke up with her. Do you think that was a wise decision, or should he have been more understanding and tried to work things out?

8. Andrea was deeply hurt when Brandon broke their engagement. She needed his support and didn't understand why he couldn't wait until she had located her birth mother to get married. Have you ever been in a situation where you needed encouragement and support from someone you love, but they did not provide it for you? What would you have done if you'd been in Andrea's position? Should she have been willing to marry Brandon even though she was still searching for her biological parents?

9. Although Brandon was not as supportive as Andrea needed him to be, her friend Colleen encouraged Andrea to follow her quest to find her birth mother. How important is it for friends to support each other during difficult times? What does the Bible teach us about friendship?

10. Lois had chosen not to tell her husband that during her teen years she had given birth to a baby and put the infant up for adoption. Many years later, when the truth came out, Orley was deeply hurt because Lois hadn't told him about this significant event from her past. Is there ever a time when a secret such as the one Lois had should be kept from a spouse?

11. Orley forgave Lois for not telling him about the child she'd had out of wedlock. Why do you think he was able to forgive? What does God's Word tell us about forgiveness?

12. As an artist, Andrea enjoyed painting pictures of Amish barns, buggies, and children. She had also been intrigued by an old Amish quilt. Do you think the reason Andrea was drawn to the Plain people's way of life was because of her heritage that she knew nothing about until she discovered who her birth mother was?

13. The importance of prayer is mentioned several times in this book, as the characters asked God for guidance and help with various situations. Prayer time was also necessary when the characters thanked God for His many blessings. How important is it for a Christian to pray? When a prayer is answered, does it strengthen your faith?

14. Did any of the scriptures mentioned in this book reinforce your faith or help in some spiritual way? How can reading the Bible and memorizing verses help us deal with life's problems?

15. While reading this story, did you learn anything new about the Amish who live in Apple Creek or Walnut Creek, Ohio? Have you had the privilege of visiting either of those towns? If so, what were your favorite things to see or do there?

About the Author

New York Times bestselling and award-winning author **Wanda E. Brunstetter** is one of the founders of the Amish fiction genre. She has written more than 100 books translated in four languages. With over 12 million copies sold, Wanda's stories consistently earn spots on the nation's most prestigious bestseller lists and have received numerous awards.

Wanda's ancestors were part of the Anabaptist faith, and her novels are based on personal research intended to accurately portray the Amish way of life. Her books are well-read and trusted by many Amish, who credit her for giving readers a deeper understanding of the people and their customs.

When Wanda visits her Amish friends, she finds herself drawn to their peaceful lifestyle, sincerity, and close family ties. Wanda enjoys photography, ventriloquism, gardening, bird-watching, beachcombing, and spending time with her family. She and her husband, Richard, have been blessed with two grown children, six grandchildren, and three great-grandchildren.

To learn more about Wanda,
visit her website at www.wandabrunstetter.com.